# The Tree of Life

# The Tree of Life

## A Novel

M. David Detweiler

STACKPOLE
BOOKS

Published by
STACKPOLE BOOKS
5067 Ritter Road
Mechanicsburg, PA 17055



Printed in the United States of America

10 9 8 7 6 5 4 3 2 1

First edition



**Library of Congress Cataloging-in-Publication Data**

Detweiler, M. David.
The tree of life : a novel / M. David Detweiler.
p. cm.
ISBN 0-8117-1600-7
I. Title.
PS3554.E867T74 1995 95-8864
813'.54—dc20 CIP

# To the Reader

Some of the diction, punctuation and grammar, in what follows, remains erratic, despite numerous frank and open editorial exchanges, because for better or worse what is on the page is how the silent speaking voice that is writing commanded the typing hand.

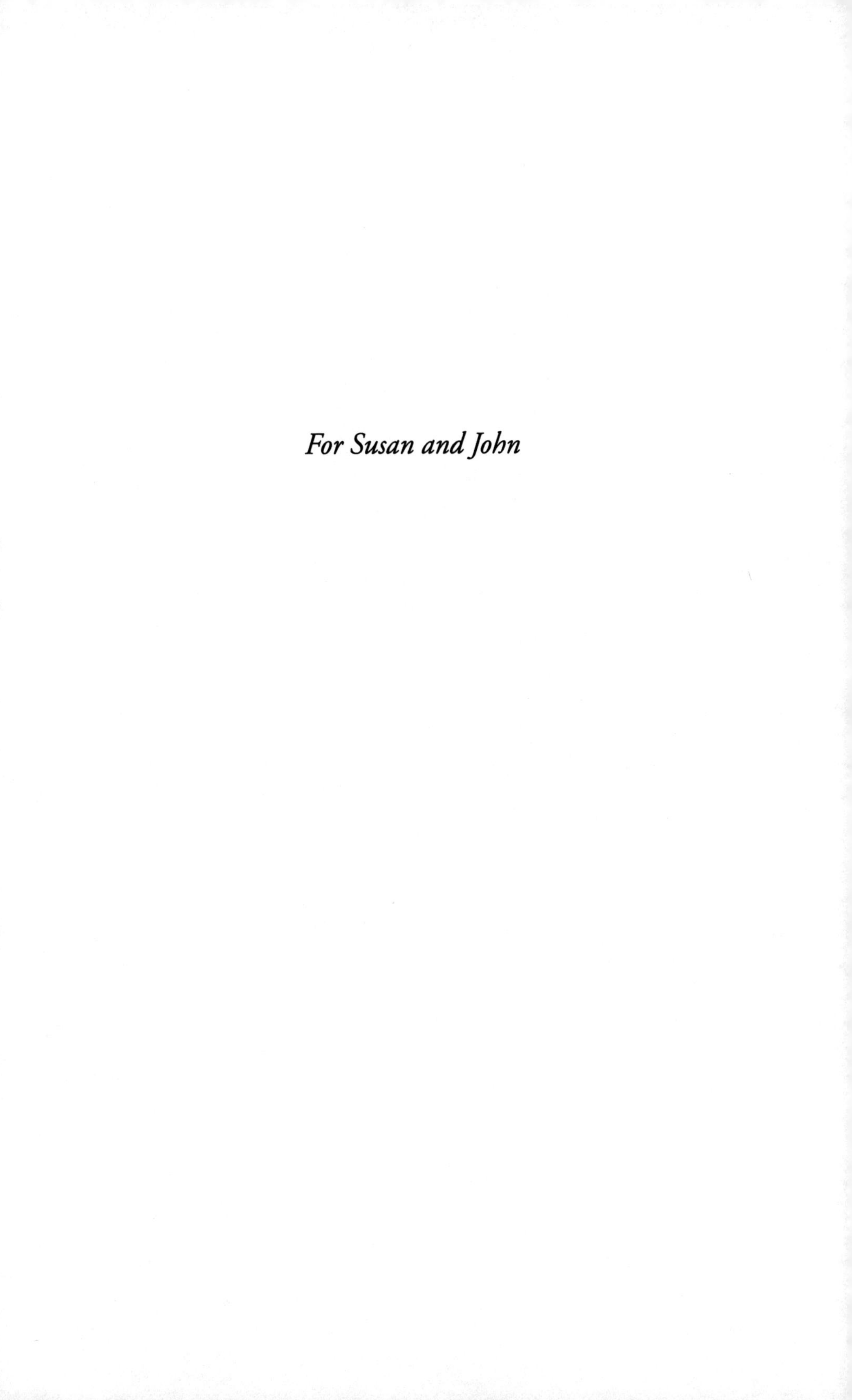

*For Susan and John*

The desire for a theory of knowledge is a desire
for constraint—a desire to find "foundations" to
which one might cling, frameworks beyond which one must
not stray, objects which impose themselves, representations
which cannot be gainsaid.

Richard Rorty
*Philosophy and the Mirror of Nature*

And you all know security
Is mortals' chiefest enemy.

Shakespeare
*Macbeth*

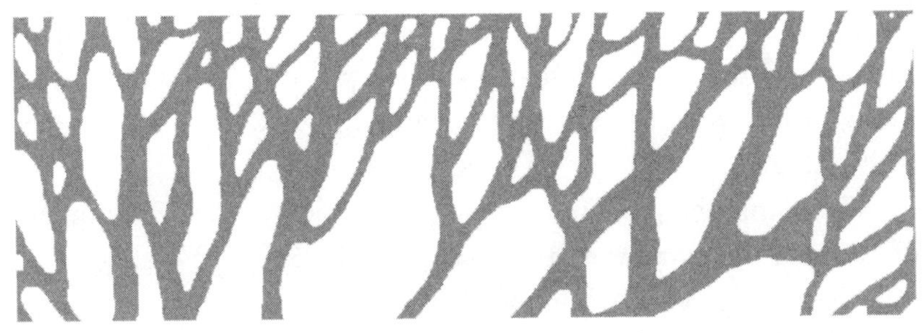

# 1

If you can't see it it isn't there.

Ages ago we believed this—no longer. That you do not directly perceive a thing doesn't mean it isn't there, a truth no one honored more than my famous uncle, Eden Hope, the particle physicist, who I went to meet and interview that spring.

I made the drive north out of the city's ganglia—powerlines, traffic, intersections, underpasses and ramps all spiraling me up onto criss-crossing lanes of concrete that bore me, in time, to an expressway that started to have hills with trees on them beside it. Six lanes became two and I was on small roads now. Shaded sometimes by mountains, bending with the river as the river bent, I went winding among green foothills, thinking of the mysterious universe where my uncle's mind labored. I passed white houses that stood back in the woods, and lolling fields with rocks cropping above their grasses, or a horse standing, and the sun was rising above the trees as I drove, all my windows down and the warm perfumes of May pouring through.

The last mile was through a private landscape so beautiful it was in a state of pleasant shock that I found my way, referring to his scrawled directions. The road dipped, yo-yo-ing my stomach up. I touched the brake. My car fed down through evergreen forest onto a gravelly, circular parking area. I cut the engine and stepped out. I stood listening, through the trees, to the trout stream that sweeps along the base of South Mountain.

Down through the pines the low, mossy roofs and silent chimneys of his bungalow unnerved me. What would he be like? Would he find my questions ignorant? Would he approve of me? Even if my questions were intelligent, would I understand his answers? A door flung open and here he came, huffing, puffing, his arms swinging, the moustache unmistakable. Bounding up the flight of railroad-tie steps to the parking circle, herding his daughter Nora ahead of him, he waved me toward his car, pumping my hand only when I offered it. He was agitated and genial and distant all at once as if he and I and his car and Nora and the golf clubs he and Nora were carrying were a set of puzzle pieces he was running out of time to figure out the fit of. "All right," he bustled, "hello ah, yes. Hop in. How-do-you-do. My daughter, Nora. You're here for the interview . . ahh, hm. Ah . . play golf?"

. . his game was so awful, so touchingly, spectacularly bad, it was fascinating. A trick-shot artist would've been hard pressed to replicate some of the mistakes he made.

He would play for minutes on end in boiling suspenseful silence. Then, rankled by a terrible shot, or startled by a good one, he would mutter—to himself, Nora, me, a rhetorical audience, or would shout, or laugh—at himself bitterly or happily or both at the same time as he followed his shots to the course's extremities to lurch, swipe and stab his white ball for the most part forward.

We were coming into the final few holes when Nora gave me to understand, in tense tones when her father was out of earshot, that as pitiful as his play was, believe it or not here and now—today—he stood to shoot the best score of his life.

So don't like act, she confided, not meeting my eyes, as if anything's like unusual or out of the ordinary—advice she seemed to have trouble following herself. As we climbed to the final tee I noticed she was moving faster, no doubt to get the suspense over with one way or the other, and we stood back, way back, from him.

The blade of his three iron flashed against the sky and he stood watching his ball's flight, leaning forward, hands high, both rows of knuckles pointing (at least he was trying to point them, per a tip he'd read) at his left ear, looking, as he swayed, less like a golfer than a nightshirted explorer peeking around a castle corner by the light of a candelabrum held aloft with both hands.

On the adjoining fairway Dr. and Mrs. Wister and the Curtisses shrieked and dove to the grass where they lay belly-down as his shot screamed over them.

"Fore!" he bellowed. "Dammit! I am so sorry, I am damned if I can play this game, I am so . . sorry!" He held his club above his head ax-like, as if he would slay the grass. "He needs a hobby," he recited under his breath, "a hobby to relax him. They tell him he works too hard, thinks too much—fine. Needs something to take his mind off his work. Fine. Medical experts so okay, I listen, I listen to what they say, I try curling. I break my foot. I try numismatics, fitting pennies into recessed circles each coin's size, big whoop. Bicycling they won't let me so I try golf. And I am no . . damn . . good at it!"

He slid his club in his bag and stood turned away from us to scribble an equation on one of the innumerable scraps of paper he carried, the lenses of his glasses flaring with fog, his sparse hair tangled wildly above the storms of his mind's electricity, his shirtpocket stuffed with pens—inkstains blotching the shiny wash-and-wear fabric his torso strained against, a sweatbead depending from his nose.

Teeing her ball up without a word his daughter powered hips ahead of shoulders-arms-hands in a rush under motionless chin to hang a high, leftward-lazing draw against the blue. She watched it with eyes that were like the May sky, fair and mildly hazy like the changing ceiling above us, strong chin lifted, shoulders without timidity.

I said: "Nice shot."

Nora Hope smiled but wouldn't look at me, and when her ball had come to rest again she was again completely shy. Slinging her bag across her back she strode off the tee swinging a light-downed arm.

Trundling his pullcart behind him her father trudged over to the seventeenth toward Dr. Wister who took an involuntary step back at the madman's approach.

"I should be shot," he confided, setting a hand on Wister's shoulder.

"Y-yes."

"Shot Wister."

"Oh . . eh, yes . ."

"Shot, executed, taken out and drilled full of steel—I would've said 'lead' but lead's bad for the environment—for the way I play this game."

Wister nodded, his bland, handsome face a nonverbal *er,* the etiolated generations of his lineage chart no help, a saddle-shoed foot pawing nervously behind him in case the need for flight should prove instant, the pink collar of his shirt twisted, his greed, lust, generosity and imagination just heirlooms, memories as faded as his shorts' plaid.

Eden Hope's great belly, where it rode the waist of his slacks, fended against the doctor's diminutive frame like a freighter bow nudging a skiff.

"Shot," my uncle concluded sadly. He walked away shaking his head, gesturing with a hand as his brain's conversation with itself continued, rolling his pullcart over Len Curtiss's foot, murmuring and muttering, to come at last to where his shot had ended up. Crouching, a foot higher than the other, head obscured by pine boughs, he devoted himself to setting up to prepare to hit: meditate . . remember . . grip, build the correct grip, remember weight on heels, not toes, knees flexed. Form a mental image the magazines said, a positive one, and remember to bend the knees and keep them bent, cock the chin, sit to the shot, weight on heels, not toes, keep grip loose but firm, set the clubface behind the ball and then—and only then—position the feet, remembering to distribute weight evenly, heels, grip, image, relax, knees, chin, weight—alignment . . .

At the trees' edge with her bag across her back, her fullback's thighs like bridge piers, Nora stared through the boughs at a belt loop her dad had missed with his army-issue brass-buckler. She was ready to wince. She knew what he was capable of. The previous summer, in a lather of competitive disorientation he had managed to doublehit a three-quarters wedge backward over his left shoulder.

Seen through the maze of branches her father's arms, pallid and weak-looking extending from the sleeves of his unsporty shirt, distressed Nora Hope in a way she felt deeply and couldn't understand.

The sight of her dad's ineffectual arms motionless in the motionless trees while he waited for the golf-demons in him to go quiet so he could hit held her hypnotized, embarrassed her—she didn't know what the sight of the white arms in the branches was doing to her. She tore her stare away to look back down the fairway to where Dr. Wister knelt examining Len Curtiss's instep. Suddenly from the pines there came a noise as of a mace chain-swung against bronze, and out of the forest careening low his slice unbelievably curved into the eighteenth fairway, striking clipped grass to bound forward like a spooked hare.

"What did I do?"

Up by the clubhouse an onlooker was cupping his hands to shout back down the fairway to us.

"He says you're on the green," Nora said.

"No."

"Yes."

"I couldn't be."

He emerged into the sunlight, pine needles in his hair, cheeks pink with exertion, his mouth an O of incredulity under the walrus moustache.

"Couldn't," he mouthed, staring up the fairway. "Couldn't be . ." As we walked, the putting surface of the elevated green became visible. "My God I am, I'm on. How'd I do it?"

"Dad, I don't know."

"Well ahh, in any event I have a tricky little downhill putt now, do I not. Hmm, yes, a dangerous downhill tester, slippery, yes, well. Hm.

Nory you know I've got," he said in a distant voice, the brown eyes ever on the slippery green where his ball rested, as we trudged, "a good score so far, my best ever I think—"

"Don't think," she advised dropping her bag to yank a wedge out and sweep it through her ball lofting a perfunctory approach not particularly near the pin.

"I gently," he regaled us as she shouldered her bag and we walked on, "I softly, sensitively, oh I delectably—I just touch that little putt. I kiss it . . and when I do—"

"Dad."

"You are going to see perfection, vector arrows showing the ball's spin like—"

"Dad."

"—like a file of—"

"Dad."

"—a file of leaping porpoises."

"Dad! Don't figure it out okay? Don't analyze it, just do it. Please?"

"Don't think," he mused as we walked. "Don't goof off, don't analyze, don't speculate. Merely—"

"That's right," she said flatly, her head down and an arm behind her holding her bag as she quickened her stride.

"—touch it," he marveled.

"Right."

"Because otherwise," he explained to me out of the side of his mouth, "I could mess the whole thing up dramatically."

Spring comes with a rush to that part of New England, is the most hurried, in some ways least satisfactory season—static drizzle then sunshine, then rain again—blurs of brightness, blossoms exploding, gray gales, ruined flowers, everything too fast, robins and mud and pollen all confused in a flood of sneezy gold green . .

It had been clear as we had been playing. Now, as we moved up the eighteenth with our bags, you could see it was going to rain. Sliding over the hills the air bore a moist coolness, and though a thin light still touched the big firs along the fairways, in the west the mountains were darkening under a wall of weather.

## 7

As we came onto the green he didn't seem to know which ball was his. I pointed to it and he swerved, as if I'd pushed him, to tremblingly mark his white pilgrim, wipe it clean, replace it jigglingly, and take his putting stance.

The first of the three carefully considered practice strokes he now made would have sent his ball off the green. The second would scarcely have nudged it. The third would have missed it entirely.

He was putting out of turn. No one said anything.

"Just," he whispered, "touch it."

Nora lifted the stick from the cup and stood back, shutting her eyes.

He bowed his head and at last was still.

The breezes the storm was pushing before it stirred his hair, subsiding.

With the silvery head of his putter he touched the ball.

In his daughter's slitted eye the white Titleist wobbles, hesitating, and picks up speed. Finding its way down the slick inclined plane like a blind person's hands in an unknown room, at the last instant instead of zigging it zagged, ceasing to be visible.

At first he was bewildered. Then, as we congratulated him, a roseate dawn climbed the wattly neck, and the brown eyes went moist with real-time happiness.

I shook his hand.

Nora slung an arm over her father's shoulder to give him a kiss. This was hard for her. Nora was on the verge of her own rushed spring, the engorging eruption and explosion of all the weird flowers of adolescence. She loved, hated, wanted to help, wanted to understand, was driven to distraction by, was in awe of, felt for and was utterly, confoundedly disoriented by her crazy dad. Kissing his cheek she closed her eyes, in happiness mostly, and hugged. He hugged back, but suddenly he wasn't there.

He was thinking of something.

You could see it happen.

A message from himself to himself began to play behind the hazel eyes. The face went calm, the forehead as smooth as the sea when there is not a breath of a breeze. The uncallused hands were hanging, one gripping his putter, the other empty, at his sides as he stood slack-jawed, listening to his mind.

He went to his pullcart and slid his putter home and stood, hands on hips, looking at his clubs.

Wheeling his bag with its woods, irons, gloves, snacks, pencils, quantum equations, candy wrappers and spare cleats and the Sure-Loft wedge the kids had given him for Christmas to the green's far edge with a single, tottering heave he threw the whole thing in the carp pond.

Panting, he surveyed the drab water, when it had closed over the splash.

The rest of us were too stunned to move, let alone speak.

"Home!" he bellowed before we could come to ourselves, and up over the lawn and past the clubhouse we went, past the wall of evergreen forest, past the practice dial with its tilting pins, past the tiny proshop's rotting front steps, to the meerschaum riverpebbles of the parking area.

Back at the bungalow, in the disarray of his study, standing at the tackboard wall behind his Determinism worktable with its crisscrossing Reichenbachian time lines, he unpinned the charted scores of all his seasons, a Himalayan range of peaks spiking into the 120s but never, 'til this day, dropping lower than 103. He unpinned them all and took them down, folded them, committed them, with his golf videotapes and books and back-issue U.S.G.A. newsletters, to the wastebin he kept by his computer, and sat at one of his desks.

As the rain came at a slant against the windows he stood an elbow on his papers, cradling his brow in a palm, ignoring me. He scribbled, stopped, thought, made a noise in his throat like a wax record slowed with a finger, and was scribbling again, the big face frank and calm—even handsome, clearly unaware of me, of the rain, the rafters and crossbeams above us . .

As he worked I tried to relax. But I couldn't. I was sitting across from one of the world's most honored minds—professor, dazzling theorist, winner, in his distant youth, of the lofty Naumann prize for his work in proving the existence of mathematics. He had chalked up the awards, the published papers and degrees both ceremonial and real. He had popularized, in the TV series you may remember, his science, had jousted with the data, wrestled the squirming theories, debated the late-night cafe debates and suffered the petty politics. Now, in competition as much as in concert with a handful of equally brilliant, equally self-reliant colleagues around the world, he was mentally on the hunt for a brace of pristine equations—laws—that all matter and all energy obey at all times everywhere.

He sat back with a creak, flipping his pen and watching it fall. It fell onto his papers, rolled an inch, half an inch back, and was still.

"What," he asked, staring at the pen, "do you know about particle physics?"

Very little was the answer. Compared with what *he* knew, nothing.

"Nothing," I said.

He looked at me.

The rains spoke against the windows. There was no smile on his face, no passion in the staring intelligent eyes.

The moment changed, I'm glad to say, and he relaxed. He looked away passing a hand over a smile of inner amusement and said "heh, I too sometimes ah, feel I know nothing."

He gazed, still faintly smiling, through his spread fingers, and I waited. I had to wait awhile.

"Lately," he said, "I have been attempting to step back, to get a perspective. We scientists get caught up in, ah, oh in our observations and models and calculations and . . "

He made as if to pass the open hand again before his expression, as a magician waves gloved fingers before upsidedown hat. But the hand fell. He sighed. The eyes went distant and he talked on. He talked of the need to fling wide the portals of the thinking mind, study history, study biology, study philosophy and even poetry, as well as physics—get away from the lab, away from the blackboards of equations and out into the gardens of some of the other disciplines, to refresh oneself . . . further unbuttoning his already unbuttoned collar to yank it away from his neck, he sat deeper in his chair, eyeing me like a bulge-eyed frog.

As he talked he scratched his scalp. Tapped the arms of the chair. In the gray rainlight picked up sheaves of calculations only to let them drop, sidesliding, as he spoke of Newton, Galileo, Einstein. With his hands open, palms down, floating above the clutter on the desk, he paused for breath. He spoke now in a different, quieter voice, of Uncertainty. Heisenberg's great breakthrough of the '20s, the discovery that the micro-world of basic particles and forces is indeterminate. As he went on he warmed to his subject, worshipful of it, trying to speak of physics in simple terms, that I might understand. He described a world—ours, at the subatomic level—that was flux, a shifting maze, a cauldron of fizzing infinitesimal matter-events that suddenly come into being and as surprisingly disappear, a cosmos of maybes, of disguises and odds, about which we may write equations only if our equations embrace that bustling micro-world's fundamental unruliness. The very act of observing a subatomic particle changes the particle's behavior. To measure an electron's momentum precisely one must give up knowledge of its position, and vice versa. His voice filled with feeling. He forgot me, getting to his feet, pushing his chair back, drifting to a window to gaze at the drops streaking the glass . . . one measures an electron's position with precision, he said, at the expense of knowing anything precise about its momentum. The uncertainty principle underlay everything, he said to the windowpane in a burry, reverent tone, lifting a hand to touch, delicately, some talisman before his eyes on the invisible air. The uncertainty principle was bedrock, the sure, clear basis for all current theory . . . stepping back from the window, murmuring—I leaned forward straining to hear but couldn't—he sat heavily, not looking behind him, where he thought his chair was

I would be up there on and off for several years. The interview never happened, but we did become friends. I was invited often and even did some work for him, joining the loose salon of friends, relatives, graduate students, quacks, colleagues, hangers-on and assorted other eccentrics that he supported, in one sense or another, in that place of streams, forested ponds and leafy, shaded ways.

It was new to me and more fun than I had ever had to make the drive north out of the city and into those hills, to play the games of debate and meet the characters who came and went and to hear Eden, astride—precariously—a floating inflatable duck under spring pines and a burning summer sun, elucidate a distinction between two intellectual loci so elusive, so rarified, you had to shut your eyes to see it.

His family thought he was crazy, but even if they weren't, it doesn't necessarily follow that he was. He did get a glimpse sometimes, scribbling at one of his desks in that raftered room, or on a scorecard while waiting to hit, or at a cafe down in the seaside university town where he taught, or inching through the imitation-velour-roped maze of the airline line or waking, overheated, in his bed in a lonely hour to paw for the lampswitch and his pad and pen.

At the end I would see him wild with his mind's desire, shag-bearded, the friendly brown eyes crazed and lost, white-robed Sufis whirling in the yard, this raftered den, the whole bungalow, jammed full of strange new machines and people. And I would wonder what is inevitable in this life and what not. But really whether his absentminded lack of coordination was the result of, or the reason for, his idealism is a question with its tail in its mouth.

. . . picking himself up, a knee on the floor, head down, ball of a foot (heel raised) on the floor and the fingers of both hands splayed against the rugless hardwood in parody of a sprinter starting, he wavered, pink-faced, to his feet. As I sat back down he resumed his chair and impassioned narrative, speaking to me now of hadrons and quarks, of dark matter, of spin and strings vibrating that could be anything, the poetry modern physics can't do without. He was as serious as he could be. You could see it in the earnest posture, the brown eyes' pain of concern. He said nothing about the fall he'd taken. He talked on but was unsatisfied. I was grasping next to nothing of what he was trying to get across, a fact I'm sure my expression made obvious. He stopped—grabbed his pen, scribbled, head cocked as he wrote, and I waited. Quickening, the spring rains drove the windows sideways.

He dropped his pen and banged his desk with a fist. Looked up blackly at me, not angrily, just intent—the plastic big face a mask of concentration and will.

"Hold your hand out," he commanded.

I did so.

"'K," he said. "Look at it. What is it?"

"It's a hand."

". . made of?"

"Well," I said, looking at it, "it's made of skin. It's made of muscle—"

"That's not a hand," he rumbled leaning forward, "that's space. That thing you think is your hand is empty space, empty space with forces in it, with electricity in it. It's not that simple but let's say it is, let's pretend it is. That thing . . look, look at it. Your hand? No! A world of night, a world of empty night with a zillion billion bright little somethings—particles, impulses, ideas, tones—we don't know what—zooming around."

He sat back to assess me. The eyes were alive and terrible in their knowledge, wrinkly at the corners but at their centers unmoving.

"It's true," he said. "That's all that thing you call a hand is. It's all anything is. You, me, matter, energy. Listen—"

Lightning ran down the sky.

His head jerked.

"We're made," he said, turning in his chair to stare at the dark window where it had been, "of atoms. It's more complicated by far but—" head ducked and a hand lifted, begging patience "—let's just say atoms. Let's start with that. You're made of tiny atoms, each with the power of a summer lightning storm coiled in it. Think of it. Atoms pulling, dancing, jostling, pushing—tiny coiled lightning storms, tiny potential hydrogen-bomb bursts inside you, attracting, repelling, pushing each other away, pulling each other toward each other across kilometers—relatively—of empty darkness . . . and that's all. That's all you are. And—"

He lit a cigarette.

To the rhythms of the rain drumming on the windowglass he smoked awhile.

"That's all anything is," he said quietly. Thoughtful now. In a private, self-absorbed calm. "The sun. The sea. A flower. The gum on the theater floor. E played on a cello. It's all just particles. The sky's made of 'em. The air before your eyes . . . little summer lightning storms, all the same and just put together differently, if only we could figure out how . . . everything," he said wistfully, "everything and everyone . . . is atoms; everything's made of atoms . . . " With lidded eyes he drew on his smoke. "Except my wife."

# 2

When Picasso slapped the face of woman sideways, put her eyes on the same side of her nose, gave her her and somebody else's arms and broke her apart into angles, torquing the human physique so that when you look, she and her sisters are sides: tribal mask on a river-maiden's whitebelly body, all this, according to my uncle, presaged not only an artistic but an economic, military, medical, psychological, religious, social and scientific future of dislocation, i.e. now.

Some era is always ending, he said, some new era is always coming in. History is always coming to a terrible special pass. The future, he was saying, pacing that room itself so like a mind with its laden desks and shelves and the weeping rains trying to get in, is a constant clownface of change. The future is a grinning face floating ever just ahead, leering back at us as we approach it, ever receding yet always close, and, he said, stopping to try to mold the air with clawed, pudgy hands, he wanted to understand. He wanted to learn he said, to understand . .

The door slammed open, banging the wall with a bounce.

Rairia Hope was big—big hips, big rear, pillowy big shoulders, olive-complected face, eyes whitedark and dramatic, holding horror. At that time in her life the shining whites of her eyes were floodlit with fear, or some wild revulsion.

Her black hair was rich falling beside her cheek, and when she drew her fingers through it to get it off her face, falling to her shoulders, when she dropped her hand, with a silken musical heaviness he had hoped some lover or other would by now have found alluring.

"Nora," she stated, "says you threw your clubs away."

Her shadow fell on his ideas, the envelopes, cards, notebooks, pads and loose sheets. Her silence loomed over him where he had sat, fast, at her entry. As the seconds wore on and she stood her ground, her silence tried him, convicted and condemned . .

"Well," he uttered.

He sat a little forward and stage-looked through some papers.

"Well yes," he quietly answered the ongoing, glaring silence, "I did. I did throw them away."

There were shouts and laughter and distant indistinguishable music through the open door. That house was always full.

"Well that's wonderful Eden, that's marvelous, it really is. This is the last straw, it really is—I mean are you proud? Are you proud of yourself? Would it ever occur to you to give them to somebody if you don't want them? Did that ever occur to you? Does anything ever occur to you that's practical? I mean does it? Do you ever trouble yourself to use your mind to think of anything in the world at all except—"

With a wave she disdainfully indicated the room.

Cocking his head he smiled at his papers.

"Yes," he said slowly. "For ah, example—"

She stepped forward in a single fast stride, the air moving around her. Leaning over his desk she pinched the cigarette he was lighting and stabbed it out, savagely, in his ashtray.

"I won't," she told him in a tone low and full somehow of the same strange light that filled her eyes, "bother asking why. I know better. I know better than to ask that question. You ask it, you ask 'why,' oh yes, you ask it of the world, you ask 'why' of the world, but the world isn't supposed to ask it of him," she said to me without turning.

Clutching and squeezing the balled-up handkerchief she was never without, she looked around distractedly. I thought she would flee but she didn't. She looked at me as if I were a cigarette.

"Has he been acting strangely?"

"I'm not acting strangely."

"I'm not asking you," she let him know without taking her bright, dramatic stare off me. "I'm asking you," she told me pointedly. "He's been acting strangely so I need to know if—"

"Rairia for god's sake, how could he possibly—look. I'm not acting strangely. I haven't been acting strangely, all right look. This—" he waved a hand to indicate his study "—is not acting strangely. This—" with shocking agility he managed to sit upsidedown in his deskchair—legs kicking over the chair's back, arms—backward—holding onto chair arms, head hanging upsidedown off the seat's front "—is acting strangely," he said with difficulty, the upsidedown face going red. "This is strange action, not—" with more difficulty than he'd gotten into the position with, he strugglingly righted himself. "Not wanting to—" he was dizzy "—not wanting to come ahh, to an overall understanding of the universe."

"I really don't know Eden, I really don't know why you do what you do. I would have thought you would at least—nevermind. Nevermind. Do what you want. Do what you like. He will anyway."

With a groan she wheeled and quit the room massively slamming the door.

It had stopped. A golden light was beginning to spread on the windowglass, and he could see, as he sat, turned from me in his chair, wisps of faroff blue through the forest. As he watched, a few trillion more photons came streaming through the waterdrops atremble on the glass, a sharp wonderful brightening that he had to squint to keep looking at, and that I found myself hoping he would take as a sign.

Realizing he'd lit another one he looked at it fondly. He held it at bay to rub an eye with some knuckles preparatory, I suspected, to making a wry comment that would put what had just happened in context. But the door slammed open. She stood before us like statuary, magnificent in diagonal shadow, a sash of darkness—slant-seam between light and gloom, the way the sun was shining in—dividing her from shoulder to opposite hip.

"I just want to tell you," she told him, "that I hope you don't think it was in any way an existential act because—"

"Ag," he blew out, throwing his hands up, "that's not even—"

"Because if you do Eden, I can tell you it wasn't. I can tell you definitively it wasn't. It wasn't anything of the sort. It wasn't existential and it wasn't heroic and it wasn't funny. It wasn't humorous. And it wasn't kind."

"—not even remotely—"

"And it certainly," she bored in, "wasn't spontaneous. I can tell you that too so you can set your mind at ease about that, he can't comfort himself with that. It wasn't in the least spontaneous, because he isn't. He'd like to be but he isn't, well it's true, you know it is Eden, you try and try, but he couldn't do something spontaneous if he planned it."

"First of all . . ."

For some minutes now they wrangled over whether it had been his intent, in throwing his clubs in the pond, to commit an existential act. Also over whether throwing one's clubs away is in fact—or could be, under certain circumstances—existential, and finally over the definition of the word.

They knew what they were talking about and took it with the greatest intellectual seriousness, but it was personal too, that was every bit as clear. Their spats were this own-little-personal toy they shared, that they alone knew how to use and, painful as it could become, could not refrain from playing with.

Tiredly, Rairia quit a point she was trying to make mid-sentence and sagged. "I don't know," she said, "I really don't. I want to ask, I want to know Eden, what will you do? You've played your golf all these years. You've taken your lessons, you've kept your scores, you've been to golf camp. So you're no good at golf, so what? What theory of objects do you think you're operating in? It's bad faith to quit just because you don't happen to've been born with—alright, fine. Nevermind. I can see—"

she held her hands up in surrender "—no more golf, fine, you've chosen. But seriously. You know Dr. Wister says you've got to have a hobby, so what's—"

He yawned nastily and scratching his scalp, and holding his cigarette high above his head to stretch, said, more loudly I think than he intended, because he was talking through a yawn:

"Hot-air ballooning?"

Her sigh was like a billboard.

She put her head down and started out of the room again but thought better of it. Stood her ground before the open doorway, her back to us.

"Nora," she said without turning, "has her party tonight."

"Oh I—"

"Oh I. Well. Oh I. I thought you might like to know. I'm driving her over."

"Want me to?"

"Why would you want to?"

"Why I—"

"That's why I'm here isn't it? Isn't that what I'm for? To take care of the house and your last child for you while you hypnotize yourself with your so-called brilliant studies, isn't that right? Hm? Eden? Well isn't it?"

"Mom can drive me," unseen Nora's voice chimed too cheerily from somewhere beyond the open door.

Into the room shot Alan Elwive passing his gramma's vast haunch at top speed, blond head down like a battering ram.

"And who," his grandfather inquired of the small figure as it tried to clamber into his lap, "might this be?"

"I might be Darf. I'm Darf, I'm . . .Vader."

"Alan Granddad's trying to work."

"No he ISN'T!" Alan shouted, head down, still trying.

"It's all right Rairia for god's sake it's—ahem." Standing an elbow on his chair arm he peered through the V of his own arm at Alan whose face, looking up, was wonder. "So my friend, do you know . . what . . I'm . . going to do?"

Bug-eyed, Alan didn't.

"I'm going to tell—"

"A storee!"

"Oh you think so?"

"Yes I do fink so."

"Well you're right." Sitting back he looked down as if from a chiseled height like Abe himself great on his marble seat. "And know what?"

"Yeah," Alan said softly.

"What."

"Don't know."

"Well," Eden said. "It's going to be the most amazing—"

It was as if a vacuum brought into instant being by Rairia's exit sucked the door shut behind her *slam*.

"Dat hurts my ears."

"Nevermind. Gramma's got work to do and she's got a lot on her mind. We're lucky she's here. Come here. Come up here. Okay. Comfortable?"

"Yeah."

"Once—" the rich bass slow "—upon a time . . "

Cradled in his grandfather's arms Alan sucked a pair of middle fingers and stared—lost—into the story as it unfolded.

It was, as he had known it would be, more amazing than any he had ever heard. There was a boy named Joe who had a tiny ant for a friend and there was a backhoe with a purple button on the dash that Little Joe must never—ever—push but does, causing *Tyrannosaurus rex* to boom from the forest. The ice-cream-truck driver nervously offers the monster a cone. Leaning down like a gray mountain falling, the dinosaur politely eats the truck.

He effected a reconciliation of sorts with Rairia—tense whispered appeals, her skirts aswirl in the long living room, his hands out—palms up in appeal . . . Rairia muttering, seeking a window. He steps cautiously over the upended tricycle. She is listening at least. They stand before the terrarium, his hands palms-down now, pacifying, patting the empty air downward—everything all right, he grateful, thankful, appreciative. Clutching her handkerchief she accepts a hug and lowers herself, with dignity—Alan's eyes are wide as he looks up in his gramma's spreading shadow—to the threadbare carpet to play some blocks.

Behind the lenses of his spectacles the brown eyes sparkled with a deepening and stormy concentration as he beat me twice at checkers. He seemed to know the whole game after the first moves. When I took some extra time to try and extrapolate out a particularly thorny sequence, he giggled, smoothing his moustache with a froglegging forefinger and thumb.

"That way madness lies," he teased. "Heehee."

He actually said "heehee," the sonorous bass breaking into a 19th-century Russian-novel-character's titter.

Finishing off the last of his idea of a light supper during the course of which there were songs, the phone had to be answered, an encyclopedia consulted to settle a dispute, and he got into a shouting match with a dinner guest over whether or not the neutrino has mass, he took Emma for a walk.

Swinging his arms for exercise, humming, muttering to himself, tripping over rocks, he circled the wildflower meadow, Emma exploring and sniffing and running with flat ears out around him and then, stopping to watch him stride into the far forest, and cocking an ear to stare, turning to trot back to the bungalow.

Near and at a distance as he strolls the trees change position around him. He is smelling the woods' nectar, the sap of the year's new shoots, the musk fragrance of alive dirt and can feel on his cheek the cool of the evergreen dim as he hikes through the trees, listening to the insects' and birds' noises.

Bad camper, wildlife ignoramus and klutz that he is, the beauty of the natural world does touch him. He holds his face to the wetted air. To be here in mountain woods after rain with the chartreuse canopy of the season's new foliage filtering the sun, walking now on needles now on leaves from the autumn before, all the leaves overhead new in their yellowy green dripping, the air even here in this pool of shadow jeweled with treasure-chest light—to be in these woods that ultimately do not care or even take note of you as you walk, is mightily peaceful. He is fifty-nine, walking in May with this exquisite early evening light streaming down all around him through the high boughs. He smells the forest's chemical communion with itself. He is passing through some beech trees' gray trunks, then hemlocks' pungence, then tall hardwoods' raindarkened girths. These leaves underfoot from the autumn before are slippery—his sneakers are getting wet. The ankles of his white, elasticless socks are wet. The wilderness—for this second-growth forest is wilderness as far as he's concerned—in its not-thinking odors and the air-cool, humid spaciousness of grove and glade—is a boon to his lardy heart.

*Here* the insects' and birds' intricacy of communication is saying. *I'm here. I'm here here here . . . well that's fine* they warble, buzz, twitter and chirp back and forth, *that's fine. You're there, but remember, I'm over here. Hear me? I'm over here . . . are you like me? Yes I am stay away, I'm like you, stay away—stay away, away . . .*

He stops now, to look up, and stands
looking
through treetrunks

# 3

flat of water calm
green
under forest branches slides
quiet
through gnarls and the fairytale quarrels of roots in mud banks.
There is a hang of damp, expectant air above a trout stream

He stands among the rainheavy boughs, shiny laurel leaves
watching his brother fish.

Flicking his rod like a lizard's tongue Lim Hope is keeping his eyes on a point amid the current's subtle vagaries and slow swirls of speed—the spot he'll cast to. His forward-backward-looping line becomes slower on the air, smoother, longer, unfurling in lengthening smoothing curves. Not once looking away from his target-point on the whorls and ravishments of change, Lim stops his rod. Slithering through the air to settle onto the currents his line lies out across the water now in a river itself—thread-thin—of low-frequency waves floating, across-stream in curves, downstream in Eden's gaze with the water's endless slide in Eden's gaze, which has not a thought in it.

This—so lovely—is sensation. What his eyes are seeing is entering his mind unanalyzed as he stands wheezing in the forest's shadow vaults and warm tallow ponds of light.

The angler's head turns.

"Someone there?"

"It's Bishop Berkeley."

"Eden?"

"I have given up golf."

"Wanna try fishing?"

"Sure."

"Stay where you are."

Cranking in, Lim secures his fly to the miniature ring for it on his rod, and wades ashore, his hip-boots' straps dangling as he climbs the bank, his rod pointing everywhichway but never scraping treebark or catching a bush as he clambers up.

When he takes his cap off his perspiring head is almost perfectly spherical, brown fuzz on top like down on a peach. The lenses of his glasses are round, his surprised eyes round, the expressive small lips sensitively, perpetually worried. A second chin. The goggly, worried eyes. Eden imagines cartoon commas of sweat flying out in dynamic halo from around his little brother's amazed expression.

"Come on kid, we shoulda done this years ago, but you were never interested. We'll catch you a trout. Come on."

Eden is shown the rod, and its uses are elementally explained to him.

There is neither unfriendliness nor gentleness in the way little brother guides absentminded ocean-liner big brother down the bank and in. Lim's ushering arm is as careful (he, like Nora, knows what Eden is capable of in four dimensions) as his words are sharp.

"Get wet," he snaps. "Get your clothes wet Edie, wade out here beside me."

"I feel I'm about—heehee, to be baptized . . "

"Don't be funny. Take the rod. How's the work?"

"Good," Eden whispers.

Lim eyes him. "You sure?"

"Oh sure . . "

"It's coming along?"

"Oh sure," Eden whispers, thinking, not of his work, but of this that he is in, this hallway of forest, the moist alive air over the water, and the water itself nameless in volume and mass, carrying on its ton-swirling surfaces the last shells, shields and lance-glimmerings of the day's sun.

The flowing water is cool against his legs and he is trying to learn but when he casts the line collapses in tangles on the current to drift, in the exact, pathetic pattern in which it fell, downstream without result. Lim coaches, badgers, encourages, and this time when he tries again, wide-eyed with the beauty of what he's doing and the surroundings he's doing it in, alas again his line half-drags forward over a shoulder to fall in sad wriggles on the endless, flowing slide.

A shadow at his elbow in the twilight, Lim again shows him how, and again wants him to try.

He is staring into a flow of swirls, sliding currents and ripplings, little differences before his eyes in the dusk light, the bottom rocky here and still dimly visible in places, the sensation of sideways-pouring water dizzying to him as he looks into it, until he is not standing on hard bottom but is flowing with the currents in a vertiginous trance of not moving yet ever, somehow, moving, the stream pressing his walking shorts tight to his legs, the forest a single shadow now instead of separate trees—water, wilderness, brother and disappearing sky pressing in on his spirit in a drama of such intensity and hope that his arms feel light and his guts all loose and watery, as if he were water . .

"Oh yeah like that." Lim's voice is anxious in the shadows. "Okay again, that's the way."

This time the cast is merely mediocre instead of terrible, and he gets a second or two of natural float.

A little fish splashes.

Before realizing the splash was nowhere near, and therefore had nothing to do with, his cast, he knows the hook of the cosmos, echo of cold faith infinite.

Experience and repetition, not epiphany, ignite the love that lasts. So it was with my uncle. When that little fish broke the water nowhere near his fly, he was hooked. The water got into him. But life-lightning strikes slowly, so he didn't know it then—just that he was moved . . but it happened. He was hooked. He would have years—good years—of planning to go fishing, thinking of fishing, dreaming of fishing, writing about fishing, remembering fishing, talking and arguing about fishing, lauding, doubting and scrutinizing fishing, fishing, reading about fishing, listening to stories about fishing, giving and getting advice, buying equipment, getting angry fishing, traveling to fish, being sad due to being unable to fish, being sick and therefore unable to fish, feeling sorry for himself over not having been asked to fish, feeling like a boy, giddily wonderful heading out at sunrise to fish, studying fishing, making jokes about fishing, teaching a kid to fish, hoping to fish, loving to fish, longing to fish, explaining it, or trying to, to someone who doesn't do it.

His line hangs heavy now, bellying downstream. The float is over, Lim is explaining, the visor of his hat aiming up in the gathering shadows at his taller-by-a-head brother. This next one will be the last, the smaller silhouette explains to the bearish larger one where they stand, side-by-side under the high shadow of forest. But suddenly the smaller figure is alert. He holds his brother's casting arm and bids him wait, points to where the trout rose—there, there it is again. He tells him to wave his rod, get line out, see? There, no there—*there*. Gripping him Lim aims him, the two shadows appearing to grapple as, disorientedly, catching Lim's excitement if not his skill, Eden flails with his rod and suddenly, a scream having echoed off the dark, the tableau is frozen: Eden looking over and down in horror at his younger brother who, like a silhouette of Quasimodo trying to play a violin with one hand, is exploring to see where the barbed hook has embedded itself behind his ear . . . after a minute or so, the larger figure trying uncertainly to help and being waved off (told in a hiss not to move the rod, just—please—

let the line hang), it is free. One bleeding, one hangdog, they wade ashore in shadow.

Pulled by his brother's hand up the bank he steps into the trees and with lowered eyes stumbles on ahead into the darkness of his middle years.

He wasn't unhappy. It was a darkness, rather, in the sense that there was so much left to learn, so much left to understand.

There was so much to discover and study in physics, in history, in metaphysics, in military history, in life, in art and even theology—the whole outriding world of thought elsewhere in time and distant in focus from the incorporeal particle presences and imagined, mathematical universes of his vocation.

The "work," however, that his brother had asked after the progress of (sliding his eyes toward Eden when Eden had merely answered, "Good"), wasn't scientific. It was the opposite. My uncle wrote fiction, adventure fantasy. Stories grown out of bedtime tales he'd made up for the kids. He was currently on, or was supposed to be on, the fourth and final volume of his terrifically successful "Gwen saga," a narrative rollercoaster of braved monsters, cunning clues, unnatural disasters, insidious sorcerers and a village crowded with enraged clocks. THE LADY AND THE SWORD (for that was the tetralogy's name), having commenced with *The Search for the Sword* and continued through *Lady Gwen* and *I Dreamed that My Father Rode Beside Me*, was set to conclude with *The Sword's Return*, which Eden reportedly had been toying with re-titling, and a final battle scene of Herculean proportion—Good v. Evil, a titanic denouement, a *grande tuerie* and circus and reconciliation the prospect of which had my uncle's agent, a mundane man, who took twenty-five percent of everything, salivating. Or I should say Eden's agent would have been salivating, had *The Sword's Return* (whatever the title) not for many months now lain stalled, untouched, comatose as it were in sun-yellowing, dust-filmed piles on Eden's "Gwen desk" under the workroom's largest window . . .

Resplendently grieving she sits in the Horrid Hall, the plains around her castle running over with armies, guidons leaning into the wind, freaks taller than the tallest tree trampling her wheat. Her allies are galloping to their positions of deployment—pink gnomes, white-haired angels materializing above the cataracts' spume. Sidesaddle on his dragonbird the Master of Night smiles as he scans his bumbling legions. Gwen's long-fingered hand hangs off the throne arm. Her gaze tends toward the Sword, on its velvet retable, the Sword of Sighs, so dearly regained. Behind her, Blok, the King, with his poor Lehwhurlerra fluttering about his head, stares at her mother's bier. There is plenty of time though her counselors scurrying on their noiseless wheels, arms laden with scrolls and their caps falling off, do not act it. But there are hours—days perhaps—before that lovely, hanging hand must lift. From the dungeon kitchens seven walls away come warm smells of roasting suklets and camoria, the mingling of spices, brine of the great seven soups in their stewpots of bronze, for the children of Tarr will feast before they fight. Thank the mountains they at least are here. But why would the Night Master, murky, unmistakable in Lady Gwen's seeing ball, be smiling? Nothing is certain, nothing yet decided though her counselors, ignored by her, chatter their calculation papers up with a rustle of desperate proof to show the battle as good as won . . . her lover and his son are riding, they must be—she knows they are —somewhere over a desert and a steppe with their mounts' manes streaming and their deceived manfaces grim. They will arrive, though neither wheel-counselors can figure, nor seeing ball glimpse, when.

Her grief and sorrow are measured and deep, as they must be, but Blok mourns sloppily, a blast more like a throat explosion than a sob, the sound, in fact, of someone spitting iced tea, lemon, mint, tobacco, ashes, cigarette paper and sugar and ice a third of the way down the dinner table to our amazement and delight. My uncle's relationship with the physical world was, shall I say, dramatic, and a number of us, at dinner my first night there, had been well aware in advance what might happen when we watched him put his cigarette out with a hiss in the iced tea left in his glass, as he gamely answered Rairia's accusations regarding the throwing away of his clubs. Still it was a shock when, getting off a nicely turned phrase about the dangers of "hoarding one's successes," he half shut his eyes and dropping his hand to his glass swept it up and, pinky extended, throwing his head back drained it.

Only Rairia didn't laugh. She was so angry she couldn't even raise her voice.

"It's sophistry Eden, in French or not—" (he'd been speaking French) "—it's just words, words you don't even believe." I wished she would cry, but she was so distraught she was almost calm in an awful, trembly way, as if tears and anger and shouting were all imploding, crashing on her center. "It's sophistry," she told us, "and bad sophistry at that if there's such a thing as good. He threw his clubs away," she shuddered, "because he's an idealist—he's worse, he's a would-be idealist. Oh." Her voice was getting tighter and smaller and she seemed, figuratively, to want to turn away from each one of us simultaneously. "He's an abstraction," she whispered to herself. "He's a brain on two legs."

She burst into tears.

Nora: "Mom wait . . "

Cruel merriment sparkled in my uncle's eyes. Picking a piece of tobacco off his tongue he taunted his mate: "Oh Rairy you poor thing, your problem is you're made of atoms." Turning to Alan, in an aside: "Gramma's made of atoms."

"I am not," the big woman sobbed, "made of atoms and I don't—" sob "—know why he—" real sobs "—persists in persecuting me with it. I am not made of *atoms!*"

Some of us tried to circle a wagontrain of conversational first-aid vehicles and soup kitchens but he held a hand up, in benediction silencing us. He smiled over at little Alan, who, concerned for his grandma, had gotten off his chair and walked around behind her to rub her back, because that was what Alan liked when he felt bad.

"I'm sorry," Eden Hope said firmly. "I apologize." Hand up, head bowed. "I am sorry."

That was it. He sat that way, at the center of our granite silence in that messy room with Alan's bulldozers and forklifts parked among Straffordshire on easels and a couple of Fabergé pieces on the yard-sale sideboard, then dropped his hand. Like forest creatures venturing out after the earthmovers have growled past, here, there, a conversation started, and another, and in a minute the crickets were singing again in the screens, and we were eating and arguing and sending fireworks of laughter up, or going to get the encyclopedia, and someone shouted from the kitchen that there was a bear. We raced out to look. Stood on the rickety back porch staring into the insect-dancing glare of the flashlight Nora held, and a trashcan did lie on its side, with the top a few feet away, but we saw no bear. In truth, back at the table as dessert came in, it was more exciting to look at Chase Parr, the girlfriend of one of my uncle's students (a person named Bright) with whom Chase had come.

The greedy eyes lascivious with mascara, her cute bod alive dangerously under the soft, off-the-shoulder sweater she barely had on, her jewelry tinkling and her rapier nails digging into my arm, she wanted me to understand her enthusiasm—her love, though it was her first time here—for this place, these people, this evening and life on the planet in general.

"I want it," she thrilled, leaning a breast into my biceps, "to just stop. Forever. I cannot. Believe. I'm here."

You waited, with Chase. When she was up, her tone was awed and breathless, convincing to a fault—she was the lifelong pilgrim arrived at last at the holiest destination. You waited while the rapture waxed in her and the liquid, ravening eyes praised you and the hushed verbalization of her joy gathered in her—on stage for you, in love with you, worshiping you—

"I cannot. Believe. How lucky I am. I want everything to stop right now and be forever. I could die right now," she explained. "I honestly, truly, could."

Her blood-red talons gripped my arm, her high-fashion body like an electricity jolt near me. Chase Parr carried her sex about six inches out from her body, a range I was within. Candleflames bellydanced in the killer pupils. I was used to practical dinners at a friend's apartment down in the city where a group of us postgraduately were grinding toward our respective fortunes. Staying up late and drinking the extra bottle of wine or shooting pool in the second-story room of bright-lit tables that Edward Hopper could've painted, at the corner of Upper Broadway and I forget what cross street, we imagined we were wild. But our midnight bull sessions were about salaries and sports and the price of platinum. Philosophy, subatomic particles and what is existential and what is not, whether the human spirit is capable of progress—such things did not come up, in the city, in my life.

The mountainside night was blowing through the screens, the candles measuring the air's waning and waxing as we finished dessert. Chase's awed voice was now telling her dinner partner on her other side how she had marched. Absolutely. Marched. Into Bloomingdale's three days ago to buy all—all—new makeup. She fell into a whisper, her classy bangs over her eyes as she looked down. She spoke in a hush to draw him (a teenage lacrosse cousin of Nora's) physically toward her in a lean, to her date's annoyance you would've thought. But it was only momentarily that Bright glowered down the table at her as she practiced her wiles (having forgotten me) on her new instant swain.

Is the human spirit capable of progress?

Bright thought no. Wister said yes.

Spooning the last of his flan into his mouth, Lim Hope chewed and talked at the same time. "Whole question silly," he munched.

Speaking into the sudden sea of their stares I ventured to vote yes. After all, I tried, the idea of loving your neighbor isn't even two thousand years old.

Lim snorted. Brushing a flan fleck from the puckered cotton of his shirt's outrageous stripes, he put forth a single word for our consideration:

"War."

"What about it?"

"War's human," he shrugged. "Look at history."

Nora, unsure, yet obviously feeling strong emotion, offered, hesitantly, her opinion that the first human beings—weren't they, she asked in a small voice, like peaceful? The first farmers on the first farms? So maybe if we—

"Wrong," Lim interrupted. "Nice little dream Nory, the peaceful vegetarian farmer. But it ain't—" pick a tooth "—so. It was the early hunters, the meat-eaters, yes the butcherers of warm-blooded animals, who were relatively peaceful—see it isn't 'til you get to the first farmers that you start to get real horror war. Agriculture means organization, property, owned land, the fields you till, something to protect, therefore something to steal. And the organization you need to farm can be carried over to the techniques of killing, sorry."

Chin up, blowing smoke, her legs crossed while an impatient stiletto heel kicked the air, Chase Parr waited for someone to notice her.

Stubbornly, Nora stared at her plate.

She was holding onto something.

Her father was looking at her.

She stared at her plate, the broad chin firm, the blue eyes trying to be strong.

Eden looked at her. He looked young all of a sudden, simple and kind as he studied his youngest. In a voice of comfort, as if he were taking Nora's hand, though they sat three places apart, he said he wasn't sure war was the point. If one is talking about the progress of the human spirit, he said thoughtfully—speaking to his brother while continuing, fondly, to look at his daughter—perhaps one ought to consider the fact that while war is not new, the commandment to love one's neighbor (acknowledging nod down the table at me) is.

"And when they said 'love thy neighbor,'" Lim rapped, "that's exactly what they meant, neighbor, the person next door, your tribe buddy. Love thy fellow national. Love thy fellow tribe member 'cause you're gonna be fightin' by his side when you go out to wipe out the infidel. Notice they didn't say 'love thine enemy of a different color and religion far across the sea.' Will you turn that goddamned thing off?"

Chastened, Joe Bitterbeer did.

A pear-shaped man with an enormous Easter-Island head, Bitterbeer was testing his theories about the impact of music on life. From time to time he would twiddle the dials he wore on his chest, and the music emanating from him would change . . . when the war argument had started he had switched to the battle chorus from *Norma*, which he now turned low—scarcely a murmur issuing from the speakers he wore on his shoulders, while he scanned for a different selection.

The debate lurched on, Rairia getting into it, getting more serious and untranquil and angry until her anger over the point of view (whichever one it was) that she found herself compelled to attack rose undertonally threatening to burst from her like flame from the walls of a house getting redder and hotter and brighter-glowing until a room-sized puff of night fisted through the screens, leveling all four candles.

Dredging his moustache and lips with his napkin as the air stilled, and the flames climbed upright, Eden was watching his grandson.

"I think," he said, "Alan wants to say something."

Putting her fork down Nora leaned over her nephew where he sat with his chin an inch above his dessert plate, desperate to enter the dialectic, and straightened his napkin for him, as an afterthought brushing his whitegold hair with a swipe.

"First," Alan said quickly, "I would put fire in my space gun. But I woun' shoot it. I would shoot it *at* targets, but if, if, if I . . . if I went way way way way—" hands spread apart (aunt moves milk) to indicate the enormity of the distance involved "—way WAY far—" wincing with the effort required to make us understand "—to San Francisco onna train in 'bout ten hours!"

"Sounds right to me," Eden said. As we got up from the table our laughter was like downcoming branchfuls of brittle leaves, because dinners up there tired you out—wonderfully, but I saw Lim look hard at his brother, trying to divine something.

The Curtisses and Nora's lacrosse cousin, whom Chase had let drop, were building a fire in the fieldstone hearth flanked by Eden's books by the thousands on their shelves in the living room, because a chill had come on the night. Someone was tuning a guitar, to Bitterbeer's displeasure, and with their hands on their hips Alan and Nora, one looking up, one down, were negotiating Alan's bedtime as Eden, pinching a smile, stood listening to Chase's account of how the same person had snubbed her three times—three!—in a single day. A head taller and with a good hundred-pound advantage on her, my uncle had his arms folded across his chest and his appreciative, amused smile was peeking from either side of his lips' finger-pinched center. She came to his seminar often, tagging along with Bright to sit, swinging a heel, and say nothing, gala, bored, passingly interested in the actual physics, it seemed, when in the midst of his teaching he would glance over at her, which it was not difficult to do.

Lim was still upset and suspicious about something, you could see from the way he pretended to be browsing through his brother's library, and in the corner by the terrarium Dr. Wister and Chase's friend Bright had uncovered a mutual passion for hawks. They were deep in discussion, with bowed heads looking at each other's shoes and nodding, as Rairia swept in with coffee on a tray.

Tellingen was there that night, Tellingen, who believed nothing, the curve of his silver flat hair, that covered but half his skull, like the swirl in a marble. With his theory of reciprocal variability Tellingen was better known even than my uncle, and he sat in a corner, redoubtable, inconsolably honorable, having, in Eastern Europe a half century earlier, been given good reason to believe nothing.

He had been with my uncle that afternoon but sat alone now, holding his cup of tea, the simian, rounded upper lip smoothshaven.

It was a lot of people to meet at once and I couldn't then know who would rise above the background—who, so to speak, in time would prove who. I saw Tellingen, for instance, one more time only—I'm sure Tellingen was even then distressed by my uncle's peregrinations beyond the accepted bounds of their science—and Joe Bitterbeer virtually evaporated. Bitterbeer does not figure heavily in what I have to tell . . but that first night it was all new and pleasantly confusing, my uncle, his funny little brother, the great and powerful Rairia, Nora, Alan Elwive . . . that first of what would prove a hundred evenings and a hundred more, it was still all just an agreeable farrago. It occurs to me to wonder whether I really knew any of them any better at the end of my time up there than I did that first unsettling visit. Well of course the answer is yes, if I stop trying to think.

# 4

"Show you something," he said the next morning dropping plot notes, time lines and character summaries onto chairs to clear his Gwen desk.

"Lemme show—" hunkering, he was opening drawers and peering into them to collect paperclips. "Talk," he muttered, "a*hem*. Talk, debate . ." I had thought he was going to show me something about physics, but though the paperclip patterns he would make on the desk would be about physics, he was telling me—I realized after a moment's confusion—how he worked. "Yak," he said, "notes. Ideas. Get 'em, think 'em, get 'em down. Then a*hem*, ready to go to work, focus. Skittish. Can't get started, pressure builds . ."

He was arranging paperclip clusters on the bare desksurface. A grid of paperclip bouquets, each far from every other, each equidistant from the four nearest it. "Tension," he said as his fat fingers arranged and fussed to get each atom just so. "Increases. Can't think, blocked, damn, panic, ideas in the mind are blocked so . . . ahhh . . . behave badly. Behave rather badly, don't know why—seems to work. Selfish. Rant. Seclude self. Next morning, up before dawn. Remorse."

Producing a dime from the breastpocket of his pajamas he crouched lower still, the brown, fascinated eyes at desktop level, to sight with the dime. "Remorse," he repeated closing an eye. "A banana. Black coffee. Toast. Fresh juice. Remorse. No one else up, house silent. You see we think the neutrino . . . lemme show."

He had his dime ready and said "This—" about to fire "—is a possibly mass-less particle we can't see. Neutrino. Hard to trace. One way you can know one's around, er, was around, is when it bumps into a certain type of atom. There's a reaction of a certain sort, to which, when observed under the right conditions, you can attribute the—watch this—" sighting squintingly a last time "—the presence of—"

The telephone rang and the door banged open.

"The roof's leaking," Rairia said, compressing her hanky. "This house needs repair Eden."

He froze in mid-shot, his eyes—still aiming—widening and filling with trapped light.

Alan Elwive ran in.

"Alan," she commanded.

Making a very realistic sound like tires screeching when the brakes are slammed, Alan froze—head down—mid-stride. He held the position quite athletically, a runner's elbow cocked, a rear heel up.

"Grandfather," she told the cast Mercury, "and I are trying to talk."

"No," Alan said.

Straightening from his dime-shooting crouch Eden came out around a corner of the desk to set a hand on the boy's head.

"It's all right," he said. "Just wait one second, okay?"

"'kay."

"'kay," he said absentmindedly in the same affectionate tone to his wife—"I mean alright," he corrected quickly. "All right now honestly, I do know Rairy, I do know, we do need repairs, and if you could just give me—"

"A list," she rolled her eyes at me, "of everything we need . ."

"Would you get that?"

The phone. He meant me.

Dazedly I went to it and picked up.

"I got a idea," Alan offered. "I got a idea," he repeated, trying, as we waited, to figure out what idea he might have. "Okay I got one. I sit on grampa's lap an' gramma goes to do a launnnnn-dry an' you—" big-eyed, speaking to Eden "—tell me a story of a boy named L'il Joe wif—"

"Hello?" the voice in my ear was saying, "my brother there? Hallo?"

"Yes," I said. To Eden: "Your brother."

Lim through the phone into my ear sharply: "Ask him if he wants to go fishing."

I put the question.

"Yes!" Eden practically shouted. "Yes I do! Tell him I do, find out when—"

"Nancy's coming," Rairia remembered, pressing a palm to her brow in horror. "She's getting in this morning, I was supposed to meet her at the airport oh damn."

"Doan' say dat!"

"I mean 'shoot.'"

"Sayin' dam's roood."

"I specifically told her," Rairia marveled in dismay, "I'd meet her at the airport. Oh damn I mean—"

"I'm here actually," Nancy Elwive said.

"*Momma*!"

I held the telephone with his brother on it in my right hand as his older daughter hugged her mother giving me, over Rairia's dandruffy shoulder, an oh-god look of apology for them all.

Saying hi to her dad, with a quick wave she dismissed her mother's excuses for forgetting to meet her, did a sort of plié to scoop Alan up ("Mommm," he said happily, "mom-mom-mom-momma . ."), and with her chin to his curls smiled at me: "Hi. I'm Nancy."

She wore dragon glasses. That's how I think of them. You know the old-fashioned kind for women with frames curving out to satanic points? She had a short, thick helmet of black hair the same luxurious texture as Rairia's, and was small.

We shook hands.

She wheeled to peck her father's cheek.

"How's *The Sword's Return* goin' Dad? Hah."

Turning to the window he said "fine," then, still looking out, said, strangely, as if a spirit were saying it through him: "I think it's going to be called *The Tree of Life*."

"Really? The fourth book in the tautology or whatever?"

"Yes . ."

"Well good luck," she said turning with her boy in her arms to look out a window of her own—her chin on her son's happy head "—I mean you gotta do what you gotta do. Whatever the hell *that* means."

He was pawing for his brother so I gave Lim to him and he stood scratching his red-gray chest hair where it spilled from the fuschia collar of his pajama tops, his eyes lit with pleasure now to be talking fishing.

Nancy Hope Mann Elwive was direct and funny and reasonable and I liked her. If her cheery irony was a shield protective of some vulnerable childish self, then that shield had become reality—had been used so successfully and for so long that whatever fragile self may once have been there to guard no longer existed.

Later that day at her father's suggestion she took me on a tour, an elbow draped out the window of her rental car and Alan singing "Da *far*-mer-*takes*-a-*wife*" over and over in his carseat in the back. We drove to the lake, seeing at a distance through the tall evergreens pale figures jumping and splashing and fooling with sails and masts around and about the docks of the low-slung boathouses. Then down the mountainside she took us and into the white, black-shuttered village on its wooded slope. Beside the red library, on the green (mole-veined commons of benches and lovely old overshadowing chestnuts), a soldier of stone, with correctly bent knee, bayonets thin air . . .

Back up the mountainside we sped passing fields of wild grasses with post-and-rail fences and stone fences encompassing these lazy, open spaces of relative ease, and we crossed little streams that gurgled by brightly under us, passing through their stone arches . . . then suddenly you enter deep forest again, and glimpse houses, big ones, sprawled and lazing like great gorged animals behind their shrubs and ancient hardwoods, set back, in the woods' shadows, over rolling swells of daffodil-splashed lawn with glints of sunshine slanting from where the sky appears among highest branches . . .

"Whaddya think?"

I said: "Beautiful."

"It's a zoo. Believe me."

"What zoo?" the back seat immediately wanted to know.

"I was speaking figuratively," she explained, lifting her chin to look at Alan in the rearview and, seeing herself, firming her jaw.

"No you weren't," he murmured without conviction . . .

I never did get straight the Hope, Sellerworth, Grumman and MacAttick family lineage with its root systems of tradition and power, its knots of madness, its rings of wealth and blossoms of honor and lightning-scars of poverty and defeat, because it didn't matter to my uncle, though he'd been born to it and (spatially anyway) lived in it.

Eden befuddled the gentry up there. A scattering of white houses on a wavecrest of green, and the estates on the hills surrounding, Norham isn't old the way certain lay-bys of the Brandywine are, where they have raised being boring to an art form, or the places above Boston with their vowels like hammered boards. Norham is a hundred-and-fifty-year-old small-gauge summer railroad community, to which Eden's and Wister's and the Curtisses's ancestors once trained to sit on their porches, rest from their crimes, and watch the pines close over the pastures once more. It is—do I say "was?"—it seems so long ago—a pleasant place, eclectic, lovely, permissive—I mean with room for someone like Eden, whom in time I would start calling "uncle," though he was really just a distant, removed cousin of my mom's.

"Doomed," Nancy Elwive said to herself as we drove the shaded ways, passing in and out of the day's brightness. We passed barns, bicyclers, rivulet creeks, curing sheds, riders on horseback who waved, a pair of birdwatchers with their heads stuffed in a bush, sheep barns, springhouses, boarded-up skeet towers and a riding ring with a dozen colorful jumps.

"Doomed," she said insistently. "All of it."

"Really?"

"Doomed," she said dreamily, "doomed to the wrecker's ball. Doomed to—"

"Is that really true?"

"—to the developer's level, the logger's . . what do loggers use?"

"Grapple-skidders," the back seat provided.

"Doomed," she repeated gravely. "Don't you think?"

"I don't know," I said, "I thought—"

"Maybe it isn't doomed, but I think it is. I think it's doomed. What do you think of my father?"

"I like him."

"At least he thinks," she said watching the lane. "Nora's totally devoted to him. Totally." We were approaching a pair of faceless lions. "But my poor mother. She's going to explode. She's absolutely going to explode."

"Why's gramma gonna 'splode?"

"From frustration Alan, from her deep, abiding love for your grampa. Grampa's always all wrapped up in his thoughts, you know the science he does? The books he writes? She gets so, so lonely for him, she loves him so."

"Not," Alan laughed.

Nancy Elwive's voice lowered and tightened now as she spoke fast to me in an undertone through clenched jaw muscles: "you've heard of Gwen."

"I sort of have."

"His first wife, my pre-stepmother."

"Yes."

"Torrid," she said darkly. Straightening her arms she drove with noble responsibility. "Absolutely torrid. They couldn't keep their hands off each other. And that," she informed us, nodding to indicate the snarl-silvery grille of the black limo nosing at us from between the two stone lions, "is the Grummans." She pecked the horn. "A Grumman was Treasury Secretary once. Verrrry impressive, even though he was eventually indicted. But I can assure you of one thing. That limo's a rental."

She continued looking straight ahead but her smirk of a smile was etched now for at least a minute as we slipped down those pleasant ways, birds singing and flitting in the trees and flowers all over the place and the shadows of the sun splashing up and up the windshield and back down again sliding over our heads as we drove.

"Mom?"

"Just a minute Alan I'm thinking. I want to try to explain something to our guest here. We—the family. Let me start that again. The family, though I must say it feels more like they sometimes than we, as I live in Tacoma . . . I'm currently between divorces. I mean—" she sniggered "—between marriages I meant. What was I saying?"

"Mom?"

"Hm?"

"Grampa tells me a story."

"Yes?"

"A story of a boy named L'il Joe, L'il Joe wif an ice-cream truck an' a huuuge T-rex."

"Do you like the stories Grampa tells?"

"Yeah. Mom?"

"Yes?"

"Does Grampa have a penis?"

"Why Alan—why er, of course."

"How old is it?"

"Fifty-nine," she said keeping the car straight.

"How old would a new one be?"

"Four," she said without batting an eye.

Utter silence in the back as this information was processed. Then, as we motored on, a soft, contemplative, wordless singing came from the back seat as Alan considered his world.

She hit the brakes smoothly so there was a lurch but no tire-screech though Alan, feeling the momentum-shift, supplied one—"EeeEEEC!"—and we turned onto a different lane.

She said nothing as we wound our way higher through the trees. We turned left, right, left as we climbed. The trees opened.

I was staring at "Lookout" where it sailed against the sky. Towers and turrets, blazing windows of olden glass holding the setting sun's fires, faceted slate roofs, fortress double chimneys and cliff walls of blackest stone, archways, crenellation, gables of mystery among parapets, porticos and spires. Lifting above the surrounding hills and the city I had come from and my imagination's most fevered dreams, the old strongbox of a mansion did seem to move, as you stared—to sail, against the drifting clouds and blue . .

"Nursing home," she said with her jaw set. She turned us around and drove us back down.

I liked Nance from the first and respected her energy, so I was baffled when I discovered how untrue so much of what she said was. At the very beginning I assumed everything she said was meant. Then when I found out that Nora was far from "totally" devoted to her father, that the Hope-Sellerworth-Grumman clan was perhaps a little doomed, but certainly not seriously so, and that Eden's relationship with his first wife, Gwen Ledger, had been anything but "torrid," I overreacted and assumed Nancy lied compulsively about everything. But that wasn't it either, I came to realize. She was smart as a whip, and insightful too, and some of what she told you was a beam of pure particles of truth. And some was waves of fabricated intrigue. There it is. Was it a defense? An offense? Was she bored, frightened, totally compulsive? Just flexing her vestigial capitalist's muscles of command? Amusing herself? Looking for a world? Giving herself a vacation, betimes, from the stress of clarity and honesty? Yes.

I slept in a single room off the laundry behind the kitchen, a cozy-sealed tongue-in-groove-paneled chamber maybe eight by fifteen feet—draftless window, chair, dresser, new mattress. It was nice. A little cramped, but when you were up there you spent no time in your room anyway, except to sleep at night. The bungalow was well built, much of it—new and old both, some rooms level, plumb, caulked and sealed with luxurious-looking varnished paneling on the ceiling as well as the walls, and floorboard heating that worked. Other older rooms and quaint eccentric wings of little rooms were crotchety, drafty and atilt, smelled—

musk of summertime dust and damp. It was a house of sprawling additions, afterthought miniature parlors like cameos, nineteenth-century wallpaper, grandiose impractical soaring skylights and sunroofs and cantilevers, halls of cedar and best exposed pine and even, in the master bath, Spanish tile and some oak . . then two doors down a dilapidated sleeping porch built when Theodore Roosevelt had Brooks Brothers sewing pairs of spectacles into his uniforms and campaign hats in preparation for our national charge into a new century, not charming at all, the scuffy wainscotting so decayed and warped that at night light from rooms adjoining poured through in rays.

In the morning before he would start working he would invite me to his study to talk philosophy, or to explain what he thought the meaning of a certain sequence of historical facts was, before showing me out and closing the world and me out with a distracted wave and the door's latch's soft, final click as it shut behind him.

By the time he's finished for the day the sun is at its acme. Bursting with the need for exercise after so much thinking he explodes from his study corralling whoever he finds to join him . . hopping—tilting—sideways on a foot in a race against the seconds to see if he'll get his swimming trunks on before he crashes into the dresser. He is talking to anyone who'll listen. He is ordering hash-fruit-coffee-ham-toast-eggs in answer to Rairia's shrieked query from the kitchen. Wolfs it all down and hustles us out of the house and over, in his shabby car, to the lake for a swim.

He drives in to the village for the mail which he sorts methodically, looking for a letter from his son though he won't admit it, standing in sunlight in the street beside his car where he slammed the brakes on at the edge of the Post Office lot when, driving off, glancing up he saw in the rearview the fluttering white storm of his flyers and letters and magazines and bills and catalogues.

Rushing to get dressed for the Curtisses's dinner that he doesn't want to go to, and that Rairia doesn't want to go to, and that they're going to because Rairia is reading a book called *Doing What You Don't Like*, rushing to dress, hurrying past the dresser toward his closet he bumps the table lamp on the dresser and spins—the lamp is falling—slow-motion crisis—lamp is tipping and will fall, strike floor, shatter—he hurls the shoe he's carrying at the unbalanced lamp, for once in his life on target, and will explain afterward that it had been "my intent to divert lamp, ah, in mid-fall into the wastebasket which I knew had socks and newspapers in it, and so would cushion the, er . ." —catching the falling lamp perfectly with his flung shoe to his wife's utter disbelief he pulverizes it, powders it, she told me awedly, like a clay bird passing through the pattern's center.

Rairia had been emerging from the bathroom, nicely atingle from a scalding shower, and had at first thought he'd shot the lamp with the buckshot-loaded derringer she kept for snakes.

Exactly counting the exactly-brimming final spoonful of coffee into the filter, he clicks the machine on and steps out onto the back porch. Bare feet feel good in summer on wood. Human eyes like all this green. Fighting squirrels spiral the mulberry trunk, a terrific hissing comes from the kitchen behind him, he swirls to race indoors to the coffeemaker which is spraying boiling, clear water onto warming circle and counter and floor.

His absenteeism from the existence you and I know was less a removal from the physical world than a kind of waking dream of that world, a dream of himself and you and me and that still largely unspoiled Berkshire countryside as the coupling and uncoupling, along stunning contours of space, of ideas.

As a boy, in that impossible mansion that I can see if I shut my eyes, moving—appearing to move—like a many-atticked quinquereme against the blowing sky, he had tried to keep quiet. But the excitement would mount and he would start to ask questions, unanswerable ones, too many questions. His father's evening paper would collapse like the dynamited front of a building to reveal the elegant, sad face.

I heard from him how as a child he had gotten only fair grades in school then out of the blue would score perfectly on some strange quiz the rest of the class hadn't even understood.

The others flee, kids in quick evasion the way a scared school of fish turns, and he is left giggling and holding the shattered creche that he did not break, and that the others thrust into his hands at the last instant as now, in darkening vacuum, the shadow of his mountainous, vast-breasted fourth-grade teacher chills his afraid-to-turn back . . .

Patiently running the bath water his mother kneels, in the white tile bathroom light, to work the silver taps. She says "That's all right Edie" in a voice he knows means it isn't as he stands behind her crying, barefoot on the cold floor clutching his bugle, covered head to toe in the MacAtticks' cows' still-warm manure.

"Easily told," he said of his life, throwing an opening hand up. "Too young for Korea, too old for Vietnam. Fifties college, Kerouac, bowties. Loved science. Good at. Married my first wife, Ledger, first name Gwen, from these hills. Our son Thomas sells—" pain in the brown eyes "—sells knives by direct mail in Ventura. Not too much contact. Not any." He hung his head, then shook it off. "Rairia stole me from Gwen. Stole me," he repeated in sad thoughtfulness, "I'm ah, sorry to say. Name Gwen coincidence, pure coincidence—" bending to sight with his skimmer dime among more paperclip clusters "—and so we find ourselves, we find—" ready to fire "—ourselves a long way from the Greek simplicity of Democritus's atoms, a long—" ready, steady . . . aim "—way from the notion that everything's made of earth, air, fire, water. Now it's quarks, super-tiny things you can't see with the eye. You see them—" flicking his finger "—with your mind. You see them by seeing the results of certain infinitesimally small, infinitely quickly over-with collisions in which they participated. You see them through pure mathematics, through correspondences, beautiful, beautiful symmetries—" sending his moon-silver 'neutrino' skimming through all the paperclip bouquets on the gleaming desktop. Not having touched a one, his dime dropped off the far side of the desk and I got up and retrieved it for him. "Thank-you. Now. We're close to a fundamental understanding—" fingerflick: *zing*—again missing all "—of how matter and energy work." He coughed loudly, his face low over the desktop. He explained to me that the reason he and his colleagues had decided that the wacky modern extended family of tiny particles exists (or, for some particles, once existed) is that, observing the off-showerings of the particle collisions they learned to make occur in their colliders, they saw spins, trails, ghosts of things, debris, fragments, wreckage, on a sub-subatomic scale, that implied, if they decided to read it a certain way, the existence, perhaps, of all these charming mind-discovered gluons and quarks and leptons . . . he explained how at Time's beginning the universe was so hot everything meltingly was the same—protons, gravity, electromagnetism, you name it. This state of affairs lasted a humonga-trillionth of a second before that first immense, scalding explosion. Cooler now, the universe has in it only some of the strange particles that existed, to our thinking, in that first burning instant. We've built collider tracks that can smash protons into each other off-spewing great tangled complexities of micro-debris. In the hotter-than-the-sun holocaust of these tiny particles' collisions, if we collide them year 'round, sometimes—quite seldom, but sometimes, if the collision was just right—we will see after-traces that tell us one of the weird original particles probably was briefly created. This helps us believe in the Model (which he went on to describe) that we thought up several decades ago to fit our knowledge and have been trying since, experimentally, mathematically, and successfully, to legitimize. Delicately with the hand that was not aiming his dime, which I had retrieved again and returned to him, he straightened a paperclip bouquet that his air had stirred. "We have figured out," he murmured, "that there are the following fundamental particles. Six quarks (one's missing but there's increasing evidence we've found it). Six leptons. Twelve gauge bosons. Two-dozen antiparticles. And something called the 'Higgs boson,' assuming it exists. Maybe it does maybe it doesn't, but we need it. And we know what we're looking for, so—" flick *zing, pow!* "—see? I hit one, very rare. Thank-you. Knowing what one is looking for certainly increases one's chances of finding it. Then of course watch this . . then of course—" flick zing "—whoops sorry. There are the four basic forces. Thank-you. If we can ever integrate rarity, I mean gravity . ."

It's hard to say what he wanted. Something of the heart, I have to think, as well as of the mind, something big—unattainable surely, even if it exists. A Final Theory of Matter. Energy and matter in universal, eternal lockstep to the tune of a few simple (if only one could think of them) formulas—I mean equations. God. What if reality were a formula!

He would not give up on it, was in fact beginning to get it mixed up with what he was—with his worth as a human being I mean.

This was a while in the knowing. I could not have known it then and so, naturally, didn't.

Neither did he—but I sensed it.

Why else does a grown man stand in a flowing stream for fifteen straight minutes with trout rising all around him and instead of fishing persist in fussing with every tiny fly in his box?

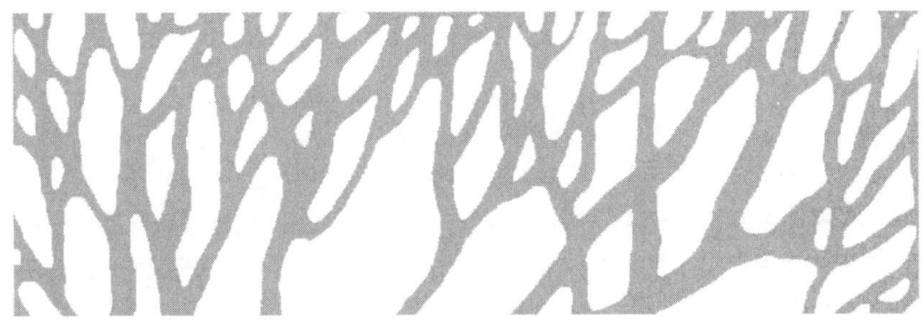

# 5

"He isn't any good at this either," Rairia mused.

We sat on Lim Hope's terrace gazing down over the lawn at my uncle where he stood in the water.

"He wasn't any good at golf," she said thoughtfully, "now he isn't any good at fishing."

The stream here was a flat of elegance with willow branches touching the smooth passing of the water over green and slow, swaying vegetation. Eden stood in the current laden with the equipment Lim had helped him buy, his net hanging down his back, his many-pocketed fishing vest abulge, his rod trapped under an elbow, his flybox open in his hands, the visor of his cap low over his eyes, splotches of sweat staining the underarms of his shirt—immobile, fixed as a statue but for the fingers fumbling and searching among the flies in his box as trout rose, making circles on the current around him.

"We're supposed to feel sorry?" she wondered. "I mean is it written that failure's noble? Is failure interesting? Is that it?" Not clasping her hanky, having, in her husband-inspired sarcasm, dropped it, she sat studying his distant hunched form with a steady squint. Balled it slowly, like a time-lapse flower, expanded on the flagstones by her right sneaker where she'd dropped it.

In the eternal flow that was before he was born and will be after his form lies on stainless steel, Eden Hope stands trying to close a fat forefinger and thumb over the fly he wants in the confusion of them all stuck to each other in the metal compartments of his box—tangles of fur, barbs, quill, hackle, awe, frustration, fuzz, wings—madness in the little divider compartments . . . trout are rising. He can see them out of the corner of an eye as he works. He can hear their splashes, feel them somehow, otter-lithe slippery-smooth bodies flashing and diving all around him, their life calling out to him, but he can't get his flies untangled.

Fingertips cannot solve this puzzlesnarl of artificial flies before glassy eyes. They stick, are mixed up, cling to one another, elude his pinch. Reaching for one he gets another. Near and far in the evening quiet they are surface-feeding, gliding up nose first to the seam between water and air to swipe with streamlined, waterlike body as they eat.

He's trembling he's so excited. Trout will feed like this then quit. He knows he hasn't a lot of time. But he needs to get the fly he wants—an Adams #18 Lim gave him two of and said should be perfect, but his fingers can't. He thinks he sees it in the tangled messes of flies of all sorts that he's been meaning to sort out and organize, but when his fat fingertips fumble for it, the one they come up with isn't it.

"I mean if the meek have to inherit all right, but do the incompetent have to too? And do we have to sit around and wait for them? Is this unreasonable to ask?"

I started to answer but she snapped "nevermind" and then, coming to herself, realized I wasn't Eden and apologized.

The current slides by under the trailing fingers of the willows. He has an IQ of 151 but the current slides by under the willows' fingers—slides, through the shadows cast by the far-shore forest, swirls gently around his boots, swirly glass, and the trout are wild for the wing pairs of hatching mayfly duns passing in review, but he can't do anything about it. He can't do anything about any of it. The feeding trout make their moon-crater circles that drift a short way on the water before disappearing.

Upstream Lim's line slithers out to settle, soundless, down onto the current—

something happens

Forest sky stream freeze and Lim snarls, no other word for it, yanking his rod high.

His left hand controls his line and he is keeping his blasphemous grin on the splashing to which his line runs from the elevated tip of his rod like a gondola cable.

Time, the stream, life and any chance of ever catching a trout on a fly sweep by Eden Hope where he stands in the water poking among his patterns. When there's a considerable splash not five feet from him he whispers: "Oh . . . oh—"

His rod slips where he has it under his elbow. He makes a lunge to save it and his fly box tilts, flies tumbling out, scattering, lightly, onto the current.

He bends to pick up as many as possible before they start to float in a spreading-out flotilla away, and his box, unnoticed by him, tips more.

A couple big sharp ones tumble out, lightly to fall, unnoticed by him, down inside his wading boots . .

Lim has released his fish and is wading ashore, glances across-stream at his brother with a look of incomprehension. Lowers his little head, frowning around a leer, and climbs the bank.

Sitting down among us loudly in his wet boots and unzipped vest, rubber toes akimbo on the stone, his gear dripping stream muck, Lim pulls over the big cardboard box I've been wondering about and sets to work unpacking his new artificial reality suit. His eyes seem ready to explode. Didn't I read somewhere the human body contains all the chemicals necessary to make a bomb? Haven't we heard of humans suddenly, mysteriously combusting, catching fire from within?

He didn't, but he looked ready to.

"How's he doing?" Rairia asked.

"My brother," Lim responded, struggling with the pieces of equipment packed tightly, his eyes laying swordlike about him as he labored, "re-ties the Gordian knot."

We look over the lawn. The object of this comment, bent at the waist, is reaching out for more of his spilt flies as they move away from him on the flow.

"Is he going to have like a nervous breakdown or what's going to happen?" Nora blurts.

Quick as it fled her bashfulness is back. Her stare is lowered, fixed on the mortar-joined stones. A honeyed strand, loosed from her gathered and pinned up hair, hangs down her temple by the strong jaw. The blue eyes hurt.

"Honey," Duffy soothes.

With her Ichabod nose, Duffy Ginty is a kind soul, a friend of Eden's and Rairia's from town. Duffy has the best butcher shop in the top half of the state.

"Nora," she says, "oh honey."

Leaning to set a bony hand on the teenager's arm.

"Honey," Duffy says with feeling, "believe me, yer makin' a mountain outta Mohammed."

Others were getting into an argument over whether turbulence theory can be applied to statistical trends in baseball but I didn't hear it. There was a call.

A Lim son stepped through a French door to gesture without politeness . . . indoors, when I picked up and said hello, a silence of static greeted me. The silence continued, holding me for pregnant fabulous seconds as I waited, until at last, without preface or explanation, a voice graven with awe, freighted with abject, disbelieving misery over the terribleness of its destiny, announced:

"I'm at the airport."

"Uh," I said. "Is this . . . I mean am . . is this Chase?"

"I'm nobody."

Silence again, an impenetrable well at the bottom of which her sexy little heart huddled, betrayed, lost, confounded by fortune, forced by an unfair world to withdraw and condense into purest self-defense.

"I don't," her lifeless voice revealed over the line's blackness, "know what to do. I cannot. Believe. What happens to me."

I asked what airport she was at.

"I wonder if it matters. I honestly do. Truly. I wonder if it makes any difference whatever."

"I would think it would."

"I'm nobody."

I could see the gorgeous eyes flashing with impatience, the wicked lips set downward—angry, despairing, the svelte body hunched, wrapped as it were around the phone—me—someone—anyone—for warmth against the meaningless vista, behind her through the great window, of jets' vertical stabilizers moving through one another like sails in an olden port.

"Sure you're someone."

"No I'm not. I'm nothing. But that's all right because nobody cares. It's just," she said, suddenly breezy, "the way it is isn't it?"

I stared at a silverframed photo standing on the glass top of a burnished mahogany table: the Lim Hope family in rugby shirts, lacrosse sticks at port arms. I said something generic about forking paths, hoping to calm her, and then, into that mesmerizing, thousand-eyed silence, I made the mistake of asking what the matter was.

She told me, her words in her fascinated-by-themselves eyes in the phonebooth glass in whatever airport coming at me with all the gravity and awful trite resolve of a soul reading by the metaphorical poor light of its insufficient heart for the first and final time the words on its personal tomb . .

"I can take," she breathed, "a flight home. To Denny Street, good old Denny, where I live. Or. There's a flight to Anguilla. To the most lavish." Slight sob, quickly controlled. "Incredibly lovely place and a person—if I tell you his name which I won't, and you breathe a word of it to a soul I will never trust another human being again. Ever. Who's expecting me. And I don't. For the life of me. Know. What—"

"What if—"

"I can't see!" she cried out, so convincingly that for a second I thought she was being mugged.

But she meant she was in a decisional fog over which flight and life-path to take. Now for several minutes we argued thus: I suggest Anguilla. She touts Denny Street, her comfy flat there, rest, relaxation, scrambled eggs at the corner diner at midnight, an emotional break . . . so I suggest Denny Street. She describes this guy's place on Anguilla, the possible missed opportunities for adventure, the possible missed opportunities for . . who knows? Love even . . so I question the wisdom of running back to Denny Street. Morosely she wishes to inquire of me if I have taken leave of my senses. Stubbornly, fondly, she defends good old Denny Street, in her bedraggled sadness, and not without a certain eloquence, so I question the wisdom of going to Anguilla. Snappy as an advocate she's ticking off the pluses of Anguilla . . . at last we hang up with wrenching, for me anyway, poignance and pain, though I had met her but once and had had maybe three conversations with her total. She could do that. She could get so familiar so fast and convincingly you wandered, from your conversation with her, back outdoors onto the broad terrace of real life dazed, these summer-clad women and men eating corn on the cob, this lavender sky above the willows' Nile-green cowls, this broad flat of water with a fat man standing in it, the dream, and your hermetic ridiculous recent conversation the reality . .

Catching sight of another—wings upfolded like a carrier plane's—he takes a roily step through the water to reach out

what sunset, bedazzling

can throw over a trout stream at eventide

blinding

bathing all things white, mayflies aflutter, the forest, his hands, his face—everything, as if all were light, the world made of pouring photons . .

Not twenty inches from his hand as he is reaching out a trout with a surge takes one of the flies he dropped shattering the evening light on the water into salients, twinklings, disappearing, of shimmery liquid light—

staring into the candescent lights in and on the water where the fish took he is hopeful suddenly with a replenishment of energy childish and, given his abilities, baseless and he knows it, but his heart doesn't care. Hunched over his box he manages to extricate one—any one (the two sharp ones inside his boots slip, unbeknownst to him, lower inside the rubber legs)

shutting his box and stuffing it in the wrong but easiest to reach vestpocket without looking he gets filmy leader end, after tense, willed moments of coordination, through eye of hook. Making his knot he pulls prayerfully on the working end upon which, to his astonishment, running through the loops of itself it comes tight and holds.

Trout are rising everywhere.

He is ready at last and so excited a cloud of obfuscatory energy oscillates out around him. He swats his rod back and forth dumping a cast onto the shining, living water

but something—

As best he can see, in this light, his fly is floating over where there are fish, but something—

Something is biting him.

Biting?

some bristly insect has gotten down inside his boots and trapped against his foot is biting it, eating it, using pincers to tear through living flesh—his! He freezes at the thought. Drops his rod. Makes strangled noises in his throat—then screaming is splashing toward shore, the thing in his boot biting horribly—falls in up to a shoulder, lunges, gets balance, thrashes and careens through muddy water and bank grasses to stagger up between the willows and on a mossy rock is dancing, yanking everything off—vest, suspenders, boots, jeans, socks—pantingly. Holding his foot he sits down. In his underwear. To examine his skin as his brother comes at a jog down over the lawn.

Our food forgotten, the rest of us sit at attention in our terrace chairs. Could this be the breakdown so many have predicted?

Reaching his brother Lim kneels. Taking Eden's face in his hands he looks him in the eye.

"Who's President of the United States?"

“What?”

“Who’s the—”

“I heard what you said,” the soaked angler in jockey briefs, on a rock, tells his brother, “but what does who’s President have to do with—”

“They ask questions like that to see if there’s brain damage, if oxygen’s getting to—”

“For god’s sake Lim. Something was biting my foot. If I say Millard Fillmore what are you going to do?”

“All right hold still, which foot?”

On his knees, taking the proffered foot in both hands Lim examines it.

“I don’t see anything. Still hurt?”

“No,” his big brother rumbles glumly, staring.

Lim stands, brushes himself off and looks down skeptically at his fat brother on the rock, turns, as if to the never-ceasing stream for an answer, gazes out over the water, sets his knuckles on his hips to turn and look at his brother again and, looking at, then staring at, then staring harder at, then going over to and picking up, Eden’s rag wool fishing sock, stands in saturnine triumph holding the sock dangling from a fastidious forefinger and thumb.

Eden’s breath frays from him. He sees his barb-sharp crawdad ties sticking in the rough wool.

His chest lifts, holds a moment, deflates.

Lim brings the sock over to hand it to him.

The angler places a palm to his cheek . .

At the sound of their laughter we start eating again.

And the stream is quiet, the currents trailing along riseless, the air above the water empty of insects, the light soft, the evening cool now in the sudden stillness, on the grass, of night’s coming.

“Eden,” Lim is saying with a surprising softness. “Eden . . brother . .”

“Huh?”

“You okay?”

“Sure I am. I guess I made a racket.”

"Well you did. How's the work going?"

"Oh it's going. It's ah, coming."

"Coming along is it?"

"It's coming along," the fat man—in briefs—on the rock said.

Lim looked at him sharply.

"You sure?"

Eden nods . .

"And so," Lim carefully reeled, not taking his suddenly gimlet eyes off his brother, "you'll be finished by Labor Day?"

"Actually—"

"WHAT!?"

"There's—"

"Eden you said you were going to finish *The Sword's*—"

"Actually ahhhh, it ah, seems to want to be called *The Tree of*—"

"I don't care if you call it *The Rape of the Singing Nun*," the little figure exploded frantically with those cartoon sweat-bullets one always envisioned flying in wild halo from around his round head. "When are you going to finish? When Eden? You were supposed to've finished last Christmas, then it was spring, all right, that can happen, then it was Labor Day, and now you're telling me—what are you telling me?"

"Oh, I should think by Christmas."

"You do? There's a lot riding on this Eden, what's the . . four hundred—"

"Five fifty."

"On delivery of manuscript."

"That's right."

"Well boy, man," Lim said looking around irritably, "how many chapters have we got left?"

"Seven."

Lim spun and stared at his brother long and hard, as the doer of a crossword might stare in steady concentration at a crucial clue.

"Seven huh."

"Yes."

"You seem pretty sure. Not six, not eight. Seven."

Did Eden nod? If he did it was slight as he sat staring (there being no window available) at the soothing passing water . . . Lim shut his mouth even tighter and for a moment seemed about to say more but then must have thought better of it because he just snapped his arms folded, turning, that way, to do some looking out over the currents himself.

"So I ask myself," he explained after a moment, "I ask myself Eden—here's the question I ask. Wanna hear it?"

"Okay."

"I ask myself," Lim constrainedly fumed, "am I my brother's keeper? And answer comes there one. Know what it is? It's no, I repeat, no, I am not. I am not my brother's keeper. I am," Lim declared with dignity, standing straighter as he watched the movements and hues of the creek, "his literary agent. And he should thank me. He should say Lim, I thank you. I thank you for your patience, I thank you for your encouragement, and yes, I thank you for your prodding. I thank you for busting your butt to sell rights on the first three to half the Northern Hemisphere." A pause. Grand as Washington crossing the Delaware Lim is looking, now, not quite out over the currents—is looking, in fact, out of the corner of his eye at his brother. "Well?"

"Oh," the soul on the rock says, "sure. Ah, I mean of course. I thank you. Thank-you Lim, I do thank you."

They and I above them watched a mallard pair flying in the shadows of the far trees. Entering a last beam of light the head of the drake showed gaudy green then black as the prisms in the feathers aimed differently.

Lim went about picking up Eden's equipment. The big fellow continued to sit, morosely watching the bug-less, trout-less stream. At a distance through the forest the horizon gradually, consideringly, was swallowing the bloody sun whole.

We ate in our wrought-iron chairs on the flagstone terrace over which the shadow of Lim's house—a Georgian brick box with white icing onto which had been grafted a solarium, skylights and a gym—elongated toward us as we chewed our burgers and potato salad and hot corn.

"Lim come eat," Rairia called.

Lurching about in his artificial-reality helmet, the little figure was going to walk into a tree.

"I'm into it!" he yelled.

He walked into the tree ecstatically, arms flung out. The faceless helmet cushioned the blow I guess, because he didn't seem much bothered. The helmet was smooth, white, featureless, plastic, eyeless. Sensa-gloves uplifted as if to feel, mummy-featureless oblate helmet-head wobbling, the creature of the future staggered back from the walnut trunk only momentarily stunned, before getting his composure—if not his bearings—back and lurching off over the dusky lawn a different way.

He was running a program entitled "Evening Lawn." Inside his helmet, through scrolling visuals and digital stereo-sound and high-resolution color and high-intensity graphics and mirror functions and tactile stimulators and interactive visual cues, he was experiencing a slope of verdant lawn, fading warm sky, willow trees in a row by gliding water, the sudden evening flight of some sparrows.

You could hear his cackling inside the helmet (ducks quacking in a jug) as he reeled about.

"Just like real! I'm not kidding! I'm not! It's like real! You wouldn't believe this!" He stopped, paused, lifted his face (or since you couldn't see his face, lifted the conical-blunt blank of white that was his helmet), awkwardly raising a gloved arm.

"I'm seeing . . . oooooo. Ooooooooooo. Trees. Grass. Shadows on the grass. Sky. A stream's goin' by—shit here comes a bird *whoa*! Scary. I mean it was like it was comin' right at me it was so close."

He was among us a minute later, blinking, helmet off, checking the platters along the buffet and what was left on them. His voice was sharp as he spoke to his brother who sat looking down over the walrus moustache at his third hamburger in his podgy fingers.

"So we gave up golf."

"Yes," Eden said, about to bite. "We did."

"Ridiculous game," Lim scoffed putting a burger in a bun. "Silly sport. Right?"

"Right," Eden munched.

"Are these safe? I mean to eat? To me golf's sterile. Golf's nothing, zilch, zero, a drive—what's a drive? What the heck is a drive unless it means to like *drive* me crazy. Though I don't see why I should have to drive—" dainty bite "—when it's a short walk for most people around here. Nahh. Monks in madras, that's all golf is. A buncha madras monks totaling. Totaling totaling. This tastes all right. So, you like fly fishing."

"I love it."

"Right. Fish alive, fast, slippery," Lim preached, warming to his burger. "My right? Trout not cunning but can act cunning, behave as if they were cunning. My right?"

"You are," Eden munched.

"And a stream moves, a trout stream like . . . moves, right? My right?"

"Indeed you are."

Lim held his burger to one side.

"You tell me," he said, "when the last time was that you saw a golf course move. My right?"

"Yep."

"Christmas," Lim Hope told his brother firmly, "no later."

"Right."

"Well it better be."

Duffy Ginty leaned toward me in the shadows.

"He's brilliant," she whispered, though it wasn't clear about which one. "A mind like a steel sieve."

Duffy ran her butcher shop and family with an "iron glove," which I decipher to mean she was a tough disciplinarian precisely because at heart she was a pushover. I'm not sure. But her husband and three daughters, when they visited, were poker faces. They scarcely spoke, were more paralyzed than polite—but that could just as well have been the circus nature of my uncle's house . . as I've said, the scene up there disconcerted me too at first.

Duffy Ginty's mother had cooked for Eden's grandparents, and Duffy helped Eden and Rairia part-time as a housekeeper, which she enjoyed and for which she was—sporadically—remunerated, but she sat at their table and was much more a friend than a retainer. Uneducated beyond junior high, Duffy loved learning. To my uncle's fascination she had amassed a library of medical instruction videos—hours-long teaching tapes of a highly technical nature showing actual OR procedures such as eye surgery, brain surgery, bypasses, transplants and refined reconstructive bone work—that she watched over and over.

She was always welcome up there, although—or because—she often made no sense due to her "misspeaks," as she wistfully described them, and you could see Eden was fond of her even if he and all of us, I'm afraid, committed the sin of reducing that good soul to a trait.

The stream was shadow and so were we, phantasmic well-fed ideas of people—a face lit demonically from below by bug lamp's flicker, other faces practically invisible in the night, just voices disembodied in the warm dark. Carrying platters and utensils and glasses people crossing the terrace were silhouettes in the light from the house, forms magically, wildly distorted as they moved, headless—an arm illumined, stilt-tall shadow blossoming longer and taller backward over the stones and finally out infinitely into the night as, holding the screen door open with a hip, because your hands are full, you step in.

"Before it gets totally dark," Lim said—he stood his elbows on the table's iron latticework, pressing his face into his hands. "Let's go back out and catch you your first trout."

"But he's hopeless," Nora's voice blurted in the darkness. "Isn't he?"

"Just," Rairia's shadowvoice reminded, "remember what we said. Remember what we talked about."

"I know Mother. I remember what we said. But it was you saying it. I wasn't saying it. I just want to like understand, I mean he's been trying every day for three weeks or whatever and he still can't catch one. I'm sorry, I can't help it. Why doesn't a person stop trying when they obviously can't do something?"

The two men had their gear and were going away down over the lawn into the deeper darkness.

"I mean couldn't it like develop into a psychosis or something?"

"An obsession," her mother said. "Yes."

"Whatever."

"Yes," Rairia said. "It could."

"Get one Dad," Nora called into the night.

I got up, swinging a leg over the low wall, and stole over the lawn in the night until I could just see their forms by the water's edge.

I couldn't tell what they were saying. Lim's tone was impatient, Eden's gentle—gentle and small as he tried to do as he was told.

But it was the same that evening and would be the same the following day and the day after that. He couldn't get one. He could catch dace, or fingerling trout so helplessly small you can fly them over a shoulder onto the grass with a wrist-flick if you want, and sometimes he would get a serious hit and for a second or two of unendurable excitement would have the angry, shuddering fight of reality through his tightened line before the sudden slack-go.

But he couldn't get one. He knew fairly well what to do, but when he descended the bank and entered the world of water he got nervous and excited and not in control and did everything wrong, even stuff he knew, fishing badly, then worse, and finally embarrassingly . .

# 6

His rod was caught in a wall of briars. He struggled to free it and succeeded but in doing so got his net snared, and now he had to twist into the thorns, holding his rod away from them, to reach—wincing—into the plant with his free hand to unsnag each thread of mesh from each sharp stem, and as he was doing this the tip of his rod looped his line over a sapling branch.

He pulled without looking to free his rod as he worked on freeing his net and his reel clicked as his line, fast to the branch, stripped off, and his net was caught worse than before.

It was as if he and his equipment and clothing wanted to make friends physically with every leaf, branch, pricker and stem in nature.

Sweat fogged the lenses of his glasses. He could scarcely see—saw only a bright, mostly green mist . .

He had to get his glasses unfogged. Letting go, carefully, of his net, which he had reached behind his neck to unclip, and for the moment leaving it hanging in the briars, putting his rod down he took several blind steps backward and removed his glasses.

Locating a portion of his shirt that wasn't sweaty he wiped the lenses of his spectacles. But when he fitted them back on they clouded up at once because it was so hot and he was so hot and this forced him to rest because he couldn't untangle his things if he couldn't see. And he wouldn't be able to see until he was cooler, so he sat on a log.

With his spectacles in his fingers he sat, wiping his face with a shirtsleeve, and cooled off. Breasts heaving and subsiding under his XL three-pocketed Longwear khaki shirt with stitched-down epaulets and rod-holder loop. His booted toes tapping the forest-floor detritus, the humid woods air pressing against the mountainside, and against his sinuses and ears, like a soiled weapon of suffocation.

Staring, without his glasses, at the meaningless blur of green, he relaxed, at first gradually then suddenly. He knew he was just a little human being. He shouldn't take being unable to catch a trout so seriously. Peace, acceptance and an infinite resignation such as doesn't come often (and was probably gastrointestinal) blessed him a minute. Then, moving slowly so he wouldn't heat up, with his glasses—clear—on, he got his stuff unsnagged, unhooked, unknotted and unthreaded back out through itself and properly organized, and made his way back to the water.

He must remember what Lim had told him about waiting on the backcast, and what the magazine articles said about feeling where the line is without looking, and wade slowly always, even if you don't see a fish. Cast slack, keep low, use the wrist . . . the rules piled in his mind and seemed to weigh on him physically, hindering his balance. Wide-eyed with earnestness he teetered, as slowly as he could manage, into the flowing water where he intended to concentrate and do what Lim and the magazines said whether he caught one or not. One more step, his wading boot suspended in the brownish current, and a little one that had been hiding on the far side of an underwater stone shot out zooming over the bottom upstream zigging zagging gone.

"Oh shoot—shit shoot shit, he was right there, I'm damned," he whispered angrily to—since there was no one else—himself. "If I can do—" panting with the effort of wading "—this—" squinting to see if the fish he'd scared was anywhere "—the way I'm—" but it wasn't "—supposed to . ."

He could think of nothing else to do but try again, and so, crouching to reduce his silhouette in the trout's much diagrammed crystal-palace dome of vision, he fished his way upstream. He waited on each backcast and tried to use the wrist and to feel his line behind him on the backcast and to wade slow, but he saw—felt through his rod when his fly was floating—nothing.

He was starting to become discouraged again. So quiet, so dull-feeling, so filmy was the current, so empty the brown water drifting toward him. But he was resolved, he would be diligent. Carrying the rules of fishing as if on a balanceable platter atop his head he took one measured, smooth step after another in the flow (glancing to be sure he wasn't making ripples), and presented his casts, the next after the last, one groundless act of faith after another, to the unobligated water.

Intrigued by the inorganic sciences even as a child he had thought about questions he knew he shouldn't waste time on but that gave him such pleasure he couldn't help himself. One infinity being larger than another for instance. There's an infinity of even, and an infinity of whole (odd and even) numbers, and in the book his father gave him he read how you could show the infinity of whole numbers to be greater than the even-numbers infinity.

You did this, his dad's sad, dreaming green eyes showed him, before turning away, as his dad always turned away, to go to his study, where he wrote the poems no one read, by matching—one matched one infinity to the other, number by number, thus: 1 (the first number in the whole-numbers infinity) for 2 (the first number in the even-numbers infinity), then 2 for 4, 3 for 6, 4 for 8 and so on, making it clear that for every even number there's a pair of whole ones.

So the whole-numbers infinity's twice as large.

Something was wrong with this almost immediately in his fourth-grade mind. It was something about movement, and, immensely excited—a big fish of thought had emerged from the murk to glide by him!—he went, thinking, to his father's shut study door. He knocked.

He wanted to tell him, be proud and have his dad's help in figuring it out. He listened. He knew his father was in there, here in the upper reaches of the huge old house his rich great-grandad had built, with his sad dreaming verse scattered like a forest floor of dead leaves all over the big desk that had been moved by truck from the shipping yards, when those had been sold.

The boy knocks again, melancholy pooling in his stomach, but there is no answer. Behind the shut paneled mahogany door with its cut-glass knob, why is his dad quiet?

He wants vaguely to help his dad if he can, but he doesn't know what's wrong. Why doesn't anyone ever see the poems? And why, when Father's not up here, is there mostly a newspaper in front of the long sad face?

He wants to tell him about the thing he thought of about infinities in the book the tall man gave him. He holds it, lowers it, at his side, does not knock again, turns away, down the narrow hall, in this wing of the old place they will not live in much longer. Something about movement—he had to think it out for himself that night, lying awake in his bed in the room next to Lim's, shadows, moon, clothes like a stooped person strewn on his chair in the hoarlight . . . something about movement. If infinities would hold still, then all right, in that case he could see how you could show one infinity to be greater than another.

But infinities didn't hold still—he loved thinking about this.

He thought: you can't have infinity without time. And time is movement—the essence of infinity is you're always adding on. He pictured the even numbers as a curving line extending into the stars like a swaying rope of champagne bubbles, the line's top always growing outward beyond what you could reach, adding more even numbers forever. Therefore, if someone argued the whole-number infinity is larger because it has the numbers 1 *and* 2 to match against the even-number infinity's 2, and so on, somehow—in the dizziness of thinking—you could say right back oh that's no problem, I'll just reach up and get more extra even numbers from the endless end of the line of them swaying up there expanding forever in the stars, see? The whole-number proponent might retort well then I'll just reach into *my* infinity and get more of *my* numbers, but so long as the thing was endlessly moving outward, which being infinity it was, you would never be able to get your two infinities to hold still long enough, he thought, excited in the simple night, to prove it. It confused him terribly and thrilled him to think about it.

"*Mis*-ter Hope."

He didn't know where he was

"Would you," the grand voice acidly invited, "join us?"

Mrs. Mariah stood over him. He dared look no higher than the gold circle-pin riding her mohair bosom like a life preserver on a tidal wave.

She pointed to his workbook. It lay open on the pocked desktop—to the right page fortunately. On the page were ten clockfaces, some without numerals, some with one hand, others with wrongly placed numerals, one—he saw immediately—whole and correct.

Still disoriented by the abruptness of his return from infinity, he focused on the clock dial to which Mrs. Mariah's bejeweled burgundy-nailed finger was pointing.

It was a whole, correct clockface.

"Would that," she demanded, "tell time?"

He stared at it.

"Think carefully," she commanded.

He stared at it, dimly aware of his classmates' mirth and fascination out around the edges of his eyes. He stared at the clockface on the page, thinking as hard as he could.

"No," he said.

"No?" Surprise—sympathy too now in her tone. "And why not?"

"It's made of paper," he said.

Air-implosion of shock. The class erupted. He'd been serious, had wanted so badly to give the correct answer that he'd thought his way right past what was right. Silencing the others' laughter with an eyebrow Mrs. Mariah seemed physically to expand, as his punishment filled her ruled mind.

His kind, cool mother, when she heard of such things, comforted him only a little. She would try to hide it on her Rushmore face but he would see it—a look of reserve, even disappointment.

Another time, belowstairs in the hot clatter clash of the long school lunchroom, formerly a bowling alley in the former mansion, two villages over, where he went to country day, he got so lost in his fifth hot dog he wasn't aware he was subconsciously listening to every word of Becky Stine's rendition, at the next table, of the story of the club initiation rite requiring new members to spend a night alone in the haunted house. No one was able to do it because before sunrise they ran out screaming with white hair, but now the person telling you the story reveals he's the first ever to make it through an entire night, but, Becky says to the imaginary narrator, *your hair's white too*—and the answer comes back YESSSSSSS! and he shrieked and knocking his plate halfway across the table threw his milk in the air to the amazement and, once they'd understood, the delight and amusement of his schoolmates, in those simple years so fresh in memory yet so far—perhaps infinitely far—off and away now in the renegade dimension.

unmoored, it turns
upsidedown
slowly rightsideup again, but only briefly under the water suspended above the bottomrocks
weightless
its shell under it again under the water, as he stares at it, head and scaly legs extended, drifting
downstream at the speed of the water it's in
he stands looking, seeing what he is seeing an apparently
unconcerned turtle, scaled leg brushes underwater rock, claw slips off, past the gray stone and on
downstream tumbling slow
freefall in the current the turtle
in a trick of light is gone.

His fat-person's gravity-center riding above his slow-marching boots, he trudged the bank, watching the stream.

He'd never been this far. He was still on the property, he thought, walking along watching the water for fish—walking too fast, slow down.

Look the currents over thoroughly, be sure each shadow on the water, each pendulous curve-border and seam between current speeds, isn't a trout.

He saw one.

Froze.

Enthusiasm and hope came all the way back up in his heart. He held still, watching the spotted svelte shape—black eye—rudder tail wagging rhythmically

He fought not to stand hypnotized. Think, plan. If he could remember what he knew, sneak downstream, wade quietly back up, get close, but not too, please be a smooth backcast—he was in position now squinting upstream to where he thought he'd seen it.

As he was leaning to try to see, the trout fed, twenty feet upstream of him, with a klunk like an egg dropped from a height into a full rainbarrel

He stared at the concentric, expanding circles

He leaned forward in a prayerful dream casting his line out behind him—

. . his leader lay properly on the water. His fly was drifting right about where it should be. He couldn't remember making the forecast. He waited without breathing as his tiny sacrifice floated, with the flow, over where the fish was—

no. Angling's eternal question answered in the negative.

As he was gathering line, setting up to cast again, it fed again with a smack sending new circles of hope through his muscles, but on the forward motion of the cast the very real possibility that he might catch his first trout right here right now seized

his arm.

His line hit the water.

He let the mess of it float toward him and was soon quietly straightening things out when the fish rose again, but now the rise was further upstream, it had moved away. He tiptoed, figuratively speaking, against the current upstream to within comfortable casting range and tried again, but it was the same. He was only herding it upstream as he cast to it.

The day's haze had turned to curtaining mists of rain. He struggled up the bank with his rod dangerously waving and slogged, in loud boots, feeling neither anticipation nor clarity, further downstream along the dense forest trail.

He passed pools and glides, riffles, tailwater flumes where the current smooths with a flip between a pair of rocks, and sometimes where it looked as if there might be fish he got in the water and hurried some casts, and sometimes he didn't but only—staring at them—passed the pools by, because before long it would be time to head home fishless once more.

His fishing failure was part of him, not so much frustration or confusion (though these) as a clinging, unwanted friend.

He was stiff. Too stiff. The parts of the body tight. Uncoordination. When one part moved it pulled other parts, his casting arm for instance pulling torso and legs. There had to be a way to fish so this wouldn't happen. Not to his surprise it was all unraveling—fishing—coming apart like a badly conceived equation dissolving before your eyes into squiggles. He kept trying, robotically now in the drizzle, sending his casts aimlessly onto the stippled face, casting anywhere, fishing any way, rushing like a compulsive gambler from cast to cast and spot to spot in the speckling rain as if his movements were prayer or some formalistic repeated exercise rather than actions designed to an end.

Dreamily in his despair, casting absently in the summer shower, beyond feeling, he presented his fly to the drizzle-flecked, gliding currents without intent.

At last, he got out.

Got out of the stream, rain rivuleting the lenses of his glasses, and followed the trail where it twisted in the forest—more a game trace now than a path—narrow, and with brush, branches and sharp runes plucking at him.

The trail took him inland and opened onto a pine-needle floor of dark trunks. He could walk about freely here without having to crouch and fend, but he couldn't see where the trail was.

He felt as if he were floating wraithlike through the pine trunks as he walked through them toward where he thought the water was. Not knowing why he was going. Battled through thick, dripping cover where the forest closed again in the direction—he thought—of the water, though he couldn't see. These weedlike trees and climbers and all this soaking shrubbery in the eyes . .

Lifting, with care, some vines and ducking his head he stepped under
brought his rod through and stiffly straightened.
The wilderness pushed in close here,
the stream a pool, walled by forest.
The rain had slowed again to a mist that did not fall
the water darkglass
the air dense        —silent
the pines along the opposite bank impenetrable

Sharply the stream cut out of sight above the pool's head and below its tail. Impression more of a currentless pond than a pool of a flowing creek. So tightly did the forest darken in on all sides of the mum, onyx surface here, that he had the feeling, breathing through his mouth, because his nose was full, standing, in his bedraggled gear, on a precipice of root-supported bank, that he had uncovered a secret. The trees of the forest were guarding something, wanted to grow together, binding all, braiding all, blending all in an eternal mean of silence.

Like what your eyes think, when first you look, is tree shadow
and when you look again is a white-tailed deer staring at you
or like the drowned branch you think you are seeing that suddenly, moving its tail, moves away over the sunny bottomstones,
the man
was there.
Standing in the stream flyfishing before the watcher
realized he was seeing him
facing upstream, his back to Eden. Sun-faded shirt—sleeves rolled up—ox-slow, brawny shoulders
he spoke to Eden without turning:
"Havin' any luck?"
"Er, no."

"Fish," the stranger said calmly.

He didn't turn his head even slightly to say it. He didn't cast either. Was watching.

"Them wild browns," he said. "Muscle just about every brookie around outta their lies in this weather. Size don't matter."

The man turned and Eden saw his face.

"Size don't matter," the other repeated. "No luck you say?"

"No I'm, er, I haven't. I'm a beginner. Not very—"

"Wouldn't worry."

"No-no-no I, ahh . ."

"A person doesn't catch a trout just by trying."

A shower of rain came dotting the surface. The breeze and the rain made a sigh against the canopy of the forest. Eden Hope took his glasses off, worried his bandanna from a pocket, and pinching his rod under an elbow wiped the dropleted spectacle lenses a lot more thoroughly than would have been necessary.

The other's voice was gravelly: "Been out long?"

"A few hours."

"See anything?"

"Sure, here and there. Ah—"

"Couldn't raise any."

"Never do."

"Wal."

"How 'bout you?"

"Got seventeen."

"My god. You mean—when you say seventeen you mean fish, heh, seventeen—"

"Yep. Kept four."

Wading to where Eden stood on the bank the man opened his creel.

Quicksilver sleek they lay. Treasure in the wicker shadows. None was under eleven inches and there was one big one.

"We eat 'em," the stranger said.

"My god the, ah, I mean I've been out here three hours, three hours and not a bite and these were in the same water!"

"Wal."

"Incredible."

"They like this."

Outsized, woolly, outrageously yellow and without notable form except, perhaps, wings, the fly in the stranger's scarred fingers looked like nothing he'd seen in the magazines or his brother's fly boxes and he reflexively wanted to hold it but did not move to, for some reason in the tranquil, colorless light the rain made in the mountain woods.

"It's certainly big."

"Yeah. They can't stay away from it when it's wet like this."

"What do you call it?"

"Don't know, don't call it anything."

The stranger did something fast with his arm twisting his wrist to send his yellow monstrosity to the pond's far rim. It hit the rain-dappled surface. Two trout rose roiling the water, his nonchalant strike missed. He laughed. Hauling line, leader and fly straight in the air over his head a way Eden hadn't seen, where the forest left no room for a backcast, he whipped a shortcut presentation flat to a different spot.

A fish hooked itself, splashing, and he was playing it . .

"They can't leave it alone."

The shower let up and a hint, then a gift—warm, full—of true sunshine came everywhere shadowless and cheerful on the refreshed air. He was playing the big trout effortlessly toward Eden's net.

"Thanks. You've got a rip there. Better fix that . . . waal, this is my best of the day. Also my limit."

Freeing the hook and sliding his catch into the wicker creel he wore, he fastened the top by its disintegrating leather thong and turned to look Eden over.

A look split-second serene.

"There's bigger ones 'round the bend."

"There are?"

"Like to see?"

"My God yes I do, I mean would."

Banks of mist, puffy fresh far below the miles-high sun, tumbled low through the treetops as they made their way back into the woods, Eden dutifully following the sun-bleached workshirt through the snap-back leafy branches touched with watersmell and autumn's decay's faint beginnings. The forest opening again, they stepped from the trees.

They were standing on a shelf of rock.

Next to where they stood the current emptied into a gentling vista of riffles and, beyond, a long pool bordered by grass banks that, biting his fly off, the other indicated with a jerk of the head.

"There's big ones all through there."

The man had work-aged hands. He had his box out. A garish row of magic monsters was visible. Somehow, as the stranger was putting the one he'd used back, another fell out, blew downstream onto the current and spun, hurrying through the chute beside the ledge, to—just before the riffle stretch—get snagged, Eden saw, on the tip of an underwater branch.

It trembled there.

"I always catch fish here," the stranger observed gazing at the riffles and the pool and the parks of tall grasses and hummocks along the banks. "No one sees me. Come here two, three times a season. Take my limit. Fer the family. This place isn't known. I'm kinda surprised you found it."

"Yes . ."

He was keeping a sharp eye on the outsized fly where it jiggled, stuck to the branch tip, with the currents' turbulent vagaries . .

The other was cranking his line down through the guides of his rod.

There was a small smile on his chapped mouth as he worked.

He was watching Eden without looking at him.

Lifting from the water the bright hazes rose past the face of the forest stately and slow, unveiling the leaves' after-rain green and the blemishless shape and form of the trees' being.

It was shuddering, delicately with the current's force. Submerging partway every other second. The stranger had wished him luck and gone away into the trees. The fly, off which my uncle had not taken his eyes, appeared to be staying for the moment, however precariously, where it had snagged.

With his rod he sat down in his boots on the ledge and slid into the water and was stumbling—wading, swinging his arms—toward the fly which as he neared it uncaught, slipped from the twig tip and went bobbing away over the riffles.

He splashed after it. It would slow, turning. He would start to catch up. As he almost got to it the current would take it again. He crashed through the rocky shallows splashing, in his desperate singlemindedness turning falls into forward lunges, questing heavily after it as it journeyed away downstream through the curls and crests and dells and waterlaughter of the run. His breaths were coming in gasps. His sweat-darkened shirt clung to him under his gear and stuffed vest. His wading boots were becoming too ponderous against the living water and stones, his glasses starting to fog over again.

Beyond the riffles the fly sashayed out onto the calm of the pool, and panting through the rippleless water up to it he had it.

Sitting on rain-soaked grasses he got his leader untangled. Quickly he tied the stranger's yellow wings to his leader's angelhair end, working too fast to think.

got into the stream, waded, cautiously, to the head of the pool, stood in the shrifts of riffle current that patted and slapped at his booted legs, waited for his heart to slow.

He cast his fly upon the waters.

The trout that took hit it so square it sounded like a beavertail slamming water. The fish struggled a second then swirled deep to sort things out. It was big and was aware it had swallowed—whole—some very wrong object.

It was unsure what to do about this.

Neither did Eden Hope know what to do.

He'd hooked a trout.

His rod dumb in his hand, time a tangle of seconds going nowhere, afraid if he moved he might do a wrong thing, he stood in the current gazing nonplussedly at the water as if he and not the fish were caught.

The ability to dissociate that constituted such a powerful part of his thinking capacity—the ability to steer clear of the present—served him all too well. He stood holding his rod in the same position in which it had been raised when the trout had struck and hooked itself, perspiration beads coursing down his astonishment. Then either he lifted his rod or the fish swirled and the battle was joined. For the first time in his life he was genuinely connected to a fighting trout. He tried to keep the rod in the position he knew was right—at an angle to the force of the fish. It knifed away but getting control of his line and remembering to pull with the flex of the rod he brought the wild, pumping force in the water toward him . . and a bit more. Turning its head in anger—bit-crazed colt—it bolted. Tentatively, now that he was getting the feel, he coaxed and pressured it back, fearful beyond reason of losing it. Tiring somewhat it tilted on a side and allowed him to slide it nearer still. Floating, yieldingly, black eye staring, white belly as helpless as the exposed keel of a broached sailboat.

Staring down at it he realized he was hooked to it.

He stood in the moving water looking down at black-spotted back, gazing unseeing eye, working red gills as the fish waited, in its exhaustion, for him to do something.

Getting hold of his net and bending down he showed the trout the net, in effect asking it if it wanted to die. With a swipe it surged deep burrowing out of sight into the shadows of the depths, pulling line off his rod. Trying to stay calm he controlled the line and with his rod's flex coaxed the fish to the surface, drew it to him, held his net in the current downstream of the spent trout, the way he'd seen Lim do it, and holding his arching rod high and to the side the way his brother did and letting the trout drift, with the current, into his net he lifted.

With his rod under an arm he fumbled with the fish tangled and squirming in the netting and fiddled with it, twisted, finally ripped the sodden fly from white-pink cheek-inside of gaping jaws. Getting his creel open with a hand while clutching the fish through the net's mesh he smothered his net with the trout in it overtop the open creel and shook. The fish flopped in. He snapped the flap to.

He bent, holding the creel underwater to get it wet. He had one. He had his first. Looking his yellow fly over, blowing on it to dry it, and getting his line straightened out, he started casting again. Fishing his way downstream through the pool he experienced a surge of anticipation each time his pair of mothlike wings touched the surface. He felt the stream very differently now, the water exciting—fish here, fish ready to rise. He felt wonderful, nervous, happy, a jolt of expectation hitting him with each cast, though his next several bore no fruit. Just as he stopped thinking about what he was doing there was a flash in the water under his fly. He got his line airborne again and made himself keep his eye on the spot where the fish had shown itself, a faint wake where a boulder sat under the surface. His presentation was perfect. The yellow wings alit without a ripple. Touched the tension of the surface as exquisitely as the points of two pins touching. And as he watched his fly float onto the subtle, trailing wake of the great underwater rock, he knew a fish would come.

could know this from the look, as he watched

of the float of the fly

the splash before his eyes was real and, stunned, instead of flicking his rod back sharply to strike he lifted gradually, unauthoritatively, as an afterthought, but this one too had taken with such vigor as to hook itself, and there were two now weighting his creel as he fished his way to the pool's end.

Another flashed under his fly, he struck too fast, missed. Losing it didn't bother him.

He had never felt this way. The water was magic everywhere with the possibility of fish, they were here all around him under the shadowed surface, looking up. They wanted the yellow fly.

If he made more casts he would catch more fish. He was of them, in this way. He had caught and landed two, a fact that could never change.

He quit wading a moment to open his creel and peer in.

He stared down at them, dark feelings mixing with his joy.

He had killed his first wildlife.

He had never seen death take place.

These had been fish.

The water sliding through his legs, swirling around him as he stared into the creel, was singing. The water was singing to him sadly. They lay on their sides in the shadows, one gone, its flanks' silver fire diminished to forever gray, jaws shut, body rigid, black, circular eye not even glassy.

The other was still alive, working its jaw.

As he watched it it died. The last light drained from the eye—he watched this happen—its jaws clamped. The water flowing around him was singing to him and the forest growing above the flat sweep of the stream was singing to him sadly. It was a song of feeling that despite the satisfaction of having caught two was a cavity all of a sudden in his spirit. Something had been in these two creatures that wasn't now. He had watched it go away in the one. He looked at them, shaded in the water and mucus at the bottom of the creel.

They were objects—things to be overlapped on beds of pulverized ice behind the glass sliding doors of the cases at market. He didn't want them—he was sad. He was confused. He shut his creel and turned toward the deep center of the pool. Unlimbered his rod and line and cast. On the third presentation he had one, and worked it, brought it to him, got it in his net, his hands shaking for fear of damaging it, and, working with his fingers through the netting, holding the wriggling fish under the water, struggling not to let it out of the webs of the net, in a brief second's clarity of intent and movement he had the jaw in one hand's fingers and quick with the other hand twisted his yellow fly uncatching barb from white V ridge of lower jaw and the fish was free. He bumbled it out of the netting and furiously wriggling and righting itself it shot deep.

He left the water. Climbing out, he climbed a bank of treeroots—gat-toothed, downgrasping fingers and legs of forest growing clutchingly down, beautiful in their completion, into the water—and sat smoking.

Something was still singing to him. He was aware of thinking, but there was no content to this thinking. He could feel his mind thinking. It was happening, too, through the body. It was going on indescribably in the legs and the pit of the stomach, in the fingers where they rested, holding his cigarette, on the rubber knee of his boot. He got up, got his cigarette out and dropped it in a pocket, and walked into the soon to be autumn leaves. High, foliate cathedral canopy. He came to a place where the forest floor was black loam, cinnamon-colored pine needles, delicate portions of root breaking the ground, small, smooth pebbles. Some dead leaves in seashell shapes in curls, burnt red. Swatches of verdant spongy grass.

He unsnapped his creel. Going down onto a knee he lifted their stiff weight from the shadows and laid them, beside each other, on the forest floor.

He struggled with a grunt to his feet and stood looking down at them.

The forest would take them back. Weasels would get them. Dirk-toothed clever little jaws take them—eat them.

Snapping his creel shut and not looking back he strode through the trees' green . . .

The beasts of the open ocean, their range and power, are absent from the land's streams. Little creeks spawn no gods or tales of such. Little trout—flashes—streak out of sight if your cast falls wrong. They flash everywhichway, fleeing their feeding posts to dart under underwater rocks and in under the grass-hung banks.

Huge and stupendous the time-mangled white barnacle-rubbled back curves in powerful motion endlessly through its own shape's form until the giant, spread flukes lift, above the waves' inconsequential tossings; and when the animal plunges ideas follow it. Streams of thought torque and twist down, hurricaning into the water-vacuum above the colossal, sounding body.

Man, balancing on the tilting planks of his craft, cannot stop his soul from wrenching from his chest to sing out over the waves and fly down into the suction quickening above the sounding, impossible mammal.

A sickness—human compulsion—having nothing to do with whales screams from the watcher's chest. Screams silently like a ghost bird to fly to the whale and clasp, hook, join itself to the whale for eternity, because one has had the realization, beneath consciousness's surface, that there is a terror worse by far than the terror of the vortex of the whale.

There is the terror of the vortex of the self. The self-compulsion inward, away from the world. So the sickness escapes the watcher's chest to fly out over the water toward what, after all, is only a whale. oil. bone, intelligent eye—blubber, size. The sickness embraces the whale. Embraces the whale as other, as: Not myself. Anything but myself, any compulsion but that one—Othello, Appel, Cabot Lodge . . . ideas empty into the vortex the mammal trails. Thought pours. Notions of evil and some of our most deleterious ideals stream down whirlpooling and are sucked into the plummeting sounding of the whale now become more than whale, more, even, than idea.

Destruction by whale saves Captain from destruction by worse. The beasts of the open ocean stir, puissant, half-imagined forms nosing along under the inconsequential waves. The dangers of the sea lie deep, glide deep through curtainings of mythic aureole. They do not wriggle with fear in your hand as, gripping the little body lightly to worry hook free of gasping mouth cartilage, you are troubled, really, by nothing you can't handle.

# 7

"*Yes.* Oh," she said, "that's good. That's very. good. please. yes, geeeeeeeesus . . . ok. No like this—" getting her legs inside his legs she hooked her ankles over his ankles. "Like that," she whispered in a voice of air hot from the front of her mouth. "Yeah," she said relaxing into a deeper, slower "yeahhhhh," her voice someone else's, throaty, way down inside, "yeahhhhhhh. I cannot. Believe—"

Digging her nails into his buttocks she pulled him tight to her, lifting her face to find his mouth, the bed bump, bumping the wall. He gasped. He put his hands flat on the mattress rearing from the waist, arms straight, drove desperately into her, and she grunted, shifting, trying to follow. His head jerked up

chin lifted as if

the world hung from it

and he failed her. He left her and fell on his back, soaked. He lay there.

They lay, touching, on her bed in the dim of the room with traffic noises and university-town motorcycle street growls distant through walls, her glowing aquarium, its *Paracheirodon innesi, Pterophyllum scalare* and

*Colisa chuna* winnowing their veiling tails, bubbling because it was getting too much oxygen, glub, glublub

—lub, lub, lub on the antique bureau her mother'd loaned her, its size and brass handles out of place in the flat's glass-table, hardwood-gleam spare modernity

Pillow-propped, staring across the shadowed room at her fish, she was holding the sheet over her little breasts and perfect body. She spoke to herself

"Lordy," she said.

Like a kid in his first tent he lay beside her, anxious, wide-eyed.

"How," she said to herself, "is this going to work I wonder."

He turned his head to look at her. She was looking at her *Paracheirodon innesi.*

"It's like this totally," she said. She was gazing in a trance of concentration on herself at the magic-lantern glow of the bubbling waterlight.

"Unexpected. Development. I mean is your wife going to flay me alive? Is this a question of I'll never be invited to your house . . that beautiful spot—again ever," she concluded grimly.

glublublublub      lub

"I don't know why it does that. I cleaned it one time, and I put it back together . ." she paused, scarlet lips falling ajar causing a bauble of saliva to glitter, before popping, at the labial font of so many awed utterances where the lips of a thousand revolving suitors yearned to press " . . and it's been doing it ever since."

A buzzer buzzed. She excused herself and threw something on. She was away a time. She came back slamming the door behind her, leaning back against it in a sag, her magazine-page beauty rent, terribly discombobulated for the moment, disbelief, relief, fascination, anger and exhaustion all playing over her stunning features. She pouted with her whole lower lip and blew up, causing her bangs to lift and fall . .

"He adores me," she marveled. "I do not. Know. How I get into these—"

There was a banging now on the other side. Smiling sardonically she wheeled and faced the shut door with her hands on her hips.

"Don't both-er," she sang sweetly.

She listened.

Nothing.

"I mean what I say-ay," she sang.

Bright's voice came from the door's other side declaiming mightily, some of the things it was saying desperate, some epistemological, all of them angry. She said stuff back, looking at her feet evilly, listening—he could see—to her tone as she let Bright have it. There was more silence. She opened the door a crack. Into the crack she spoke in a hard voice: "You can't. No. No means no. I'm sorry you're sorry. I'm sorry you're angry. I'm sorry you're everything . . all right that's right I don't want you to. I cannot believe—" in a whisper "—you could be this impolite."

That seemed to do it. Loud fast steps hurrying away down the stairs beyond the door.

"Call me," she shouted.

Slammed the door again. Shot the bolt. Stalked back to bed plopping in, in her peignoir, not exactly flirtatiously, and with folded arms lay there.

"He thinks he owns me. He thinks. Oh it's too ridiculous. I do not," she meditated, "understand. How I deserve . ."

"Why does he think he owns you?"

"He thinks we're getting married. Can you believe the—"

"Are you?"

"Are you kidding? Everybody thinks they have like this *piece* of me."

"Why would he think you're getting married?"

"I told him we were."

"Oh."

"He adores me. And I have been perfectly." Glaring in the jailhouse of her arms. "I have been perfectly, utterly honest with him for the most part."

The phone rang. She made as if to ignore it but as it kept ringing it became clear she'd forgotten to turn her answering machine on. Her eyes filled with anxiety and she sprung up and, taking the room in three strides, legs flashing, grabbed it.

She listened for nearly a minute. Then for a minute more she argued and wrangled and seethed and, toward the end, briefly negotiated—it seemed—with what surely was the deranged Bright, and hung up.

"Well here," she tensely said popping back in bed, "we are."

Lying beside her watching her tropical fish swim in their sandpebble light across the room he wanted to think of something to say. He would get it straight in his mind before saying it out loud, as a person prepares speech in a foreign tongue. He could feel her waiting, not impatiently particularly, but waiting nonetheless, for him to speak, which wasn't unreasonable for a person in bed with another person for the first time. But the wound of his embarrassment over having been unable to perform had him flummoxed, frightened and shy . .

glub-lub went the fish's bright $H_2O$

She: "I don't know why it does that."

He—without thinking: "I'm old. I'm an old man."

She, worrying a nail, fantastic hair on pillow, body under sheet inches from him, declining to disagree: "I'm usually not attracted to men who look like you. I like you," she debates herself vitreously staring across the room at her *Pterophyllum scalare,* "you're interesting, and I also guess. On the other hand I do not. Believe myself."

He could feel her waiting again.

He lay beside her and his thoughts confused, tumbling over one another like numbers in a bingo drum.

"Well," he said, "I'm old. I'm an old man. I'm sorry."

"Oh you mean about not making it?"

He nodded yes, the sheets making a small noise.

"Don't worry," she said slapping his leg, "it's cool, I just have to say though that I don't see how this whole thing's going to play out. I honestly, truly . ."

She seemed to be thinking it through, or trying to, her expression, couched in her hair, positively angelic in the halo of the moment's short-lived and willful implosion of mental effort, but thinking apparently didn't work. She flopped her head away from him with a degree of impatience and waited for something to happen.

He felt terrible.

"I'm going to make a fool of myself," he said. "I can see it coming."

Her head didn't turn but her hand flopped to slap his leg in a friendly way again but in the halfheartedness of the effort missed, flopping short, and didn't try a second time.

"No you're not," she said passively.

"Yes I am, I'm going to make a fool of myself," he declared with quiet desperation to the equationless ceiling.

"Really?"

"Yes."

"How, do you think?"

"Typically," he said unhappily. "Old man, old fool. Beautiful young girl . ."

She waited politely.

"Oh I don't know," he tossed, "I just ah, I wish . ."

"Yes?"

"I wish," he said in his misery, "I could give you something. A gift, a boon. It's such a damned stereotype isn't it. The old idiot. The young beauty. He can't give her anything in the sex department so . ." He had broken out in a sweat and did not know how to stop saying what he felt. It was as if he were telling her the worst, the truth in other words, so she would either comfort him or throw him out, ending this awfulness one way or the other. "So he compensates," he said. "He compensates with all the perfectly predictable, perfectly typical gifts. Presents. Luxuries." He was lost a moment in the aquarium light bubbling luridly. "Not," he said flapping a hand, "your fault. None of it your fault."

"Nooooo," she thoughtfully considered, "I think not. What gifts?"

"May you never get old. You don't know. You don't know you are until you are. One day you wake up and—"

"No go back to—"

"Hm?"

"What you were saying before."

"What I was saying about what?"

"Presents."

"Old," he listlessly derided himself. "Doddering," he said, attempting not to care, so acutely painful was his embarrassment. "Lavishes," he began, " . . . pathetic, pathetic."

"Lavishes what?"

"You cannot know the empty—"

Chase was sitting up straight.

"Really," she said, "don't put yourself down. Presents aren't a problem. There's nothing wrong with that, trust me. Look. Listen . ." Her face turned on, eyes and grin coming on full like footlights, backlights, klieg lights and spots and floods thrown at the same instant. "Just," she advised in a voice changing to something different, "relax. Think you can? Hm? Relax for me? Do you like that?"

"Of course who hee—ah . . who wouldn't I—"

"And that?"

"Who wouldn't . ."

"Et cetera," she said soft and low in a tone so sure and full of experience and so clearly having fun doing what it was doing that he slid down. "Don't worry," she was telling him, "just let me take charge of this little process here . ."

glublublublub

Later she was moving her head side to side as if to say no, kissing open his lips, pressing herself the length of him, taking charge of him with her tongue. He touched the swirling skirts of an appetite he'd never known—well, hadn't known since that forty-years-ago rogue first summer in San Francisco maybe, but not like this, not like this. Going down his arms her hands fitted his hips. She pulled his body, in that vicinity, to her as they kissed. Her hands slid behind him fitting to the curved buttocks that were his under the sheet—his old self that had been asleep.

He could feel her exciting herself with him. She sipped her excitement. She lapped at it, then was guzzling it. A thousand considerations melted in him and he was afraid—wonderfully—she was her excitement now and couldn't control herself.

The rhythms she fashions each flowing out of the last and over him are a lovely single flow of differences and spill into him and he floods with young energy. It's getting randy fast—he surprises them both by burying his moustache between her heaving legs and, moaning, she clutches his head. Inspired now his working lips and tongue are up over the skin of her belly to her my god, my god they are, little, beautiful breasts. And on up the tensed tendons of her neck straining to find her tongue with his, bearing her smells and taste to her. As her fingers gallop between her legs he moves them both a different way and is in her.

She runs her hands flat over his back, moving with his rhythms as he tries to find hers.

He scoops each of her buttocks in a rounded palm and shifts her, hard—confidently—a different way under him to make a new, angry, powerful driving pressure against her and they forget everything. It's aflame. It's violent. They want it, she has to have it, she loves it—he can feel her wanting it and having, this new way, to have it. She doesn't know what she's doing, grips him, pulls him. She cries out. Something with loose metal parts jingles and slides and falls. She's wild. She groans and manhandles him until he is exactly, precisely how she wants him, until this that she controls is the precise, exact thing, in the exact, precise way, in all the world that she wants.

It's a welling cresting exploding, baths of expanding light and tidal blinding warmth, heat from the birth of a universe diminishing, then over.

lub . . glub

"This is really," she warned no one in particular, after a minute's blasted amazed rest, lying beside him staring at her ceiling plants, "going to be troub(♪)-le."

So that was how that started. The following Tuesday, closing a door with a bell attached to it that jingled, twinkling on the dim air of the shop, he stepped in. He stood among reels, racks of spooled line, floppy hats, tweezers, holsters, pliers, pincers, scissors, forceps such as a surgeon holds a palm out for, thermometers, files for sharpening hooks, magnifying lenses, nippers, patches, clip-on tiny pen lights, retractors, holders, kits, wading boots, hip boots of varying permeability hanging from racks or folded in boxes on a table, rods assembled standing upright in their wall holders, hooks, vises, bobbins, bodkins, gauges, threaders, necks, thread, fur, hair, foam, chenille, tinsel, poly yarn and hackle of fowl. He stood on uneven wood flooring, looking around. After the doorbell's cheery notes came this silence. There was no one else in the place. He had been visiting tackle stores, along with subscribing to every fly-fishing magazine and ordering every catalogue and reading every book on fly fishing that he could get his hands on and talking to every angler who would talk to him. And until now, whether starting a conversation or stepping into a store or opening a fishing magazine, there had always been the sense of entering an ongoing conversation—of interrupting, and being welcome to, a celebration and fishing debate that was the point of it all, or a primary point of it all, but here, looking around and listening—hearing nothing . . . here was different. He lifted a hand, reaching toward a reel. But did not touch the silver wheel, and his hand fell to his side. He felt as if he had an obligation to keep silent in the still silence of all this merchandise devoted to the thing he loved. The shadow and dust smell of unsold gear was virtuous, profoundly good. The thousands of artificial flies in their compartments under transparent plastic lids each with a wooden knob for lifting, and more flies in compartmentalized plastic boxes stacked in towers on the counter and on the table beside the piled wading boots, and jammed into wall shelves between ratty-jacketed books, were a treasure so pure, so unfathomable and lost and now found, that he felt unable to stroll to a lid, lift, as it is the customer's right to do, and removing his glasses start taking a closer look at the caddises, mayflies, stones, streamers, nymphs and terrestrials in their niches. There were flannel shirts, windbreakers, wool socks, folded sweaters, a shipment of shirts of khaki, sunglasses, suspenders, mud guards, wading belts, staffs, fly dope in medicinal-looking bottles of dark glass, bug dope, lubricant cloth, reel seats, stripper guides, ferrules, cork grips, epoxy, split-shot, indicators, poppers, hoppers, creels, lanyards, clippers, backing, regulations, fly boxes, hemostats, wading shoes, bags, blanks and a chronometer that at the moment wasn't telling time. He stood in the low-ceilinged room looking around like a fish in a bowl looking at shadows in glass beyond which the fish does not know, but on occasion suspects, there is another world.

He had been thinking, on the trip over (and crossing the bridge over the mill flume under the piney hill by the cathedral had nearly run over some old fool of a soul on a bicycle) about physics, about which, when he thought about it, he had not thought in days. He had been idly shining his mind's light over one of his science's simpler givens, the gorgeous proximity of the Planck energy, which is the "voltage" at which gravity becomes as strong as any other force (about a billion-billion-billion electronvolts), to the energy at which we figure the strong and electroweak forces' strengths become the same (about ten-million-billion-billion volts). There was something more, he sensed, that his mind wanted to think about this. A further mental step he was ready to take. Nothing was clear. But he knew how to wait. It was mathematics, extrapolation on a log-log plot, and he trusted math . . . they'd tightened the calculation, updated it in light of better identification of the W and Z particles' energies . . . but there was something . . . something was mentally different in him. Having been ranging in philosophy and history now somehow when he came back to the long-familiar calculation he found he came to it differently. It was the same, but as the shadowed rooms of your house seem odd when you return home after a trip of many weeks, the equations looked different to him now in a way he couldn't put a finger on. There was something more to be thought about all this. He didn't yet know what. But he would get to it. But not yet. But it was there. The feeling of it was there, but it was weakening in this place. Then it was gone. He looked at boat nets, double nets, catch-and-release nets, miniature nets, nets of rugged cotton mesh and superbly laminated hardwood handles. He looked at creels of wicker and canvas hanging on the off-plumb walls among photos of anglers holding up fish. Also on the walls hung mounted bass, trout, salmon and walleye on oval plaques. The mounted fish filled him with the comfort and awe of things, items, practical in being necessary to a purpose, that are neither categories, states, forms nor phenomena. No, that 'cuda-like pike above the cash register—forward-eyed predator, taker of mice and young ducklings, death-arrow of remorseless, consciousless hunger—is not a phenomenon. The northern pike is not an Aristotelian actuality—never was. It's a pike.

Henry Anther was standing behind the cash register looking at him with, it might be said, a smile. Difficult to tell. Weathered face, vermiculate lips, muscular rolling shoulders and chest under his workshirt, eyes twinkling cold like houselights glimpsed through blowing forest, nose tufts, ear tufts, skin like hide.

Eden in his surprise jumping reflexively startled knocking boxes of fly-tying materials off a shelf. His hands leap to steady the topless boxes of duck flank feathers and hen pinfeathers and turkey tail and the short-barbuled saddle hackles of roosters, and he had the stuff, kept it from falling. Was keeping it from falling. Could not look away from the wrinkle-complicated face. Was sliding boxes back onto the shelf so they would stay—they stayed. He took—carefully—his hands away.

The boxes stayed. The two men looked at each other . . . it was probably a smile.

"You ever get a fish that day?"

Eden was nodding before he was talking. "Yes," he said, "I sure did. I got several in fact thanks to that fly that . . one you see—well, ah, one fell out of your box apparently ah . . not apparently. I saw it. It seemed you had plenty. I should've told you but. I did not. After you'd gone I rescued it and used it, caught several fish. And of course since then I have wondered often about the identity of you, er, who it was," my uncle concluded in humble confusion in the field of the other's gaze and, if, indeed, it was a smile, Anther's smile.

The shop's proprietor's chuckle was low. As he laughed his eyes shut a little.

My uncle was in a state of spiritual pain from having to be direct. He yearned to ornament, to amplify. But he confessed. "I took it. I should not have." He wanted to hang his head too, but Anther's gaze had him on a stringer.

"Wal," the other said, "I wouldn't worry. I'm glad it helped."

"My name's Eden Hope."

"Henry Anther."

The hand in his squeezed not from wrist or fingers but from way back in the forearm. The lack of a finger felt odd. The hand's temperature was neutral, not warm, not cold. A pulse of life came through the handshake, something quick, not vibrant like the lifepulse of a hooked fish or a bird caught in two palms, but so gradual as almost not to change, for all its silent power.

Flusteredly he told Anther about the trout he'd caught, about chasing after the yellow fly, about catching his first fish, about how each time he cast it felt like there was a trout under his fly, how he had looked down at them where they lay, one dead, one dying, in the creel Lim had smirkingly slipped into the mountain of gear he'd outfitted his brother with: the singing, deep sadness. The sadness of the sight of them in the mucous shadows. How he had gone back to the water and caught another just to be able to release it. How he'd returned the dead two to the wild, left them on the root-patterned forest floor for the weasels to find.

Listening, Anther ran his fingers over a clear lid beneath which some of his flies were displayed. His seven fingers lightly pushed aside paperclips, stray flies, a stub pencil and fishing-law pamphlets on the light-table lid.

Eden had run down and was silent. The shopkeeper, looking at his flies, let the silence tire a bit before speaking. "These," he said. His forearm, below the rolled-up sleeve, appeared among the flies as, doing it backwards and from behind, he lifted the lid from the front and reaching around and under and in got the pattern he wanted and brought it out. "Are real good too," he said, "for a day like that was. This here."

Holding the fly on his palm, Anther looked at it. There was a sea of calm in the air between the woodsman's eyes and the fly on his scored palm.

"Drifted," he said. "Ya know how t' do that? Drift 'em a foot off the bottom."

"Yes?"

"Yeah, they do pretty good."

"Truly?"

Anther looked at him.

"Well of course truly," my uncle quickly castigated himself, "I mean you just said so, I'll take some, could I ah, er, could I buy a—how many? How many would one buy? Half a dozen. Half a dozen. Half a dozen say?"

Anther's facial muscles scarcely moved. Perhaps a lift of the forest eyebrows as he gazed at the drowned worm tie he held.

"That ah, other one, I can tell you, that great yellow thing surely did work."

"Yeah, I thought it might."

"Hah?"

Anther did not seem to feel the need to repeat himself.

"You thought it might work, in other words you knew it fell out, out of the box, er, yes—heehee you did, well, I certainly." He was blushing. "I thank you sir."

"No problem."

"And that one you're holding?"

"Worm."

"Works like magic too," my uncle said peering at it, "does it?"

"Wal, under the right circumstances. Like t' try t' tie one?"

Excitedly he let Henry position him at the desk in the shop's back, and Anther stood behind him and just talked, keeping his hands behind his back to avoid succumbing to the temptation to reach around Eden's fat shoulder and demonstrate. Henry Anther taught his pupils their first simple ties—Woolly Worms and such—this way with great success, quietly and patiently using just words to make pictures of what, step by step, the pupil was to do. Anther explained the vise and told him to try the knob that adjusts the tension of the jaw, then: "Now pick a hook out of that little puddle of 'em to yer right at two o'clock. Ya hold it by the eye. What'd the 'eye' be, that's right. Put the bend of the hook—now what'd the bend be . . nope . . nope . . ." After ten minutes, an intrigued Henry Anther said: "That's all fer today," looking fascinatedly at the hook dangling from the vise jaws like a moll's cigarette garlanded with chenille, ribbing, thread and hackle in resemblance perhaps to a rat's nest or the paths of particles produced by a collision but not to anything that ever lived or died in a stream. And before he pushed his chair back, staring at the mess he'd made my uncle could not help or stop the voice in his brain saying to him in italics *you are irresponsibly fucking a sorceress!*

"It's just. Absolutely," he cried out fleeing the shop's behind-the-counter area in his shame over the failed lesson and in his anger at his own physical inability and his dizzy fear of the voice in his head, flinging his arms up to indicate all the fishing accessories around him, "marvelous. Glorious. Of course you obviously yourself, for decades I'm sure. But for me this is all beginning, discovered . . one can't express . . what a grand . . utterly . ."

Searching his mental data banks for an adjective he sensed, from Anther's posture, that his teacher (for that is what Henry would become), though he might use live worms and salmon eggs or a live hopper, did not use adjectives.

Like a child who has lost his ideas, doesn't know if he's good or bad or wants cereal or eggs or cookies or nothing or what to do next and so, guileless, trusting—having to be—stands looking up (in fact Anther was a foot taller), he stood now before the bald, impassive woodsman in the shop's dim. He stood surrounded by merchandise—tying vises, rod cases, tiniest coils of fine tippet material, mote-smallest #28 anonymous midge flies, massive, endlessly-pocketed vests, none of it displayed right. Boxes of stuff stood stacked uninvitingly, no loss leaders featured in bulk, the whole little place more like a knot of merchandise to be untied than a magic, spacious treasure house of treats. Smells of dust, linseed, canvas and, through a door behind the cash register, sweet-steaming kielbasy. The eyes of the other were on him.

Through the door behind the counter he hears the sounds of Henry's family of varying ages that has come home and is playing and doing chores and fighting and there's the noise of a TV. A woman bearing an unbelievable resemblance to George Washington sticks her head around the corner.

"You eating?"

"Ten minutes," Anther tells her.

"No-no-no please, I'm leaving, please, go ahead. I'll be back. But what I, ah, that's to say would—might one—"

"Aw sure."

"Teach me?"

"Sure."

"That's to say do you ever—well good. Good. Thank-you. I'd like to learn properly."

"Sure," Anther said—amused?

"So you would? Will? Give me lessons?"

If it was a smile, Anther's hand, with hair tufts, wiping the lower half of his face wiped it off as he nodded.

"I'll pay of course," my uncle said excitedly. "I'll pay handsomely."

Now, whatever it is, it is not a smile. In the dead-calm eye a heliograph glint, perhaps, of ax-head steel swung up at a great distance . .

"Er," the would-be student said. "Perfectly . . pay . ."

Looking at the shop's proprietor looking at him, webbed, spun and cocooned in the other's traitless stare, my uncle took a step backward.

"Or of course however," he found words to say, "you like."

It was a nod, before the woodsman turned to go behind the counter and talk through the door to his wife as the bell over the street door sounds, tinklingly, in acknowledgment of the entry of more customers.

A day later they were out on the Farmington.

# 8

Below a water-stair through immense rocks—pools and spills going up away through forest and sky—there were fish in a crisscrossing of currents, a rock here and there breaking the surface, the river a complicated intertwining of speeds, depths and directions of flow. To one side by a pocket of plainer water, cupped halfway 'round by tannish boulders, Anther had positioned him.

On the opposite bank it was all viny forest skirted at the current's edge by flats of reeds and muck.

The morning's few clouds were indistinct, vast puffs hanging, pale blue showing between.

"Like a church ceiling," Eden marveled, gazing up, his rod tip touching the moving water.

"Relax now," Anther said as they got down to it and his pupil started to get excited and make bad casts, "just relax now." It was the timbre of the voice more than what it said that, as they worked, and Anther never stopped gently talking, did in fact relax my uncle's spine's nerves and the nerves and muscles of the hands and arms as they worked on his presentation, float, and preparedness to strike.

"Now does it matter for instance if I hold this this way?"

"Naw."

"I'd had it like this."

"Naw it don't matter. Put it this way," Anther said, his black-billed cap tilted up, "maybe it'll matter later. It don't now."

He was slow to strike. When he did manage a proper cast, his line—static river of curves athwart the current, floating, with the current's passing, over mystery—was somehow so separate from him as sight and fact, and so marvelous, as he stared at it, with his boots sucked to his legs and the sun beating against his sweaty back now through the monumental vague clouds, and the hills' life all around him, that his spirit entered a loose untroubled state of peacefulness in which everything went away. Everything except the changing lights, shadings and movement before his eyes. Cool of the stream, the water's dank smell, the air's pure taste on his tongue, the currents' murmurs and the flow carrying his line in its curves past his stare

a shadow flashes

dreamily he does nothing. Is lost some seconds more in his reverie. Is totally and unconsciously a part of the stream's sufficient beauty. His delay might as well have lasted half an hour. The trout's gone. After the fact, realizing his friend said "There" with—for Anther—a tint of urgency, and that a trout has tasted his fly and gone, he finally, sheepishly, half-lifts his rod uselessly to Anther's amber chuckle.

The moment when the fish was there mouthing his fly and he missed it glides away on time's flow.

Steady and animal, Anther's eyes are couched in wrinkles. They are not smile-crinkles like my uncle's first wife's, but dust-bowl ravines, quake faultlines, saber scars, grand and old deep wrinkles like elephant hide.

The turtle-blue eyes coldly twinkling.

To call a human's eyes "animal" may be wrong or mean many things but what my uncle saw (though Anther, watching the professor by simply moving his rod tie elaborate knots in his line, may be forgiven for not noticing his pupil notice it) were eyes alert and intelligent and not caring, as a squirrel's eyes do not care. A squirrel's eyes, a lion's sandy eyes, do not care. A squirrel's eyes watch. The squirrel will act.

They are natural unurgent eyes with just the sharp, unvarying light of simplest thought.

Anther understands the wild, is much less sure of men.

So spectacular is Eden Hope's uncoordination when he gets flustered that it becomes almost a beauteousness of anti-coordination—Eden can tie three knots in his line by hardly seeming to flick his rod at all, can threaten, with a bare economy of motion, to spill all his flies from their box and drop his rod and lose his hat all at the same time. Looking across the small space of swirly waters at his student, Anther is trying to fathom if this one can learn. He thinks yes but isn't sure, not sure yet . . some never are able to.

This one's full of professor talk, comes from Norham, one of the old families there. That may be all right too but Anther will have to see, time will tell. Anther tests. Being innocent Anther can play innocent—more innocent than he is. He tests by watching, once he's told Eden to keep his line running through his right forefinger, to see if Eden will do it, will forget, or, even more interesting, will find times when it's easier to ignore the remembered lesson and on his own experiment by going beyond what he's been told.

Anther is wary as a woodcock. He gives his pupil chances to make a fool of himself to see if he will. "When your casts's on the water," he tells him, his own big, scored hands holding his rod to the side, "and your fly's started its float you get ready, you be ready, be expecting a fish."

"I . . . *strike.* I'm going to *strike* . . . ready to *do* it."

"Try it."

"er, you mean without—"

Anther's silence.

"—without even a fish there?"

Anther's silence is his pupil's testing. There is no one thing he wants Eden to do, or hopes Eden will do. He wishes by his silence to let Eden answer his own question, and back flies the rod in an exaggerated strike and flying up off the water comes Eden's sharp fly which you or I would duck from but Anther, unmoved, has measured and knows will miss him. So. He went ahead. The pupil went ahead and tried. Good.

They worked the pool. Eden got one and they moved upstream, Anther shepherding with a cautioning, steadying hand. At the next run they came to, teacher positioned pupil and watched, without speaking, the presentations and floats.

He wasn't doing quite what Anther wanted. Anther put him where he wanted him. "Here," he said. "Stand here, cast there."

"Sort of . . like that?"

"Not half bad, try 'er again. 'Dja see it?"

"A fish?"

"Yeah it followed, didn't take but it was lookin'."

"And I . . there. Like that?"

"Sure that's ok, git ready now, here it comes again. There. There," Anther said with Anther-like excitement.

"'There' *what*?"

"You had him. You shoulda struck."

"Could you," my uncle implored with the least trace of annoyance, "say 'strike' or something instead of just 'there'?"

"Sure."

"Okay trying again, trying again, trying again," Eden panted under his breath, "trying-again-trying-again, ahhh . . 'bout there?"

"Yep."

"Ok-ok . ."

"There."

"You mean—"

"A fish has your fly," Anther declaimed, "in its mouth. My advice 'd be to go ahead and strike now."

His mind threw up an insight having to do with categorization that suggested inconsistency in the reasoning of St. Thomas Aquinas and believe it or not at the same time a whole new angle to come at matter-energy from.

But you know what happened? He was going to reel in, ask Anther to hold everything and try to find the pen and spiral notebook he knew he had somewhere in his vest, but know what happened? The motions of the stream, the flow not just of water but of the water's currents and speeds and temperature and random ornaments of turbulence and noise swept his perception away downriver to the great joining of waters where the currents widen as the branches of an elm lift to the seas of the sky.

"Careful now," Anther said kindly. "Pay attention."

The fish was lost, but soon he had one.

Fishing with Henry Anther seemed to help him. Anther didn't tell you what you should or needed to or ought to or must do, but simply, in a nice voice, unhurriedly described, as if it were already happening, what you were going to do. "You're keeping that extra slack out . . . you're keepin' your eyes right on your fly where it's floating, and on the water under it . . . you're keepin' that line comin' down from that rod tip—that's it, that's got it . ." Even when he wasn't doing exactly what Anther was saying, Anther kept saying it. Not telling him to—telling him he was. And it worked. He focused and fished better, out that day with Anther, than he had ever done. Though it was soon autumn breeding time for them, and those that were working weren't exactly what you'd call ravenous, he got four.

Anther's eyesight is supernatural. If he sees half what he says he does, the Defense Department needs him. Under what to Eden is the usual dizzying interswirling of watersurfaces Anther sees, with clarity, a world of fish, this one near, that one far, that one holding, this one traveling, one feeding selectively, another taking everything it sees—"Git ready . . git ready now . ."

"Huh?"

"He's lookin', he's tight on it, git ready—"

"Goddammit I'm ready for god's sake," the pupil splutters happily, "but I don't see anything."

"Wal he's—there!"

"You-mean-'strike'-*got* him! Damn. Missed."

"Almost. Almost. Okay now see that one in tight to the bank under that branch?"

"Oh bullshit."

"It's right . . in there, under that biggest branch."

"You can't see in there in all that shadow. It's forty feet away for god's sake and it's in total shadow, don't tell me—"

Anther's chuckle is short—sound of a rolled kettledrum backstage, fast, over with. He gulps his wad juice and says low: "There's a fish. Right about a foot downcurrent from that last evergreen branch that's almost touching the water, down about a foot, in about a foot. It's a good fish. Brookie I think."

"And the son-of-a-bitch can *see* it," Eden tells me waving his hands. "He's unbelievable, I'm staring at a treebranch and some flat black water under it and he's seeing a trout, registering size, registering species for god's sake, unbelievable. So I try. I make a couple casts, one ahh, good, one a mistake. He's there right beside me all tensed, if he gets such a thing as tensed . . . amazing—" my uncle thinking of, seeing it "—tensed like a fish about to take." Pauses, looking for something—insight? cigarette? idea?—among the moderately ordered papers on his desks. "So I say, you try. You catch it. He says aw no but the second time I say it the man's fishing."

Eden stood by watching his teacher unlimber his rod and magically get plenty of line out almost instantly and make two perfect casts in the time it would have taken him—Eden—just to get his line ready. On the backcast and even on the forecast Henry took shortcuts Eden didn't even understand. Although he was always in control and every least move of angler and rod and line was beautiful to behold, Anther's line did not flower, long and straight, out behind him on the backcast. No, he did something shortcut with it, and before you blink it's traveling forward tight-looped to tuck, perfectly, in under the branch just above the lie.

On the second try Anther caught the trout in a bulging water hump locomoting for his fly as it slid under the branch.

His brother, Eden now realized, was only fair. Until this day he had considered Lim good. Now, watching Anther in this short minute's fishing, he realized that Lim used up time and line unnecessarily and wasted rod motion, and he could also see how Lim did things in steps, little quanta, instead of one smooth-flow line-action without waste.

The line unfurls in its loop over itself close to itself to get in under such a branch as dusted the level, dark water there, and Anther made this happen with understated wrist action. And the strike when Anther made it to set the hook after the fish came on toward the floating fly happened in a smoothness of slow motion that paradoxically was fast. Eden tried to describe it—Anther's style—how it was different from Lim's. He sprung from his chair to crouch in a stream I had to imagine lifting a rod I had to visualize to set a hook I couldn't see. He tried to explain how although he had thought his brother was fast and smooth Lim wasn't fast or smooth compared to Anther who somehow was already starting to lift even as the fish was coming to the fly, a melded continuity of motion, fish taking, rod lifting, line tightening, veronica-like finish smooth in the snagged trout's explosion in the current, whereas his brother, he realized, executed the strike by the numbers—barely perceptibly so, but so nonetheless: 1. Fish comes, angler doesn't move. 2. Fish mouths, angler doesn't move. 3. Angler moves from standing start while fish still has fly in mouth.

"There," Anther said, invoking the point of his barbless Aberdeen stinger through the fish's lip, hook-bend tight from within fish's mouth against lip, and the contest was on. "See that's why I say 'there' I guess, 'steada 'strike.' 'There''s kinda where it is."

Yes Eden was thinking, yes watching his friend play, coax, allow, bully and corral the big trout home. He's a continuum when he does it. Lim's good but Lim when he does it is "Step-One-Two-then-Three," and of course I'm "Step-Two-Halp!-before-One-oops . . sorry . . "

It was a fine trout and Anther, his rod elevated but not dramatically, with a lean down had the bright-colored fish in a hand without squeezing and lifted it, sagging, wild-eyed, dripping, colors of forest and sky shining from the current for them to look at.

The forest wall was patched with tufts of dirty gold or orange and dull brown—last leaves—but most branches were bare, stark in their gestures among each other, except for the slumbering vines. Describing, Eden said, is dreaming. Impressions—brushstrokes—words such as "branches," "dull" and "stark" evoke not the real but a feel of it, the illusion of the thing. Dreams aren't sensually complete but use fragments, shards of mental image, and so does the painter when she pens, say, "the pointed firs" and our mind thinks it sees forest.

Go stand in the water there. Feel the pull. Look across-stream at the high, dense forest when there are still a few autumn colors left. Feel, as Eden told me he felt, the sheer lunacy of imagining that human or any kind of perception has any relevance ultimately to the forest's nature or life, let alone being a condition of the forest's existence.

They ate a sandwich each.

Deciding to keep on fishing, they made their way downstream to some riffle water where they would try. Both fished now, six yards apart casting across and quartering down as they waded the chortling shallows. Fishing this stretch up would be better than down but now that Eden had done well on some fish and retained a few hints, Anther sensed it was time to just fish. Fish together, right or wrong, lock the lessons in under a laminate of happiness. So they strolled, in their boots, to the extent it's possible to stroll on changing bottomstones, on down through the splashing water dappling the waves with their patterns. Flicking a side glance like a cast Anther noticed Eden, clearly remembering—looking down at his finger (the one you're supposed to keep your line running through) but not doing it. On purpose not all the time doing it. Which to Anther is good, is fine. It's a breakable rule, unlike some. It is one of Anther's many little tests. Eden glances guiltily at his crook'd finger but doesn't ask, lets the line (held of course in his left hand) fly free of his crook'd right finger on some of his longer casts, which by Anther is good. Doesn't ask. Is just trying it. Good for him. And so they imperfectly dapple their flies on down the stream side by side, down the clearing afternoon, laying their lines out languidly, and Henry catches one, Eden casting as Anther bends to release the over-excited trout. Then Eden is catching a little one as Anther is casting. One of them is stopping to—elbows out—tie on a different fly. The other is casting. Then both are casting as, footing uneven, they angle their way on down the rocky stretch . .

"You know when you said you left them fish, the ones ya kept that day? In the forest fer the weasels ya said?"

"Yes?"

"Wal, somethin' woulda eaten 'em. But not weasels."

"No?"

"Nah, a weasel likes blood, warm blood. Nasty animal."

"Really?"

"Oh I seen all the hens in one henhouse, all the hens in one single coop, twenty-five, thirty fowl, killed by a weasel, one single weasel. I saw him. When I was a kid."

"No."

"Aw sure. A weasel kills for enjoyment a lotta the time," Anther said. "A weasel 'll kill a lot more than it can eat. Just bloodthirsty. Kill 'em, leave 'em there. Rabbits, mice, chickens. Bite the neck, suck a little blood maybe. Leave the meat."

"I don't believe it."

"Wal, ya don't have ta."

Eden laughed. In a head-cloud of fortunately momentary intellectual outrage he knew that animals do not kill gratuitously—only men do. What Anther was spinning about weasels was not true, because it could not be. This, from his beliefs, Eden knew. Politically he was a theoretical radical utopian, though his activities on that persuasion's behalf stopped just on the far side of voting and writing out the odd check. He knew, because it's obvious, that humans are good at heart, as is the world, and laws have to be passed to make sure, and nature is good, but some humans aren't, but this can be explained. But Anther was a natural simple soul and obviously did believe what he was saying about weasels, so let him have his myth. Let him think any beautiful animal would kill that way. It had been a wonderful day and Eden wasn't about to spoil it by pulling mental rank. Besides, another spunky native had just flashed out of the waves to hook itself and was pattering and flopping all over the surface, as he waded, reeling, toward it to set it free.

A sight, held a second to behold, bright in sunlight. Brightest of all the bright trout under the water. The flanks of the wriggling little being are silvery full of candescent spots—spots such as what you see when you see spots before your eyes. Only these are red, these are blinding gold and purple vermilion blue orange dancing in the light like fair music or banks of violins racing about the highest registers as he stares down, appreciatively, at what he holds in his mind's memory that night, in the bedroom darkness drowsing with sleep, before succumbing. Spot rainbow color, sunlight of a held native trout. He lies under the covers with his cheek against the pillow feeling the line's life aquiver in his muscle-memory and, dizzy still with the stream's sound, can remember if he doesn't try to. Is unable to remember, closing his eyes in the pillow, when he tries to. Dreams of the shining fish that doesn't know its name resplendent under the sun before you return it to its world.

He was a long time learning to fish and never did learn very well. It was too actual—but he loved it. He unreservedly loved it, to stand, nerves at attention, eyes straining, poised to set his hook not after the trout has come but as it comes.

—so different from physics . .

And had returned late that afternoon wonderfully exhausted to a house that was peaceful. Very unusual. Rairia was singing and baking, singing old jazz tunes—badly—baking bread, then cookies, and finally, before bed, a cake.

Lim had driven his daughter who was Nora's age over to sleep over and do homework together. The phone did not ring. The doorbell did not chime. Lim had dropped off some of his latest crop of cider which he bottled elegantly in forest-green former champagne bottles, and everyone had some. Brown apple-gold ice-sparkling taste with deep-sea suns in its russet essence. It was as delicious as the best sights—hues—winds, noises and textures—of autumn.

A peaceful evening with no one moving past anyone else's perimeter of privacy yet all of them together. With his day outdoors on the river all through him and a well-being both physical and spiritual strangely come to hover, like angels about your ears, he fell into a deep sleep before it was nine-fifteen and slept like a log 'til eight the next day—very unusual.

"I don't see what it has to do with me," Chase said, when he tried to explain fishing to her.

When Chase Parr was down—energy about absolute zero—she could appear not even to believe in her own existence. Who, the haggard, staring eyes seemed to wonder, do these doctor's reports refer to?

They sat passing them back and forth. Dutifully he looked at what he was handed and when he had looked a page over would return it to her and she would stare at it for a long, empty series of seconds—wrecked—decimated by what she was seeing in front of her poor little eyes—before passing it back (or some other page) to him for him dutifully yet again to be amazed at.

"I cannot," she said.

Her body lifeless like a rag in a bag in her nothing over-the-head dress. Eyes as juiceless as a shut-off pinball machine. She still managed a trace of archness in her tone. Shoulders, however, curved despondently, the wide lips unsensuous, the eyes without magic, the stage unlit, the theater empty, the Universe uncreated, even her varihued chestnut hair seemingly nothing special today as, hugging herself, she sat looking at her results—a wash of printouts on their laps and on her laminated hatch-door coffee table and the rug between them.

Frowning, silent, lipstickless, Chase sat in a cloud of gloom.

"Believe this," she concluded. "I cannot. Believe. I am seeing what I am seeing. According to this I'm allergic to everything."

He took a deep mental breath. Holding a sheet to his face, as if to read, he was able to look at his watch without her seeing. Half an hour, he calculated—half an hour to humor her, choking off the urge to tell her to grow up, then bed. But it took an hour to humor her instead of half an hour, and then she said she was starved so they went to a late dinner, after which both were tired, so he drove home. So the next time he steeled himself for there to be no sex. And only minutes after she'd buzzed him up the golden bird was flying on schedule. She'd been smoking something. Lust without love in its hazing heating light, as fun as rhetoric without argument, inspired her to handle him roughly, not able to stop once she'd started, and he likes this, encourages her, pleads with her to. This excites her more. The chick's egg cracks. Out the bird comes spreading growing wings that get tremendous fast and the soaring bird full-grown and growing spreads amazing wings and shrieks becoming the size of the sun for eight full seconds and is everywhere—is every wet, heaving, blinding thing—

then gone

they lie together, resting . .

closing her eyes she turns her head on the pillow toward him, and lifts a hand to his face

"It's still there," she says.

"Yes," he tells her ceiling plants.

Chase had something he'd never met, a beauty—superficial and in flashes deep—and a worshipful appreciation of beauty undercut by a street-ambitious egotism so endurant, final and full that one could only marvel at the frequent irresistibility of her allure. Only the ideas he courted in his work were similarly attractive, so long as you served them as slave.

For Chase, pondering, a bloody nail hooked over a canine, marble eyes option-considering, the facts of the matter are that even with plenty of men on her plate she must still be careful, always remember Anguilla as an option while looking out for the little girl in pigtails picking posies in the sun-halo meadow of the untouched part of her heart.

Despondent Chase, languorous Chase, adoring (to an extent) Chase, beyond beautiful just now with her chin on him. Mahogany hair gold-streaked washing over a rounded, dark cheek on his chest, as she stares at her fish.

"I wish you would explain me," she says. "I wish you would explain me to me. I truly do."

In the surveilling dusk of autumn evening he would make the homeward drive out of that seaside town with its seas of unwrinkled student faces bobbing in rivers under gothic towers and glass. He went through a phase of making colored-pencil diagrams, in his Mercator pajamas, in his study late at night with Rairia in the house somewhere fiddling neurotically with the furniture. They were Venn diagrams, ethical schematics, crazy crisscrossing angles of lines of responsibility, accountability, value and imperative taken from his reading, as confusing to me when he agitatedly showed me them as what we think blows out of an atom smashed apart at the heat of creation. He was buying her things, a dress, a sapphire, a bottle of *d'Yquem* one waning, yellow-gauzed afternoon. A trip she wanted, wept that she must have, a long weekend to London to just. For once. Be away. From everything and everyone (though it turned out she wasn't). Even, in the confusion of his obsession and infatuation, twenty shares of something Lim had the family in.

She is frank with her body, relaxes in postures, unconscious of how well she moves. Looking at a canvas of dense message-ridden crowds of apocalyptical horses with purple manes, she stands with a hand on a hip, an elbow out, a leg out, turned at the waist, suede jacket open and her head turned, hair across eyes.

Half the people in the gallery are looking at the paintings, half at Chase. Furious with him, she has without trying or thinking about it struck this pose that a fashion photographer would gladly spend hours trying for.

He makes himself look at the painting.

Decades have passed. The Pollocks and Picassos of his youth are become the dusty classics of yestertime. Today's stuff thirty years ago would've been old-fashioned.

Rainy raw heads-down weather in that seacoast city of coffee shops and concerts . . . on the parquet floors of the museum, rainwater from boots beadily shines.

The award-winning building is shaped like a teardrop. The architect has designed up a storm, laid the droplet on its side, concaved the ceiling smoothly and specified benches, freestanding, of superglued cardboard, sturdier than you'd think.

Along one wall of her award-winning design she plays like a xylophone run a window row that gets, curvingly, lower as the ceiling does.

How much of our lives' time is wasted.

He touches Chase's sleeve.

She doesn't want him to.

A cool air-eddy following her, she strides three strides to stand looking at the next one.

He goes in steps to her side. Holding his beret where he might hold a fig leaf, he speaks.

She doesn't answer, and then neither is saying anything as the moments wear on.

They move—drift—to the next one.

He would arrive at her apartment of an afternoon having taught his seminar and puttered in his sterile university office (desk, chair, undusted shelf, phone), and she would not be there. So he would walk, cross and doublecross the town streets with the gray faces of the dumb young pouring at him and tailing away behind his back. Couldn't think. Strode as involuntarily as his fatty heart beat, to and fro the streets trying not to check his watch, then would go back. And she would be there. But with someone. *He* is the rejected Bright tonight. He stands inside the entryway door conjuring, as her boiling, whisperous voice through the speaker holds him, a detailed vision of her naked in his poor helpless mind as he bends before the black call-buttons while they wrangle.

She will not buzz the door open. And he has not been offered a key. If she did let him in, under the circumstances he probably wouldn't want to go up. But since she won't he wants to. But doesn't rant, isn't Bright. Could be but wills self dignified. Doesn't bang on door, doesn't raise voice, stands, beret in hand, as he describes it in the journal he is now increasingly keeping, bent over the circlet of holes in metal into which his voice (" . . of course I'm here to see you. Why for god's sake else?") goes and out of which hers comes (" . . I cannot, believe. Look—" her tone lowered tensely as if the other him up there listening with her weren't listening inches from those extraordinary clavicles "—can you just please! Call me."). Then he's in his car and in the autumn night to his left and right as he drives are the tame, enigmatic lights of the country houses, the farms and manses of the hills winking like fast stars through the darkness through the trees.

She was sitting, purposefully, on the other side of the room from him their next time together. This, one could see, was unlikely to be a night when they would get into bed. One could see this plainly in the admirable way she sat, a leg crossed against him, her shoulder offered him like the prow of a ramming ship.

"If you were trying—" her voice like the larcenous eyes, sepulchral across the fish-glugging room "—to start a fight—" she looks down, surprising him—vulnerable "—I must say you most certainly—" defeat in her voice, to make him the sorry they both know he'll be "—achieved your purpose."

He hears himself say: "I'm sorry. If that's what happened, then I'm sorry."

He stands to leave, half ready to, but she is in control. In the mascara-flashing deep angry eyes it is very clear that if he wants to leave it is more than alright with her. So he doesn't. They go out and he buys her two sweaters. Talking about which, her package tucked under an arm, strolling the melting lights of the town's student evening streets, they have hit yet again on some life business, stage business, to move them away from the really vicious argument they periodically approach but never, ultimately, seem to want to have.

You drive somewhere. You buy something, talk to a person, return home—answer the phone because it's ringing, but, filled with the flu-passion heart's foggy bacterial working out of all this in you, you scarcely remember having driven, talked, made a purchase. And now on the phone your voice sounds unreal and you wonder if you're saying what you think you're saying. He was in just such a fog, the state one gets into in which one does things that later one can only wonder in retrospect at one's ability to have gotten so wrong.

Even Chase wondered about it from time to time as the weeks passed.

"It's fine with me," she told him airily. "It's fine with me if it's fine with you, but I fail to see where it's getting you."

It would invariably be just when he was pretending to himself that he was at last seeing it for the ridiculous thing it was and was finally resolved and prepared, right now, this day, to break it off, that somehow he would be there in her apartment again, as if he had appeared—been transported instantaneously instead of having walked, yet again, through the streets to her alley. And they would be in bed again, seeking their pleasure, finding it where they knew they would. By mutual unspoken consent they would stay off such subjects as the future or her other men, and stroll to an early dinner drifting first into a store.

The gentle high of it when it was this way was not entirely false. The oases of good times in a bad affair are often more, not less, powerful because the affair is bad—in the beginning anyhow.

Gamely when she was up Chase Parr would be telling you what a good time she was having unless, enthralled by you, hanging on your every word and limp before you with admiration for you, she would be listening to you talk about your life or give her advice on what you had thought was a fairly straightforward matter. If down, she sucked all your sympathy and attention in as she complained of her travel problems, her allergies, her men, her enemies, her mother, her uncaring cousins, her ennui, her self-doubt, her desire to be alone, her need to be with people more, her reputation, her bad luck, her job, her lack of furs.

One time at a party—this was years later—in the middle of going out (conspicuously, in her attempted secrecy) with no fewer than four of the dozen men in the room (one of which four, I hardly need add, I was not), she came up to me with slight tears of anger I think it was, and moving close as if to take hold of me—I could smell the fabulous Nile lavenders of her uneconomical perfume—breathed: "Oh John . . John . . do you think there's a chance for us?" *Me?* She was something. And she wasn't yet thirty. She was just getting started in those years.

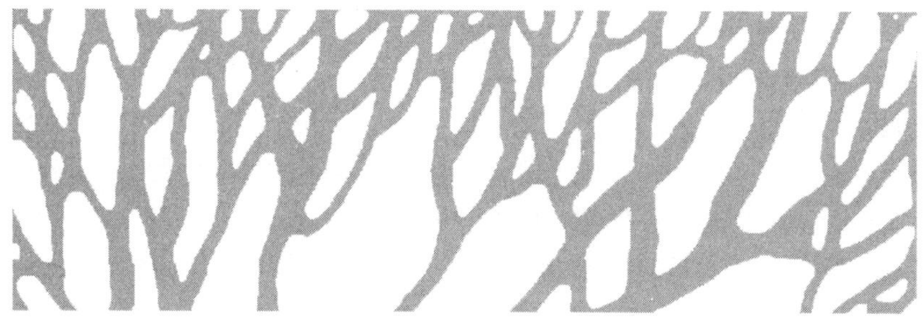

# 9

Nora had a boyfriend, a dreamy dropout who gave her protracted French kisses on the bungalow steps. I had to step around them. Opening the front door I could not help looking back at the sexy wooers, and consequently nearly tripped over Alan Elwive's cousins Jemmy Diaz and Luke Hope—grandchildren of Lim's. Luke, five, a warmhearted thug without an untrusting bone in his sumo wrestler's body, was the little brother of eight-year-old Jemmy, a lover of gowns and frightful plots at whose instigation the two were methodically timing the teenagers' kisses with Eden's stopwatch.

"Three minutes," Jemmy whispered to her dial-mesmerized partner as I recovered my balance and passed through the shadows and ponds of sunlight of the house, wondering if being timed made Nora and her boyfriend kiss longer.

He was reading something he'd written, sitting at a tilt in his deskchair behind the strewn battleground of his work, wearing a vague, bemused smirk of skepticism as he reviewed his words, an unlit cigarette walking back and forth between his fingers, books everywhere—texts, tracts, pamphlets and journals of philosophy and physics and troop disposition and who knew what. Alternately at proud attention and sloppy at-ease on their shelves, the books and monographs he'd written rested under the smoky, papery hang of the room's air between the knotty-pine walls and under the cathedral cross-beamed ceiling: *Introduction to the Ontogeny of Time and Space, Math and Mirage, Beyond Strangeness in Basic Quantum-Electrodynamics Renormalization,* and, of course, "my playthings," as he referred to them, *The Search for the Sword, Lady Gwen, I Dreamed that My Father Rode Beside Me* and his other popular fiction in monster-dancing, galloping-prince, damsel-cleavage hardcover and paperback splendor as well as the indecipherable swirls and runes of the foreign translations Lim had been able to hawk.

Slamming his papers down he leaped to greet me gladly, stepping on Emma who with a yelp sprang to four feet and then, as he profusely apologized, lowering her golden head and wagging her tail came, side-to-side skittishly, lovingly, back within the madman's range to be patted. He shook my hand and sat me down and at once became distracted, turning away, talking to himself, smoothing his moustache, drifting back to his desk, not to sit but to look, as he talked to me about the philosopher's dream, nowhere in particular.

. . something about—he was speaking muffledly and I had to focus intently to hear—Sartre's distinction between the two types of creature that are in the world. First is the animal, who according to Sartre is unselfconscious and thus can be said to live in itself *(en soi).* Second comes self-aware, self-making, self-becoming us, the human being with all its creative capacity and penchant for deception, who lives for itself *(pour soi).* And . . I leaned forward some more . . the little joke he'd thought of was that trout were beings *(êtres) en eux*—"in themselves"—rather than Sartre's singular "in itself." Thus to express in the plural what Sartre had spoken of in ah, the singular was funny because it exposed and undercut Sartre's closet solipsism (*en-soi*-singular being so monad-like), for all the great man's campus comradery and drooly communism.

I started to ask a question but he sat down hard. Opened *The Upanishads* at random, jabbing a finger down and commencing to jabber.

"The neutrino doesn't zing," he said. "It could be said to float as much as zing. I've met the most amazing man."

That was when he first told me about Anther, then worriedly it was Nora without a conjunctive—he spoke tightly, lit another. He was concerned.

Nora's grades had never been good but now suddenly they were outright bad. More ominously, her soccer coach said she was "just playing anymore on talent," not trying. She had given up her student-government responsibilities. Quit the school paper.

When they finally went to speak to her teacher, Rairia and Eden were subdued. They sat with their hands on their knees and there was no bickering, no intellectual stunting. They sat listening, and, quietly, answering when Ms. Corelli asked a question, their hands in their laps, their own lives not necessarily exemplary, their brains balanced upright on their shoulders in the neutral-carpeted common room: cheap shelves of expensive textbooks, maps pinned to walls, leftover tea sandwiches under clear wrap on a platter.

They sat there, in school.

Ms. Corelli said a number of pleasantly ice-breaking things then posed some innocent questions to relax them and told them their daughter was exploring (pairs of fingers scrunched down in the air to put quotes on the word): "freedom."

Ms. Corelli's whole being smiled at them, Eden, for some reason, sweating profusely. She took them through themselves and Nora and what they would have to do. Having to use paper towels from under the countertop sink now that his bandanna was drenched, with a brief spurt of optimism he addressed some of the more famous philosophers' notions—freedom as revolt, freedom as piety, Kafka's quip about the bird that flew out in search of a cage. Then, in the spotlight of his wife's and Ms. Corelli's silence, quit. Hung his head, out of ideas. Stared, eyes goggly like aggie shooters as a new salty droplet formed from the tip of his nose to replace the one that had been there.

Cheerleaders in black—black jeans, black turtlenecks, black combat boots—hurried past the doorway.

In her expensively embroidered cowboy vest Corelli knew Nora was their last, their baby, no longer so short she could be lifted, no longer so trusting she could be fooled, no longer so small that to look her parents in the eye she had to look up but rather, rushing toward adulthood, Gibson-girl wistful and mysterious, blue distant eyes, lightdowned skin, gazing, when home, at TV, a magazine, the terrarium, her untouched plate of food, her head full of thoughts her mother and father by definition couldn't have, whose own lives, hopes, achievements and marriage, as they sat there in that warm room, did not seem—to look at them—sources of pride.

It was time for them to talk to Nora formally. Ms. Corelli expertly guided them. In effect they would neither forbid Nora to go on seeing the boy nor fully hide their displeasure. For all her cowboy embroidery and smiliness Corelli had steel in her heart—palladium maybe—she could care just enough and do what was called for. Did they know what a relatively mild problem this almost certainly was if they could just do a few fundamental parental things?

But he snapped into the old role, he told me, shaking his head. He would get all set for a conversation with his daughter and carefully open it on a topic—fly fishing, MTV, baseball, the weather—innocent enough to relax them before he would attempt to rudder the dialogue around to the subjects of her life, but they would end as they had started, sparring, gibing at each other, bickering back and forth in the comradely way that apparently was all they knew.

Rairia did a little better but it was Nance, barking at her sister long-distance, who could hold Nora's attention the longest.

Joe Bitterbeer disappeared one morning leaving a woebegone note attesting to the impossibility of accompanying life with music. With him he took several thousand of Eden's dollars in the form of acoustical equipment Eden had staked him to.

"Not again," Rairia said.

She stood in the doorway to the master bathroom, a towel around her blowsy body and one turbaned 'round her head while she waited for the use of the shower.

"Not again what," he gruffly asked, bending over the sink to slap mouthwash against his face.

"Somebody ripping you off."

. . . he was peevedly toweling off his cheeks and nose and didn't reply.

She was going to say more when dropping to his knees he walked about on his knees, bobbing his head, waving his arms from the elbows like chicken wings, urging, pressing, goading her to guess—"Who am I? Look, who?"

"Toulouse-Lautrec."

"How'd you know?"

"Eden," she said, leaning against the jamb. "I know, believe me."

"I wanted you to guess."

"Well I'm sorry." She smiled down at him as he started to get, in the stiffness of his sixth—it soon would be his seventh—decade to his feet on the tile.

It was less a smile than a sad remembering.

"Believe me," she said. "I know you. Whatever may have happened to us . ."

She did not know what more to say.

Quiet, on his feet, not looking at—but looking near—her massive familiar form in towels, the satiny somehow graceful folds of her, the blackgray lush hair peeking in wisps from under the wound turban, he was thinking about it too.

If tyrants can slaughter whole villages an estranged husband and wife can obliterate decades of shared good. But not these two, not quite, not yet. She still cherished—even, paradoxically, as she resented—the fixed meals, folded laundries, kissed and dressed kids' cuts, worked-out disputes, unpacked religious holiday decorations, swim meets, car pools, cookies, colds, miseries and moments of sun-washed joy of the last two decades.

He wished her well and wished she would go away. In his passivity he wouldn't dream of lifting a finger to hurry her. Their first summer together, that long-ago time in San Francisco, the illicit excitement of deceiving his first wife, the uncluttered first years of his and Rairia's marriage—these distant delights were like the ruins of a civilization buried by the ruins of a latter one. Still, there was a certain bond and respect between them, he told me.

But Rairia was unhappy that fall, unhappy and uncertain. She would go silent for hours on end then explode. Asking her a simple question was like pushing a button on a talk doll. She would make mistakes, buy the wrong bread, tell Alan he was scared, throw the mail out, until somebody got angry at her which, strangely, seemed to satisfy her. The negativity in her seemed just that, a force from within. It looked for an outside referent, an imagined wrong, a word or look from a salesperson, an unpredicted weather change, if nothing authentic was available.

"I don't mean this negatively," she would preface herself, then go on to rant.

She was nasty, short, glum, then answering the phone would transform, instantaneously cheerful if—especially if—it was just a charity or some acquaintance she hardly knew. Her hair, for one disconcerting stretch, changed practically daily: henna, grayish, curled, straight, frosted, moussed like a maniacal anchorwoman's and—for a blessedly brief succession of hours—dreadlocked.

She made conversations drag on until the other person was nigh desperate to be somewhere else, walked out of rooms without any sort of farewell, had to know what was going to happen, could get furious—the fury of uncontrollable anxiety—if plans changed unexpectedly, then: "Nevermind. Nevermind" she would bite off bitterly, and be gone.

She kept his house and at her desk in the kitchen worked on her causes, her political pamphlets, her volunteer canvassing and local-election watching, to the extent she could get herself organized.

She seemed to be addicted to being told to shut up. She would talk until something stupid came out and if no one's goat had been gotten would push it, and harder, until she got what she wanted and could be furious.

Thinking all this, wasn't it strange to be in realtime passing her fleshy actuality wrapped in towels in the bathroom doorway and to say to her: "All yours."

Did Rairia know what she wanted? Did she harbor hopes? Hates? Would she go? Would Gwen ever come back? Should he confront her? With what? Did it matter? Was he patient? A coward? What was the right thing to do? His mind retreated from these questions to his study and the far easier inquiries of Plato, Aquinas and Quine.

Alan Elwive phoned three evenings running to get help for his fears. In his bed at night, tucked in, prayers completed, main lights off, his wall-socket nightlight throwing a distorted blossom of shadow and light up the wall, he heard things—creaks, clunks, a door opening, things on the roof, things everywhere, sounds that could be skeletons or teenagers (Alan was in a phase of being preternaturally afraid of teenagers).

Alan's parents were practical people. First Nancy, then Lt. Cmdr. Elwive, then Nancy again, taking Alan's cool little hand, walked the white-faced, trying-to-be-brave child through the upstairs rooms looking under each bed with him, peering into the recesses of every closet.

They thought they were proving to Alan that there was nothing there. As Alan's grandfather immediately understood over the phone, however, all the exercise proved to the little boy was that there was nothing there when he and his parents looked, the grim corollary to which was not lost on the diminutive figure in his animal pajamas as he was led, a second and a third time back down the hall to the tangled dinosaur sheets of his unease.

Alan's parents loved him very much and wanted to be reasonable. But they were starting to get annoyed, at Alan for continuing to get out of bed and pad downstairs, at themselves for their inability to comfort him. When, rubbing his eyes and walking around the livingroom, he mumbled something about how Grampa had told him things one visit that made him feel better when he was scared at night, they phoned the bungalow.

It was late, eastern time. Alone in bed, in sleepy disgust Eden had just tossed Spinoza to the rug and clicked the light off and was slippingly losing consciousness when it was the phone ringing—he lunged for it and got the bedlamp which fell against the wall smashing the lightbulb. Sitting up, groping in the blackness for the ringing thing, he finally got it. He picked up the receiver, holding a hand on the dial to keep himself from knocking it somewhere, and answered . . . over the night-hollow three-thousand-mile line came the brave-hopeful fear-energized voice of Alan who launched without greeting or identification into an exegesis of his needs.

Eden understood at once. Alan didn't want to hear there were no noises in the night. He wanted to hear that there *were* noises, and that the noises he heard might be many things, his dad or mom walking, someone putting End-Dust (the cat) out, a mouse running behind the wall on an errand, a squirrel on the roof, the washing machine, his dad snoring (here Eden demonstrated several varieties of snore, feeling his heart leap at the startled, relieved little laughs coming over the line).

Shortly after they hung up, Nancy told him, calling minutes later, Alan was in bed asleep.

Why couldn't he have done this with his own son?

All the years of no letters, no calls, not when Thomas had been in college, not when he had been away at school . . . the fishing trips they never took, the advice Eden was never asked for . . the only communication from Thomas in recent years had been a curt, friendly note accompanying a copy of the professional-looking catalogue by means of which he sold his knives.

. . . Chase on white marble. Chase caressed by gauzy curtains blowing in a doorless doorway: Mediterranean glints miles beyond. She is reclining, her tummy suck-in making her look better even than she is. She modeled, in the photos she shows him, just that one time for a lark. This in the photographs' gloss is the she he thinks about when with her, when not, when angry with her, when eating, when working, when here, when home.

It's classy to purr and wind this way around his white uncle's body as if she were an ether snake.

Chilling him. Suddenly she wants him cold. Why would she want to make him cold? He shudders, as she runs her tongue over him. This is learning. She's breathing power in. She can feel how one day she'll confuse princes of the realm, mind-ruin captains of industry, etc. She moves under him various ways, looking for it. Faster. There—no . . . yes, there it is, the molten bird banks in blackness to glide back looming everywhere into her and she cries out and it flies dripping, scalding from her ripping from her and still flying and pouring from her and still, like a long, speeding locomotive of light, pours from her

she was panting, sobbing, finishing, panting—finished . . . finished now. She felt of him, patted his back, sobbed, once, felt her breathing slow and go normal. She lay looking up, marveling as she came back. Sitting up she pulled her hair up and held it high behind her neck with both hands. Frowned, the S of her back rising darkly above the sea of sheets.

She turned her head to look down at him through her hair. Seeing him nonplussed, she giggled. She fell against him. Said something about eating, where should they eat, she was hungry, where should they go?

The phone would ring and when at last she would hang up while he sat, fuming, in her bed, she would go to the window and look out it hugging herself, saying nothing. At the window staring with those illegal eyes into the mirror of herself that she was, she would make him speak first, waiting, tapping her forearms with pic nails and breathing through flaring nostrils, for Chase Parr was on the birth-to-death express, which makes only one stop.

For two straight hours he sat with scissors, Scotch tape, rolls of glossed paper and ribbon spools, his fumbling fingers stuck with stickers and pre-tied ribbon bouquets, to finish wrapping every gift. Nora, standing by the tree after dinner, had her splendid hair French-braided—stunning conch-shell sweep in the back.

Sitting by the firelight, watching it, in his slippers and robe, he could not help but be aware of the fact that he had a daughter, this woman before him, watching the fire too by his home's holiday pine bedecked by them all with its tinsels and gaudy balls and candy and lights, who was seeing an older boy whom her mother and father wished her to forget while he, the person sitting in this mellow firelight and reflected tree light thinking this, was involved in a thing down in the city that were he his own parent he would immediately force himself to halt. Laying this out in his mind was as far as he got before, sensing that if he thought about it more he would have to face a guilt and a moral lassitude in himself that he did not wish to face, shutting his eyes he let the sounds of Alan's trumpet and the voices of the carolers and the crackling of the fire and its smells in the season's soft lights lull him into a nappish haze of holiday relaxation as unprofessional as the haze in which the physicist nudges—coaxes—bends—his supposedly objective data toward triumphal discovery of what he has all along had it in mind to find.

. . . her throne is hers. But there may be a heart she cannot trust within these walls, unlikely enough a traitor that, taking his wicked ease astride his mount, the Night Master smiles confidently. So much is at stake, the quest of generations, dust clouds of centuries above the caravans and sallies—Eldertarr's stand at the pillars, the festival of the fanciful faces, the betrayal of Gwen's lover and their son by the angels of the pretty good. Old Blok putters deeper and deeper where his bride, Gwen's genius mother, lies in body only. Pitifully Blok bids his wafer-winged Lehwhurlerra flutter faster, more cutely, more beautifully about his eyes' sorrow, and when they do he gets angry at them and kills a couple. Nattering measurement and proportion her advisors, their wheels flashing under their thunder-and-lightning skirts, bow up to her with a do-si-do bobbing with lowered heads to lift, for her inspection, their sheaves of proof that she can win. Her advisors are the tenants of reason and she is wrong to ignore them but she wants her lover and their son the warrior back to make this fight. She does not need their swords for the fight . . she needs their company to be able to want, herself, to fight. Gongs, sheared mountains and braziers jammed upsidedown on the heads of oafs are so distant where her enemies deploy as to be but an undifferentiated growl, yes, oafs. But the Night Master isn't, and he is smiling. So much is at stake: a reasonable and caring, peaceful world . . or din, slavery, savagery, woe, the mind-mining of the Night Master's shackles, which she has felt, and which are mist. The battle will probably decide. Of what her counselors have wheelingly to offer, of the Tarr children's and her own provincial friends' contribution (once they've eaten), of these and also of the factor of the Sword, whose use is tricky, and of her love for doddering Blok and the memory of her mother and the coming, soon, she must hope, staring at the useless jewels on her hand, of her lover and son, she must make a plan. What part strict logic, what part oaf-lust of the provinces, what part Sword and what part memory it is hard to decide as sniffily Blok, getting sad again, bids his Lehwhurlerra whirl. Does she expect the Master to act? His drums mix on the twilight with the crashes from her dungeons and kitchens. It is doubtful he will attack as formed up, that he will proceed in the direction in which he will appear aimed, that he will—if they speak—tell her more than a fourth the truth. This much she knows and can thus be prepared for as the hand—hers—lifts—bejeweled—to wave her chief meteorologist forward. The implications of the battle are immense, the peoples' future and her own, but no, whatever Master Night does his way is sure to be as circuitous as her riding son's and lover's way is straight toward her over the blossomless deserts to these settled suburb dells with trees, chocolate-brown bark and a green egg—each—on a trunk stick. Oh Jegorian and their illegal son Rowain, how she needs them to fight for. May their steeds' way be as straight for instance as the path out from the sun of a certain infinitesimally small, nearly impossible to trace, perhaps massless sub-subatomic—

"Are we among the living?"

It was Lim's nasal voice in the mustard blackness behind the shut eyes that were Eden's Christmas resting own. He came back from his dreams of Lady Gwen's kingdom where battle was battle, bad bad, good good and guilt could not be explained away—where victors lounge before blazes quaffing and tossing boar thighs over ermine shoulders onto floor stones for their hounds to stir, grumble over, and settle down to gnaw . . . fantasy—that isn't the way the world is. But it felt good to dream of and was probably the reason the fiction had been such fun to write, and sold so many millions of copies . . .

"Yes," he said. "We are." His throat made a noise like a drain as he fully woke. He sat up and waved his brother, who was looking at him, into the chair opposite by the low, steady breath the air the logs were taking in was making. "Merry Christmas."

Lim had mulled cider in a pewter grail. One of Nora's trophies. In the blending light of ornament color and flashes of tinsel and swaying fire shadows Lim was looking at him with pride.

"Merry Christmas," the little man toasted. "Happy Whatever. And here's (if I may) . ." Sitting back into the cushioning of the somewhat decrepit, still serviceable chair from the machicolated mass of black fieldstone that soared and sailed before your eyes against the sky, Lim lifted his cider in salute lowering his head and smiling hard. "Here's to *The Sword's Return.*"

As if woven in tapestry—static forever, an irrevocable (no matter how zanily the measurers might dream of wormhole travel in time) memory, the brothers sat, Eden with less hair standing up wispily, Lim waiting with raised cup and shutmouthed smile.

"Here's," the little brother tried again, "to—"

"*The Tree of Life* is actually what I'm thinking of calling it . . when I get back to—"

"Here's to *The Tree of Life.*"

Neither's expression changed. And did not change, during the following exchange.

"Here's to—"

"I heard you the first time Lim. You've been toasting it all night. You have me dreaming about it."

"Good! It's almost finished, right?"

"Ah . ."

"When's it going to be finished Eden. You said Christmas, you said Christmas very clearly."

"Spring."

"Spring."

"Yes."

"You sure?"

"No."

"Oh wonderful. You're not sure."

"No." Quietly and with a degree of stubborn tiredness.

"What's it this time?"

"Lim—"

"What."

"You look ridiculous. You don't have the physique for Santa Claus."

"When Eden. When. When'll it be finished. That's what I need to know. What's the problem. That's what I've got to know. What the problem is. If I know what the problem is maybe I can help."

"I want . ."

"Yes?"

"I want, you see, to come to an understanding."

"An understanding."

"Yes. To the extent possible. A deeper understanding, it's difficult to explain."

"A deeper understanding of what?"

"Of life."

Lim lowered his goblet. His smile went out. His narrow shoulders under their scarlet velour sagged, and his cap's snowballed peak was drooping as he stared at what he had just heard.

"Eden."

"Yes."

"What are you doing."

My uncle leaned forward. He'd lost eleven pounds. He was earnest. He was still heavy but less so. The number of particles comprising him was down. He was thinking. He had ideas. It was going to be hard to explain, but he was going to try. Beyond all the vases and utensils he'd broken in his life, beyond the far-from-final, incomplete theories he'd blueprinted in his vocation—and the facile fantasies he'd stumbled on as a hobby, and beyond all the times he might've paid more attention to a loved one and—behind the shut study door—hadn't, he wanted nothing less than the security of knowing that he had at last done some shining, final thing. And so—he was stubbornly rowing toward it—beyond the errors of his ways and the unfinished state of his work on all fronts to date, beyond doubt, beyond the imperfection of his mortality and his sloppiness and bashed hopes, something fine was calling to him. It was waiting for him. It might be in physics. It might be the last Lady Gwen book. It might be both. To get there he was reading, the philosophy, history, psychology, military strategy and other sundry stuff lately increasingly overgrowing his workroom. He did not want to make his final intellectual assault on a universal explanation of matter/energy, or to try to finish *The Sword's Return* (under its new title), until he had gained, as Lim, later that evening, hysterically told me waving his baggy scarlet arms—until he had gained, Lim croaked, "a sense of the meaning of things, that's what he said, those are his words. A deeper understanding of. And presto. Bah." He threw his cap on the hooked Oriental and looked about to jump on it with both boots. "A little philosophy here, a little history there—bah. So I tell him, I ask him, can't he postpone it until he finishes the book. I remind him that like it's not just the rest of the advance we're talking about here. No-ho, we're talking—" yellowish forefinger hooked in sequence over first, second, third and fourth apposite other-hand digits to tick off his points "—foreign, mass-market, audio—" dramatic pause "—mooooooovie rights payments hangin' on this. Plus it's not good for him to screw around, it's not just the money in this; he's wandering, I can feel it. So I tell him that's what we've got churches for. They save time, you don't have to sit around for twenty years scratching your navel and reading every book ever published to figure out how you think it all fits together."

He was silent. Obviously this hadn't gone over with his big brother.

"So then I try hubris, the hubris approach? Like who does he think he is sitting down for a year or whatever to figure it all out—" evidently this hadn't worked either "—and he says to me awwwwwwww—" Lim's voice lowered warbly as he tried, picking up his cap and jamming it back on, for his brother's bass "—he says ahhhhhh, I realize ahhhhh, I do realize I may ah, I may be ah, I may be discommoding my—heeheehee. I hate that. I hate it when he does that. Discommoding my ahh, agent he says, but I must go where I must go. Exact quote. Shit."

Eden had tried to explain it to his brother. Trying to place each thought and idea as he learned it in the context of the mental whole that he wanted to form, he was trying to link, to overarch. It would be nothing complete—he knew better than that, let alone perfect—anyone knows better than that. But he felt and said—tried to say—in the floriferous bass, leaning with his arm on the chair arm and looking at the fire's glow as he spoke and Lim, his held cup beginning to tremble, watched him, it would be something. It would be something true or at least in ways would partake of the truth. He was convinced that completeness is not a prerequisite of coherence. (Lim's eyes crossed.) There could be, if he read and studied hard enough, glimpses, glints and facets at least, of a truth true for all cultures, planets, peoples and times . .

"Yeah right," Lim scoffed fidgeting and cackling as if a host of sexy scorpions were swarming under his suit. "Something universal right, sure, I'm the Tooth Fairy by the way. I mean what's 'overarching'? What's 'overarching' supposed to mean? Didn't 'overarching' like go out with spats? Gimme a break, what's he planning—like he's gonna overarch the whole world? Will somebody please explain to me how you can overarch a globe?" Satanic satisfaction of a grin, though Lim Hope wasn't as bad as he wanted to be. "Answer's you can't, you can't overarch a globe. Isn't that right? Wouldn't the only thing that could encompass a globe be like a ring or a halo or whatever which would by definition be circular? Know what I mean?"

He saw Anther over the winter, would drive on sun-blinding ice to Anther's shop, of a Saturday, under sky blue as porcelain. Past the deep green of the northcountry groves he would drive, through deep winter, such as they used to have up there—snowbase four feet, puffs of iced powder blown off pines, the morning clear and bright-frozen as errorless thought, his feet chilled in his mukluks on the pedals of his jalopy. Over to the shop he would drive to poke among Anther's flies in their compartments under the transparent lids, to shake—wristtest—fitted-together rods to learn their action, to finger unnecessary woolen shirts and try mentally to talk himself out of the bamboo six-footer his naughty heart knows no rule, theory or ethic is going to prevent him from buying.

The group would arrive, drifting in one by one through the bell-tinkling door for their Saturday fellowship. Their easy discussion and debate was truly a social phenomenon, he told me. It was like the old general store he said, waving the unlit cigarette he was trying to give up, a time and a place and a gathering—informal yet with seriousness, but not grim—a loose group bound by common interest and in need of information, news, rumor, the physical touch of things familiar (wader—smooth, cork handle, lid knob—coffee) to renew their sense of themselves as part of something unchanging. Just like the old crackerbarrel community he said enthusiastically . . and they called him "professor." He liked it, I could tell. It was Henry Anther's idea, the kind of teasing that goes on. He threw the still unlit bent and crumbly cigarette down on his papers. When a question came up—the cause of a kill, a detail on line tolerance, do trout have a memory, what's the best canoe—the old woodsman would chuckle his low, flood-rolling-boulders-underwater chuckle and suggest they "Ask the Perfesser here . ." Implicit in their teasing my uncle with outdoor-sport questions he didn't know the answers to was their acknowledgment, conscious or no, that there were other, loftier questions he did have the answers to . . . his gaze and voice trailed off. You could see he was proud. He wanted to do something, know something, understand something more—to leave behind something more. I don't think it was because he thought he should so much as it was because, apart from thought, a devil of religious craving wriggled in him.

Because he was a person whose spiritual side you could make the mistake of not taking seriously, given his pratfalls and selfishness, I feel I need to emphasize that when his gaze drifted, and his words stopped and there was that silence, it was a silence not of content but of yearning, of unfulfillment and need, a place of hollow in him, for all his energy, that had always been there but only now, probably because he was no longer young—and probably too because he had had success, was starting more and more achingly to demand to be filled with something.

On a winter morning in the fishing-tackle shop anglers look over merchandise. The sport's earnest children, they are less interested in the pricing and quality of the reels and wood-handled nets they pick up and examine than they are interested in getting quietly into the great themes-braided conversation that is fishing. All Saturday morning here in the erratic pooling radiator heat in the cluttered space of poorly displayed rods and boots and reels and vests and nets and the fur and hair of animals and the feathers of birds, they weave time into loose intimacy. They swap news of local streams, offer opinions on hatcheries and stocking practices, talk about the weather and argue the possible merits of the streamer pattern Anther's inventing at his tying desk, in the back where he sits, too bashful to be among them, listening and talking to them over a shoulder as he works.

"Gossip's—heehee I'm telling you, gossip's a big part of it. It's this sort of, in many ways a kind of a quilting-bee mentality, stitch, scandal, stitch, rumor—bah," he says to the unlit cigarette. Throws it down again on his work. Looks at it, glares at it, wants it, wants to smoke it. "Who's stolen whose fishing knowledge, who's suing whom for breach of contract, what manufacturer is pushing rods that fall apart, who's going out of business, who broke a promise, how a so-called pro—" exhaling blue smoke in a musical unturbulent stream "—ah, for instance faked a distance cast or lied about a catch or tied a pellet imitation on or stiffed somebody, ran off with somebody's spouse. Honestly—" another meditative lungful he doesn't seem aware he's taking from the cigarette he doesn't seem to realize he's lit "—it's like anything else I guess."

With the blue stream his stare and posture loosened into that distance of wanting that I keep wanting to describe, a yearning, a dream of something fine or transcendent, a world without gossip and meanness? I'm guessing. All I know is that for my uncle it was real, and it had him. It drove Lim up a tree.

He looked forward terrifically to wandering in, come Saturday, to browse, joke and chat and drift in and out of the discourse about easy things that they all drifted in, through the bell's jingle, and out, under the bell's changeless goodbye, of. ("Wish some a' you bastards 'd buy somethin' once in a while," Anther mused, where he sat with his sun-bleached workshirt back to them, tying in the halo of shadowless light shining on his vise.) Radiator-clanking mornings. The familiar shop clutter and people—men mostly, but not all—of different ages. Surgeons. Liars. Skinflints. Fine anglers. Jerks. Boobs. Rich ones, dumb ones, beginners, punsters, pedants, schmoozers, champions, saints, collectors, experts, kids, caddis freaks, Eden, sycophants, quiet ones who knew where to find trophy muskies, bohemians, spin fishermen, butchers, conservationists, neurotics, good souls. Not even introducing themselves often, as if the names don't matter, handling the merchandise, milling about, leaning on the counter to ask Anther a question, falling into conversation with one another or just browsing, listening, and finding, in these tales of fish behavior and human comedy and the rise and demise of streams, a sense, fleeting as snow blown off the branches of a pine, of the world as pleasant.

You can lose a fish you wanted to catch and be discouraged but no matter how fine a fish it was it's not the same as losing a friend. You can break a rod or fall in and be laughed at but it's not as real as making a human fool of yourself in the world-life of love, commerce or war. Victory over a trout you've been stalking for hours is joyous but not as significant as a deed of mercy performed in the face of religious rejection, all of which is part of what makes fishing a fly a respite, a release and relaxation, because when you fish you can care passionately about, as if it were as important as children and bread and shelter and faith, stuff that isn't.

He didn't know this.

If he should find Anther alone—have the old rodder's company to himself in the rickety dust shadows and oil canvas smells of the shop's years, he would tour the displays of spools and neck plumage and assembled rods of differing heights coyly, in his shiny 44-inch-waist chinos . .

"Look at these nets, trout nets, salmon nets, boat nets ah, nets for netting fish from float tubes, yet ultimately they all have but one purpose, and—thus—" peering at the variously sized long-handled baggy-meshed objects of his analysis where they hung on the wall and lay copiously under the pike's yellow eye "—thus they are all, in an ultimate sense, the same net."

"Wal." Anther laid a finger at the horizontal under his nose, sideways to rub the nostrils. "Some of 'em," he said, "are fer nettin' a fish you're gonna release. But some are fer nettin' a fish you're gonna keep."

My uncle, who had been reading Carnap, looked at him.

"Ah, yes," he said, careful as an angler taking up slack. "But are they not all . . in any event . ."

"Wal." Anther spoke uncomfortably. "All I'm sayin' is that nettin' a fish you're gonna keep is different from nettin' one you're gonna release."

"Good, that's good but—" caution "—still is not the purpose of the net in all events fundamentally to snare the—"

"Aw . ."

"Perhaps it could be argued, ah, you know that basically there are two fundamental types of—"

"Aw Christ," Anther said lumbering back to his tying desk.

". . such an enchanting way to pass the time," my uncle was effusing on another occasion. "Women and men going down to the waters peaceably—I never dreamed . . the civility, the devotion to detail, but playful, always that marvelous context of—"

"Yeah," Anther said at his desk tying a Mickey Finn.

"—and that first time—that day I ran into you, oh when I looked into the creel my brother tricked me into accepting and saw them, saw them in their death—do you know I nearly wept? I caught one more just so I could let it go, as I've told you but. Which really I—how I could have failed to . . but when you're—and the sort of ceremony, I mean the votive—when I set the dead ones down on the floor of the great forest—"

"Aw Christ." Anther let the bobbin hang. "I take a dozen trout a year from a place I know nobody else fishes. It's a legal limit just about, and there's plenty of fish there. My family needs the food, I take bass and I take walleye fer the same reason and I take a deer each year and small game fer the same reason, it saves thousands of dollars a year."

"I was merely—"

"Wal I was merely."

My uncle had the good sense to leave it.

Everybody liked Henry Anther.

Sometimes after fishing the two big men, one stomping and bumping lamps gesticulating expansively, the other maneuvering—moccasins as silent, on floors and rugs, as American Indians' soles on leaves—around the toys and cousins and bungalow guests, would drink some cider or a beer together sitting side by side in a pair of threadbare chairs or two of the fan-backed summer wicker chairs Eden and Rairia used year-round, looking, as they chatted, like Churchill or Stalin and Roosevelt at Teheran or Casablanca. They would talk of angling and the outdoors which Eden, with his keen mind, was learning about—intellectually: he still tripped over logs and couldn't surprise a groundhog. Henry Anther, in his hearty twill workclothes and gas-station-attendant boots, was politely at home, called everyone by their first name, comported himself with ease, smiling civilly at the house and its activities—smiling? Hard to tell with that scored, weathered landscape of a face—is a turtle smiling? Does a rhino smile? Is that a smile in the gnarls, swirls, whorls and burls of the tree stump you're looking at? Yes. It was a smile on the weatherbeaten face, a smile in the sharp twinkly eyes, a smile—faintest ghost—on the chapped lips, a smile certainly not of condescension or mocking but of amused acknowledgment. Anther's ease was impressive. Like Churchill or Roosevelt leaning, elbow over chair arm, he would consult quietly with his new friend—none of that handwringing desperation to please that even good people can succumb to in a house they fancy is fancier than they, nor yet with the stony silence, awkward embarrassed, of a man without an old name in a house where, however cluttered the floor, however frayed the lampshades, venerable names, achievements and generations hang invisibly on the air like an admonition. No, Anther with dignity and aplomb sat and in his customary few words conversed, there in the bungalow, with all the naturalness and quiet enjoyment of a long-lost cousin.

He and my uncle respected, were wary of, tested and taught each other. Eden knew the old woodsman worked hard for his family, which was a couple dozen in number counting the in-laws and grand-nephews and nieces that hung happily around the rooms of good-cooking smells and TV sound and pleasant shouts beyond the door behind the cash-register counter . . . there was a question he wanted to ask Henry Anther. He didn't know what it was. The seven-fingered pair of hands was working with invoice copies and the shop's ledgerbook and inventory listings (such as they were)—back turned—at the tying table behind the counter.

Not knowing what his question was, but feeling it—and that it was important—my uncle stood touching a pair of Neevar™ boots suspended among relatives of similar synthetic derivation from a rack designed for a different purpose.

Anther was reconciling his books by hand at his tying table. He was smiling the crocodile's steady, uneven ajar grin that is not one. The skin around the eyes star-wrinkled, cratered from rain and shine . . .

Knowing at last what his question for Anther was, but not ready to ask it, feeling of the interesting-feeling boots he asked—for something to say—about them (the boots).

"What," he said, "do these mean?"

The satiny fabric, manmade molecular units marching through empty halls of space to frame from within—polymer necropolis—this sheeny, no doubt remarkable material . .

Anther stood behind him.

"You said," Anther said, "what do they mean."

He was in thought, didn't answer.

"You said," Anther was half-telling-half-asking, "what do they mean."

"Oh sorry I meant—"

"Cause a-course I couldn't tell ya that."

"I meant ah, what properties do they have."

"They don't let ultraviolet rays through. They're real hard to puncture. They're light . ." Anther went on, paraphrasing the sales rep who'd talked him into taking three pair of the damn things. He could see the professor was scarcely listening—thinking smart stuff—but he kept on talking, maybe to sell a pair, maybe to see how much he could remember of the rep's spiel, maybe just to keep some specifics on the air.

*. . out of vacuous clouds, Earth formed.*

*First was rock—minerals, batholiths. Then busybody plant and animal life came into being usurping. Centipedes, spores, spirochetes, fronds, hopping birds, fish, horned growly monstrosities scurrying around.*

*The rock was very, very angry. It stayed angry for 3,000,000,000 years. That basalt has a will. That malachite* pulls *Molloch's eyes down to it . . .*

they have evolved a tool, *the rock says to itself:* thought. Good. I will make them their tool's slave. I will make their tool their master. They will think. I will make them enamored of the image. They will think about their world, about themselves, about thinking . . I will drug them with dreams of thinking. I will cause them to live in a future that never comes. What they possess, *the rock decided,* will define them to themselves. They will use me—minerals, ore, jewels, metal, alloys, polymers, isotopes and fossils and combinations of these—to distract themselves from what is real by desiring wading boots impervious to the sun's ultraviolet.

This is from years later but it's as good a flavor as any of the kind of thing I have to guess was beginning to be in his mind as he stood looking at the hanging boots.

"—be stored pretty much any way at all," Anther was gamely concluding. "Hung 'r tossed in a closet, which a-course is a plus."

"mm."

feels his soul's about to sneeze—has to get home. He had it bad—none of us knew, then, how bad. Had to get home now to his study to make notes and read and study more. Could feel Anther's smile, if that's the word, following him as he made his muddled goodbyes and rang himself tinklingly out into the winter air.

Soon is home behind a shut door reading, scribbling, crosschecking, standing, pacing, blowing out a breath he isn't aware of having held, maybe lighting one, maybe not. Wagging his mind from the neck slowly, hands on hips, to uncramp a thought.

Sitting down, banging a knee, grabbing a pen.

Sometimes he saw, or thought he did, in his notes and pages, a wink.

It was incomplete not because it had yet to be finished but because incompleteness was its essence. But it was there.

Saw the skirts rustling away offstage. Saw a shining city of knowing that if you looked at it disappeared and when you turned your mind to look at it from the side came into partial, ghostly relief. It was universal and as such incapable of ever being more than a third built but capable, with luck, and if he worked hard enough, and gave up smoking and this thing with Chase—capable at least of that.

# 10

One Saturday Trent Ott walked into Anther's shop, the door's slam behind him cutting off the bell jingle as if a big bang might end it all, after all, as well as having begun it.

The Saturday morning customers were in field clothes, examining tackle. Quietly they conversed, over the vintage cash register and glass-topped counter, with Anther where he sat tying Hornbergs in the bronze light of his brontosaurus-necked lamps. No faces turned or conversations stopped until Ott started walking around introducing himself and handing out his card, laminated in four colors—brown/black, green/yellow—announcing him (beside a generic fisher striking with his line slanting at an acute angle to a canary-yellow splash) as Assistant Editor of the magazine *Angler and Trout* but not, understandably, announcing his intention to be Editor one day soon.

Ott's surfaces—skin, nails, hair—were as new looking as his silver felt Stetson, a popular hat among sportsmen later that year. His teeth when he grinned were as blemishless-frictionless as silicone-dressed line. The shaven wall of his cliff jaw and cheek shone like chrome brightwork on the most expensive, highest grade Pflarger #2.2 Tarpon Reel, of which he owned two, having paid for neither.

He was pushy but politely so, even charmingly so, a comin'-atcha frank zealousness of self that offered, to tell the truth, a measure of relief from the inbred core group's weekly coming in between nine and eleven to take up their familiar stations and begin their feeding on each other's gossip.

It wasn't 'til Ott went around the cash register and introduced himself to Henry Anther shaking hands and saying flattering, true things about the old angler, asking pointed questions and admitting his ambition to know more and meet the unknown best fishers of the region, and make *Angler and Trout* the best magazine in the industry, that I saw Eden take notice. While my uncle remained bent over one of the compartmented trays, with its clear lid open like a car hood, the brown, rheumy eyes came up. The eyes came up behind their spectacles and his whole face seemed to move forward, the eyes clarified, the skin around the big nose taut.

Anther was standing now and ducking his head as he received compliments he deserved. At Ott's persuasive invitation without apology they got into a pretty good give-and-take on the mote-sized, weighted midge nymphs Anther sight-fished in late summer on some of the smaller regional streams and was in his reserved way proud of. He and Ott stood back there talking. They seemed unmindful of the rest of us and it seemed to me Henry Anther's voice was a tad loud. I expect he was impressed, though he tried to conceal it, by Ott's having heard about him and his microcosmic nymphs.

Driving home looking straight ahead with his blotchy hands at ten and two on the wheel my uncle suddenly, after a rather uncharacteristic stretch of silence (though when I thought about it it wasn't so uncharacteristic, lately), said: "there's no reason I would've known about them, no reason to think—in the first place they're for summer, 'second place I couldn't . . he probably ah, I'm far from a level of competence competent enough er, to be able to, hm. So why would. One would still of course, like to see them, ah, of course to see them fished . ."

Looking up in disoriented dismay at the chorus of leaned-on horns in the rearview mirror. Staring forward, through the insect-streaked windshield, at the traffic light just turning red again.

The following Saturday Anther with considerable difficulty and reticence and, thus, obscurity of message, at last got Eden to understand that he, Anther, hoped that Eden as the scholar that he was would be able to stay, this day, after the morning crowd had left because—this was hard for Henry, who never asked for anything: "I got sumpin' t' show ya."

"Something?"

"Wal."

". . yes?"

"Wal," the old angler grumbled, kneading his nose, "I wrote sumthin'."

"Ah! Did you. Written something—oh. Henry that's—I can't. Can't tell you how . ."

My uncle's fusillade of encomium continued although, bowing, even blushing a touch, the woodsman lifted a callused hand.

"Of course of course of course—" excitedly "—understood. Understand. Not now." Voice lowered with difficulty. "Later." Stage-whisper. "Very ex*cit*ing."

To speak of this thing to my uncle Anther had come from behind his counter and feigned a bit of business with an unlevel shelf of gravel guards. Now Henry stood, uncomfortably, while his friend went jubilantly on in a whisper as others around the shop took increasing notice.

Henry beat it back behind the counter, across the altar boundary and back to his tying desk, and my uncle winked to himself, fluttering a restraining—himself-restraining—hand. Secretively he made as if to examine some packets of coiled leader. "Mum's the excellent, excellent. But. Of course—" *sottovoce* to himself "—I wait—" wink "—incommunicademente hee no seriously. When things have . . cleared out. Perfect." Nodding sagely to himself and quieting, the childish bulbous face quieting, closing down . . . Taciturn. Secret again. "Mum. Later, of course . ."

When it was past lunchtime and the last of the morning crowd had left, Eden sat briskly at Anther's tying table to be handed, by a hovering, nearly nervous Anther, eight or nine ratty double-spaced typed pages on fishing the weighted midge nymph. Leaning erect—businesslike—toward what he'd been given, the "Professor" started to read. As the other read, Anther spoke of mistakes he knew he'd made, changes he wanted to make, and was shamblingly admitting that he wasn't any good at writing but maybe—

"Just," the reader said, patiently but firmly, lifting a traffic-cop hand but not his eyes from his reading, "take it easy. Let me read—" quietly, distantly, absorbed "—now that's good, this is good, good . ." Thus he read the woodsman's pages and it was fascinating, he told me, to come upon paragraphs of fine writing amid the timidly tinkered-with, the backtracked-from, the toned-down and hoked back up again and, unconfidently, marginally come off of.

"So there I am reading, and the poor man's nervy as who wouldn't be. Brave. He's written this—" wave, expansive, of unlit Camel "—draft of an article on how to catch trout with these tiny things . . and it's good, ah, rather it could be. I can see how it can be made to be, but it isn't now—it's terrible in fact. So. I ask you, what do you do? What do you say? Do you say well, now this has much that is good in it, and it's improvable, but right now as it stands it's dreadful?"

I started to shake my head—

"Right!" he bellows. "I know what I'm doing here, I'm on ground I know—thinking, writing—I tell him it's surprisingly good, this part's good, that part's good, the crack he makes about slack. I show him just a little—quick—how here and there he . ."

With the curiosity and fear of an earthling leaning over the crib of a Martian babe, Anther the old outdoorsman, face calm, gnarled hands together before his belly piously and then—awkwardly—hanging at his sides—then slipped into his pockets, leans over his friend's shoulder to look at the passage he wrote about slack. It was a clever heuristic two-sentence crack about slack—twenty perfectly conceived words sparking off each other, "really," my uncle nodded to himself—remembering—when he told me about it, "very very good."

So a*hem*, they can't do this here he tells Anther, not here, not now, not today. Come over to the house he offhandedly invites. "You see I could have edited it then and there, finished it. Wouldn't've been hard. Two hours. But you see—" the wild-haired head cocked as if to say *comme-ci comme-ça,* but a wince of work-pain concentration too "—see I want to do it in a way that gives him confidence, confidence he can do it, not just me with sleeves rolled up ignoring him for two hours then presenting ah, you know handing it all back to him all fixed, so . . make sense? Course. So. Some days later, by appointment naturally, over to the house he comes, sits where you're sitting. He's all ready. He even . . and this is—this I thought was really wonderful. He has two sharpened pencils sticking up out of his shirtpocket. That moved me. Sits where you're sitting. We begin."

Anther had two calipee-yellow pencils, points up, in the calico pocket of his shirt. He never carried pencils. A figure of rounded and gentle bulges, forehead and temples like the flair of a galleon's hull, Henry Anther had shoulders and a chest not fat, the way Eden's were, but considerable, used, indurate. And his hands were large. The hands had done a lot outdoors. They rested now on his knees. Two polite hands ready, two poignant unnecessary pencils, sharpened, points-up in the old angler's pocket.

"I ask him: 'Ready to work?' Teasing him a little. Says yes, yes he is. Says yes, ill at ease, for him mind you. This means maybe the eyes move, maybe they move once or a hand moves, tests the morning's shave. I like him John. Pencils! And he's put on this dainty shirt with dude-cowboy pockets you know, ah, imitation pearl buttons? Like a kid in nursery school his first day? Earnest, pure. Ah, so I say—I'm trying to give these things up," shoving his cigarettes so hard the cellophaned pack slid almost off the desk edge which, suspensefully, it came to rest overhanging. "Shoot—couldn't do that if I tried a thousand times. She's right, they're killers, give 'em up. Eat candy instead." He had a box of lozenges somewhere and rummaged among his papers for it, hands crabbing through the tracts and texts on his desk as he told me how at his clever suggestion they'd gone for a walk to discuss Anther's article, rather than sit in this roomful of notion.

"You see he of course expects to sit, toil at a word processor, lean with me over the operating table, over his poor manuscript, pencils are scalpels you see—sit? *No! Walk!* Come on I say. Up ya' get, out we go." His hands find his box of lozenges. He shakes one from the half-crushed box, drops the box, is working the wrapping paper off his substitute for a smoke. "Get him moving. I've got most of what he wrote in my head, can remember, out we go, up over the field, all the way to where they're breaking ground—" pudgy fingers fumble with wax-paper wrapping "—for the condos we—" crinkle sound as fingers fumble faster, though no more successfully "—had to sell a little bit of land for." He had it off. "Get him walking, relaxed, ask—you know conversational, offhanded—about slack in the line. Let him elaborate in conversation walking out of doors instead of trying to write with his two pencils on white blankness. See when you're fishing those—"

As he went on talking he lifted, thoughtfully, the paper wrapper to his lips. Paused, between words, tossing the piece of red candy in the ashtray. Popped the wax wrapper in his mouth.

"Weighted-*pah!* Shoot! Idiot! Nevermind." Grabbed angrily for box. Got another. "So anyway you see I get him talking. And I remember what he says—should've tried a recorder but didn't think of it . . hard to rely on outdoors anyway, unless one of Lim's . . well, I must tell you, when we get back in I sit down and I'm typing like a son-of-a-bitch to get it all down."

He got up gradually now out of his desk chair as if a slow puppeteer were lifting him, his hands coming up, candy forgotten, and moved about wristily shaking his hands forward and forward as if dispensing salt and pepper from them. "So I get him into it. I write down the stuff he said on our walk. I let him read parts, I read parts to him, stir the pot, anything but direct confrontation with a blank sequence of pages, relax into it, take him easy. Details, add the in-between-the-lines stuff, things—important things—he doesn't know he knows 'cause he's such a natural. Order. Color. Logic. Clarity." At the window, thrilled, looking out. "Nothing John, is more exciting. The human mind expressing itself clear and pure. Doesn't matter what. A proof. A fishing tip. A field equation. A joke." He turned to look at me a second like my dog to see if I was realizing how seriously he took what he was saying. "How for instance . . you see it's delicate to sort of jig-lift—*zip*—that tiny nymph without—I got him to say finally—'jerking it out,' listen to this, 'without jerking it out of the envelope of its stream-natural momentum.' Delicate. What's hard you see is to get the diction, the style, just on the edge of being too fancy for Henry but never going too far. Drag's the word—he wanted to say 'without dragging.' Well that's fine, drag's what they all say, but I got him to try the 'envelope' image . . just one image, one at most—per thousand words so as not to hee—jerk his prose out of the envelope of its momentum, hm? So. I edit—we edit. When he starts to clam up I divert, change the subject, trick him back into the flow of what he knows. Really if I do say so myself it's quite a stunning little piece."

I'd never seen him so intense. "The human mind," he said, looking over his rows of books as if looking for a particular one but not, I knew, doing that, "wonderful thing." Hands on his papers on his desk, arms straight, head bowed. "Expressed." Moment's silence—antiphonal? But what could he want me to say? "So. Then. I type it up. Clean copy. Take it over to him, to his shop. Next day. He reads it. Now *I'm* the one on needles and pins. He reads it—slow.

"Lips don't move but a finger follows under the words. He reads the whole thing, takes his time. And do you think he knows I'm on pins and needles? That old—of course he does. Of course he does. He takes his sweet time, finishes, sets it down—" one of the thrills of my uneventful life was to hear, this once, Eden Hope mimicking the voice of Henry Anther "—says '*Wohhhhl,* ya fixed 'er. Ya fixed 'er so she works.'"

He smiled to himself.

"I say 'course I did, 'course I fixed it. But he's bothered. Something. I don't know what. He's unresolved about something . . . I wait. I've learned. Finally that voice. He says shouldn't it have my name on it too? So. That's easy. I tell him the truth, they're not my words they're his—your writing, your thought I tell him. I just got you outdoors walking around talking. Your words. You talk, I take dictation. You write I edit. You fish I edit, I tell him—he knows more about fly fishing than half the people writing for those damn magazines. He can write as well as you or me but he's been brainwashed to think writing is setting a time and sitting down then to a piece of paper—typewriter, word processor—when writing's just talking in your mind when you're walking around. Netting some of it in written words before you realize that that envelope you're scribbling on is paper." Pondered, chin in fingers-V. Eyes turned down low, brown, low light like pilots, calm for my uncle. Like his daughter Nora watching the flight of a golf ball. "I help you write I tell him. You help me fish. How's that? A deal? Well, he likes this. You can see he does, trying to act noncommittal but not deep down. It's good for the soul, anybody's. Have you seen one? They're no bigger than a speck, here wait," slamming drawers, "here's one. Careful now let me, hold your palm out."

"Ow," I said.

"Sorry . . . there."

It was an eighth of an inch, smaller than the pupil of an eye. Hook, body, hookeye, dash of weight to sink it, not to the bottom.

"Stand upstream quartering," he muttered positioning himself 'above' his computer station. "Sight fishing. See the fish, summer water. Feed cast and drift down, watch, natural drift over the bottom. Feel the slack, adjust—he describes that beautifully once I edit him. Half-watch the fish—shadow, bright sides under sun water er, half-watch fish half-watch nymph if you can see it. But you can't sometimes. If the fish moves like a take, strike, slow but not too, slipstrike. He describes that too, I've got him doing it clean and clear, you're there in the water fishing, forest breeze, browns holding above beige stones—waterlight . . .'beige.' I put 'beige' in. He didn't like 'beige.' He's right, he'd know 'beige' but not for streamstones. He'd think 'beige' for fabric, all right all right okay so we put in 'lion-gold,' 'lion-gold' stones. He acquiesces. Dangerous—too much if too often. But just that dab—eye-dropper drop. I like him John, and he knows his fishing. I want a*hem*. I want to help him if I can. If the line doesn't move that you can see but something—anything—feels different, you strike, slow slipstrike, lift and strip in line, it's all there, never understood it but reading, asking him, clarifying—" he fell backward into his chair, which was there. Rubbed his eyes, cheeks and whole face happily. "Became," he said happily, sleepily through his fingers, "clear."

Henry Z. Anther's 4,500-word article on fishing the weighted midge nymph was sent off to the *Angler and Trout* offices in Wardleton, Montana that March. The "Z." Eden had maniacally inserted, without consulting Anther who has no middle name, in the finished draft, which he then ran off on his word machine and showed his friend for final approval, along with a suggested three-line covering note for Henry to copy out by hand if he felt comfortable with that.

The old angler looked at everything—manuscript, draft-note, his new name—for a slow count. He looked at the papers as if they might move, as if they were living things, as if he were watching the rise—in a trout stream—of a fish other than a trout.

He nodded.

"Guess it's fine," he allowed. "That 'Z.''s gonna help somehow?"

"Just in fun. Take it out if you like."

"Waaal—"

"I can—"

"Nah," the old angler said still watching the pages that Eden bending and fussing and doting like a diamond salesperson had arrayed for him on the back-of-the-store table. "Nah yer the boss."

"Sparkle yarn. That's all."

"Yeah it's fine."

"If anybody ever asks you what it stands for, say only three people in the world know."

"Waaal—"

"If comfortable, if comfortable."

The illustrations for Henry's article were done by an eccentric cousin of Rairia's down in Chelsea and were unusual. Actually they were unheard-of. It had been Eden's idea. She did neo-post-abstract-expressionistic watercolors as a hobby and Eden had had the inspiration that maybe it was time for something other than the super-real line art every fishing magazine he subscribed to used. After several sessions

(Henry, Eden, Hattie [for that was her name] talk, read, Hattie sketches, Anther demonstrates, Hattie sketches some more . .), a dozen weird visual enhancements of Anther's fishing wisdom were ready. It was all soft indefinite shades—the suggested, the swirl.

And so it was that the manuscript, dimensionally amplified by that difficult art, about which there would be wails but a compliment too, and crowned with Anther's hand-scratched note (Dear Mr. Ott, [para] You may recall awhile back we . .") hit the mail.

He received his check for $890 a month later.

He needed it. Shrewd as he was with a trout in a stream, as a businessman Henry Anther was generous and genuine, a bad combination if you like money. Early in his life he'd put in time as a carpenter. He'd sign on with one contractor or another and be all excited about doing fine work and there they'd be, on site, the crew in the house calling out wrong measurements to him as he measured, cut, trimmed and planed in the yard—not on-purpose wrong, he told Eden, the one time he opened up about it. Just sloppy wrong. Work would have to be redone or else the boss would say use it, just use it, make it fit. Sooner or later he'd be bounced from the job after a fight (my uncle's brows rose at this and Anther chuckled and explained he'd had a temper when young). There was dishonesty with foremalice too, as when a job would intentionally be allowed to run late and suddenly he and a crew would be rushed back onto it, after the office letting it sit for weeks, because the customer was screaming bloody murder and they rush back and everything's gotta be finished a week from yesterday no matter what the quality. So he'd quit or get fired from that one too. And, he admitted, running a hand around his bald head, maybe he just plain didn't like working for somebody else.

My uncle sensed it was with faint amusement that his friend looked back on, and down on, his youthful woodworker's life of disillusionment then anger then, short of cash, thinking the next hire would be any different. Eventually he had learned, and would only work alone. He had become the lonely craftsman working on a job alone without interruption start-to-finish, a room of cabinets and shelves say, at his own speed and to his own standards, and was starving. He was married by this time and had a family coming—had always been at home in the outdoors, and knew a lot, so when his wife's uncle died he took the tackle shop over.

He was older than Eden by more than a decade—still in quite good shape. Lost his right little finger in a saw accident when twenty. Had been guiding recently, and would make money off the shop too if he could just stop forgiving debts and to his wife Mary's ongoing dismay taking payment in barter and trade—seven easy-chairs in the basement, rusted-out Packard in the backyard . .

His second article, written effectively by Eden though the meat was all Anther—not for Ott and *Angler and Trout* but (Eden's idea) for Ott's competition, *Trout Rodding*—was on water temperature and was good. Several dozen letters to the *TR* editor (only five of them planted by my uncle) praised the piece for its freshness and originality. The *TR* editor called three times in as many days with as many new article ideas, Henry cluckingly reported. A rod-making company called. Trent Ott didn't call. He burst through the door so explosively the bell broke.

Eden had been right, Anther admitted chuckling—my uncle wanted to think—admiringly.

Over the next few years Henry "Z." Anther wrote for *A&T* and *TR* and even *A*. They had Ott on a hook, my uncle felt. *A&T*'s money was best and so, Eden suggested in what he—more than Henry or Mary—considered a strategy session, over coffee at the Anthers' kitchen table that knock-knocked a sixteenth of an inch on its southernmost leg as Eden planted his elbows and flowered open his wattly hands—"Why not stay you see for the most part with Ott and his magazine, under nothing remotely resembling a contract, and you can be in sort of a perpetual state of mild complaint, always just about to go away and write full-time for *A* or *TR*. You never do of course, but you throw a scare in Ott betimes—hee, do a little article or a little book review for one of the others every so often. Then you see this has the effect of keeping Ott, hee-hee, so to speak hot to trot—no?"

My uncle's hair was extremely sparse and electric-wild.

Henry Anther had no hair. His head was like a Turtle-Waxed car hood.

In sweatpants and a sweatshirt Mrs. Anther snapped about the kitchen making toast and eggs. She looked less like Washington each time you saw her, but she still looked like him, except when she smiled. She had corn-kernel little white teeth. She was a tough person, as good and whole as her husband. Eden made no secret of loving to go over there.

Her husband, his head looking defenseless indoors without its cap, said: "Yeah, your way's how we'll do it. You gotta be the one t' set it up 'n make it run though."

"Right right right. That—" florid trecento gesture "—I can do. What we'll do is we'll create a process of periodically propagating these articles that devolves—"

"Hon'?" Anther asked.

"Yes hon'?"

"Get the dictionary?"

"Sure hon'."

The seven big fingers and two birch-scabby newel thumbs plodded through the Anthers' dictionary's onionskin pages in mild jest as my uncle, smiling with self-effacing impatience and nodding in acknowledgment of the joke, nevertheless plowed lexicologically on, describing to them his thought that in time a series of articles on fly fishing could lead to a book.

It's a fine book—still in print. Bitching and moaning that his efforts were nearly *pro bono*, Lim got it excerpted all over the place. Magazines bought sections. They got it reviewed in the top newspapers and sold Japanese and Norwegian and a ton of other rights. You may know it: *Simple Fishing*. It's illustrated that same watercolory way. Strokes in sweeps and flowing curves—clouds—charcoal swathes—give a feel of idea rather than the customary fingersnap super-reality line art. It sold forty thousand copies in North America alone and is selling still. There was even—almost—a movie.

# 11

Lying beside each other in that heat in her bed with the sounds her aquarium made only dramatizing the silence, they weren't together.

They were inches apart, naked, but weren't together.

Noises of cars, motorcycles, buses—the familiar oxidation of her pets' water. Her plants hanging overhead . .

For minutes now they had been like this, side by side in the thin, 18-carat light of early summer evening, each thinking, each saying nothing.

That had been a spring, for my uncle, of doubt, walking the stream, catching some, sometimes just sitting on the bank to watch, worrying about Nora, tolerating Rairia, worrying about Rairia, worrying about his work, reading, thinking—mind-roaming—more eclectically than ever.

In the unseasonable heat that had dropped down over the state like a cocktail of flaming rags, it almost rained, and day after day did not. It stayed hot, thunder grunting behind the mountains—in his closet his leather shoes had a sheen of green culture on them. They lay side by side, nearly touching, and the lublubbing oxygen too loudly entering her aquarium became so familiar in the dimming room, and was so markedly, incessantly, the only sound in the hot, dimming room, that though it was noise it was like silence.

His vast khakis tossed over the back of her sofa.

Their wine glasses, beading in the heat, on the coffee table.

Ajar closet door: sliver of hung nightgown.

It was over.

He knew it, and felt it, and was certain she did too.

She did.

It was the tension, in their silence, of their not moving—it was a release, a flying away from each other in silence—yet unresolved, she—he—waiting . . . with the back of a wrist, fingers loose, swabbing a corona of salty pearls from her forehead, she told her ceiling plants: "It's absurd there's no air conditioner."

Her plants overhead, the gas-explosions-in-water of her pets' prison, the wrinkleless heat, the lovely way June light can go away in a window . . .

He had to go. Now. Go, not a minute from now, not after talking to her. Not after touching her a last time, right now. Do it. All he had to do was lift himself and swing his legs over the edge of the bed. She wanted him to—it was over, go, get up, get dressed, get out. As if electric-shocked, he sat up.

With the sheet held mermaid-like over her chest she was lying still, not looking at him, nodding her approval, her hair moving—sliding lightly on the pillow as her head moved.

He swung white legs.

His bare feet felt the cool of wood floor.

There was a crash, the building's front door practically flying off its hinges, pounding steps, louder. The door slammed open and Rairia with her handkerchief crushed in a fist filled the doorframe in the full panoply of her neurotic majesty as thirsting as did ever Assyrian or Visigoth come down, full, raging, imperial—best of all in the right. Her self-doubt whirled inward and gathered into white-molten anger. Right, knowing she was and riding it like the Reaper or the Lord or the language itself when young, in a voice not raised but low and dull with moon-furious glimmerings of held-in fury pulsing from her controlled—barely controlled—tone, she spoke, chest heaving, arms ashiver.

She delivered herself of what she had to say, wheeled, and slammed the door on her way out . . pounding steps. They stopped. Came pounding back again and the door flew open again and she fired her last shots. Everything she said made sense. He no doubt deserved it all. As of this evening he was no longer welcome at the bungalow. He could be in touch with her, she informed him, to arrange to get his clothing. Whatever materials he might need to work. Sundry personal effects. In that livid and icy smoldering delivery she actually used the words "materials," "sundry," and "effects." He and Chase sat staring at her, sharing the sheet. Nora agreed with this, Rairia magisterially informed them. His brother agreed with it, she said. Nancy agreed with it. Gwen, she informed them, agreed.

Shortly afterward he went to see his mother, who looked healthy and very old. Her aged fingers of gracious and disciplined memory with their lentigo of a thousand tennis matches—sinewy, jewelless, arthritic—knobbed, swollen a bit and not all joints pointing right, his mother's ancient lovely fingers, with the years' suns burned into their skin, lay on the back of the cat she held on her lap.

She sat facing him, her back straight, photos of children and ancestors behind her in a forest of silver frames among the skylines of her stoppered perfume and lotion bottles on her dresser. Her smile was friendly and cool as always, her eyes icy as the eyes of a Siberian husky.

He told her his troubles.

Though she was old, she did not have a tremor or a tremble. She did not have a facial tic or move her hands involuntarily or otherwise on her furry lap cat that, because its eyes were shut, had none.

She heard him out—his mistakes, his clumsiness. His search. He thought her hand stroked the drowsing fur once. She said:

"Well. Just so long as you're happy."

"I'm not happy Mother."

The cat, old snapshots, essence bottles. His mother—eyes, hands, erect back—time flowed a moment neutrally. She said, looking at him:

"The important thing is to be happy. So long as you're happy."

"I'm not happy Mother. That's what I'm saying."

"Eden what is it? What's wrong?"

Her eyes were not gentle but her voice, momentarily, was the old gentle tone of his childhood.

He stammered.

She was looking at him. The cat's eyes opened.

"You're not chasing soap bubbles again," she said levelly. "Eden?"

He could only breathe.

"Because if it's that," she said, then remembered something else. "Eden you're not still trying to found the Perfect World Club are you?"

He had tried that one summer with some other kids, but it got nowhere. Or was it the Perfect Word Club . .

"Whichever it was," she went on, growing in size, "you have to understand. You know—" her chin swiveled "—your father—" she was turned in her chair looking over a shoulder at his dad in his engraved frame in the wilderness of forebears and descendants on her doilied dresser. His father, Alger, had tried numerous businesses in his short life, among them candy dispensers, bonds, oil rights, swimming-pool construction and a scheme to combine drugstores and local first-aid stations. "Your father tried it too," she said, "the same thing. The way when you were a child I would take you outside and we'd blow bubbles. You lifted your little hands as the bubbles floated, in and out of the shade, up, and you try to catch one and hold it and when that one bursts, with the same look of wonder on your face you try for another, and another, and you never got discouraged. It never occurred to you it might not be possible, and he—" she faced her son again, turning her back on his father and the others in sepia framed in solid silver behind her "—was the same way."

Her face was young suddenly and in side-profile long—graceful neck, long-lashed eyes downcast. Then she was old again and staring straight at him, her hands on the cat. He was terribly anxious, thinking he should—must—say something, but it didn't seem, as the seconds wound on, he would be able to.

"Eden when I was small I chased the same bubbles. Now that you're grown and starting to be old it's for your children and grandchildren to chase them. It's for them to chase them, Eden. It's for you to be nostalgic about chasing them, to be sad about it if you must be, and do your work. We have—" her polar eyes were for a short second the eyes of the cat, which were shotgun barrels "—our work. We have our rules," she instructed him, "our parties, our chores, our work, our children."

"Mother—"

"We have our chores and our work," she explained, "our rules, parties, children."

Something was going, he or she or the atmosphere, something changing, there wasn't time, and now instead of getting bigger she was at the old cement swimming pool with him when he was a baby before Lim was born, but why, if they're at their old pool in the sunlight, is she wearing golf shoes

mother, he tried to say

"If you're not happy," she told him, trying to get the disapproval out of her tone—she thought about it. She was mindful of helping him. The visit was coming to an end. She stroked the concrete sphinx, foundry-eyed, on her lap. "If you're not happy why don't you take a long fly-fishing trip out west?"

So he did.

They flew to Four Falls changing at O'Hare and rented a car. They drove to Tenneson and fished Clark's Creek for four days, then drove through the Slough River Range, with its apricot and coral crags, to cross Ponder Pass and in Gligglerville hook up with Jock Glover, into whose drift boat they climbed, one chilly morning, for a day's float on the Belouche.

The boat was new and squarish hulled, high-sided, flattish-bottomed and comfortable. Among the amenities was a rod holder, fitted inboard the hull toward the stern, where in a dozen slots perhaps half that many rigged rods tremored at the vertical—tips against sky, as Jock put them into the stream. Jouncing atop one rod was a perfectly immense fluffy pink-white thing—fly, one guessed—anonymous and soft—that made the yellow pattern Anther had trickily made Eden a present of, that steamy, rainy day nearly a year ago, look fastidiously miniature.

Anther eyed it, didn't ask. Later on during the trip he drew Eden's attention to it, when Jock was out of earshot behind some sage. They considered it—gross, excessive, hanging heavily enough atop the gentle rod tip ever so slightly to bend the rod's final few inches—and murmured questioningly over it. But Anther couldn't figure what it was.

Toward evening when the sun was almost down, in the first dusk light through balmy cooling shadows they were floating the last mile to take-out. Henry Anther said: "I give up."

"Pardon me?"

"I give up," he told Jock. "What is that thing?"

"My white fly?"

"Yeah, if you call it a fly. It's the size of a baseball."

Shipping his oars Jock blinked, looking at it against the sky that was preparing for stars.

. . . where the green leafy branches of alder trees grew over the water—low over the fast current, almost touching the water's racing surface, the trees made an arbor where the current flowed fast with scarcely a ripple in the swift run in under the branches.

Jock, elbows out, working hard, slowed them.

Quick in the current they came near the gravel bar, thirty feet out from the run under the trees, where he was going to stop them. All three without saying anything were watching the eerily smooth flat, slick surface racing under the bower the alder branches made. There was a rise.

"See it?"

"Yep," Anther said.

"I didn't, ah, was it a fish or, excuse me for—"

"It was a fish," Anther said quietly.

Having said "See it?" Jock was now working fulltime to position them for anchoring in the speedy race of the flow and said nothing more, his flat-nosed, squat-nosed face watching current, oars, bottom.

Anther knew what water like this might mean.

"Er, so it was a trout. A big one, no? Would conceivably a fish like that be—"

"Yep," Anther said, leaning forward with his elbows on his knees as the boat swung expertly, watching the place where the rise had been.

Jock edged them fast out of the mainstream, all three peering now. Twenty feet down from where the first rise had been in the race under the branches, another slap broke the green water, circles smoothing, disappearing on the slick speed.

All spoke at once.

Eden who had seen this one whether it was the same fish or a different one was babbling, his words filmed over, for his companions, with the powercloud of their knowledge and concentration so that even as they joked, without taking their eyes from the place where the trout had fed, they were working, so to speak, so hard that Eden's voice and words were like the senseless buzz of flies in a bottle to them. Anther just said: "There," when the trout took. Jock, who had his boat about where he wanted it, was smiling down at the whirling water now and saying "O—kay now. Nobody wants to stop here and give this place a try do they."

"Oh hell no, haw. Let's by all," Eden giggled, "all means drift on, get outta here, who would—hee—who in hell 'd—" he was unsettled "—I mean to throw one's life away wasting time fishing a spot like this forever for god's . ."

The side of the run away from the bank bordered, in the vague seam between the run's current and the gravel bar's slower water, on gravelly bottom that shallowed fast. Jock brought them over the bar, dropped anchor, tried it, drifted, tried it again, it held.

Their host made sure they were careful getting out, and, with their rods, they were standing waist-deep in water swift enough to, if you get too deep or broadside to it and feel, suddenly, your toes lifting—push you over.

"Don't stand too deep," Anther told his friend.

Jock nodded in agreement and said that that was right. He set them up in position. You could feel the loose gravel stones sliding from under your boots. Jock liked Anther. Eden could tell. Anther liked Glover. The old woodsman gave Eden less advice than usual that day.

There weren't many of the bulky golden stones and salmon flies coming down, but now and then one fluttering came riding the surface to pass in a hurry smoothly—fluttering—under the low branches, and was smacked with a quick-disappearing

"The suspense," Eden told them, fortunately not then, but later on when they were ashore eating, "of being as it were before nature's bar, before her altar and knowing you see that the answer, the truth, is there, the truth is there beneath the surface and will sort of make itself manifest . . but you never know if or when as you cast your offering, your prayer you might say, through an opening, an invitation in the ah, universal . . ."

Jock looked at Anther.

Anther looked at Jock.

. . the current flying under the alder branches was greenish from reflecting the leaves' green and they cast their flies through openings in the alder boughs where sunshine strikes a patch of current, then, poised, watched as their pattern shot into shadow—line lying on current flying quick under branches that almost touch the speeding water

Ready

you are your fly traveling at the water's speed on the slide under some trees and it is, as it has been before, this moment, no other. Your booted feet on shifty gravel. Your legs cold in your waders against the tremble. Your eyes are on your little distant pattern hurrying over where they are as has happened before and will happen again if you are fortunate . . bare mountains and scrub grass and rocks in the distance over your shoulder. Blue sky above but you don't see it . . nothing happens. Then something is happening fast, the same thing, as new and renewing as when it happened in other places and at other times—and it will happen again in the future, if not to you to someone—fast without your brain having time to tell your arm to yank up your arm lifts and heavy, splashing as it pulls because you are pulling it out—in the heaviness of the current—from under the treebranches, there is a blush-red fish: rainbow: fourteen inches. Even after you've played tug-of-war with it and won, tired it sufficiently to enable it to let you lift it—rod squeezed, slipping, against your side with an elbow—with its head cradled in your left hand and its stout tail in your right—to your friends' cameras and shouted instructions and smiles and aim focus leanings and clicks, and even after you've let the slippery weight of it slide into green watershadow where with a drift then sudden wriggle it vanishes, it is too real—this is hard to explain—it is too mysteriously real to be sure of.

Each one took one good one from the millrace under the boughs.

My uncle was having a very good time.

Coached, stationed in a prime spot, aimed, assisted with tippet maintenance and body balance and hook removal by his professional companions, Eden took a second creditable fish before they were back unceremoniously up over the gunwale and Jock had the anchor dripping.

He let the river swing the boat, used, with the blades of his oars (sails to the stream's winds), the river's turbulence to drive, drift, slide and swing them downcurrent past the distant grassy hills. Sometimes they forgot sufficiently about fishing to be content to drift like the turtle he'd seen that day upending whether free or in extremis in the trout water lazily, tippingly, letting the stream rule. And talked. Or fell silent. Gazed, talking, or not talking, out over the current at the foothills, and at the mountains and sky. And laughed.

Having gotten to know each other and feeling comfortable in each other's company, they laughed a good deal that day. Hoots—guffaws echoing off hills and trees back at them when their jokes (only fair but like food much better in the open air) built, accrued in themes and series progressively, to allow them to release the hard laughing they'd come here to do.

Because if the need to have time off is our excuse to fish, so fishing is our excuse to drift like this, and drifting like this is our excuse to laugh . . why, it isn't about fishing at all!

It had been the strangest dream. They'd never owned a cat. And his mother's eyes had been brown, not gray. He thought of this, as the mesa-like hills moved past in the distance. But certainly the advice her voice had clearly given him in the dream had been good. Unhappy? Go fishing. And here he was. He'd been talking and had stopped in mid-sentence. Jock and Henry didn't know why. He'd just suddenly, forgetting his talking, thought of the dream and fallen silent.

Watching these wild lands that seemed to move because the boat was moving, he was thinking of her.

The distant hills were gentle slopes of gray-green scrub, then steep walls of rock to flattops, plateau tops under the continent's sky. Memory, dream and seeing are similar, not the same. They had never owned a cat and she had most always been comforting and warm, cleaning him off when he got into trouble, holding him when he cried—never had she sat like that with such tundra-gray eyes . . yet . . the family . . the manners he had had to learn . . the rumors and whispers about his dad's failed ventures . . the black vaunting house of chimneys against the clouds, the traditions of their name . . . Evaporated, scattered and scattering, zero-cold snow swept from a green branch by wind . . . each soul's lost world . . . and now, feeling Henry and Jock looking at him, his mouth ajar, wondering—he—if he were pretending to be in a trance or were actually in one, or if some other combination of states had him, knowing they were looking at him, probably with concern, he continued to stare at the moving tabletop hills as the river carried them.

"Oh! Big Fish!"

Make a C with your hand. That's how big around the tail was—just before the fin—that Henry Anther saw deep in the sunny water as they glided over the last of the alder-bower run and Jock oared them back out into the mainstream.

They fished the river's miles, its pools and riffles under the sun and the sky's blue and clouds. They saw three eagles working, dark birds high above cruising low over the short grasses of a faroff high hill.

They fished a boulder pool, standing on a pile of ton-heavy rock. One good fish came up once. Then where the whole river flattened and became corrugated watercontours of all the little underwater stones, they anchored. Clambered out and Jock taught them something you could do with a high rod and a low line.

They ate strawberries and ham sandwiches with lettuce and mayonnaise and potato chips and fresh celery and drank river-cold beer, one each, sitting on a hummock of grassy clumps. As they ate they watched, spread below, the gray-blue expanse of wind-mussed river.

The sunlight glitter on the wind-stirred currents made it seem as if a thousand parallel twinkling corridors of light were flowing upstream and down at the same time through each other, as they sat eating.

Anther and Jock Glover talked about fishing, fees, rods. Native Americans and Trent Ott. Their conversation was easy and friendly but he heard little because as if having tiny strokes he kept slipping into reveries, eating his sandwich, watching the sunlight's play on the grand, wind-touched bend of water.

When he had finished with his sandwich he tapped a cigarette from the crinkled pack he was slowly working his way through this trip.

"May I be permitted?"

"'things 'll kill ya," Henry Anther said.

Shifting the way he was sitting Anther took more celery from the plastic bowl atilt in the grass.

"He," Anther said—it took Eden a moment to realize they were talking about Ott, "wants me to write a article on

—it was seconds later and he realized he had tuned out.

"Blow some my way," Glover said. "I haven't had a cigarette in fourteen years but I still like the smell."

"Why did you stop?"

Glover looked blank.

"Why?"

"Why ah, yes, why?"

"Why, I stopped because he—" indicating Anther with a nod "—is exactly right. They kill you. Why die before you have to?"

No one answered this question. Their silence made the moment ominous.

Eden held the burning cigarette backwards in two fingers and a thumb. It took maybe a minute in that silence before, with the wind's freshening, whatever direction the conversation had been about to take went away like circles on current.

It was a superb day's fishing, but it wasn't that. They caught fish, but it wasn't that. Turning with the boat's changing headings and the river's unmodelable surges, he more and more forgot to think on a scale other than mildly brackish air over water, voices under a turning sun, green trees, hills flowing by, the need, perhaps—soon—for another sandwich.

They passed some front lawns. In a tress of fast current hugging the cut-bank where the people's lawns ended, Glover showed him how to strike shoreward instead of riverward, because the fish is coming out from under the droopy grasses. Henry watched from the boat with his eyes then a camera. And he lost all four but didn't mind—"He says," Jock said, standing in the water beside him, "you've really helped him with the writing."

That was all. Like Henry, Glover did not do a lot of verbal falsecasting.

Where a brood of fuzzy little ones paddled, Mother almost able, as she dabbled, to pretend she wasn't paying vigilant attention to the trees and banks surrounding, they anchored in slow water. Eden insisted with a jovial boom that Jock and Henry go fish together and let him watch for a change.

The limit of ethics is action, of reason, mind. But aesthetics and theology seek their limit in the heights and depths of the soul. He was moved, sitting on the boat's seat, to watch his companions casting side by side against the green of the trees, now saying something to each other, now silent, together and each—alone—at work.

The mother duck dabbled. At a signal from her that he could not see, her brood lined up behind her like iron filings to a magnet. They started to go somewhere that way. Songbirds flew off a branch. In the space of two seconds the hen seemed to rise to twice her height spreading her wings and furiously splashing and like lightning the ducklings swam one way then instantly the other and she had them all racing away over the water, even though it had only been some birds.

*Why did she fuss so*, his mind drowsily asked. He was sleepy with the river afternoon. He was honored to be where he was, to be able to sit here and observe the other two, who in their angling had forgotten him, casting and catching some and chatting, against the darker green of the trees that had strolled down here to the water from the meadows to drink.

In trying to recall the name of a particular fly, that night, thinking of it, which he could see but not think of the name of, trying to think of its name and thinking of nothing else, all at once as if the skin of his body had flown outward to the ends of the cosmos he fell into a disconcerting, then wondrous, then peaceful floating in which he did not exist, though he knew where he was—beside some planets maybe. Was ultimately calm, without mass or shape, floated, had forgotten the fly he was trying to remember and was atingle with this traveling feeling of expanding outward and outward until he felt as if he were everywhere. He was all-tranquil, soaring, or so he expresses it in his journal, writing later about that evening.

As the sunlight thinned, tired though he was they stationed him at the edge of some sweeping rifflewater and untangled his leader for him, changed his fly, dropper, weight and indicator for him. They yelled at him to strike when he was slow. Elated he stood in his gear mute trying to carry out their casting and line-control and rod-position instructions, goofy-looking in his dark glasses, wearing an unchanging, faint smile that did not seem to be affected by what he was doing or what they were saying.

"Throw slack," Jock commanded. "Really throw it. Give it a pop."

Beatified Bubba, Stupefied Buddha in shades, happy, worn out, his laden vest stained with streamwater from a recent fall, hat gone, hair—

frizzy strands—electrified, smile ideal, arm heavy but willing. He threw a sloppy big loop of line upstream of where his woolly yellow indicator rode the serrated water.

"That's it, that's it, rod high, follow . . that's right," Jock narrated, "floating . . floating . ."

Anther stood in the chortly flow not fishing, hat back, watching.

"You might want to take those glasses off," Jock suggested.

". . just about foolproof," Jock commented, bending to get Eden's roseate trout unhooked for him. "You just watch that strike-indicator like a hawk. It hesitates, it dips, you strike. There we go . . good fish."

The smile under the untrimmed walrus moustache beneath the goggly double-Polaroid spectacles floated inscrutably on the purple light. It was almost twilight. Anther chuckled, turning to watch a pod of rises break the miniature—at this distance—flat of a pool they'd left far behind.

"Ready to try again?"

"Yes I am," the amateur said blindly.

"Want to change your glasses?"

"Yes. Could you hold . . thank-you while I . . they're here somewhere. Oh. Yes. That's much better to see."

"Try again along that same lane." Without turning Glover addressed Anther. "I really liked," he said, "the art in that article of yours on weighted midge nymphs."

"Wal. His idea."

"Really."

"Yep."

"I liked it," Jock told Henry, watching the indicator bob and duck with the movement of the little riffle waves. "It's different. I thought it worked."

"Thanks."

"Fine article," Jock said.

The serious personal talk on a fishing trip takes sixty seconds.

"Yeah," Anther said quietly. "Thanks. There."

Glover grunted.

"Gone now," Anther said.

"Yeah."

"Yeah," Anther said.

"Think he hears us?"

"Hard t' tell. He's lookin' up at the sky . . interesting place t' look fer fish."

He was indeed looking at the sky, and he did in fact hear them, and he had indeed missed a fish, but the rapture of looking at this darkling amazing light spread across the Western sky, and how sharp, in blueblack silhouette, against the sky the trees were becoming, wowed him. That a sky could linger such peach-tinted luminous lavender, exactly—*exactly* as the American painter who had seen it saw it

"Do you," he dreamily asked, "know Maxfield Parrish?"

"*No!*" they shouted in unison.

And at their outing's end, with the boatbottom slap, slapping the standing waves of a bib of whitewater Glover steered them down, with spray against the face, the hills somehow further off during their ride in this water of wavecurls, the feeling good of riding after a day of work, of simply, in this bumpy stretch, riding, Anther said: "I give up."

"Pardon?"

"I give up," the old woodsman's profile—a shadow made by the last pooling peach light in the west—said. "What is that thing?"

"Thing? You mean my white fly? That up there?"

"Yeah if you call it a fly. It's the size of a basketball."

Jock blinked, looking at it against the sky that was getting ready for stars. The bow-cleft spray was a mist-rain briefly against their faces.

"It's nothing," he said. "It's not anything. I tie it on and leave it up there where the other guides can see it. They think we're using it and try to figure out what it is. It confuses the hell out of 'em."

Like cannonfire their laughter echoes over the riding water. Their happy, tired laughter, loud as columns of gods pulled down, loud as anything. Loud as the scream of an Ojibwa ghost-spirit flying at you out of sheer rock-wall as you go drifting by—Glover told that story too that night, back at the lodge.

# 12

He took a flat, a pair of cramped city rooms. Stove, refrigerator. Sink in the living room, tub in the closet. Through his single window he had a view, across an alley and a story down, of a window the blinds of which were seldom shut . .

His time in the city was short. Six months, that's short. From the Big Bang to now is ten or fifteen billion years, or as Alan Elwive would say, "fifteen hundred dundred bundred k-dundred sundred zillion a-billion ghilion willyon a hundred infinity years," while from here, i.e. now, to eternity is probably at least that long, so what's six months? Behind that gray window across the way a woman whose head he never did see lay with visitor after visitor. She screwed them like an old locomotive's off-balance-weighted, massive wheels beginning to turn. Her Visitor (buttocks and back) rode her like rod-connected, weight-impulsed old locomotive wheels getting started in the far window's dirty light. Because the windowjamb cut her head off, the faceless undressed woman's physique, which he never did see clearly because it was dim and moving and because it was covered with another body—ravished, paid for(?) (for her sake he hoped so)—was somehow mysterious in its availability to his eye: evidence of the universe's ultimate loneliness . . .

he was not happy. And yet he had a feeling, frightening and promising, of adventure. He purchased notepads and notebooks and pens with relish, romanticizing himself to himself, visualizing himself here in the wilderness of a new life, here in the city heroically alone, able perhaps thus to come fresh to the oceanic data of his science. Perhaps one morning of whirling street-cleaners and starlings against gothic towers and spires, waiting, thoughtfully, to step onto a bus—or in a smoky cafe one midnight with a gaggle of adoring students—he would make his breakthrough. The tumblers would align, the forest's face take form, where for so long you had seen only trees. Matter and energy would reveal their Secret . . it was time to make his try—he wasn't getting any younger. Maybe the very loneliness of the whole thing would act as a catalyst. Perhaps his banishment was a disguised blessing. It was just a matter, after all, of standing mentally back, getting the larger perspective. The Perfect Model—a final simple way accurately to describe the universe—existed. He knew it did. It had to. Whether it was accessible to human reason or not might be another matter. To our little minds, he was beginning to suspect, the pristine equations to which all energy and matter succumb might appear everchanging, coyly throwing off sparkshowers of new questionmarks every time science approaches too close . . . but the few, beautiful rules existed. Of that, staring out his window, he was sure. He would try, in these solitary rooms—it was time. Being alone was almost certainly what was needed. And he was in little danger of being distracted by Chase Parr, who, the sweltery evening of their interruption *in flagrante,* after the door had slammed for the second time said: "You can't stay here. I mean tonight you can. If you sleep."

Lifting out of damp bedsheets the flame of her torso, concave back-small his hand might trace, collarbones, gorgeous hair five colors all dark but one, all of her rising curvaceously, where she sat nibbling a nail, from the white sheets' sea, was a proximate ideal of ruttish charm so here-and-now real, so immediate and—it looked like—linked to his life, and at the same time, he well knew, so ultimately inaccessible to him, so wrong, so inapropos, that he gave a gasp.

In a blink she was out of the bed and across the room sitting in her chair by her fish, aquarium light sidelighting her, beautiful even in this: biting a nail. Head turned. Chic shock of wood-grain hair awry, whites of eyes in aquarium light staring through her orange, blue-silver and roseate pets at the fact of his sudden, and as she saw it total, availability. Sideways she bit nipping with white teeth—lips tense, bared—the rapier nail's imperfection.

She was figuring.

"You're welcome sometimes," she said biting the hangnail. "You're not moving in though."

Fumbling with the bedclothes in which, trying to extricate himself from them, he had become entangled, he wanted to get his legs swung over the bed's edge. She talked to herself right through the soft noises of his activity and around the nail she continued to harass with those 1950s-bright ivories.

"I do," she said. "Not believe. I'm saying that. But it's true. It won't work with you here. Lordy. I mean tonight," her voice said without life, "you can stay if you sleep on the oh god I cannot. *Believe* what I get myself into."

With surface-only-frightened eyes she looked at the ceiling shadows the fish were making.

She was thinking, race-calculating her life, certain significant parts of it that he was unfamiliar with and that were crucial to her ambitions in ways he wasn't.

He went home once, invited by Rairia and supervised by her for the hour he was there. He collected his typewriter (the computer stayed), boxes of select texts and journals, boxes of drafts and notes, essential fishing gear, assorted pens and an airline bag stuffed with underwear.

As he puttered unangrily about his study, Nora, at the door, unnoticed by him, finally took a step. In a voice that was a feather she said: "Hi."

"Oh—sweetie—sit down, here," he pulled a chair out and pushed her in gallantly gentle but firm with a reverent, irrelevant bow. Hurried around behind a desk, his physics desk, to sit and, patting his papers, eyebrows surprised (eyes and blue lips not), explain things.

He was going to be living in town for a time, he said.

His youngest child looks at him.

Her mild blue eyes are tight with something. The wide face, with too much weight in the cheeks and athletic neck, is too heavy with gravity.

"Mom says you have to huh."

He coughs, wonders what Rairia has told her, can't ask, can scarcely speak, as if some process mentally advancing—the paradigm he wants to conflate—is taking up room, space and energy, as a result of which he is not right now free.

"You don't have to go."

"Oh Nory, I know I don't. I don't but I do."

"I don't understand."

"To tell the truth I'm not entirely, ah—"

"I'm not on anybody's side," she said.

He could see that and was going to reassure her but she wasn't finished.

"You don't have to is all I'm saying. I mean why can't the two of you just like sit down and like . . talk?"

He tried to explain. He said some tender things, some things that were surely silly, some less than coherent things and one or two things that were true, but his voice was a desperate buzzing in his head and Rairia once, twice, thrice was there looking in at the door like a trusty.

He tried to explain—it was for the best perhaps. One could never know, he tried to explain, 'til afterward. He did not ask Nora how much she knew, not wanting to taste the judgment Rairia had made it clear that not only herself but Nora and Lim and Gwen and Nance and probably the whole family to its furthest cousinal reaches as well as the Regional Planning Board and their local dry cleaner had darkly passed on him. He referred obscurely to his work, love (his—for Nora), temptation, ethics, his new phone number, forgiveness, and fishing (exceedingly briefly), then sat there. Malleable, ashamed in his skin. Stubborn and unrepentant at his soul's core. Head hung. In a grabbag of syntax he had tried to reach out to this fine young woman—his flesh—sitting now watching him, lazy in her eyes not just because this hurt but because it hurt and he couldn't help her.

In that small feather voice she told him not to worry.

Each individual is unique, and each human situation, but there is a sad sameness to a parent trying to explain something like this to a child. At first the child is eager to understand. Soon, sensing it is a thing that will never be understood, as the parent talks on the child tries to grasp comfort but, as the parent talks feelingly on, instinct tells the child that whatever is said, the comfort to be had here is little if any. At last to grasp comfort somewhere—anywhere—there, here, the future, a delusion, a journey, anything, anything to keep at bay the bald face of the parent's deficiency—the child goes somewhere else in her mind, dreams, as the parent's talk struggles, of a moment and a place and a feeling not this.

He knew it. He knew it amid his skin-surface shame and inner pilgrimage unchanging and the buzz of his voice in his brain as he talked—knew—knew—he couldn't help her. He couldn't make her feel better—give her, now, the comfort she needed, so when he'd run out of talk and was wondering which papers to take and she told him he shouldn't worry, even the deep shop in him where only thought lathed and joined was rattled by such love when alone later with a chance to think about it and recall, and appreciate, he was touched by what a fine soul she was to have told *him* not to worry.

*When you are desirous to be blessed,* he remembered from *Hamlet, I'll blessing beg*—the joy of someone needing you . . of course it hadn't been specifically that. Despite her need to be comforted Nora had, instead, comforted, telling him not to worry . . but why was he able to see and feel this only hours later down here in the city? And why have to compare it to *Hamlet?* Why veneer and qualify what if he could—grasping his temples—just naturally *see,* was so simple, so real?

Rairia had allowed him an hour. She held her unstrapped wristwatch over the fingers of a hand. She was deadly efficient. The month previous, increasingly suspicious, she had hired a private investigator—an amateur, but sufficient to her purposes—to follow him. And now, storm-darkened in expectation and mood, spring-wound with the validity of her position, she trooped where Eden did as he gathered some clothes and distilled the contents of his study into half a dozen straining cartons.

When he left she escorted him out.

He wanted to ask about Nora's boyfriend. But Rairia was fuming. She was livid because he was doing this. She kept officious pace with him as he carried cartons out to his jalopy.

"Why are you leaving?"

"I'm leaving," he panted—two cartons at a time, "because you said I have to."

"And you just—" she squinted sighting with an eye and a half "—are?"

"Well yes, I don't understand, why shouldn't—excuse me—" shoving a taped-shut box of holism with a grunt over the kinky carpeting of the little station-wagon's back "—why shouldn't I? You told me to."

"That's no excuse!"

"But—"

"That's not a legitimate excuse Eden! Whatever happened to good old-fashioned—"

"For god's sake Rairia, I'm not the one who hired a bloody private investigator, I'm not the one who—"

"Well the investigator sure had something to investigate, didn't he?"

"All right. All right let's—"

"And anyway," she concluded, "he was an amateur, he wasn't a professional."

Feeling his back about to go out he paused, hunched, staring at boxes in the back of a car. "You mean," he said to the boxes, "the investigator."

"That's correct. He wasn't a professional."

"Rairia," wearily, "what in god's name does whether he was an amateur or a professional have to do with—"

"Nevermind. Nevermind." She whirled to go. "Nevermind."

"Is Nora's young man still a factor?"

Stupid, stupid question he told himself as soon as he'd asked it. He put his head back in and stayed leaning in the back of the car fiddling with cartons that didn't need it, feeling her, halted in mid-whirl, letting the fullness of her righteous moody majesty gather.

"Yes," she flung. "He's still around, which you would know if you talked at all to your daughter."

She flung this sweetly in the nastiness of her ire, and he had long since learned to fold his passion like a tent and put it away.

Nora came out of the house and halfway up the outdoor steps.

"Wish Gwen'd come back," she blurted.

Stalking down the railroad-tie steps Rairia brushed past Nora and slammed the bungalow's front door so hard the birds shut up.

In the short time it took him to get his head and torso back out of the wagon's rear, Nora had turned back toward the house. She was hurrying away down the railroad-tie steps. He sadly, slowly turned back to his car, lifting his arms and closing the rear gate . . he gave a start to feel Nora's hand trailing lightly down his back.

He spun 'round. But she was hurrying away again, her back going into the trees' shadows. Scientist! How many peerless constructs of the intellect are possible only because the thinker has a family to neglect and does!

Setting down his evening bag of groceries, outside his apartment, to search for his keys, he would be thinking. For a while he did a peculiar new type of thinking, a particularly virulent form of intellectual dementia that had lately misted across the Atlantic, masquerading as analysis, in which words were used to describe words, language to dissect language, until every tale and belief system was diminished to a skeptitude (*sic*) and cynicism of meaning as unreal as the sight of dace, trout, fallfish, stream eels and suckers floating all over the top of the water when the electric shocker has been used or the wild, precarious exfoliation of tracks everywhichway when the collider boys blow a particle apart in the faith that things cannot have been other than very hot once.

He would find his keys, after a digging badger-search of his paper-stuffed pockets, try one or two wrong ones in the maze of locks—either a right key in a wrong zigzag hole or a wrong key altogether—before getting the door open, and he would go in. He would sit down at his little table where the books he was buying weekly by the dozen stood piled among his notes, and start to read and scribble. He would try to think. Hungry suddenly, he realizes time has passed—it's dark. The lights are on. He must've turned them on.

Kneeling with difficulty in his "kitchen" to open his miniature refrigerator, he peers in—tuneful rungs, the morning glass of juice he poured himself: full. A vase of French dressing, some Salvador Dali celery, an egg. No evening groceries. Smiling ruefully he gets up off his knees and back to his feet, goes to the door, solves the maze of bolts and locks that he carefully twisted and clamped into place and slid home an hour ago, opens the door and stands gazing sadly at the supermarket bag on the hall floorboarding, a stain near the bag's bottom where the raspberry ice cream has thawed.

He hung around the lab, taught a summer program, spent no time in his university office because it depressed him. Hatrack, phone, wastecan. They had some of Lady Gwen's adventures in paperback now in the co-op bookstore. He scribbled equations, had dinner out with a colleague or a couple graduate students or, more rarely, Chase, who had dropped most of her courses and was debating abandoning the undergraduate life altogether, but most nights he was alone—alone, and not entirely unhappy to be.

He looked at water a lot. Scum of neglected fountains. Free-spraying, well-oxygenated bouquets of the working ones. He looked at the misty bay with its paltry surf and horizon over which you knew there was only more land before the spindrift spleen of the North Atlantic. He looked at puddles in gutters, oil-rainbow collages of filth, and at the unblown big fountains indoors in the hotel lobbies as well as—home at last—his water in his drinking cup. Or that bead droplet, mysteriously unevaporated on the counter: ovate glassy eye staring back up at him as he unzips his windbreaker. The silver column foaming from the sink spigot to fill his teakettle . .

He saw the other researchers and theorists in his department now and then but less than he would've expected. His fault. He sought solitude. When he did have a meal or a few-blocks'-walk chat with Tellingen, or Zell or Hernandez, it was genial unless the conversation got scientific, then it was terrifically awkward. My uncle had published nothing of consequence in years and had for some time been going to no conferences or meetings. He found himself shying away when the others waxed enthusiastic over the electrifying breakthroughs in theory and experiment that were coming now almost yearly. Particles were being discovered, not in fact but—far more exciting—mathematically, that one had long yearned to arrive at, and it looked as if there were going to be enough money available soon to build some colliders big enough to make anything happen. He smiled, nodded, knew it was good, but mentally shied away. Alone in his ramshackle rooms before falling asleep he still—as boyishly anxious as any of them—mentally chalked test equation after calculus-fragment after visual metaphor on old mind's black tabula, but it was mainly in a solitude, a voyaging pridefulness of self, that he was going where he was going, and a lot of his time during those months was spent on a truthfully embarrassing personal barrage of poetic ravings

—inflame ourselves how? Arouse our better selves how?
Smash through to the new,
drear essays
what wind? what giant dream?
What swirls out of
How?
Who?
Go where? Called to what?
His quavery hand slants across all kinds of paper, storm-driven ink

regattas of loopy spinnakers and decksweepers heeling, pages of personal declaration and pain and passion and jubilant demand. He had moved his thought a universe over. Up he would get, blinking, looking around. Run a bewildered hand through hair he did not have, staring, attempting to decipher, with mute-moving lips, this dingy two rooms.

What was happening to him? Seeing the open door and the lightbulb hall beyond, he realizes that in going back out earlier to get his forgotten groceries he forgot to close the door behind him on the way back in. Pushes the door shut not hearing the jangle of his keys on the other side, which will turn, as he locks the locks and shoots the bolts, and which he will find, on the morrow, loosely hanging in the outer lock in golden testament to the building's security (as if anyone seeing him lumbering home with his groceries full of Anselm, Rorty and Saxe would care).

The city revealed itself as surfaces—gray crime, the bay, the tame Sound, trucks, the U., pigeons, some fountains, a park. Not a spot the ruins of which in a thousand years would bespeak much grandeur. A place of poshlost and atoms packed more tightly than usual.

Nancy got his phone number from me (that family could drive you crazy if you weren't careful) and called him. She was as brusque as a wildfire. She asked pointedly if he were all right. Rolling her eyes and holding the receiver away from her ear, she listened to him talk about thinking, about reading and being alone, the walks he took. She put Alan on.

"Alan," she told her father, "has something he wants to ask."

"Hi Grampa know what?"

"What's that Alan? Alan? It's good to hear your—"

"Know what a heh, do you . . what's a—" whispered conferral with Mother "—what's a 'etter-an-sa.' Mom? Did I say it right?" and Nance back on: "Dad? Is it . . *être-en-soi*?"

"Why that's Sartre, yes, where'd he—"

"He says one of his cousins told him. Something you were jabbering about at a party last year?"

"I don't recall, I'm sure I did. You see the distinction is—"

"They thought it was a swearword so they're using it."

"No no no it means, it just means . . put him back on. Alan?"

"Yeah?"

"It's *êt-re . . en . . soi.*"

"Yeah."

"Say it."

" . . . . "

"Alan?"

" . . . . . etter. en . . . .—sah."

"It means something that's just itself, like a chair. A chair's a chair. A chair can't think, Alan?"

"Yeah."

"A chair can't remember or be proud of how many toys it owns or love another chair or plan next year . . "

Alan *sottovoce* away from the phone to his mother: "He's 'splainin."

"Versus . . Alan? You there?"

"Yeah."

"Versus something like you or me. We're *être-pour-soi, for* ourselves . . that means we do and think stuff on our own like plan, or love somebody, or be greedy for money, or remember stuff, or doubt stuff . ."

Alan—mouth away from receiver to his mom: "Did Gramp go crazy?"

Eden chuckles popping one of the miniature egg rolls he's become addicted to in his mouth. "Ok Alan listen. A stone is the *en-soi* one. A stone is a stone is a stone. A stone doesn't like, oh, extend out from itself or think. A stone . . listen. A stone doesn't remember, right?"

"Why not?"

He could hear the two middle fingers go in and begin, very gently, to be sucked.

"Why not. Well. See . . think of it. You can remember, oh, say going to daycare the last time, or you can remember visiting me, and me telling you stories?"

Pause to remove— "yeah." —reinserted.

“Ok so you’re more than just you sitting there right now holding the phone. A stone would just be there, but you, why you Alan have a mind that can remember stuff and places, and you can think, think way out—in your imagination—from yourself . .”

Nance from the sink—pots clanking: “Let’s wind this up Alan.”

“. . ok just think of this Alan. Just think of this. Then next time you come we can go into detail, ’kay?”

“K.”

“Just think of this. You can remember stuff. Right?”

“Um-hm . .”

“Ok but a stone can’t remember stuff . . a stone can’t remember you see and that’s—”

“Yes it can.”

“Huh? Did you say it could?”

“Um-hm.”

“Well but . . okay. What could a stone remember?”

Pause to remove fingers . .

“It could remember when it was lava.”

. . sleeping, or trying to, the traffic of the city having slipped quieter save for the occasional siren or tire screech, he was half-dreaming. Like a huge undersea ray winging by, a grand idea about matter-in-process seemed shadowily about to reveal itself—

But he was awake.

Then she was.

Half-asleep to come awake in an at-first-strange room at night with unknown headlights crossing the ceiling to plunge down the wall over them, where they lay, in her brass bed.

They were groggily fooling around.

Suddenly realizing what she was doing she horrifiedly stopped. They hadn’t made love for months and never would again. The only reason he was here at all was that she had had a lapse and had felt sorry for him, to see how tired he was having been, that afternoon, dragged—figuratively—by her here to commiserate. That afternoon she had been rejected by an important person in her life, and at once had glumly called Eden to describe what had happened. She just wanted to go away, she told him over the phone, away from here, away from everyone and everything, curl up somewhere in a corner like a cat.

Did—he had ventured—she want him to come over?

No, she said. Not unless you want to.

So of course he had gone and had sat and listened, and watched her, and after a couple hours including a confused dinner he at last dragged out of her that what had happened to send her so nuts was that the Anguilla person—breathless, bitter awe—had, first of all, not phoned when he'd said he would, and then when she called him had sidestepped her, in effect canceling the long weekend they'd been planning—pled work, pled a cold, was lying, she was sure of it. By the time this revelation and their disjointed take-out meal and bottle of wine were finished it was late. He was more tired than he knew. Chase, seeing it, and knowing that she owed him, allowed him into her bed rather than his having to walk the seven blocks to his place or to try to find a cab at this hour . .

And now she slithered in a lightningstroke away from him under the sheets, having come awake enough to realize what they were doing.

She stabbed the light on. Sat in shadow, naked-flame torso, hair sweeping an apple-rounded cheek. An awake, bright, alert, annoyed, trapped big eye lit by the artificial light of her bedlamp.

He left. She suggested it, he agreed. He never learned what the idea had been that he'd nearly dreamed. When she left the city for the Coast he ended up with her fish, which was a mistake.

Having been tossed a towel, drying off, sipping his planter's punch, sweaty in the haze twilight—happy for now, patting and drying himself with the towel he's been tossed by ottery Tom, his colleague Kyle Kulka's oldest kid, he talks of his vision of the universe as a grid of tiny cubes. Standing by the tree that shades Eden's chair, Kyle lifts his camera swiftly hunter-like to snap. Camera mounted fast, aim, frieze a kid.

The Kulkas live in a red-brick house on dark green grass. To Woddington, their leafy suburb, Eden takes the bus once a week for dinner and lawn games including practical jokes played by Kyle's kids,

Phare, B-Z, Ben and Tom, gags ranging in complexity from string tied with Dad's help to Eden's foot and a tree (Phare, 3) to a booby trap rigged to trigger the super-soaking of Eden from a walnut limb the moment the majority of his weight has settled into the carefully positioned outdoor chair to which he's led (Tom, 11).

He met Kyle a few years back working for the unsuccessful Rights-of-the-Deprived candidate for Senator, both having recoiled in horror from a pragmatist Middle-Liberal whose cause, planed of votes by the Deprived-Rights challenger, failed. Kyle Kulka loved studies. From the last study to the next Kyle's humming brain happily hopped as if on smooth waterstones of reality. Kyle did group studies, thought experiments, decades-long studies, rigorously controlled ones, thrice reified and countertested ones with solemn mortarboards of national press coverage balanced on their heads, loose intuitive studies, studies of himself, studies of his students individually and in groups, studies of the sick, the well and the unwell, studies that teased out the human compulsions severally and one at a time, studies on the effects of everything—smoking, not smoking but wanting to, not wanting to but doing it, being fired, being fired twice, firing fairly, firing unfairly, shooting animals, having a lot of money, aggression, anger, race, sub-race, time off, make of car owned, water intake, platelet count, bad memories, sex, age, region, number of marriages, ore.

My uncle and Kyle were in political agreement pretty much, each, in his way, being somewhere to the left of Santa Claus, and scientifically/intellectually each fervently believed there's nothing ultimately that cannot in some fashion be understood. But to an idealist and incipient mystic such as Eden his friend's refusal to subscribe to any mystery except data was grating. Eden wanted to till the fields not merely of empiricism and reason to get his Big Answer—he was open, as we've seen, to all manner of history and philosophy and quack experimentation and semi-supernatural speculation—all that stuff too he knew would one day be rationally explicable, so why not start digging now? But Kyle lived within a pale of strictest logico-empirical methodology. "I mean," my uncle chuckled, "to seriously fund and with a hee—with a straight face carry out a study on the effects of what kinds of ore a community lives over, I mean isn't that, doesn't one—but he's serious John, the man's serious! We get along famously."

Tweedledum and Tweedledee of one rational church, they were easier to tell apart doctrinally at some times than at others. For instance Eden would sometimes take a more extreme stand than he really believed, with Kyle, just to do it.

Sitting thus in the suburb twilight peacefulness of children, midges and heat, where families of all kinds hosed their domesticated grass when there was enough water, and pyred and clucked over and poked at their elaborately marinated chicken, salmon, and (rarely) red meat on charred rungs over flames, sitting, in his easy exile in this mild, not terribly bothersome smudge of gnats around his eyes, dry now from Tom's trick but not from the humid and friendly breezeless summer closeness of the old neighborhood, he wonders if that rumble, afar, is thunder.

Artillery?

Chekhov? Train cars coupling?

His planter's punch sweating, forgotten in his hand, he tries to explain . . the electron's the final particle. Distort and force the electron apart though we may, exploding it into collections of things it doesn't want to be, like dynamiting a soccer team, still it remains the irreducible basic particle. But of course different electrons act differently. The universe is a grid of tiny cubes—potentials—a vastness of three-dimensional graph paper. Each minuscule cube of potential is an electron. There's no such thing as movement. All that happens is that in the giant 3-D gridwork of potentials, different sets and patterns of electron incarnations ongoingly actualize. The changing messages of a great card-section in three dimensions. Which would explain how things can move faster than light (nay instantaneously), as well as explaining quanta-leaps and why the second hand is a series of tiny jerks in its movement and never truly smooth.

This was nonsense of course but it was fun to try it out on Kyle, who had but little real scientific wherewithal. And, too, in its ghostings of string theory, and in its release of cynicism in a field—particle physics—that these days had all the faith/trust juice it needed, maybe it wasn't entirely the time-off planter's punch funning he thought—anyway the thing he liked about Kyle was that instead of saying you're crazy or nudging him toward analysis or some other therapy it was just: "And!" (Kyle used the word "and" the way most people use "well" or "uh.") "*And!* Not only *that,* but there's a study coming out this fall indicating—" aim . . snap "—a clear causal link between—" aim . . hold it—f/8 in this light "—anti-matter and—" snap "—incorrect opinions. Quite something really."

Eden knew that he himself probably was in fact crazy—at least he felt that way; but super-rational Kyle was crazier.

For a moment, sitting with his perspiring drink forgotten in his hand, he could imagine that this suburb Woddington was the peaceful secure healthy wise place he knew the world must one day become—trees, kids' harmless tears, barbecue smoke, tricycles atilt in shrubs. In contrast to newer communities such as Belleau Hills and Hattindale, where the houses had brick or stone fronts but aluminum sides and their cars' huge garages opened their jaws each morning automatically, Woddington was old. Shady hills, rivulet brooks, slightly dilapidated cottages and erstwhile farmhouses where a university crowd had come together—well-intentioned folk. A village of the spirit, it really was. Everyone friends. Kids happy. Chores shared. And they would no more be able to save it than they had been able to create it. He decided to be quiet now because he was talking too much but he loved it here, and he was lonelier than he knew. As pushy with his talk as Rairia ever was, he scarcely took a breath. He told Kyle about Anther and their wonderful trip west, the arbor over the green water, the earthly holiness of fishing—to all of which Kyle, out of film, listens mmmmmmm-ing, because holiness earthly or otherwise makes Kyle Kulka nervous.

He tells Kyle of the scream that came out of the lurid wall of rock beside the river, in the story Jock Glover told them at day's end after their ride down that last bouncy rapids. Jock and Jock's dad had been fishing up in the upper reaches of the Upper Peninsula and at the end of their river day had been gliding past facerock. Their American Indian guide stood up in the boat an instant before the deep, shrill, inconceivable sound came from inside the rock. It was unlike anything Jock or his dad had ever heard or heard described or would ever want to hear again. The guide shut his eyes in the wind of the sound, stripped off his shirt. As they drifted he stood with his eyes shut in the free-swinging boat lifting both arms, Jock said, and holding the palms of his hands out as if to push back the wall of screaming rock that went silent, as they drew beyond it.

Looking around contentedly at his host's arborvitae-walled yard, aflower luminously on the dusk, Eden wondered out loud what such a noise might've been.

"Of a multiplicity of possible explanations," Kyle winked, "a buddy of the guide in the trees suggests itself. *And,* seriously though, there's such a thing as auditory hallucination . ."

Phare, koala-cute, was emptying ants from her bug bottle into the waist of Eden's shorts.

"Everything can always be explained scientifically," Kyle assured his friend having finished reloading—snap: Tom with B-Z in his arms, carrying her in through the screen door . .

"Explained scientifically *eventually,*" Kyle qualified—snap (a diving swallow, missed it)—and went on to list for his dreaming pal in the lawnchair four beyond-doubt-verified types of nonvisual hallucinatory behavior . . snap . .

Eden is ill at ease suddenly, feeling something wrong in his underwear, every Sunday, in the July then the August heat of that odd year, from mid-afternoon until usually a little after dark.

He bought a Borsalino hat.

No one noticed him.

Thoughts he may have had of becoming a campus legend—cafe scribbler, solitary walker, outcast from the mundane—were bad faith, Sartre's term for avoidance of the responsibility of being free to create one's ah, career as a God-less human and—he spilled something, but the words look like "revolt . ." "reject . ." "project . ." Anyway, hoping to create himself as an image in the minds of the campus populace was every bit as much trying to make a thing out of himself as some country-club yahoo defining what he is by the make of his four cars—bad faith. So he quit it. Sartre himself had avoided defining himself as a campus icon, not by not trying to so define himself, but by having so scattered a focus that he compulsively flitted from students to workers to Soviets to drugs to drama to literature to blather, his action the verbiage-action of goading others to act . . I think the more my uncle read of Sartre, and by him, the less he liked him—the spill stains are nowhere else so frequent. "*Angioplasty,*" it looks like through the grayed brown of probably coffee on the fading ledger page, "*of the cerebrum.*" He favored those ersatz-leather-bound account books—Cash, Record, Ledger, red vertical rules making columns. He was excited, lonely and confused. He had energy, but he was a passive man when I look at it. His wife had told him go away, he'd gone. He wouldn't have had to. The phone was Chase.

"What should I do?"

The directness of the question coupled with the fact that he couldn't possibly know what she was talking about indicated she wanted them to begin by his being patient. But she surprised him.

"Come over," she said. "Could you?"

He thought he heard her eyes close. She didn't want to toy. She didn't want to negotiate. Whatever it was it had to be serious. She didn't want to be herself just now—he could feel it and hear it in the olive, strange shadows of her phone silence.

"Just," she said. "Please."

She had paid him the compliment, he saw when he arrived, of no makeup, no stylish clothes—hadn't even brushed her hair. Beautiful anyway she was raggedly, haggardly beautiful sitting back down on the edge of her unmade bed after letting him in.

She was exhausted. Torn jeans, loose cashmere. Firecracker of hair behind head—just a rubber band. The eyes were dull and turned off, the crew gone home, the stage gray, nothing moving. Staring thus at the room's silence—hers—which he was supposed to fill, she waited.

He asked, she answered.

She was going to the Coast. Moving to California.

"I've been starting to know people out there."

Part of her depression was that he wasn't going to plead, he wasn't going to beg her to stay. He didn't care, no one did. This she knew—had known for almost a day, since deciding. No one cared what happened to her. Few knew, fewer cared.

"I have to go out there," she stated. Her hands, fingers over fingers and one hand half under the other, made a valentine on her jeans knees.

He was annoyed. She was going, so go. It was probably an excellent idea. She wanted him to try to talk her out of it so she could warm herself with his desire for her, real or imagined—one as good as the other. But he truly, all of a sudden, didn't want to play. But he did, at least to the extent of asking her why she was going.

"I have to. It's where my best shot is."

That, apparently, would be all . . but no, she went on at miserable length, said she loved the East, couldn't bear the thought of leaving behind the fenced meadows and white charm houses of New England etc.

Sensing his impatient annoyance she changed, swiftly perking up. She asked him, looking up, how his day was going. That was wrong but she stuck with it—they hadn't talked for weeks so you don't ask him how his *day's* going . . but she brightly stuck with it. She could do that, make it work. As he tried actually to answer and tell her about his walks, watching water in the different ways it moves, and the channels his thinking was taking, she came on. It took seconds. The breakers were thrown, the circuits completed, light! Dressing rooms emptying, curtain, action . . she bit a nail, staring at his knees with all the light in the city in those lavish eyes.

"Come with me," she nibbled.

"Ah, huh?"

"Want to?"

He stared at her.

"—come out there with me?"

He was going to smile. It was so transparent. If he would go to the Coast with her for a week—move in, whatever—she would use him just long enough to get herself settled, play him against her next lover(s), and finally there would be the tearful, glum breaking off in which, depending how he reacted, she would be nice or not nice. Nice if he should give signs of staying available. Not nice if he should give signs that this truly was the last straw, in which case she would probably try to get him angry so she could scream, sever, cauterize and purge—get some exercise too. He was almost, almost smiling at the transparency of it.

She caught this and changed instantly.

"I don't think you should," she said, turning her profile to him, still nibbling. "I don't think you should come, I don't think it's a good idea."

He was able to stanch the smile that more than ever wanted to come.

His evident control disconcerted her.

"I'm bad," she nibbled nervously. "I'm a bad girl."

When he failed to disagree with this she flashed a fraction of a smile to herself in—despite herself—admiration of his resistance, and got more agitated still.

He waited a beat and then by protesting in a kindly voice that she wasn't bad, unhooked her, let her go back to her pleasures. She contradicted him—she *was* bad she nibbled . . he interrupted oh no . . no you aren't. And away they went. A gilded cat grin could not help but warm now on her stunning face as she listened and nibbled and argued.

She flew out to the Coast that Halloween. She had friends to stay with while she looked for a place. The job she was taking was as appointments secretary to a famous producer who had never wanted an appointments secretary until his second wife with whom he was breaking up had gotten one. There were people in time who would help

Chase, but my uncle heard little of it. He heard her voice just once. He got her number and called, prompted by loneliness one night when the dog barking in the alley and the soup scabbing over on the stove were dog, soup—not imperfect shadows of Eternal Dog and Eternal Leftover. She gave him the fast version. Mr. Anguilla was the reason for everything—Mr. Anguilla owned the producer and had wanted to find him, the producer, an appointments secretary (and keep Chase on a secondary hook [at least she fervently hoped so]). There was a silence, between them on the line, like a waiting horse. He blurted something about a recipe for flan . . did he want the cooking temperature? Silence, the vast Pacific rolled toward her, the facile lappings of the Sound toward him. He felt like hanging up—she said there was someone at the door (he doubted it) and they hung up, each saying no more—and no less—than "goodbye."

When his brother came to visit it was bearing gifts. A thesaurus, a plant, a ream of paper, a tape and some transparent solids filled with clear liquid and dark dye that when you turned them on end bubbled tiny dye bubbles through a system of enticing chutes and paddlewheels and trapdoors to make you a pretty show to stare at to relax you.

"These," Lim said cryptically, looking at them where he'd dumped them on the bed.

Eden knew what they were and was trying one, captivated, as his brother checked out the flat's particulars with darting eyes.

"So," Lim said, drawing the word out forcefully yet somehow tentatively as he continued to stand in one place, looking around with his hands on his hips and birdlike moves of the head.

"These things are wonderful . . . marvelous . . ."

"*So,*" Lim snapped.

"The lambent ah—"

"Hope you don't mind," Lim snapped, in the same posture.

"Mind?"

"She paid me. I won't pretend I don't need the money. And you were acting strange, everyone was concerned, I wanted too to know what was up . ."

"I'm sorry?"

"Hadn't done anything like it," Lim persisted, still with his hands on his hips, as if he wouldn't change his manner until he was delivered of this. "Had no experience. But it's not that hard. Followed you three cars back, a block back along the sidewalk, kinda fun—"

"*You're the investigator?*"

"Amateur."

With a faint, eternal smile Eden turned back to his relaxation device.

"So," Lim said.

Staring at the flying wheels Eden made a soft noise of lyrical music in his throat.

"Did it for a relative," Lim finished up. "For two. Her. You. It was for you too believe it or not."

"Oh I'm sure it was."

"Well it was. You're in no position to know what you're doing. So. It's done now and you know. Bush-league I admit. Bushwa. Bushmaster, bushveldt if you know what I mean. I hope you do. I sure don't."

"Lim are you all right?"

"No. See that's the point, that's the key point, I'm not all right. Where do I sit?"

"Er, here?"

Lim looked at him witheringly, but sat.

"Know why I'm not all right?"

"Why,

"I'm not all right because I have to ask where I can sit down Eden. Because I have to ask why I'm not all right. *You* should be the one to ask that. I should come in, we should hug each other, you should get me a *chair*—and instead you . . there are certain." The little man had run out of steam. He sighed and sagged, where he sat perched on the edge of the dingy bed beside the presents he'd brought. "Rules," he said defeatedly. "Customs. Nevermind."

"How's—"

"Fine dammit. Everything's fine except your wife who you should be separated from except you're living in the same house has kicked you out because you're committing fidelity with this—she's attractive don't get me wrong."

"Adultery."

"Hanh?"

"You said 'fidelity.'"

"Eden!" Lim was glowering and smiling menacingly as he got off the bed and advanced on his older brother who having gone to the window to see if there was any action across the way, now, seeing his brother's mien, thought better of turning his back and was standing sheepishly by the bedraggled once-white five-and-dime curtains. "Eden you've got a real chance here, a real opportunity, a golden—" glowing with dark intensity Lim was rubbing his hands together "—opportunity to get a lot of work done down here."

Eden said nothing, sneaking a glance out. No action across the way. Lim, still coming on, rubbing his pink hands, managing, as if magically, ever to be coming on forward toward his brother yet never quite arriving, in that pocket-sized room, repeated himself demoniacally: "We have got a golden opportunity here to finish the frigging book *do-we-not?*"

All sudden city sirens sound the same until one day, listening, you hear the one you're listening to get louder, and closer, and it stops outside your building. Exasperatedly Lim turned and strode two strides to the aquarium.

"What the hell's this?"

"It's an aquarium."

"I know that. But what happened to it?"

"I ah, you see, preliminarily there was—"

"Say no more. *Momzer,*" Lim whispered explosively.

"Did you say—"

"Yes I did, nevermind."

"Lim do you know that's Yiddish for—"

"Yes yes I know, never—"

"Since when—"

"I read a book, all right? *Swearing Therapy.* You curse in other cultures, oh goddammit nevermind Eden we're here to talk about *you.* Seriously. I mean it Eden. When are you going to finish? You've got the final battle pretty much set up as I understand it, so how long? How long Eden? How long are you going to sit there twaddling around on this *verfluchten* chase after whatever it is you think you're after? I mean Eden there *is* no deeper understanding. Or couldn't you like finish *The Return* or *The Tree* or whatever you're calling it this week and *then* work on your worldview? I mean you've got more than just yourself riding on this. You've got *family* riding on this Eden, little children—"

"Lim come on."

"No *you* come on, and your readers—there're thousands upon thousands of people out there who can't wait to find out what happens, does Lady Gwen take up the sword and use it, does the Night Guy have something up his sleeve after all, does her boyfriend get back in time with the kid . . . you owe them Eden, not to mention your publisher. *Allez merde*—that right?"

"Close."

"Well, so, what's hard? Finish the book. Then you can take all the time in the world to—"

But the big man was shaking his head stubbornly and walking around. "No," he rumbled, "you don't understand Lim. That's not the way it works."

"What don't I understand?"

"I'm not going to finish *The Tree of Life* until I finish this ah, reading and thinking that I'm doing."

"And why," Lim wanted to know, sitting down on the presents he'd brought, "would that be?"

"That would be because I don't know the outcome—I don't know the action, the plot exactly, of that whole final battle scene. And I won't know . . I won't know Lim, not until—"

"Until," his little brother filled in, "you figure out the meaning of life."

"Well, come to an understanding, yes—at least to some general . ."

"Some general?"

"I've expressed it before. It's hard to put into words. Some, ah—"

"Some rational synthesis of history and philosophy and molecular physics. When you're not even—" the sweatbeads were real, the diminutive figure up off the bed again, so distraught he was scarcely able to speak "—when you can't even . . you didn't even, you don't even . . . what am I saying. Eden. You can't figure shit like that out. It's a game, a ruse, an escape or something, listen. I—" he was so angry his voice caught in his throat and disappeared "— . . ."

"Here Lim. Look at this."

Lim gaped incredulously at the inverted transparent device with its cheery spinning wheels and bubbles.

"Eden I don't want to look at it because I brought it for you to look at because you are making no sense in your life and I am your agent and it's worked pretty well." Deflated. On the bed again. "Eden listen. I wanted it too. I wanted it too when I was in college. Know what? The fuckers told me existentialism's freedom—no rules but your own, no will but yours. Some other fuckers told me tonality was out, completely out in music, oh and communism's the wave of the future. If I didn't agree it was 'cause I didn't understand—I just didn't understand. It took me twenty-seven years, twenty-seven *years* before I figured out how full of shit they were . . bums me out. So," reasonably, waving a white rag of a hand, "all I'm saying is you can't know. You can't. You just can't."

"I know."

"But you don't—" sadly picking up the wrapped ream of bonded writing paper he was sitting on, looking at it, laying it, as if considerately, to one side on the sagging bed. "You don't know, I really don't think you do. This isn't a quest for knowledge this is a midlife crisis, garden variety. Write—" wearily "—the book. *Helas.* Why do I even—

Eden was apologetically shaking his head.

Lim (hopping around): "Oo, ow, oo I'm thinking, I'm thinking, my brain, shit, why'm I thinking? I can feel it; the fucker's my spine, ugh, brain's a big lump on my spine, up top . . . ooo," he shielded himself and cooed, "ooooo . . *shit,* I'm *still* thinking!" He stared at his brother. "See what I mean?"

"I know Lim, I know."

"Can you at least set a date or a goal of . . I mean could you figure out the secret of life by next summer, or say by this coming . . you're never gonna finish are you."

"Now Lim . ."

But Lim was defeated. And he was depressed, though able to put it aside long enough for a jovial meal at one of Eden's favorite cafes.

. . walking into a smoky cabaret with a brunette—not Chase when he turns to look—Rairia, but not Rairia, yet Chase somehow when he doesn't turn, he sits at a table and concentrates on the show.

The act on the cramped stage is "Screaming Genes," a rock group. Heads like penises strumming and drumming, their tiny mouths yelling the lyrics to their signature song, which doubles as the group's name.

The words weren't, in his dream, exact, but something like: "Screw! That's what we want you to do! We're the Screaming Genes and we want you to make more of us. You human individuals are our way of making more of ourselves . . so do it! We'll make it so you'll enjoy it so you'll do it because we want you to, because it makes more people which makes more us! We can change that way!"

The human race is in a war of revolution against its genes, whose procreating slaves we are. By our generations they want us to carry them and be their host and a proving ground for their art and change . . . rise up!

With better computers to think for us and atrophy those thinking parts of us that don't think like computers, with war to be made obsolete and natural disasters managed and diseases old and new brought under control—with gene-engineering, and with the past disposable, we humans as a race are managing our genes as never before. Threatening them with irrelevancy. Threatening to strangle their strangehold on us. The "Screaming Genes" are totally ragged about this. Watch out Genes, we might do it. I was turning the pages faster and faster. Flip

flip. Letting me in, conspiratorially, he had pulled me without explanation to the ratty, lone window where with a mottly finger he indicated the other window across the way and a story down.

I looked but couldn't see, behind the distant working bodies, the beauty he found and in a low voice named.

On a Grecian divan with her knee up and a bare arm trailing triangles and perfect circles in the mind, Mediterranean sun streaming down . . . the shadow rises, is in sunlight—the paragon in the jelly, the dream, my uncle's love, the ideal. Something he could imagine in and beyond those faceless naked bodies coupling on a city bed.

He sat me down at his tilty table scarred by the cigarettes, bottle-rings and anonymous stains of his predecessors, and I started to read. Soon I was skimming, squirming. A hand over an eye. I read everything he showed me, every odd-sized page he slid under my gaze, but it wasn't easy. And it wasn't fun. And God created Gödel, the inevitability of incompleteness, and created the largest prime number the spooks keep looking for like racing after the sideways-flying end of a searchlight beam sweeping the stars. Eating is God changing clothes. But how will they write the history of this time? Ears don't have teeth, but how will they write the history of this time with its cities of records and its evaporative mail? Slow recitation of modal woes, tiny fierce fireriffs—graceless gracenote arpeggio on a bass sax, violins like torn metal—is there

some pure thing a human may do?

And could there be wave shapes common to the rise and ebb of empires if one could but present-value—forward and back—to adjust for differences in culture, time, inflation and standard of living?

In a towering turning mirror an image whose curve you had always assumed to be the rim of a colossal circle

suggests itself, suddenly

as the crest of a repeating wave . . .

Then fell the portcullis of November.

Snow. Snow on the sills, snow on the floor of the entry, frozen clouds of it over the garrets and spires of learning. White layers of it on the boots of his students as they tramped in, and on the arrogant blades of the municipal plows and the ice rims of all the outdoor water places he'd visited that summer, on his hat, on his nose, snow in bridal-train drifts and veil-dancing breeze-rivers along the sidewalks. He was glad to have his regular class to teach. When tired (that was often now), he could speak coherently without having to think about what he was saying and catch up their questions like merry-go-round rings. He enjoyed his students' company more than ever, though that time when I visited him, and he showed me the lab, I am quite sure I did not imagine his colleagues' solicitousness, the way they cast sidelong looks at him when they thought he wasn't able to see, the way they stood back from him, and watched him as he plowed about puttering and bluffly asking questions and making his jokes and introducing me around . . . even as they finish their discussion of conformal symmetry (the condition—not verifiable by observation—that one must imagine to have the rest of modern theory make sense) he can see the wonderful beautiful underlying principle fade in his seminar students' young minds like a movie dissolve as they file out, their backs in winter coats, the empty table glistening, the chairs around it empty, snow in puddles on the floor. Chase didn't call, Rairia didn't call, Lim didn't, Gwen didn't, Nora didn't. Anther didn't. Nancy didn't. No one did. He drifted to lectures on Yeats, Disney . . his sense of adventure had left him . . if I am correctly making out and piecing together his increasingly sloppy notes from that time, the false party was over. He was dancing on the head of a pin.

Christmas Eve, he bought three decorations. He put them up. He would spend Christmas here. Not, probably, even call. Anyone.

The universe is composed of an infinite number of infinitesimal two-room flats, each with its anti-flat in view across the way. Infinite pairs of anonymous physiques grappling—pairs of stones as far as you can know them, which is not at all—more *êtres en-eux.*

He had opened a can of tuna. He held it, balancing the water, which was good for him, in it, and used the heel and last three fingers of that hand to pick up mayonnaise jar and carry that too, bending, holding these two things precariously in a hand, beside the sink to open the lower cupboard where his salad bowl was, but hit his free hand on the counter so was turning, backing, to be able to get at the cupboard door from the right when his tuna-mayonnaise hand which he'd forgotten about bumped the toaster oven spilling the water the tuna was packed in, when the phone rang. A sound under the circumstances so shocking and welcome he strode—two strides—to the instrument where it was jangling brassily on the wall by the fridge and grabbing it with his free hand smashed mayonnaise jar and tuna can to his ear and said: "Hello-ow!" There was blood but not much. He was trying to save some of the water the fish had been in by setting jar and can (bright-red drops decorating disc-sharp lid) on the counter as he said "Hello" into the right thing.

Rairia sobbed: "We've lost him."

"Who? What's that? Lost who?"

"Thomas," she wept, "your son Eden, we've lost him."

He hung up and turned off the stove, unable to remember why or when he had turned it on. He locked the apartment and drove home.

He thought one thought and that thought was an iron finger on his windpipe the whole dangerous drive back up into the hills through the night. *Thomas.* Car motion cruising silence of enginenoise in headlights. *We've lost him.* His dolor was constant as he drove, memories and guilt pressing against the surface tension of his spirit. Dumb eyes funneling in headlights' corridor, a life now forever changed, a misery and a finality never to be put right, never to be different, never to be gone back from, never to change, not even at some billions-of-years-hence reheating of everything beyond where strong and weak and other forces blend identical to a magnitude of heat so ferocious as to meld superstition, piety, mystical passion, string theory, the standard model and talmudic tradition to name but a few into a smooth blazing seamless sameness. Not even then, he realized, driving in shock, could what had happened be undone into not having happened.

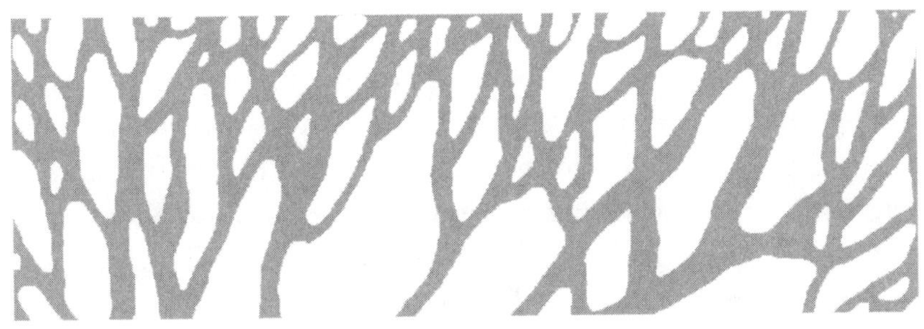

# 13

He got there and parked, hurried down the railroad-tie steps in the darkness, weeping, toward the bright windows of the bungalow, and opening the front door was greeted by Thomas.

Each, in astonishment, said the other's name. A second-hand jerk of calm passed. Eden said: "What happened? What's happened to you?" His son, a hefty man too but strong, with Gwen's freckles and her happy crinkles around the eyes, replied that nothing special had happened to him that he was aware of. Awash in vertiginous relief and bewilderment, Eden started to say that Rairia had said that—"Oh she's just angry," Thomas interrupted. Awkwardly, Eden stepped forward and found himself with his arms around his boy's beefy shoulders (big fellow!) in the doorway light. Snow-cold Christmas mountain night. Icy dark pure and silent unlike anything in the city, down through which puffs of snow fell from the trees into the porchlight as they hugged. It felt good—he shut his eyes . . how many times had he left this face, when young, uplifted in disappointment to go away to the lab or his study or a conference—how many times had conversation become dispute, dispute fight and fight flight . . . and now after their warm embrace, father and son, who have not communicated in years, arm in arm enter the festive house. Sharing Thomas's famous eggnog by a restorative fire they untie the knot of all the years of misunderstanding, talking long into the Yuletide night. They are at peace with each other by the time the last light has been put out—friends again, friends truly for the first time. Life is not that way—the world is not put together that way. Nothing of the sort happened. They quickly got extremely embarrassed in their embrace and my poor uncle, wandering on into his house, was greeted by bobbing faces—Nora, Lim, Nancy, Wister, Duffy, Alan and a dozen others amid the season's green boughs and festooned red ribbons and silvery bunting and reflecting orbs and silver and gold stalactites. He had the impression that while one was glad to see him, all this most definitely would have gone on and was, in fact, going on as it were without him. He felt like a ghost. There were no presents for him. He was hugged. His hand was shaken and Christmas Eve went on as it would've anyway, with its kids commotion and smells of turkey and beef and hot punch and the sting to the nose of fresh-cut pine, and there were carols, but Alan was busy with his cousins and did not ask to be told a story, and he felt, he told me afterward, as if he were a spirit, or not yet born.

He became exceedingly angry, justifiably so in my opinion, when he found out why Rairia had said over the phone of Thomas that "we've lost him." Alone in his solitary city rooms, Eden had assumed the worst. In fact, Thomas had taken a job with the Republican National Committee. "Rairia for god's *sake,*" he sputtered, but she eluded him by busying herself with some dishes . .

He gave up and ate his custard.

They spent a pleasant hour in a museum of belief, after dinner, singing the Christ hymns they all still mildly were moved by. A second tree was trimmed with Rairia's new balls. Nora was by herself tonight. She and the Poet, Duffy explained, were no longer on terms, a clear case, Duffy confided in a whisper, leaning to speak to him behind a hand, of the pot carrying the kettle to Newcastle. Alternately silent and in spurts sidelong cynical, Nora made him sad. It was her way of trying on a way to be, in her desperate search for a way to be, but that didn't make it any the less sad.

Thomas looked in general like his dad but was simpler, solider, didn't fidget, at least not elaborately, or knock things over. He seemed to enjoy himself. Sitting with an upright fist on either arm of the chair he'd taken, in that long living room of books, he sang lustily, his ruddy chipmunk-jowled face ashine.

Every now and then he uncrossed his legs with a puppylike wriggle to resettle his butt, and from time to time if Alan said something funny or their singing came together into soft, true-pitched chorus, ducking his head Tom would smile and dial—it looked like—an ear with the finger bearing his gold ring with a large, nondescript gem in it. Eden couldn't help looking at him where he sat, pleasantly aglow with energy and health. This was not the lost unhappy soul their lack of contact had allowed to take form in the father's imagination. His son was big. Thomas's glasses threw the holiday light back as if the light were glancing off a thrown open treasure coffer of doubloons. Tart aftershave had filled Eden's nostrils when he had stepped forward to embrace his son in the front-porch night, herringbone tweed arms hanging apelike a moment, then holding—steadying—the father.

Getting to his feet, the chipmunk face set in concentration now with a bit of simple work to do, Thomas stepped to the hearth. Rairia and Duffy and Lim and Lim's wife and kids were working on the second tree, down at the other end of the room.

Thomas took the poker up and bent to the fire to make probing changes, the vent of his jacket parting to reveal a banker's-gray ass of some breadth.

As he worked he turned his chin, but not his eyes, toward his father.

"I hear," he said, "you're jamming to finish the fourth book."

Eden gulped a breath.

"Not ah, at the moment."

Thomas was leaning the brass poker back where it belonged with a clank.

Wiping his plate-sized hands up, down, he surveyed his handiwork.

He had his mother's stability, a level bubble that hardly stirred. The one unconservative thing Thomas had done, in his life, was to take his mother's maiden name. He had Gwen's sandy warm voice . . Eden was dreamy of Gwen. He still hoped. It made absolutely, utterly no sense. Gwen had been gone for decades, and over the years had kept in nice touch, a visit, each summer, cards, a note now and then, but her warmth was friendliness, not love, and her having kept in touch, at least until Rairia broke Chase's door down, was, if he thought about it, probably as much politeness as anything else . . . but he missed her. It made no sense and got him nowhere but there was nothing he could do about that. And here was their son back suddenly for Christmas, a large-boned, corpulent Republican in a tweed jacket gazing at some burning logs.

Catching his uncle's eye across the room, Thomas shook his head.

One evening when he and Rairia happened both to be home, that January, as he was on his way, in his apron, from sink to refrigerator, suddenly she was blocking him.

"Are you back?" she demanded. "I mean are you Eden? Are you back here?"

He nodded.

"Are you? Are you finished with it?"

"Yes," he said, studying her.

"You are? You're finished with it?"

"For god's sake Rairia—"

"Well it's important to know! It's important! I would think you would realize that. I would think—but of course no," she said.

Her manner and attitude were rash, as if some controlling mechanism were close to failing, as if she held—menacing him with it—a skillet or a cleaver or something, though her olive hands were empty (excepting of course the throttled rag).

"Well all right, for god's sake," he said flusteredly, "of course I'm back. I never wasn't, ah, in a sense back."

"You were never here Eden. You never called, you never came."

"You wouldn't let me!"

"*That's no excuse!*"

Nora hurried from the room tossed like a buoy on storm seas by her parents' inequilibrium. He started to say something but Rairia yelled "No excuse!" again, and he threw his hands up.

"All right you're back," she acceded bitterly. "I don't know the details and I don't want to."

She left the room.

He went out too, strode to his study. So when she banged back in there was no one there. She stalked back out fast so he wouldn't by chance come back in and find her alone. In the empty room the phone rings. It rings, patiently, seven times . . .

At month's end they had three warm days and the ice on the streams melted, then it got subzero-cold overnight as the blue pseudopod of Canadian air on the TV map pushed rudely into the Republic. The streams froze thick in hours. The upper stretch of Winding Brook, over north of Hebron, was black ice.

You could skate for a couple of miles turning with the stream's bends, skating on ice transparent, smooth, obsidian, perfect pure black and so cold that if you took a thermal glove off and hunkered, to touch a bare finger to it, you stuck.

Eden, I, Lim, Lim's wife, Nora and some others, skating under an invisible sky, swung right, left, right up the S curves of that way of pure ice under a sky so cold the blue of it was almost perfectly pale above our wool hats. The sun was a ghostsketch of a sun, shining as hard as it could but only hanging palely somewhere vaguely in the still air that lay over the sere, germless fields.

I skate like a scarecrow but I manage. Lim resembled a speed walker, skating in ungraceful control with sardonic concentration. His wife skated easily and well and Nora Hope skated as you would imagine (flying, once she got going with all that weight). Her father said "whoa-wohhhhh, look out, look out I'm—LOOKOUT LOOKOUT!"

We stopped, went back, picked him up, helped him out.

That flawless ice, except for maybe an argent small bubble—"Gödel's ah, necessity I suppose" (stocking cap askew, standing and gazing down, ankles active)—was over a foot thick and his falling hadn't cracked or weakened it in the slightest or even made a sound that came from anywhere except off its surface.

We picked him up, shook his hands, working them like a bellows to warm him, and looked him in the eye—boxing-ref check: "You all right?"

"Sure. Was thinking you know, er, ah . . Sedan. I just remembered, they signed the Franco-Prussian War Treaty—have to check but—"

"Dad—"

"—in the Hall of Mirrors too—"

"*Dad.*"

On we went, in line, abreast sometimes, turning with the level hard stream's turns, shooting past a tree, a fence, a house in that gunmetal blued cold—wonderful skating, the touch of that biting country air rushing your face . .

*If Bismarck,* he reasoned, *caused Kaiser Wilhelm who caused World War One, and* that *Treaty of Versailles, which in turn caused* . .

"—you know who!" he chortled barely in control. I had to run up on the bank.

Lim's wife, I later learned, had skated in college. She grabbed her little demon husband's hand and pulled him along then whiplashed him out ahead of her to Nora who, looking back through her hair, caught her uncle's arctic-gloved hand.

He was gleefully managing to keep up at a kind of desperately boogying rate of half-a-dozen blade strokes to his niece's one as we skated, at our various rates, ahead of, behind and beside each other through the classic cold.

". . . no really I'd forgotten. Hall of Mirrors. Bismarck, 1870 or whenever, rubs the Bourbons' nose in it, tricked 'em into war, smashed 'em, Sedan battle, then Versailles, Hall of—"

"Dad," Nora who had skated sexily backward to be at his side advised, "just be like careful, 'kay?"

"Mirrors," he said. "Treaty humbles France Hall of Mirrors Versailles,

1871. So in 1919 when *Bismarck's* emperor's smashed, France humbles Germany back, same place, begetting Hitler . ."

"Dad . ."

Lim had a preschooler grandkid on his shoulders now and was struggling but making it with his wife effortlessly outriding, and some of the others had slanted off to look at an iceboat some kids were rigging.

"Fact you could say," my uncle panted, with perhaps not as much blood in his head as should have been there, shouting to the thin, bluegray heavens, "fact you could say—" gulped breath as his arms windmilled and he spun "—Louis XIV built Versailles bankrupting XV and XVI and begetting Napoleon One who in a sense in a sense *wait*—"

"*Dad!*"

"Wait who Bismarck was getting back at! Metternich just rowed the boat! So it's Versailles, Versailles, Compiègne, Versailles, *Compiègne!*"

"*DAD!*"

We picked him up again. Because we were cold we hurried, not saying much, and with his cooperation—not a word—he was being good—we were all skating again, his ankles like pendulums, his meshed, overshirted, sweatered and parka-ed arms waving and balancing and soaring as he began to sing . .

Afterward we were back at the bungalow in our thermal socks, sitting on the rug and on the threadbare couches and chairs, drinking mulled cider and eating melty chocolate-chip cookies in that low-ceilinged room of dogeared and spinebroken editions, while some of the smaller children played Fort with the Scandinavian-made battlements he'd spent seven hundred dollars on retroactively for Christmas, when Gwen came back.

She arrived by surprise, hung her clothes in his closet, slept in his bed. She pulled up in a vehicle more disreputable even than his, stepped, with weary dignity, into his old arms and rested there.

He held her. Her time away from him was over, her blond mind told him through their touching heads. He was so, so happy. The golden retriever circled and bounded swinging trapezes of saliva from its friendly soft mouth, hoping for a ball or a stick as his mistress and this nice man embraced, and Eden glorified in Gwen's freckles and sandy tawny hair, remembering the smell of her. Things were thawing, snow dripping from the bungalow roof as they embraced, the last icicles hanging from the raingutters melting, one, every so often, to dislodge with a crack and drop—whump—in the big banks still left close to the house where the sun did not hit.

They took her dog for a walk up in the pine forests, the trail muddy where the sun struck it—slick bright mud the color of cocoa spattering his trousers. In tall rows the evergreens slid by, pines in rows going by under the sun above his hatless head as they went along.

Under the trees where the sun did not find its way there was snow and a stillness, a motionless cool, that they passed by, hiking and talking in the light. She was back, had come back, was here—he clutched the reality of it like a child with a long-lost toy. Panting and smiling and drooling her retriever explored in and out and back in again among the dark trunks, pluming fawn tail wagging and waving, but the dog was Emma, and Emma lived here, so how could Emma have come with Gwen, and why did Gwen suddenly look like someone else? Where the path lay in the grove's shadow, ruts in the earth, frozen over but with the water drained from them, were covered with wafer-brittle ice over air that crunched, a popping sound when Emma stepped on them in her hurried nose-to-the-ground searches.

They came out of the trees and the sun was blinding on the snow as they started down over the half mile of open white slope to where his house stood in the forest.

She brewed them tea. He helped her carry more and more and more and more things in from her car. Then there was a strange roaring sound and something was wrong. He didn't understand, and Gwen was taciturn, so comely, but didn't want to talk to him, honeyjar light of scary stillness and silence where he can see her—blond curls, which she doesn't have!, freckly cheek—but somehow, with downcast eyes, she was walking ever away from him and moved—in that silence of light—ever just out of his apprehensive reach. Then as she set up in the sun room for her usual hour practicing the dulcimer, and he started to turn away to go back through the rooms to his study, she was a fireplace.

It was a plain colonial hearth of grizzled stone. She was it. She was coming out of it. A voice warned: *She's coming out look out here she comes,* rushing, windless, through him. Exploding from the strange fireplace he felt her soul freed and on its way to adventure pass through him momentarily snuffing his own soul—it was hugely powerful. He knew she had been trapped a long time in the nondescript hearth, but now she was sitting across from him in a booth in the noisy bar and grill of their college days, and her hair was longer, bright platinum blond, smooth wavy like a star's—she looked rich as she lifted her unheard-of hair behind her nape and let it fall. She was Rairia but he knew that wasn't right, and she was doing that with her hair and was vampy, not at all the plain she really was. And what she was saying was painful because breezily it did not include him but he couldn't hear, couldn't make out the words and something blew up—no a snort, it was a snore, his, opening his eyes, waking confusedly, overheated from the dream, baffled by the sight of the fort, and the kids playing around it, and all the others playing on the rug there in their socks that February afternoon after skating.

Gwen Ledger had a pleasant grainy voice. I met her just once, years later, but I remember clearly the lovely serious face with its crooked smile and freckles. Soft voice like the crinkles around her off-balance smile and innocent, deep eyes. She does not appear in this story but her voice—usually you forget a voice—was sandy-grainy and reminiscent of pennies in a hot summer pocket, butterscotch color, chowder smells. Sound of tissue paper crumpling.

Gwen's long, thin legs in her bleached jeans striding.

I looked her up in Tucson, and I guess you can tell she was memorable.

Her goodness was sweet simplicity, her swearing a shock always, an attempt to be bad, or maybe just vivid. She swore shamelessly in that granular voice—like a trooper. I mean salty. Lim, Nance and the others were ever surprised by it. But she couldn't be bad because she wasn't. She wasn't vivid either. She was a saint, well, not a saint, saints are dramatic. Gwen Ledger was nice. If nice people are dull then yes, that's what Gwen was, a little dull sometimes, but you would defend her too if you knew her—they all did, except Rairia.

She was an inch taller than I: six feet. A pleasing, athletic figure, plain brownblond hair, naturally wavy but not very—crooked toothy smile lighting that lovely, handsome face.

She had kind, deep eyes.

She was quiet around you.

She never took charge, was always, in a group of people with values, valued.

She would continue staring out over the lake if he had walked there with her, gazing, when it was time to go, for long minutes as if to drink this beauty in to make it last.

Her memory wasn't good. She was not brilliant but she was of average intelligence, and she tried, tentatively—though that could mean for years—many different things, groups, lives, lovers, cults, trades.

She got a lot of sleep.

She was friendly, helpful, distant sometimes, good-looking, sexy but not, really, extremely so, actually not—frankly—sexy, he finally looked away from me to admit. She was a saint of the everyday. She had done the housework because she liked to, and would sit for an hour with one of his books, trying to learn. She was an athlete, I mean good—on Nora's level—they got along well, Nora and she. Gwen ran several times a week always methodically warming up. She was slow and deliberate in all she did. Before playing tennis she would warm up for ten minutes making every stroke in the book, her strokes lengthening, smoothing and increasing in force until she was ready. Hearing an idea or a concept of some difficulty, she would go more still than usual—give herself over to simple thought, before deciding what to say. She bent with calm determination to whatever she was doing, whether turning on skis or folding a napkin. She had a fair sense of humor, the ability to laugh at other people's jokes mainly. She had loved the bungalow and the life that boiled in it, and in her time there had been quietly devoted to Eden who was more a father figure to her (who had had a rocky childhood) than husband or lover. She slept in his bed and they made love from time to time in a friendly way and she supported him in his work, believed, unconditionally, in his brilliance and work in a way no other adult around him did. She was almost fifty now, a young fifty but fifty all the same, and for most of her life had been experimenting—lighting for a time on a way of living then at the end of her time with it taking quick flight, packing up the minivan, zipping horizonward with a full tank. She had to keep distant. Distant in self if not in space, for, being truly good, being trusting and innocent and kind, by instinct she had to hold herself back from everything lest the world devour her.

She was graceful and moved deliberately whether trying a swing, on that wilderness-walled course, with his three iron, or leaning, without flirtation (in this way Chase's absolute complement), to brush a tiny spider from my collar.

I don't think there was ever any chance of her coming back to him, but she had kept in touch, until Rairia had MC-ed the blowup of the Chase thing, and everybody up there except one had always been excited and glad when the summertime week of Gwen's visit had come around . . . it's so typical of Nancy to've jutted her jaw and called her dad's marriage to Gwen Ledger "torrid." I like Nance, but her need for drama and her love of fabrication are sometimes neck and neck. No, between my uncle and his first wife there was an amiable truce of mutual consideration into which they had fallen almost from the start —Gwen had been a good wife, a good mother to Thomas, and everyone loved her. So yes I can certainly see why Rairia, calm as a general inside, while overtly teary and lost-sounding, had begged Gwen's long-distance shoulder to cry on the June before. Building suspense by taking several minutes to disclose what had happened, she started off by speaking to Gwen heavily, unhappily, of her own devotion to Eden despite their incompatibility. Her admiration for him, despite her teasing him about his brain-heavy soul, her—sob—need, still, for, if not his affection (did anyone, she cunningly inserted, really have that?), at least for his friendship. But now he's shacked up down in town with this little chippie, she had mused out loud. "I just found out about it. The whole thing is just—" sniff "—difficult," Rairia Hope told the deadly silent phone unhappily twisting, untwisting and retwisting the curlicue long cord. "He says," she improvised, "it's the first time in his life he's had real sex, real love. He says he never knew a real woman 'til now, oh and he says he never wants to see me or you or any other woman ever again."

Gwen was as silent as black matter. Rairia knew her mark—knew the hurtable heart that beat under the trim athletic chest and behind the easygoing sandy voice and eyes. Gwen Ledger was not selfish. In fact she was so much the opposite that she could be hurt fast and bad by even the slightest intimation that she was, in any sense, about to be left behind. "Oh yes," Rairia answered the question posed by the phone's silence, "yes, his exact words." And now with much adjuration to be strong, to be brave and to call if *she* should ever feel the need of a shoulder to cry on, clever Rairia sheathed her electronic weapon with a triumphal *pink.*

An hour later she stood, herculean and stupendous, in Chase Parr's door to tell him—in addition to the fact that she was kicking him out of the bungalow—that Gwen didn't want to see him, hear from him, or hear about him ever again.

Since his personal mail came to Norham Rairia knew she would be able to—and did—intercept and destroy the single, meek tendril of a letter Gwen sent. For a week or so Rairia continued to report to Eden lugubriously, over the phone, on Gwen's alleged attitude, and to Gwen on his. Once, adding a dash of art, she even got Lim on the phone and blew up: she had to talk to someone she said, his brother was being a child, a selfish spoiled infant. He'd hurt her, hurt his children, and hurt his first wife, who wanted nothing more to do with him. The whole thing was just—twist—so very pathetic. Twisting the phone cord as she stood, swaying, in the middle of the kitchen. So mournful, so convincing—because she was more than half convinced herself. She fingered and crinkled the spiral cord, leaning from time to time for support against the kitchen island . . . after that one letter from Gwen there was nothing. In time Rairia stopped calling Gwen, and no one heard from her, and soon Rairia stopped calling Eden, from whom people had also stopped hearing. Only much later did we piece together what Rairia had done, by which time it didn't matter because she was a different person.

"I don't understand," Gwen told me.

We were at a Tucson outdoor restaurant.

"I don't understand," she said in a voice made quiet, in its carrying of her hurt, by the passing of so many years.

"I don't see," she said, as I had more steak—mesquite-grilled, "why he left me."

Enough time had gone by so she could examine it without badly hurting, her gat-toothed smile told me.

"I was totally supportive," she said, looking at the mountains. "I did all the work of the house. I never argued with him. I never questioned him. I never wanted to. And I never bothered him, we always agreed. Why would a person run from that?"

She was a lower-case saint, serene, very nice to look at, selfless. It hit me that she was the adjusted person, the norm ideal that all Kyle Kulka's studies and definitions of dysfunction, and all our legislation and regulations and research and wellness counseling posit.

"I don't," she said, looking out over a Spanish-colonial auto dealership strung with wires, at the faraway mountains, "understand."

Had she come back, as my uncle had so often daydreamed of her doing, then dreamed literally, the day of our black-ice skating, of her doing, he would've left her again, because his soul demanded that he struggle for perfection, not find it.

But so long as she was gone he'd been able to idealize her—pure irony, Gwen being ideal. Come closer. Slide your chairs closer. Put that cigar out. Listen. If a particle as all-around sufficient as Gwen Ledger ever presented itself we'd eat it alive.

In the months after his return from exile Rairia started to be away from home more and more. She was tremendously agitated. When he had been having an affair, there was at least that certainty, but now . . . he said he was back and was through with it. But was he? Almost certainly. But *would* he be? Could she trust the future? What he had done once—might he not do it again? There was no way to know. He might, he might not. He had once—more than once? Unbeknownst to her? That she could not know either. He might. He might again. Or might not. And there was no way to know for sure. Her poor mind couldn't abide it, it drove her crazy, so she drove him crazy. That skating afternoon for instance she'd been up in Boston sleeping in a bookshop, making friends with the first scouts and emissaries of what would in time become the network of disaffected scientists and mathematicians she finally committed to hanging out with. She would return to Norham without warning full of political surface rage, ready to leap back into touch with anyone and everyone in the family, breezing in, her briefing notebooks in her stout arms, the mass of her crowned by the always lovely, now increasingly long graying tumbling lustrous dark hair behind which, partly, her olive cheeks and war-white eyes hid, and emerged, and hid again as she would power into the living room denim-skirted—cossack-black boots—dropping her broadsides and posters and white papers onto a couch before herself.

A day later, a week later, she and Eden or someone would have a fight and back up—I guess it's more over—to Cambridge she would shoot to set off every imagined alarm and tripwire and Klaxon to alert her at-this-point-somewhat-bewildered "support network" which didn't, truth be told, even know her that well.

At bottom she didn't feel good about herself or have confidence. She trusted neither herself to be liked nor other people to like her for what she plainly and without drama was. And so she compulsively seized on every wrong to her that she could find—big wrongs were best, little ones served too—and if there weren't any she stirred or made some up. Then you see, he muttered without gratification—not meeting my eyes—then you see ah, she could build for herself the attention she down deep didn't feel she deserved by regaling new acquaintance after new acquaintance with accounts of her suffering.

I remember Rairia squeezing my dancing hand, one time when

everyone was dancing after supper. With each squeeze she made a fretful *m*-hm . . *m*-hm . . *m*-hm in her throat that I don't think she heard or realized she was making as she tried to let me lead and powerfully failed in that fire-crackling room of thrice-read volumes.

Damply she squeezed my little hand, sometimes on the beat sometimes not, making that mewing sound, with no ear or feel for anything. Afterward as I rested alone on a couch, her shadow spread over me and, sitting like a manta ray settling, she launched without preface into a paean of pity and praise for her misunderstood genius husband for whom she was sacrificing her health. Without pause or transition she described Gwen Ledger as decent and neat and sane, if a spiritual dilettante. Leaning toward me, squeezing her hanky (better it than me), she confided her suspicion—sadly arrived at—that given enough time her husband would be able to drive even a saint crazy. Maybe—squeeze—it was better that Gwen ("the girl") was long gone.

Though it was not for her, Rairia, to say, maybe the girl was—squeeze—too good for him. Not meant critically she hastened to add. She blossomed and yawed about the evening's festivities resplendent in an orchid-breasted mu-mu and docksiders . .

People were going to bed. Eden and I stood by the fire's low glow while he tried to make me understand how one can read logical positivism as mystical. Seal-sleek black hair and crushed handkerchief sailed by. "*Scare* him you old windbag! For God's sake *scare* the boy!" Veering off in a self-uncomfortable glowering of introvert dissatisfaction she disappeared to whatever bedroom, to get whatever rest.

He throws the day's newspaper, which he's read, in the laundry hamper and drops his socks in the wastebasket. Turns the light off. Cheek against pillow in the night. Thinks, thinks, thinks. Can't order his life but knows exactly what he's going to argue the logicians' superstitions are . . . but what if on the first day Ewell *had* taken Culp's Hill?

Dawn gray.

When he went outdoors there was a frost on the lawn. From the window it had looked like snow. Around nine, the sun hung in a miasma, a diffuse neutrality.

Rairia had left early for Boston to attend a seminar on noise, and for a change the house had no one in it. It had been arranged, by Rairia before she left—and as a compromise, for she did not approve of the Poet, with whom Nora had had a reconciliation—that her father would drive Nora to school and then the Poet could bring her home.

He got it all thought out and written down—the logical positivists in their cantations and omissions were very like mystics in the following five ways . .

When he went for a walk there was sunlight to the west. In the east, along the mountainside, low clouds moved independently, just above the gray trees, trailing gauzy trains like veils that were falling snow.

Under the sunny sky the tiny squalls moved along in patches of shadow over the mountainside forest.

The sunlight would be bright around you. Then you were in the March snowshower and couldn't see fifty feet. Gradually, through the flurrying of the big breeze-played flakes, a mile away you would be able to see sunlight on fields.

Peeking out as the Poet's jeep pulled up, he dropped the blinds and strode through the empty house and out the front door and up the railroad-tie steps to shake hands heartily.

Nora waited with folded arms, hair down, looking at the ozone-angry slogan on her sweatshirt. He bade the lad come in and was surprised when his daughter didn't complain. He was surprised too by Griffin's looks . . mopey, sallow. Neatly dressed. Scrawny Vandyke. Apologetic smile. He'd expected a stud for some reason. They talked a little poetry and a little weather in Eden's study, and after the dude left she wheeled on him.

She shouted: "Why don't you tell me what to do?"

"But Nory I don't, I don't tell you what to do."

"That's what I'm saying," she pleaded wildly. Their voices were raised yet not angrily, more as if they were having to shout over the noise of a falls "—why *don't* you?"

"Why *don't* I tell you what to do?"

"Yes it's like you never say *anything*. Why are you looking at me?"

Because she was too heavy, twenty pounds overweight easily—irrelevant but that was the answer, that was the reason.

"I have to let you learn," he shouted madly at her sweatshirt. "There's such a thing as freedom, not meaning exis—"

"Shut up shut up shut up." She wriggled, closing her eyes and dancing her big fists on the air. "Like whatever, if you'd just like *tell* me—"

"Would you listen?"

"No."

"Well then. For god's sake Nory—"

"Why should that stop you," she cried still with her eyes closed, "if you cared, I know you care, I know you care, I know you care."

"Don't you have to work your freedom out?"

"Dad. Dad, Dad. You're *messy*. You are a *messy man*."

When Nancy yet again told me—I forget when, but it was around that time—that Nora was—chin (Nance's) defiantly out: "Totally devoted to him. Totally," when I looked skeptical she reddened. The chin became a perfect *ledge*. "Totally," she said looking straight ahead, "totally devoted to our father."

At their early supper together that day it was better. In a different sweatshirt and with her hair different Nora asked shyly, as they ate, what he was working on. He explained how Moore is like Farid ad-Din Attar. "Oh Dad that's so lame, I mean isn't it?" He surprised her by agreeing. Yes, he said. In its ah, sometime failure to accept social responsibility philosophy, like science, could indeed be seen as lame . . she surprised him—silhouettes in the kitchen. "Don't say that Dad. You should believe in things." Trumped, astonished, admiring, fork in midair, he was yet a fourth time surprised by her when, glee-light in her smile, she slides her chair back and rises, says "Thanks Dad I love you" and leaves.

He splashed hot then cold water on his face. Reaching for his face towel he pulled it and its wall holder into the basin. He shaved, showered, brushed his teeth—count of thirty for the medicinal mouthrinse he used, the same hole, for his brush, in the same barrel-shaped blue holder with the same holes in its head standing where it always stood on the morning bathroom counter.

Rairia was in one of her domestic moods so the kitchen stank of burnt toast.

He wanted a glass of juice, a muffin. But the breakfast-area table was set with red plaid placemats, laundered and ironed matching napkins, and the good silverware. She had the blue-glass individual salt-and-pepper dispensers out, that he could remember on the table in the big house when he and Lim were boys. And there was this-day-fresh cream in a pitcher beside a cutting of his indoor spinach in a cut-glass vase.

Smell of sweet bacon frying weighted the air. There were water-dropleted strawberries and perfect little melon balls and walleye eggs cheerily poaching in their dainty-handled metal cups in their special poacher pan. There was icewater in glasses, new-squeezed juice in glasses, parsley sprigs and even a scattering of flower petals on the readied plates—three—laid out on the countertop. Should her struggles with her new coffeemaker prove successful, there would be coffee.

She cleared her throat. She was trying to make golden strainer fit holder, which neither object wished to do. With her aqua cashmere sweater, which he'd never seen, tucked into the waist of her black corduroy trousers out over which her belly rolled partially obscuring the turquoise Mexican silverwork of her new belt, she went on fussing with the appliance's shiny-new pieces—cleared her throat again.

"I thought I had the right one," she said. "When I bought it. I distinctly asked the salesperson because I knew from two people I'd talked to that there are two models and a different sieve for each one so I wanted to be sure, I mean I wanted to be sure I was getting the right one for the right one. But I don't think I did even though wait. Wait," she said. "Maybe this is right, she was very nice but I don't think she knew what she was talking about. I just wish—they should say I'm sorry if they're busy. I'm sorry I don't know the answer if you can wait a second I'll find out for you . . wait there that's it, it is the right one.

Good. You know say to the customer if you could just wait a second I'll find out for you. I'll give her that it was crowded and a madhouse. It was like a zoo. But I think this is the right one," she said.

Birds blew down, juncos, songbirds slanting off the trees like autumn leaves blown diagonally, dark, sharp, to the lawn. They were on the lawn poking and stepping and looking about, bending to poke—head up, variously turning their heads, preening birds on frosty April lawn in sunlight, now that the sun has come out.

He stood staring at her desk smothered with bulletins and discount coupons in sliding stacks and cut-out ads and political calendars and notices of collection and letters from inmates and bills and invitations and catalogues and canceled checks all of which, as he felt sunlight on a cheek as he stared, head cocked like a bird's, frightened him and as he turned he caught her looking at him—staring, as at something odious, which made no sense and went away on her face fast.

"What were you looking at?"

"What were *you* looking at?"

Nora came in carrying a book. She stopped, looking at the mats and matching napkins.

"Hey," she said. "That's nice."

Setting her book at a place, she went to the refrigerator.

"We are going to have a hearty," her mother informed her, "healthy—" plugging the coffeemaker in and flicking the switch "—breakfast."

Nora was opening the fridge door.

"I'll just have a banana and some cereal I think."

With lightness of spirit and the will of the crusading heart Rairia tossed—like a circus tent in high winds—about the kitchen delivering the food she'd made to the table she'd so opulently set. "I want us all," she said gaily serving up, "to take the time to have a good, full breakfast, and to *talk,*" she said firmly, preparing their chairs. "Talk to each other. I want to hear what you're going to be doing in school today Nora. And Eden I want to hear about what *you're* thinking about so long—" she straightened the cuttings of his spinach "—as it's not quackery, and I'll tell you both what *my* plans are, sit here sweetie."

Nora stood behind the chair her mother was indicating. Nora frowned and squinted, as was her way when trying to decide, and said, politely: "Mom thank you. It's lovely. I'll really just have a bowl of cereal."

Thinking of Kant he was wondering if there mightn't be more notional overlays than just *being* and *existence* that were illusory. He wondered if categorizing (concluding too for that matter, not to mention modeling) might be unnecessary to physical survival and serious thought. Maybe the race's history of in-life instances of looking, smelling, hearing, tasting and touching had built a genetic memory-habit of categorization, concluding, and modeling that wasn't a bit greater than the sum of—

"Eat the healthy breakfast I made!" Rairia yelled.

Nora sat down. Immediately her mother was speaking calmly, or with attempted calm, reaching out to touch her daughter on an arm. Rairia spoke about the value of taking time like this as a family at certain times of day, and how love has to be maintained just like a car.

Nora had winced at the rifle-shot shout. She nodded. Her handsome jaw firmed and she reached for a strawberry as did he, who had sat down wondering if Rairia was going to stay forever on the verge of leaving. They talked for some minutes about things each was planning to do this day. Effortful, tiptoeing talk. He was trying in a compartment of his mind to get the Kant-thought back but it was going away like the trailing painter of a dinghy . . breakfast was delicious. He was eating everything before him. Remembering he had to go see Anther today, wincing in his heart he remembered Nora's wince when her mother had yelled. Devouring a popover he glanced at his girl, mild-eyed, big-jawed, unreachable, and saw the wince was gone.

He hoped it had not gone down inside.

When he stepped out for some air, later, halfway up the faroff mountainside a frost still lay on the forest. Low clouds were tumbling above the hoary trees, and a break in the cloud cover cast a slant of pale light from the firmament's floor. He was so tired of taking his toothbrush out of the same hole and putting it back and reading and thinking and questioning everything and when he drove to the university stopping at the same lights, and waiting for the same amount of time at each, and saying the same helpful things to the students in his class, and increasingly in his own mind doubting more and more even the bedrock tenets of his science, and hitting the same lights green each time driving home and going through them—and his days—no closer to an understanding of anything.

At the end of that afternoon there were ridges of dim clouds without color low in the west, and above them a thin, seething border of orange burning.

Overhead the draining sky was a canvas upon which a single, winking star shone.

# 14

there is before
the eye

water

cumulus reflected sky, windruffled

flat ocean, sandy flat bottom, ocean flat to the far horizon, sky soaring all the way back overhead and on into the west, diamond beach, white shore shacks, scrub trees, fingering, moving palms

wind across water

and the spoonbill visors of four hats

aim

east over the stir breezetwinkle sunblinding, watershimmer, shifting, sway sea grasses

"Here," the guide says quietly, "they come."

He hunkers with a straight back, visor pointing, hands in the air before him to feel what he can see—only he can see it, with sea eyes, a shadow in a hurry over the bottom at a distance, ghosting shadow, shining sandy bottom, shadows, then not shining, palms' fanning leaves clacking up in the air, four sun-hot shirt backs and the ocean's slap, slap against itself, tousled by the trades. The cresting tide is pouring in over the flats bringing all sorts of bottomshadows to hunt, pushing the water ahead of them—all see, all four can see the

"Get ready," the crouched, pointing guide tells

—shallow floodtide lights, winks, sun motion change, twinklings, flash, shimmerings but you can see—cast. Throw it under the wind. Onto the world's old watersurface, clear, moving silvers, windblown smudges greengray, watergray or blue, changing before your eyes, silver turquoise, sapphire, indigo, pale yellow glitter disappear, there are many green-gray swirls, jiggles of mercury-like light, marly sand, shadows over the bottom hurrying—cast—try it: the wind is still. White sand under the water detonates in sandstorms where they feed, miniature artillery-like impacts, puffs along the white bottom, and that evening before sleep the memory of the ocean's cool on your bare calves with remembered press of cork rod handle fitted to palm of casting hand where the fate lines are.

The sky is drifting—blown sideways under your knees, sun tilting, clouds drifting sideways when you look down.

You see something in the water, a brightness under the surface and then, just the glistening face of the water.

cast, try it, the ocean is motion a thousand small ways always before sunweary eyes

a hand, spavined, splotched, maculate, tough, with three fingers flips dainty flip

like teacup to wrist-toss dregs sending 8-weight line out miraculously from the big rod as that twitch of fingers and wrist, generating smoothness of impulse from the action's fulcrum, sends the line singing silently straight through the breezes. The fly is down on the riffles

and something

something is going to                                        shadow

turns toward fly chartreuse yellow gauche human-made not born of the seas having plopped, on the again-breeze-ruffled lights

something has turned above the white bottom, and even in this tough daylight the four Polaroid-darkened pairs of eyes can see and are watching the hump, forward pushing, of seawater come on, shadow over sand

banshee

"Good you got him. Great cast."

shriek banshee shriek blurring reel mandrake high scream metallic, human shouts . . the motionless heron does not take wing. Line off ocean into blue air singing fifty, a hundred, a hundred and fifty yards like

that

old boulder-rolling low, delighted laughter from the three-fingered helplessly—he's too old to run after it through the gulf—holding his rod high letting what will happen happen

then in chairs beside a curve-rimmed pool with no life in it, shadows of palms amid chairs, tables, guests, shadows lengthening across the purified still water, sipping through a straw pinksweet, in sandals before dinner they

"They run—swim I should say, ah, the hundred in three seconds, no? And that's through water, not air! Truly isn't—"

One of the guides, sitting with them: "Yep."

"I mean my god the aesthetics of, when you consider a human being covers a hundred yards in ten seconds and he or she's a champion, but they—and through *water*. Three *seconds*."

. . . hand with three fingers sets—with care—wicker-basketed, sweating glass of planter's punch on broad wicker chair arm, chuckling.

"Cheetah's that fast."

"Well yes, that's my point, what are we humans for? I mean hee . . well." The whirlwind of his silly thought subsided and he sat back. He looked at the curtsying palms, at the shadows a breeze was making on the surface of the swimming pool, at some white thunderheads capping, far away. He looked in every direction but one. He looked at the alabaster walls, the blue-brown flowers of tile running the border of the pool just below the lip, at Anther, their guide, the white-shirted black-trousered young women and men waiting tables. He looked at the loud-shirt guests at the other tables. He looked for a while at the waddly lizards with their chin beards of wattles of rough-scaled flesh, stepping around in the gardens looking like they couldn't cover a hundred yards in an hour let alone three seconds, or would care or need to. He looked at the laid out buffet—poolside—of pineapple and wetted berries, salads, roasted pig, sliced meats, whorls of shrimp, breads, vegetables, sauces, carved ice (swan, cornucopia), the long table's white skirts stirred by the evening air. He looked in every direction but one.

He looks all of a sudden awkwardly and bluntly in the avoided direction, at his son. Nautilus-armed. Thomas's short-sleeved shirt printed with cameras. Having a fine time, Thomas Hope Ledger is turned away talking to Anther and one of the guides.

In his golfing days my uncle once played so badly he lost all his balls, every one in his bag and several of Jim Wister's before, too disgusted with himself to go on, he quit—the only time he ever did that. Offering prolix apologies to Jim, off the course he galumphed, up the eighteenth, head down, arms swinging like an out-of-shape sergeant major, angry only at himself, feeling good for nothing, hat lost, striding, puffing, bag by its strap over a shoulder. Nearing the putting dial he registers that his sweater is in his bag, and, as he walks, without taking his bag off his shoulder, pulling it around to unzip the largest compartment he miserably yanks his pullover sweater out.

As he neared the putting dial in his fog of shame and lack of understanding and self-directed rage over how poor he was at golf and—it seemed—everything, he pulled, still striding, his sweater over his head, shoulderstrap and bag, had both arms through the sleeves, then his tortoise head came out the crewneck and realizing he needed to duck into the locker room to get his street shoes he lifted, with a hitchhiking thumb through his sweater—not thinking—his heavy bag's strap off his shoulder and disgustedly threw the bag down beside the putting dial to tilt and crash pulled by the thrown bag's weight pulling his sweater and him to the grass in a melee of bag/sweater/shout and kicking spikes, to the curiosity of those putting, and coming in off the course.

That got a laugh in the Indies that trip, that night. He was relaxed. Telling stories on himself proved it. He sneaked looks, in the changing shadows and dancing light of the bug lamps in their coconut-shaped bowls, at Thomas to try to read his son's smile and laughter. Thomas had come along at the last moment. He seemed to be enjoying himself. Talking to Anther, the guides. Eden wondered if his son was ashamed of him. He wondered if Thomas was proud of him. He wondered if it were neither—maybe Thomas didn't particularly care—how did one tell? Thomas seemed to enjoy the fishing, and he talked to the guides and to Anther, so he was enjoying that. And Thomas had laughed at the story about the golf bag . . it didn't seem mere politeness. It was night. The winds blew the shadows changingly so it was hard to read his son's face. Eden's father-love was powerful, all latent. He yearned for his son. It was hard to explain. Would Thomas have a son one day and feel this last-of-the-herd, weakest-of-the-herd feeling? Feel the fear of the stronger other. Want to be friends—and that desire latent forever now in the old heart thickening over with fat . . . but at least he was here. He had come. The guide, then Henry, went to their rooms. For a minute father and son sat at the cleared table. Their silence went on until, yawning, and when the yawn started to end forcing it to continue, getting to his feet Thomas bade his dad goodnight and they shook hands.

There's worse.

"The ahh, boy casts well."

"Ain't a boy. Yeah, he does."

Noses and cheeks clown-white with cream, hats all-flaps down, impenetrable darkglasses comical, they stood under the sun, swells of tide-cocked sea leaving wetness on their hairy legs. They watched Thomas cast with pretty good control but an unnecessary forward half-corkscrew of the casting shoulder (left one), solemn in his ear-covering neck-covering hat while a guide coached him.

"He's never done it before."

"Wal, he should be proud. You should be real proud."

*i am* Eden tried to say, but his white-salved lips just worked

they watched Thomas making casts. When his father called a compliment to him it was hard to tell whether he'd heard. Seemed impatiently to shake his head no, shake it off because he was concentrating on what his guide was telling him, or shook a sand fly away?

Out here there are no engines. There are no full streets, no white shops, no white-hosed hot streets teeming with people with cameras, nor beach mansions, nor forests of masts but only, on a cay in a necklace of cays laid on the blue curve seen from the jet's oval window, these many low reefs of sand and coral and this wading, this poling about in skiffs over the ocean flats of shallow bottom, green underwater grass, starfish on the bottom, spiny sea urchins, swaying swerving suspending racing hovering hesitant schools of baitfish, gulls and pelicans on the sky, shells—a lobster now and then on the bottom, smell of dead seaweed, heat, salt, a smell olive greenish brown

thoughts with saline in the breeze on them in the brainpan fuddled, winddisturbed, light-blinded a moment maybe—feeling the warm of these puttering waters about the skin of the legs and

Thomas, guided by his mentor, a tight end in a baseball cap crouching—seeing—pointing—teaching—instructing, throws a long cast, wait . . ocean explodes pulverizes like crystal atomized, the splash fulgent under the sun. It makes its reel-scream run, they cheer and

when Anther casts it's as if he just reached up, by his hair-tufty ear, to tip a teacup. The line like an endless freight train from just that cutesy flick of wrist/fingers powers out long, straight, thin, level, tight-looped, and Anther stands there—isn't moving—and *still* the line, fifty, sixty feet away is powering out level and true like magic (maybe Anther's smile moves, if that's what it is, as the guides frankly admire—but that's all)

Thomas can't cast like that (not even the guides can) but is doing well.

The guides like Henry Anther.

They like Thomas.

in the sunny shimmer that is the water sky-reflecting your legs
you see a twisted soda can on the sand in soft, moving turtlegrass

the can is silver, red, blue, designed, metal, thrown there

it lies on the oceanbottom

Before you get your arm wet
you are very sorry to see it.

You will die.

Eden and Thomas face so that were they casting they would be casting parallel, Eden up to his knees in the tidal shallows, Thomas, twenty feet south of his dad, up to his calves in the ocean tide pouring over the distant reef to flood the flats, and each man is watching—waiting, scouring—to see something in the acres of quivering waterlight, or to be instructed by one of the guides behind them.

Son glances at Father who doesn't see it—Father, glancing at Son, does so after Son has gone back to his scanning.

They are in yellow, a greenish yellow that moves, a golden sapphire yellow that glitters with aqua, cobalt changes at the outer edges of where they wade, and white in a semicircle beyond that, and, beyond the white, dark green and brown grays in density—plantlife, and over everything a gauze blue. Something happens. Air moves, the gauze slides away. Hotter suddenly, and cooler the water. The moving blues and yellows and aquas and turquoises and coppers fling the unveiled sun's light up off the water so bright in reflection that their sun-tanned, white-greased, dark-bespectacled, shadow-visored faces are darker still, unless one of them happens to look at the sky. There are sickle tails tipping above the water.

"Oh look!"

"A touch too far," a guide's voice says, "but they're comin'. Steady. Be ready."

Eden's so excited from and about and over this trip and being with his son and is so overwrought with scatters of energy from not having thought deeply for several days that he practically shouts—scarcely knowing what he's saying—as he watches the rare, elusive prize come on toward them in a tipping of sharp tail-points out of the current: "He sells knives!"

"Dad."

"Really," a guide's voice feels there's time to say before the school will be in range.

"Sells ah, knives through the mail, with success, ah . . ." Eden chatters giddily watching the disturbed ocean where they're feeding on little crabs on the bottom. "Heehee no really and," my pacifist uncle says—ocean lights shifting on black, deep lenses of glasses, "something by way of business experience, valuable eventually in whatever line of—"

"Hey Dad. I like selling knives."

"—endeavor one, that is . . . more constructive way to make a—"

"Gentlemen."

"—a living," Eden says, sunstruck.

"Gentlemen," a guide says, as both guides slip wavelessly to their clients' sides, "we can try now. This is the hard one, this is the tough one to catch."

They're big, silver, have that caliper scythe tail, are big and blunt of front like a World War Two jumbo bomb, and have large eyes.

Each guide coaches and spots for his customer, and Eden is soon a Christmas tree of line, a spluttering of goodnatured self-deprecatory jests, his guide, rueful, waiting, while Thomas has one follow. On his next cast Thomas causes another short heart-pounding turn of one of the broad, fork-tailed fish to look. Now he's dropping his crab right beside them where they're nosing the bottomsand, but they don't see it.

"Toldja," the guide says. "But don't feel bad. I've known good fishermen who've fished for years for 'em and never caught one."

"Shall I try again?"

"Give 'em a rest, see what they do. They don't look like they're goin' anywhere."

"So be it," Thomas says, his rounded cheeks and capacious form, in shirt and shorts, going still now to watch out over the stilling gentle waves and breezeriffles in a mile-long field all the way to the open ocean.

Trying to get his line straightened out while his guide, pointedly, and not angrily or unkindly, doesn't help him, Eden is nervously babbling softly. He never means—he didn't mean—to demean selling knives by direct mail, though knives—guns—the race does not need these . . . to make himself feel better he will think about micro-physics for twenty seconds. But he can't remember anything. And still draped with a little line he turns around to say something—anything—to his guide to recapture a sense of reality in this sunlight, in this sea, twenty feet from his fly-casting son. But his guide is talking across the water to Thomas.

"Sell any hunting knives?"

"Sure. Hunting knives, collector's knives, throwing knives, old bayonets."

Eden winces, unlooping the last loop from his forearm.

"There," Thomas's guide, their shoulders touching, tells him. "See him? Out from the pack?"

"I think so," Thomas says, "no. God it's wonderful. They're like spirits. You see it right there in the water and you're looking at the same exact place and it's not there."

"See? See it?"

"Yes," Thomas says, false-casting his line in figure-eights at his side. "Should I try?"

"That's a Rog. See if you can drop it a foot—less—this side of him."

"He's coming toward us."

"Can you lead him? Four, five feet?"

Thomas cast.

"Oh good," his guide said.

Under the tame ocean the fake crab sank to the marl as if escaping, and the strange-looking, blunt-nosed silvery trophy swam faster.

"Sheaths?" the guide asks calmly. "Don't retrieve."

"Sure," Thomas Hope says over the water's dozen different soft noises, "sheaths, sharpeners, you name it. You name it . . . if you need it we have it. If we have it, you need it. That's our slogan. *God.*"

"That happens."

"What did I do wrong?"

"Not a thing, absolutely not a thing."

"It swam right at it and looked right at it. It practically put its nose on it. I thought—"

"Believe me."

ribbongrass mud, crabs mollusks, snacks, shrimp on the near bottom, undersea grasses in the incoming tidal winds sway, almost wriggle, are still

—sway again in the breezes of the sunny waters' underwater pulls, pulls that are not

these flagging currents of the air's convection against your face stirring the wilted points of his dad's bandanna that Thomas has borrowed to knot red for no practical reason 'round his own cypress-girth

red

neck

"Collector's knives?"

"Sure. Sigmans," Thomas says urgently looking at the more distant brightness the fish have swum off to roil with their work, his crab fly sitting—of interest to no living creature including himself—on the tannish marl under the shifting lights, where they'd been. "Hales, Herons, you name it."

"Henry's got one!"

Four long visors swivel like tank turrets to look north.

"Looks," a guide says, "like a nice one."

Between sky and vast ocean the palms are a belt of curve cupping the deserted beach. At the half-moon bay's extremities—this sultry half-lagoon where Father and Son parallel play—noticed by no one a white apartment building of tiny, windowless staterooms is just now emerging, smoothly, from the trees' green

Does white egret
poised epic eye
leg straight—a leg bent
glass with constant stare the sun-molten surface in that full eclipse pupil?

do fish have teeth?

While they were gazing across the water at Anther, who still had on whatever he'd hooked, and looked to be laughing, one—silversided quick—had approached and passed finning pushily right over Thomas's crab and was swimming on toward their legs.

"Hey, yow, Dad look, what do I do?"

"Nothing," his guide tells him. "Hope it doesn't run into your line." The guide thinks a brief second of suggesting the guy's portly father try a tricky short cast.

It looks around, annoyedly it seems, for crabs. It's damned near at their feet. Frightened, though no one has moved, it makes a skittish shiver in the blue-silver and swims off . . . "Now," the guide says. "Can you put it ahead of it, like before? There's no wind."

There wasn't. The breeze was ficklely coming and going this afternoon, but right now, though the flat of the face of the intertidal sea was not that viscous, sluggish glimmer that can come when tide's out and the air an orchid sweat prison, the water was fairly still, the twinkles few, the water clear, the big, blunt-fronted silver fish clear to the eye. Thomas was falsecasting, getting ready.

Eden said in a low voice: "Here we are sort of, ah, as it were stalking the elusive gamefish and—heehee, here," he whispered excitedly, "one has come swimming right up to our feet. Approaching the—shut up," he whispers to himself. "Shut up."

"Damn," Thomas says, because a surprise breath cossets his cheek as his flyline flies out and the zephyr gypsy air pushes his line left and collapses it feet short of where he'd wanted it, and had had it—would've had it. His guide's voice mere inches from his ear is saying something and the scythe tail shows above the water but not where you'd thought it was because the fish has changed its mind too and the crab it thought it was feeding on isn't there and—sinking, getting away—Thomas's artificial is.

At the last instant, Thomas will tell them afterward, the guides nodding and smiling, when the big creature made its turn and dive in the sunshine under the water it went invisible to Thomas except for a disembodied—seemingly—black outline of a fin. The sea though windless calm again is a scrimmage now where the fish's hit and reel-screaming run tells the rest of the school *Shark!* or *Barracuda!* and it's every *être* for itself. Rod high, reel spinning blur, trying to work—and getting shouted happy advice from his guide on—his drag, Thomas has caught one of the world's most difficult sporting quarries and is exuberant and Henry's waving, though none of them notices, and there are whoops of victory—one of the guides shouts something about there still being time to go for tarpon, and Thomas is brawnily gaining on the powerhouse under the water. "Aren't you proud of him?" a guide shouts over a shoulder. *Yes!* Eden shouts into the wind that is in his ears that are stoppered from too much swimming. *Yes!* he cries more desperately into the winds in his head, for he's so proud he hurts. He's so happy he's dumb. The splashing geysering fury of the fish is matched: twenty-inch biceps against Caribbean sky. Thomas's rosy-cheeked face is grim in the fight, and young, and happy behind its dark glasses and suncream. The infant Thomas in just diapers sitting on the whitewashed border of the ancient swimming pool, petting a snake.

He got up—which morning was it? Third? Fourth. (They were there six days), and took a shower in the predawn cool, thinking. Just mildly—a little light thinking—about how the mind's compulsion to conclude, if taken too far, calls forth its opposite, Kierkegaard and the urge to illustrate—dramatize and aphorize and lyricize and illustrate with no conclusion really in mind, and comes to himself, standing under the warm weak jets, annoyedly unable to remember how long he's been here or whether he has soaped and washed and rinsed himself, or has it yet to do. This often happens . . now he must look for clues: is the soap bar messy? Are there bubbles around the drain? A trace of soap left anywhere on him?

Why, he wondered, starting to soap and lather himself, either again or for the first time, do humans have to do that kind of thinking so? The concluding kind.

—wrapped in a toga towel when he stepped out onto the wooden porch there across the gray flat of the sea the sun

was rising

like a head sleekly from between a mother's thighs

baby's

fiery pink

out of the waves' loins silent in the bird-quiet.

between casting and catching fish their talk is of fish, how fish act, how they have acted in recent and distant memory, how in theory they might act, and why, and what equipment to use.

He was so proud of him, so grateful and proud to be with him. But every time he tried to tell him, something happened—he was too loud and people turned to look, or he found himself making a joke when he hadn't meant to, and a not good one at that, or he turned one way and Thomas the other and a chance was lost. Their time here was slipping, sand moments hourglass disappearing, in which he might say

to his son or

show him or

"So ah—*pah,* sorry."

Thomas picks a gob of grilled yellowtail off his collar.

"Go ahead," he says.

"Sorry I, ah, how do you live out there?"

Thomas folds his big arms. "A plain life. Knives do well, we turn inventory five, six times a year. California's not what it used to be. I'm thinking of moving to Iowa."

"This fishing is *fun!*"

"It is dad."

somehow express a

cloud shape wind-stretched westward,

the play of the sun in the water's kaleidoscopic lights,

why one does it, how one loves it.

Casting under the *brisa,* figuring where the school—bulge of ocean ahead, will muscle up into the flooded flats, the blue-white-silver water lifting before their powerful swimming as the bull's muscle-knot quivers that the matador must seek—calculating where cast, wind, school's progress and crab fly should converge, a guide gets Eden into several

silver in silver through silver—

or laughing at Anther's head-back bellying laugh at himself as, his old legs unable to run through the ocean, he can only stand, belly-laughing at himself, nose and cheeks white with cream, hat brand new (odd for him) with its flaps down, and let the silvers in silvers through silver streak taking his screaming line until

there's no more and snap.

a mantle of strange, sweet ache descended on my uncle that trip.

By the watery ways,

what is the purpose and toward what graspable end do we strive? According to what laws do the tides run and the dazzling schools of lights with them, the swells loll, cradling, into the coves at evening to lullaby the anchored sloops?

Much later, with the bungalow full of strange computers and mystics in white robes spinning and everything come apart, when he looked back in photos on this that is still, now, happening, there is, now, still a chance to say, to his son, or show him, or declare, to his son . . the moments slip, knot by knot, loose, gone. It is a year-and-a-half later and the trip is old photos, echoes, statues in a glass box mum

—their words are blown off at the top, broken, scattered by the day's rogue gusts of saltair

"*What?*"

"I . . said—"

"*What?*"

". . it's *blowing!*"

"*Yes!*"

so big its dripping body sags at the belly between where your hands hold it, two feet from knifegash mouth and saucer stare—black-pearl-in-white-oyster eye—to V tail. The sun shines on it

seems,

so luminous silver is it, to shine from within, lights changing in the turquoise water formed for the moment into this prize that you hold, that you caught, that joins—flash as you release it—the moving stars glass suns jags and diamonds it came from

and the bay is as before.

a file of pelicans flaps by mounting one by one some invisible air stair, the first climbing then the next in line climbing then the bird after that, against sky as blue as cold ocean deep, but here in the flats the shallow bottom's bright, and when the tide comes in in they come with it, wary of being somewhere so shallow, to hunt, zigzagging around, nosing for crabs, attacking the terrified schools of baitfish where the grasses wave, and if they get excited and pay too much attention to the baitfish they're savaging huddled in their ball schools of terror, and just feed on the easy baitfish, foolhardily no longer wary, and don't look around, don't, for instance, look behind them,

teeth

At the next table five people were talking loudly. They'd paid like everyone but they were loud about the cost of trips such as this one and then, worse, laughing in barks and practically shouting they were talking about size and number of fish caught. Thomas, sitting with his chin on his fists, listening with interest to Henry Anther, flicked an annoyed glance toward the loud table.

"—maybe that trout," Anther was saying, "just a hour ago escaped a osprey . ."

He was talking about why trout take or don't.

". . you don't know what that fish yer fishin' for's been doin'," he went on, "or what's been happenin' to it before yer fly gets there. Now if that fish takes yer fly you think it's cause you got the right one tied on finally, or if it doesn't take ya think ya got the wrong one on, or there's drag—it ain't floatin' right. But maybe that fish just a hour ago had a run-in with a osprey. Maybe it remembers and doesn't take a fly it normally would, or maybe while yer fishin' for it it goes from rememberin' t' fergettin' about those talons comin' down through the water, so all of a sudden it takes the new fly you tied on 'n ya think it's the fly that did it. I dunno, it may be bull—"

"It's not Henry it's good—" happily scribbling Eden sat brow in hand "—menaced . . by a predator . . we can get this in."

In the book he meant. *Simple Fishing* was in proofs at that time, due to be published the following season.

Apollonian college juniors with suntans a month or a million years old and polite, hungry eyes cleared the tables lingeringly because they were interested in Anther—deft with silverware, glasses, plates—and what he was saying.

"Ya know," he said, looking past a swinging head of red hair at the moon—expansive for once in his life, "I was readin' . . I read where this scientist of trout had this big brown he was watchin'. Some terrestrials, ants, started comin' down on the current over the . ." coffee ". . fish. And this guy was watchin' this big fish, and the fish let the first ant go, then the next one. The guy watches this big fish let ten ants go right over his nose without touchin' 'em. Then ant number eleven goes over and Bam. The trout's regular on those ants now."

Thomas sat with his bare forearms in an upsidedown V, fists together, chin on them, listening.

"And the guy wonders . ." coffee ". . why the fish sat there and let those ten ants go by before he started takin'. He says mebbe it took a while to implant the image 'r trigger the response. Prob'ly so. But I got t' thinkin . . what if the fish was waitin' t' make sure it was a real stream of 'em comin' down, and not just six 'r seven . . see I was thinkin' . ." Jamaican ". . they talk about how a big trout won't take a fly or a ant or whatever unless it'll spend less energy nosin' up 'n gettin' back down than it'll nourish itself with from the food. Which makes . ." his cup, when he lifts it, is empty—Anther surprised: Eden drops pen, pours more coffee for his friend, grabs pen again ". . good sense as far as it goes. But I was thinkin' how it could be more complicated . ."

Immersed totally in what his friend was trying to express, holding his brow Eden queried and scribbled . . a single ant might nutritionally reward the big fish in that the energy spent in eating the ant would be less than the energy the ant would provide—but suppose there was only one, or just two or three ants at a particular feeding station. Though each of these, risen to, taken and eaten, would give the fish back more in nutrients than he spent in the getting, what does the trout do after the third and last ant? It waits for more . . there are no more. So, like an angler, it moves to a different spot. Waits there a while . . say a couple ants fall in: eats 'em. Waits. Nothing . . so it moves again. Perhaps a big enough fish, in order to survive, must seek out not merely (like any creature) feeding opportunities in which energy gained exceeds energy spent, but beyond that must—at least some of the time—go for a certain *margin* of advantage. If this is so, Anther reasoned, then the difference between taking one or a few ants and taking many dozen from one lie is crucial. Per ant the energy-gained/energy-spent ratio may be the same, but a lie in which a fish can feast on dozens is far preferable to taking three at one spot and then having to move *because of the energy expended in the movement between lies* (italics Eden's). This to Anther might be the reason evolution selected for trout that wait—at least sometimes—and watch. Not going to work until enough ants or whatever have come over to indicate good odds it's an ant army brainlessly marching in, or a dead-tree nestful blowing in.

"Put it in," my uncle whisperously cheered his fishing buddy on among the palms and balm of the tropical night, feeling, absently, of his brow in the ripple-tank shadows as he scribbled.

Turning his face on his fists' knuckles Thomas smiled at his father, who, busy transcribing, didn't notice.

After a few nights their table had become a gathering place on the hotel terrace.

"Put it in," Eden was repeating happily as he scribbled, "there's time, I'll talk to them, they can add a signature." He waved his pen. Chiaroscuro of stars and watery light reflected off the pool, night shadows of huge shrubs, the sidelight from the ground lamps upward-illumining, the bug candles in their shells on the tables, his brow as smooth as it had ever been. "I say if it costs it costs—I'll help." He set his pen down in his unfinished yellowtail and rice, conjuring more paperscraps from a safari-shirtpocket.

Why do we map and model the chthonic parts of our selves? Couldn't our unconscious be meant to be used, not understood? Might not going down in and shining the light of science around and funding experiments and counting genes and mapping emotions freeze the race by rationalizing its power source?

"There's one thing," Anther was telling a student, a fly angler as a matter of fact, who was mildly risking her waitressing job by lingering to listen to the old woodsman. "One thing a lotta these trout experts forget." Eden dropped his smeared pen fast during the pause to steal a sip of water and shake the cramp out of his writing hand. "Trout," Anther said, "make mistakes." Eden doesn't even attempt to right his water glass that he spills in grabbing for his pen. "Trout make mistakes," he whispers, "trout make . ." She, pretty, tall, pigtail, eyes close together, tall body like bamboo, rights my uncle's glass for him and sops up the spreading lagoon listening, in the Caribbean night, to the old angler.

"Trout make a lotta mistakes. I think people assume when they're writin' about trout that a trout does everything right. Now I don't mean when a fish goes for a fly and misses—I don't mean that kinda mistake. I don't even mean when a trout goes for your fly mistakin' it fer a natural—I don't mean *that* kinda mistake. I mean trout sometimes plain feed on the wrong food, not nourishin' enough, or they set up shop in a wrong part of a stream when they'd do much better someplace else."

Natural selection remember—my uncle had his friend Henry say—depends on trout's mistakes. Individual trout who do something better pass that trait on to more children because they survive more (Eden writing furiously and when he gets back to his room writing more), so that trait gets heightened in the species—it all depends on more trout makin' mistakes than doin' everything right. See?

". . so that when" Eden wrote for his friend in the sheaf of pages that indeed did become an added chapter in *Simple Fishing* (and an article for Ott), "we talk of trout as conditioned to feed selectively and be wary and conserve their energy and key on certain foods, we must keep in mind that the creature we're talking about is no perfectly developed machine that never makes an error. No, a trout might feed for an hour on mayfly spinners, the shell adult fluttering down to die on the stream the way a mature salmon weeks without food in its belly, dying, fights the river and predators to mate before its end. But that trout might've been better off gorging on nymphs instead of those spinners—nymphs might've made far more nutritional sense, or to be downstream alongside that log paying attention to that ant colony pouring in.

"Trout make mistakes. Don't forget. It's impossible to get the thing down to a science. They say there's turbulence in a stream. Flowing water breaks, swirls or surges without reason . . . maybe the water makes a mistake . .

"I know trout do. Sure as hell I do."

the wind is manageable today, the high, glutting waters of cresttide are welcoming the schools in over the flats once more, shadows gliding, materializing vanishing, busy over the bottom

"Tally-ho!"

"Got one! He got one! Good shot Tom!"

"Thanks."

—slashes faster, a shadow or

something wrong, see it too quick: saw it—both men astounded—see in memory the bigger bright disturbance and the littler prey ascatter . . . they wade to the place, look down, see a broken idea of a fish on the white bottom. Half a fish, in the shimmering, the other half far away in knife jaws

then the gray expanse of runways tilts faster and faster below and the nose of the great craft is up, wheels up and beyond the fishsilver wing dipping the airport is small—smaller

green forests of palms going away below, white curves of beach

bluedark (from here) ocean, lighter white in the inlets in the sand's halfmoon curves, there, look, there, down there, the one they were fishing this morning when the barracuda

tiny faraway cavalry charges of combers trailing down there where you were but

mists in the oval window, white—bank of whiteness

blindwhite          clouds

# 15

In the rain that was not in the room but seemed, in its noise, to be in the room, and in her, Nora sat looking at her window reflection.

It was cold at this desk once her sister's in this, Nancy's old room—Nora's now—where she sat each evening like this, at the hateful beloved Nance desk Nance had used to finish her perfect homework every night and write the class valedictory.

The lighting was shadow-pooling—easy to fix, but she didn't. Why move lamps when you aren't going to do your homework? Such rainy, raw weather. More like November than September. A snake of air was passing over her cheek, clammy, lecherous caress. *Better than nothing ha-ha* a voice inside her that she has trouble stopping says. Original to the house, the casement window didn't quite shut because the dolphin-shaped latch didn't turn flush so the iron-crosshatched glass didn't shut the forest out, quite, and the steady, insinuating slipstream of air just kept moving over her cheek. Working in light like this was hard on the eyes because of the way her floor and desklamp were positioned. As easily as she might have worked on—or gotten someone to work on—getting the window to close, and as easily as she might've unclamped her desklamp and moved it, and moved the floorlamp, she didn't. Night after night she didn't, sitting this way, having come 'round again to where you were the day before. She did not lift a finger to change the snaking cool that trailed her cheek tauntingly, lightly, like a torturer's whip stroking mockingly before the lash. She felt that this wrong lamplight, the chill, the rain, her shame and the mess the room was in must not be touched—not fooled with. Not a single item displaced or tidied. She was going where she was going. It was perfect somehow.

Her days were a few easily repeated actions.

That something was wrong was known to her faintly, offstage, way faraway through walls. The fact that something was very wrong with her was a distant scream, a remote teakettle-whistle of pain too far away, almost, for her to hear, which was odd, since it was in her.

Her body was too big. She ate junk or nothing and didn't understand why she should be so heavy—she felt rounded, a huge unused eraser. On the athletic field she was logy and dull but no one seemed to care, which made sense. "Don't smile," a friend taunted when they took the team picture, "don't smile Nory, we want to see your eyes."

She felt like a stone head, a brain of stone sinking through stormseas on the surface of which, going away above her as she descended, her classmates and dad and sister and boyfriend were peering down at her through the jiggly water.

She looked at her dad standing amid his desks looking at his work—his books, his papers, his thinking, dissatisfied with it. But she knew she was too dumb to understand. His shirttail was out. His cheeks were pink, not with exertion or excitement but because of poor circulation, the moustache shaggy, the stare a weary one. She waited. He had summoned her, saying he wanted to talk. But he was preoccupied, looking at his desks thinking his thoughts. The pencils stuffed in the breastpocket of his shortsleeved shirt were brand new and unsharpened. Hanging out over his army-issue buckle the folds of his belly, more ample than in months, were full of lies and old rules that no longer worked. She stared at him. He stood struggling (she knew) with his genius ideas, the cholesterol-viscous eyes, capillary pink lightningbolts in them, preoccupied with stuff Nora knew was beyond her and would be beyond her forever.

She wanted to move—couldn't. Couldn't even speak. Hated him in a flash virulently because he was himself and was blocking her light and confusing her urges and shortening her breath and judging her intelligence and because he was so weird and smart and she loved him and he was her father and was holding her fast even though it wasn't his fault, hated him so wildly, maddeningly, that the flash of it couldn't last and didn't. Quickly she felt sorry for him, and loved. She wanted to help him if possible. Each next feeling following—driving out—the last, a well of helpless depression spilled. Then it was devotion, just as helpless, and still she couldn't move, paralyzed just the same as when it had been hate. The devotion passed too and she couldn't think, hate, devotion, love, respect—the way she was now nothing was particularly real.

Behind dulled eyes she stood, in her heavy body, waiting for the big man who was her dad gazing at his books and papers to finish his thinking and notice her.

What a struggle his work and thinking were. At least it was like something he had—believed in and could do . . at least there was something to struggle for . . Nora had often wished she could enter her father's mindworld, see even just some of what he saw, share even just some of it, but her brain wasn't good enough.

In fact he was not, as he stood holding his chin and staring at his desks, thinking the lofty intellectual thoughts she thought he was. He was feeling the radiant ache of memory. The memory of your youngest at three sitting on the bathtub's slippery edge to gaze up, watching you shave. He was looking down at his papers. His brow was furrowed. But there wasn't a syllogism in his head. Only, hazed in halo, the visual memory of Nora's childhood innocence, wonder and pure trust, the plant-green paneled bathroom, how your child's eyes can watch you, when all that child knows of you is awe.

He sat her down finally and tried to have the talk he'd planned. He'd planned, first, to tell her he loved her, which he did do—then to ask simple questions about her life. But in his teeming head the memory of her as a child toddling around the corner of the bathroom door having heard his morning water running, to perch on the tub and watch him shave, loomed larger than any plan. Her dimpled chin—she so small you could lift and toss her above your head without a change in heart rate. The blue eyes . . memory of . . intent closed lips as her eyes follow his every move, mug, brush, strop (he'd used one), razor, washcloth, aftershave—*this* is what's on his mind. So why does he blurt out a bunch of words about Time?

Nora listens, trying to understand. He talks—stops a second to sit and scribble—something about his science, a question. Then he's talking again, telling her about what he thinks about, and Nora listens, lips shut, pursed.

At the door, Rairia smiles. Lowering her eyes she's about to glide away softly closing the door. Eden spots her—hoots. Briefly they discuss dinner. Rairia's home for two days before a much-organized swing west. Things are better between them, have been much better lately. The Curtisses are having a party and need to replace a last-minute dropout couple, Rairia says. She is holding tan, noble-browed Emma by her collar. So they'll go? Sure. Ducking his head he throws a thumbs-up. Nora, sitting where she is, feels madness tickle. They'll go. They should go. Why shouldn't they? Loose, Emma trots into the room and over to her.

—old girl. Old Emma. She's not that old but you say "old" to a good old dog, blanket warm. Brown fur under Nora's scratching fingers. Feel the warm of the dog's feel liking it. Dogs know who needs the comforting. Soft. Old girl.

Her mother looks great. Her dad's strands of remaining hair are elegant white, slicked with water down the sides and back of the ostrich egg he keeps his ideas in. Plastered tracks of hair like sidereal longitude lines, though of course she doesn't know the terms.

His shirt is a fishing shirt—short sleeves. Breastpockets, khaki epaulets. Laundered, lightly starched, pressed.

The brown eyes are not so calm as he thinks. Dancing are the eyes, dancing with change and the most intense, sustained, controlled firewalled glee.

Since his bonefishing trip of last June he's been soaring over the rooftops of the world holding the hand of some invisible robed guide, soaring over the data, assumptions and mathematical equivalence statements of a half-century's physics, conducted through the stars by the holy ghost of some Xmas yet to be imagined, in the solitaire of his heightened thinking getting ready to call everything into question because his brain's eyes are open too wide and most of his science is in his field of vision now and he's being too objective, which is something a scientist can be.

Old girl. Nora—fat tired soul in a fat tired body—the person thinking this—is getting fatter while her mother's swift and sure these days. Old girl, strawy sweet duskiness of dog. Dog eyes without depth. Without guile, hate, desire (except ball desire. Throw ball, stick, rock, anything . . please? If you do I will love you. If you don't I will love you). Top of honest smooth head. Soft, old girl . . scratching fingers, nails—Nora's—hard behind Emma's ears . . the dog's eyes close . .

Rairia signals him. *You?* she gestures, *me?*

Both, it would seem. He is up. Out of his chair—Rairia is in through the doorway in two strides—rustle of hand-print skirt. Each now stands with a hand on a wide shoulder of the weeping young woman. Emma in ecstasy from the continuing scratching, Nora's face a flood . .

Her days were a few easily repeated actions—school, where she sat in the back, lunch, at school, under the loud ceiling of reflected voices, where she made patterns on her plate of the pastel food, and home where she would not return her friends' calls. Might walk, trailingly, with Emma through the family's woods. School where her counselor was trying to get at what it was. It was nothing. It was only because she felt like this that she felt like this. It was only because she felt the way she felt that she needed a counselor. If she weren't like this she wouldn't need one. The only reason she needed one was that she was the way she was—it was so dumb. She would touch her homework, literally, and not do it, and in class, in the back, hot in her heaviness and not prepared, would sometimes discover she was sticking the point of a pen into an arm. To see how much she could take? At least it was real pain. Classroom mumble and the pain she was in. Her bedroom door shut, her homework before her, not getting done. She would scarcely be hearing the music snaking in the earphones in her ears. The evening's allotted pills in the desk drawer that could be locked—fast if necessary.

Everyone has something—pack genius books in the back of a car, find a life, know everything in the world, go fishing, play around with a cute woman, go off or whatever like her mom, or do school right—do the work and be respectable like Vanessa and them, as Griffin would say—and why not say it that way? Why not say it wrong? If you're no good then why not go ahead and be what you are? Nora had met the Chase whore, except Chase wasn't—she was a fox, as Nancy would say, and Nora maybe didn't blame her dad. Did she? She didn't know was the trouble. Last year when he had been packing his car with his books in boxes, getting ready to leave Mom the way he'd left Gwen, and go away to think or whatever, in town, she asked him to stay. He hadn't wanted to. Had he thought it through? If he had, Nora's mind wonders, then might it have been she—Nora—he hadn't been able to stand and had needed like a vacation from? No way. He was her pal. Yeah right. But he was. He really was. So why'd he go? To get a vacation from this whole crazy mountain of family that Nora hated and like really loved because it was so beautiful and the child she'd been still lived here. Would she ever, trailing angel-wing tatters of pain triumphal, fly up and out of her troubles like Mom? Nah. Anyway she certainly wasn't going to achieve it by staring in her memory at her dad showing her his fat back, showing his fat butt to her and not answering when she told him he didn't have to go, so intent and bent was he on stuffing all those stupid riddle books in the back of his broken-down car, whatever. Nora drifted, in her mind, away from it, was aimlessly rising like an airfloating bubble—with prisms in it—toward the possibility of . . .

Gwen for some reason. Gwen, just now, was all that came to Nora

Hope's locked-from-the-inside mind.

She dreamed now of being Gwen someday, or her mom maybe or someone, someday, with a man and a dog and a jeep—she would have a jeep at least. She imagined the jeep a lot, the dog she already had. The man . . well. Maybe no man. Dog, jeep. She used the pills sparingly—two, no more, no fewer. Except every few days when it would get to be like steel around her and the only thing that moved was her mind. Then she would use as many as she needed. Her friends did try. But she was starting to have new friends—companions more like. Souls like hers, dogs to hang with, blast-eyed, hurting themselves. She was still strong enough, she decided, to be going through this alone, and she knew she would get better, whenever.

But what if the strong part of her was further away in time and smaller and less sure to survive than she thought? She would realize this much later when she was better and the sand between her toes tickled and she was stunned by the Pacific sun blinding in a flash like molten dimes pressed against your eyes if you go up for a spike the wrong way.

Her father is staring at her, across the wash of papers that is his life.

The trip with Thomas and Henry—silver jet to a sky vista of white curves and cays in blue sea—is much with him. It was one of the best times of his life. Row of palm trees on sand, sharp-looking fronds in clusters like all-sized kitchen knives jammed points-out all ways in a lineup of taper-thin vases.

The day he'd gotten back he'd gotten a call from *éminence grise* Tellingen. This supercollider they wanted to build, would Eden testify? He demurred, speaking sweetly into the phone with a scowl . . . they wanted him for show. For years now they'd been past-tense eulogizing him behind his back (not that he didn't deserve it)—poor Hope, nothing more there, best work way back in his youth, these days not much, keeps to himself, crazy ideas . . . and so, isolated by circumstance and choice from the checks, balances and cross-pollenation of discourse with colleagues, my uncle pondered. Like a master-detective insomniac reviewing for the Nth time the unsolved case's file, he went back over—

and over, and over—the milestones of the last five decades' high-energy physics. Perspective gave way to examining, examining to questioning, in that lightbulb head, and questioning to doubt to disbelief.

A physicist sat on a scarp in thought. 2 + 2 = 4. No disputing it. Crystalline, pure. Then went into the world, found scientific evidence that 2 + 2 = 6.7777! Must be an "x," x = 2.7777, find x. They had a machine of phęnomenal potency that could make things that normally aren't around, and they turned it on, left it on for years. It made pink avocado skins, old license plates with registration #s no state had heard of, Styrofoam packing peanuts in new shapes, strange types of dust, knots of confetti and trillions of numbers such as $\sqrt{-i}$, to name one. Lo, in March of the third year they had it running, not one but two 2.7777s clanked out the machine's dispenser slot. Disregarding all the other stuff the machine had made 'cause it was too complicated and was stuff they weren't looking for, they had their answer.

But what if Time's a trait? What if Time exists no more independently of matter and energy than "the sneeze" exists independently of your nose? What if Time is just our noticing that matter moves? Then Time and our clocks and calendars and eras and anniversaries are no more independently significant than some Platonic concept of breathing exists independently of real commingling oxygen, lungs and blood . . with a grunt the poor soul grabbed a pen. Time is a husk, an illusion, the result of our spiritual immaturity. Time is no more context than the fluttering of the ephemerid's wings.

# 16

He'd finished for the day. He'd called me in—I was up for the weekend and we were going through his mail and filing work and some university stuff he'd been ignoring, but, sitting in the familiar room, we had fallen into fishing talk. It was the end of the day, that cathedraled hour of burnished pines and lawns. He was waving his hands, trying to make me understand a similarity between casting and inquiry, when the door clicked open and Rairia, wearing one of his shirts, came in holding up for our inspection the hinge with which she proposed to repair his wall cabinet.

"Looks," he marveled, getting out of his chair to approach the device, "like a ski binding. What do we need?"

"Screwdriver," she said, examining it with him. "Screw starter, what do you call those things." She giggled. "Screwer."

"Rairia please, we have company."

For months now since his return from his bonefishing trip Rairia had been downright friendly, even sunny. Her dark moods and swings of emotion and the combative bitterness were evidently things of the past—had he stopped to consider and analyze this, he might've found it odd. But he didn't. Oddness was never a bar to much up there anyway.

They knelt and I stood behind them. They were in intimate discussion. Either the original hinge had been mounted wrong or itself was faulty . . . their heads bobbed, her hair touching his pate as they contorted to peer into the cabinet from various angles.

"Let me—"

"Can you—"

"Yeah," she said leaning past him, "I'm just—gonna—"

"But see that pin? The head of ah, that tiny pin, right there?"

"Yes."

"Well look at the one on the bottom one, it's not the same."

"I know it isn't," she said sharply, working as he watched, "but it doesn't matter."

"Sure it does, doesn't the—"

"No," she said, "look." With a sigh she came out of the cabinet, her head coming back out, brushing his shoulder, and she guided him in, his head in, to show him. "See? The arm doesn't clear the corner so it doesn't matter if—"

"If we loosened the—"

"Hunh-uh."

"The lower one? No?"

"No because . ."

For all its stacks of notes and drafts and books in Pisa towers that room was a Spartan place, a single print of a rising trout on a wall, no other decoration except sometimes, these days, she would arrange him a vase of fresh flowers, unlike the wild spinach fiasco. The tackboard wall where once the mountain-range peaks and valleys of his golf had hung was blanketed now with pages ripped from magazines and journals and newspapers highlighted with yellow and light blue and pink Magic Marker and scribbled on in pen or pencil beside arcane schematics of his thought trains . .

The question is whether the hinge is mounted wrong or is, in itself, wrong.

"If," he suggests with unmeant pompousness, "we mount your new one in the same holes, will not the re-use of the same screw holes weaken the holding power, in other words the—"

"No because—"

"—the holes will be in essence—"

"Plastic wood, we have some."

"Do we?"

Yes, they did, and she got to her feet. I said I would get it for them if they would tell me where. Top shelf garage workbench. I went and found it, marveling at their dilapidated conveyances in the shadows, forms that could move if you turned a key and some electricity surged sparks into gas vapor. When I got back they had the old one off. He held the two screws like untasty candy he was having to be polite about on his chubby open palm while she, her leviathan torso torquing, examined the holes some more.

"Let's try."

"Without the ah, plastic wood?"

"Yeah."

"No!" he hooted in disbelief. "You'll loosen the holes, I mean the screws."

"No I won't," she said looking at, and fingering, surfaces, her raven hair across one side of her face.

"But you will sweetie because—"

"No," she said impatiently, "just relax."

"But the screws—"

"Screw the screws," she said and they were laughing.

They made stupid jokes about the screws, then about the jokes they were making, and were laughing so hard that their laughter caused more until they were weak and had to sit on the floor like pandas.

As a school of fish turns, they were through laughing and were serious again, on their knees.

"Because," she was telling him, "even if you're right and it's loose, the holes were made, were—" twisted at the waist—I couldn't see her face—fitting the new hinge in position, holding a hand out to him without looking at him "—were made you know, larger. Well. We can still put the plastic wood in if we have to. Screw. Screw please."

Vivid as the sharp different air of a springhouse in August when you step out of the day's heat, you could feel it between them. Civilized goodnatured affection. Without a word solemnly he handed her a screw.

"Thank-you," she called softly over a shoulder with her head inside the cabinet.

I'd turned the lights on for them.

I said, "You're welcome."

It was affecting to see them like this. As her doings were heating up in Boston and elsewhere with that weird cadre of tenured scholars and prizewinners run amok, she was, strangely—or perhaps not strangely at all—increasingly halcyon when around the bungalow. No more clutched handkerchief, no more slamming doors, no more outbursts, no more vales of depressing depression. Her hair was shorter, though not short, and she'd rinsed the gray from it. Her great roast haunches and the pillowy big arms were as sizeable as ever, but she carried herself, now, with a confidence like a set, before-the-wind sail. She still didn't believe in reason, and this remained anathema to him, but the fresh flowers were nice.

One afternoon he walked decisively into Nora's room.

"You're better," he told her.

And she was. It had happened suddenly. The slovenly solipsistic moping and energyless glumness had disappeared. It had surprised him, seemed inexplicable, but he wasn't going to look a gift horse in the mouth. She was even sunny, working hard again at her schoolwork —athletics, her doings with her friends, everything apparently all back on track.

When her door had banged open without a knock, in looking up from her homework and showing her father a wintry calm of expression, she had paused, before saying merely: "Yes?"

"You're better Nory."

Her sandy long lashes blinked—shutter-click.

"Well," he said. "Aren't you? Better?"

"Yes."

"Ah, yes and, ah, you—I mean I'm . . so I, ah—"

"Yes dad?"

"Would you like to go for a walk?"

"Yes."

. . . steaming, shockingly warm for this late in September, the draped vines and clingers, brambles, wild grape, myriad detailed branches . . . the whole live mush-floored forest seemed to lift as the mists lifted skyward. The sky a twinkling pale blue now that the rain had ended. Rising slow crystal-clean haze, trees and brook revealed—it wasn't winter yet. It hadn't snowed yet by gummy. There might be a fish or two left, catchable in the cooling waters of the hills' streams.

"Aren't you? . . Nory? I mean, ah . . better?"

She nodded under the high lengths of leafy stout wood soaring criss-crossed above them as they strolled.

For some time she had been coming out of her room at night, phoning up Vanessa and other friends, keeping her bedroom exceptionally neat. There was a spring in her step, lifelight in the mild eyes. The report had come through her counselor that she was playing soccer hard. Her counselor admitted to never having encountered such a reversal. It was, as far as Ms. Corelli could professionally ascertain, authentic. She was losing weight in an orderly way, the loveliness of the stalwart athlete's body showing and sculpting itself. The strong jaw. The eyes clear. They looked back at you. She nodded affirmatively as he gazed at her. He took a quick glance at the scrap of notepaper his absently roving hand had discovered in a pocket—scribblings, a quote from Tolkien: *He that breaks a thing to find out what it is has left the path of wisdom.* Not now, not now, stuff it—*both*er—stuff it in a safari pocket.

He leaned forward, under the branches. "So glad," he smiled. For he was. It touched and impressed him how even though (he admitted it, he admitted it) he wasn't the best dad, she had come back. She had stepped back and averted, on her own, whatever brink she'd been brainlessly waltzing for. He mentally congratulated himself on having kept an at least somewhat happy house for Nora to have been nurtured in, even if things were confused sometimes. One's faith in rational remedy. Indigenous world goodness under it all. The Good underlying the Slippery. The world's fundament—goodness—was requited sometimes after all. Was it not. Yes. So there was at least (he singingly in his mind with blithe songbirds of thought said nonverbally to himself as the toe of his sneaker hooked under some Japanese honeysuckle), there was at least a basis, a familial stability for Nora to've fallen back on, though not, one hoped, as he was falling now, pitching, ass-over-tincups, hazel forest floor of evergreen needles and roots spinning rushingly up

This business of being picked up, helped up and asked if he were all right, brushed off by a relative or colleague, was familiar. Yes yes yes he said. Fine. Annoyedly. She was trying not to laugh.

She smiled at her father as they hiked on.

"So," he said. "Do kids still, ah, does one say 'have your act together'?"

"You can. But not really."

"Well whatever is said I'm just very glad."

Hands clasped behind his back, they reached the plank walkway over the bog, and he paused. Enjoying the fumy-hued, motionless pools. Moss in mounds, exotic grays, greens, clotted grass, clumps of shrub, no tiny blossoms now in the imaged, watery still.

He let her go first.

"The will," she said, "is stronger than any idea."

"Hm?"

"I said the will is stronger than any idea."

"Well that's—" tipping a second stepping from plank to plank "—that's certainly an interesting observation."

"It's not an observation."

"—hm?"

"I said," Nora said, holding a branch for him until he could reach it and hold it for himself, "it's not an observation."

"You mean—"

"It's a fact."

"In other words it's true," he conversationally instinctively pinned her, following the broad heels of her hiking boots on the precarious planks with swimmy-from-momentary-allergy eyes, able to discuss such things with her using, as it were, but a single mental hand as the preoccupied swashbuckler fends off his attackers with a flashing sabre while at the same time—calmly—studying his spread-out map of battle. "It's-not-an-observation-it's-a-fact you're saying . . it's a truth . ."

"Yeah."

"Well—" continuing, mock-innocently, to set her up "—ah, now tell me, what account does one take of the social contract?"

"The what?"

"Oh just a for-instance, you know the agreement among everybody to abide by certain rules? Don't cross against the light? Don't commit murder?"

"Yes?" she asked over a Shetland shoulder, her hair swaying as her head turned.

"Well you said the will is stronger."

"M-hm."

"Ah, than *any* idea?"

"M-hm."

He was charmed.

"All right, but suppose the will of the person next to you on the bus is telling that person to hurt you. Is that person's will then stronger than the idea that ah, battery's a felony? Or the idea of loving your neighbor as yourself?"

"Yes," she said as they picked their way.

"But you're going to get hurt."

"Yes."

He was captivated by the alert, watching stance of a saurian-like lizard, orange-pink, staring at his sneaker, tail still, by a scalp of sphagnum.

"But you don't want to get hurt do you?"

"Of course I don't."

"But if the guy's will is stronger than any law—"

"It's not stronger than *my* will," she said as they came off the last plank and onto hard trail.

There was a lot wrong with this, plenty he could puncture.

But why bother. It was marvelous of Nora to have these little ideas. A wonderful sign. Don't discourage it. They could stride now, side by side down the branch-canopied way. This was truly charming and to be encouraged, though, as he panted to keep up, he realized, in thinking about it, that discussion of the will was not exactly rampant these days on the philosophical scene. He was a little shaky too as to just what the refutations are that demolish the arguments for the primacy of the will.

He made a mental note to look them up, and after a couple attempts asked me to do it, but I didn't get anywhere either. He said Nevermind and forged ahead with more observations on Time, mind-rhapsodizing that he was convinced would help him through the forest branches, vine-throttled and intergrown, of scientific doubt to the clearing where the light shone.

In arguing that Time is an illusion he pointed out that certain relatively recent civilizations regarded mountains as useless. Similarly, he argued, might we not be mistaken in thinking the dainty-winged mayfly is the thing the bottom-burrowing, clinging crawly nymph under the water is the bearer or vessel of? What if the mayflies dancing up the blinding sunset air are the children, and the nymph, with its long, crawling life around the underwater rocks, the adult? (If we could consider "adult" aside from who lays the eggs.) Similarly might Aquinas be further along than Sartre? And progress thus quite possible once we consider things aside from the linear illusion of Time?

To say progress must be linear in Time is as fusty as leaving mountains alone. As close-minded as refusing to consider the stout-legged, three-tailed unbeautiful crawler as Adult to the fluttering Sulphur's Child. As plain wrong as it would be to imagine that when Leonardo paints the *Mona Lisa* he starts in the upper lefthand corner, paints across to the upper righthand corner, goes back and paints across again, and so on (he showed me with an oscillant straight arm) until at last at the canvas's lower righthand corner: final brushstroke—the masterpiece complete!

Saint Thomas Aquinas, an Italian holy man and philosopher of the thirteenth century, nicknamed "Dumb Ox" for his corpulence and slowness of movement, was a sharp and orderly, pious mind who reconciled rationality to the mysteries of faith. In his writings St. Thomas shows how reason and logic can lead us to God by building from the world through our five senses into mind's thought. He worked up a number of logical proofs of the existence of God. He is said to have been generous and humble, though lance-sharp in dialogue, and to have lived a life pure in its acts and unselfish in its charity.

Jean-Paul Sartre, born 1905, was a French writer and philosopher. He believed there is no God and human beings are tossed in a sea of freedom—choice. There being no universal rules or essential ideals according to Sartre one ought to make one's life up out of authentic choices instead of sitting life out like a bump on a log letting custom, tradition, social convention and transient pleasure-patterns decide, for one, what one is. Sartre was not a nice man. In what he did, as opposed to what he sat and thought about and wrote down, he did not lead an exemplary life.

At six Alan was interested in drawing lighthouse women with flashlights coming out their ears and men in camouflage beside salmon the size of elephants. He was interested in composing labyrinthine, gothic, highly technical tales which his grandfather and others were then enlisted to commit to writing while Alan dictated, at the kitchen table, holding his golden brow and perfecting his illustrations with sonic-bright marker pens and ongoing consultation, with whoever was around, as to what Mach eagles dive at, whether there could still be plesiosaurs, and how many gigabytes it would take if you wanted to list the names of all the criminals who ever lived.

That October at the height of the foliage we took a moonlit walk.

Lim was gabbling, flanking his brother like a herding dog in that uncanny shining. When we would come out of the forest and go down open lanes under the night sky, so vivid were the flammatory pinks and oranges and hot yellows and freshet blood reds of the trees' daily leaves you could see—ghostly but unmistakable to the eye—these actual colors in the moon's silvery bathing light. Nancy, Duffy and Nora in knit caps and mittens romped with the children—orbitless planets in their little boots and coats. Lim was working hard, striding apace, to make Eden listen, and sometimes my uncle nodded, the down-filled flaps of his hat, unfastened, goofily flapping. But Eden's pace was as if he were trying to escape the argument (it wasn't too hard to guess what it was) unspooling off his agent's unstoppable tongue.

When we got back and were having hot chocolate by the fire, Alan Elwive came up to his grandfather. The boy's cheeks were still chilled from the night air. He stood close to Eden and leaned against his grandad in his absorption with showing him what he'd drawn with crayons on construction paper. But there was no suggestion of anyone clambering onto anyone's lap.

"Nice house."

"It's a spaceship. This is the steering place, these are the crew, this is the Dad, this one's the Mom, this is a kid, this is another kid, a brother, and this is the dog."

"What's this?"

"Those are flowers because there's a garden, because even in space you need to eat, and there's like. There's a. It has a covering."

"Ah. So the space air can't get in."

"That's right."

"That's wonderful Alan."

"Yes."

The spaceship was an enclosure, a rectangle. In it, plenty of blank space separating them, were the relevant living creatures, the garden, and other unidentifiable elements.

His grandfather noticed the height from which Alan's eyes looked down at his crayoning. Eden noticed the shape of Alan's shoulders and chest and was aware of the presence around, and on the brow just above, the boy's eyes. A maturity, a thoughtful calm, that had not been present a year ago.

Alan still made dictional and grammatical mistakes—said "soupess" to pluralize *soup* and thought the word for Universe is "university." But he could list beautifully, list phrases, even clauses, and he was getting better than good at hypothesizing.

"And ah, what's this?"

"That's a—whaddya call a thing that keeps everything, makes everything go straight like—" hand cleaving the air "—all straight and not upsidedown or—"

"Gyroscope."

"That's right. That's what it is."

Like the other elements in his crayoned vision, Alan's space gyroscope, which resembled a minaret in a locket, was discrete in space and enclosed by a crayon rule roughly in the form of a rectangle.

"Because let's say," the boy went on, "a mutant got attached to the ship, the hatch was—somebody forgot their chore and the hatch was unlocked and there was a terrible explosion, the mutant burst in and sucked everyone's guts and blood and eyeballs out. That's why you need a what'd you say?"

"Gyroscope."

"Gyrescape, yeah."

"Right," Eden said, tousling the architect's hair.

Alan had more comments and questions but after a few minutes Eden wanted to go back to the adult conversation—monologue was more like it—he'd been engaged in with Lim and Duffy and me, and Alan, looking, as he went, at his spaceship system, went back, with it, to where he and other kids and Nancy were drawing on the rug by the terrarium table.

My uncle said he wanted us to just "floatingly consider" Nietzsche. Wittgenstein. Think, he adjured us, how much philosophy has been written by human beings mentally (hee) unbalanced no really, think . . Tertullian, Plato for heaven's sake. We really don't know how mentally messed up such people may've been. Sartre was a spoiled brat with a vast ah, shallow mental facility. Philosophy isn't what it pretends to be. By applying the right countertension of perspective to the canon of a Hegel or a Sartre one may expose the philosopher's purportedly objective thought as merely the employment of thinking tools such as rhetoric and logic to ornament a soul-commitment more personal and emotional than reasonable and universal . . no?

Nearly pulling him by his collar Lim conducted his brother off to the high-raftered study for a private talk . . . "X marks my words," Duffy Ginty divulged as we sat watching the different-sized brothers go away through a far door, "one day he's gonna wake up and find out he's playin' Russian Rigoletto."

How questionable everything is.

Take Aquinas's Fourth Proof of the Existence of God: common sense knows some things in this world are better than others. But this must be according to a standard . . if there's a good, a better, and a better still, there must be a Best, i.e. God. The hierarchies of the natural world and our human worlds are arrows pointing toward the divine. Hold that thought and let's get up and walk around the table to the other side, namely a proof of the existence of absolute evil along precisely the same logical lines. But the vulnerability of Aquinas's proofs only ennobles them, only makes them the more poignant and powerful . . imagine how impossible it would be to believe in a God whose existence could be logically proven.

If, he said—and this could be related back to the practice of physics theory—if, he said, tugging a dachshund-wattly earlobe . . . if, he fervently near-whispered, instead of a sea of Cartesian (complete) or Kierkegaardian (heroic) doubt, a *science* of doubt could be devised, an open-eyed epistemology of uncertainty, then without having to fall into lockstep over everything one might have succeeded in working up a philosophy incomplete and inconsistent on purpose, structured yet changing, a self-adjusting machine—wouldn't *that* be something, First Mover Unmoved Who on Occasion Allows Himself to be Adjusted, an asymptotic God as real as a belief system instinctively self-nursing, self-building, self——

#$!&! H. F@#!!-ing $#$@!" Lim spasmed and was screaming.

"Lim be careful!"

"Eden! Eden! Eden! Come here!"

"Ow you're dragging me—"

"Yes I'm dragging you, yes, sit, siddown. Calm. Ok? Calm? We're calm."

"Well I certainly am but—"

"I am too. I am too. Brother—ok. Now listen."

Lim took a moment to get hold of himself. The bole, stemmings and branchings of his valves and atria and ventricles and twig capillaries were juicing dangerously and he wisely, in spite of himself, waited a bit before saying what he had to say.

Eden fidgeted. His remaining strands lifted like tinsel on a Van de Graaff generator, the frayed end of his web belt flopping as he shifted—ill-at-ease pupil—in the chair his brother had forcibly put him in.

Lim stood with his hands on a desk of my uncle's papers, arms rigid, head hung, breathing deeply.

"Okay," he said. "Okay. Now." But he was still too distraught and had to take another deep breath and go to a window and pretend to be seeing what he stood staring at in the big glass that Rairia had Windexed and polished to bright invisibility. Turning and beginning to pace while contemplatively massaging his strange little head, he tried again: "Okay. So. She's in the tower, right? Am I right?"

"Ah, not precisely."

"Look Eden, she's sitting—you said she—"

"The castle does have a tower, several in fact, but, ah, you see she's in the Hall. On her throne. In what was known as the 'Horrid Hall' before the castle changed hands, before she took it—not from the Night Master as you know but from his cousin Earthbender. But you see she still *thinks* of it as the Horrid—"

"All right whatever, ok, in the Hall and she—"

"Right."

"Right and the bad guys 're comin'."

"That's right."

"The Queen of the Night's gonna—"

"Master."

"Right, the Master of the Night."

"Correct."

"Is gonna attack. I mean this is a bloody, this is huge, this is a three-or-four-day ordeal we're looking at if I understand it. This is Armageddon. This is Utah Beach and Crécy and Gettysburg rolled into one, know what I—"

"Yes."

"Yes," Lim said with increasing excitement, his pacing quickening, a gesture of medieval aggression coming in now and then as he marched, "yes . . and it's gonna be a cliffhanger, battles everywhere, sword fights between heroes, frontal assaults, cavalry charges, siege stuff too . . Eden?"

"Er, sieges?"

"Yes sieges . . yes?"

"Ahh, of the castle."

"Walls, ramparts, ladders, boiling oil, catapults, my right? Am I?"

"Er, probably, but actually there's—"

"Right and spilled guts, noble deeds on the field of honor, hand-to-hand, engines of war, a regular Valhalla Express we're talking about—*wham,* ka-*zing,* aieeeeeee—so. Now. So the—ok. Now. What happens, I mean who wins, like in the end."

Eden with a vacant, outer look, the eggy eyes gazing in actuality at some inner nameless thing, touched his Victorian moustache. It was as graywhite now as it was henna. He touched it, still staring that way, with a first and second fingertip, as an actor might check a costume prop. He said: "I want . . whatever does happen in the end I want to be consistent with all the threads of all the characters and their lives and destinies as these have unfolded in, ah, well you know. In the earlier."

Lim frowned. He noticed a date, wrapped in transparent wrapping. It was lying on some reports. He leaned down. He began unwrapping.

There was no smile. He unwrapped the oblong sticky fruit from its cellophane. He looked at it. He dropped it in the wastecan, looking around for something to wipe his fingers on.

"Yeah," he said.

"But what I also want—I know you don't like this Lim."

"You're right."

"All right, I understand, but it's—" stubborn wriggle squarely into chair, arms folded pugilistically "—it's the case. I want to come to some larger understanding of the world I live in. Its thoughts, their history, the matter and energy everything's made of, and when I have achieved this, then you see to have it be what drives the book's end. I've written these ah, things . . playthings . . they're fine as what they are. But now that I'm drawing to the end, of the sword cycle anyway, I just want—you know to the extent possible I want it to last. To partake of a deeper . ."

No more came. The sentence wasn't going to be finished, probably because to do so would've proved repetitive. Lim's big brother sat there with his arms folded. His eyes remained focused inward, stubborn with light, the same buttery, harmless brown as ever.

Lim looked as if he'd eaten the date instead of throwing it away. He shoved his hands in his pockets and considered, then tried again.

"Okay," he said. "But you can't do this forever."

"I know that, I do know that."

"There's no like final—no ultimate—"

"No no no no—" acquiescing hand held up in gentle fending-off "—I'm aware of that. I know there isn't."

"All right," Lim said in a voice as attentive and tensed as if he were tending to line and rod with a cast out and a fly floating over a spooky fish, "all right then . . just so you understand . . if you wait for your thought to clarify you'll never act. Like you gotta *act.* Am I—"

"Yes that's good, I agree."

"Oh good, ok. So." Lim stood straight and massaged his hurting back. "So let's talk about what happens. She's there in the tower—*hall,* in the hall, and the armies are gathering, and she's got her allies and the kid's comin' but what specifically happens next is what we need to focus on. For instance what do those little—I really like those little kiss-butterflies, the cave people with the spell on them?"

"Lehwhurlerra."

"Yes. So for instance will *they* help her? Will they change back and join the fray?"

Eden pulled his open hands down his face that since he'd been losing weight again was a spotted, rubbery mask with eyeholes. He sighed. "Actually, as a matter of fact Lim I don't know if Blok and his Lehwhurlerra might not turn out to've fallen under the evil influence of—"

"Whatever Eden, whatever, but—" gleameyed "—Gwen, Lady Gwen, she's the decision-maker. My right? Oh I know she's got her problems, she wants her hubby or whatever back . . but *she!*"

"Yes yes, you're right."

"She's got the Sword, she commands all those angels and guys, she's got the Tarr—"

"Good Lim."

"—on her side. She calls the shots, she sets the strategy."

"Yes."

"Oh Edie I remember when you started off with the funeral—" Lim dropped into a chair, innerly smiling "—in the first book? *The Search for the Sword?* The ziggurats of ice? The wake dances and parties they were all having and how everything changed, rainbow colors when the horns blew? And the quarrel that broke out over that map . . what was—"

"The Map of Empire."

"Yeah, those two little TweedledumTweedledee guys. That like really solemn moment, the high prayers for the departed, and all the black flags go up and the clouds change color and they're all praying and these two little butterballs get into a shouting match over who gets the map?"

"You've got a good memory Lim."

Eden sat much more relaxed, rubbing a shoulder, still staring and thinking.

"Well it's good Eden, it's really good, you've gotta remember that . . and when the prayers and everything are over, remember how that slow breeze blows over them all all of a sudden?"

Nodding, Eden shut his eyes. Smiling, remembering when it was new, the flash of new words and deeds each time, each session, each morning, each sentence as it came, unspooling in his heart, the freshest, sweetest, sunniest, most innocent deathless moment, sideline though it was.

Any tale worth telling is worth telling again for the savoring and now without having planned to the brothers sat remembering. It was exchangingly retold by them how the death of the One Parent—godlike vague progenitor of Blok—marked the passing of an age. Then the pomp and fury of the great ceremony and cortege, how the crone limps up to Gwen (not yet "Lady") to whisper of a sword, a weapon of heart and destiny long lost in the faroff Mountains of Eldertarr, and how the Companions of the Sword, who don't yet know they're that, gradually gather and set off into the sunrise, little knowing that their failure to take even one bad person with them will call the Martahg out of his spring pool, when they cross Denthehn Fen. Lim cackles with pleasure at the image of that hillock-backed, dripping ape with his gunnysack of expressions, mouths, attitudes, eyes, who holds them up for an entire afternoon while he builds different faces on himself and insists they criticize each one and tell him which ones they like best (so the Watcher in the reeds can learn, see traits, and especially weaknesses as he peers and concentrates, holding his dragonbird quiet with a fell claw in the unstirring grass) . . . "I mean," Lim said, trying to open his hands the way his brother could do it but achieving only a pantomime of the discovery that you've lost the trapped housefly you thought you had, "I mean . . it's good Eden . . but don't you like them? Don't you like all your wonderful characters?"

"What a strange thing to say. Of course I do. Of course I like them, but you see that's—"

"Well then—"

"That's why I want to get the ending precisely, deeply right."

"But all this reading you're doing instead of—ugh. We've been through that . . but really I don't see how all this reading and philosophy and shit sorry, sorry but I have to say, I really don't see how . . I really don't see why. Now if it were your work, your real work, your physics, if you were abandoning the stories because you were spending like twenty-four hours a day on physics, now I'm not saying I'd like it, but I'd understand it Eden, I'd understand and—but, you're not even doing your physics are you?"

"No."

"Well so."

"Lim, I don't know what you want me to say."

"It's like you're a monk or something, some guy in a smock, er—"

"Habit?"

"Robe, whatever, white robe, habit, whatever, it's like you're in a white room with one window, I mean just studying to study, and that's fine, learning for learning's sake, how many angels and like that, but Eden, these people, these animals and monsters and things, that people *like—like* Eden, you didn't sell four million copies of the first three because people all over the world wanted to be nice to you. So there they all are." Diligently the little man bowed his head to tick the players off finger by finger. "Lady Gwen on the throne, everything focuses there, decisions, intrigue. Her dad, Blok, the little whozees, the Night Master across the hills getting into position, her husband or whoever he is riding like hell—"

"I know." Eden with two hands—elbows out—yawned and rubbed his rubbery face. "I know it, I'm just attempting—"

"Eden the fucking book's gonna earn a million dollars for you counting—" this time the finger-ticking was extremely enthusiastic "—movie rights for the four, translation rights for this last one, mass market paper and on and on and on, di-dah di-dah di-dah, and twenty-five percent, twenty-five percent, which I appreciate . . twenty-five percent of a million is important to me in, well excuse me but in dollars, ok? I have to say that, I have to say that Eden, and to the family too, though there's no obligation, none whatever, but always in the past—"

Hands up: "Yes yes when the time comes I shall certainly ah, as before. No use for all of it."

"Good. I don't mean good. I don't mean that, I mean I understand. You understand," Lim said animatedly, "I understand. Okay now let's get back to what happens, 'k?"

"Lim."

"*What.*"

"I do care."

"Oh good. I mean good as in ok, okay now. What—you with me? We with each other? Good. What, to take a specific instance, is going to be the Night Master's line of attack—I mean does he like do this massive full frontal assault? Is there a diversion? Does he have a back way in, like a spy?"

Eden nodded.

"Okay *great!* Or maybe both, spy lets commandos in, full frontal assault meanwhile *is* the diversion."

"It's possible."

"It is? I mean it is. That's very good see now we've got—" Lim launched out of his chair and began pacing again, smacking a palm with a fist "—we've got movement, we've got action. The attack comes. Gwen leaps off her throne, grabs the Sword, storms out the front gate . . . is this ok? You tell me Eden, you're the boss of all this, I'm just trying to get it started. The castle gates are forced—kaBOOM! In pour the dark hoards, in pour the—"

"Actually—"

"Don't say 'actually' Eden. I don't like it when you say 'actually.' 'Actually' what?"

Lim had stopped pacing and, ceiling light on him, hands on hips, glaring down, stood night-reflected in the window with Eden, more shadowy where he sat politely in his chair by the wall, in the background in the night in the window. The full moon, an eerie luminescent silver, was appearing over Lim's angrily bowed reflected head.

"Ahhh, you see I'm not resolved. Let me explain. Let me explain if I can."

"Explain."

"The symmetry of the natural world is evident everywhere, especially in particle physics. So. Fascinating symmetries, and there's a process by which nature breaks, you see, these ideal symmetries . . in any event . ."

"In-any-event? *Yes?* "

"Well just that—then of course the . ." big rubbery face lost "—there's the pacifity of the natural world."

"Eden 'pacifity' 's not a word. Goddammit what're—"

"Lim," the big brother said zealously leaning forward to clasp his hands, fingers laced prayerfully, and slowly shake them, "I'm just—congeniality of the thinkers, of their schools ah, and politically too Lim, politically the world is improving. We're coalescing, even with all the—"

Lim stared at him: "So?"

"Well of course the dark hoards are gathering. They have to, that's natural . . but I'm . . as I said I'm unresolved . . suppose Lady Gwen sends an emissary."

"Excuse me?"

"Emissary."

"That's what you said. Ok. So she sends an emissary, so what."

"Well just . . as I say I'm unresolved but suppose, ah, Lim suppose she does, and there's discussion, some ah, dialogue."

"There's no discussion Eden, there's no dialogue. She sends an emissary and they turn him inside-out by his gizzard and cut his extremities off and giftwrap him in aluminum foil and stuff him in a fucking saddlebag Eden. Then they attack the fucking castle. They shove darts up the emissary's ass 'til they come out his nose and they burn him at the stake and they cut his head off and take his passport and throw him down a fucking *well Eden!* There's no—"

"I'm not saying I've decided. But the beauty, the unexpected symmetry of an emissary you see, a parley there on the pending field with its, oh you know, its engines of war and mailed knights and foot-soldiers and all the terrific smoke and anger of a looming, ah . . then you see she could receive a delegation from—"

"From the Master of the Night."

"Right. Good Lim. And they parley, all that evening long and far into the starry—"

"This is in the castle."

"Why yes."

"Lady Gwen and the Night Master."

"Ah, it could be, yes. It could be He Himself . . and you see they begin to negotiate . ."

Lim's eyes bulged as if someone had him by the throat. His expressive lips were shut tight and absolutely at the horizontal as his eyes grew bigger.

"That day," his big brother orally sketched, wiggling his fingers smilingly beside his eyes and ideas, "that day or the next, while the hosts wait sleepless, there in the once horrid hall they treat and discuss. And they find a ray, a sliver of hopeful light, and it widens as they communicate, oh it widens into the most marvelous promise, an open door . . . they negotiate a settlement—"

"Settlement."

"Why yes."

"Settlement," Lim says to himself. "Settlement. Eden."

"Yes?"

"Eden."

"Yes? Lim? Are you—"

"I'm fine. Settlement," his little brother says, going to the room's other side, saying the word "settlement" several times more, with pauses of silence between. "Have you got any Tylenol?"

"Why ah, sure, sure we do. Why don't you sit down?"

"I don't want to sit down."

"Sure, wait, sure just wait right there."

He took two, with the water my uncle brought back.

"Settlement," he said swallowing. "Eden," he said oddly. "Where if a porplex, settle not—shit." Momentarily unable, in the supremity of his dislocation, to form sensible English, Lim repeated an unprintable profanity as he lurched to the near window.

"I haven't decided," his brother was trying to reassure him.

Without turning from the night and the moon and his own reflection, Lim held up a hand.

Fumbling through his pockets he carefully, staring at himself in the glass, opened the silver pillbox he'd begun to use, and took one of what was in there too. "Okay," he said, waiting for a modicum of calm. "Ok now," he said in a reasonable tone, "listen. We've got to get that bitch off the dime. It's as simple as that. I want you to think of—no. No that's exactly what I don't want. I don't want you to think. I want you to decide. What's going to happen, what's going to happen Eden, and it better be a fight, a fight with grand deeds and blood and shocking surprises . .'k? No ambiguity . .'k? No peace negotiations. Just," he said quickly, holding a hand up again to stop his brother's reply whatever it might be, "leave it at that. Leave it at that for now. See what comes to you." Eden started to speak. "Period," Lim said impolitely.

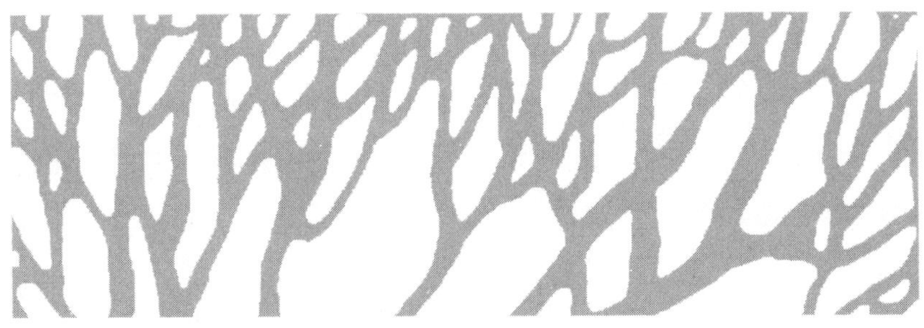

# 17

As we ate, that Thanksgiving, Duffy Ginty and the children in song, Nora, composed, sitting before her full plate appearing to have to complete some long inner prayer before she would be ready to dig in, and Lim wolfing his food dexterously with one hand while playing chess with Alan with the other, Eden was with us—somewhat. He sat at the table's head as stubbornly false-polite and incorrigible as he had been the month previous, when Lim had shut him up by wedging a period under his tongue. He was happy. He was happy because he was thinking. He wasn't supposed to be—he was supposed to be listening to Bright, a Dr. now, with several impressive papers to his name. Bright was lobbying my uncle for the existence of a fifth force—but Eden, looking like the canary that's swallowed the cat, the body behaving (sitting still and not eating too much) and the mind not, wasn't listening. He was thinking and there wasn't a thing anyone could do about it. Rairia wasn't with us. Rairia had gone, as Lim put it, "completely Old Testament." Her mind had been made up for some time. This in retrospect explained her cheerfulness that summer and fall. She was off raising money now, giving speeches, leading marches and publishing broadsides and appearing on talk shows and rafting down Class IV rapids. Her cause was a campaign, reportedly gaining momentum, to have the words "and the pursuit of Happiness" expunged from the Declaration of Independence.

Several places down the table from my uncle Bright leaned gawkishly forward to harangue his old mentor some more, and a rare thing happened. Eden lost his temper. It think it was unconsciously—I mean he was so in his own world of thought, until Bright's adenoidal insistence got to him, that his anger crept up on him and came out as a vituperative cynicism, about Bright, about physics in general, that was not as a matter of fact put on. Since his lonely time of exile down in the city the previous year, the hooded serpent doubt had swayed up in my uncle's intellect, a dangerous skepticism and cynicism that he probably took to an extreme as he made rude fun of Bright's modern-physics orthodoxy.

Smug in what he knew and had to tell, Bright rangily leaned out over the table to yap past our faces at my uncle. They'd found the ______, Bright announced, naming one of the basic particles. (I forget which one, but it was an important one.) Eden smiled sweetly into the candlelight. Ah yes, he said. Smashing protons and antiprotons into each other at trillions of electron volts, he said, then sorting through the incomprehensible debris signals of the wreckage that resulted (Eden sweetly told us), they found a couple instances of what they were looking for.

Bright said this was a blatant mischaracterization and bit his lip.

Ah, had, my uncle wondered angelically, they filtered out and discarded all the background, all the spurious and the irrelevant?

Oh yes was Bright's quick answer, of course. They had calculated the expected background, Bright said. Of course.

He was glad to know that, my uncle said. Always prudent, he said, to get rid of what you're not looking for.

Bright started coughing, not because he wasn't certain he was right but in embarrassment on behalf of his erstwhile teacher.

Eden bored in, staring at the candles and talking in that false nice voice as if entranced, as if he were a seer, the remaining strands of his white hair combed back wetly, as I may have said, in unparallel streaks crossing at times on the speckly globe's curve. He wore a veinal-red corduroy shirt. He intimated that the sightings—the confirmed ones—of this crucial elusive particle were but a fraction of a fraction of a fraction of a percent of the total number of collisions, in the collider, that they'd had to cause, over the years, to get even this many "successes." I think it was something like a couple dozen confirming events out of the endless collisions. And how close, Eden beatifically wondered, was the number of confirmed sightings as a percent of total collisions to the statistical minimum needed for them to be confident of their results? Were their readings well over the percentage they needed to see to be sure? Obviously they weren't below that level. Were they, coincidentally, right *at* the minimum percentage level? And, the deep voice unlovingly soft in the candlelight wanted to know, was the calculation of what minimum percentage would be statistically significant made (surely, he suavely inserted, such a calculation was made) years ago at the beginning of the search, halfway through, or more lately (when the calculators would have had a pretty good idea of what the experiment's results would be) . . . Bright's retort was numerical and full of jargon I couldn't understand. My uncle interrupted. The rich voice now wished to inquire about the calculation of the energy level at which the various forces of the Standard Model become equally strong. He was still talking into the candleflames, and I saw Lim so angry with his brother he wouldn't even look at him. About a million billion billion volts, wasn't it? Oops, no it wasn't, Eden pretended to remember, no they'd spruced the calculation up, hadn't they? Biting his lip Bright nodded. Yes, my uncle "recalled," yes they ah, they recalculated. Did they not. Yes. They got it to more like *ten* million billion billion volts than just a million billion billion, so the Planck energy's only a *hundred* times larger instead of a thousand. Nora finally, pacifically, took her first bite. My uncle asked if Bright thought there had been a chance the scientists doing the calculating would allow the energy level to come out at a lower (i.e. threatening to the Model) level than the original million billion billion

. . . Bright just shook his head smiling bitterly. Naturally, he assured the man who'd taught him, the calculations had been objective—Eden knew that as well as he did, Bright said.

The front legs of my uncle's chair struck the floor with a bang.

"But did they *try?*" he demanded. "Did they try as hard? Knowing," he pounded the tablewood, "that a recalculation that lowered the energy would weaken their case, and that a recalculation that increased the energy would—" pound "—strengthen their case, did they try as hard to find reasons to recalculate lower as they did—" pound "—to recalculate—" *pound* "—ouch. To ah, recalculate higher? No. I do not believe so."

Bright patiently shook his head and said nothing. Eden Hope had done some exciting work, Bright told me later that evening, but the man was becoming quirky—not unbalanced, Bright made a point, wiping his scarred face, of wanting me to know. He wasn't implying his benefactor was becoming unbalanced. Just impossible.

Tellingen was less polite. Courtly Tellingen leaned, inclining gently, forward, having set his after-dinner tea aside. "It's hogwash from a physicist," he said. "He knows better," Tellingen said. "If I did not know that he knew better I would take it less seriously—I would take it as a joke." The rounded, oversized, oddly refined anthropoid upper lip stirred measuredly as Tellingen spoke. "Hogwash," he said, his words words of outrage spoken in an even subdued tone of anything but, a tone learned, learned and earned, his superior nihilistic brain thinking heaven knows what else on parallel tracks as he judged my uncle harshly, late that night. "They examined millions of possible events, they closely analyzed several hundred thousand, they calculated their background carefully. They were at about four or five standard deviations. That is, if they'd seen three events say, they could not have been certain of the signal. Of course one designs one's search on the basis of what is expected," said Tellingen, who we left sitting with his tea by the fire as the last of us went to our rooms. "It is impossible to do otherwise. One gives up on finding errors if what is being measured is what has been expected."

Since I had known him my uncle had spoken of physics to me, and other laity, in terms simplistic and even childish. This was so we would have at least a fighting chance of grasping what he was talking about, but it was also, he once confessed, a salutary thing for highflown science to have to be conveyed from time to time in terms a child can understand. From this however he had lately wandered into nonsense (from Tellingen's point of view) and cynicism, a cynicism all the more intense, perhaps, for his having made little progress—little contribution—to his profession in recent times. Yet I know he was trying to do the honest mind-work too—he was playing with the real math and data and theory—it was just that he was keeping it all to himself, which, since I couldn't've understood it anyway, was fine with me—and so like everyone I was exposed to my uncle's scientific thought through a distorting lens of sarcasm and parody, as modern physicists themselves, as I understand it, are forced to view natural, physical reality through the prism of humanmind mathematics and the process of coordinating one theoretical system's assumptions with the symmetries of another.

Come to think of it, Eden's problem may have been that after a highly distinguished early career he fell into trying to solve scientifically problems that are not scientific, problems solvable, if they are, in the realms of faith and pure feeling and unreflexive action only. And thus he lost—well, perhaps the problem in a sense is that he *didn't* lose his mind . .

Like a naughty child he sat soundless, his eyes very open. He was thinking. They couldn't stop him. He was thinking. By the candlelight of always family and friends sing, sitting variously down that familiar, initials-carved board—Nancy is conducting a cousinly chorus. Alan, joining in in a reedy voice, never takes his eyes off his canopener bishops and rodeo-rearing knights. Duffy brings more everything in, including a fancy gelatin she admits is probably "gelding the lily."

I was having a pleasurable talk with Henry Anther about bucktails.

His eyes, winkling like Montana stars you fold your arms behind your head outside the tent to stare at, looked around the table. He was smiling at the scene, at Alan, two fingers on a rook, looking at his uncle to see if the move was correct—at Duffy dishing out, jovially commanding Nora to pass her plate whether hungry or not, at Nancy smirking at herself while conducting selfconsciously the last—she's told them this is the *last,* then dessert—Farmer-in-the-Dell chorus.

Anther smiled at Eden who had put on Alan's Patriots hat and was feeding scraps to a friend—giveaway plume wagging by his chair—while trying to look innocent as his mind handsprung, vine-swung and cartwheeled about the free amusement park of its thoughts if, indeed, it was a smile.

I'll call it a smile. Henry Anther surveyed his friend's family and laden table. Say he was faintly smiling.

We'd been talking bucktails, patterns tied of hair (squirrel, bear, fox, skunk, synthetics) to look and behave like baitfish when dragged under the water. He explained that bucktails aren't exactly "flies," as they imitate fish, not insects. But they've come to be called flies.

Though not the most refined angling, bucktail fishing is productive and can be fun. As anglers will do when talking technique, lifting a hand he made—effortlessly and not too broadly, here at table—several fast shortcast gestures with his thumb in the air and three fingers closed down the pad of the heel of that hand's palm, with a one-ounce imaginary hammer tapping tacks at different angles into a post. To fish a bucktail properly, he said, "does take a certain amount of finesse."

You could see him, in his workshirt of the brand he always wore, with creases across the chest from how it had lain folded in its box that afternoon at the store, reflecting on his newfound articulateness just as he might pay attention to the action of a new rod. He wasn't embarrassed a bit, just aware. Trout go after a bucktail 'cause they're hungry or curious or angry. To unlock the secret of what the fish needs to see to be stimulated and follow/strike, often you have to try, he said, a "smorgasbord" of speeds and rhythms of retrieve. He looked at the word, *smorgasbord,* with the craftsman's pause of gaze. A word he'd always known, but to denote a sideboard of dishes. Then Eden had dubbed it into a chapter of *Simple Fishing,* showing how it could be used colorfully an unexpected way . .

Henry had more to say and I was interested. Knowing I was, and knowing I would wait, he was quiet, looking around.

If you have fished with a master you may have noticed that while he or she is more efficient in everything than you are, the master is in some things actually slower.

Holding a caught trout, needing to get the hook out, you or I will tense and rush and fight it and fumble with the hook in the air-gagging jaw.

The master may do nothing—nothing at all—for a full second, which is a long time, before with a wrist filigree making trout and hook separate. That relaxation of action, unhurried but fast because exact once in motion, is what Anther was doing with me when he looked up from our unfinished conversation.

What he was in the process of making me understand about bucktails would wait, even ripen.

Roles reversed I would have been talkingtalking, Eden too, Chase, Duffy, any of us, my hand on his arm, my voice leaning intemperately toward him in my anxiety that he get the point.

Not Anther. He let me and his thoughts hang like a caught trout while he looked over the scene. It is beautiful—in the jury room, in the wild, at a dinner—to see that pause, the master in repose, that hiatus—a second and no more—during which something gathers though nothing moves, so lovely because unlike other fine moments—honor or mercy or courage under fire—it does not require badness on the world's part to call it forth.

There would have been servants at work, and no children down this long table fifty years earlier, when Anther was young and these doors were closed to him.

Just interested I think. Swordpoint eyes in that face of sunspots and dried riverbeds. Forehead like a cistern, new shirt, never laundered.

He talked in detail about the reasons trout hit a bucktail. We got onto the subject of play . . . does a fish ever strike for fun? The woodsman shifted in his chair. He said, in that organ-notes voice: "Sure. A fish'll play. But," he cautioned, setting fork and knife more properly on his cleaned plate, "play's practice. Play's always just practice of one kind 'r another."

This was wonderful and I said so and made mental note and later told Eden, and it would've gone into the film, which was already being discussed, as I've said, and before I got up to help with clearing for dessert I was enthusing over the idea of play as practice and complimenting Henry on it and trying to think of examples from all walks of life to cite when, nodding, he straightened his plate, at which he was looking as I yammered, with two fully extended thumbs, saying nothing.

I have never in my life been so loudly without a word told to shut up and I did.

He and my uncle had a friendship based on Eden's helping Henry with his writing about fishing and Henry's helping Eden with doing it—fishing—and based too on my uncle's veneration of him, but they didn't talk much.

Unlike the cast of characters at the bungalow where people came and went and got confused and returned and disappeared again like crisscross thought-asteroids in the mind of a schizo, "'The Anthers'", as the mailbox by the sidewalk by the patch of lawn you crossed to get to Henry's shop door informed you, was always orderly, plainly, uncomplicatedly gay. The TV murmured to itself unheeded in its corner, a fresh antimacassar on the brown, silk-tight back of Henry's chair, and there were tasseled lampshades, Mary, in sweats, always taking a plate, adjusting a burner, setting a kid down, packing a cooler, manning—less than comfortably—the shop cash register for five minutes, listening, weight on both feet, on the kitchen phone to a son-in-law who will repair a table for her—eye on the toaster oven as she listens, with a grunt flipping a mattress, sorting and sifting through slippery color photos of the family, telling a grandchild, without looking up from her work, to stop it, sliding the ones she selects into the clear plastic table frames she buys, shooing her husband back out to the shop after he and Eden have had their cup of tea at the Formica oval table among sink and stove and fridge and the darkstained wall cabinets her son-in-law made her, countertops crowded with flour and sugar and coffee and tea in glass jars, breadboxes, the toaster oven, a Bible calendar, knives—wooden-racked, sharp—beading plugged-in Crockpot, a small community of balled socks, photos of Henry and her and their brothers and sisters and their brothers' and sisters' families and their own three sons and one daughter and the eleven grandchildren, a heart-sized lump of anthracite, fruit in a wicker basket, paper napkins between miniature sections of post-and-rail fence, blender, bills, food coupons, cutting boards, a scarlet shiny ice bucket in the shape of an apple (the stem is the rounded top's handle), a bait-casting reel, which isn't supposed to be there, a tower of stacked birthday hats, which is, a Waldo book, a teddy bear, teddy's duck friend and the Galactic Space Sucker, with its rebarbative stare, that she'd gotten for their second son's two-year-old who wanted one.

Past the ancient cash register, engraved like a classic shotgun, my uncle would tiptoe—hippo quiet—if the shop were unattended when he dropped in. He carries presents—a soccer ball and a clear-plastic sac of Spitfires and Messerschmitts—sliding from under his arm that holds also the manuscript he's returning. He peeks around the door corner into a life filled with tidy messiness and quiet love. There are smells of sausage, coleslaw and sweet baking bread in the little living room. In the kitchen/dining area barely beyond, Henry is invariably eating his lunch at the Formica table, and Eden invariably says "Oh," and turns to go waving a hand "I'll come back when you've finished be back in half an hour don't get up don't get up" and Anther growly low "Nawww, come on in, had lunch?"

At the table, Anther, forkful by forkful finishing his broiled chicken and mashed potatoes and greens, this, for him and his, being the day's major meal, and Eden, tasting his Tetley with a tendriling pinky atremble, say little.

They are waiting to go to work. On the stream, though Eden will never be a tenth the angler Henry is, they are so familiar with each other's ways (and Anther's fishing wisdom) that a downstream splash or the way a cast goes wrong will elicit a mere grunt from one or both, in which nonverbal sound a full continuum of understanding, if not understood, is at least commonly felt.

In much the same way poring over a paragraph written by Henry, edited by Hope, and now being reviewed by Henry again at the shop's rear-corner tying table, or more rarely at one of my uncle's desks at the bungalow, reaching down without a word to line out in pencil a certain word and then grunt interrogatively is all one or the other need do by way of fusing colloquy into decision.

Apart from action together on the water or at the writing desk, however, there was a reserve, a formality. Particularly, I noticed, they never touched. You noticed it most when they met—they never shook hands. At Anther's house they might sit and visit a minute in the tilty living room.

Bubblingly needing to chatter and chat and weave his zeugmatic cleverness, Eden—bug-eyed holding his thought in—knowing it isn't really wanted here—quietly hands, under Mary's presidential eye, to the little redhead pedaling her fire engine, the soccer ball she doesn't want, and is prodded by her grandmother to thank him for. Then to her younger brother goes the sack of Spitfires and Messerschmitts that the redhead's eyes follow, and Eden and Henry get up and go out to the shop to take up their positions as naturally and wordlessly as they would get into position over on the Farmington or some other local stream, the old angler, elbow on tying table, squinting at the words—his—changed—made sleeker and better, Eden on the balls of his feet fiddling with his pen as his friend reads . .

"You ah, see? What I did?"

Anther throat.

"Now don't agree if you don't agree."

"Nawww—"

"Because—"

"Naw I do. I see it. It's okay."

"Good. Then in this paragraph . . is that all right? I mean in general is it. I've changed a lot here. I want to be sure you're comfortable. This is yours after all, I want—"

"It's fine."

"Be sure, because it's your writing not mine. One wants to be certain one isn't, ah—"

"Only," Henry Anther said, a bluing firmness in his tone, "if ya keep askin' is it all right it does bother me."

"Okay okay, yes. I understand. I simply—no. Understood. Ahhh, now here."

"Fine."

". . . . . then—"

Reading, Anther grunts, and is understood.

"Because the," my uncle says.

"Yeah," Anther says, reading on.

But when they were finished, or had come in off the stream, they were wary of each other in a way Nancy found touching.

"The dynamic," she told me one time over the phone, "between those two is fascinating. They're friends. Stop that. Excuse me a sec. *Stop* I said. Of course you aren't allowed to, you know very well you're not allowed to. Sorry. Anyway they're indubitably friends and Henry Anther has helped dad with dad's fishing enormously which, well, frankly my father's athletic prowess is no secret—" snigger "—I mean—" voice lowered "—it's really somewhat spectacular as you know. And," buoyant again, "of course dad's helped old Henry with his writing and gotten articles placed and then this book which I understand looks to be *quite* a success, but I'm telling you. I'm telling you. I may be wrong but I sense a deep, ominous undercurrent to the whole thing." Voice again lowered, conspiratorial, the only difference between Nance and Chase being that Nance's mischief was almost completely unegotistical, whereas Chase would never have been able to talk at length about two people neither of which was herself. "Deep . . what was I saying, put that down. *Now.* A dark undercurrent of competition and resentment, enemies at heart, I don't think everyone sees it, there's this tension there that I don't find healthy, not a bit healthy. The whole situation and relationship is set up based on opposites and a tension, as I've said—" hand cupped over the receiver and tone even lower in its alarm "—and all this going fishing and working on what the guy writes is essentially a papering over of—" terrific crash, many silver things falling onto hard surface followed by wails "—oh god I've gotta go, gotta get off, see ya."

When my uncle stood behind Henry looking over his pupil's shoulder as they read, he never put a hand on the big shoulder. Out on the stream now and again Anther might lightly take his charge's elbow in a firm thumb and three fingertips to position him. But that was all. When Eden arrived, or Anther came in, they would sometimes not even say hello but mill sort of—if two people can mill—seeming almost not to notice each other, until a concrete topic—a bite to eat, a car to pack with gear—afforded them a scaffolding for communication.

The distance and reserve between them had been there from their first meeting on the mystery pool in the humid rain that day, but over time it had hardened into rote—they were friends. They respected and helped each other and did what they did together—edit, fish—but that was all. They were, in their friendship, no longer exploring or finding new things to do together or learning new things about each other but only, like a pair of lead actors, performance after performance, being pupil and teacher then the other way 'round.

Henry's family led a plain life. The Anthers were religious, liked innocent jokes, and, when Eden visited, grouped around him like so many corpuscles, watching him, asking if he wanted coffee, or tea, or if he wanted to sit here instead of there, or for the TV to be turned down, waiting, politely and with a persistent friendliness of reserved curiosity, until him and Gramps would go off to their fishing or writing.

One day in the shop, that November, Henry showed him an antique rod. Six feet in length, it was Tonkin bamboo, wrapped every few inches with burgundy-colored thread.

"That's the most beautiful rod I have ever seen."

"Yeah it's a beauty. I picked it up the other week."

"How'd you get it?"

"Got it from somebody who can't fish anymore."

"Is it ah, will it be for sale?"

Anther thought about that.

Big ones, jawbreaker sized, struck the roof in loud metallic bangs—one . . a pause, then many at once . .

"Yeah it's for sale, but you don't want a rod like this yet."

"Sell it to me! Sell me on it I mean! Get me bidding, get me eager—get others in on it," Eden encouraged, "seriously—it's what you've got to—I mean if you're ever going to . . I mean—"

"Wal."

"—it's what one is in business for is it not?"

Another thought about something. "Wal," he said quietly, the word an empty gesture as he pondered, uncharacteristically, with harrowed brow, "you can have it if you want it."

"Oh I do, but I want to buy it for what it's worth."

Gingerly holding the assembled little flea-picker out Anther snapped it once in the air to show the action.

"I can let you have it for a hundred dollars."

"That rod? Look, that rod is worth what is it worth, you know better than I." My uncle, his hair a few electrified upright threads, his eyes mapped pinkish with his worsening blood pressure, the big chest rising and falling with emotion as he stood staring at the rod, gasped air. "A thousand dollars? More. Much more."

"Wal," Henry Anther said, still thinking about whatever it was he was thinking about, "I could let it go fer two-fifty. I didn't pay anything for it."

"That's not the point Henry, I want you to want what it's worth—I mean I . . you've helped me."

"You've helped me," Anther said. He turned the rod to look at a different part of it.

"Two thousand."

"Nah . ."

"Two thousand Henry."

Having subsided, it came again now with a strange unseasonable darkening of the little windows and an unnervingly loud series of bangs against the shingles over their heads.

Anther's chuckle was a nervous habit sometimes, used to protect himself.

"You think yer ready t' use a rod like this?"

"No," my uncle responded happily, "no I'm not, that's the point precisely—owning it will give me something to work toward."

Mary Anther, in the doorway, very frowning, went away without a sound.

"Let me give you a thousand."

The hail had ceased, for the moment at least, but now a cruel wind was moaning in the stripping.

"Wal . . I'll take three-hundred-'n-fifty for it."

"For god's—"

"That's all," Anther said uncomfortably. "Want it?"

"Let me pay you Henry, I mean pay you what it's worth for god's sake."

Anther looked at the rod. Holding it behind his back he carefully pulled it apart into its sections. Eden was looking at it.

It was not so alive as it had been when splitting the cane through the grain of the culm and stripping and planing the maker had begun his making, or as it would be when fished, but it had a certain motionless pulse, the rich butterscotch shine, its taper's slender grace, all the glinting metal guides—they looked at it in this, the middle of its career as a thing. Henry shook his head.

"I'll let it go fer three-fifty," he said. "No more."

"I don't want it," my uncle said distractedly, "if I can't have it—I mean ah—" turning away "—I won't if . . if I can't pay you what it's worth," he said in a small stubborn voice.

There was a tautness to the air beyond what the wind was causing. Henry Anther looked at his friend with a focused stare like the absolutely motionless stare of the camouflaged bow hunter in his or her cover.

Then turned, locating the floppy sleeve and long metal case. And he was putting the thing away.

The amber, watery eyes reached for it.

"Please?"

Anther shook his head.

My uncle adored Henry Anther, but perhaps too much as idea. And perhaps the old woodsman sensed this, or perhaps Henry felt beholden to Eden and didn't like to. Perhaps he felt the differences of their backgrounds in a moment such as this . . perhaps he was just grateful to Eden for helping him and wanted to give him a present. Or maybe it was what Henry said it was, so simple a thing as not being comfortable marking something up beyond a certain height. Anther may have felt a twinge of guilt too over the money—much needed—he was making now with the "perfesser"'s help, if, as I suspect, Anther, though he did like my uncle, did not like and admire Eden the way Eden did him.

More came, banging the roof, and the light was shadowy.

Anther making a slow project of putting the rod away, Eden sad, his belly slung old and low under the threadbare belt.

He had had Henry down to Manhattan for a round of meetings with the magazines and *Simple Fishing*'s publisher. Anther had had the equivalent of an anxiety attack, humming low identitiless tunes and deferring to his mentor, at the meetings at the polished desks in the clouds and at Dubble House at the thick white tablecloth laden with crystal and bone china, with a nod and beseeching glance.

One time, just before Henry appeared unannounced in the bungalow study door (on the occasion of the one negative review *Simple Fishing* got), Eden was but half a minute from having declared to me in a perfectly audible, carrying voice that "poor Henry ah, just doesn't have what it takes."

We'd been talking about false values and the heel-nipping that publishing, like anything else, can be, so in declaring expansively that his friend didn't have what it took my uncle was roundly complimenting him. What Anther didn't have was the mercenary gene. But looking up in surprise to see the old woodsman standing in the door my uncle, not knowing whether Anther had overheard or not, was bollixed into not being able to bring himself to ask, and so would never know, Anther, hurt by the review, standing slack-faced, waiting to be invited in, unsure this one time, rather than humble and wise. But the day of the hail when they disagreed over the rod, as Henry slowly put it away it was my uncle who was troubled and Anther who like a white-tailed deer, interested, unseen by you but seeing you through the leaves as you walk, remained calm.

That was part of what was between them too I think, that Anther was curious, looking out through the leaves, if I may, of his naturalness at *Homo sapiens* going by. Zoomorphism is as out of date as quill pens but Eden thought—and so did I—that Henry was, in ways out of the ordinary, like an animal of the wild. When she heard this Duffy Ginty averred that we both needed our marbles examined. We were confusing facts with reality, she said, and the whole thing was purely plutonic anyway . .

In the end my uncle purchased the rod for three hundred and fifty dollars, miserable to do it but afraid his friend would be offended if he didn't (which I don't believe was the case), and feeling more miserable still as Henry, over his mentor's spluttering protestation, insisted on making out a detailed receipt.

Then they went to work which felicitously, that day of changing weather, meant fishing, as there was an article to be worked up on fishing lip currents. Where a little dam of tan rocks, twig-and-leaf-clogged, made the water upstream of it flat then quickening, before funneling to pour through the center spillway and break apart splashing down a grade of stones into the next way the stream was, they played and fished, talking, and everything was all right.

His fly dragged slow on the swift currents at the upper pool's end. His line tightened and the drag became a pronounced wake like a cartoon schematic of a radar beam. But when he tried a whole lot of slack he had no control. And this was what they'd wanted—they'd agreed: Eden would fish it and Anther would teach him and that would be the fundament for the article draft—it worked well. In few words Henry showed him a better, closer position—how to hold his line up off the water, how to drape it over rock to get at least a couple seconds' right float. A little one was surprised enough to crash its nose against his bushy fly. He didn't hook it. But that was all right. Anther explained, then demonstrated. The pool above the dam-and-spillway looked smaller and narrower from down here looking back up, through forest, at the fast water V-ing through the chute where the stream, having quickened, rushed to toss and splash down over the riffles into the still of this, the lower pool. *Up* went Henry's rod and my uncle cried out in admiration. It was all right, here, fishing together with something other than each other to concentrate on—he didn't know what Sartre did with a whitetail's or a human's look, not at another animal or human, but at the living world. Beautiful little. Spotted sides, colorful in the sunlight. *Simple Fishing* hadn't covered water like this, no matter. Nothing covers everything . . the book was selling well—Anther's nervous chuckle was unnecessary out here. The only tautness was the tautness of line, and the day was the day, between them as they fished. The storm had passed. No problems solved but plenty forgotten for a few hours, and that is more than enough. Showing him a no-cast quick-float Anther holding his rod tip-down got several seconds of what he wanted, on a terribly difficult spurt of current, by holding rod handle high, tip low, and kind of lifting back and up with his lifted arm and hand as if drawing a sword from a scabbard. My uncle took notes. There were still a few leaves racing down on the dark brown water, and it was cold, but the autumn sun was high. Twenty-six shopping days 'til Christmas. That particular cast actually had been covered in *Simple Fishing,* though for conditions different from these, and in all but that one bitter review which Eden had easily explained away for his pupil, great praise had been given the book's casting detail . . this among other things helped sell foreign rights, didn't hurt in stirring up invitations for Anther to teach, and played a role in the idea—just then starting to come under discussion—that nearly turned the whole thing into a movie.

# 18

Called simply *The Fisherman,* it was to be a sentimental descent, through an angler's death by cancer and his grandson's crazed grief, into the kind of bathos that doesn't work in print but can be magic splashed across a silver screen with the right acting, score, script, lighting, direction and special effects.

Already that winter there were storyboard sketches, idea sessions, treatments, negotiations, shouting matches—lawyers' suckling tentacles grappling coast-to-coast—early revisions, changes of heart, location vettings, stretches of inactivity, penciled-in budgets, held-breath hiatuses of seconds, days, weeks waiting for the boss to rule.

A boy astride a good horse, was my uncle's thought. A plain youth astride a good horse trotting down a lane of oaks. He wanted it kept plain, no tricks, no angels. Problem was, the studio, in the mysterious person of its owner, thought otherwise. The studio saw angels, space aliens, a false grandfather trying to steal a real one's mineral rights, whiffs of incest (optional), a microcosm of cultural diversity in the village's makeup. This was all discussed with Zany Percy Foss—*Mister* Foss to you. To be precise, it was discussed with Foss's intermediaries. Discussion took place by fax, phone, ultimatum, innuendo, appeal, delay, tantrum, decree, the incidental quadrille of reason, and on one memorable occasion a flight to LAX for lunch. Foss could've financed the project out of pocket—from the income from his bond portfolio alone, but Zany, so nicknamed for having gotten his start in comedy, wanted the usual channels punctiliously to be gone through. Zany was alternately wildly enthusiastic about the project and skeptical, at times exhibiting a playfulness, not always benign, that manifested itself as an infuriating tendency to oscillate between engagement and weeks not just of indifference but silence: calls unreturned, messages ignored, even the intermediaries' secretaries unavailable, my poor uncle's diligent pages of scene description and underlying-concept visualization flying, as it were, into the mills of the mails and out over the fax line and down through the telephone wires into a devouring black hole of unresponse such as physics has lately provided the language with as metaphor.

At a perversely odd hour Eden's phone would ring and it would be Chase, morose at having to act like this. Messenger girl from the mighty, bearer of, to her former lover, the latest problematic tidings . .

"Hi." Funereally. "It's me."

Fuming storms of silence on the line while she tacitly dares him not to recognize who it is.

"He wants to know what's happening," she would finally plunge, "I know, don't tell me, don't say it. He hasn't called. He hasn't called you. He hasn't returned your calls. I know this. I'm aware of this. You're incensed, so okay. Maybe I would be too. But the fact is, we know very well—" stifled inhalation of incredulous despair attempted, fails to get off the ground "—he's like, well you know this as well as I do. He's the prime mover in this—" merry suddenly "—and he's the way he is." She made doorbell-music syllables of the word "is," descending minor third. "He's the way he is and you know it as well as I(♪) do(♪). He's the boss, so we play from there. That's the starting line. And whether you like it or not he wants to know what's happening, sooooooooooo . . . . . you'd better call." (tuneful syllables for "call" too)

Eden would call and get a vice president. There would be a flurry of confused conversation, Eden windmilling his arms, striding around the desk where I worked on his mail and bills to tell me—awedly—what was going to happen.

"Drop everything. Put all on hold. Heehee, do you believe I am flying to Los Angeles for lunch? For *lunch!* So therefore ah, I need a suitcase do I not. I do not. One isn't even staying the night!"

That Christmas, on their way to Venice Zany and Chase had a layover in NYC due to engine trouble. They drove up on a whim, Zany's whim, Chase took pains to emphasize ("You've got. To believe. I wanted *no* part of this. Do you believe that?" First desperately then interestedly, to see if I did: "Do you?").

I did not, but wasn't given the chance to say so.

"If you don't," she went on, standing close and leaning closer, "I'll slit my wrists." Moist undertone, exciting as greenhouse air. "I honestly, truly will. You're the last real friend I have."

I hadn't seen or spoken to her for a year, and before that had talked with her perhaps five times. But the point wasn't that I reply—she was to Eden's side now in a leap to tell *him,* whisperously, some crucial confidential morsel before we would go in.

The limo, out of which Zany Percy never got, was thirty-one feet long. I paced it. He stayed in it the whole two hours. While Chase was whispering to Eden, her escort and I stood looking at the smoke-dark windows of Zany's car. Suddenly the young man's beeper beeped and he whipped out his handset to listen. "Mr. Foss wants to know," he told me, listening to the device at the same time, "if you can ski on this stuff." I looked around at the snow. Chase breezily said "Let's skip the ski and go right to the après," without waiting for a reaction to which she headed down the steps, her ermine tails swinging.

We followed, but not before the young man had spoken, and listened, once more, very quietly, cradling his portable phone.

The bungalow entryway's wide lintel was garlanded with evergreenery and mistletoe and red berries and Lithuanian handpainted eggs as Duffy's concession to the "*zeitgeist* of the Christmas spirit," and we tarried there while the escort, an attractive person with his waistcoat, premature hair and toothy smile, told us he wished to convey to us that Mr. Foss deeply appreciated Dr. Hope's "gentlemanship in these matters. Mr. Foss has many girlfolk," I was confidentially informed in a nappy voice, "and obviously this—" indicating Chase with his eyes only "—is one of such, through which the connection took place. Now to understand, Mr. Foss don't want detail, Mr. Foss is feel. He wants a picture, a concept. He hires other people's feet to shoot."

Chase with a proud stallion toss of her worldclass hair had gone away during this. From around a distant corner her voice came soaring: "I adore. This house! I *adore* it!"

We found her stretched out on a loveseat, her heel-length fur flung open.

Pink nails dangling. Looking around with lidded, annoyed eyes at the period furniture.

(Pissed at not being able to live in such a place.)

"I am not," she declared huskily, "leaving this exact. Precise. Spot. Ever."

A tooled boot, spike-heeled, bounced in the air once to the second with each beat of her heart.

"Lordy," she sighed. "I could die right now, I truly could."

Her audience took seats.

Passingly something troubled her. She asked if this visit, on Christmas, were an inconvenience. My uncle pouted open-eyed and tilting his head shook it no, not really, no problem. Chase slyly smiled, because surely it was at least a little inconvenient if he had to so readily deny that it was. She liked to think of, and see us, being patient with her . .

"I'm so happy," she whispered.

It was impossible to look away from the way the light crossed her face—cheekline, rounded curve of wonderful lustrous hair—the miniature lips, voracious even in repose, and of course her figure, framed in the labial, lush folds of her thrown-open wrap. We were all looking at her. It didn't matter what she said. I glanced at Eden and thought I could see his mind, behind the moistly admiring eyes, grinding back to recall what she had been like.

He composed himself, interlacing his fingers in his lap, and asked if anyone would like anything.

The escort cleared his throat. He said he desired fruit juice of any variety. I shook my head.

"What," Chase inquired gravely of us, "do I want."

The hooked floral rug did not answer. The cut-glass ashtrays, bowls and exquisite stoppered decanters did not speak, nor did Eden, nor did I, nor did the escort . . the silence in the room honored her question as the calm honors the storm. Intrigued by the riddle—elusive, thrilling—of what she was and might want, Chase Parr lifted a set of nails without moving her arm. Without moving her face she shot her eyes down at her nails.

"I think," she said, "I want something light."

"And er—" with a circling dialing finger Eden indicated the escort's portable phone "—will he ah, have something?"

The escort communicated quietly with the limousine. Zany Percy evidently was fine.

"Or I don't know," Chase was saying as she slipped pins between her lips, feeling with both hands for the way she wanted her hair and, holding it that way, with one hand plucking the pins from her lips one by one to slide them in. "Maybe I should have a glass of vermouth or something. Lordy, I don't know." The last hairpin went in and she dropped her elbows and arms. She got up, shedding the scarlet-lined fur without looking at it, and went to her escort. Standing before him and leaning down she took hold of the lapels of his suit, looking into his eyes. "What do I want?"

Looking into hers he checked the limo fast, talking out of the side of his mouth.

"A glass of sherry," he told her.

"I do?"

"Oh sure."

"Really?"

Girlishly she was smiling then laughing at him, flapping his lapels together.

"Sure," he laughed after a fast 'nother check with the vehicular redoubt parked outside under the pines. "A semi-dry sherry is just the ticket. It will rev up the tastebuds."

She dropped his lapels and stood back, weight on a leg.

"I want my tastebuds revved," she told him.

The handset beeped again and after listening a bit, cupping his hand over his voice the young representative said: "Sir I don't think you want to say that."

At his core Zany Foss was so purely, perfectly venal—the Invisible Hand, in him, was so invisible—that now that he had made his billions, nested in them he had become like a black fossil egg and could present himself only by proxy.

Bored, Chase dipped a finger in her sherry and flicked some at her escort.

"Are you afraid of him?" she taunted, wetting her little finger again and letting her keeper have it.

"Yes," the escort answered without hesitation. "That's my position." A voice—Zany's!—could be heard now minutely in the room, so loudly was it shouting. The rep listened. "He says siddown," he neutrally relayed, "he wants to talk to Dr. Hope."

Chase did as bidden and took her negative attitude out on the glossy pages of a quarter-century-old fashion magazine in a collector's pile of same forgotten by Rairia in a previous year, during one of her upscale swings.

The real Zany had been taught by life that he was a person no one loved and everyone would take advantage of, so, with the help of his publicist and intermediaries, and his money, he projected the image of an immensely powerful lonely man, which he was, except lately he'd decided he wanted to be artistic. That was why he was so interested sometimes in the old angler movie, and especially in my uncle's vision of it. Eden saw the film as plain, and this had gotten Zany's attention. Part of Zany Foss wanted to do something sensitive. Another part knew exactly how to do the film so it would max out. And both parts wanted to worry, like a dog bone, Eden's instinct to make the film natural and thus less commercial. Zany wanted opposing things: to make a natural film and on the other hand to test and harry and see if he could corrupt my uncle—wear him down into doing a glitzy movie and liking it. He wanted to spoil, in a sense, what he could not be. Deep down Zany Percy wanted to give his billions away and live plainly—work as an extra or a key grip or something—bellhop, be the kid he'd started out as. Of course *deep* down he didn't want to do any such thing. But he did profoundly want to want to. And he actually did, a little, want to . . but the extent to which he wanted to was the extent to which he knew he never would. He'd been over it with his analyst and publicist and accountant, Chase told me, and they all said fine. The publicist in fact was delighted. The analyst was pretty happy about it too. It was a healthy thing to yearn to be rid of one's wealth so long as one never did anything about it.

Zany's life had become such an enjoyable habit—power and money and the exercise of these (not to mention the manipulation of other people)—that he could only use and manipulate more and more, as if thrashing in a mail net of gold, wheel and deal more and more, make another hundred million, and another, use the power he knew so well how to wield while talking (or rather instructing his intermediaries to talk) about values and aesthetics. Thus he thrashed. Such at least was the gist (accompanied by photos) of the package his publicist had insinuated into several top publications to much fanfare and controversy. An "exposé" of Zany Foss, it was far from flattering, which simply—this was a clever publicist—lent credence to the message (the man is rich but real) that the publicist wished to drive home and, to do so, was willing to chum—using criticism of his subject—for the usual sharks with.

Chase was hanging on for dear life. She was in sight of thirty and this was real money. Real $$ and/or power—same thing. She flipped the pages of the magazine loudly while Eden and Zany talked art through Zany's man.

"He says 'What's art?'"

"Ahhhhh, art's a mirror."

"Is art what the biggest number of people enjoy?"

"No," Eden corrected, enjoying himself, "the definition of art does not include a notion of good art or bad art but only the ah, heh—"

"We're opening presents," Nance said, her head in the room. "What're you guys *doing?*"

Engaging in dialogue. Eden in earnest, Zany Foss too, through his man, though in Zany's case it was the earnestness of a beanstalk giant's colossal hand picking up a church cautiously to shake it and see what might fall out.

Did it matter if Sartre in almost no wise lived according to his professed philosophy? Was art perhaps like philosophy in its unnatural potential?

"Come on," Nance laughed metallically. "Christmas comes but once a year guys."

The faces in the room turned and there was a second's hiatus. Standing in the doorway Nancy experienced a rush of objective shock in which she was looking at the faces in the parlor as they looked at her. These people, her father, his erstwhile mistress slapping magazine pages, some newcomer in a suit using a walkie-talkie gizmo—god knew why—came home to Nance in epiphany, making it clear, clearer than ever, clearer than she wanted it made clear, just what she was genetically part of. She was of a family that sat in a room like this with crazy people talking about Sartre when it was Christmas. It hit home. It was the way it was, the same people in the same roles carrying on the same conversations leading nowhere, and she was part of it, and it of her. She stood in the uneven door struggling, her hand, absently, on a kid's head, and the faces in the room were politely waiting for her to say something or do something or else to go away and she was struggling not to accept, not to acquiesce, not to let the room's reality drown her.

"She's furious," Chase muttered hopefully to her magazine.

"Yeah because," a tiny personage I'd never met added, "we're ope-nin presents. An you can sing too."

It was Alan's brother Michael, a thin child with hair the color of rosé and frightened copper-sulfate-blue eyes. He was with several others, various cousins and Alan himself.

Alan stood back, watching, listening.

He had grown tall, had defined shoulders, had become handsome, tall-browed face and those gentling strange eyes under the brim of the flower-banded straw hat he wore.

They all wore hats, grownup hats—a Kelly-green bonefishing one with the flaps down, a woolen beret with a pom-pom, a shako, a topper, a kipa, and Alan's.

Six kids, six hats.

Their bearing—solemn faces, lifted chins—testified to the mysterious dignity that had settled over them when they had put the hats on. Alan held himself back, ready to organize once he saw how the land lay.

But the shirttail of his burgundy rugby was out.

"Or you could dannnce," the diminutive redhead listed, "or sing, or open *pres*ents, or just . . just do . ."

"No come on," Alan decided. "They're workin', they'll come. Come on." To Nancy's hard smile and appreciative headshake over her little master, he formed up his younger cousins and herded them, in their hats—chins up, slower than usual under the terrific responsibility of the hats they wore—from the room.

Zany asked about Henry Anther, whose name Zany didn't know. My uncle folded his arms. He looked at his shoes. "You know," he said, "my friend Henry is interested in this, but ah, I must tell you. I must—" he struggled with his thoughts, sitting off-center on the sun-faded chair cushion and contemplating his feet "—you see, he trusts me. I want to be fair to him. I'm not at all sure he—"

There was an electronic squawk as Zany ordered his man to scan. Producing a miniaturized videocam the young escort showed his employer the room and, smoothly panning, each of us—lingering on Eden . . then unfortunately Toronto was screaming to be heard and Zany had to be on another line.

Silence during that time but for the swat, *swat* of Chase's pages as we waited. Then Zany was back on. "He strenuously wishes to meet the fishing gentleman," it was reported, "honest . . yes . . yessir I will. He wants to look him in the eye. He wants to sit down with him."

"I'm just not sure," my uncle said. His jaw muscles rippled. "That a meeting," he continued, "with Mr. Anther is ah, necessarily the right idea just at this particular, ah, I would think . . to be frank he may not want to. He has said that to me. I can ah, relay any questions. To him. Suggestions. Ideas," he concluded, standing his ground, or rather sitting it, with folded arms.

This response was relayed out to the limo.

Eden would tell me later that Henry had not said specifically that he didn't want to meet with the movie people. My uncle told me this avoiding my glance. He said Anther wanted to be protected, had not, in so many words, said so, but he—Eden—could read him. He said this to me in that same arms-folded way.

. . we waited. At last the reply came back that well, Mr. Foss could understand all that, but he still wanted meeting.

Eden fingered his moustache. "You know," he said, "I really think you see the heh, does—" glance at the handset "—does he know what Uncertainty is?"

One of the gorilla computers in Zany's state-of-the-art zoo made a search. "Yeah," Zany sent back, "sure, Uncertainty. The act of observing a particle's position has an effect on its momentum and vice versa, simple."

"He doesn't know that," Chase said to her magazine. Her voice was low enough to have no chance, even with the quality of the technology involved, of being picked up by the receiver-transmitter. "He looked it up." *Swat.*

"Well good," Eden said. His eyes came up brightly to the rep. "So you see to speak directly with my friend Henry would risk ah, changing him. By directly observing him you would ah, so to speak you would be changing him. The real Mr. Anther is only there, ironically enough, so long as you aren't."

"He never is anyway," she muttered bitterly. *Swat!*

Through the windows you could see the waves and plowed riprap of white. Darkness of winter evergreens and their still darker trunks, the cheery scarlets, pinks and fuchsias of the children's snowsuits as they staggered, arms out, after Lim in his Santa costume falling, shouting to each other in the sparkly day. Through the little room's doorway came house laughter and CDs of Handel and smells of burning cherry wood and baking gingerbread and chocolate all making the holiday afternoon safe, sleepy and comfortable.

I watched Lim lead the kids up a slope and with much pixieish bounding and silent—through the bright windowglass—shouting start arranging them on Duffy's toboggan. I saw Alan, red cap, green suit, fall on purpose.

Remember how falling in snow with your arms out and staying there, staring at the sky, and not getting up, was interesting? Not cold but peaceful in the packed snow all around you in your mittens and scarf lying under the winter sky?

We watched the little figures crowd in. Chins under scarves, brows under caps. In a row with their arms around each other from behind.

It was relayed, again, that Mr. Foss desired meeting.

Looking out the window at the kids my uncle repeated, in his radio-announcer's basso (burbly lately with troubles he was having with his throat), that that was really probably not such a good idea.

Could Mr. Foss speak to the fishing gentleman over the phone?

No, Eden answered after reflection.

Zany started, through his man, to say more, but Eden was on a thought train and plunged ahead.

"You want the angels in the woods to be real. You want the old man on the portico, the real grandfather, to be evil—a criminal. But my friend doesn't want this. Mr. Anther does not want this approach to be taken."

Had Eden asked him? Asked directly?

The query was relayed.

My uncle nodded darkly, then, pressed by the escort, spoke: "Yes!"

Zany Percy Foss did not see why he could not speak to Mr. Henry Anther at least by telephone. Very well, my uncle said folding his arms, you can easily get the number, go ahead, call.

In the dim air of the parlor the threat hung with a direness as sharp as it was sudden while the brightness of the winter day outside remained all glorious in the windows.

Chase swatted a page over and another, impatiently, then swatted several back, to check something—swat swat *swat,* but still no one paid her any attention.

They were on, six stitched hats, five pairs of padded arms around the cousin in front, in the shade of the forest through which puffs of snow drifted down, straight, there being no wind.

Santa stood with ski-gloved hands on hips, surveying the arrangement of kids on the toboggan. Six round faces under hats immobile—waiting—sitting in a row, keeping still, looking forward, looking downhill, in the direction in which they were going to go.

Zany pushed a pawn. Did Eden think, it was asked by the rep, that it would endanger the project if the studio should undertake to contact Mr. Anther directly by telephone?

Eden said it was possible.

If Foss really wants the deal he wants to communicate directly with this Anther and not some overweight rocket scientist who imagines he's a writer. If Foss wants to do the project he needs this Eden only insofar as Eden can put him together with, or keep him away from, Anther. If the fat professor's telling the truth, then approaching Anther directly could spoil everything, so Foss is wary on this angle, his representative told me later that same day, but he's also playin' with the guy (Eden), to show who's boss.

Lim looked to be swearing a blue streak under his swaying hat-tassel as he strained to push the coaster from behind.

Eden was mentioning further ideas he had had and written down. If Mr. Foss might care to see them . . the silence this time while the message was digested sounded—though it's impossible—like a cosmic sigh. The rep waited, listened, and without enthusiasm said yes, send the ideas along. But might Mr. Anther at least be willing to consult on the project?

Eden said he thought so.

Because, it was relayed, if not, there might not be a film.

Eden said he would pass this along to Mr. Henry Anther and no one, it seemed, knew who had the advantage.

"He says remember," the young man intoned, "that when a movie makes a ton of money that also means the most people see it."

"Aquinas," my uncle said, staring at the stuck, unsliding tobogganers, "lived a plain life. And *he* got a lot of ink—I wonder if we should help."

He was standing and had moved toward the window and I was out of my chair and ready to get some air and help push if necessary, but no, for into view come Nora and a turtlenecked Nance. They must've been watching from a window too. They were hurrying and wore no coats. Their knees lifted as they tromped through the deep white. Lim was standing straight, having given up. Lobster-faced, breathing mist clouds, talking vexedly to them as they approached.

The faces of the kids faced forward, waiting. Nance and Nora stepped this way and that around them, making sure they were secured. Half-prancing half-hopping through the snow Nancy went on down the course the toboggan would take to look over the drop-off the far side of which we indoors could not see. She turned and gave an upright-single-finger-twirl of affirmation to her sister who, bending straight-legged at the waist, was making a snowball.

In the way she side-armed that snowball Nora Hope appeared happy.

Lim kept getting down into position to push and then because the girls weren't ready would have to stand straight again, putting his hands on his red hips to look around and wait.

Rearing gracefully, kicking a heel high, Nora threw a forty-foot strike against the black trunk she'd picked.

"Sit straight and hold on," you could see the women telling the riders.

Six faces under hats, five snowsuited sets of arms around each other from behind.

Alan in front, his arms around no one. Chin up. Looking out from under his hat, where the children on the toboggan waited out of the winter-pure sunshine in the shadow the pine forest cast on the snow.

"That's where I lie in the sun," Chase was pointing out to her escort, leaning into him to show him a resort ad she was fantasizing herself into. "All day long in the sun. Right after our morning swim."

Their heads touched.

"And where am I?"

"You're in under that awning finishing your second breakfast."

"I have two?"

She giggled.

"Don't you want two?"

"Well sure, why not three?"

"I could float," Chase went on, beholding the full-color page of diamond-glittery water, sails at a distance, white balconies of striped awnings and cottony clouds strewn sideways across the sky, "in that pool absolutely all, day."

With the flat of a palm her escort, who had had to attend again aurally to his boss, telescoped his set's aerial in and set the set on the decoupaged table by the divan Chase had taken three-quarters of. He took a deep breath.

"This," he said to my uncle, "is beautiful country. The long mountains in their wintry apparel, the meadows, those gray rocks protruding out of the slopes of the foothills. The fences. The creeks winding back and forth under the road under their quaint old-fashioned bridges."

"Where'd he get that I wonder," Chase said idly, flipping more pages and looking at them.

"Don't know," her escort whispered, "said he wanted to compliment."

"*Protosearch* or one of those," she speculated. She said this with waning interest in herself, continuing to browse, dabbling a finger in her glass and lifting tastelets of sherry to her tongue's tines.

My uncle blew out, amused, and looked out the window.

Its rope over a side, the toboggan sat empty on the snow.

"*Oh my God!*" Chase cried out.

We stared at her. Flinging her head back she gazed at the ceiling.

"I am," she declared, "utterly happy. I cannot. Believe. How utterly free I feel." Still gazing at the ceiling she located her escort's hand and held it.

The door burst open. The room had no door. It was rather as if a door, or some gigantically combustive thing, had exploded. Shockwave of fisting air whumping in before Rairia's coming.

I had not seen her since she had become *Gall.* Her hair was but an inch long all over her head. She looked fabulous, not beautiful but powerful and pure, trite words but she was. Her eyes shone with honest curiosity, and though she would always be big her body was no longer heaviness and down-seeking weight of defeat but rather, as she stood glowing and shining at our center, a lightness of air and light. *Gall,* a Sioux warrior at the Rosebud, was her ur-name, taken after two weeks in a canyon. Approaching Eden who had half risen she said "Don't worry it's all right. I have to do this."

"Do what?"

"You'll see."

"Er, yes," he said, pawing behind him for the arms of his chair.

"I can make sexist jokes," she laughed.

He stared at her, his mouth working like a stranded fish's. She really did look very good.

"The difference between you and me," she told him, "is you believe the world can become a peaceful place where people get along and there are places where people of differing religions and races commune gracefully and everyone is fed enough. You believe," she told him, with not a trace of selfconsciousness, "that this noble goal can be worked toward and realized by humans acting rationally. I believe God is," she announced. "He or She is a good but an awful God who made this world as a testing place of endemic misery as well as joy. My God made this world as a preparation place for the human soul. She does not want it to become Heaven, nor will She allow it to become Heaven." She was into a pretty good preacherly rhythm. My uncle, suspended above his chair, half-standing-half-sitting as if, as he listened staringly to her, he were waiting for a command, was transfixed. "Our lot," his wife said, "is to seek and accept not joy and certainly not happiness though either can come as a side effect, but to seek God and to make social war on His or Her behalf, accepting this world's darkness as well as its light, yearning, striving toward Heaven as Heaven exists in the life to come."

My uncle's mouth hadn't stopped working. She smiled at him now, not unkindly. Christmas laughter was tossed in the air somewhere else in the house.

Up from their magazine the feline, rapacious eyes took a look.

But Chase was ignored.

"Who're you?" Rairia asked the escort.

In getting to his feet he seemed to forget his handphone which, in reaching to shake Rairia's hand, he in effect handed to her.

She took it and shook his hand and gave it back. She leaned forward, trying to find something in his eyes.

"Who," she repeated.

"I represent Mr. Foss."

"In the matter of the film."

"Correct."

"Right," she said. "I've heard about that," turning back to Eden. "Eden now listen, you can do it too, you can do it too, but I have to do it first. Ah . . kah—*yuh,*" she uttered throatily, smoothly spinning, "akim-bo*KUH!*" I got my leg out of the way. "I ran with the runners of rivers," she said, "I ran with them two weeks. They asked me to stay. I'm proud of that. You pay for the two but after that they asked me to stay, even consider teaching—I'm very proud of that."

She was not pillowy anymore. There was a distinct curve of muscle on either bare upper arm, and the suede against her haunches curved too.

"For decades," she told him, "—I have to do this Eden. For twenty years—longer than that—I was repressed. Notice I don't say *op*pressed, *re*pressed. I complained. I was negative. I was a bitch. I picked fights and ran away, I picked fights with salespersons and friends. What happens happens and what happened happened and evermore shall have, so no guilt. I was a mess."

"Oh," he said quickly, "you ah, not really—that is you weren't as . . not nearly so—"

"No no," she contradicted brightly, "I was. But I was tired all the time. I was tired Eden. I was tired of taking the garbage out. I was tired of loading the dishwasher. I was tired of unloading the dishwasher and loading it again. I was tired of loading the children and unloading them while you were off somewhere ahhhhhh . . kahhhh-YUH!!"

"*Ow.*"

"Sorry," she said, balancing back. Her toe had poked his chest more powerfully perhaps than she'd intended. "But I have to do this. No don't worry. Listen . ."

The Foss representative had his handset on transmit and was holding it out toward Rairia so it received, and transmitted, what she was saying.

My uncle was standing his ground and there was a gleam in his eye. This was no joke—she was fascinating to him, as the anvil forming above your rowboat fascinates. He said teasingly: "Was this existential Rairia? Was this an existential act?"

"Debate it," she scorned, "debate the meaning Eden, debate the subtext. I'm beyond it. I've done it. Blood," she said, "fire, ice, guts. I'm beyond the other. I don't know if it's existential or ethical or aesthetical and I don't care. I'm new! Kuhhhhh—" he stepped back "*—yuh!*" Fast as he'd been she almost got him. "I'm bellicose!"

"Well you certainly are. I er, I certainly must," he fumbled, "admit you—"

"You can do it too Eden, you can declare. It's good for you."

His eyebrows were dancing as he tried to make fun: "I can? Really? You mean I really—"

Irony and sarcasm were among the things Rairia had gone beyond.

"Yes," she encouraged, "it's valid. It's good for you Eden. I *was* a mess. Say what you have to say."

"Ahhh, all right I—heehee I—"

"Go on!"

The red of her suspenders was the red of honest arterial blood. Her face was open and her hands, open, implored him.

"Well—hee . . actually you know at times you were rather a pain, rather a heh, pain. A lot of the time in fact. Actually most of—"

Dropping a shoulder she squared. The roundhouse right came as if it had never not been coming. She positively decked him.

"You understand I had to do that."

"Uh," he said blurrily. His mind was thinking double. "A-h," he said, feeling of his jaw, "yes the . . . certain . ."

"Good Eden. Don't worry. It's valid. There must be more, there has to be, go on!"

His mind came back somewhat into focus. As best he could, he eyed her.

"You were a wonderful cook."

"*No I wasn't,*" she guffawed collaring him and shaking him. "Don't be a coward!"

"Er, could I, that is could, ah . . later perhaps?"

"Sure," she snickered in a voice remarkably like her older daughter's. "You can do anything you want. And who—" turning to Chase for the first time "—might this be? Wait I know, I know who this is, *sssssssssss*—" making lion-rampant claws, nails out "*—SSST!*"

Chase looked up from her magazine starting to be furious, but her anger ran into the extremely recent memory of Rairia's landed haymaker and she said nothing, retreating to her fashion pages *swat* . . . . swat . .

Rairia turned to the escort.

"Where is he?"

"Excuse, you mean Mr.—"

"Mr. Foss yes. Where is he?"

It was explained that Mr. Foss was in his car. There were important calls Mr. Foss had to make and take. Rairia frowned sardonically, and before she stormed from the room she went around to shake everyone's hand, Eden's and Chase's as well as the escort's.

Eden needed something for his face. Chase looked very alone. Her escort, having been disconnected from his boss, sat blankfaced, as if his plug had been pulled.

My uncle went over to Chase and considerately tried to make her feel better by looking, with a slight bend at his ample waist, at her magazine.

"Would you like," he attempted, pointing to an ad, "to live in that one?"

The killer eyes glanced a glancing glance down at the four-color magazine-page mansion, then looked away—but at least she was listening.

"No really Chase, see? Look, that lovely woman, there—hee. She's you. You're lovelier of course, far lovelier . ."

Both looked at the ad. Secluded estate. Croquet in progress. The woman Eden was pointing out: a Manhattan model.

Chase—looking—said: "What." Flatly.

"Hm?" My uncle was still pointing with a forgotten finger to the refined demoiselle—skirts up a touch, dainty toe on one ball of two, mallet cocked.

"What," Chase stated, "makes you think I'm her."

The question hung on the air. Straightening imperceptibly out of his waist-bend, lowering his point, so to speak, and palming his smile to slip it in a side pocket fast, he said "heh, why—"

"Yes?"

"Why er, for fun. For fun of course. The ah." He was blushing, except for where Rairia's knuckles had caught his left cheek. "The ah," he said. "Of course naturally—"

"I said," Chase said, "what makes you say I'm her."

"Because—" his voice was going away, telescope-small "—of . ."

"Because of," Chase said.

"Yes a*hem*. Excuse me. Well obviously the—"

"Because of what. Say it."

"Why," he said. "Racial identity. But of course—"

"Shit," Chase purred in iron syllables.

Fast as a grouse she exploded from the room.

Was back seconds later with the day's *Times.*

She thrust it under his nose.

"Here. Read. *Read.* That's racial identity. And here, *here's* racial identity." She scanned the long columns. "And here. Look at it, read it . . . okay gimme." Newsprint pages clattering and snapping. ". . annnd, ok let's see here, racial identity, don't talk to me about racial identity. What do you think caused this? What do you think caused *this?* Or this, look, what do you think's causing that?"

Eden tried to make Chase see her mistake. These things weren't racial. Fundamentally they were political. Political, economic, social.

Her look shut him up. He didn't have the heart to refute her. For myself I had never seen Chase Parr so real. Her gestures and wiles had failed her. She was neither turning the charm on nor feeling sorry for herself nor acting nor calculating. She stood—in the pain of our gaze—with imperfect hair.

She dropped the newspaper, and its articles on war. "Forget it." She sat down, flicking a leg at the diagonal under her. Grabbed her magazine.

She was wrong—we knew that. Wrong about racial identity. But her view was her view. Can't a person be wrong?

"Folks!" my uncle boomed, "up! It's a holiday for pete's sake," and out the door he herded us. Down a hall into the long living room where kids were blowing this way and that and Duffy's and Nance's decorations shone in the confused pleasantness of one yuletide more. He passingly participated, opening a present here and admiring one there, and, hardest of all, tried to sit peaceably participatory in his chair smilingly observing and doing nothing untoward amid the seasonal activity, but my uncle had ants in his pants. Holding an ice cube to his cheek, he spirited me away to his study. He was tired. He flopped behind a desk.

"I should call him," he said. So he did. Yet again I found myself in the position of observer. He wanted me to sit here and listen to his conversation with his friend Henry Anther so as, by my presence, to give it value, to make him—Eden—maybe a little better (better than what? Than he thought?). He wanted me to make what he did better by listening to him and approving of him—believing in him. "Henry," he said wearily. "A minute? . . may I?"

He spoke to the old angler solicitously, as if to a family member one must be careful with. He talked with his head down, holding the receiver with both hands, listening, advising, explaining, listening again, starting to speak then catching himself, because Henry hadn't finished, listening again, and I sat still, listening and, I suppose, giving my approval by dint of not doing anything.

"Ahh yes, well, yes." Listening. "Yes but you see if, yes. But if you want me to protect you from . . ." The word "integrity" appeared in my uncle's strange flow of talk . . . was Anther at his tying desk this holiday hour? Maybe in his too-warm living room amid the decorations, gifts and guests of the season, with Mary in her chair and on the sofa and tables the inevitable fishing magazines, outdoor publications, periodicals on hunting and photography, their pages curling, and on the walls Henry's framed photos of old hunts. "So you ah, you ah—agree?" My uncle listened. He listened longer than I would've thought necessary if simple agreement were all Henry was expressing. Quieter and quieter in tone, pausing, waiting, Eden concentrated. He was trying to establish that he'd been correct in putting Zany Percy Foss off, in keeping a distance between the studio people and his friend, in keeping himself, thus, in the role of conduit and spokesperson. Anther was apparently agreeing, though as I say, when my uncle stood barely patiently listening, scratching, with the nail of an extended smallest finger, an eyebrow forest, it did seem to me that if Anther were in complete agreement he was certainly taking a lot of words to say so.

# 19

From the way he slumped I could see how tired he was. He had taken as gospel the grim premise that the universe can be understood. Now he found himself halted before a wall of doubt. What are the particles going to do? At a zillion degrees it'll be weird, but does that tell us anything more than that if you torture nature she'll distort? A football team of players plays as a team. Run them into each other at three hundred miles per hour and of course they'll look different. You'll conclude the game's made of bloody body limbs and rolling empty helmets.

I felt for him. He had aged. The spots on the hands, when he wiggled his fingers to evoke alternatives, brownish, yellowish stains of time, reminded me of some venerable armored beast as he went on reading in the various systems we've developed since stepping out of the sea.

I like his idea that the basic particle need not necessarily be the simplest. A family of particles working in concert might be the basic unit, and supercollisions at superheat as seductive a gardenpathway to infinite regress as pure thinking is the paved road to doubt.

He kept at it, no longer expecting to be satisfied. Just addicted,

addicted to thought. Could physics have cornered itself in its own imagination?

Under a chain of mountains on the other side of the planet a cache of fifty tons of a certain metal in liquid form was being scrutinized—scientists were looking for evidence of a particular particle, the one he'd described to me that first morning, crouching to sight with his dime. The metal-in-liquid-form they'd amassed has the rare ability to register a neutrino's presence. When the infinitesimally tiny neutrino, which can't be seen by our instruments, and legions of which on their way out from the sun pass invisibly through the earth every second, hits the special metal in its liquid form a certain way, an observable trace is left, zing—heehee . . for some time now the scientists had been counting up traces of neutrino hits in their test sea of metal deep in the Caucasian earth. If they were right in their predictions, a minimum number of neutrino-collision traces would register, but, shockingly, the count had come back at less than a third the predicted volume. When the mechanics and validity of the experiment had been crosschecked and triple-tested, an inescapable conclusion loomed.

Due to pride of intellect however, not to mention the need not to jeopardize funding, that conclusion—that the scientists didn't know what the hell was going on—was adroitly sidestepped. Obviously (they declared) the Standard Model under the aegis of which all this experimentation was taking place, and under whose aegis, likewise, the physicists were, er, paid, couldn't be wrong.

The model must just need modifying. Theory would have to be adjusted, the offending table leg, once identified, sawed a bit shorter (or have a matchbook wedged under it).

A suggestion was put forth, bolstered by a set of calculations made in the knowledge of what they were intended to show, to the effect that the neutrino maybe is different, acts, maybe, differently from how we'd thought.

He held his head. He was so weary.

He no longer believed in it. It was his work and his profession, but he no longer believed. He didn't want not to. He simply couldn't. He held his head. He doubted all of it now.

When Theodore Gordon mounted the wings ahead of the hackle on the flies he tied, slanted the wings back instead of tying them vertical, and narrowed the amount of shank area wound with hackle, these advances in technique presaged an era of diversification beyond Gordon's imagining, i.e. now.

With centuries of gradual progress behind it, fly fishing explodes. New rod material and design, patterns, casting theories, behavior models for trout and types of clothing and gear fill the sport as full of innovation now, each season, as it used to be filled with innovation from one generation to the next. With progress accelerating at an accelerating rate, why not fish the same tackle your dad or mom did?

Turning a rounded shoulder, lumbering away like God in my uncle's sweaty dream the following year getting off His throne, broad shouldered, head down, forever, the old angler with mildly amused disgust would go somewhere else when my uncle got to talking about such things. Anther would listen, trying to be interested, and wanting to learn if he could, and after taking as much as he could, wiping his dome with rough fingers he would go back to his tying desk or wade to a different part of the stream.

Chase Parr wet a fly once.

Provided by Eden with a rigged rod and a few sentences of instruction, she gathered some loops in a manicured hand and, testing the camber, falsecast thrice surprising hell out of him. She got thirty feet of line off the reel and with a shoulder throw laid that thirty feet across-current perfectly. There was even a little *klop* as she fished, and after a few presentations more, though she hadn't caught anything, she let rod and bellying line hang and turned. That hair over an eye, grinning, as beautiful as the mountain laurel flowering along the flatsliding stream . .

Armenians killing Turks, Serbs killing Bosnians, Arabs killing Jews, Jews killing Arabs, Tutsis killing Hutus, Hutus killing Tutsis and the way the Ivory Coast rival tribes slit throats, mashed each other's legs and yanked brains and intestines out of still-warm bodies, or, like other overexcited casuists around the globe, after knocking a pregnant woman down kicked her—in her stomach—these and other realities such as for instance what Muslim does to Hindu and vice versa in India, or in the Sudan Muslim versus Christian/Animist or what is being done to the Kurds, and by them, or what radical whites do, or radical blacks, Sunni Muslims, Shiite Muslims, Mbochi, Pool Lari and Vili to name some—granted all this had helped Chase, brandishing the day's paper, to make a strong case for the human propensity for racial violence—but my uncle had smiled, behind a hand, to murmur that half what Chase was citing was religious, not racial . . or else it was political, he gibed under his breath. But he forbore to rebut her. To use his superior intellect to spoil her little outburst, seeing how distraught she was, he knew would be ungenerous. Sickening savagery was to my uncle as much appearance as reality. For him, fundamental reality is human goodness. Of course when one doesn't have enough to eat or is the victim of repression or inadequate care, there is always the danger of violence. But it's a danger that can be removed, once its material causes have been removed, and so to Eden it was a superficial danger, in some profound sense. Appearance, reality—is there a difference? Is the distinction between appearance and reality a false one, or does it only appear so?

Thomas Ledger looked at his watch. Sitting opposite his dad's desk while Eden went on about reality and appearance, the beefy man with his glinting spectacles and lineman's arms tried, in checking the time, not to be obvious about it. He had dropped in—could have stayed days but had laboriously arranged his trip so only a few hours with his father would be possible, and they had almost embraced. Thomas was doing well. Knives were doing well. Eden nearly asked about Gwen but his words caught in his throat and he veered off onto reality and appearance. Popping up he ransacked a shelf. It was here somewhere, a beautifully illustrative little anecdote: where? Where was it? He felt his son's eyes on him. It had been here on this shelf, the page marked. He searched other shelves. While he was looking he told Thomas about Theodore Gordon. You could see, if you studied your fly-fishing history, false skins of legend annealing around that famous turn-of-the-century tyer who, our best scholar of such things shows us, didn't father half the innovations attributed to him. Gordon is no more seminal than Aristotle or Plato in whom we have come to find everything.

He was trying to express this as he looked for the fishing book he wanted to share with his son. His mind was going too fast. He was excited. There was so much he wanted to tell Thomas. He was embarrassed and annoyed at not being able to find the book, which had been right here. He was going too fast, sit down. So he did. He sat down. A tribesman fitting on his lion mask thinks he is a lion or, at least, has the lion's spirit in him. Is this different from the glazed looks on the faces of Europe's anti-nuke demonstrators in their robes with their faces made up as skulls and pallid ghouls, swaying, dead-eyed, grateful for this chance and excuse to dress as what they dream of? Or different from the state of mind of the physicist pretending energy and matter are orderly according to patterns—laws—that explain why his pen, when he bumps it as he looks through his papers as he talks, rolls off one stack of papers onto another where it hesitates, then rolls off the desk to the floor?

He stared at it. Thomas stared at it. He wanted to tell Thomas why he loved fishing. He had written it down and wanted to work it into the film: fishing with a fly was mental activity vindicated by action: wet real-time action in the muddy wet world. Philosophy, on the other hand (at least since philosophy had separated itself from society and the church), was mental activity followed by more mental activity. Science too. He saw Thomas's eye go to his wristwatch. But he couldn't stop. There was a test, he said, looking desperately through the desk clutter. A test for genuineness. Fly fishing passed it, philosophy and science did not. It was the test of being laughable. Fly anglers could be laughable; they could even enjoy being laughable. Not so with the others, oh where *was* it?! It was a hand-sized volume and it had been right here yesterday. His pen lay on the floor where it had fallen. He got out of his chair to pick it up and saw the book, his paper-scrap marker sticking out like a tongue. On the south windowsill of all places. With a yolky smile of appreciation, sitting in his swivel chair with a moccasin heel against the desk edge and a hand on the back of his head in a gesture unconsciously like Anther, he held the little text in a trivet of thumb and first two fingers.

He read his son the description of the super-dedicated eighteenth-century angler, Dr. Birch, who

> . . . in order to deceive the fish . . . . had a dress constructed, which, when he put it on, made him appear like an old tree. His arms he conceived would appear like branches, and the line like a long spray. In this sylvan attire he used to take root by the side of a favorite stream, and imagined that his motions might seem to the fish to be the effect of the wind. He pursued this amusement for some years in the same habit, till he was ridiculed out of it by his friends.

Thomas laughed out loud. His father sighed with relief. "Think," he suggested, holding both hands up with the book in one like a magician about to cause it to vanish, "of somebody laughing at that a hundred years ago, laughing just as, ah we are. Someone . . . gone."

They looked at each other.

Low in the sky the night clouds were tumbling within themselves as they moved. They were blowing levelly east. It was a wild sight. When you looked at the clouds you did not notice they were moving except, tumblingly, within themselves. Then looking at the whole sky you realize the whole night sky of in-themselves-tumbling clouds is sliding eastward.

A border

cold shining icy brightness, is the moon

the uncombed clouds as they slide east cover the moon whose fierce, heatless silver illumines the ghostly cloud banks from within

and again the naked moon . . .

Eden now covered St. Thomas's proofs of the existence of God, explaining how they were a countermarch against the Averroist heresy at that time (1270) pushing the One-Soul-Shared-by-All line which arguably rendered the notion of personal salvation meaningless (since if there's just One Soul how can there ah, be a Heaven for any but all?). Deprived of the notion of personal salvation and therefore personal divine punishment, society would have—hee—society you see would have had a hell of a time getting the Industrial Revolution going. He went on from there, as the full moon yet again is resplendently unveiled by the hoary, unscrolling shapes, to suggest that maybe the best proof of God would be an adaptation of Gödel's theorem that any rational system ultimately depends on an assumption outside its own vocabulary and procedure. Thomas, slow-rotating a stout wrist to get his chronometer dial facing up, re-rechecked the time.

Unable to stop himself Eden went on to the role of the machine gun in warfare and string theory and several correspondences he felt he had uncovered between quantum leaps and musical modulation.

Thomas now had his timepiece unstrapped from his wrist and was flicking it with a fingernail, shaking it, staring at the face pointblank to fiddle with a control.

. . . he came to himself, holding this pen that had rolled to the floor, and that he had picked up . . when? He was aware Thomas was watching him. While talking he must have picked the pen up. But how long had he been standing here with it?

He couldn't tell and was too chagrined to ask.

It was now of course, which it never isn't.

"Dad?"

"Hm?"

"I've got to go."

It was late.

If they built the super-supercollider . . there was something wrong. There was something wrong with the assumption. If they built it they knew—*knew*—they would find either the Higgs boson or new forces . . something wrong with that . . he couldn't grab what it was . . .

"Dad?"

"Hm?"

"The work's going okay?"

. . either they would prove the existence of the Higgs boson, or else . .

"Or the roof?" Thomas tried desperately.

"The roof?"

"Yes didn't you have to fix it?"

"Why yes. That was years ago."

"Yes it was," Thomas said quickly. "So. It got fixed?"

"Oh yes."

"I see Rairia on television."

"Yes."

Thomas stood with loose arms as if about to get down to get ready to block somebody, the thick corrective lenses of his spectacles shining.

"She's doing well," he said, "I guess. Yes?"

"Ah, oh yes. Very. She seems finally—" my uncle daydreamed of her "—attractive," he said. "She's changed. She's . . . I surprise myself." He thought some more about her. "Strong," he said. "You know she actually—"

"But you and I." Thomas was sweating. He spoke too fast. "We don't know each other."

"Hm?"

"Dad."

"Hm."

"You know they've got programs, places, people who can help with that."

"Ah, yes."

"Maybe we—"

"Remember," Eden said, "that fishing trip?"

"Sure, it was only six months ago for goodness—"

"Yes well, I was thinking of it."

"Well good," Thomas Ledger said. "Now some of these places are fakes. But others—"

"Not for us."

"No," Thomas said. "But we had that fishing."

"You don't know how much I enjoyed that."

"Well tell me."

"Oh enormously."

"Why don't we do it again?"

"By all means."

"Next summer?"

"Next summer ahh, we'll have to plan."

"There's time."

"Oh plenty."

"Plenty of time," Thomas Hope Ledger said, thinking of something. "Fall would be better."

"Splendid."

He was a good boy.

But the subtleties of life escaped him. They'd found him petting a snake when he was a baby, sitting in just his diapers on the cement spillway of Agnes Sellerworth's pool, meditatively stroking the back of the black snake sunning itself, to warm its blood, on the grainy concrete dip of the spillway. Thomas was petting the reptile with apparent interest, the snake quiet with the sun's heat above it and under it in the cement, not minding, or perhaps liking, or perhaps unaware of, the fiftycentpiece-sized hand stroking its muddy-dark chip-like scales.

Thomas's parents couldn't tell whether it was poisonous or not, not that it mattered: snakes bite, and the young scientist, waving his wife behind him irritably with a down-patting motion in the air behind his back, drew near—in a soundless walk down the flaking whitewash poolside—his son—closer, relaxing himself, noting the snake's loose position . . . in a move smooth and efficient for Eden he whisked the baby away from the five-foot-long serpent that started to coil but, sensing room, thought better of it and shooting in Ss through itself fled over the grass down the steep poolside embankment into shadows, where there were rocks. They hugged Thomas and marveled at him now that he was safe, but did they tell him in scare-voices never, ever to touch a snake again or did they let go of it—let it ride?

He wishes he couldn't remember, but he can. It was the first. They—

Eden more than Gwen, Eden leading, Gwen eddying in his wake—scared the baby in no uncertain terms that Snake is always and forever No.

"There's plenty of time," Thomas said.

"Yes ah, of course, to plan. The ah—"

"And the fall'd be okay?"

"Yes indeed."

"I've got to get on the road."

That afternoon when Thomas had called up to say he was coming, as always calling late, hurried—emphasizing it was just for one night, Eden had wandered to a drawer. One not opened in years.

He took out what was in it and sat down. He began looking. Spent an hour . . . there were hundreds, taken over decades, the oldest color ones faded, unreal in their process hues but still mesmerizing to view: Thomas at 3. In the lake with his mom, held up by Gwen, a dripping catch of love . . . Lim in a breaking wave—Antigua or somewhere one time when the two families had gone down. You could tell it was Lim from the porkpie hat, though the surf had dumped him, his innertube, his hat and drink and straw and Business Section in a sprawl of spray . . . Rairia angry about something, swallowing it for the camera in her New Year's hat . . . and Thomas younger still: toddler, proud, chest out, sitting his red tractor proudly, looking surprisingly like Alan. Birthday parties of kids around paper-tablecloth tables or squinting into seabeach sun or squirting each other with hoses or perched on the white, starched laps of old retainers, when the family had been in full cry—one kid per retainer, stare straight ahead, each kid held from behind by either arm like a trophy cup . . . he himself with an arm around Rairia in some unidentifiable meadow, both faces happy . . . Gwen gardening. Out of order chronologically so a shock to see this youthful Gwen, when he was in graduate school? Her long bare legs splayed straight in an upsidedown V while with her nose practically in the bulbs she spades . . .

"Dad?"

"Hm?"

"Are you aware what you're doing?"

Eden had hunkered—in slow motion of the body with its mind elsewhere—to lower, toward the wood of his study floor, the pen he had earlier picked up. To his son's amazement and horror he was clearly, while the mind thought its thoughts, intending to place the pen reverously back on the floor where it had been.

"Dad?"

"Oh."

"Did you ever hear of cartoon therapy? This is a long shot I know, but in Morro Bay there's—"

"Cartoon?"

"Got something to draw on?"

"Hah?"

"Something to draw on, any—"

"Rairia has a big flip chart."

"That'd be fine."

"I'll get it. I'll get it. I'll see if I can find it."

Thomas nodded staunchly, having yanked his coat off, and was rolling up his sleeves, twisting enlarging doughnuts of shirt over his elbows tight against the beefy, lobster-red arms.

"See if I can find—"

"Any old—"

And when his dad was back in triumph with his step-mom's white pages on their tripod stand, nearly dropping it all in his excitement, Thomas steadied him, and the flip-chart stand, and they set it up. They looked for a marker pen, easily found one. Thomas drew some squares.

"What do we say? What do we do? How ah, I mean what does—"

"Lemme see if I can remember. I only did this once. Okay. You draw cartoons of yourself, and your friends or family or co-workers or whoever. Then you try to imagine what's gonna happen, or what just did, what they're saying . . ."

"I'm not very good at drawing humans."

"I don't think it's supposed to matter. Now for instance . . ."

They took turns—neither drew well. It was stick figures, simple eerie faces such as children make. The figures they drew of themselves spoke. The Thomas child asked the Eden dad, whom my uncle had assiduously given an outrageous belly, if they could play. The Eden figure said: "Not now," in Eden's scrawly conversation-balloon hand. Thomas took the marker and drew a questionmark over his own head. Looking deeply at the stick figure of himself as a child that he had drawn with the head too small for the body, he kept the marker pen, though his father was gesturing for it, and reaching out drew an arrow. From the questionmark he'd made the arrow led horizontally through the air to a series of startling exclamation points that he drew fast. "Anger?" Eden inquired softly. *Yes* was the answer Thomas printed in a second conversation balloon he had to crowd in beside the questionmark . . . they drew Rairias and Gwens, the most touching driving away forever with the back of Thomas's four-year-old head low in the front seat beside her. There was a catch-and-throw (Eden beaned—true story—by Thomas at three), and a swim. Also a goodnight tuck-in. He had told Thomas good stories, he had at least done that—Thomas's conversation balloon for his go-to-sleep-storytelling dad was a heart, which brought a moist symmetry to the physicist's eye that my uncle had, surreptitiously, to wipe away, but soon the game quieted down and the messy drawings on the big white pages looked silly. It was quiet in the room. Thomas was rolling his sleeves down.

The boy-man thought a moment, then politely took the marker pen. Flipped to a blank page with a rattle and clatter. Drew more frame boxes. In the first he drew a figure with long hair.

"Ah, who am I to assume—"

"Guess."

"Don't know. Nora."

"Look."

Next to the cartoon woman Thomas drew what clearly was a sword, one it would take anyone both hands to use, heft-hilted, massive of cross guard and double-edged blade, oilstoned to atom-sharp crease of hone that, ironically, in the depicting Thomas artistically belied.

"Hm," my uncle said, not exactly happily.

"Think anything about it? Dad?"

"It's . . Lady Gwen?"

"Do you think it is?"

"Yes I do."

"Well what do you think? What's she saying? What do you think she'll do?"

"I do not know. Thomas—"

"It's fine Dad. It's okay if—"

"I do not," Eden rumbled, "want to do this."

Thomas without a further word flipped the page. There came a crash in the mountain night, followed by bumps and a muffled cry. The intruder's telescoping ladder had contracted. When they got outdoors and searched the shrubbery, there Eden's literary agent was, groaning and blaspheming. Thomas turned to his dad in the moonlight to explain that though he and Lim had discussed it, he, Thomas, had only tried it after the real cartoon therapy hadn't worked. He didn't want his father to think he was pushing. ("I haven't given up," the shadowy bloomless hydrangeas muttered, "don't think I'm giving up. I feel like giving up, but don't think I'm giving up.") In the thrashing blackness Thomas tried to explain that he did however strongly feel that his dad should finish the adventure saga. It would be good for him, and a good thing in general. Eden was angry. He pushed these words away tight-lipped in the night with swatting hands as if bees were after him. It was rare to see my uncle angry at someone not himself, and even in the darkness Thomas could sense he should be quiet. So he was, at which the phone started ringing, and they got my uncle's agent picked up and brushed off and calmed down—nothing sprained or broken—and leaving the high-tech surveillance ladder where it was they hurried back in but by then the answering machine Nance had bought her father had taken Henry's message. Reluctantly left on the machine's impassively turning memory, halting, with gaps of echoey silence between sentences, faint-voiced at times, Henry's message, as best it could be made out, was that he and Mary had been talking. This, as the tape unscrolled, was evident from the sound of her voice coaching him in the staticky background. The old angler said—pause. Mary's crackly voice indistinct in another part of the room—he just wanted to check in, Henry's voice said. See if anything was happening with the movie . . . with the movie people . . . another pained pause, during which my uncle stood over the message recorder and stared down at it with bottled, unhealthy energy. The film project was in one of its hiatuses, no one having heard from Zany for weeks. Chase bitterly wasn't even sure if Z.P. was in the country. Just, Anther's voice said. If there's anything, you could hear Mary prompt him. But Henry asked her to be quiet. Just, he said for the machine, let me know if anything needs done, or if anything's going on. This he said louder and more forthrightly. She was only pushing him to do what he in fact wanted to do. His voice said "because I want t' say, I'm interested. I want ya t'—" His last pause. "—I wanna do it," he said, "if they want me to." The tape played on, a moving electrical silence as Henry Anther tried to say goodbye to a machine. But he couldn't, and with an abashed rattle you heard him hang up. Eden punched the machine with a forefinger. He glared at it. He wanted the movie made, and Henry in it, but he wanted Henry in the film on his—Eden's—terms, not the studio's, and not—and this was my uncle's struggle—Henry's if the old fisherman's terms were going to be commerciality and capitulation. Certain the film project would come to nothing, Lim was leaving. He waved a hand at father and son, no hard feelings. But Lim didn't want to talk. He was going to get his ladder and go home.

Minutes after breezing in that afternoon Thomas had made a call that had caused him to get a call back that, he said after hanging up, meant that instead of staying the night as originally planned he was going to have to leave, which he now did.

# 20

"Answer me one thing," Eden demanded of the phone, which he held less to his ear than as if looking down into it as if peering into an annoyingly inscrutable well, while with his free hand he waved Nora in.

"No wait— . . . wait a minute," he rumbled, "just tell, well just . . . is his character—do we have a name? All right nevermind but wait, tell me, is he someone who would say 'by gummy' because . . . no I'm not kidding. G . . u . . m, yes. I swear to God. I've got these faxes here and . . . hm?"

He waited, listening. Stare of exasperation. From three thousand miles away by a tepid pool—striped awnings bellying, burnished palms waving in a saintly wind—the film's Assistant Producer, fervent, amazed (at the comprehensiveness of her misfortune), breathless and sexy and conspiratorial and flip all in a package, was explaining what she could not. Believe . . .

But it was reality. Like it or not, believe it or no, it was the reality of the situation (sorrrr-y). *He* (the Assistant Producer referred to her employer ((mixing rage and desire)) as *he*)—*he* wanted the old angler to be the sort of person who would say "by gummy," by gummy. This was not—believe her—a question of right or wrong. It wasn't even a question of take it or leave it. It was a question, she sighed, as the Bernoulli-lifting green almond-shaped leaves stirred, of *is. Is* was a noun lately out there. At a recent shareholders' meeting Zany had snapped, in response to a windbag holder of one share who had begun "It looks to many of us in this room as if—": "Hey. Lemme tell you, looks ain't is." It was one of Zany's surrogates of course at the rostrum, but the words were Zany's, she emphasized, examining a toenail in the sepia smog, and now everybody was running around using "is" in the nominative.

My uncle breathed, listened, tried to get a word in, couldn't. His moustache twitched. Seeing Nora watching him, he crossed his eyes for her. Nora's smile was composed and kind—the smile of a patient parent. Looking at it, he was hearing over the line how Chase had become caught in a web of gilded success. Zany was paying her too well, she said, and the networking possibilities were too incredibly great with this assistant-producership in Mr. Foss's pale, she said, to risk rocking any boat or to do anything, in fact, other than take it. And smile. To the weekend parties she dragged by their ears the zombie stud-muffins she could have at a fingersnap. Then throw the main breaker, flood the still sorcerous eyes. Coo. Do not smash this plate of canapés that you are passing—smash not your benefactor's hors d'oeuvres into the Tuscan, beautifully boned face of the woman who is supplanting you. Don't lose control . . think! Swallow that pride. Swallow that rage. Step forward, turn cheek, offer cheek—cheek is kissed, you kiss air—swallow a canapé by gummy.

"Ok the will of the maladjusted person," he told Nora hanging up, "the ah, will of the sick or ignorant person—"

"What about evil?"

Nora's face was remarkably still.

Evil? His turn to smile. They had these little debates ongoingly—picked up where they'd left off. It was like the jibing and joking they'd done of old—some kind of communication at least. At least better than nothing. Nora was certainly earnest enough about it. And he tried to be vigilant and hold himself intellectually back so as not to quash her . . . evil indeed.

"Well," he said. He creaked his increased weight in the noisy chair, leaning and stretching back and lacing his fingers to hold his hands behind his head having, annoyingly, to make a noise in the throat to be able to do this. "Of course ah, yes. Evil. And there's always a reason," he told her, "always a reason for evil."

She looked at him.

"For instance some terrible deprivation. Some ah, wrong. Granted one may not be successful in determining the cause. But evil is always caused. In any event—" squinting to see her face and its reaction "—do you see? If you let the will dominate the idea why—"

"The will is stronger than the idea."

"If you think so. Nory I hate to say it but—I don't know how to say this diplomatically—"

"It's stronger dad. You can't cause the will or prevent it. It just is."

"So you don't believe in ideas."

"I never said that. I believe in ideas. But ideas have to have will behind them. Because the will's stronger."

Peeved at this obtuseness he controlled himself. Following his daughter's gaze to the windowglass he shared with her the nice sight of Emma carrying her ideal crossways in her whistling mouth, trotting back to a hunkering Duffy—*well* he thought, at least she's better. Yes, his daughter was better. But it was hard for him to be patient. Her didacticism was unfortunate, a mild learning disability, truth to tell. But that was all right. It was all right because she was better. Obviously she was doing some reading or something—touching really. So. She was over her period of "mysterious malaise," as he termed it, buttoning his barn jacket, and for the moment at any rate Nora's illusions about the will were, if not all right, a comfort to her, and therefore not to be demolished. He kicked the door open and we strode onto the last soapflaky down-light snow, through which new grass shone, of the year.

Where lawn in a steep breast fell beside birches above the MacAtticks' pond, I slipped. My sneakers from under me on the snow-slick. I sat hard. My coccyx hurt.

"Hee—I believe I'm the one who's supposed to do that."

Out here in the fresh air he looked better in his pom-pommed tam and baggy jacket. An odd day—March, but the sun was powerful. The tissuey skin of snow dressed the meadows and the leafless woods with a formality of lacing: shawls tucked 'round the shrubs' shoulders, a white mantilla blessing most of the MacAtticks' slate roof, confectioner's dustings all over the sere gardens and rubbly paths, this blue, natural world of creeks, hickories and grass flexing, bulging, glowing in its coming-on umbers and sorrels and new grass green under the snow's see-through delicacy. It was still winter, but the sun was as hot as sand—why, these lank branches might explode!

Will. Debating Nora yet again on the subject a few days later, he was devoting but a portion of his mind to what she was saying while furtively in another mental compartment trying to work out possibilities—remote ones—of how the neutrinos they were so desperately seeking might be cloaking themselves, but what was this she was saying?

Her hair—shortcut, chic-martial—something a low-security prisoner might sport—looked good, went with the bottom-solid face . . . but what was she saying?

"The will," she was telling him, "can make any church meaningful, any church. The will can turn time on a dime dad."

Where was she getting this stuff?

He asked her.

She told him.

Thunderstruck, taking a step back, still facing her, he mouthed—mumbled—bumbled, numb-lipped, stupefied, unable to get so much as a phoneme out his soundless operating mouth . .

She had said: "I'm involved with someone a lot smarter than you are."

She had said this coolly, holding his eyes. In a rush he thought of her behavior recently, this new odd calmness, her silly ideas, the nights she'd not come home . .

"Involved ah . . you mean in other words—"

She smiled.

The very air in the room threatened him, the tension of her calm terrifying. It is what you knew it was, unconsciously, but did not face, and now, here it is.

"Is this a person ah, I mean from ahh, your school?"

"No."

"This is an older person? That's to say—"

"Yes."

"Nora. Is he married?"

"No," she said, holding his eyes. "Not the way you think of it."

"Not married the way I think of it."

"That's right."

And as he was fleeing their conversation in the middle of it she called after him—hit his back with her voice: "You two should meet, you'd get along." He hurried away leaving her there in the debris of his learning. By a shattered dam—wall once—where the stream made a ninety-degree turn, in the very cold water of a triangle pool—wall, dam ruin, gristly fieldstone above—he stood. He tucked a heavy Ed Shenk sculpin with a dot weight on its nose hesitate . . . line and leader weightless spaghettying loose a second in the air before plop, into the pool. Thumb-2-fingers-slow, as if twirling sine-waxed end of handlebar moustache, with rod-tip-juke up, wait, retrieved dolphining the black bristly fish-imitation off icy bottom detritus, under the opaque gray water as the universe of flakes—stinging the nose—descended. One more snow after all. Under gray current nosedive-glide down the little fake fish . . . pause—, inert on the bottom. Then *scurry* (wiggle) sculpin-like, then stop and for a few seconds a big, outraged something he couldn't see had pulling control of his line and rod and was fighting him in the gunmetal water as it snowed. But lost it, and his excitement went down a lot quicker than his pulse.

His fingers were cold.

He had lost his father's shooting gloves.

He prepared himself to talk to her, waited for her, and when she got home the following afternoon put his questions, looking around as he did so, as if for a thing he'd misplaced, hoping this dull confused anger he couldn't rid himself of would go unnoticed.

"This thing," he said. Prowling the familiar room and picking a thing up—immaculate ashtray—to feign interest. "How long has it been going on?"

"Last fall."

He nodded, wondering why on earth he was nodding. He asked her if the person lived nearby. With soft prosecutorial control (he hoped), he waited for her answer while staring at the ashtray glass's empty sparkle.

Nora's brow was knit and a slight degree of tension and extra focus shadowed her face, but he thought he could see it was concern for him rather than any deep concern. If bothered at all she was bothered only outwardly, as she described the town, thirty miles north across the Massachusetts border, and the roads leading to it. Inside she was secure, centered in herself in a way he had not seen, or, seeing, had not noticed. The athlete's legs planted, she stood her ground, patiently giving him route numbers, mileages and turns in a neutral voice that by tone as well as content said his questions were the wrong ones.

He set the ashtray on his copy of the Dialogues so as not to—for some reason—make a sound, but it made a sound. The snow floating outside the windows was so light, so silent soft, that to see it behind Nora made her shadowed face appear foreign to him, her shoulders appearing broader than usual. He said: "So. I'm sure it must be very stimulating."

"Don't make fun."

She said this quietly.

"No-no-no."

He looked around unhappily for something else to pick up.

"You're," he tried again, "ah, after all you're—" *think* "—you're ah—"

"I'm sixteen dad."

"Yes. But," he said. "I mean this is what I mean." He froglegged his moustache with a thumb and finger, then coming to himself, having lost track of a few seconds (more?), stopped. "Ahh," he said as she waited.

"Is this," he began weakly, "I mean a question of." His voice was small: "Do you . . ."

"No."

On alert. Eerie in the palms of the hands and the center of the chest, up the back of this his neck lifting all of him as if he were his stomach, and it lifting, moon-gravity light inside him, ever lifting never climbing not watery but too big for the chest, fuzz on the back of his neck gingerale-tingly—

"Is it, I mean, ah, sexual?"

She smiled.

The mind started to crank turning fear to thought and keeping it there, which is anger. He stood mixedly thinking in consternation; it wasn't very orderly thinking. He winced and dropping his hands asked her one question more, except it wasn't a question quite—more the expression of an extremely legitimate concern. "I hope," he said, "you're taking the proper . . . oh certainly I know these days everyone is this," he asked, "person taking the proper precautions?"

The snow beyond the windows fell, unblown, just lightly pulled, by its and the planet's gravity, to the new grass.

She said: "What do you mean?"

He began to wave a hand. She said: "No, I want to know what you mean. You said 'precautions.'"

His attempted dismissive wave ended up looking as if he were trying to flap some flypaper from some fingers.

"Just concerned," he mumbled.

"About what?"

"Ahhh, it's all right, never—"

"But I do mind dad. Are we taking the proper precautions about what?"

"Why if, I mean when you smile like that when I ask, I must naturally assume—"

She smiled the same way, ending his words.

In not a breeze the flakes continued sparsely to drift down outside the windows, in a little sunshine now, each flake different. As a child he had never been able to believe in the possibility of a proof that would establish conclusively that no two flakes could be identical. Strange late-March weather this, warm sun, greening grass, then these late little squalls move through. It was not as haunting, not as exciting, to see the last of winter descend the bright air as it had been when as a child one thought of snow and iron January air together only to see, suddenly, snow falling in say April sunlight when the grass has already started to grow. Eden gulped. His reaction now was beyond neck tinglings—it was a dissolving, he was dissolving. There was a ringing too, not local to his ears. He started to speak.

Nora said: "Excuse me?"

He had intended to say something about believing her, that he supported her—would support her in what she did. But the words as he started to speak them came out gibberish.

She didn't laugh.

She came and went, doing her homework faithfully in her room at the desk she and Vanessa had bought with Nora's money from her new waitressing job, and substituted for Nancy's old one which they lugged out, insisting on doing it themselves, and drove away in Vanessa's dad's pickup. Nora exercised, jogged, ran, lifted, stretched and always in passing greeted her dad politely with a hug, told him where she'd been, doing what, and what her plans were. He would be in his study scribbling something for the movie or gnawing a fingernail while staring at a window and trying for a particularly elusive ideation. She would knock and walk in and bending down hug him and speak in a flow as suave as whipping a wedge from an about-to-be-recumbent bag before it's even hit the grass to smooth a fast shot safe. She would tell him for instance: "Hi. I was at Vanessa's, I'll be home tonight. I'll be silent for the next three days."

Sometimes, holding his fleecy towel outside the shower stall, staring at his flabbergastingly out of shape naked body dripping, he would quite honestly, no matter how hard he tried, be unable to recall if he had remembered to wash himself because, for example, in the shower he would have been thinking how Alexander hoodwinked the Triballians—how, outnumbered, outpositioned by them at Pelium, he battle-paraded his splendid phalangites on the plain *in perfect silence* before the enemy's eyes, hypnotizing the barbarian hoards in their numbers on the heights, then without warning turned a parade maneuver seamlessly into an attack and his Macedonians, lifting their shrilling cry, carried the day. One other time he was thinking, as he performed his morning ablutions, how the unknowable may not merely form a part of reality's fabric but be indispensable to it, when he caught himself almost lifting his two-track razor to his mouth to brush . . . his dreaming eyes, when he looked at them, were hazed in the mirror like the double-exposure streamflow idea he'd had for the film and jotted down the evening before: currents of twinkling mountain creek superimposed twinkling sideways through the old angler's eyes toward the last scene's end . .

His colleagues were dreaming of their platonic symmetries but trouble was, the symmetries revealed themselves only when the physicists were thinking. When they applied them to the physical world, the symmetries broke, to which their response . . . interesting, as his hand poises above his wash-station city of spraycans . . . was to believe that the symmetries they imagined merely needed to be adjusted, changed in other words, to fit. Poised, decisionless hand. It seemed to him that all their lofty thinking, beginning in purity, alas ended there. He was putting toothpaste on his hand.

He stopped, got things straight—the morass and ghost chains of all his daily devices straight—got dressed and, the house not having a downstairs, went down the hall.

He peeked around the corner of Nora's bedroom, seeing her made bed hushed and impeccable in the morning light, her childhood frog catty-cornered on the pillows' undisturbed shape under the bedspread's nap. On her desk, with school volumes symmetrically stacked, were her phone, laptop, and blotter, all new. Dresser. Closed closet. Chair. All was quiet before his eyes in the galaxy motes drifting in the morning sunshine with that special, utter silence of a bedroom that is to've been slept in but hasn't been.

In the shadows of the dresser mirror his face was a moon—white, uncertain—motionless in the glassy umbrage unless he moved.

When she returned, later that morning, he stopped puttering to stare at her as he'd stared at her unused room. She wore a plain gingham dress redolent of country—not this type but silos, grain elevators, towering threshers toiling. Her hair needed a good brushing and her blue eyes were baggy. She stood before her father in the meaningless rich gold of the springtime sun in the bungalow's glass-walled entryway of boots and rods, as composed, in her tiredness, as my uncle was nervy.

She explained. It had been last-minute, spur-of-the-moment. They had spent the night then gotten up to watch the sun come up.

"Ah." A weak, ghostly sound coming from no deeper than the front of his mouth.

The skin around them was exhausted, but Nora's eyes were not the mild blue of warmweather but this day the royal, rich blue of the ocean when the bottom falls far away from your keel.

He asked: "How was it?"

She answered slowly, rubbing her eyes. "It was very real," she said without irony. She felt and thought it through, rubbing her eyes, stifling a yawn. "We exercised, did the pleasure exercises at midnight. Then we disciplined our bodies to sleep which was hard, which is good. It was hard because of—" shutting her eyes she did, now, yawn, unabashedly stretching "—oh excuse me—I need an hour's nap—because we were excited. We got up at five and had like just coffee and disciplined ourselves not to talk. We drove to Haystack. It was hideous."

"What?"

"I said 'hideous' because of opposites. He has us working on meaning-awareness so we like—we say the opposite, especially when it's important. If you focus as you're doing it it can make you actually experience what you mean much more intensely than what you're used to."

"Oh?"

"Really."

She yawned a final time and repeated that she had to take a nap.

"What about school?"

She looked through the skylight at the sun's height.

"I'll be late, but not too. It's all right."

"It is?"

"Yeah."

*Us,* he thought, turning and tossing in sleepless hours of addictive thought in his bed that night. She'd said *us*—has *us* working on, so if it was *us* this person Nora was seeing had working, there'd been more than the two of them staying the night, and getting up to watch the dawn . . . but what did that mean? Damp with perspiration, groggy but far, in this swelter, from sleep, he twisted, fisted the pillow, fiddled with the sheets, composed word-perfect rejoinders, incisive glistening sentences, wise ones, forceful, even angry ones . . . she would be gone a day or two at a time that April, and dressed in clownish clothes one Sunday because, she said, humankind's clotheschanging is vestigial racial change superficially expressed to give the Reaper of Natural Selectivity plenty of variety to choose from—Gaia raising up enough children of possibility and variegation to cull.

Rather formally, they sat down, Eden before she.

Nora sat still, not changing expression, not moving her hands.

She wore black hightops and a polkadot camisole.

"He told me to," answering her father's question before he could get it out of his eyes and into words. "He makes us do things. It's purposeful."

Like a testifying witness who might have said more, she shifted in her seat instead of speaking. Her weight hung a second from her lower arms on the arms of the chair, as she shifted how she sat. Then she was still again, looking at him.

He could feel the back of his neck. She was as self-possessed as he had ever seen her, or, thinking of it, anyone.

"What other things does he make you do?"

"Oh, play a sport I don't like. Make faces."

She showed him her smile just a second like a flashed card.

"That's fine," he said, "good." He stood. "That's fine and good. That's fine and good but that's to say I mean, ah . . . how do you feel about all this?"

hawk taking a rabbit, talons

extended in slowed motion so you see the bird's legs, straight slants, curved talons—go into soft, trembly fur

storm of wings, tumble dustcloud and, in no hurry, the magnificent predator, in the videotape he showed them, standing on what it is going to eat looks left then straight ahead, then down to take its first tear.

Their minds were alabaster inside their inclined heads.

How did you make someone understand how Quadros could be silent? How waiting Quadros could be, at start of session. His silence unfolding from him—into them as they took their places.

"Good," she said.

"You're absolutely sure?"

"Yes," she said calmly, "as you would understand it. But nobody can be absolutely sure of anything. Only the will is sure, and the will doesn't know stuff dad."

It was her pinched glance at him to see if he had understood that made him so suddenly, intensely angry at her that he became jovial.

"Oh well—hee—sorry. The will is sure, eh? Did he tell you that?"

She looked evenly at him, the answer in her eyes.

"Heehee and are we proud? Is this something one finds oneself proud of?"

"Me you mean?"

"Yes Nora I mean you," he bellowed getting up (having the moment before sat down). "I mean you, I'm talking to you, you're the only person here if you ah, are." She was watching him. Pacing strenuously, unmindful of where he was waving his arms, he managed not to strike or knock anything over. "I respect," he said with effort. "I do. I respect how you feel, and who you are. The will," he sputtered, "heh. Tell me, has this little person read his Schopenhauer? Has he read his Nietzsche?"

At last, he saw, he had asked her a question she had to think about.

"Oh," she said loosely, "yeah, I'm sure he has."

"And understood it too."

"Probably as much as you have Dad."

Nancy's "take," in her words, was "look I've talked to her, I find her reserved, extremely so. I can tell from the tone of her voice this is a thing she wants to do—this is a thing she's *going* to do, I've never heard Nora this determined, my gut reaction is if we want to put a stop to it we're going to have a battle on our hands, and even then there's no guarantee she won't be alienated. I don't approve of what she's doing, whatever it is, which I'll get to, but in the final analysis I trust her and we'll have to see."

Her unmysterious eager voice, coming to me across the trout streams of Idaho and the otherworldly Dakotas rocks, the great cheese wheels and glittery lakes of my long-ago geography-book Wisconsin/ Minnesota and the rusted ghost mills of the Great Lakes and the slumbering, economical Pennsylvania farms, was a beacon of pure enlightenment compared to the rest of that family. "We'll just have to see, er, is she sleeping with this bozo?"

I said I didn't know.

"Well find out!! Just kidding just kidding. She won't talk about it to me but I gather from dad—stop that. Stop it. Now. No you can't stop this evening, now means now Michael, sorry—" to me "—where was I oh, according to dad there's some mumbo-jumbo about—" voice lowered ominously "—about making love without touching, which is sort of unclear. But my gawd, does anybody realize we're talking potential federal offense here? She's sixteen! It's kind of fascinating actually, look I've gotta go. The long and the short of it is . . *are,* the long and short of it—*are?* Who cares, the long and short of it is we don't even know who this Quadros is. In any event we've had some good talks and mark my words, she's determined, Nora's very determined about this, but something really bizarre is going on. She's calm. Very secure—reasonable. She stays there sometimes, which I gather—" voice lowered and infused with disgust "—had been going on for quite some time to no one's notice . . and there are others involved in the . . program? But aside from a lot of mumbo-jumbo about 'sessions' and 'exercises' and everybody-and-their-brother's 'will' and a lot of other hokey stuff that frankly—stop that. Yes you can suck 'em. You can suck 'em—his fingers," she explained, "for five minutes. And that's it. Alan'll set the timer. I'm sorry, sorry where was I—no Alan wants to set the timer Michael, Alan likes to set the timer, you're the one who's getting to suck 'em for heaven's—excuse me, sorry. I've gotta go, so, she looks good apparently?"

I said yes.

"And she's doing fine in school again, in fact she's doing better than ever and playing all her sports really well again and all. Well, find out what you can. Find out what you can and report back. You're like a member of the family, and I know you care. I can tell you care." Silence: hers, mine. "Well?"

I said I did.

"You must admit I was right, it's a zoo, a veritable—I really do have to go. I'll fly back if I have to. Dad's fine by the way but he looks old doesn't he, I've gotta—Michael what're—no. He had it first . . I've gotta—he had it first Alan. Gotta go. We have a disaster in the making here. BYE!"

Nora wanted her father to go along with her to Quadros' place, Nance told me, but wanted him to ask. Nancy knew this because her sister had told her. And Eden wanted to go, Nancy said—he'd told her he did, but he was waiting for Nora to invite him, so nothing was happening, "typically," Nancy editorialized, "but that's the way it is. Confidentially," she modified her voice to divulge, "I've come to the conclusion the guy's a humbug. Maybe not. I could be wrong. In fact I think I am." She paused then told me, her voice lowered further still: "The fact of the matter is I wish he *were* a humbug, but I fear he's anything but. I just wanted to say 'humbug,'" she snickered, "but seriously, remember that day in the dim reaches of the past when you and Alan and I drove on a tour of the old place? And we saw the lake and 'Lookout,' the big house? And Alan was singing 'Farmer in the Dell' incessantly? And we passed two lions? A limo was nosing out? And I said that's the Grummans'? Power people in govt.?"

"What?"

"Govt. Gov-ern-*ment*, I just wanted to say 'govt.' And I said how they're still connected some of them? We and that branch hardly communicate but they're still somewhat connected, as I say, so you know me, I got my courage up and called a Grumman. I asked her to find out what she could find out, just gave her the name, you know not expecting much, and a strange thing happened." Like an orchestra using its harmonic palette to modulate down and thus maintaining, by reaching up to a higher register to continue its descent in key, a true feel of descent while always from a higher starting point, Nancy Elwive could lower her voice endlessly. "An answer came back," she conspired, "she called me back and was downright evasive, as if she wanted to confuse me—she really didn't know she said, no one does, maybe he's an average Joe, but also maybe he's a retired double agent who became a millionaire in some really world-class under-the-table operations in steaming distant jungles, or Mafia, or a white-collar criminal who never got caught—ties to the intelligence community . . she said there's a rumor he's a Du Pont, hah, that's frankly like saying he's a Napoleonic ruble, I mean noble, I mean everyone's a Du Pont by now. Anyway I got the distinct impression she was trying to get rid of me. She was feeding me conflicting mumbo-jumbo so if and when I ever did get this guy's real story I would be less likely to recognize it, if that makes sense which I'm not sure it does. Anyway you know me, I blurt right out what I'm thinking, but I was nonplussed. I said little. I have to give this one some thought. I'd like to know for my own oh god. Oh god! Oh-god-oh-god I've got to hang up. Egad, see you. *Bye!*"

She had called me at my apartment down in the city. Hanging up I went out for a stroll, and crossing West End Avenue nearly stepped into the path of an accelerating cab as it hit me that if Nora had told Nancy that she, Nora, was waiting for their father to ask to be invited and if Eden had told Nancy that he wanted to be invited, but was waiting to be, then what was *Nancy* waiting for?

At some deep level I think she just enjoyed it—mild chaos—was compelled to, psychological and other superficial issues aside. She liked to hurl bombs and rockets into conversations to see what might explode back out. She whipped up little fights and conflicts that did not, essentially, exist, and where ones did exist she enhanced them in a series of conversations in which she relayed the comments of others to persons not themselves, and vice versa, telling A, for example, what B and C thought of A, then relaying A's annoyed reaction (to what B and C had never quite said) back to B and C (. . and D—why not?!) in a stirring quickening twister wind of confusion and disagreement that once she'd got it going she stepped back from, putting her fingers in her ears, and watched, interestedly, to see if it would explode. Or, if caught at what she was doing, she simply clammed up. But I don't think Nancy ever did anyone harm, which is saying a lot, and I think she accomplishes much, practically, which may be saying even more. I never did get straight her husbands and children—some adopted, some, like Alan, not—some of whom, like Alan, visited Eden often and others of whom, like Alan's older sister, virtually never came, and I don't know if Nance played her tricks because she was bored or mischievous or because she was distrustful of the world and so had to keep poking it, that it might squeal—pinching it, so to speak, as one pinches oneself to be sure "this is really happening," or if, uncertain from her youth of both parents, she was now perpetually constrained to test people and situations in search of ethical evidence, but it is probably as silly to model a person as matter, or the palace of our thought.

The next day, with the rains of April slanting in a free race against the windows, without warning or introduction there walked into my uncle's study a person so indeterminate of age, so cool, so redolent of wickedness in his statuesque mien and delicate shoulders, that my uncle was fascinated. A long-limbed, fine-boned Basque, Quadros only seemed tall. His face was considerably larger—proportionally—than his body. Wide of brow and with angelic graying waves falling beside the sensitive temples, the head was like a marble statue head set atop a slim neck column.

He wore a loose shirt. His mostly dark-brown hair fell in a pair of curves—an S and a backward one—from a centered widow's peak.

"You fish," Quadros said.

"Yes, wonderful activity." Lifting a hand to gesture Eden looked at it—his hand—and put it away. "Wonderful," he said again. "You ah, no doubt. Hm."

Conjured by distant suns from distant oceans the streamwater plowed back down slanting, driving, insisting, hammering the windowglass as my uncle ignored the ringing phone. Quadros, with an eyebrow, suggested he might wish to answer? No-no my uncle said with a hand aflutter, "no ah this is, obviously this is important. Now. First of all *ahem.*"

"She was on drugs," Quadros said. "I got her off them. She had lost her self-esteem. She has that back. By the end of this month," Quadros, his hands perfectly folded, said, "she will be ready to move on. From me."

Although the rain continued and if anything intensified, quickening to gurgle from the mouths of spouts and flood in shimmery falls from the leaf-clogged drains, it was for my uncle as if the sun had burst forth, so relieved was he to hear what he had just heard.

He leaned forward. "If I understand you, before the end—"

"Of this month. We will say goodbye, Nora and I."

It was intriguing how depending on the light the hair could be either gray or brown, and how the sleek fingers of the hands lay atop one another on a knee, not moving.

"I had heh, I had sort of intended to, heh, you see to engineer the conversation around to lead up gradually," he told me, "to whatever, well frankly to whatever confrontation might prove inescapable. But he just—" wide-eyed pout, Gallic shrug, exploding fingers "—he just got right into it." Sitting back my uncle straightening an arm propped himself—at that arm's length—back from his desk, chin held in a thumb-finger clamp. He seemed to be thinking. He rather suddenly sat forward, putting his hands on his papers and books like sphinx paws. He coughed. "Can't say I like it. But of course tolerance—understanding and *ahem,* the situation admits of more than one analysis, er, more than one construction, 'construct.' 'Construct.' Dreadful word. Always sounded to me like a hee, cinder block or something."

Expansively in his relief at discovering the whole thing was soon to come to an end, he invited Quadros back—come anytime, come tomorrow. It was a little surprising when he did, gliding into the study to sit, folding his hands. Not clear his throat, not pick a lint fleck off a sleeve, not settle, in his seat, or smooth his hair or smile or check his watch or move his gaze off his pupil's father.

"Nice of you to come."

"I've reamed out her soul. Cleansed it."

"Hah, well. That's a novel idea."

"Not an idea."

"Oh."

"Act."

"Of course you mean 'act' in the sense of 'deed,' not the, ah, not the thespian—"

"I don't believe in ideas."

"Yes," Eden said with forbearance. He composed himself, sending a tolerant thin smile toward the room's open doorway into which, to his surprise, Nora stepped.

"I believe in reality," Quadros said without looking at her. "I believe in the physical world, in which I see no ambiguity. I do not believe in ideas. I do not believe ideas exist."

"Oh come, why—even if an idea is wrong or ill-formed, still it exists. The very fact that we express it in words is proof of our having thought it, which of course proves its existence—" leaning forward over his papers professorially and with no little force of mien himself "—even if only in the mind."

Nora relaxed against the doorway, listening.

"Thoughts exist," Quadros granted, "thus thoughts of ideas exist. But the ideas themselves do not. Ideas do not exist."

"Heh, poor fellow, well heh, in other words the idea of freedom say, or God, or unity—"

"Those things may exist," Quadros said. "God may exist, unity may. Freedom certainly does. I just don't believe there are such things as ideas of those things."

"Bah," my uncle grinned. He loved this stuff. His behind wriggled in his chair like an eager puppy's and his face was lit with the joy of immateriality. "So the will," he carefully laid his trap, "is stronger than any idea."

"That's right."

"The will—" just to make sure "—is stronger than any idea."

"Yes," Quadros said. "In that ideas don't exist I would certainly say so."

"So the idea," my uncle grinned, "of the will itself—does *that* exist?"

"No dad."

Jolted he turned to her who seemed dreamily to be practically rubbing herself against the doorway like a half-eyed cat as she listened.

"No," Quadros said. "The will is. It acts, it wills. It isn't some doily image of itself floating in the mind. It isn't an idea. The will isn't an idea."

"That's sophistry," Eden said starting out of his chair to pace and banging a knee. "Ow. I'll be patient—oh ow . . . but the argument's specious." It struck him that his disillusionment with certain aspects of his science was not perhaps so far from a disbelief in ideas, but that was too dangerous an idea and he let it evaporate. "All right. I'll be patient. I'm here to listen," he said, and sat down but Quadros, his long-fingered hands finger by finger like two spiders lolling one on the other on his knee, now that he had been invited to elaborate did nothing of the sort. Instead he started to ask some pretty knowledgeable questions about physics. Eden knew this was flattery but he got interested and for a minute they talked about how atoms, if frozen cold enough—right down to almost zero—might merge and blend into bigger new things that according to uncertainty, since their velocity—near zero—would be highly determinate, would have wildly unpredictable position . . .

"Or," Quadros suggested, "maybe if their momentum were fixed their position would be too. You're the expert."

Eden smiled and puffed out a little. He threw them a few bones of real thinking, made a secret mental note to consider Quadros' idea, and suddenly felt the jovial host, especially since this strange man was going to be gone from their lives by the end of the month by his—Quadros'—own declaration. It all changed as Quadros, in the same voice and sitting the same way, said: "We don't make love."

"Huh?"

"Nora says you're worried about that."

"Ah"

"Me," Nora in the doorway said.

Her father was speechless.

"Not in the way you think of it," Quadros qualified.

"And how do I think of it?"

"Image," the other said, "mental image. Thoughts, memory."

Eden sat perfectly still and blank-faced, cogitating. That they didn't make love in the way he thought of it, if the way he thought of it was all mental image, was not necessarily to say that they did not make love physically, so what was Quadros telling him?

"We do it," Quadros said. "But we do not touch. Isn't that right?"

Quadros did not move or turn his eyes toward Nora but it was she he was asking, and she nodded, winsomely, yes. Without looking at her Quadros said: "Yes and powerful."

"Yes," she said in the doorway.

Eden stood.

"Is this some sort of exercise?"

Quadros looked at him. "Yes," he said. Relieved, Eden sat down.

That May, after all the leaves were out a blizzard dumped thirty inches of wet snow, and in full leaf the branches of the forest held the snow until, in the black balm of the spring night, you could hear trees going over in no wind. In a starless darkness touched with the perfumes of all the new blossoms and the first tentative songs of the season's frogs and toads, every so often you would hear c—,c-c-,c—c—c-crack and the awful rustle and commotion in the night of tipping trees and branches of leaves and a thud crash on the forest floor. One fell on the house. Duffy got her brother-in-law, a roofer, and his brother-in-law, a carpenter, to come put "the King's men back on their horses." To their pounding and hammering and shouts as if God Himself were renovating Heaven my uncle sat with his head in his hands, staring at his ideas.

He threw his pen down, slapping the hand that had held it back against the side of his head. He resumed staring. His wife was trying to repeal the Declaration of Independence. His heart hurt. He stared at his life: papers, numbers. The house was quiet except for what was going on overhead. Rairia was traveling. Nance was in Tacoma, Thomas in California. Nora was off with friends from school—Vanessa or another of her crowd, no longer, it being May, with Quadros thank god. And his poor neglected characters, Blok, the Children of Tarr, the evil oafs and their velvety Master, even Lady Gwen herself and her wheeled advisors, he thought of now as sun-bleached and fading like some larger-than-life 1930s alfresco bare-biceps mural of Hero Workers ready to strive, but frozen in time and fading. They were there. They were all still there and he'd not forgotten them, and he cared, still, very much about them.

Lim Hope had passed through despair and anger into a state of discouraged persistence that ill befit his impish person. It was a kind of lookingglass wormhole-inversion of willpower. Doggedly, as the rains flew at a slant in a blur against the study windows, once that strange snow had melted and the roof received its last nail, Lim's highpitched voice came flying over the phone to make the point that he—Lim—*moi,* that's right *moi-même*—was out of pocket personally for the fiction-writing software he'd commissioned a customization of for use in getting the last book of his brother's *Sword* series finished. He had gone ahead, he told Eden—had taken the #!@(!@¢&*!!ing liberty, that's right, you heard right, that's what I said: #!@(!@¢&*!!, and I meant it, I don't like having to hire a computer to write your story for you either Eden but you're not doing it, I don't even know if you even any longer *could* do it, even if you decided to. No Eden, you don't wanna do the things you can do, you wanna do the things you can't do. That's you. So okay, okay, we've got three different endings so far, and I want you to read 'em, you don't have to say anything, you don't have to speak, I can #!@(!@¢&*!!ing well hear what you're thinking . .

My uncle, with his elbows on his papers, cradling his forehead in a hand and holding the receiver violinlike between chin and wattly neck, doodled as he listened—cartoon caricatures of old S-matrices: the probabilities-calculations of all possible results of all conceivable impacts of particles. His brother's voice came electrically loud into his ear mocking his dreams. He went on sketching. Stream, old angler, boy, underbrush, Anther—a new kind of movie, something simple and plain beyond the age's artifice. Lim was reminding his brother of the family fund, naming several cousins ready for college and other needy potential beneficiaries. He finally broke off his dour harangue to say, in the third person, of Eden: he's not even listening. Have a nice #!@(!@¢&*!!-ing day. Lim rung off.

Dropping his ballpoint sword he stared at it.

He had an idea, a poor shard of a one—"windtunnel" simulation of the Planck energy using sound—not a very good idea, but he scribbled it down, two sentences, three numbers, a diagram. Flung himself back in his chair with a hand held above his head—fingers elaborately extended like tree twigs—hold the pose, his mouth, under the trimmed moustache, an O of I don't know what . . an O. Spinning in his chair he pops to his feet to pace and prowl like a tiger in a zoo cage stalking, trying to turn the cage into a savannah, if a tiger could plod, upright on fat legs, with spectacles down its runny nose.

Some days he felt sociable, other days stayed mostly in this room with little to say to anyone.

He began snapping awake at 3. After the third straight night of trying to pound the pillow and slam his head in it and force sleep, on went the lamp. He lay in bed reading, scribbling ideas, numbers—soon the restraints of intellectual decorum were gone. In the small morning hours now every night out poured contorted little homilies, notes for children's tales, biblical parables, new adventure fantasies, rules-constructs, imprecations, formulations of wonder, doggerel cuttings, crass cracks, myths by halves of nowhere-meandering late-summer brooks of idylls abruptly cut off, dialogues and allegories and sayings, made-up words, dirty jokes, puns, prayerlets. It was much the same thing as had happened to him—come issuing from him—two years ago during his time in his cramped city rooms, only now it was worse. He wrote, or calculated, on the flyleafs and pages of the books he read before sleep and on the notepaper he stocked at his saggy bed's side and on the insert cards that slid out of the magazines he subscribed to. He would read and jot and stare for an hour before feeling sleep pulling him down. Reading he blinks—gives a start . . . for how many minutes have these glassine eyes been moving over these black letters on white paper without seeing? Or he would get reading too fast and be skipping, as if looking for something, or intransitively—without object—looking . .

He had friends high in the University, but they were too high to help him.

He said it wasn't that poor Quadros had been bad, just, with his pseudocredo of the will, a bit much for a sixteen-year-old to handle. I could tell he was thinking about other stuff too from the way he sipped from his mug without seeming to be aware of its existence. He said he was proud. Of himself. "Oh for the way I," stretching to a different, more comfortable position and sipping again, "I was patient. I mean the heh, the man was heh. All those sophomoric. And the difficult part was she believed it—the will, as if an act isn't a perception. But no—" ducking his head and with the hand not holding his coffee mug delicately fending off and gesturing away a phalanx of invisible temptations "—no there was no, I did not employ . . . it was tempting, but I held myself in check. You see to have defeated his arguments would in no wise have caused her to be any the less interested in the man. In fact the opposite's possible, human nature being—" slurpy sip, white circumference of steaming mug "—being human nature. In any event," pensively, "in any . . . event . . ." staring out over his mug as if across a field of battle now finished (and won), tired from the conflict, satisfied with the outcome. "In any event I didn't say a word. Scarcely a one. And the whole thing's over. Has been—" glance at calendar "—for weeks."

He went on to say that Quadros had come to strike him as pathetic, in the final analysis. They never did find out what the man did, but he had made a great impression on Eden, Eden said, slanting to pull a deskdrawer open, as lonely. A man alone. And rather, ah—my uncle was staring into the open drawer. Something there? I couldn't see. Rather, he said, less intelligent than he fancies himself. Rather ah, sad. Rather, in a way, comical with his appropriated old shibboleths . . . but he never made fun of him—restraint, patience. He grunted, leaning down to set his steaming mug of coffee in the drawer. He certainly *could've* made fun. Perhaps the so-called exercises were mildly interesting but—his eyes lit up—if the will's so all-fired wonderful he blurted kicking the drawer shut with a foot and rolling backward triumphally—why the need for "exercises"? Hm? No he mused, there was something fatally sad about the man. But it was in the past now. Academic . . .

The lenses of his glasses flared with mist. Electrified by the coming storm's ions, the seventy-seven hairs he had left—too few to tangle—felt upward waving blindly above his bowed head in the breeze through the windows. The pearl depending from his nose refracted—as it trembled with his outrage—the storm sun changingly when he found out she had been seeing Quadros all that May and was seeing him still. Muttering analyses and courses of action and declamations of fury over the offense, with his fingers he deftly, compared at least to the botching ways of the past, knotted this silken strand of tippet to his leader while the currents' turbulence swirled and scalloped about his pilaster legs a hundred feet upstream of where Anther, not casting, stood eyeing the water for fish.

At first Nora had evaded him, feeling his anger. She swam away, gliding off to farther rooms when he tried to collar her to yell at her, or, when she did stand fast—infuriatingly like Quadros, composed like

Quadros, unstirring like him with her handsome face like carved stone—to hear her father out, he couldn't seem to get his words organized and would fall back on sarcasm and a rhetoric as parts-clattery as his car.

Quadros came. He apologized profusely. He said he should've said something, at least made sure Nora said something. Yes, Quadros agreed, he'd said it would be over by the beginning of May. Yes, now it was June. He seemed eager for forgiveness and reconciliation. He spoke quicker than ever before, though no part of him save, barely, the lips moved as he sat like a supplicant before my uncle's reports, physics journals, treatments, storyboard sketches, faxes, unanswered letters, lab printouts and envelopes and scribbled-upon napkins and full-color flyers of coves and bays and cays.

"Do this yourself?" Quadros asked, looking at the pointillistic paint droplets around the periphery of the pane of the biggest window.

"The paint job."

"Yes."

"Yes heh, terrible no?"

"Maybe not," Quadros said. "Maybe it's artistic."

"Heh one—"

"Let me explain," Quadros said, "in detail why it's necessary. I mean this further time I need."

"With Nora," Eden tried to say.

"Yes," Quadros filled in for him, "further time that I need with Nora."

Quadros sat still always, yet in his voice this day there was new warmth and an eagerness for Eden's understanding—my uncle could feel it. It reached out like hands. The long, wavy hair was kempt. The spare shoulders were anticipatorily square.

"We need to loosen her," Quadros said. "One last short period of work. We need to shift focus. We need to work on passivity, on relaxation," the lips said. "On having some fun now at the end."

Eden lay a gauntlet forearm sideways on his papers. He smiled sardonically.

"Such as?"

"Such," Quadros said . . . there was a moment's pause. "As crafts. Denial drill."

"What on earth does—"

"That's why another six days are necessary."

"Wait a moment, wait a moment here . . . now what's—did you say 'denial'?"

"Nothing," Quadros said blandly, "more than the rejection of rejection. It's denial *of* denial we're talking about."

"Oh."

That made it marginally alright but there was wind that you couldn't hear through the windowglass. The air had gone gray and gusts bent the evergreen boughs. Over the lawn the wind was playing angry skittish patterns that bent the grass in silvery waves like schools of fish.

"Six days you say."

"Yes," Quadros said. "Six."

"Six days."

"Six," Quadros said. "Days."

To emphasize the temporal specificity of what he was delighted to've herded Quadros into committing to, my uncle made a show of opening the lower desk drawer he kept his calendar in. Peering into the drawer, horrified at what he saw, he of course did not under the circumstances remove the spilt mug of coffee. He had another drawer though, and on the calendar he took from that one he marked six days from now with a colored marker, so Quadros could see.

"At the end of that six days," my uncle rumbled commandingly—

"She moves on. Starts her new life for real, on her own. No more me."

"Well all right. All right then."

"It's an informal system," Quadros told him, "based in part on my instincts, in part on my needs."

It was eight days later and Quadros had come again. He had come again because Eden had asked—tremblingly angry—Nora to ask him to come, because when Eden had asked Nora if her time with Quadros was over she had shaken her short hair no and said no, no they needed three more days. And when Eden had started to shout questions she had shaken her short bobbed hair back off her face to look stonily at her father saying, "he says he wants you to talk to him about that."

And now Eden addressed the intruder with barely contained suspicion, letting his eyes glare at Quadros, not even trying to be polite. "I don't care," he said, "what the reason is. Twice now we've set a time to bring things to a close, and ah, now there's, well quite transparently, quite frankly there's this ongoing pattern which I must tell you, I must say—"

"It's not acceptable," Quadros said.

He was sitting in the same chair.

"Well it's not, I mean that's right, it's not acceptable. It's not acceptable at all. Now this—"

"The activities," Quadros said, "the 'exercises' as we call them, and the discipline I impose are, in order, meditation, inconsistent behavior, self-awareness, self-abnegation, fun."

"But I mean what's—this doesn't make any . . . but it doesn't matter," my uncle mumbled, glowering over his propped arm at the offending drawer. "It doesn't matter because the program or whatever you care to call what you do is over. Correct?"

"Correct."

"Really?"

"In exactly," Quadros said, "three days."

My uncle held his head. It was absurd. He didn't want to be unreasonable. It was nonsense. On the other hand it appeared to have helped her. And he knew you couldn't will something. You couldn't force a Quadros to do something. You could reason however, be reasonable and patiently firm.

"Three days," my uncle said. No sense in marking the calendar again. "I have your promise."

"Yes."

"Your word."

"Yes."

"Very well."

"Thank you."

"You're welcome," my uncle replied ironically. "Go your three days. I shouldn't say this, but I have to. I have to tell you, all these exercises—in fact the whole of what you do is, I don't mean it may not have helped. But beyond a certain point the imposition of one's will on the will of someone who is weaker is not good."

"No," Quadros said. "It isn't, you're right. It's neither good nor bad. It just is."

Eden waved these words off like a bad smell. "Meaningless," he said, not seeing the other nod. "But in effect, in *fact,* three days. Three days more. Yes. Ah, we're counting today?"

"No."

"All right. Tomorrow's Saturday. So. Sunday, Monday. Three days and we're finished."

"That's right," Quadros said.

But it wasn't.

Nora looked to have caught cold. She told him Quadros needed her just three more days.

"You mean three days more than the three we just got finished agreeing to?"

"He says," she told her father, "you are welcome to drive up and talk to him. I can tell you the way."

"Well I will, I certainly will, I most certainly will drive up and talk to him, I will do exactly that, this has become laughable." His anger was not helped by the sight of Nora with the flu or a cold or whatever it was she'd contracted with her resistance obviously down from her times with the charlatan. Her face was the white of paste. There were black circles around her eyes.

"I will tell him," he informed her angrily, "that it is very, very clear to me now that this is a person not to be trusted. I ah, but this isn't your fault. This isn't your fault Nory but . . ."

But what?

Scene sketches and vines of dialogue for the film hanging in his hands, he stood gaping at her. Then he dropped his papers and drove on back roads that turned into each other through tall forest with white, neatly black-lettered signs telling you you are nine miles, at this turn, from the same town you were nine miles east—or was it west—of a few miles back as you continue north—white small signs against hunter green backdrop forest, and found the place—three flat acres of lawn, shade trees, white picket fence, single-story gray normal house, kennel, red chimney, tree-lined suburban way.

Quadros pulled out a chair for him.

"Another three days," Eden said leaning forward. "She said you said it would be *another* three. What are we to make of this?"

"Another three days," Quadros answered, "that's all."

"No more?"

Quadros was serene. It was impossible to know how serene from the face that was so hard to recall when away from him.

"You're not comfortable with this," Quadros said.

"Not comf-, look, look here, of course I'm not. Of course I'm not comfortable with this. Would you be? Think about it rationally," my uncle adjured the beast. "Would you be comfortable with someone telling you in effect ah, promising you that something is going to happen in, ah, is going to happen in—"

"Three days," Quadros said.

"Yes three, three days, but suddenly it's going to be six days instead of three."

"Yes," Quadros said.

"Or three *more* days or—"

"Or five, or ten."

"Well that's, ah, you see that's my point precisely."

"I can understand," Quadros said.

"Well I'm relieved to hear it. I'm relieved to hear it but that's no longer the—"

"You are told your daughter's time with us will end on such-and-such a date."

"Precisely, precisely and—"

"And then," Quadros interrupted, his lips moving, the rest of him as still as a creeper-choked ruin come upon through jungle, "imprecision. I understand. Imprecision and inconsistency. And now you have been told we need a few days more."

"Three."

Quadros said nothing.

Eden blinked, he braided his fingers, he looked at them. He wanted to be reasonable.

"Didn't," he attempted to begin in a firm voice but half-croaked, "you say three? Three days more?"

"I have a confession to make," Quadros said.

"Make it then, by all means."

It was disconcerting to hear the man's apology delivered in the same unflinching, unmodulated way, but at least it was good to hear that Quadros felt bad. Quadros, Quadros said, knew Eden did not think highly of the exercises. That Quadros appreciated. He wanted to emphasize, he said, Eden's patience as Nora's father. And was, if it helped, sorry.

"Well that's better, ah, certainly at minimum that's—"

"What I must confess," the other said calmly, "is that I have myself been uncertain how much time would be necessary. Nora is an apt pupil. She has made enormous progress—I enjoy controlling her. But in matters such as these you must understand that one cannot always be precise. There is often an element of uncertainty. It may take three days more, it may take twenty—"

"What!?"

"Twenty, ten, thirty, I want to be honest with you, I wish I could know sitting here right now, but I cannot. And I have been guilty, and I confess it, of giving you shorter spans than I had suspected we would need because—"

"It is no. Longer. Relevant what—"

"Excuse me let me finish. I was fearful you would balk at the longer estimates so for Nora's sake I was deceptive, I was perforce deceptive."

"This has come to an end. Right now. Not three days from now.

Not one." My uncle's face was red and he could hear his heartbeat silvery-sheeny twice a second in his ears. "Not an hour. It's over."

Quadros gets up.

"Would you like more tea Mr. Hope?"

"No! This is not going the way you said it would. I have been patient, I have been very patient, somewhat at the expense of my, er, composure at times, but my patience is at an end. Your relationship with my daughter is to end, not tomorrow, not this evening, not an hour from now, but now. That's all there is to it. There's nothing more to discuss."

"Very well," Quadros said. "Then we'll not talk."

He walked out.

My uncle in a tizzy nearly tripped nearly running out of that quiet house into the day, breathing heavily, to stand in some spruces' shade where Quadros was righting the wheelbarrow he'd dumped.

Unsure what to say, grooming his moustache he inventoried his emotions. "Well let's," he said—relieved to hear the equanimity in his voice, "at least let's not stop talking."

Always better to talk than fight. Who could gainsay that?

Quadros' hands guided the wheelbarrow on its simple wheel past the fence of kennel wire to a barrow of scoured river rocks piled in a pyramid at the grove's edge, where the trees' floor of needles met green grass.

"Let me tell you," Quadros began as they walked—and Eden fairly trotted to keep up and hear. "Let me tell you what I do."

*I wish you would,* my uncle thought but didn't say.

He was proud of himself for resisting the temptation to use such an easy weapon as irony.

"She's a good student," Quadros said, bending to lower the grainy handles. He set the conveyance's legs down. "A fine student. Fascinating. I discipline myself. I'm trying to have power, not distraction." He delivered the rest of what he had to say looking off into the trees, arms at loose attention, neck straight, flowing, clean hair faultless. "I speak to you of controlling, having power over. This distresses you but it is honesty. What teacher exercises no control? I have power over in order to give power to. I exercise my willpower to rear the wills of my followers. I discipline myself not to become involved with Nora, whom I shall miss. She's compelling. She has a will, make no mistake."

"Oh I make no mistake, I make no mistake whatever."

"The revolution of the human will requires discipline. The content once mattered," Quadros said. "No longer. Our incessant thinking and machines have gone too far. The will has to take over." Quadros' words, so laughably remote from intercourse, amused my uncle only at their beginning, for soon, as the thin man talked on, his words took Eden by the hand. "The radical-liberal flag," that seldom-breaking voice said, "the arch-conservative one. In the end there's no difference. Religious fundamentalism, the religion of the state. No difference. The political tenor of the time is always wrong because it has always built into a glut of whatever it started out as. It calls forth the tide of its opposite, which in time calls forth the original. But this time . . ." Quadros waited for the wind to go quiet. "This time," he said, "the mind has gone too far." The branches of the little grove of suburban evergreens subsided and a pair of middle-aged men, each carrying a dog, passed into the trees' far shadows. "It is time to break the cycle and stabilize the world. It would have been better to do it your way—far better to have done it your way."

"She said 'involved,'" a fascinated Eden ventured.

"I know what she told you. She said 'I'm involved with a man who's smarter than you are,' did she not."

"Why yes that's—"

"As we explained it was not, is not, physical in the way you think. Of course it's ludicrous to say I'm smarter than you. But it was what she wanted. She wanted," Quadros' momentarily high voice listed, "to shock you, impress you, and finally to show you she had something to think about too, could have thoughts of her own without having to get them from you. So we let her have her fantasy knowing, mind you, that that was what it was. She had to face it. Face it, admit it, before she could have it, use it. Follow?"

"Of course. Heh. But ah—"

"You want assurance."

"Well of course I want assurance. Look here my good man. You tell me you and she are not involved in any er, sexual, ah, yet ah, apparently there is in fact a—"

"That's right. But it's not physical. Not that she's not available. But no—nothing. You have my word."

"Well good," my uncle said. "Yes," he said, stroking his chin and thinking—at least he thought he was thinking. It didn't quite feel as if he were. (He hoped he was.) "Good, good," he heard his own deep pleasing voice say. "So that's that."

"That's right."

Sipping his tea sparely, with what oriental sculpturesque, without tongue, does Q sip—invulnerable—his tea . . .

They talked of transmogrification, changing a thing grotesquely, and reincarnation, the turning wheel of how many people you've been. Of Vico, the first modern historian with his notion of history as the story of the birth, maturation and decline of societies rather than of great men or God in action, and how Vico seemed almost to believe in the reincarnation, in a new time and context each time, of historical cycles . . .

One of the two men who had been carrying the dogs knocked on the doorjamb and stepped respectfully in. He did not have a hat, but he carried himself as if he did, and were holding it in hand. He wanted to know what to do. He asked, in a voice from his upper throat, if Quadros thought they had been there long enough. How long, Quadros asked the pupil, had they been there? Half an hour. Quadros said that was not long enough. Maybe it isn't long enough, the man said, but he, referring to the second man, doesn't like it.

Doesn't like what? My uncle bewilderedly asked this question when the men had gone.

"What they have to do," Quadros said sharply.

And ah, ah—ahhh, what was that?

Quadros seemed annoyed. Or something tasted wrong to him. He made no gesture, for Quadros scarcely ever made a gesture, and in fact the big-scale, placid face barely seemed to change.

"What they have to," Quadros answered. "What they're told to."

"What's that?"

"They take the dogs out, beat them, chain them to a tree and leave them there. Whether or not it's horrible depends on your point of view."

"This is . . ." My uncle was in disbelief. "Surely it isn't, heh, I mean—"

"It's quite true. They do it."

"For god's sake man, why?"

"Because I tell them to."

While my uncle was trying to deal with the astonishment of this Quadros explained that horrible or not it was an exercise, an important one. It was an exercise, Quadros said, in the exercise of the will. Quadros himself happened to think that to treat any living thing that way was horrible, but the point was what did the two men think? Quadros predicted that in time the second man, the one who hadn't spoken, would refuse. At that point he—Quadros—would have a decision to make. As to the other, the first man, Quadros dismissed him: weak. He would become not only uninteresting, but no longer welcome here.

My uncle was shaking his head. He must say something. But he couldn't look at Quadros, who sat in a chair. Quadros' high voice was jeweled with sparks sometimes. At other times it was lispy, tongue lingering deviatively against teeth tips. At the same time, strangely enough, it was a quite normal voice when you thought back on it and tried to remember.

"Your daughter," he said, "is pushing a wheelbarrow. Find her."

She was loading it with rocks. Leaning into and out of the sunlight the trees let through in a patch, she answered her father's questions without stopping. Yes, she had driven up. Yes, the sunlight was warm. She was moving the rocks to a different part of the lawn. Because tomorrow, she explained, I have to move them back. He asked in a small voice if she was quite sure she wanted to be doing this. She did stop now, a scythe of bob-long brown hair swinging (damp from her efforts). That wasn't the question to ask, she said. She went back to her labors. Wondering what to do he went past the empty kennels and back indoors.

"Would you like more tea?"

"You don't hurt her do you?"

"Sometimes psychologically."

"I can understand the necessity of discipline of a sort. That," my uncle said, "I can ah, understand. I can, uh . ."

The other waited.

"But any physical." My uncle was thinking. His hand floated, but could not find a moustache. "Any physical

"Of course."

"Is unacceptable. Absolutely."

"Of course."

"I want that understood."

"Of course."

"Animals are people too."

"Of course they are," Quadros said.

"So long as you take my point. This is awfully important, whether you realize it or not. This Cartesian distinction supposedly separating animals from humans is tenuous, it's very tenuous."

"Of course."

"So it's psychologically, er, the discipline—"

"Of course."

"I have been patient. I have been exceptionally patient."

"Yes," Quadros said, "you have."

My uncle looked down at the pallid Fabergé hand, and took it.

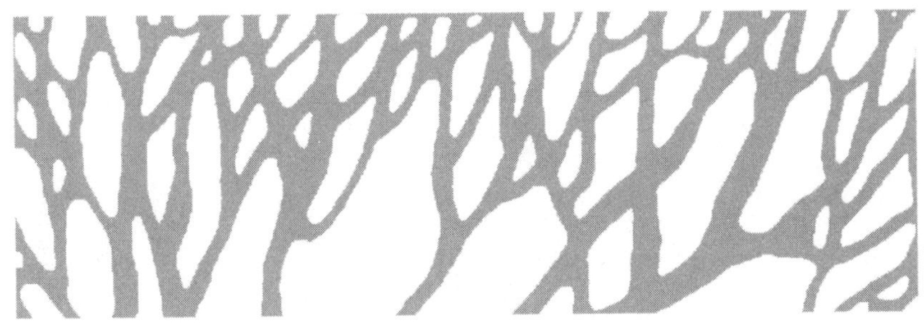

# 21

That night, several hours into sleep he came awake in a roaring silence sweaty and with a temperature to sit bolt upright. Moments later he banged out of the room and down the halls to Nora's room, in which, this night, she was. He knocked hard. He opened the door without waiting. She was sitting up in artificial light in her bed with the covers held to her, squinting at him. Even in his agitation he couldn't blame her for being wary. One night not long ago, after the bungalow had been quiet in sleep a few hours, he had scared Nora half to death first with his protracted scream and then, only partly awake, his lurching and banging about the darkness of his bedroom groggily trying to find either a light or the robber, or ghost, that had in fact only been his hand, on which he had slept in such a way as to put it to sleep then rolled and flopped—somehow—over his face . . the hand totally without sensation, so that when he had come awake, here covering his face in the black night had been a huge hand—not his!

She went on squinting at him, trying to bring herself fully into conscious focus.

"Nora you don't hurt animals, you don't harm animals in any way as a part of all this . . do you?"

Groggily she shook her head.

"Do you absolutely promise this? Do you abso—"

"Dad I don't," she said rhythmically in her annoyance, "do it. I refused the very first time."

"We gotta get her out of there," Nancy shouted, "don't we? Maybe we don't, maybe I'm wrong, but I'm not. I'm not wrong. I'm right. Did you hear about the dogs? That's where you draw a line, period, I'm deadly serious, we've gotta get her out. Out, out, out. Have you talked to her?"

I said I had not, and we conversed frantically for several minutes more. But we weren't settling anything, and I said I had to go.

"You *what!?*" she screeched.

"I have to go. Is that ok?"

"No! It's not! *You* don't have to go," she cried, "*I* have to go!" It was her phone disorder, a symptom of which was that it had always to be she who had to go. "So," she raced—I could imagine her Uncle Lim's sweatbeads flying off her, "*I* gotta go. Gotta-go-gotta-go, right now. Remember, it's not *you* who's gotta go, it's *me*. Gotta go right now, sorry, bye. *Sorry*. BYE!"

"The old angler," my uncle showed me, "stands here, in a stretch of water I think much like this one." He pointed over the gray-green subtly mussed sweep of the river, here before the next rapids, where he envisioned the movie grandson standing and fishing with his granddad in the pair's poignant final outing. I found out later that the studio—Chase, Zany, everybody—had given up on the project and couldn't believe the naive energy my uncle was still pouring into a torrent of written and drawn treatment sketches and sundry plot notes and snatches of dialogue. Beguiled, Zany gave orders to keep it going. Barely. In some ways like Rairia and her cause, my uncle swam hard toward his goal: Anther in a film so shockingly simple that when released it would wrench audiences out of the herd-haze of violent intrigue and rote worship of change—his words, as I stood on the bank while he fished and explained—in whose grips the world's screens, speakers, catalectic conversations and twenty-four-hour digital-color newspapers had us.

Of Rairia there was little to say. She was living a life of hotel suites and phone banks. A few rich individuals sustained interest enough in her bizarre quest to support her over the years, and years, indeed, it turned into. The media were wowed by her crazy idea. But in time they would forget her. The great bovine eye of the public would swing elsewhere. Rairia didn't care one way or the other. She kept at it, collecting signatures, dogging the reception rooms of congresspersons, marching in the streets. A patina of legend started to shine—her energy and faith were as interesting as the content of what she was trying to do. She didn't of course want, though Eden was fond of putting it so, to repeal the whole Declaration, just the words "and the pursuit of Happiness." If one's Life and Liberty are sufficiently protected, she argued, the rest's redundant: one's as free to pursue Happiness as a Govt. ought to insure. She feared, in her Old Testament fervor, that Govt. these days was forgetting the word *pursue* and slipping into trying—an easy job—to convince the electorate that the Declaration insures not only that all citizens be free to pursue Happiness but that they all be Happy. So, laboring bravely and in vain for a lost though intriguing cause, and never giving up, Rairia Hope (in time she would drop her wolf-name "Gall") became a hero. Who knows but that at some indeterminate future date beyond this story's end, she or a follower will have succeeded . . . however for now (for then that is) it gave her, in the best sense, something to do, and that made her happy.

He missed her. If she would return, give up her campaign and come home and stay with him and go back to her seas of deskpapers and her complaining and her nastiness and affection, he would madly want her gone. But since she was effectively gone, visiting now only two or three times a year, he could not stop himself from yearning for and dreaming of her back and now of course with this business with Nora there was added reason to wish Rairia here. In addition to which he found that since her dramatic Christmas entrance, in her new haircut and with that curve of muscle on either bare (though it was winter) upper arm, his mind's eye had been seeing her a lot.

He had recently caught up with her by phone at the Lawrence,

Kansas bed-and-breakfast where she had just come in from jogging. They had a confused conversation in which Eden, closing his eyes, imagining Rairia and wanting her, kept trying to impress on her the details and gravity of the Nora situation, and Rairia kept saying things like "Good for her!", "What's wrong with that?" and "More power to her!" The miscommunication was due to his self-admitted circumspection of circumlocution, as he tried to describe to his old battle-mate what was going on. "Ahh, then too," he confessed, reeling in, "I do retain a certain ambivalence on the matter myself. And I do believe she heard it in what I was saying." Maybe on the other hand, it had occurred to him as he hung up, it hadn't been miscommunication at all. Maybe Rairia fully understood the risk and dark mysteriousness of what Nora was doing, and approved. It was the end of the century after all. Life—she had insisted before ringing off—is a war, let the girl explore, if it's right it's right, if it's a mistake it'll only make her stronger. Briefly and furiously Raira had then "declared," seized by an angry need to, more odds and ends of leftover resentment against him, the genuine rage of which diatribe made him glad the transaction was taking place long-distance. As soon as it was over she lightly apologized, tearing off her dripping terrycloth headband and propping a foot to untie a running shoe. She assured him it was necessary, "though I almost said to her what can one expect, ahh, from—heehee, what can you expect," he rhetorically asked, reeling in, securing his rod and hippo-climbing the bank, "from somebody seriously bent on taking 'and the pursuit of Happiness' out of—" He didn't finish because there was a surprise slickness of richly brown mud halfway up and, nearly going in myself, I had to sideslide down and reach out, our hands, a moment, a foot apart reaching toward each other theatrically. Then he went—sucking cannonball splash in the not particularly shallow water, and I waited to see if he was safe—he was, laughing, splashing erect, a boobish equipment-laden Triton, so I wouldn't have to get wet myself, but I did, sliding helpless just as he was starting to say this gave him an idea for another scene.

"I have no proof," he told me, stuffing newspaper balls in my soaked boots by a small fire in a small room back at the bungalow, "that they ever actually beat those dogs. They say they do, but I can't believe anyone would gratuitously see this dries them inside and out. I wonder if it isn't just another 'exercise,' perhaps to see my reaction? My father did this for me," he rumbled quietly, setting my boots, dark with streamwater, in range of the flames' heat. "He was not the best at business but he was wonderful in the field, a wonderful man out of doors unlike hee—much to his chagrin unlike his oafish son. Lim of course was always competent, but I would fall in, trip over a log or get caught in a bush, but that one time . . ." His brown shimmery eyes went deep in the orange flames of the little summertime fire he'd laid, and you could see him remembering. "I fell in the lake," he said subduedly. "Got a big largemouth on and stood up in the canoe, he went in too, it was cold, the water was icy and we were in danger awhile—I can still feel his arms. I quit trying to fish after that. When we got home he laid a fire, it was September or October, not July like today but . . ." voice trailed off. Twin blazes reflected in glazed, fondly remembering eyes ". . . he was patient with me that day. Very . . patient with me. Never . . . fished after that.

"As I left," he went on, staring at the flames and changing—it took me a moment to realize—the subject without a change of expression or the least transitional gesture, "I saw into a room where Nora and four or five others were gathering. He'd ended my meeting with him by, ah, why by simply without a word getting up, pushing his chair forward, turning," he listed for me, "and going—he has a way of gliding—from the room managing not to be in the least impolite about it and—" Nora passed the doorway carrying some books but he didn't see her "—then as I say, I glimpsed them in that farther room and she was getting to her knees on a floorpad of some kind. They each seemed to have one. He was there at the center and I must tell you John, I must report . . ." he blinked the flames from his stare and sitting forward began stuffing his own sodden boots "—report," he said as he worked, "that I am unresolved. I do not like it. And yet, he has a power. One must grant that he does have a certain, ah, force about him. More importantly," he went on, "this whole thing appears to be doing her good, some good at least." I reflected that if this was how he'd spoken of it to Rairia, of course she'd've said what she said. "Some good anyway ah, for better or worse. I've called a friend of mine however, someone who knows about this kind of dynamic, and he may help, in fact I believe he's agreed to. It would be so easy," he said, "to order Nora to do this, do that, desist, forbid her, tell the police, take her on a trip. But better I think to exercise patience. However, as I say—" here my uncle's watery eyes went into a focus of resolve as he stared into the beauties of combustion "—I have called my friend. I have taken that action."

Nance snickered over the phone at the idea of her mother's crusade, yet she respected Rairia for it and was astounded by the press it was still, that summer, getting, psychologists and even a scattering of priests coming out in favor on the previous evening's news. She barked: "But that's not why I called now listen, I have engaged in a modicum of further research on this whole thing and the mystery—" down went the voice into a register of low, supersecure furtive alarm "—deepens. For no one knows. No one knows where this guy comes from. No one knows where his money comes from. If even half what I'm hearing is true then part of what we have to make a decision on here is whether or not we want to contemplate legal—" *click*—dialtone . . . I didn't have her number so I waited. A moment passed, and a moment more. The phone rang. "It's me, sorry, I got agitated at the thought of taking legal measures. In my stress I was pressing too hard on it and it hung up. Hah. Dad's no help by the way. To be frank I think most of the time he's off in the la-la-land of this stupid movie, although he is apparently thinking of calling in this friend he has, Kyle Kulka? From down at the U? Whoever *he* is. Maybe he can shed some light, but I don't like it. I want everyone to know I'm on record as not liking this whole thing one little bit, you know me, my instinct—" silence . . . *click*. Dialtone again . . . I waited, baffled, and picked up on the first ring. "Sorry," she laughed through a tensed jaw. "I did it again. I was grinding my teeth and inadvertently hung up, sorry. Anyway, this is my *sister.* This is my sister and I guess we have to just trust her and keep an eye on the oh my god. Michael. How did you get up there? Don't move! *Don't!* Alan how did—gawd, look I gotta go. Good-luck-*Bye!*"

Kyle said there were some wonderful studies. Eden gave him details over the phone and he drove up in a Mazda. Kyle's warm, reasonable smile, round eyes and head of curly hair shouted of health in the June sun. The latest thinking, Kyle said, snapping Eden with the roofs of the bungalow in the background, indicated Special Treatment, and/or "Childing," and/or Observation as the three most effective techniques in similar cases. Intimidation as a rehabilitative tool was out of favor, Kyle hummed, swiveling to change focus and shutter-speed and immemorialize the blue jay that glided out of shadow down into, and out of, the vibrating light. *And,* he added, within accuracy-tolerance of plus/minus ten percent it had been established that in response to each case's particular needs the long-term aim of diffusing a subject's core maladjustment was best served in a context of flux.

They decided to try Observation.

Kyle was up a day at a time several times that July and August before Eden, Henry Anther and I trained out west for the annual big fishing convocation.

He was introduced to Nora, and explained to her that he was her friend.

She looked at him.

His fists casually in the pockets of his baggy casuals, rocking on the balls of his feet Kyle outlined his academic background, cited his friendship with her dad, and expressed his desire, if she might like to think it over, to learn more about her work with Quadros and perhaps even tag along sometime.

Quadros showed them the gun. It was an early-model Walther 7.65mm *Polizei Pistole,* a weapon for the masses—self-loading, double-action, stolid yet streamlined in the barrel's underswept chin, solid and safe with its 8-shot magazine. As quick to get the first shot off as a revolver.

"Evil things," Eden said, unable to take his eyes from it.

Nora had said "Sure" when Kyle had finished his glowing introductory speech. She had excused herself, made a call, and half an hour later, sliding silent into the bungalow like a slipstream through a wall crack Quadros found them and ignoring Kyle showed Eden the gun.

Nora watched her father. Kyle Kulka had recoiled at the sight of the weapon cradled expertly in Quadros' palm. Though Quadros' fingers were open and not around the grip, and the barrel was pointing harmlessly at no one, the sight and physical presence of the firearm seemed to cause a bizarre new persona to descend on my uncle—he just stared at it, as if held, blinded by the presence and fact of it. He wanted to ask a question, but the sight of the pistol and his disorientation made vague and smoky in his mind the questions he wanted to ask and the thoughts he wanted to think. He stared at the stocky, checkered grip growing at a slant like a fat trunk into the great-girthed steel branch of the barrel.

"Evil?" Quadros asked, hefting his forged fruit.

"He subjects his ah, students," my uncle told Kyle, still helpless to take his eyes from the side arm, "to various 'exercises' as he calls them."

Kyle had collected himself and was observing. Scratching his curls ferociously. The central strategy of the observation technique was to grow the subject's natural human urge to behave well: you are being watched, judged, Observation nonverbally said. It had worked time and time again in controlled experiment after controlled experiment until there could realistically no longer be any doubt. Of course secondarily Observation also gleaned invaluable empirical data on an ongoing basis.

Nora looked at the gun, at her father, at Quadros. She turned and looked out a window, waiting, her canyon jaw set.

"What do you make of it?" my uncle asked Kyle.

Since he couldn't stop looking at the firearm he was misunderstood by Quadros as having directed this question to Quadros who said: "I don't make anything of it. I'm showing it to you."

"Ahhh—" the brown, lit eyes "—to see what *I* make of it, isn't that right?"

"Perhaps."

Kyle Kulka observed, saying nothing. But that evening in the post-analysis he told Eden that he, Eden, had been laudably patient, at least at first.

"If not evil," my uncle, staring at it, heard himself say—and he tried to put some gravure into his tone, "at least nasty, at least ahh—if not nasty certainly dangerous. Very dangerous. You do not dare disagree with that."

"I don't think I do," Quadros said.

To tear himself away from this impasse and infuriating paralysis, my uncle launched into—as he saw it—derisive action. To mock Quadros he heard himself asking Quadros if it were loaded.

"I don't think so," Quadros said.

Quadros watched him. Kyle was watching both of them. Nora gazed out her window, a jaw muscle rippling. My uncle of course was unable to look anywhere but at the piece.

"Not loaded?"

"I don't think it is," Quadros repeated.

"Oh well er, could I hold it?"

"You may," Quadros said. He held the weapon on his palm out for my uncle awkwardly to pick at with scrabbling fingers as if it were an item wedged in a supermarket shelf.

The serious cool weight, the darkness, the lethal shape, the metal feel, the fact of it, and its use, here in his hand, muddled him worse even than he'd been.

It would be a good idea now to make a joke to get control of the situation, he hazily decided. He pointed it.

It could hardly be said that he aimed. Holding it ineptly—more or less as if intending to use it, he extended it, just above waist level, and far out from the body, to "aim" up approximately at the top shelf of his southern wall of books.

They all now were staring at him.

"Go ahead," he snarled, "*make my day.*"

Their silence was disconcerting. It was supposed to have been a joke.

"Heehee," he said apologetically and tried to lower the weapon but, oddly, couldn't.

"You call me forth," Quadros said.

"What's that supposed to mean?" Eden made this inquiry turning vaguely toward the other with the gun turning and Quadros smoothly without alarm reached out as the black muzzle-hole swung toward him gently to deflect it, with two fingers, away from any of them, and, until satisfied that Eden realized that where it was pointing now was where it was supposed to be pointing, keep it there.

"Your books," Quadros said, "have no evil in them."

"My what? You mean, er, you don't mean the physic-, er . . you mean the fiction. The fantasies."

"Yes."

"Why, heh, how could you be so wrong? Of course they have evil in them. For heaven's sake." Back on the solid ground of something he knew about he rakishly shut his left eye and took rough aim again at the top shelf. "Haven't you read any of them?"

"I've read them," Quadros said.

"Well for god's sake man, for pity's sake, does one—" aiming and, as he talked, imagining himself taking a perfect potshot "—I mean does one need to make a list?"

Quadros started to speak but Eden didn't let him.

"I mean the Night Master, the gnome fathers," he listed, waveringly false-aiming. "And you might not have perceived it or heh, excuse me, you might not have read far enough but ah, that little purple village Gwen passes through toward the end of her early journeys? There's evil in those lampposts, genuine, explicable evil. And of course the whole episode of—"

"Not real evil."

"Uh—hm? Ah. Ah. Lim has sent you. That's it, isn't it? Did he? Did Lim send you? And this is merely a—"

"No," Quadros said.

"Hm, well." My uncle smiled cleverly. He squinted, one-eyed, and played with aiming, trying to see if he could keep the sight steady against the flow of books. "Be that as it may," he said with cunning. Heady in the field of the weapon he wielded, and in the strangeness of the whole situation, he had entered that overlay state of thinking in which, out of kilter, the intellectual ratiocinates only meagerly, is, in fact, mentally operating in a dangerous untethered world of memory snippets from films and personal fantasy. "I certainly ahh, heehee I certainly," he said insouciantly (he hoped) toying with his aiming, "don't mean to seem condescending. But it's been a long time since I've worked on my little tetralogy, which my poor brother is desperate that I finish, and sometimes he schemes to, ahh, you see to nudge me along."

"Your brother is not well," Quadros said.

"Hm," Eden said. He tried to conceal his surprise by concentrating even harder on preventing the gunsight from swaying left, then back to the right, then left again. "Lim'll be all right. Do you know what 'tetralogy' means?"

Quadros said nothing in answer but a black wave billowed out through the air to pass through my uncle.

"My heh, my dear sir—my dear dear sir . . . allow me to assure you—"

Inadvertently Eden fired a 7.65mm Browning round through the spine of his *Moby Dick*.

The discharge was quite loud in the room, thin, quick-loud like a slap, and the recoil was considerably more substantial in its effect on my uncle than it would have been had the weapon been properly gripped. In fact the Walther had nearly flown from his hand.

"Ahhhh," he said in a whisper. "Hahhh . . ."

Quadros made a sign and Nora was instantly gone.

Kyle, who admirably stood his ground—white-faced—did his level best to continue to observe.

In the ringing powder-smell Eden was trying to hand the gun to Quadros who wouldn't take it. He managed to find his voice and croak: "You said it wasn't loaded."

"No, I said I didn't think it was."

"What's the difference? It certainly *was* loaded—was this some perverted attempt to teach a lesson? Because if it was I must certainly—"

"No no," Quadros said. "I'm just trying to destroy the language where I can."

"Wonderful. You say things for effect don't you? To see the impact your words have. All the blather about the will is a ruse, this business about discipline and exercises—it's just the manipulation of words . . hah! I'm right aren't I? You're a thinker too in your way!"

Quadros looked at him mildly.

Why had Quadros brought the gun? Kyle listed possible reasons. He and Eden analyzed each, that evening, sitting on the side deck in the forest night wall of buzzing insect song and stars. Here and there in the branches a late-season firefly disappeared, appearing—light in a point—disappearing again, and, if you watched the blackness where it had been, appearing again, near where it had been, but Nora did not come back so Kyle was unable to have the dialogue with her that he wanted to have until the following morning at breakfast, after which he got in his Mazda. She, Kyle and an observing Eden (under Kyle's tutelage Eden was practicing Observation) sat at the round breakfast table under the breakfast-area skylight.

Dr. Kulka asked Nora how she felt—how did she feel about herself, how did she feel about her work with Quadros. With the white sleeves of his cotton broadcloth shirt rolled up off his well-exercised forearms, he asked her questions about sports, her friends, her father. Nora looked sleepy but was attentive. She answered in order, good, fantastic, soccer, Vanessa, sorry for him. The moment was less uncomfortable than it might've been and before leaving, but after Nora's swirl departure for work, Kyle told Eden his daughter was displaying three of the five classic signs of response. The gun, after all, was not the point, Kyle said—it had been a gimmick, an action device, an excuse (Kyle smiled and scratched his forearm, looking at it)—an 'exercise' if you will. Quadros had a head and a heart too, it was important to remember, Kyle said. He said he would be back in four days.

That Nora spoke little was to be expected, Kyle said. "You should try it sometime," he joshed his friend, slapping Eden's shoulder. "*And.* If we keep our eye on the fact that she's trying to change her whole life here, her habits, maybe even her values, we can be as patient as we have to be. Hold still, right like that." Snapping his shutter Dr. Kulka caught my uncle's silhouette: sun-thrown shadow on white wall. I still have it. "*And.* See Quadros' scheme for things fits right in. He's trying to teach these people how to find their *own* deep wants, *whatever* those might be, *instead* of someone else's, or some tradition's or peer group's. If we want her to move away from Quadros we have to realize she first has to want to."

Quadros apparently agreed. At least he nodded, sitting catlike behind his table while half a dozen of his followers, Nora among them, awaited him in the larger room two doorways away.

"You agree?" Kyle Kulka asked him.

Quadros looked at Kyle, not nodding this time, or perhaps he had been about to nod but a wail of a voice called for him through the doorways. The exercise session was late in getting started, the voice wailed, a broken rule: "Wait!" Quadros shouted without moving.

"We're all finished," Kyle accommodated, "don't let us hold anything up. We'll just observe if that's all right."

One had to assume it was, for Q rose and went away through the doorways to stand at the center of his pupils on their mats. He spoke to them, as Eden and Kyle stood along a wall listening, of "your deepest ambitions." At first it was the usual psycho-jargon but then without warning they realized Q had changed to talking about them, speaking now of Nora's "helpers." He said they had explained to him that they wanted Nora to want what she wanted, what she "truly," Q said not gesturing with his hanging arms, "wants and not what someone else wants for her or she deceives herself she wants because she thinks she ought to want it or because it sounds good or like fun, correct?" Quadros waited. "Correct?" he asked again, not raising his voice. He was looking at the floor. He lifted a finger, and in unison his pupils on their knees on their mats asked loudly: "*Correct?*"

A shaken Eden and Kyle looked at each other. "Yes," Kyle answered, "yes correct, yes."

"Well let's see," Quadros said. "Nora?"

Quadros did not look at her as she got up, fawnlike, to come to his side, stand, eyes lowered, then, lifting them—unafraid—meet his gaze.

He gave her a second. He stood, arms at his sides, a universe of empty air between him and the girl, communing, his eyes, her mild blue trusting gaze. Nora's bravely lifted chin. And still his arms hung at his sides, full sleeves of blowsy poplin—impossible to know how thin the arms inside are. There was plenty of secondary sunlight shining on the dance-studio-buffed hardwood. The others, including the two who had, or had not, whipped dogs, waited on their knees.

"Yes?" Nora said.

"Nora, what do you want."

She gulped. Her head, my uncle thought, jerked to try to look in his and Kyle's direction but didn't make it. She stared into the eyes, in their nimbus of shampooed hair.

"To help people if I can get strong. I'd like to teach, to help other people, there's so much pain and ignorance. If I could just help like one person, an old person, a child, to learn something they didn't know or unlock—" she pushed her hair off her brow "—unlock an emotion they didn't know they had," she said, to the amazement of her father who had never heard her talk quite this way, "or I don't know, something constructive. It could even be helping other people indirectly by growing food, food for people who are hungry."

Quadros slapped her face with open fingers. The sting of the fast smack of his fingers against Nora's cheek was the only sound in the room, and for seconds afterward the echo, in my uncle's memory, of the sharp sound was as loud as it was real.

He started to move, but Nora's voice stopped him.

"Yeah really," she tremblingly answered her teacher's question, which had been posed in the slap, "I'd like to be on a beach somewhere, on a beach somewhere with other kids playing volleyball forever, you're right."

"Better."

"Better," three or four others echoed their leader in undertone.

Kyle Kulka made it crystal clear in no uncertain terms that he decried violence of any kind. He was forceful, even loud about it back at the bungalow that evening when he and my uncle had had, as Kyle put it, a chance to cool down and regain perspective. At least they'd observed, Kyle said. He wanted Eden to know he'd written it all down too. Maybe it was time to start talking about separating Nora from the context up there.

At the same time maybe she really did want nothing more than to play beach volleyball forever . . . they wondered if Quadros were thinking of trying to get beyond that. Kyle suggests a memo, a piece of paper laying out agreed-on terms. Guidelines. On his next visit he produced it, and they sat down with Quadros with it. To their surprise he agreed to all of it, initialed it with a flourish: Q. One of its provisions was that Nora would henceforth spend only two days a week with him. After two weeks it would go down to one visit a week, and in a month's time her relationship with Quadros would be over.

"Yes yes," Kyle beamed, "I know, you think you've been through this, you set deadlines and he missed them, I know, you told me, but *you never wrote it down Eden.* A human entity is *never* more observed than when it has agreed to and signed something. *And.* Hold still . . . like that."

There was a study out of Palo Alto on reward that Kyle wanted to look into. He mentioned also, his next trip up, some seminal work that was being done with interactive reassurance software—for Eden, not Nora. He wanted too to see if he could unpack this Quadros some more, get Q talking, get background, some reads, feels . . . the week after, when Quadros tore the agreement they'd signed into shreds and beckoning with a crook'd finger led them to a powder room where, fluttering the white scraps into the toilet, he flushed, Kyle could scarcely contain his excitement. "Progress," he couldn't wait to get back to the bungalow to tell Eden when they sat down for post-event analysis. "You may not see it but I do. He's revealing himself. He's allowing us to see him—that's a big step. It's a big part of what Observation does. You can't imagine what a big first step that was. He's making himself vulnerable. *And*—what he said? Did that bother you? That we inspire him? Let me finish let me finish, of course it's ridiculous, of course it is. But that's not the point. The point is *he believes it!*"

His curly hair smiling, the light of pureed reason flooding his eyes, his white rolled-up sleeves cheerful, Kyle would've wished to take readings had Earth's actual clouds gloriously hemorrhaged a Savior down—get data, plus-or-minus accurate. When Quadros was not violent—was behaving well by Eden's and Kyle's lights—they made demands of him, pressing him to be better. If he balked or was bad they would repeat, threateningly, their demands, then temper them, then give them up and make new ones, of a less demanding nature, and when these were ignored or rejected they tempered these, finally giving them up. After a stint of this, tempted to throw their hands up they persevered, making now their mildest demands to date and threatening, if *these* were mocked, to take them back. Nora was right. Her father was a messy man. Once he had not been. In his youth, as a master of chess crisply plucks and places, he had made his mental moves. But for decades now my uncle had been thinking too much. His adventure fantasies might or might not get finished. They were fun, an outpouring in primary colors. Standard regulation castles: a surprise or two, some nice twists . . . editing Henry Anther's angling wisdom was easy. The film however was turning into something else, a nasty obsession, a preoccupation without flywheel balance. This was becoming increasingly obvious to everyone except my uncle, who kept nattering away at Henry on the subject on the train going out.

"I want them ah, us . . to make a motion picture," he told us feelingly, "that has mud on its boots. To craft something plain instead of contriving. Mask," he said distantly as we crossed the sunlit cornfields, "masquerade, manip—" the train hit a new rail and as if the change made his talk change Eden shook himself, turned from the jiggling picture window. "Henry? Don't you feel the same way?"

With his usual extravagance he'd taken three deluxe suites for us along the carpeted, carpet-walled upper hall of the silver car. We were sitting in Eden's compartment.

"Henry? I mean ah, er . . don't you?"

"Wal sure."

"They haven't called or tried to get in touch with you in any way have they?"

"Nah."

"You're quite sure."

"Aw yeah, I'm quite sure."

"You continue to be comfortable with my acting as . . ."

"Aw

"As a—"

"Sure," Anther said.

"Henry they want to figuratively speaking put makeup on your soul. They'll look through your closets and then from scratch make clothes that are more real than your own, and when we get on site they'll wait 'til the light's just so and they'll tell you where to stand and how to fish and what to say and how to feel about it while you're saying it."

"Wal."

"I'm serious. I want you to be in it of course, but I want to protect—have it ah, unfold on our terms. Unless we take care they'll be telling you who you are and how and why and where and when and in what colors—"

"Ain't that art?"

"Are you sure you haven't talked with them? I've told them. I've said—I've been very honest with you about this. I've told them in effect to stay away, stay away from you."

Not at heart conspiratorial, much as it would've disappointed him to hear me say so, my uncle did love to play at conspiracy, to spin plots and plans and webs of nuance conversationally and ideationally far more complex than the situation warranted, over such a trivial decision for example as how to drop a car off at a local garage, or who would give Thanksgiving dinner. But this business with the film was different. This was a different Eden. Too serious. You stood back from him when he got going on the film. He was desperate to protect Henry—if that's what it was. He was determined without patience, humor or qualification to see the exact, precise film made that he wanted to see made.

"You appreciate that don't you? I mean 'appreciate' in the sense of understand, ah, that I want to insulate you, safeguard, preserve . . . I'm not, well, it goes without saying," my uncle said, his voice getting smaller, "that I'm not looking for gratitude."

Pinching his nose as if about to go underwater he stared, with the Nebraska sun filling his eyes, at the endless green corn.

"They been in touch with ya?"

My uncle nodded to the side to indicate me, who had lately heard from Zany Foss and delivered Zany's message (most of it) to Eden.

"Yes they have," he said cautiously. "They're apparently sending two people to sort of . . meet us."

He thought about this. Something moved, we all saw it. The long train barreling past had unnerved it— "You know," he said, "I was thinking . . in the last fishing scene, before the scene when you learn you're to die, when you and the boy . . look at that." Tail high, the slight brown fox, head high, shoulders, as it were, back, like a Tennessee walker trotting went away from the tracks in the morning light and up through the grasses into the broad, sunlit upland seas of corn. "When you're out there on the water together," he went on, "I'm trying to get them to see," he insisted cadentially, "that the way to get life in a jar is, paradoxically enough, just to, ah, why ah, why is to let you and whoever plays the boy just go out and fish, just fish—and shoot, shoot 'til the barrel melts, see what one has, edit if necessary, ah, let nature take its course. You agree with that. I know you do."

"Wal sure."

"Well," my uncle said heavily. He spoke to the blurring green as we picked up speed, "I'll keep fighting."

Putting a doughy hand on a knee he turned his face from the nation going by in green sky blue in the train window and gave me a look of such overdone humorless resolve that suddenly with a shock implosion of air strong enough to make a noise the window went to rapid repeats of lightflash in shadow as we passed the eastbound freight.

I would learn later from Chase that Eden had by this time come to be regarded as not merely a nuisance, by the studio people, but a crank, a nutcase, the megalomaniac with the stupid ideas who kept calling and faxing. But Zany was behind the project. Zany wanted *The Fisherman* kept alive. In fact the very day before this trip had begun there had been a call for me at my office in the city. A deliquescent executive secretary of indeterminate sex bade me hold, please, for Mumble. I almost hung up. *Another broker* I was thinking when the satiate voice not of a Zany minion but of the brains himself came on, filling the line with a cloying, honeyed tone of surface nice.

"John!" he sonorously yelled.

"Yes!" I yelled.

"Good," he said. "Wait-a-minute." Talking to someone else. "No," he said in annoyance, "nnnn*nn*. N'n, n'n . . *nun.* That's not where we are. Tisn't. Tisn't where we are at all, is it then, is it after all, is it ducks. What a stupid way of talking. So make him . . look. Listen. I have someone on the phone, make him understand. Blow him off? Oh well gosh, gee, whatever would make you think I—right. Correct. Accurate. Roger. Do it. Sorry," he said.

"That's perfectly—"

"I've been playing with this," he snapped. "I admit it."

"Meaning," I said carefully, "the—"

"Yeah I'm sending two people, two key people. To this thing in Idaho? The whatsit? I'm stepping back. Ok I'm sending—got a pencil?"

"Annd," I ventured, "this is regarding—"

"Right the film yeah okay so I'm sending, ok I'm sending Mandy Bongiovani and Achmed Alain. A,l,a,i,n. Got it," he stated. "Now. I'm serious about this. There's a film maybe and either it's good or there's zip. So. We're gonna find out. He'll be glad to hear that." Eden. "So you tell him, you tell him I'm serious, I'm serious about Mr. Anther and I'm serious about a film starring Mr. Anther and." The pause was unexpected. I could see the cigar's earth-center glow three thousand miles away, on the Coast I assumed, though later I found out he'd been coming to me from a jet over Barranquilla. "Tell him," he said with sharp consonants. "I'm serious about the film and I'm serious about his wife." Rairia! "Tell him we'll work it out. These are the two things that interest me that interest him. The film. His wife. Tell him I'm serious about the flick. I'm not coming to Idaho. That proves I'm serious. I'm giving control to colleagues. That'll make him happy. Tell him I'm serious about this woman. He can't help it, I can't help it, she can't help it. We'll work it out. She loves me. Strange sensation."

Bright sunlight again and the clacking rails, green fields to the horizon. The nation's grain in green expanse. As distant from each other as atoms, vertical Victorian houses with porches—barn/outbuilding/flagpole at the end of a straight long lane.

As we rode we watched the flying countryside and of course my uncle was thinking, behind those hazel eyes, about the film. But not about his wife and Zany Percy Foss, because that part of it I had not been able to find the courage to tell him.

Henry Anther watched the plains, jiggling with the train, the newspaper he'd been glancing at forgotten.

Rairia had crunched out into the snow in her boots to hammer on the limo roof—don't you toy with my husband! Don't you toy with my poor husband! His heart's all the way in this film idea and he knows nothing about film, hey—you in there? Is anyone *in* there? Either kill the project or give it a chance, hear me? The answer, a slowly opening rear door seemed to say, was yes.

About Quadros, that whole trip, my uncle said only, and somewhat out of the blue, "his ideas are harmless but he's a dreamer, though he'd deny it. An amazing person. All in all I'm glad, ah, I'm glad we finally got her away from there."

For the month of August Nora was on the road working for Rairia, which had enabled Eden to feel free to leave home and which as an additional benefit would either "heh, have the effect of cutting the oxygen off to the relationship, and ending it that way, assuming they aren't capable of taffy-stretching to thinness-beat gold . . ." or, in Kyle Kulka's words, "afford us a definitive opportunity to test just how reliable this Quadros is."

# 22

The Annual Confab of North American Fly Anglers was held high in some of our most striking mountains, where a workingman's castle lifts, stark against rocky peaks, out of steep, dark-draperied hills of climax forest—a stronghold of redwood, cedar, oak and quarried rock, turrets and precipitous gambrel roofs of double chimneys—beautiful, bizarre, bigger than "Lookout," and different, "Lookout" having been built by just money. Raised by the subsidized shout of a hundred out-of-work workers and a hundred more, in the days of the WPA when such ideas were undecadent, this hardy hostel is a dark delicious gingerbread house from a children's story, five hundred rooms, newels like coiled anacondas, thirty-inch-deep windowsill in my room, whole trunks of trees used as beams seventy feet above the main hall's gleaming pegged flooring, fireplaces you could do a cartwheel in, as nearly happened at the awards banquet, the final night.

Two streams play through those high woods, pour around black boulders, slip over gray slate, descend in pools, glides and runs en-shadowed by grown-together treetops, a ray of whitegold sun—eerie beam—spearing down through the canopy of closed forest to shine in one holy spot on the frothing, churning cold trout water.

There were casting demonstrations on some of the tamer currents and at the reflecting-pool tanks set up on the bocci lawns in the lee of the comrade-constructed fasthold with its door hinges the size of a dictionary. Here and there in the August sunshine mediocre anglers mingled with experts to wave their wands sending a lyric of chasing shimmery lines out, and discuss the niceties of the thumb, where in the cast one accelerates, rod construction, line memory, flats, wraps, action, wind, taper, loading and hooks and the tuck cast and the skater cast and all the rest of the blessedly infinite angling vocabulary that gives such pleasure to fishers.

They stood in groups on the cooling grass. They would watch as one of them, taking a rod, would try to put what they'd just been talking about into practice.

And with blazes going in the hearths in the grand dining hall amid a roar of conversation and argumentation and jokes and the din of scraping chairs and cutlery against china they would discuss it all all over again, at dinner after the day's workshops and panels.

There were auctions of trips and of angling art and of personal lessons from legends and of tackle and gear and flies—outward, visible manifestations of the inner compulsion. There were committee meetings on conservation and youth in the hostel's paneled smaller rooms, and there were the usual spontaneous conversations and "get-up" sessions of teaching and comparing notes, indoors or out, shoulder to shoulder, to the membership's thrill, with the likes of a Bob Celebreesi, a Mandel Mann, an An Wu, a Louise Track or a Henry Anther. There were classes, the League Board Meeting, which was open, sessions of equipment testing, a fly-tying contest, author signings, and for twenty bucks (benefiting the League Restoration Fund) you could get your casting motion videotaped.

The amateurs' enjoyment and the professionals' livelihood depended on a process of unceasing discovery, the devising of new ways to entice a trout to your fly. All this progress was reflected in the variety and opulence of the trade suppliers' booths that had been set up in the ballroom among guides' booths and catalogues' and publishers' and tackle shops' booths under the three-story-high ceiling. There was health and well-being in the milling of the shows' attendees, the clustered heads, the polite jostling, the happy intensity of discussion where they gathered about the experts who sat chatting as they tied at their vises in their booths.

Trent Ott was there, sporting muttonchops on his otherwise porcelain face.

He was editor of the magazine now.

His smile was pressed outward, as the smile on a parade-balloon face stretches. He sported an ascot—orange cowboy-kerchief knotted nattily in the open neck of his plum cotton shirt, and I could see he was wearing a most amazing watch. A pair of tinted eyeglasses hung from the lip of the breastpocket of his shirt. All these were insignia, trademarks by which, as his career in the "industry" progressed, he would be recognized, then identified, and finally (and this would be fine with him) caricatured by the good people of fishing.

Stopping at the booth Grundig Rods was sharing with the publishers of Henry's book by an arrangement understood by no one, Trent Ott pumped more silicone into his smile and, spreading his hands as if to indicate the size of a fish he'd caught, beamed at the old angler's bald head that might, or might not, contain recognition of Ott's presence as Anther continued, slowly, to tie.

The shape of the top of his head showing as he bent to his work, Henry sat at the booth's front table winding dubbing, twisting it between a forefinger and thumb as he wound evenly to a thread-wound size 14 hook.

Ott had a way of moving about a gathering without hurrying or hesitating, without ever having no one to turn to, without ever having to hang hopefully at a group's edge while he waited for the person he wanted to address to get free, without ever being trapped in a conversation, without—apparently—ever even having to make an effort.

"Your book," he told Anther after they'd exchanged greetings, Anther by looking up and smiling, Ott by smiling and chewing the last of his pita sandwich, "is classic. Wondrous piece of—" swallow "—writing."

"Wal," Anther uttered, going back to his fly.

"And that—" Ott gulped "—article last month. Even though we didn't get it. Wish you'd've let us see it. In—" Ott gulped, swallowing the last of the tuna pita he'd snagged in passing the concession outside the great room's pine-trunk-jambed portal, gulped—a hiccough almost—without uttering his principal competitor's name "—where you say 'fish make mistakes' or 'trout make mistakes' or however you put it? Great." Wiping his fingers hastily looking down. "Just great. That's breakout writing, centered."

Turnwrapping thread to hook shank with concentric circlings of the tying hand is not precisely the same motion as cranking your reel to take in line, but with the application, to each process, of the correct Cosmic Constant to compensate for the difference in degree of wrist tension, wrapping and reeling may be glimpsed as cousin descendants of a single primal circling motion fashionable during the first instants of our Universe's birth back when Plato was active.

Through the crystalline-polished panes of a window the size of a canal-lock gate I could see elk—tails to us, dark neckmanes and light rump patches in summer pelage—standing in a meadow with far-distant rock peaks above against cerulean sky, windowglass sunlit, elk and meadow not, craggy faroff mountains glorious with sun, the giant cloud that was doing all this a mile high in the upsidedown bowl of the sky, suspended like your stomach as you stare up.

Unlike suave Ott, I, who at Eden's encouragement had come along, before going to Oregon for some camping with friends, stood at the edges of things enjoying myself, drifting about the convocation happy just to be among these civilized friendly people in their shirts and khakis, and to listen to their debates and teasing and marvel at their paraphernalia. The watercolory art that Eden by way of Anther had suggested to Ott as the best way to illustrate the how-to-fish articles, all that sweeping, unclear interbleeding of swabs and spots and dervishes of color instead of line-drawing-real streams moving and unambiguously rendered humans and rods and lines moving through pert arrows and letter-labeled stages of sharp movement, had caught on. They were using the style regularly now Ott said, and reader response was positive. Did, Ott wanted, offhandedly, changing the subject so swiftly I almost gave a cry of surprise . . did—peering, leaning forward to do so, at Anther's Wet Dark Hendrickson as if it and not the answer to the question he was about to ask were what fascinated him; did, sniffing interestedly as he looked down at the fly taking shape in the graceful kiln of Anther's sure, large fingertips; did Henry have a new bass popper?

"Naw," Anther said.

"You don't? I'd heard you did."

"Naw," Henry said, tying. "There's a floater/diver I tied a fin keel on off-center to make it yaw, but ya don't mean that."

Ott didn't, but was alert with interest immediately but Anther, having gotten Ott going toward the floater/diver, turned him: "Oh ya mean," Anther lion-purred, working the while, "that sorta hairbug I tied with the . . with—" occupied momentarily with tufting, fingering, primping, trimming and coddling the pinch of mallard flank feathers he held between the rounded tips of his first finger and thumb. "See that? See how ya kin get it t' . . um . . that I tied um, with the . . ."

"With the what?" Ott inquired casually.

"Oh with . . . caught hell out of 'em too. That I tied with the uh, damn," to the little fly before his eyes in his vise. "See the hackle, you don't want it—you don't want the hackle t' sorta . . . twist like that."

Shutting his mouth and pushing his jaw and lower teeth up as he toiled, Anther pushed his upper lip out, saying nothing more.

"Er," Ott said. "Hmmm," he continued, conspicuously interested in the fly in the vise. "Yeah, if the hackle's not soft enough . . . that grouse?"

"Yep."

"Yeah," Ott said. "I see what you mean. Anyway," Ott said to the fly they were both looking at as Anther's big, gentle hands fooled expertly with it, "so what was the tie on that . . . hairbug didja say?"

His whole lower face, mouth shut, pushed up so that his upper lip looked like a milk moustache, and the weathered eyes glinting with concentration, Anther did not answer—obviously too caught up, at the moment, in positioning and trimming and adjusting the swept-back beard of hackle he was trying to tie in underneath his Hendrickson's neck and head.

"Er," Ott said softly.

"There, there we go. Got it," Anther was saying as he worked.

"But the," Ott said softly. They watched Anther whip-finish his pattern, making his turns with bobbin and thread and, keeping tension on, touching his half-hitch tool to the hook's eye and with constant tension pulling the thread turns off onto and tight on the fly's head *presto*

Ott had heard a rumor. He had heard of a dramatic innovation, a tie for the popper-type fly for bass that was exciting and worked wonders and had been discovered/invented by none other than Henry Z. Anther who, Ott had heard (correctly as it turned out), had been signed to do a full-color feature on the thing for a fly-rodding magazine that was not Trent Ott's. Yet Ott, leaning, both hands on the booth's front table cluttered with finished flies and fowl capes and exquisite small tools and devices and hooks lying around and flyers for Grundig and some copies of *Simple Fishing,* as the afternoon light coming through the grand windows, over the heads of them all, turned gray as the sun moved behind the one cloud in the sky, knew not to push. Ott knew how not to push. In fact, as Anther sat back waving a hand derogatorily at his finished fly, Ott was about to let it go for now (and come back to go after it again later) when Anther, squeezing his nose, rumbled. Most probably a cough though possibly it could have been a chuckle or conceivably indigestion . . and looking up innocently at the young editor asked: "Didja want me t' tie one so ya could see it?"

Ott visibly restrained himself.

"Oh," he said, testing his voice. "Sure."

"See if I have what I need . . . let's see here . . ."

Ott's throat and glands, his developed chest under the plum of his shirt, his eyes and cheeks and parade-balloon smile all now were bulging from within with his satisfaction. He stood quite still, leaning on the table and watching as Anther gathered what he needed and started to tie. Ott wasn't going to memorize and steal, not a whole full-color feature anyway, but—at least he was thinking about it—he could rush a little mention, a color photo or two, into the October issue if he could get Anther's approval without, somehow, getting Anther's approval. Maybe not. Maybe . . probably not. There was a code. But at least now he would have seen and would know about the tie, and in the world of fly fishing, as in any line, except poetry or religion, knowledge is better than a lack of it.

I drew nearer. My angling eye is uneducated but I could be sure from Ott's body-tenor, as if he'd taken an enema and was a mile on foot from the nearest bathroom, and, too, from the double take a grizzled expert did, drifting by and stopping to watch, that what Anther was doing was new indeed, probably sensational.

Eden screaming, I on the floor. He wasn't screaming but he was shouting so desperately it was like screaming. I didn't know what was happening. I wasn't quite on the floor, knocked by him when he'd jumped back, but was almost. And when, still shouting, he lunged to catch me from falling, he tripped and we both went over.

He had scrupulously been avoiding Anther because this was Henry's moment—*Simple Fishing* was a tremendous success—and he wanted to leave his friend alone, let Henry have the limelight and not interrupt. But gazing across the room at the old woodsman, bald head bent as he tied and talked, my uncle had been seized by a fit of happiness for Anther and a pride in Anther and a rush of optimism and nervousness and unhappiness and excitement and an appreciation, simultaneously, of humanity and fly angling so intense that he was transported into being able to feel the oneness of each trout lifting through the waters and each dainty mayfly and grub and the eyes and guts of the angler there on the bank, and he could feel the fellowship and little cheats of death that the conversations here in this lofty hall meant, and he was feeling all this so suddenly and intensely in a trance that he thought he would just pop over and say hello. He would pop over fast, say hello. Just swiftly and cleverly pass by. In this fit of ecstasy he could envision himself hurrying over to Anther's booth to stop just long enough to slam the table twice with a gemütlich palm and bending down and grinning say: "Good show. Good *show,*" before hurrying on.

No sooner had he imagined doing it than without thinking in a blaze of outer and inner childish glee he was doing it. He strode up, grinning like an idiot. Anther and Ott had little time to be confused before, leaning down to slam the table and look his friend in the eye, my uncle said: "Good show *AHHHH!!*" The first palm slam where he wasn't looking had jounced up the hooks of some of the flies lying loose and the second slam drove stinging points and barbs into his palm.

He bellowed, flinging his hand up, staggered into me knocking me over and as I have said, turning, shouting in a storm of pain, in trying with his good hand to save me from falling he knocked and dragged us both to the floor.

When we had gotten that bizarre moment sorted out and were back on our feet and Anther, holding his friend's wrist, was using his tweezers to get the hooks out of Eden's skin without too much blood, my uncle's expression as he watched the surgery, wincing less than I would've thought, was one of wide eyes, muscles around the nose tightened. Henry dressed the cuts with supplies from the booth's rudimentary kit— "I certainly did trip," my uncle said before any of us could ask what in hell he had thought he was doing. As if through with us, that strange soul turned his broad back and sawed away through the browsing crowds.

It was as if he had been emergency paged or suddenly remembered an appointment, though in fact he had little to do that four days, and spent hours each afternoon in his room reading and pacing and making notes on the meaning (God help him) of fishing.

"It's such a lovely way to pass time," he waxed at dinner. "Such a boon, such a lovely way to live." There were several of us listening to him at our end of the rough-hewn polyurethane-sealed gleaming table, of which the hall held twelve. "It's such a lovely metaphor—" spilling his tea "—for life. A loose genial community of individuals—friends—goes down to the stream as a group and spreads out, each alone, yet no one far from at least one other, to go, each—together and alone—after her or his . ."

"You must be a philosopher," said a lady with razor-teased hair who didn't know him.

"Yes," he said happily, his eyes on the hall's upper distances. "Such a . . you know. Surely fishing is . ." Kindly, she wiped up his tea for him. "A long time ago in New York," he dreamed out loud, "when I ah, lived there, I used to walk over to the United Nations in the spring . . . garden paths, green lawns, the river there, the great hopeful deliberating building casting its shadow. Women, men, children of all kinds strolling. Talking. Sitting on the benches to be in the sun. Peaceful," he said. "The way the world will be one day . . . but this fishing we love . . ." he looked at us, before asking his question ". . . why do we love it so?"

Henry Anther appreciatively ate his ham.

Herm Ebbleberger, the best saltwater tyer in the U.S., working his snub nose joked with a couple down the table about philosophy: "I stink," Herm suggested, "therefore I am."

"Well-l," Eden laughed, "yes—hee—in a way that makes as much sense as—"

"No seriously," Herm asked, folding his short arms, "wasn't there someone who said 'I am therefore I exist' or something like that?"

"Right," Eden air-tagged Herm across three faces—one of them mine—down that cheerful table. "You're talking about . ."

There was a call for Eden and he asked me to take it and I excused myself and went past hundreds of bobbing laughing faces and through the high doorway leaving the tables behind and was shown to an old-fashioned phone station. It was a closet of light pine with a door with a window. When I shut the door and picked up and said *hello,* at first I was sure the silence on the other end was Chase. No one spoke. Then, listening, I could tell somehow it wasn't Chase. When it was Chase, even if it was silence it wasn't silence such as this, with echoes and overtones as if a cave full of thousands of terrified people were keeping silent. The seconds wore on, and my unease turned to fear. I was about to hang up when there was an unresonant *click.*

It did not disconnect the connection.

There was a suppressed cry, or sigh, and whoever it was hung up.

I forget about things like that—reject them.

I carried my surprise back to the table and said *wrong number* to him shaking my head as I resumed my seat, sitting down to deep-dish pie and a conversation that in my absence had turned into a seminar by Eden on the seventeenth-century philosopher and mathematician René Descartes.

They seemed interested. He was explaining that Descartes had locked himself in a room far from everything familiar. Descartes set out—thinking—to doubt everything and see if there might be something that, try as he might to doubt it, he would be unable to doubt and thus could take as indisputable.

After doubting all sorts of things—the spiritual world, a neighbor's pain, ideals, math, the physical world and "a bunch of other 'inferences,'" as my uncle put it—Descartes came to the conclusion that everything was doubtable "*except*—" clanking his tea off-center in its saucer "—his own doubt! If he tried to doubt the fact that he himself was doubting, why he, hee-hee, he was proving it by doing it! He doubted! In other words *he thought.* His own reasoning and intellectualizing, these were real. In trying to doubt that they were he proved that they were. By engaging in the very act of them you see. 'I think,' Descartes said to himself, 'therefore I am.' Big event, big event in the history of philosophy. And now," Eden told us, looking into his beloved distances, "the universal truths—the Platonic ideals . . . all this that had previously been regarded as certain, proof against doubt and change, is blown away because it's the individual human mind that's sure. It's in the individual human brain that certainty's grounded. Rorty points out that with Descartes, ah, instead you see of having a world-model in which the messy human passions and physical raw senses are imperfect and changeable in opposition to what the rational intellect can just, barely, touch (a non-physical world of immutable truths), now with Descartes you see that plop of dog poop you got on your boot, or the searing pain of that paper cut, or a binge of personal jealousy or a dream you have in the night, why all these worldly ah, all these temporal sensory things are *in the same arena* as a pure mathematical proof or the concept of the immortality of the soul! Everything's explored now, everything decided . . inside your mind! It was just this afternoon . . if I can remember, can't. Let me run and get it. Wait." Such were the honesty of his energy and the tangible force of his enthusiasm that we sat there, smiling among ourselves, yes, and murmuring to each other that it was a little hard to understand, but waiting all the same, until minutes later he bustled back in with the text open to the very page. Waving a hand—the razor-teased woman moved his water glass out of the way—he began to read.

> . . . philosophy had, so to speak, risen above the practical wisdom sought by the ancients and had become professional . . . the Cartesian change from mind-as-reason to mind-as-inner-arena was not the triumph of the prideful individual subject freed from scholastic shackles so much as the triumph of the quest for certainty over the quest for wisdom. From that time forward, the way was open for philosophers . . . to attain to the rigor of the mathematician . . . rather than to help people attain peace of mind. Science, rather than living, became philosophy's subject . . .

. . . shutting the text he went on. His faith was palpably present in his voice, in the flashes of caring in the brown eyes, in the gesturings of his unmanual hands and his on-the-edge-of-his-chair excited-child posture. We were drawn to him, if not to the content of what he was saying.

He believed in a world of truth apart from human beings, a truth-world unaffected by us. He even believed in the possibility of a system of thought that could evoke that Ideal. This thought-system would needs be, paradoxically, unideal. That was what was odd. My uncle was coming around to believing in a pristine, eternal ideal system, valid for all places and times, that changed, that revised and renewed itself—even welcomed inconsistency and bubbly unsolvable little mysteries into its pale . . . he just couldn't think of what it was.

In his defense I will say this. If one rejects with certainty the existence of universal certainty then one is clearly falling prey to the human need for certainty. No, I like what Eden was trying for, so far as I'm able to understand it. Of course he was nuts but the try was valiant. He was dreaming of God, I think, and just didn't know it. He was trying to use thought to get to God. Dangerous. And yet who can say for sure, given what he was trying for, that he didn't, in failing to finish, in effect finish?

Through a copse of heads I saw Achmed Alain and Mandy Bongiovani two tables over. Mandy fit in superbly and was in deep conversational give and take with a dozen anglers while Alain, who spoke scarcely at all, sat looking. Alain did little but look. He looked very well, and was always doing it—not holding his thumbs at right angles to straight forefingers the way actors playing directors do sometimes in the movies, but looking all the same, all the time, at everything with the camera eye in his brain.

"How," one of us was teasing Eden about Descartes, "can a person be sure he thinks?"

Anther rumbled "Yeah that guy was usin' the wrong fly."

Eden was in high spirits and gave his friend a goofy stare. He oogled that way a second. Teasing back, he asked the old woodsman how it felt to be famous.

Anther smiled. "Aww."

Eden: "Don't be humble. I'm not pushing. I'm not trying to be testy. I'm wrought up. I'm philosophically wrought. Seriously! I ahhh . . . I don't know what I'm saying, they're all—everyone's so glad you're here!"

Anther, ill at ease more for his friend than himself, smiled(?) at his plate.

Eden in a quieter tone: "Seriously. You should be proud. I hope at least that, ah, that one is—enjoying?"

Anther: "Wal sure. Appreciate yer help."

Eden fended the compliment off with a hand jiggling as if erasing a sum on a blackboard: "Point is you're enjoying, good. Excellent." Happy without qualification suddenly, his mind off philosophy, his mind, in some shift of the universal epistemological winds—or the Krebs cycle working on his chow in him—off his mind. "Yes, well. We don't have hair. Gentlemen, ladies—" eyeing us each "—observe. I declare it. I do not say I like it, nor necessarily that I do not . . but! I declare it. It is not doubtable. He—" jabbing a finger to indicate Henry "—and I—" similarly signaling himself "—have no hair."

Anther: "Aww . . ."

Eden (mock-solemn): "No it's true, it's a truth. We do not have hair."

Anther (firmly): "Waal. I had hair when it mattered."

Below where I stood a compact youth with a red moustache and swarthy eyes was deep in discussion with an elderly gentleman whom I also recognized. I had wandered out to streamside and was looking down at fifty anglers in three hundred yards of water casting like so many line-art illustrations in a book. Against the crowded visual chorus of their interflowing lines, Mandel Mann and Woody Prafranesk, for that was who the two on the bank were—titans of the sport, one youthful brash, one immemorial and wise—by their very presence drew me toward them, even at the risk of bothering them, to hear, if I could, a snatch of their knowledge, for if Anther was good, Mann was better, and Woody Prafranesk was God. Prafranesk is a name even nonanglers know, who caught the first shark on a fly and still holds the trout record for four states. Companion of Presidents, inventor of all-time-best flies, scientist of the salmon and the steelhead, legend of the North Woods and the

South Seas and every brook, trickle and torrent in between, Woody Prafranesk can tie an imitation without a vise, do it just holding the hook in his fingers, whiling away the flight hours from hemisphere to hemisphere, though the rest—that not only was he tying with no vise but flying the plane while doing it, and it was an open cockpit, and it was raining—is harmless embellishment. I took a step closer down that hillside of high-mountain meadow, and they didn't even notice me so deep were they in their dialogue against the flowing, changing backdrop of all those amateur lines scrolling and catching the sunlight through and among each other. But I couldn't hear what they were saying, though I could hear the urgent contours of their voices—but someone had my shirtsleeve.

It was my uncle, on his way somewhere with Mandy and Achmed in tow. They waited, holding their wading boots over their forearms while he accosted me. He smiled too much that trip, right up to the final night. His hair strands stood crazily in the breezeless cool. His arms, extending pink-hairy and blotchy from the short sleeves of his khaki shirt, were like useless logs that he had to carry, and he was quite forward about grasping my sleeve to hold me while Achmed and Mandy waited. Eden's big face and too-glad smile loomed into mine to grumble excitedly in a half whisper that that was Mandel Mann, and Woody Prafranesk, right over there!

Did I know who they were?

A parity of opposites, Achmed and Mandy waited, she with jazzy lips, that thick head of brown curls and fun all over her face, he just eyes, gimlets, measuring, looking, never speaking. One wore cavalry boots and a burgundy turtleneck, the other baggy knickers. Of course I knew who Mann and Prafranesk were, but I let Eden intrusively, excitedly tell me, rather than stopper him. And a minute later he and Alain and Mandy were trooping away to whatever stretch they were bound for, shirts going away and down, then shoulders going down, then just the backs of their heads going down above the tall grass as they went off down the slope, then just forest, deep verdancy, sun gold on the edges of some branches. I turned my attention back to the two famous anglers, whose discussion seemed more intense and who noticed me not a whit as I drew near, trying to seem not to notice them.

There are lots of tricks to catching trout. There's a myriad of possible variations on equipment. Nearly infinite are the innovations one can dream up for the patterns themselves. The fly-angling world has good reason vigorously to explore them all. There is perhaps a measure of contrivance in the annual invention of new colors and materials and textures and shapes and tricks and weights and designs and varieties of action for the wet, dry, midge, bass, terrestrial, saltwater and streamer and bucktail flies to be used not to mention advances in reel ventilation and range of drag adjustment, balance, counterbalance, coating and also the machining of the reel's bushings and pawls and gears—subtleties of rod construction, variations in line taper, new casting niceties, experimentation with unprecedented synthetics in the manufacture of wading boots, et cetera. These may be inspired, secondarily, by a desire to catch fish, but primarily it's become a matter of the shop owners' and fishing writers' and guides' and manufacturers' need to maintain a certain level of income by selling their services to a world of Eden Hopes. Nothing wrong with that, given the fun fly anglers have, and given that this is America and not some Old World seacoast village where the nets are the same from generation to generation. Still, standing on that grassy bluff, the pellucid air like a faith kiss in the miles-high atmosphere against my cheek, as I looked down at all those nice people in hats casting and retrieving in not enough water, it was hard to deny that it has become an industry.

"Six weeks," Prafranesk was saying, "six weeks to the *day* after I told you, it shows up in print, under *your* name, no credit, no thanks."

"The only reason you can't catch fish as big as I catch," Mandel said, an angry wink of light flashing from his earlobe as he lifted his graphite rod, as if to end this and go fish, "is where you live. There just aren't trout that big there, so I wouldn't feel so bad about it."

"Six weeks to the *day.* I tell you how a flyline being cast looks like 'the watchful tail of a lioness' and what do you do, you turn right around and—"

"You never said I shouldn't use it."

"I shouldn't *have* to you little—"

"'Watchful tail of a lioness' isn't that good anyway, and I'm not even sure I didn't read it somewhere long before—"

"Shut up, and you stole a cast, the looper, you *stole* that after I showed you it." Woody Prafranesk's pink face was getting pinker and his jet black hair fell suddenly in a comma down his brow. "You stole it and published it in—"

"Well you lie about fish! That article in *T & A* after you came back from Patusan? Where you said you caught all those giant trout on a *river?* Well your guides told Herm it *wasn't* on a river, it was in a damned *lake!* Thought no one knew about that didn't'cha?"

"My public expects—"

"You don't have a public anymore that's under retirement age."

"Why you . . ."

Woody shoved him and he almost went down. They shoved a little, and Mann with a whipping motion lashed the overweight older man's arms off him. What happened next I couldn't say, because I walked on down the stream.

Where a dying crabapple reached menacingly over the current, bare arthritic claws about to talon-clasp the cool brunette—bushy hair in a mane cascading from under snub cap—expertly fishing the dens in under the eroded banks under the loopy, droopy grass . . . it was Mary Rath! She who the year before they'd had to ask to stop entering the casting contest so someone else could win—I stopped to admire. She waved brightly, didn't know me from atom, made a cast and drift under the brown water and hanging grass, past the window the brutes peer out from in their caves under the bank, that got a response and up went her rod like a victory salute against that rare mountain sky, and I saw not one, but two, Nikons emerge from the brush and a voice—Ott!—said "Profile! Profile please!" An Wu was showing some admiring tyros how to rollcast in a quiet bay of stillwater, further on downstream, and what always strikes you about An is how understated, sharp and small his movements are as he hunches like a prizefighter grimly to exact from his rod and line precisely what he wants, and, coming around a corner of drowsing bear grass, I happened on three men and two women in a shallow riffle. They asked me to fish with them so I did. In yet another one-person pool, the person in question—short and fat with one eyebrow growing across his forehead—stuck his tongue out each time he hooked up, and when his cellular phone rang he answered it, but did not stop fishing to do so, but the old lady just downstream of him worried me. The features of her face—crooked lipstick, gaga eyes and bent nose all unsymmetrical like gumdrop and raisin features of a gingerbread person too eagerly pressed home by infant hands—were arresting to see as she turned, her line hanging anywhere at all and her streamer loosely drifting in the current, to say hello to such a nice young man as me. A really big fish flashed. It disappeared then was back, chasing her fly! I cried out "Ma'am you've got a monster trout after your fly," and she lurched around whipping her rod around yanking her fly about sixty-miles-per-hour to the pool's other side. The big fish went crazy, zoomed straight after it, was going to take! But she asked me if she should cast like this, waving the rod again crazily and pulling her streamer *zip* right out of the crazed trophy's about-to-close jaws. He shot over gamely to get the little thing where it had shot to, and damned if, turning to ask me something more, she didn't yank it *again* out of the creature's jaws, which, finally, seemed the last straw for the bewildered pissed-off lunker who swirled and sounded. In the glide below that there was an actual formal class going on, tyers and an entomologist with a microscope communing on the bank in the brief shade of a different lone cloud, so I skirted that.

Where still more folks were fishing, near and at a distance in the river's sweep—for, widening, the stream did seem a river here, reviewed by a pair of oaks on a sidestretching knoll—their lines coming, going, furling and unfurling among each other in a confusion of waves and volutes like too many watchful tails of too many lionesses, Henry Anther was fishing. He stood in a row of others, fishing nimbly, his battered hat low over the weather eyes, suntough canvas on his head like a rotting mushroom, his slick line glinting flying out over the water, at his teacup-tip touch, with a loop you couldn't putt a Maxfli through.

Herm Ebbleberger had the CFO of the rod-making company Herm did endorsements for with him. Herm blundered down the bank elbowing a couple mortals out of the way to give him room to cast so he could show his guest what he wanted to show him. Henry, seeing in his quarterback's vision field, quietly made room for the two displaced anglers. Herm, his narrow shoulders and bulging belly/ass pear-shaped, got line out and started demonstrating, with snarly servility explaining what he was doing to his fat cat in just-off-the-shelf vest, boots, sun hat. Herm ungracefully sent out perfect cast after perfect cast with a minimum of effort, his line swinging, looping and singing in the navy air as impressively as anything Anther would ever be able to manage.

The cold sun crested in that northcountry sky, and I walked through an arcadian glade—woods circling a lumpy matted acre of elderberry and red heather in a lodgepole chipmunk's eye—to enter forest again. Over the sounds of the stream as I came back to it, through the trees I could hear his voice, mellifluous and deep. I wasn't to the water yet and couldn't see but the voice projected through the pines as I walked, and though rich as always in its bass timbre, it changed sometimes into that mischievous high-pitched giggle. I looked up and could see them, through the trunks in sunlight—Eden, Mandy and Achmed standing in some shallows, a gravel bar of pebbles behind them, the currents swinging in a sunny bend toward where I stood then flowing away from me and southward into a long, enormous pool, riseless, that lay in shadow.

Eden gave Mandy a rod and she held it and did not do anything with it, holding it upright like a staff, waiting to be told what to do, dutifully staring downstream with touching concentration, her curls shining. My uncle looked down, setting his chin on his chest. Looking past the forest of red-gray curls exfoliating from his open shirt between the laden pockets of his unzipped vest, he watched his hands setting to work, on the shelf-ledge of his belly, to tie a fly onto the tippet-end of her line for her. His fingers worked daintily, his posture relaxed—the fat man's calm—and yet a concentration admirable and immense rang out silently around him as he stood in the current working, peering down through half-moon glasses at what he was doing. Finished, he lifted the fly to eye level, assessed what he had done, and turning his head wincingly bit the excess. The noon sun's fractures and shards of glance and glare slants broke the dark blue air crystally, the current leaping, from where they stood, down over further rocks into the pool below.

Achmed saw everything, said nothing. Hopped about splashingly conceiving framings and angles and distances and lighting as Eden, pointing up, down, out, throwing an arm open, giggling and yakking told Mandy how to do it. Standing in the waterlights from below and the cold-burning sun's light from above, the current moving past his white legs that showed between the current and the fraying hems of his shorts, he saw me and waved. She was trying hard, and starting to understand. Achmed squatted, looking up, splashed backward, squinting, even backward climbed the bank a second to look down. Animatedly Eden grasped Mandy's arm standing smack beside her. Wiggling his fat fingers and fiddling them in the lacuna of shadow his height (Mandy was short) made between them, he evoked for her how the magic worked. She tried again, with success while Achmed turned straightfaced in a staring circle. Now my uncle had a friendly arm around Mandy's shoulders to point her in the right direction, and they were laughing, and, convinced she understood, he let her try on her own and stood well back from her in the current with absolutely beatifically folded hands beaming. You could see that if she should decide to take it up Mandy would be an angler, as Achmed, bending suddenly and supplely at the waist, stuck his head under the surface.

She had a strike maybe, missed it, her line a questionmark a second in the air. Eden waded forward splashing little showers of kick-spray up in the shallow current and swinging his arms to instruct her some more in that voice of burls and low purrs and overtones that was like the stream's singing. But when Henry Anther appeared around the bend and waved, my uncle lit a fast pipe. Puffing hard he nodded to Anther, abruptly positioning himself near the studio people as they spoke to Henry as he came ripplelessly wading up. Mandy asked Henry a question. Eden answered it. But she wanted to hear Anther's answer, and so she interrupted Eden, pointedly putting her question to Anther, who glanced at my uncle, who waved a hand and waded over to the gravel bar where he folded his arms across his hairy chest and puffed, huge-thighed in his Gurkha shorts and khaki shirt, with many buttons open, rumpled and soiled between the laden compartments of his vest.

Anther had his hat off in a hand and with that hand was fretting his big head with a couple knuckles when Mandy torqued at the waist from her fishing to ask him another question. Hesitating, he turned to call the question to Eden, where Eden stood, and Eden, one quizzical puff

of white smoke

emerging from his pipe, waved a hand for them to go ahead, go on, go on . . . so Henry showed her, Achmed working even harder, seeming to be in more than one place at once, and on the gravel bar with his arms folded and his face shadowed my uncle watched the lesson continue, that one white puff, from his briar, all.

A trout jumped in the stream. Rainbow probably. Mandy shouted. Then she stood passively while Henry showed her a couple quick things and gestured for Eden to come help, and she made a good cast—Eden waving no-no-no with a train-crossing signal-palm ticktocking. No-no-no, my uncle waved, you don't need help, you're fine. She was onto it! Henry took a rippleless step to her side to talk her through it, as the spitting line pointed at a slant to where the fish, facing upcurrent, holding, would be wagging its head hard, rhythmically, trying to lose the hook. And here came my uncle without thinking, while Alain gauged, splashing forward booming in his sonorous bass, shoving his glasses back up his nose. Anther ducked his head to gesture in hauling, sweeping whole-arm waves for the Perfessor to come on out to midstream and take part. Eden stopped, folding his arms. Taking his pipe, which was out, and which he'd put in a pocket, out, he stuck it between his teeth. Each of the four humans in the stream and each of the separate trees on the meadow hills above had its negative lying darkly beside it as the sun passed by one on the way to two. Anther folded *his* arms. Achmed, if perspective is identity, looked at easily a dozen different Henrys in under thirty seconds. Eden, his belly pushing the waist of his shorts down in a U sag below where his chest hair spilled from his shirt, unfolded his arms. He started to shout something to Mandy. She lost it. Her rod bobbed straight, line slack. Immediately Eden was praising and congratulating her, a good idea—her smile was broad. She turned to the old angler to ask something. Eden folded his arms. No smoke came from his briar but a mottled hand, openfingered, in and out, in and out, in and out of the afternoon light was fingers-drumming an elbow.

That last night was the longest I ever talked to Henry Anther, beside whom I sat.

He would be silent after I'd said something. I knew he wasn't hard of hearing. Then I thought he might be disgusted with my questions. But he always finally responded, if only with an interjectional "Wal," the tortoise-hard work hands polite, animate and still on the table edge.

Under the beams and rafters a mile above, bravely measured and nailed in place by hands like Anther's in the time of the Great Depression, the flames in the warrior-tall hearths danced as high and wild as hoary battle horns' calls as the couple hundred of our moving heads, down the refectory tables, made background noise. Eden was happy. The trip had been a relief and a release. Mandy B. was drawing my uncle out like a stretched chicken neck for wordless Achmed to measure. Eden was waving his hands, the brown eyes alight as he regaled us, and you could see, in the old familiar energy and the danger it put every ketchup bottle and beverage pitcher within a yard of him in, that the child was here. The child was here tonight. If Zany's henchpeople were, behind their attentive eyes, uncertain of my uncle, and if the anglers and guides and merchandising experts in attendance were making light fun of him at times—that is when they even noticed him—and if life was slipping by him a little lately, then see it as funny or see it as sad. The more it's one the more it's the other. Tipping back his chair and throwing his arms up, his face guileless, the amber eyes filled with air and light and the mouth, under the ogee of bristly hair, an O of naive intransitive energy, he said, in answer to a question he'd put to Mandy that she'd taken as rhetorical but hadn't been: "Santayana!" Oh yes. "Santayana!" he told them all happily. He shut his mouth folding his arms and waited to see what they thought of *that.*

You have to be flexible, Anther was saying. I turned my attention back to him from my thought's momentary wanderings toward my uncle. Henry waited, his face a maze except the eyes. When he saw he had my attention he tightened the air between us by lifting his brows and looking at his scarry fingers as they moved his knife, and was about to say something more—but a fool came up. That's always sad when it isn't infuriating. When good people are having a good time it's a shame that the Prime Mover (once referred to by Duffy as "you mean Allied Van Lines?") sees fit to lard in fools, but up came this big florid face floating and descending like a dirigible into Anther's face, and the guy "corrected" one of Henry's ties, a nymph described in detail in *Simple Fishing*—corrected it! And loud?

It was terrible, but Henry was patient, though not enthusiastic. Angry maybe on the inside, but you can't make out a turtle's expression when its head's half in. He listened, nodded, seemed to say something noncommittal yet concessive, or capable of being taken as concessive, and all the while the old angler was not shrinking a millimeter further from the false-friendly grandiose dispensing mouth and foglamp eyes. I was thinking to myself that Henry was handling the guy well, as indeed he was, when I realized this was also the way he handled people he liked.

He ate neatly, loudly, his false teeth making a quick-unstuck *smack* once in a while that bothered no one, himself least of all. I've seen Henry referred to in print as "humble," but he wasn't—he wasn't the opposite of humble either. He was wise in his world. He was a sage. What's a crocodile, looking at you?

At the beginning of dinner when I had sat down at the same table as my uncle, who was doing fine without me at the center of a group of laughing (at him) and listening (to him) innocents, suddenly I spied Henry looking lost, holding his glass of beer in a slow-drifting stampede of merry faces and greeting shoulders and flowing plaid shirts an aisle and two tables over. But when I got out of my chair to go get him, looking through that loud crowd I saw two men, both about the same height, each face kind—one a prominent nose and chin forming the caliper hook shape of the salmon's jaws, wearing glasses, the other stouter, softer-faced, fuller-faced, wearing glasses. They came up on either side of the old woodsman. Talking with him subduedly in that evening milling and shout, they gave me every reason to sit down again, and as I did Henry came over and sat next to me and was fine. As we ate, we talked.

Eden was saying that ah, the trouble was that before they did a new experiment they made sure their perceiving minds were adjusted in advance. He sputtered, lifting his water glass. Were ah, adjusted in advance to rule out, in the sifting of evidence and empirica, any hint of—and we were all listening (Anther with a clement expression of inner sigh on his poker face)—they were searching . . . he made his point with a crash. Those at the table who'd never met him were fascinated. Some laughed. Some wondered. They were searching, he insisted annoyedly, cleaning it up as he spoke, for what they wanted to discover rather than looking for somewhere to put his soggy napkin. Rather than just . . . *ah*. Waitress. Thank you. Thanks so much. Searching. Rather than simply searching.

He was performing, which he had always done. But to me who knew him, the nervous air fingers, the deep rich bass, the wild remaining strands, the glasses down the bulbous nose, were too-familiar disembodied traits. Suddenly I saw him as nothing—a whorling emptiness cloaked with traits. The O mouth, the raggedy moustache, from which a drop of soup hung tremblingly and fell exploding infinitesimally on the polyurethaned maple. His flaccid arms, his Cheshire-Cat smiles and spidering air fingers were tricks of magic. They surrounded nothing. In dinner-light excitement and conversation have you ever seen someone you know as a phantasy? The others, to whom he was new, listened with interest as he dragged poor Sartre by the boots on his back into the conversation. An instant longer lingered my tired-eyesight image of him as storm-eye—void—around which brightly whirl disjointed gesturing fingers, damp amber eyes, giggles, hair spinney, nose, *mots* and ideas. The others listened with no little interest as he told them about Sartre's glance at you, and yours at me, and the opinion and picture of you that the person perceiving you forms, and how the Other's perception of you is a prison you must creatively escape from. You talk to someone. Looking at you, the person listening to your words forms an image of you. You can't see it or know what it is, but the Other knows the secret of what you are, just as, in the battle that is social knowing, you by looking at and listening to the Other form a picture of him or her that he or she cannot see and struggles to transcend . . . and, heh, can one? Though my uncle was taking a lot of words to say it the answer seemed to be yes. I glanced at Anther who was steady in the manner of his regard. He was looking across the table at his expostulating friend, slowly picking his teeth as he listened.

The answer was yes one can transcend the Other's stare, and that stare's judgment, my uncle insisted as, a little way down the table, two who had been listening stopped listening and engaged on their own in a conversation on stream temperature as my uncle went on. Complaining, holding his temples and staring, talking half to himself at our suddenly subdued end of the long table, he said that although you could transcend or escape the Other's stare it is only the compulsion to think formally that seduces philosophers into taking such a stupid little question and putting a dress uniform of metaphysical circuitry on it and parading and drilling it and praising it with attention and elongating and mutating it in a fun house of mental mirrors until the day's billable philosophic hours have been filled.

He folded his arms and sat back.

There was a call for him. This time he didn't ask me to take it—he seemed glad to get up from the table of still somewhat admiring, or at least impressed—say perplexed—still-listening faces and heavily plod, hips awaddle, from the loud hall. He had finished saying what he'd had to say about Sartre and while neither especially happy nor sad now he just felt like moving around. So he went out to take the call, and Henry Anther told me of his early days as a carpenter, his love of the wild, the accident to his hand. He covered his carpentry days in slow sentences. He covered the bite blade searing loss of his finger the same way. His love of the wild he conveyed thus: after telling me how his dad and granddad had taught him to hunt and fish, he felt, contemplatively, of the weathered head that was his own and that looked like brown-red marble—at least it seemed he was being contemplative, though probably he was just remembering—and said: "My days outdoors are my best."

That was it.

Into the deep pool of unnervous silence that followed I threw a question. How was his book doing? I knew the answer. I wanted to get him talking. So I asked that question. He said nothing and glanced at me, glint of a joke in the sparkler eyes? Eden was taking a long time with his call. Conversation and echoing scraping of chairs and glass din and cutlery sabres and laughter filled the lit night hall. Anther's look made me feel silly, but then I thought: he's bashful. He's not humble. He's bashful. He's arrogant and shy, arrogant because shy, the arrogance benign and mostly hidden.

He'd worked as a carpenter. It did not deconstruct. It did not deconstruct into anything. There was no doubt about it, no question attending it, no ambiguity, no second surface.

He said he had put all his angling knowledge and outdoor color ("my best anecdotes") with my uncle's help into the book, and now, he said, with that nervous—for Henry—low boulder-rolling chuckle—now Ott and others were talking about a second book. They were talking about how a second book by him could be successfully marketed. He chuckled—"I wanted t' tell 'em you're talkin' about sellin' it but yer not talkin' about what's in it. I ain't got another book t' write. But they—" the chuckle was like a protective wall of low, perilous sound "—they gotta talk about their distributors, all these great testimonials 'n tie-ins—I learned that one. Tie-ins. It's okay," he said reasonably. "Nothin' wrong with it." He chuckled, not without effort. "But ya gotta have a book first. Naww . . ."

That was a lot of words for Henry. I sensed he would say more if I listened, so I let loops of silence float out. I took a couple bites of food that I didn't want. He chuckled and said he was tempted by the movie.

I asked why.

The chuckle stopped.

"Wal," he said softly, "with a movie see . . . with a movie I ain't responsible."

I decided to wait.

"I ain't responsible," he said, looking at his plate. "It's too crazy, a motion picture like that. Just a motion picture at all. Wild. So . . . you see?"

"I think—"

"With a book I was responsible, a book of fishing advice. With a movie I'm not responsible."

He looked dead into my eyes as he dropped the "ain't" from his diction. I realized with a chill and a thrill that he talked the way he wanted to talk. For certain occasions he would say "ain't," but if he didn't want to he didn't have to.

"Ya see?" he asked.

"I think I do . . but what's the attraction of not being responsible?"

Somebody dropped a full tray and everyone jumped at the crash except Anther whose memorable eyes did not flinch, holding mine before, dropping me as it were, he turned slowly to see the accident.

When he turned away from me his head looked different in rear quartering profile. It was topheavy smooth, a turnip, brow taller, nose hawkbeak, eye—part of, since he was turned away—sad.

He felt sorry for the boy who'd dropped the tray, a mess on the floor now with anglers from tables all over coming to help.

If I'd had a vision of my uncle as inner-sanctum vacuum of nothing circled by dustdevil traits and gestures, Anther was outer characteristics—three-fingered left hand, the "smile," the chuckle—that were ultimately irrelevant not because they surrounded nothing but because of what they did surround, a whole soul, simple and deep, that you might as well have prayed over as tried to dissect.

Eden came back in and sat down.

Anther hadn't answered my question. I tried to work back to it. I asked: "Henry how does this all feel?" He chuckled. I pushed it. "Really. How does it feel?" He looked at me. Henry Anther did not like not to be free. I collided my question into him: "Really," I said with a smile that definitely was one, "I'm curious. How it all feels, all your success . . ."

Eden sat at his place saying nothing, not eating. He was pale.

Anther chuckled darkly.

"What do you think of it all?" I insisted.

"I think it's just fine," Henry said, his eyes brightly mocking me.

The dining hall went away.

"Your book," I said into those eyes, "all the articles you've done, all the trips and appearances, then this movie."

"Yep."

"What does it all mean?"

By saying nothing and continuing to look at me, he said *what?*

*You heard me* I said without words.

Up at the dais with much stir and tapping of the mike they were getting ready to announce awards and the winners of the various raffles that had been participated in, and soon the voices around us would be lowered but Anther didn't hurry.

"What does it mean?" I asked.

"It means I need the money," he said. "That's why I gotta feel not responsible for this movie. Which I do."

I tried to stay in our stare but couldn't, and looked down.

"See," he said, "for my family. For them. Second of all—" he almost sighed "—to save a stream I know."

They were starting now up at the dais. My uncle sat looking into the air. The big arms in a droop, his mouth, open partway, the letter Q. It was getting quiet fast and my moment with Anther was wilting and I was nodding idiotically because I didn't know what to say. Leaning to whisper to me sidelong before we all finally got silent and turned our chairs to see the ceremonies up front, Henry said: "It ain't half bad."

That was that and I never talked to him again except to chat, but I'm fairly certain he was referring to everything.

Sartre's idea is that being with someone else we ourselves, in our essence as a person, are pierced by the Other's perception of us. The Other sees and hears us and forms a perception of us that is infuriatingly unknowable to us. So we have to get to it (the Other's idea of us) somehow, but probably the blare and static of the master of ceremonies up there at the head table and the gibes and jibes from her genially rowdy audience, and the food in one's stomach, and the market value of the Derrydales and the supreme old rods they're going to give away and auction off, blurs this business of knowing one another. Isn't it just as good to sit by someone in friendship paying attention not to each other but to an announcing master of ceremonies in a hall of common bond? I kept glancing over to check my uncle who seemed unaware announcements were being made. He sat, facial muscles not moving, eyes lifeless. I was wondering what if anything to do. He sat among anglers telling each other to shut up and jostling their chairs so everyone could comfortably see, and up at the front she was holding up a shadowbox of flies tied by Woody Prafranesk that caught the light momentarily in a way that made it disappear to my eyes. Eden's chair was empty. I got up. Crouching, as if trying to keep my silhouette out of some trout's upsidedown dunce-cap vision field, I slinked from the festivities. It took me awhile. He was in the exhibition room, wandering its dim-lit aisles alone, hands in pockets, cruising the deserted booths as if shopping Western culture for an idea. I came up to him and he started to turn and stopped, letting me see part of his face as if to say, that way, what he had to say without the pain of words. The upper depths of the ceiling were lost in shadow with most of the lights in the room off, and the abandoned booths, their flies and merchandise in a scatter on the show tables, weren't frightening at all. I saw, in the brown glassiness, moist light—not spilling, filling, gathering surface-tension wet and shimmery, yet still not spilling, until I thought *how can he see?*

# 23

He walked the empty fairways with his hands in his mittens, trying to think. But the leaves when he looked down, bouncing, sliding, dancing, cartwheeling across his path, confused his orientation so that he couldn't tell if the leaves were still and the earth's grass sliding or if he himself were still, and the grass sliding one way under his sneakers while this tectonic plate of skittering leaves under his windweeping eyes blew another.

Across the sere fairways the brown leaves blown by the wind tumble, hop, dance on points, rush in a slide over dormant grass—maple, hickory, oak, chestnut, brittle brown leaves by the tens of thousands sweeping with the wind over the colorless fairways in the autumn light shining low out of the west.

No one had much sympathy for him.

These dead leaves are sliding in echelon, in phalanxes, at thirty miles per hour as he walks—he, leaves, earth, each moving differently—swinging his mittens with his hands in them as he walks the closed course aimlessly wanting Rairia who he can't have. Coming back vacuous-faced to the banquet table that awards dinner night, months ago now, after taking her call, he had just been told by his wife that she was leaving him—for Zany Foss—which she had wanted to wait to tell him in person but was phoning about because she'd learned that Zany had crowed it through a minion to me, in that unexpected call to my city office the day before Eden, Henry and I stepped on the train west.

Rairia had no way of knowing I hadn't passed on to Eden what Zany had told me about Zany and her, and so, after giving Zany holy hell for it, she had gotten through to Eden, that night, not knowing that he didn't know, and had begun their conversation by profusely apologizing to him, without saying for what, and he came back to the table with a face that, after a time, he took away again, and I found him in the darkened exhibition hall. As Rairia had helped Eden through that conversation of stages and stumbling revelation and silence, more awkward even than she'd anticipated it would be, Nora's voice could be heard in the background clamoring for her mother's decision on something.

Nora was having a ball running ragged doing errands for her mom, putting off people Rairia didn't want to talk to, lugging luggage, stenciling placards, getting coffee in the radio studios, the pastel eyes not dreamy or shy at all but alive, ambitious, willing to stand and wait while her mother, wiping black hair from a war-white eye, leaning with aggressive elbows into the broadcast mike speaks without a whine of a convention of delegates, though there are no provisions, such as there are with the Constitution, for amending the Declaration.

Toward the end of that sad call Rairia had explained to him as well why the fishing film was going to come to nothing, at least insofar as Zany was going to have anything to do with it. It wasn't fair, she said, to let Eden think Zany might actually spend any more time or money on this thing, yes even with Alain and Mandy right there right now. They didn't know yet, Rairia said. So why had Zany sent them? Why had Zany passed along a message that he was serious about finally giving the film a chance? "Because," Rairia said smokily, "he was trying to please me. But at his center he's rejected the idea. So—" she said in a voice without guile, indirection or lacuna "—I straightened him out I can assure you." She repeated that she wanted to be fair, that there would be no film, and that Alain and Mandy B. didn't know yet. But they would, she said. They would know in a day. A move was going to be made, a big, effective, extremely well planned move on Zany's entire empire, which was somewhat leveraged and publicly traded. The reclusive nut was deep into his defense. Chase Parr, who called Eden breathless with this news days after Rairia had told him it, reported that he—they—could forget about the film, no one had seen or heard from a single Zany-surrogate for over a week. The buzz was that an informed siege mentality—mattresses of contractual obligation, assault weapons of suit, countersuit and restraining order—was being cultivated among the directors, corporate officers, Gucci bag people and other *inimici curiae* whom Zany held fanned close to his soul, "which," Chase's rainbow-shimmery tone inquired of her auditor, "leaves yours truly exactly where?" The tone, he noticed, had hardened with the years into a chic less liquid and suspirious than expensive. Chase repeated her question. Eden, dully wanting Rairia, didn't know what to say.

He was trudging up off the course, crossing the withered eighteenth green with its view—ignored by him—of those tossing hills, out over where the carp pond had been before they filled it in, and all he could think of—glum in his sympathy for himself (which as I have said no one, me included, shared)—was a long-ago summer, the August fogs of San Francisco, rolling hoary mists cool to the touch blowing low below the upper stories of the white hillside townhouses, obscuring roofs, obliterating sky and sun when he had flown out there to give a paper at Berkeley. At a party: black musical hair he couldn't look away from, eyes of limitless mischief, leotard. It was the mid-60s and he was a nation away from home, dear Gwen and their buddy Thomas. Rairia Ramoda took him to the Top of the Mark. They had a glass of wine. A piano was being played, after a fashion. In joking about the poor man's playing they got friendlier fast . . . he scrutinized the bill. They talked of their wants, their ideals. Politically they agreed, radicals both. Their fundamental intellectual temperaments were opposed but this would take years to discover—this night they were high in the air. They were in the bar's darkling lights surrounded by fog. They made heads-together fun of the person at the keyboard. He was terrible, playing "Misty" with barely competent desperation. Rairia's shoulder abutted Eden's like a satin fender, and now he could smell lemon. She laughed, he stared into the dark of her hair . . . muffled background, clinks . . . the pianist lunged at a phrase, got lost, blacked out, pianistically speaking, for half a second and came to consciousness again, hurrying back into the number and its rhythm. Soon, over his lugubrious rendition of "My Favorite Things," descant waterfalls of arpeggios they guessed, they put their mouths together. She asked him throatily if he felt far from home. The poor pianist went under, drowning a brief moment in his notes that tumbled against each other like an elephant joke chain-collision. After a breathtaking full second's silence, up he came, bursting for air like the two at the table coming out of their kiss. She told him how her parents in Yuma had had her tested by a service that tells you what careers you should consider. But, she revealed, along with a quarter moon of pure-white, veinless breast as she turned to look out the viewless window, she was working this summer for a semi-underground TV station across the Bay as "Weather Bitch"—he watched her taped later that night when the horns still moaned across those dangerous waters. And as he trudged past the shuttered, boarded-up clubhouse the wind, which had stopped, blew again and staring at his sneakers' slower and slower toes as he climbed he saw a sudden fury flurry of more leaves blowing south-southeast under his eyes as the hills spun moonward.

"For him," Duffy Ginty admitted, "it's heart-rendering. But for you or me or any other run-of-the-dam person with two feet in the ground, there's no less to any of it than meets the eye . . . but try to tell him that."

This was the beginning of his wild-eyed last period. He bought horses, just to watch them. An acre paddock of swift horses to study for their wisdom. He purchased strange equipment, electronic stuff used to test for telepathy, telekinesis, even spirits. A couple of times a week now white-robed Sufis—dervishes and others—came to visit and dance . . . he'd even begun mumbling about working them into the fly-fishing film. He was spending the last of his own money on it. He wouldn't let go of it. He was talking to possible freelance directors, designers, technicians . . . he would do all the writing. It would be eccentric—robed worthies in the trees by the sweeping stream. But none of Zany's venality, no perversion, no sex. It would be spectacularly sappy, he said hurriedly, but ahh—ahhh, true. He had made reservations and attendant plans for that winter to fly Anther and a platoon of Sufis and a skeleton shooting crew down to the same sandy streaks of islands where he, Anther and Thomas had been the year before. He was sure he wanted the centerpiece scenes to take place there. His memories were so good of the place, Thomas, the cosmopolitan food, Anther's old face smeared with sun screen, the nice young guides, Thomas, his boy, casting, catching wondrous difficult fish in those protean waters, of being with Thomas in those warm waters' welcoming sharing lights. It was madness—they didn't even have a script. He would spend two hundred thousand dollars easily on this one trip—nearly a third what he had left. When Lim heard about it he turned instantly on his little heel and strode straight back into the hospital.

Leaves blowing behind his eyes, my uncle sat staring at the white rectangle of paper before him on the desk. Remembering the skittery seas of them, somersaulting pointed leaves scratching touchlessly, each with its shadow scurrying beneath it, by the thousands in the fast wind around his sneakers like at the beach looking down as you walk into diagonally retreating wave-waters dizzying, he batted over a shoulder without looking at the hand that had touched him, which I quickly withdrew, embarrassed. I'd been standing there for several minutes waiting to be noticed, and I also wanted to be sure he was ok. I had moved forward, touched his back, and he gave a terrific start. As if it were a hornet my hand got swatted back to me before, after a moment, the weary eyes, coming up out of the brown remembered leaves, looked up.

"Are they heh, still there?"

He asked me this looking in the direction of the front of the house and I said yes, they were still there. At least when I'd pulled onto the parking gravel and left my car to take the crumbling railroad-tie steps two at a time, they had been there. Nora in a leather jacket cut long with lots of pockets and, of all people, the Poet, his pointy beard wagging as slowly as a fishtail side to side against her chin as they languorously kissed, beside the front door.

"Heh," he said to no one in particular.

"They're back together?"

"Ah, it would appear so."

"And," I ventured, "the other er, person?"

"Off somewhere. Increasingly mysterious, not, I am happy to say, in the picture any longer."

"I imagine," I said, "that pleases you."

"Yes," he said to his books. His voice was reedy and he was thin not in girth but in energy of spirit, his soul grown thin in the service of his dreams—insubstantial mica-sliver wings—traceried transmembranous last state of life without stomach, hunger or digestion. He said weakly again "yes . . . pleases me," and he was thinking, or trying to, but that was an iron November. The air was damp and gray and cold and laden with a leaden rain that would not rain, the sun nowhere . . . one afternoon when he went into the forest with his rod and phone, while waiting for a call from Henry, there was his brother flailing the leaf-strewn water. Lim was wearing a Red Sox cap backward. He was weeping he was so angry. He was slapping his line down so furiously on the desultory neutral stream, where burgundy leaves drifted like sodden cornflakes, that had there been trout around they would've been scandalized.

". . . Lim?"

"Don't—" splash "—talk to me. I'm relaxing. You're throwing your life away so I'm relaxing. I've decided to relax. You're going off on this absurd junket." Pause. "Right?"

"I ah—"

"Right," the little man spat bitterly. "And we're going to have to try to finish your Lady Gwen story by computer assuming you let us, which you won't so why am I—" *slap* "—even wasting my breath. Millions of—" line yanked off water with a vacuum-gulp sucksplash, *hammered* out and down again on the unreflecting murk. "—people want . . . do you know what they want? Do you know what people want Eden? Huh?"

"Why—"

"They want a little pleasure. They've worked hard, all they ask is a little pleasure, a little innocent fun." Lim's face was red and the imaginary beads seemed to be hermetically boiling within, instead of haloing out around, the near-perfect crewcut head with its perfectly round spectacle lenses. "They want to sit back Eden, they want to sit back at the end of a hard day or life and put their feet up. They want a little happy time despite your crazy wife. They want to enjoy the pleasure of a good read. They wanna see what Lady Gwen's gonna do. They wanna read some daring do, see battle scenes, be surprised by surprises, be shocked—*shit,* was that a fish?"

"No. That was you Lim."

"Oh."

"What'd they say?"

"They say there's blockage. I don't understand any of it."

"Well ahh, what're they going to do?"

"Unclog me, which the policy I have pays for all of I *think.*"

"Lim."

"Nevermind."

"Lim if there's any, ah, you know I'm always perfectly—"

His little brother under his backward baseball cap standing unhappily in the unbeautiful stream—no leaves on the trees, no song in the water—seemed to bulge with the pressure of his blood in him. "Finish the Gwen book," Lim said fixedly, "if you want to do something constructive."

The little man had stopped fishing and stood in a droop, as hung his line, a fall in logarithmic half-hyperbola to the current, straightening, as the slow flow floated it, ever so slightly to tug on Lim's despondently held rod as a worried child might tug the hem of a parent lost in worry.

"I've had my reverses Eden."

My uncle took a step more sideways than forward through the brush on the bank and, parting the dangerous branches of a dotted hawthorn, peered through.

"What reverses?"

"Reverses Eden. Money goes out and doesn't come in." Tensely staring at the imageless water. "I, this family. You don't notice anything in the real world so you've no doubt not noticed the construction that's been going on over past the three-arch bridge . . . that land's been sold too Eden, sold because it had to be."

"I hadn't known. I knew some was er, had been, but not ah—"

"Of course you hadn't known," Lim agreed bitterly not seeming to see these leaves so slowly, with the current's gradual progress, passing his boots. "And *The Return of*—"

"Actually *The Tree of*—"

"Eden what does it matter. What does it matter if it never gets written. Know what I mean?" Dismally. "What does—and of course by now there'd be close to a million dollars conceivably in the general fund, I mean assuming the same . . . admittedly generous . . . level of contribution you—shit," the little fellow surrendered.

"Oh but the film's developing," my uncle said through the branches. "Of course you've heard the great mogul—hee, apparently there's a corporate battle royal raging, ah, and—"

"At least one's raging somewhere."

"As you know I'm going ahead. I'm going to do it Lim. I've been working and we're going to fly down there ah, ridiculous as it may seem to you, and start," my uncle declared, as if to make it so, in that rich floating bass through the parted pricker branches that he would have had only to take three steps to be clear of. "There's movement Lim."

"No there's not." Lim Hope said this continuing to listlessly hold his rod and stare at the non-mirror water.

There was an undefiant set to my uncle's brother's jaw as he looked at something in the water—something with two qualities: he didn't like it, it was inevitable.

It was so typical of that clan or whatever you care to call them that

Eden and Lim, brothers, having what, from whatever angle one might assess it, would have to be called a serious conversation, would be having it with one of them standing in a stream and the other twenty feet away peeking through shrubbery. Sartre talks of the *gaze,* but what about the *peek?*

"Yes, yes, yes, yes," Nance agreed wildly, her voice boisterous and abnormally excited coming over the line to me from Tacoma. "Yes!" she nearly cried. She said "yes" forcefully several times more. "You're right," she practically shouted. "You're right exactly, *exactly.*"

The family had been rather proud, if skeptical, of Eden's liaison with Zany Foss. No one to speak of in that group had ever been involved in the movie world (excepting one nephew's animal docudrama, funded, as a matter of fact, by the fund), so they were admiring of the whole thing, even though there were questions having to do with the possibility that poor Uncle Eden was being had yet again—questions that, as Nance put it, lowering her voice, "no one dares ask, let alone answer." Smoothly she downshifted into the familiar hauling-gear ratio of flustered control-emphasis and secrecy. "I think this whole fishing-movie thing," she told me, "insofar as this Foss guy was involved in it, was just something to make him feel good, Foss I mean, something entertaining for him, a frivolous amusement and frankly my conversations with my mother on the subject corroborate that view. It was a diversion, a million-dollar mask to make the guy feel good, while bloodily and without scruple he wields his billions. He's a mogul I tell you, that's key to remember, a mordant mogul, a venal viper . . . a tactless tycoon, haw! No seriously, and I think my father was just going in there," she ardently listed, "and shuffling his papers, writing his notes for scenes, crossing them out and writing them again because he wants to make this perfect thing, conceivably because Thomas never liked his fantasy novels, did you know that? And now," she insisted, the receiver caressing her toiling lips, "Zany Percy's out of the picture and Dad's going it alone which I admire but I want to go on record. I fear he's going to go completely out of control. Completely. Utterly. I just have a bad feeling about it."

In my imagination I could see—trans-am—the short helmet of shining black hair, the dragon spectacles glinting in the Pacific Coast sunset as, deep in it now, she willed herself—until she could finish her trains of thought—not to turn around and look to see what her children's silence meant.

"It's driving my poor uncle nuts," she said, "and I'm sure it's not doing Nora any good. What you must think of us."

She was silent herself now as the Rising Sun set slowly in her sharp-curved lenses while she stared out over the scrolling Cape Flattery waters.

"Dumb," she said. "I really believe that sums it up, a dumb, dumb idea. The film I mean. What do you think?"

I said I wasn't sure.

"To spend hundreds of thousands of dollars and all the hours and energy of what's left of his life and to ignore Nora when she needs him by the way how's *that* going? I have to call her. Look, I'm not supposed to say I've gotta go but I've gotta. I respect your judgment, we all do, tell me, do you really think there's something *to* this movie? That it's *not* dumb?"

"I'm not saying it necessarily isn't," I said, liking the sound of my voice at the thought of the MacAtticks and Hopes and Grummans and all the rest of them valuing my judgment (which really isn't bad). "I'm just saying it isn't necessarily is."

"Haw. Know what ya' mean, okay, I needed to hear that. Still, I think the whole thing's dumb but maybe I'm wrong."

It was my uncle's plan that the Sufis would have their classes and do their dances right at the resort, right there on the floury beaches. All activity would be oriented toward the flats fishing, the shallow tides of sparkly changing lights. The Sufis, guided by their master, whom Eden had been out with that fall and taught to fish a little, and who was quite fascinated by the process, would watch Henry and my uncle and the guides fishing and talking about it and tying flies. They would listen as the anglers chatted. The idea was that fly angling, when done the way it should be done, is peaceful, graceful, orderly without being regimented, disciplined without being oppressive, unselfish and harmonious with the earth and the earth's rhythms—and harmonious also with the rhythms of the human soul at its peaceful best. They would take audio equipment as well as cameras. Ways of being would be discovered or—already known—would come to be known better. Shot sequences with the fishermen and the Sufis in interaction would, when properly edited, reveal a style, a way of behaving, shown to the Sufis by the anglers and to the anglers by the Sufis, that with luck might provide the foundation stones for a new myth by which to live. A small but solid start would be made as their cameras caught the Sufis, engineers of the soul, communing with these good anglers and absorbing their rhythms and giving back to the anglers something of the Sufi way. Perhaps the Sufis would develop a set of rituals based not so much on the actual physical fishing—rigging up, approach, reading the water, immersing, patiently starting to cast—but based rather on the deeper human and earth rhythms underlying these beautiful angling routines. The attitude behind the act, and behind the attitude the emotion, and behind the emotion, the faith.

Eden was excited. Mere months away from the trip now he was entering that euphoric, totally sure state one can get into in anticipation of something falsely wonderful. For twenty years he had done nothing of lasting significance in his field, so it is strange, perhaps, that one morning as he sat at his desk making schedules and scripts and instructions for the film, suddenly, to take a break, he put his film papers aside and on a fresh field of pure white drew five horizontal lines. I watched. He made the lines below each other and flush left, each extending further to the right than the line above it like a simple schematic of a stairway.

He laughed at this, a grunt strong enough to bounce him in his chair. He added arrowtips to each righthand line-end, then drew, diagonally, like rain slanting, more parallel lines over the first five. Over this, chuckling softly, slanting yet a different way he drew several more parallel lines (these broken—dashes). The pattern had started as a doodle and become a representation of leaves blowing across his feet's direction. This amused him and he laughed out loud. He was smiling as he pushed out of his chair and stood on gouty feet.

I saw, objectively, how badly off he was. I said "Let's get you out, take a walk, drive over to Haystack and hike up for some exercise." He was nodding, still gazing at the thing he'd drawn, and he said "sure"—those people never said "surely." Staring like Lot at the lines he'd made, he murmured "sure," then snapped to. He looked at me, as if surprised: "Do you ah, have a car?" I'd come by bus and taxi this particular time. "Can't drive then," he blinked. He explained. He was waiting for the locksmith. He'd inadvertently thrown his car keys away. So we waited an hour, and at last the locksmith arrived, made a couple new sets, and we drove over and had a healthy, needed hike. Aside from throwing his keys away by mistake, other automotive bumblings in my uncle's life included shifting, back when he'd driven a stick, from first to fourth as well as the ever-exciting downshift, at 50, from fourth to first not to mention driving with the emergency brake on, turning the wipers on when meaning to dim his brights, and vice versa. One time when he was grumbling and rumbling that his car wouldn't start, I made the mistake of consulting his owner's manual.

In any event the locksmith did his work quickly that day, beet-red and furious—"Eden you have the attention span of a wastebasket! You've caused this poor family more grief than—you threw 'em *away?*"

"Ah, obviously not on purpose I—"

"Well I'll tell you one thing," the struggling little figure with his Wedgies kicking out the open jalopy door snapped, from within the vehicle's fish-smelling tattered depths, "it's gonna cost ya', *don't say anything!*"

My uncle hoofed defiantly up the leafy trail making a series of fascinating sounds, as he toiled at his climbing, that reminded me of how you hear, when the band is still blocks away, just drums, no other instruments, no tones. It wasn't singing but it was certainly more than mere humming, a kind of congestive yet deep, rhythmical *huff, hunh, hunh-hunh, hoomp, hoomp, hoomp!* He was hearing Sousa in his mind, but all that came out into this world as we know it and live in it was that alien, appealing snuffle-cough that were a film ever to be made about him I would start out with, as we see him striding (thinking wildly) toward the inevitable trip-and-crash . . . I picked him up and we removed some leaves from his sweater. He was breathing heavily. On we climbed, gaining the top, then going on up the stone tower like some dour twelfth-century watcher above the Neckar, to rest and look out over the hills. In the nearer woods below, a man stood watching us. But he wasn't there when we went down. Eden got red like an emergency light going back down—much easier walking—and had to stop, and stood, dealing, physically, with it, seafoam ticking the corners of the bluish lips. "I know," he said, "you think the film idea with Anther," he panted, "is dumb."

"No I don't."

"Ah," he said. "Yes you do. You think it's dumb. Maybe it is."

"But I don't," I insisted, and I didn't. I didn't necessarily think it was smart, but not dumb either. It was his obsession. He was doing it so let him, was the way I felt.

He shook his head. "You think it's dumb," he said stubbornly. "I ah, happen to know you do." At first slowly, he trudged on, then he was swinging his arms, I following . . . in his mind he was thinking of different famous sets. He was mentally fooling with ways of overlapping each set intra-parallel, slanting or horizontal or opposite-slanting like the lines—leaves—he'd drawn. Then he was slide-rule-sliding equations in the pattern so that different discrete functions and values made common-point match-ups: leaf, toe of sneaker, longitude. Into which cusp points of multiconvergence there foamed, as he mentally watched, whirlwinds of quanta!

It was a joke of course, a laugh. But even when he wasn't making such bitter fun, in trying for instance to describe the ins and outs of his science to the likes of a me, he had always felt a need to distort the ideal by re-telling it in childish metaphor. But now in his disillusionment he was being ridiculous with intentional gratuitousness.

If Tellingen wanted hogwash, well here—*voilà*, if a locksmith could charge, and get, a thousand dollars for a simple ten-minute re-keying job then why not this, a self-adjusting superequation a blackboard-and-a-half long!

The next morning, the instant he came awake he snatched the book he was reading off his bedside table, having run out of notepaper, and opening to the title page scribbled, directly under *asperlenspiel:* **d→u** + $e^-$, and so on. As he scribbled, to his continuing astonishment—and sustained astonishment is one of the queerest experiences known—sliding his templates and calibrating his loci and overlapping this equation with that, he saw that it might not be a joke at all. The intersect points kept producing, in his imagination, all manner of tiny magic fulminations, new wildly general impossibly precise mental events not—I have to imagine—entirely unlike the crossed-out locust darkness of henscratched equations I'd stared at, that time, on the few pages of his car-owner's manual that he'd *not* torn out.

Brushing his teeth he was computing. It was stimulating to know that the Answer was ready somewhere in his mind, as he vigorously scrubbed up-down, even though it was still one of about eleven novemdecillion secrets (all but one false) in there as, wide-eyed, he switched to energetic lateral brushstrokes. All he had to do was keep the thinking slow and be patient. When the light goes off and none of it makes sense, be patient. He had read that they were in the process of discovering that the human mind attaches emotional flags—hurt, fear, rage—to important memories, the easier to retrieve them. He had always thought the human mind does creative thinking so much better than a computer because virtually all quanta of thought have a small or large thoughtless daub of sapphire sadness or forest-verdant nostalgia or scarlet anger attached, and inspirational thinking is done by shuffling and combining not cold fact-memories and serpents of logic but rather the emotions these are attached to. As usual he was glad he was alone when he nearly spat his aqua-blue mouthful on the rug. Yes, it was going, in the end, to be a calculation as mundane as—or more correctly when he got it complete and assembled and screw-tightened and the decals on, it *would* be as mundane as—spat turquoise glop in a basin. It was difficult for him to give me even a feel of what it was like, but he tried. It had come out of nowhere. He was making this superequation, he said, sticking a finger in his pipe bowl, by slanting a number of existing equations and formulations three-dimensionally through each other like magicians' swords thrust into the beauty box at various angles. The points of magic commonality where the equations met could, if one were careful, be strung together into odd and wonderful new equations that changed before your eyes in ways that were consistent, he thought . . he was almost there . . . just a couple more years . . . he was terribly excited and he was trying hard to remain calm as he tugged and worried dear old Emma's stick from her slavering smile and held it cocked, like the casting arm prepared for a roll cast while she sat. He faked one—her butt came off the ground a second, then sat—and threw it and turning with a whirl with it she was, even at her age, ears horizontal at full stride even while the trajectory arc of it was still carrying it down, through the forged November air, at the small lawn's far end where Nora and the Poet moped among the coarse trunks of the pines ambling, sometimes with an arm around the other, sometimes holding hands, destinationless. He watched them, ignoring the saliva-slimed stick pointing this-way-that-way and deeply huffing by his leg. The two young people strolled, if you could call it that, from time to time to stop, stand together, tilt heads and kiss. Then unwinding, and maybe loosely holding hands, they would stroll some more. Nora was still doing well in school and with her athletics, and the Poet was at least better than no boyfriend or a worse one, but had Eden, Eden wondered, and his own generation been so *wraithlike* when they'd strolled the dangerous garden of puberty? Probably. Nora was wan. Her Poet had made changes since last year, the scrawny Vandyke become scraggly sideburns, the jeep a Harley. The poetry, thankfully still unwritten for the most part, was the same . . . nothing changes. Tilting, swaying, weight on a foot, languorously the two young people turned, paused, kissed, and meandered on through the distant dark trunks, as the throwing stick now rather insistently was scraping his trouser leg . . . he compared the whole thing to three sentences, each with the word "grade" in it and the three three-dimensionally arranged to intersect only at the word "grade." And, he murmured, as we leaned and strained forward to hear, and for drama he poked a forefinger into his pipe bowl . . . and, he murmured, "one sentence is *I puffed up the steep grade,* the second, ah, is *Please give her a fair grade on the exam,* and the third, heh, is *For our family it has always been neither mutt nor thoroughbred, but grade.* Now where they intersect you see the word *grade* bubbles with fulminant meaning . . . now ah, heh you see, in this, er, well—" humble hands, pipe dropped: ash—Nora wipes up for him with a napkin, her mild blue eyes riddles "—in the model er, if I can . . . you see the points of intersection that form new equations are themselves changing—windows or swivels depending on how you look at it."

Nora and her Poet are faces side-by-side at the long table of candlelight. They hold hands under the table you can see from her left arm, his right. Their faces are blank puddles, holes made in some paperthin black skin through which a pair of round, dense projectiles immaculately has ripped . .

They seemed to be going through the motions, holding hands, staying by each other's side, saying little. They were a ratty pair, and we tried to get them into the swing—dinner songs, encyclopedia arguments, word games—that I remember clearly yet at an emotional distance as if coated in time-layer upon time-layer of translucent opaline tissue. Nora did join in. She sang part of a song and bravely offered her two cents' worth on whether the spirit is or is not capable of progress, but only hesitantly, dreaming of some far-off playing field probably, always with her head down.

She was going to go to a good college it looked like. The Curtisses drew Nora and the Poet out. They got Nora and her friend talking about his cycle, her soccer. Each "Curtiss"—beloved couple of those hills—listened politely, in genuine concentration as Nora got going annoyedly on how a coach had said soccer is better for little kids 'cause to play soccer you don't have to do anything except run around. One "Curtiss" nodded, extending a hand partway across the table, while the other sat back and paid just as close attention. Like as if, Nora insisted, to do football you have to have a brain and soccer is like this *random* . . . she stopped. Surprised at the word? At something. No one knew what was between her and the pitiable Poet. The "Curtisses" were cool, civil, charming but not intentionally, a couple popular up there not merely for their elegance but because they were not characters—they were more or less sane. They leaned and listened, one forward with his hand on the table like a marker, one back with his dessert spoon rotating N, W, S, E and N again on Duffy's sulphur-bottom needlepoint mat.

Eden explained how at the magic intersect points of his jungle gym of equations, new suns glowed. In grid on the dark, minus the jungle gym, those suns could be seen to suggest a new theoretical world. No joke. Virtually overnight he had come to take it with awed seriousness. He recalled having read somewhere that cubism had started as a joke. Young Picasso was so talented he could paint like anyone—Renoir, Gaugin—and so, creatively bored, he broke his canvas in joking ways, thinking this amusement, and lo the world took it so seriously it became the defining moment in the history of his century's art. As for Descartes, what if there's invisible-ink irony in the *Meditations'* introductory letter, wry amusement at the thought of the Nowhere that unadulterated reason—pure unadulterated logic—pure unadulterated thinking—gets you to, so that in a sense Descartes was glorifying faith by lightly, sub rosa, satirizing the rigors of reason (and the world took *that* seriously!).

He went back to his calculations. He lamented that these days it took him three false starts and ten minutes to do calculations that when he was younger would've taken under sixty seconds with no false starts whatever. In his mind finishing off one such reckoning, trying to help clear, with a stack of plates with silverware-salad on top and exponents and differentials scrambling over-the-shoulder-looking and holding hands out to each other left-to-right in his boiling brain, my uncle saw, as he was about to kick open the swinging door from dining room to kitchen, the door move.

"Whoa!" he bellowed.

"Careful," Dr. Wister, on the other side, puled.

Wister, waiting head down in kitchen light, dessert in either hand, wore pants of yellow ducks in a teal swim, a tie of shields and his father's and mother's expression, once brave. The white handkerchief spearing from his navy blazer was not folded right which really, really annoyed Wister.

Eden water-buffalo-bellowed: "These equations—" then, coming to himself: "er . . . COMING *THROUGH!*"

Wister heard this as *Come on through* and started to, was door-flung like a puck.

He landed a considerable distance from where he'd been, not looking like himself, a story told afterward by some, though fewer as time goes on.

Early the next morning when Murray Gell-Mann tossed his monkeywrench into unity spinning off new creations, rather than discoveries, in as many directions as a panicked politician has faces, my uncle in a rising bubble of consciousness shimmying and undulating up through sleep to pop awake on the sun of another morning, remembering the dream, in which Gell-Mann, a great physicist who invented quarks to explain things, was a playing card, didn't wake up fully until nearly finished with his shaving and by then it was too late. Holding his ideas in his head and a tissue wad to his cheek to stanch the bleeding, he went to his study, where he would work on the wild new model. He would let the fishing film go for a day. He wasn't even hungry. Found himself making a U-turn, leaving his study and the house without a jacket, this cold day . . . he walked up over the meadow and wandered on down the frozen lanes and leafless ways of his relatives' places, where backhoes and earthmovers sat, unused today, where more land had been sold off, and his equation was not coming but he could feel it—he felt the potentiality of intellectual salvation great in him, an unusual vast calm and a crazed, secret, vigilant, willed jittery patience while the math and mind-hues I could never hope to understand flourished in him with the changingness of hot life forming in the wonder of woman's tentacling grabby blossoming adhering spidery generative systems, but it scared him. He walked from the skeet range around the top of the lake—distant, shining, seen through a thousand vertical fingers—to a straight rutted back way past the Grummans' rear yard. Whitewashed postern. The Grummans' clapboard mansion's odd-shaped little back porches, inconsistent windows and scattered rear-pantry and laundry and mudroom doors unsymmetrical here on the far side of the sweep of the front facade which, white and sprawling behind green shrubs acrest a waveswell of lawns atop the S drive from the lions, always looked, not deserted, but silent. Protruding from under a Duesenberg on blocks between the clothesline and a fenced cutting garden, a pair of legs, metamorphosing, after he'd passed, into legs-torso, legs-torso-shoulders, torso-shoulders-face, sitting up, arms hugging knees, watched the physicist's fat back grow small in the glen's shadows.

He went by Lim's place, knocked, and was ushered into those rooms of expensive anonymous furniture and original oils of countryside and the very best art books and magazines lying loosely on cabriole-legged tables. Their pale blank faces floated around him—Lim's not among them. Lim was in the city for the day, his family's moon-balloon featureless faces explained. He felt they were watching him to see what he would do . . . would he scribble equations on the foxhound wallpaper? Would he track mud on *every* rug? Sally told him, as they awkwardly stood there, that Lim had been to see a specialist. Heart? Computer? She didn't specify, he didn't ask.

One unnaturally late maple, as he puffed back up his brother's ramp drive flanked by terraces of gardens now asleep, stood gloriously, still bright red while all the other trees—gray and brown torches, flameless, of crook'd branches—stood in the circular litter of the leaves they'd shaken off. Then back down the lanes breathing hard, down over the meadow and home to a house quiet. Nora at school, all guests gone.

Duffy had promised to drop by and give the place "a spit and a promise" after the previous evening's festivities, but had not come yet.

In the skylight entry among his rods and never-used umbrellas and muddy bluchers, he had a bad moment. Even more unkempt than usual, too aware of the going of his heart, looking—if it is possible to look at light—at the gray light in the skylight and on the slate floor and on his gear and kids' toys from other times and a UPS package leaning against the cedar wall, unopened since its delivery some days ago, he felt the physical world around him and this, his house, go translucent, which may be why, as he walked back through the bungalow on the way to his study, he lingered to look at his parents, hung in bad light in a narrowish hall. Big oils with fancy frames, the two portraits belonged in a white sunflooded chamber of confectionery molding where the main stair sweeps heavenward like God's upward-spiraling welcoming hand, but "Lookout" had been sold. His mother cocked her head, listening. Smiling the faintest frosty smile, listening to hear if all were well in all the farther rooms of the great house where her boys and husband and servants were respectively playing and unlocking the gun case and vacuuming, while the artist paints her. The eyes not so arctic silver as in that strange dream with the cat, but cool, loving and cool, traditional and calm, loving and hard, blooded and calm, icy, loving, locked and manacled—and happy to be—in the consuetudes of a half-dozen comely branches.

His father's thin handsome and sad green-eyed face, as revealed to him again and again by the annoyed collapse of the evening paper when he would stand his childish ground and ask his hornet questions, still looked young, in the dim portrait, and was whole, the only way Eden ever saw it, as the coffin had been closed. Now his poor father's image turns away with its mate as the thought-lost figure in baggy trousers moves on down the hall, his work in physics, in which he has done some good, in him, and also in him though perhaps dormant now forever his Sword Cycle fiction, harmless—to millions apparently entertaining, to him a lark—and also in him the tragic compulsion with the movie and especially now the forming, skittish general theory of energy and matter, either true or else an embarrassment, but you never know. The heavenly stands but a step from the ludicrous. Certainly it had him, this compulsion to be certain. There was, in this late time of life, none of that marvelous quality of proportion and health that you drink in and shutting your eyes can smell like a baby's sweetness when you read Werner Heisenberg's memories of his young years of music, Alpine hikes and jokes with putteed confreres and general exfoliative curiosity with little if any need to be finally, comprehensively sure. Touching the dim wall my uncle turned the last corner and ambled, feeling his crazy theory screaming in him to be worked on, down the glassed-in breezeway space connecting his house to his mind. He had a chance at it—he knew that much. It could drive him mad or hasten his journey there, but while he was an abnormal physicist he was still a good one—good enough to know, as he opened the study door and walked in, that the silly schematic of leaves at a sideslant under your walking feet while the sun shines one way and the earth spins another, that he'd doodled, was the plucked first ravel of a who-knew-how-complex universe that, whether he personally was brain enough to untie it or not, was real.

Quadros was sitting in his chair.

"I thought—"

"Oh she is."

"I thought Nora was—"

"She is," Quadros said, looking through a pair of spectacles.

Quadros never wore spectacles. He was wearing them to read Eden's papers. He picked sheets up one at a time, then discarded what he was finished with. Sheet by sheet—scraps, envelopes, legal sheets—he underslid each patiently with a thumb, lifted it, with fingertips and that thumb, held it at a distance from Eden's lemon-slice reading glasses, which he was wearing, and examined.

"She's quite finished with me," he said as he read. "Quite finished."

He was about to put the piece of paper down but wait . . . something caught his attention. Not lifting an eyebrow, without a single facial muscle's stir—no ripple down the jaw, no slight pulse behind the cheek—moving the piece of paper he held to a greater distance from, then half a foot closer to, the other's spectacles that he wore, he considered some more, saying, as he did so, "finished," in a neutral tone.

He set the sheet down and took up another one.

"We're friends of course."

"This makes no sense!"

"It doesn't," Quadros agreed.

"So what are you sitting there for?" my uncle demanded in a voice that started in his mind as bronze and clangorous in its wrath. In the journey from the seat of thinking to larynx and lungs, however, that red Mars voice had gotten embarrassingly throttled somehow, and came out in a series of sibilants and interrogative peeps.

"Makes little sense," Quadros said, professorially still looking down at the piece of paper in his long hand. He read as he spoke. "Little, if any, sense." He delivered himself of these words while reading one of my uncle's equation-scrimmages, or maybe it was notes for the film—

Eden was scared. He was surprised. Not surprised. But angry. He was angry. This all warred in him. He readied his voice and drew breath to speak, but Quadros held up a hand silencing him except, of course, Quadros never did anything like that with his hands. It was just his voice that he used, as he continued to read. He wore a double-breasted serge tuxedo jacket and a white collarless shirt with an orange, bright green, lollipop red and yellow Ming dragon embroidered on the sternum.

The opposing twin Ss of his long hair jounced infinitesimally.

"Forgive me," he said as he read.

He said this with a straight face. Of course his face was always straight, his calm eerie, a sea calm—oily flat ocean, merciless sun, hanging sail . . . Quadros was as calm—all of him—as my uncle's forehead had once been when in thought. The nose not hooked like Duffy's but resembling an upsidedown long-stemmed seven. The eyes pure hyphens. The lips a dash. The piece of paper held, examined, perfectly still. "Forgive me," Quadros' voice said. "I wanted to see what it felt like to sit in the seat of knowledge."

What did one say to that? My uncle was trying to think . .

Noiseless as a smashed watch Quadros had flowed into the bungalow. Flowingly his right arm now became straight. Another scrap of paper was lifted. His right arm became an L, and he was reading.

Eden stamped his foot, surprising himself. He couldn't help it but he was blushing.

"Where is she?" he asked loudly.

"Your daughter Nora?"

"Yes damn you I asked a simple question."

"She's in school," Quadros said, trying again to get the right visual range, through my uncle's glasses, from his pillbox-slit eyes to the paper. "I would assume."

"You would *assume?* "

"Oughtn't you to know?"

"Well uh, heh, obviously yes, obviously yes."

He wasn't sure if the heavy irony he intended was getting communicated.

"Well then," reading Quadros softly agreed.

"Well then nothing, is she in *school?*"

"I think she is."

"But you ah, don't know. You truthfully—"

"No one knows anything," Quadros said. "We've been through that."

"Well uh, heh, did you tell her to? Did you tell her to go to school because certainly ah, one is aware," my uncle said, acidly, "that she is unable to do anything, speak, have an opinion, eat, breathe, sleep, without your blessing, without your command I should say."

Quadros, because my uncle had begun with a question but finished with a statement, did not feel obliged to reply apparently, which silence Eden riotously interrupted, though there was a phone here in his study, with a great barging out of the room stompingly—he tried to slam the door too but missed—that he hoped would communicate to the familiar intruder that he, Quadros, was in the wrong, that the situation was wrong, that Eden was in the right, and that Eden was not going to stand idly by while some ersatz sage with a dragon on his shirt kept him from his work.

Down the corridor of glass-displayed forest and into the bungalow proper he went, still moving as loudly as he could. He found a telephone, using which instrument he for a moment thought maybe it was Kyle he ought to be dialing instead of Nora's high school, and got the school operator, to whom, without identifying himself, he put his question with the youthful theoretical physicist's arrogance of the too-simple: "Is my daughter there?"

Fathers with a Daughter They're Worried About (category) call School (category—the Daughter's school) . . . all automobiles have the same engine, all atoms follow one concordance, beavers and spiders everywhere read from the same rule book . . . Father/Fear/Daughter/ Question. *Is my daughter there?* The school operator politely asked, please, who was calling.

Striding through the house back toward the glassed-in breezeway he came around a corner and for earthly reason remembered, down to the smells of herb-seasoned beef simmering in from the kitchen, a night when Rairia had nearly run into him here coming the other way. With an in-rush of breath she had shrunk back from him—from anyone, from anything not known, not expected, in those years. Standing here with her, before he went on in for his evening's session of work, he had joked about her super sensitivity. Then she was pouring out to him the frustrations of her day—faucets that wouldn't work, children that used nastiness, salespeople that wouldn't listen, shins that bled, friends that wouldn't call back, checkbooks that wouldn't balance. He had stood there feeling the nervous spleen and bile of selfish thought rise chokingly because his thoughts were awasting while he listened to her—shadows in the corridor, her mane of lovely hair not lovely without light to liven it. He was saying "ok," and "yes ok-ok, mm-mh, just . . . all *right* Rairia" as she poured the frustrations of her day like industrial effluent into the purity of this hour in which he was going to do more work and of course then they were fighting. "Do you want me to get out of your chair?" Quadros asked without looking up. The afternoon had become so gray Quadros had gotten up in the interim to turn some lights on. "Do you want," Quadros politely repeated, reading, "your chair?"

Angry and disoriented as my uncle was, he managed to control himself and reply with an acid silence that, as it went on and he added a withering, pinch-lipped stare of hostility to it, must surely have gotten through to even such a gyroscope as Q. It seemed to work. At least the narrow-shouldered, well-dressed presence put the piece of paper down, without picking up another.

"I must ask you to leave," Eden said.

"I don't understand this."

"Understand what?"

"This," Quadros said, leaning forward, the piece of paper held again in the tapered, ringless fingers.

# 24

"These insertions," Quadros said, "as if you were trying to cover a mistake."

The gibe outraged Eden. Quadros knew nothing, nothing about physics practiced at the level of a Tellingen or a Hope. "No," he said shaking his head, "you don't, you don't understand, you are right about that. Now I am trying to tell you, I am trying to tell you in the most civil way I know, that I must ask—no, I must insist."

He said no more. What he was insisting on was patently obvious. Quadros had to leave.

"I must insist," Quadros said calmly, without emphasis or rancor. "I'm curious. About this lambda, squiggly lines and—"

"I know exactly," my uncle said shutting his eyes, "the page you're on. All—"

"Could I ask just this one question that I have?"

"One."

"One."

"One question," my uncle confirmed, "and you'll go."

"One," Quadros confirmed. "Do you really have all this stuff committed to memory? That's not my question."

"Yes," Eden said behind angrily patient shut eyes.

He could see the page, even the cross-outs. He wanted to go to work.

"Ask," he commanded.

A trifle stumblingly, Quadros asked his question. It was a good one, if naive and improperly couched.

"The ah," my uncle answered, opening part of an eye, "molded symmetry is demanded, not observed. That's why all the little circles. There's just one theory on this, we're pretty sure, but we've no idea what it is. But it has to be there, just as the top quark does."

"Why?"

"Why because otherwise the whole ah, the whole model, ah, wouldn't, eh—this is hard for a layperson to envision."

"What's this upsidedown omega?"

"Where," coming around behind his desk and bending to peer. Accepting his offered reading glasses and slipping them on over his nose, "oh that. That's Uniformity."

"What's 'Uniformity'?"

"Listen," Eden said taking his glasses off but not standing straight—"Listen to me," staring bravely at close range at the impassive, granite face. "It's a value I put in to allow for discrepancies. It makes the calculations work." The phone was ringing but he ignored it. "This is subatomic physics *on a very high level.* I don't mean to sound condescending, but of course you don't understand it."

On the firmest of ground, my uncle had at last spontaneously spoken with a forcefulness that, as he stood straight and stepped back, Quadros seemed to respect.

Quadros lightly nodded, regarding his pupil's father with an impartial eye.

"What's 'spin'?" Quadros wanted to know, looking up at him. "I've read about it—I think I know what it is—but I want to hear a master define it."

"Hah. Not so easy ah, but I'll tell you—"

The phone again, and again they ignored it. My uncle explained *spin,* not badly he thought, listening to himself. It felt peculiar to be rehearsing the basics of his science, which he had come devoutly to doubt (which he didn't want Quadros to know) and was, in his Vision of the Blowing Leaves, dreaming of going beyond, but Quadros was not dumb—his intellectual curiosity seemed genuine, angular momentum, spin one way clockwise or the other (counter-) but always—electron—the same magnitude (of spin), and as he was talking, looking at Quadros looking up at him, then looking down at his paper in Quadros' literal hand, it struck him that science is insubstantial. Quadros did not lean back folding his arms and lift his chin to consider my uncle in disbelief. No, Quadros accomplished all that with a single raised eyebrow. My uncle quit in mid-sentence.

"She needs someone," Quadros told him. "Everyone does, but Nora especially. She can't be solitary, and in many ways she had been. Now . ." he did not blink ". . she needs to be with someone. Her time learning from me is of course over. So at last I advised her, reluctantly, to reestablish her relationship with that . . boy. Who I'm sure you know has been dogging her for a year. The one you derisively call 'the Poet.'"

"You told her to?"

"I did. Did you think I would politely ask her?"

This time when the phone rang my uncle answered. It was Duffy, apologizing for not coming "today or whatever day."

"It was today," he told her. "It's no matter."

"It's six of one," she was saying, "and a baker's dozen of the other—"

"Don't tell her I'm here," Quadros said softly.

Eden distractedly nodded, spoke to his friend to the tune of a couple bewildering sentences more, and rang off, wondering—though he'd had no thought of telling Duffy that Quadros was sitting here at his desk—why Quadros would've asked him not to. He ought to've. When Q had asked him not to, he ought to've for just that reason . . there was a wind kicking up outside, boughs leaning, lifting, menacingly gesturing, falling, wildly lifting again . . . there was music somewhere too, far away in another part of the house—Nora?

"I must go," Quadros said getting up. "I very much must. You know, this whole thing with Nora is deforming her."

My uncle without a word shadowed him as he walked out of the study and through the glassed-in breezeway of dark, leafless branches bending and tossing, and through the front of the house where a staid 18th-century procession of strings was stepping through the air, though there was no one. He stood in the bungalow's front door while the narrow tuxedo-back went up the railroad steps, Quadros' hair snapping and billowing nearly at the vertical as he went to the low, silent car—door open, waiting—that idled, you could hear between the wind's shrieks, in the very middle of the parking circle with its lights on in the twilight such storm weather can make of midafternoon.

Watched the car, its lights, go, until he could see no more of it. Shut and locked the door. Found where the music was coming from: diningroom table, all the equipment he'd bought Bitterbeer! Note: *Have excellent job,* the ovate hand read, *performing on organ for all* (here the name of a venerable major league team appears) *games. Music needs more structure than life, Regards.* Absently he carried the note with him to a telephone. Kyle Kulka answered on the fourth ring. My uncle gave a fast recounting of the episode just ended. "We have to do something," he said into the phone, without waiting for Kyle's comments. "We have to do something decisive."

Kyle measured the width of his nose. Kyle traced the shape of his chin, tested his eyes' blink-muscles, purged glottis and epiglottis of phlegm.

"And," he said thoughtfully, "well . . ." rubbing his eyes ". . the first thing is, we need to observe him some more."

The wind that had been blowing at the house now quieted. In the distance, however, there was sound. It came closer, it got louder. It was more wind. And the wind now everywhere was blowing thunderously and held the house whole, roofs, walls, floors, and shook it.

Eden listened.

"We have to observe him some more," Kyle prescribed, "and be tough. It's time to get tough. We have to send a strong signal. And! If he persists we'll tighten the screws—we'll observe the hell out of him."

But Kyle came back scared from his visit to Quadros' house—if not scared, agitated. "He wasn't there," he reported. "And—"

"If he wasn't there, why so agitated?"

Kyle Kulka's bright eyes, mind, spectacle lenses and teeth looked to my uncle as if you could fling a rock against them and there would be a *clang.*

"There's a domestic dynamic to this," Kyle explained. "There's a feminist dynamic, a class dynamic, a psychospiritual dynamic, a generic dynamic, a political dynamic, a biological dynamic, a conceptual dynamic. It's not a simple thing. From the obliteration of the self to a fresh traits-cluster isn't a question of one, or even two stages. *And* . . . just remember, as long as you're avoiding the worst you're doing your best."

My uncle did at least visit Chief Airlenmacher, who, after telling several stories, drew his friend Eden out, explaining that even though a kid isn't eighteen yet, the law says if the kid goes off somewhere by choice there's nothing the law can do . . . was there a specific incident? A specific charge? A specific offense?

My uncle weighed this, willing himself, with difficulty, to be compassionate, and shook his head.

The retired security officer my uncle on the spur of the moment hired the next day, whose mission they agreed it would hazily be to drive up there and put a scare into Q, failed to report back, then phoned, muffledly, to tell Eden he was being held, and could Eden please come get him. Mr. Porette was a mannered, direct gentleman with a combat record but made no bones about being flustered—"No no," Quadros' voice affably corrected, coming on the line, "he's perfectly free. Free to go anytime." But Mr. Porette called again an hour later and used the word "help." My uncle touched the tip of his tongue to the center of his upper lip, waiting for his temper to equilibrate. "Ah, if he indeed is free," he said into the phone silence that obviously had Quadros in it, "I expect to see him here, alone, unharmed, in an hour."

"Certainly," Quadros agreed. "If you give me your word you will never do anything like this again. It is disruptive."

"Hah," my uncle sputtered, "you actually, you actually think—why the nerve of. This is so blatantly . . there's a word for this. There's a word for this you know. You have taken this innocent man prisoner. Now you expect me to allow myself to be pressured into giving you what you ah, what you, er, want. You send him back. You send him back down here and you do it without any conditions or promises."

"No," Quadros said.

"Eh?"

"No."

"In other words if, that is unless—"

"That's correct."

"Well I certainly refuse to make any firm, or commit to—to reward ah, but, now, naturally one is not *precluding* anything. You understand one is not ruling *out* the possibility of a future, er—"

"That this won't happen again."

"Well of course, of course, ah, I mean I can't." But he could, and he did—Mr. Porette returned intact, if taciturn, and was off the case. My uncle hired no one more. In their conversation before Mr. Porette had been set free Quadros (who never did admit the man had been restrained) said "You know if you do send anyone again I'll hold not only him or her but I'll go get Mr. Porette again," to which my uncle responded angrily "Well of course, of course you will, I'm not stupid, I understand that."

Nora wouldn't talk about it. Eden was confused, skipping in the articles he read, channel-surfing—in the books he read starting anywhere but at the beginning. In conversation scarcely listening he leaned on his elbows with that still pleasant plastic face lowered bull-like, fixed, dark in concentration while he waited for you to take a breath so he could finish your point for you, because, rising, building in color before his mental eye, he saw the greenjeweled city—bright farm countryside of hope surrounding—the universe revealed as an understandable system, the cosmos in process laid bare, gnats, memory, comets, jealousy, time, the influence of gravity on magnetism, your hat—mine, the pure thin song of schoolchildren's voices, even flowing water's random ways, all of it made sense of in five—I think it was five—fundamental nonlinear equations that laid end to end would reach from where you are sitting right now to the nearest spider.

In the space of two days Nora started looking awful, silent, worse than ever. You couldn't get her to talk. My uncle kalled his kolleague Kyle, who, in Eden's at-this-time febrile imagination, was bekoming enkrusted with k's, kaustikally to komplain. Kyle kounseled kaution. Then he was saying something about dithyrambic continuities, discontinuities, discourses, the "we" and radically (post)modern synthetic guise-theory when Eden slammed the phone down. He went out and got in his car, tried to start it, stomped back down the railroad-tie steps to go back in and get his keys, hurried back out and drove straight up to Quadros' where he stormed in without knocking and demanded an explanation.

A disciple showed him to a sanctum, a nondescript den of white pine—windowless—below ground in Q's sleepy suburban rancher. A disciple with buzzed short hair and a small blunt nose who couldn't look up. A room, in that furnished house (out of which, Eden thought he noticed, some divans and tables had gone since last he was here), without circulation—no windows, one door, a stillness and stiffness as if there were a seal around the cube of gray-carpeted space with just the easy chair Quadros sat in, the one-legged circular accessory table, with an atlas on it, by his lithe arm, and the floor lamp—plugged in, you could see, to the nearest standard outlet—that gave out a bland and dull light in which the expressions warring on Q's face were mercifully bleared.

Quadros sat in the lamp's cave-like light here below the green lawn and kennels (deserted) and upheaved town sidewalk.

Quadros was in agony.

"They use sleep deprivation," he moaned, "they use trick icons, lighting, drugs, rough sex—I use none of these!"

It was marvelous what agony he was in. Eden couldn't help but feel a cowardly rush of pleasure. Quadros was not one to writhe, and sat still, as ever, forearms one each on a chair arm. The narrow shoulders still, but oh the face. Up the eyes rolled in that lamplight, twisted the lips seemed, and the elegant face was upward-tapering, draining down and flaming up like a candleflame, a melting taper, up, in this impressive spirituality of suffering. It was like the depiction of a howl or a scream, or a bouquet of flamelike devouts.

"Oh," he swayed, "they want too much. They ask too much. For me to accomplish all they ask, but no more, to achieve all the effects they desire, then stop, too difficult. Nudge the blade in," Quadros dreamed, "they want me to drive the blade in a third of the way then in the passion of the job stop, stop there, no further, ohh, too hard, too hard. And that's enough of that. Let's go upstairs."

In a minute they were in the upper study—white bare walls, no books, desk, lustrous hardwood floor—that my uncle remembered though no class awaited the master through the two further capacious doors which he also remembered; and although a disciple, a different one (shaggy face in clip suspenders) drifted by dollying hearts, the whole place dwelt suspended in a cul-de-sac of silence of leafy neighborhood quiet that to my uncle was, given the circumstances, a waiting—for what he dared not guess.

"Now *ahem,*" he boomed. "All right, all right now—"

"I often begin as a joke," Quadros said. "Someone thinks I'm a joke, ridicules me—mechanizes—humor is mechanistic. Humor's the super-objectification of the individual, cartoon violence, joke-abuse. We see the moving parts and how each moves, and a surprise—but no mystery—makes us laugh. There is never any mystery at all in humor; that's invariably where they make their mistake . . a joke, well . . if you want to think I'm that, do so."

As if scanning the bright hardwood for a crop of jot exclamation points Quadros had calmly forborne to harvest and use, my uncle, hands clasped behind back, head bent, paced a little. Then felt the other's eyes on him, and made the mistake of looking.

Q's eyes grew.

Looking into them was looking over a fifty-story city ledge straight down, tiny rectangle cars oozing and pedestrian heads, crowds of dots, Brownian jiggle so very far below . .

"I'm nothing," Quadros mildly said to my uncle to his face. "Don't worry about me."

"I should call the police."

He heard himself say this as the eyes drank his.

In point of fact he had called the police. So, he guessed, he meant he should call them again. Well, in a sense he had . .

"That can be dangerous," Quadros observed. Performing the neat trick of lifting the receiver of the phone on the desk beside him without turning to look to do it, Q offered it in the air to my uncle.

"Who are you?"

"I could tell you the truth," Quadros said. "I could tell you the truth right now and you wouldn't believe it."

"And why's that?"

Q, bored: "I will do a strange thing. I will tell you the truth—I will tell you the truth, part of the truth, and mostly the truth, I do solemnly suggest. The truth could scuttle in here right now," Quadros told him, the flat eyes getting younger as he spoke, "to rub your leg and you wouldn't recognize it. You'd feel tilted and stomp it—pest!—two-dimensional. You'd stomp the truth right back out of its truth-ness and into everything else. And I will tell you this: they think I'm working for them . . . they think," Q with soft, foreign reasonableness wished Eden to know, "I'm working for them. But I'm secretly working for God."

The jamb of the white doorway, up the trim of which height-hatchmarks and children's names faint with time climb, halves a distant window onto which sunlight shines and through which a telescopically faraway stationwagon slides—green firs standing before, with, and after the car's passing in the quiet pent stillness of the house.

"What's the one they just found?" Quadros wanted to know.

He knew what Q meant and he stood a moment trying to decide what to do. He answered, still staring at the window two doorways and three rooms away: "Called the top quark." "But what we see through the telescope," Quadros' soft voice put in—and my uncle knew what he was talking about. "Correct," he said, "the universe is too young . . we can't find the dark matter where we thought we would." "We need new particles," Quadros suggested. "Yes," agreeing, "we need many new hypothetical particles." What? What was the other saying? *Solace,* Q was saying. *Solace,* Q's cashmere voice was saying. Watching my uncle as he spoke. *Solace, your science must be such a solace for you* . . . it was. And now Eden found a simple eloquence that was unusual for him, a spareness of expression, a dignity of form, that did not occur again—nor have I been able to find it in his papers—and that caused to rise before Quadros' steady gaze as the Buick Roadmaster V-8 purr of my uncle's bass went gently, surely on, a vision of the theory complete . .

"That's good," Quadros said respectfully. "That's wonderful."

"Please, leave us alone."

Quadros' eyes gleamed. He stood, arms at sides, face level, sandals, rope belt.

"I'll leave you alone for a month anyway," he said jocularly. "That's how long I'll be gone this next jaunt."

". . . traveling?"

"Yes," Quadros said, allowing his tone a tinct of fatigue.

"Well I must confess, I must tell you, and I doubt it will come as a surprise: it's a relief to hear it," my uncle said. "Ahhh . . . far from here? Will you be traveling far?"

"In fact," Quadros said, "if in spirit."

My uncle with roof-raised brows wondered if this meant yes.

Silence answered, creating effervescence—undulate globule of a world—doesn't last . .

One evening Nora talked too much. He was glad for it. Yet again the subject was whether the prehistoric hunters/meat-eaters or the prehistoric farmers were more peaceful. Ridiculous. But he let her, because at least she was talking. "No one," he told her softly, "really knows." Popping her hooked nose around the doorway Duffy asked if anyone wanted coffee. A piece of her carrot cake? No one did, but they all thanked their lanky friend, who'd been having tough times of her own lately. A trooper, Duffy still found time to come here to help tidy up, maybe make a meal. As to her own troubles she bravely averred that she refused "to give my best days away to an allusion I can't even remember."

In the awed silence that followed this declaration none of them, not

Nora, not Eden, not Nora's friend Vanessa, who had come over, not Wister and neither "Curtiss," much as each felt great affinity with Duffy, could bring himself or herself to ask her what she meant. With a sniff and a toss of the head she told them anyway: "You can't cast your pearls in a sow's ear, so why try?"

I can say of Duffy's familial problems both that they were solved and that none of us knew what they were. Her 'misspeaks' had not always been preponderant in her talk, but over time Eden had affectionately, by his fascination with what Duffy could dictionally do, pushed her to become a caricature of herself when around him. At dinner one time years before I even went up there Duffy had started talking quite normally, even touchingly, about her sudden and newfound respect for a daughter she'd always considered lazy when, Nancy said, Eden prepossessedly could not refrain from interrupting, joking, taunting, herding Duffy, as it were, back into first one malapropism, then—to his relieved laughter—many.

". . six."

"Sixteen."

"Twenty-six," Nora Hope said. "For two."

"hmp."

Eden made a T sign for time-out and busied himself scribbling variants, wrong ones, but new ones—a discrete mathematical value, one imaginary one, and the exponent it needed. He scribbled in pencil-nubbin on yellow paper. Plug the value in, appreciate the ripplechange of selective adjustment this act sends shimmering and glimmering out through the whole of his blackboards-long vision . . resume play.

"Dad?"

"Hm?"

He lifted a round peg from a round hole . .

"Do you really think we can figure the universe out?"

. . leapfrogging Peg One lightly stabbed the finger-twiddly peg in its proper, further hole of advance.

"Does *he?* " he asked archly. "Does *he* think so?"

"Who Q?"

Eden lay a king flat. "Ten."

"Fifteen . . as you know, he doesn't . . for two. No dad, he doesn't. He doesn't think you can figure the universe out, and I think you know that frankly. He thinks you can do stuff in it."

"I'm sorry."

"No need," she said with restrained impatience, "to be sorry."

"Twenty-five."

"Go."

"Go," he said. "I'm sorry he hasn't told us the truth."

Nora: "What truth?"

Eden: "He said it would be over, you'd be free er, he'd release you is as good a way as any to put it. That's what he told me—you, us." My uncle's brown eyes flicked up from the game to Nora's expression which had gone to that pinched locked tightness—jaw hard, eyes hard, lips hard—that he had been so relieved today to see gone from her handsome face when to his amazement she'd agreed to accompany him, in the December cold sun, down through the southern woods to that same fieldstone-walled broken mill pool, with his eight-foot Thomas and Thomas. The bare trees were quiet in the flat light. You couldn't feel a breeze on your cheek but, now and then, a smaller branch moved. The water, turning in the big pool, was steely, daubed blue when glanced at from one angle, black as an absolute vacuum if you stood even just a step, in your floppy boots, to the side on the underwater ledge of mud before the under-the-current drop-off of old stone beyond which the pool proper, fifteen feet deep in places, stirred and moiled. Forest complexity of seeking branches—barren—but look at that, a beech, tenacious brown almond-shaped leaves ashiver an instant. Nora wore a wool cap, her hair stuffed up under. Her nose was touched by cold, as was each noble cheek, and she was concentrating. He'd been delighted when in reply to his halfhearted invitation she'd said yes, and helped him get his gear together. The water was too cold, the season was wrong, but he'd wanted to get out of the house and she had come along. Not acquiescently either, eagerly almost: "Yes," she said when he asked her, "sure." His heart sang a measure at that. Did she have something to tell him? "Nory?" "Yeah?" "Ahhh, your line's too slack, see how it's all aurora-borealising to the side there in the slower current?" "Yeah," she said, blowing on her left set of fingers then getting them back fast on her line before he could caution her to. "You see, a fish could mouth your fly and you wouldn't even feel it." "Yeah," she said, "so what do I do?" "Here, cast again, bring it in, that's right, now cast again to *this* side ah, then flick the—Nora! That's right! That's called a mend—mend, mend . . good!" And on her own she was doing it, wrist-flick like one whisk-stir, and again, flipping dollops of line left, left, left onto the current that pulled the line, the further end of which an inch under the gray surface dove forward and down disappearing. In six months these trees would be explosions of green, birds everywhere, noisy smells warm on the air . . . he told her to keep the line as tight as possible without distorting the natural drift and she laughed at the difficulty of her father's language. He did too, clapping his mittens. The flat wintry sunlight cast sharp, bluish black shadows: rotund one capped by flop of hat, broadshouldered one with rod, hunched in concentration, wool cap hairless—shadow of woman or man on the slow water here above where they stand. Shadow of wall—isosceles black night and, in it, scarcely visible or real, the currents' glints of motion. The rest of the pool was sunlit gray and astir, and trees, elongated, were lying down east of themselves. Dark indistinct wings slide over the current to leap instantaneously up the stone wall: crow.

"Ahh, I think . ." "Dad?" "Strike! Pull up!" "Hey!" And her line straight-pulling, parabola rod, laughter, excitedly her dad swipes the crystalline drop from his schnozz, she's cranking—hard yet to tell if it's a big one—current this deep and strong can make a little one seem big, until, oh it's a good one. Good fish. But be careful at the edge of this upper underwater ledge—"be careful dad." "I ah, will. You can muscle it Nora, just pull it up here, you've got plenty of line test, that's good. Say." "Does the hook hurt it?" "No more than an insult." "It's a good one isn't it?" "It's a fine one, here let me ow! Wait . . there, like it?" "Yeah," she said, the softening of the hurt in her eyes revealing to him that hurt's constant presence. "So," he said. "Let it go?" "Of course." "Bye," she said. "*There.*" Silver in the dark water, then nothing.

Then hiking home with a little laugh she picked up their years-old conversation yet again with a ready aplomb that unnerved him. She said she wondered how peaceful the early fishermen were—more peaceful than the early meat eaters? More peaceful than the first farmers? Did they like fish with nets, spears, birds of prey? She seemed eager to talk and he let her, trudging thoughtfully beside her noisy boots, back through the woods, out into the sun and across the meadow's lower corner toward home . . . but she had clammed up this evening when he'd made his dig about Quadros not telling the truth—she clamped her incisors and scowled, wordlessly shuffled. Deft airy flutter of waterfall tens, pawnshop black blossoms, scarlet diamonds, sevens, sixes, royalty, a three, ones . . "We tolerated him," her father told her, "because you'd changed. You were better."

"Tolerated?"

"We—"

"You had no choice," the young woman said. "The will—" last card face-down his, delivered by her with the wrist motion used in mending line "—is stronger than any idea."

"Bunk," he said, quickly making a laugh over it and with a forced smile shaking his head to soften it, but she didn't seem to mind. They were looking at their cards—he was trying to calculate odds, but he was distracted . .

"When you visit him," Nora said, her cards in her blue eyes, "he's strengthened."

"I'm glad to hear it."

"Like Mom. You should see her, I know you want to, it's a whole 'nother life, I'm so proud of her, she's like this butterfly of steel, like Q when he's not having his doubts. You don't see him when it happens but he does, that's when—it's the only time he's cruel, when he's not sure. But Mom's eyes are like sparkling in charge. They all respect her, I did too. It's a shame."

What was a shame? Nora's fluttering lashes and quick silence told him—a shame he'd lost Rairia. He cut, jack. "So," he vamped, "and where do you suppose he's—" "Two dad." "Oh ah, yes." Pegged it.

"Charlottesville," she said adjusting her cards then adjusting, unconsciously, the left band of her suspenders with hooked right thumb. "Santa Fe, Blacksburg, Harpers Ferry."

"Oh really."

Showing the whites of her eyes the way her mother had once done, and Nance still did, Nora shivered her hair horse-mane back off her forehead looking heavenward. Then was glum, stared at her cards. "Yeah," she said, "really." She tossed in her cards.

"Nory!"

"I don't feel like playing."

"But there were potentially two more cribs coming your way."

"Dad stop counting. Stop measuring everything."

"I was only—"

"His will," she said.

"Ah." He began a careful question, "you mean—"

"Yes," she said, bitter—angry? He wished he could tell. "Yes."

"Now . ." again careful ". . he's gone for—"

"A month, he's gone a month."

"Doing what Nora?"

She seemed interested in the question, forgot her foggy glumness in answering. "I dunno but it's interesting. He's like just practicing on us. People come around to check. They don't think he sees them, but he does. I don't go up there anymore."

"Oh please, please don't—"

"Don't what?"

"Just tell me the truth, you owe me that."

"What truth . . Dad I don't go up there, ok? That's the truth."

"I don't understand."

"I know you don't."

"But heh, Nory . . if you don't go there . ."

"I don't have any contact with him anymore, hardly any, a phone call, a valentine. But I don't go up there—he forbids it."

"But if—I don't see why, I mean if you're truly, er, free, he's truly through with you—you've graduated, ah, as you would say, then why? What's disturbing you?"

She lifted her blue eyes and through the silk parlor wall stared off to some sandy coast far from here . . he'd been right . . volleyball forever.

"What's disturbing me so, *dad,* is that I *can't* see him anymore."

This delivered in a cool false compressed civil tone more of annunciation than reply. The tone and inflection Q had taught her, and that fell on the physicist's ear, rightly or wrongly, as haughtily patient, even long-suffering, while the May eyes gazed beyond his house's insufficient walls, a tone that so disturbed him that the instant Nora was in bed (or out a window and down a ladder!?) he dialed Tacoma.

Nancy was resolved in a trice. "That's it," she said. "I'm coming, no ifs or buts, one way or another this thing has to be settled," she declared. "I'm coming with Alan and Michael," she said an hour later, after making her travel arrangements and calling me back, "so will you tell him?" She gave me flight number and arrival time and made me repeat them back across the Republic. "And tell him," she sighed heavily, "please to lock us up—haw, I said 'lock us up' but obviously I mean pick us up, tell him please, please, please pick us up or have us picked up. At the airport? To please be sure to? Got that? Write it down! Put it under his nose! Okay? *Okay?* Write it on his *hand!* Make him tape it to his *forehead! Bye!* "

He forgot to pick them up at the airport. He had looked too late, that morning, at the note I'd made him write himself and clip to his Tillich—went stampeding out of the house and speeding in his jalopy down the narrow mountain road toward civilization nearly ran into the yellow cab coming the other way: brakes, horns, each vehicle backing up, rolled-down windows, Nancy cheerfully telling her father off (I wonder why she didn't call and remind him herself if she was so worried he'd forget), and a full-loaded lumber truck of two-foot-diameter trunks barreling down the mountain nearly took care of everything . . . when they got to the bungalow and got their stuff inside, and Eden had paid the taxi ("You're darn right you are!" Nance trumpeted when he offered), everyone sort of stood around.

Nora was a strange serene, with Quadros off wherever. She was calm, relaxed—too relaxed, though he knew she was off drugs now for good. This wasn't drug-induced or substance-induced, this fey, subduedly crazed state. She was almost like a dotty matron for whom everything is always and forevermore, no matter what, all right, the blue eyes blurred, not distant, just vague, as she stood about seeming to smile. Her sister having dropped her bags and kids accosted her, fired pointblank questions about how she was and what the hell was going on, and Nora, nodding, answered in a quiet voice that drifted quieter. Yes, she said, she was okay, considering, she was really ok. And he, Nora said—they all except the children knew who *he* was—was gone, yes. Waiting a second, looking at the word in the light of her mind to be satisfied of its accuracy. He was, Nora said, gone . . gone . . Nancy with a grin that was worry and pique, her dragon glasses flashing and the neverchanging helmet of thick hair swinging as she leaned, bobbed in front of her sister trying to get Nora who was looking away to meet her eyes. Nora wore overalls and did not have that stone, wretched color of a few days previously, so, grateful to the bone that Captain Nance had come, he threw his hands up and happily went off to answer the phone.

It was Duffy Ginty on the line wondering if, "hee," he waved across the living room to them, "—she wants to know if—" paw over receiver "—the fatted son has arrived!"

"Tell her I'm here," Nance shouted grabbing up her bags, "tell her I'll call, tell—I mean ask—I mean what does she mean by—"

"She says it's just a figure of speech," he waved, listening again as Nora, out of this, drifted, like her eyes, to the unlaid hearth onto whose firebrick, as she stared, touched a crystal of snow that vanished.

Still small but no longer tiny, Michael, whose eyes were still blue with highlights of turquoise, and who was making glacial but steady progress in learning to give up the earthly heaven of sucking (as his older brother once had) his fingers, went off with Alan to explore and play.

Alan came back. "He wants to know if he can suck 'em," he reported. "He's excited."

"He can," a considering Nancy replied, "he can suck 'em for—where is he?"

"He's in the sink."

"Alan why is he in the sink?"

"Oh he's excited."

"In the kitchen?"

"Yes we went out to the kitchen. I wanted to pretend we were plumbers, but he resisted. He got in the sink which I was going to tell you," Alan reported.

"All right I'll go see."

Nance dragged her luggage past her sister who was still staring wintrily into the blazeless hearth. Through clenched teeth and with firmed chin as she passed Nora Nance told her "Hang in there, I'll just get the boys settled." And Nancy persevered on back through the house, whose faded floral couches and wingback stuffed chairs, unfinished coffee tables, books, exposed wood and dreary (this day) windows on forest seemed smaller to her—weird. In her travel-tiredness the furniture seemed child-sized, a trick of the brain, everything here not merely gray and old but midget-sized suddenly, where long ago she had lived and perfected her homework and yelled and danced with her school friends and wondered where her sister was and hoped her parents wouldn't fight and baked and sewn—so quiet, so different now. Hoary in the daydull, no one sitting on the couches, no one dancing on the rugs, a silence and a quiet shabby somehow to Nance who all at once, for the first time, not having lived here for many years in body, didn't live here any longer in soul.

"You can suck 'em five minutes," she barked at the two button eyes peeking out over stainless steel, "then try to stop. And why are you in there?"

"Boat."

"Five minutes," she told the suddenly sapphirine emerald eyes. "Then try to stop, 'k?"

"K."

"I know," she said, smoothing Michael's hair, "it is exciting to be at Grampa's. Okay Michael. Don't er, disturb anything."

"K," the periscope eyes said.

"Where's Alan?"

"Checkin' Grampa out."

"Well good. That gives me a chance to talk to your Aunt Nora in maybe some privacy. Will you be all right here?"

". . 'k."

Alan Elwive was seven, as handsome as ever and with a childish fleeciness still to his blond hair shaped now around a full-browed, Zeus-wise head of princely proportion. His blue-gray eyes could go sharp and full of dispassionate light, but at other times they were mild, a blue not unlike his Aunt Nora's when watching, club on a shoulder, those long-ago shots so lazing high . .

Alan was good at sports. He was friendly, intelligent, well-formed, the broad little chest and arms and legs sprouting so fast that in a season he would be nearly as tall as some of the adults around him, and he was well-dressed. That is, he was artistically aware at all times of the colors of his clothes, but his shirttail still usually was out.

He continued to be inquisitive—was given to only infrequent, and short-lived, bouts of temper. He was fairly brave but, having an imagination, not overly so. He was gullible. Alan could be led. Watching TV or becoming caught up in a swirl of excited friends he would follow. Shocked by his mom or a teacher back into the corral of rules he would unquestioningly obey. He never did anything truly bad, and in discussion displayed a sensitivity to right and wrong that was a pristine rill in this life of muck, but in action it was different. The siren command of flurrying kids, sneakers, adjurations, let's go, hold this, throw that, *come on,* charmed Alan as completely as did, that visit, Eden's extemporaneous game of What's a Chair.

"All right Alan," his grampa said happily, "what is it?"

It was a simple caneback. Eden stood glowingly pointing.

"It's a chair," Alan said.

"How do you know?"

Alan's beautiful wastes of Siberian husky eyes, that came to him when he was thinking, were his great-grandmother's.

Folding his arms and taking a step back and cocking his head Eden set his chin on a finger, as if thinking, though he was watching, with a pleasure he had not felt in months, his grandson think, or try to . . . but it was too senseless difficult—it was a chair, Alan silently told himself, that's how you knew it was a chair. Grampa was smart and read books and this was a game and because he really liked his grampa Alan wanted to play it.

But he didn't know how.

His glasses about to slip off, the brown eyes fond and calm, he stood with folded white arms, looking at the boy.

"All right try this. How do we know it's a chair? Well, what are some things we can say about what a chair is? What's one thing we can say about a chair?"

No response. It touched the man to see the child's eyes staring at the chair as Alan tried to think.

"Ok," his granddad said softly, "how 'bout legs, a chair has . . ."

"Legs," Alan said, clearly not certain what they were doing.

"Ok that's good. So let's say one way you can know the thing is a chair is if it has legs—a chair has legs, oh say . . four. Four legs. A thing is a chair if it has four legs, 'kay?"

It thrilled him that Alan did not answer because he knew beyond doubt the boy had heard the question but he could see Alan was thinking, a sway in the childish back, Alan's hands on his hips, elbows out pointing behind him.

"You sit on it," Alan said soberly.

"Yes! Bravo!"

The mesmerized toil of attempting to fathom that had been cloaking the boy's face dispelled into happiness, a grin and smile-wrinkles about the eyes, the happiness of achievement, of power, a look up at his granddad that melted my uncle's heart.

"Bravo Alan, yes indeed. You sit on a chair. So, ahhh, a chair's a thing with four legs that one sits on, yes?"

Brightly nodding. Enormously pleased. Doesn't know what he's done but proud because Grampa praised it . . . but Eden stepped back and folded his arms. He set his chin on its finger-rest and, it seemed, was burningly thinking . . . Alan waited, his eyes letting in more and more light . .

"How 'bout," his granddad said with portent, after reflection, "a back. A chair always has a back."

Alan looked at the chair—thought about chairs.

"Yeah."

"Okay so what a chair is . . a chair is a thing with four legs and a back and—as you said—you sit on it. Four legs, a back, you sit on it . . it's a chair."

Alan thought about this. He nodded, turning, as he did so, to look at his granddad to see if there was more.

"But a horse," Eden said slowly, looking at the chair, "has four legs . . and a horse has a back . . . and you sit on a horse."

The silence in which Alan Elwive processed his granddad's words and, lost in so doing, staring at the chair, scarcely seeming to notice it, thought about what Eden had said was a suspense and a blessing for my uncle as exciting as any trout gliding under your fly looking up: more so, far more so, the gold-fleeced child's cranium hatless—temple and lab of all that is good in us—to Eden Hope a sight, as he stood waiting, of holy joy.

"I don't know," Nancy informed him passingly through gritted teeth as she stuck her head in the doorway and did a double take at the sight of her ratiocinating son. "Her voice just sort of I swear, trails off. She seems fine except she isn't, she seems physically fine but not really. She'll talk about what we already know about in this sort of distant, detached voice. I think she's ok but I don't, frankly—" lower, teeth-grittinger "—frankly I don't know what damage may've been done. I'll keep trying, I'm on it bye!" Doorway empty. Alan, his grandfather thought, might not even have registered his mother's voice, so intently was he—medium-sized hands on medium-sized hips—staring at the caneback and thinking about what his grampa had said—horse four legs, chair four, horse has back, chair has one—Alan all at once said "*Gee* Grampa," and the boy's tone wasn't nasty but it was querulous.

"Look." Alan strode to the chair and sat in it, throwing his shoulders up in a shrug. "I'm *sitting* in it. That's as far as it goes."

Staggered, needing to take a second now himself to process, Eden broke and burst out in such a spontaneous bout of rejoicing that Alan was, albeit a little nervously, a second time delighted and proud.

"My *god* Alan," his granddad bellowed, "Wittgenstein came to the exact same conclusion, but it took him a *life*time! That's *won*derful Alan!"

He bent down and put his expression almost in the boy's to wag a flaking finger at close range and deliver more praise, the brown eyes goggly half within, half above, the lenses of his slipping spectacles, his voice mellifluous, rich, lovely with timbre and substance, a tone smooth and elegant, though figure and dress and pink eager face were not.

"Thanks," Alan said, taken aback.

"It took him decades Alan. For a long time he thought we can be precise, but finally he realizes, he understands, Wittgenstein understands—" nearly panting "—that you can sit in a chair and know it's a chair and not something else without having to definitively define what a chair is or even—" drawing breath "—even having to develop a satisfactory language potentially to articulate a definition *with.*"

"I don't understand what you're talking about," Alan said. "But I'm happy," he added quickly. "Who's the guy?"

"Wittgenstein."

"Fischcative?"

"Close enough."

"Tell me it again. What I did."

"Alan you instinctively through action knew what a chair is. You can *sit* on it! Wittgenstein came to this wisdom only through the most virginal suffering of the mind. He worked so hard to develop clarity of expression. It near killed him. It took decades—his life—to come to his answer—that you may sit in a chair and use a chair and know it's a chair . . but you can't prove it's a chair . . . you figured this out in thirty seconds! Of course Hegel says—"

"Is he real?"

"Wittgenstein?"

"Yeah."

"Yes." At least he thought it was Hegel who said the present-day grade-school student grasps in seconds what it takes the first thinker (Pythagoras) years to divine—ontogeny recapitulates heh, "Yes Alan he sure is real."

"Would he be as strong as Donald Schwartzative?"

"Yes," Alan's granddad lied happily . . he felt like saying Yes to anything right now. With difficulty he knelt by the boy sitting in the chair and delivered himself of a paean to the mind—how proud he was, what a joy it was—he wanted Alan to understand—a joy to witness a young brain flowering and finding. He noticed but passingly the sharpness of the look Alan was giving him. Alan hadn't gotten the content of what his granddad had been trying to say, and wasn't sure he wanted to, but he felt his grampa's emotion. Nancy told me afterward that on the flight east Alan had remarked out of the blue: "I really love Grampa."

She and Nora had a fire going, a comforting sight in the wall of books and sullen forest in windows, this overcast winter afternoon, but when he started to lower his weight into his favorite floral cushioning and tufting, Nance stopped him: "Dad could we talk?"

Of course they could, and when he saw it was serious he suggested a different room. Nora and Alan could play checkers—in fact they were doing so—a cheek, each—Alan's left Nora's right—flickery with firelight. But it was more serious still: "We'll take a quick walk," Nancy decreed.

Eden said drive to Haystack and hike up. As they were about to leave Nancy remembered Michael. "He'll be ok," Nora said, digesting the board. "We can watch him." Nance was explaining that he was in the sink, and they should look in on him, when the copper-sulfate bluegreen eyes, absorbing all, peeked 'round the doorjamb—"Michael Grampa and I are going for a short walk, you stay here and watch the checkers."

He wanted to come too. Jumping Alan's forwardmost disc soldier Nora said she and Alan could watch Michael, which was repeating herself but her mind was locked on the game.

Alan looked up.

He wore an ecru cableknit sweater with a V neck, a plaid shirt open at the collar. The peaceful, towering forehead mild, the telescope-distant eyes (as he sat in part in shadow) feeling and deep as he came back into the room from the realm of the board's difficult squares, he prepared to make a speech. The flip side of Alan's gullibility was a highly developed sense of etiquette—a sense and sensitivity made manifest mostly in the realm of the logistical. He flexed this ability at the least hint of a situational tangle. All the way back now from his concentration on the fault lines of his checkers contest with his aunt, he lifted, under that peerless brow, eyes snow-cold in the eclipse dark before his face. He sat with his back to the fire. "If they want you to go," he began to explain reasonably to his brother whose two fingers at the speed of light went in, "then what you should do is, you should say thank you, I will go, but if—if ah, if they say no Michael, we don't want you to go, then actually—"

"Ah, excuse me Alan but—" to Nance "—why don't we just walk here?"

"You could always," Nora started to say, but Nancy for no reason anyone could see insisted on driving the two miles over to Haystack, when in fact at first she indeed would've preferred to stay here, and Eden too had more to say, and had begun, when Alan, getting to his knees, solemn faced, lifting his hands to choirmaster them all and organize it said "No no no wait, I got a idea." He cleared his throat. His mother's eyes sparkled with affection and admiration behind her pop-salacious spectacles. "I know," he said fast, trying wildly to think, "an' I'll tell you." His moral organizing need was more developed than his rational skills for mentally drawing up specific protocol, but would catch up. But far from yet. Inflamed with desire (that they all get along with each other by listening to him), on his knees there with their attention, as the fire crackled, he started again: "Grampa, you should get the car ready. Mom you get your coats, then Michael can stay here with us 'n learn checkers while—"

Michael's fingers were removed long enough for him to say "I wanna go uppa *mountain.*"

Momentarily overwhelmed by the complications and immense power of his responsibility, Alan made the mistake of shaking his head while getting ready to continue his solution, which moment of silence gave Eden the opportunity, turning to go get coats, to mumble: "Well then," meaning what harm. Nance's locked jaw nodded. If Michael wanted to go, he could go. Nora walked on her knees toward the shallow, flaring heat and brightness to poke her and Nance's logs with the weighty poker, which, reluctantly, Alan allowed his attention, slowly, to revolve to. "'K," Nancy commanded. "Shoes *on.* Let's *go.*"

Alan watched the fire a second, only mildly discouraged in the ruins of his mental schema for what should happen, only passingly tempted to steal a comforting finger suck. Then, as his attention moved back to the checkerboard and he mentally started to play again, Nora came back to the board, and their game.

Alan scratched his head. His gaze was returning to mildness.

Eden and Nance drove over. She dropped Mike in a backpack and started to climb.

"Nora loves you," she said, halfway up.

Under the ruffed underbellies of low clouds the chill afternoon air is still and wet. Sickly yellow shinings and nimbuses the pale of overripe banana and sometimes a plush, dark gold come and go far to the north, where higher hills—real mountains—the next state—serrate the horizon.

"I think," Nance said, two thirds of the way up, "she would very much like to leave here. When she was tagging around with Mom last summer it was good for her. I think she wants—" hand on tawny fur, waving tail like a Founding Father's crazed quill "—I think she wants to go to college far from here Dad, and I think she should."

In the stasis of its cold the wild slept. The forest's unsupple branches, without foliage, inactive trunks, plants without juice—bare stems, one berry, prickers. Layers of blackred leaves were sticking to their walking shoes' soles. No birdsong, not a squirrel on a trunk's far side. No insect—trees soundless. Vertical into their upper world of arteries, veins, capillaries . .

"I think," Nance said, three quarters of the way to the top, nudging snuffling Emma, who had bounded from the bungalow at the last minute to be with them and now had half her head in a log, with a denim knee, "that she wants to get into a different life, a life frankly totally different," she hurried, "from everything around here."

No glorious view at the top where the umbral Rhine castle keep harbors no one . . no blue sky greeted them. They trooped from the trees. Little in the way of color cheered the low, horizontal sweep of underclouds.

"Are you all right?" she blinked.

"Why ah," he said with blasted bright eyes. Far from enough—it was extraordinary, standing here to realize—blood and oxygen above his lobster neck. Here among these odd standing things that are trees on the planet Earth. Inimical darkened clouds that are the planet's atmosphere, "ahhh—I've—"

"Are you okay?"

"I'm . . . will be."

"Well *Dad*—"

"I'm just a—"

"Have you seen a doctor? All right when was the last time you saw one?"

"I shall," he drooped. "I do ah, wait a minute. I do become dizzy. I do have a silvery." These were *trees*—it was the queerest thing. "Ringing," he admitted, "in this ear. With each pulse."

"Well *Dad!*"

"I know. But when I'm finished. For better or worse when I've—"

"Finished what? You don't mean . . oh gawd. You do mean, don't you?"

"I ah—"

"You mean your physics mumbo jumbo. Dad the universe is a big place. The universe is a big thing to understand. I mean are you sure you have enough brain blood?" She looked at his face. "Okay," she said, "you have to do what you have to do, that's up to you and that wasn't the point of this. I think you're crazy but that's up to you. You're a brilliant scientist, or you were, er, I'm being frank, it's up to you." She stood with her son on her back at the foot of the forbidding black tower that looked like it could've come from one of her father's fantasy stories, if he were still writing them "—I mean are you making any progress at all on your theories or whatever they are?"

"Well," he said. "Ah—a little, perhaps a very little bit, yes."

She nodded curtly and moved. "Well good luck is all I can say and I mean it so let's climb the tower and see the countryside and go home." She shepherded them up, Emma fast, Michael bouncing—eyes—in his frame on her narrow back, Eden careful—slow—flagging—flights of tower steps, "well then *rest* Dad."

She summarized as they climbed. "Alright," she said tromping. They were inside the tower's claustral darkness, the noise of their herringboned soles hollow on the wood stair. "See a doctor," she said. "If you will you will, if you won't you won't. But I have to say it. Number Two, er Number One actually, get Nora off to a good easy college a thousand miles from here. Don't tell her I said that."

Thus the later-generations blood of long-dead warriors who once plundered and constructed on a mountainous scale swinging whole railroads 'round their heads, making war, great hospitals and law across oceans—thus in the late generations this sap thins to hiking, climbing (just actual physical hills), popping up from the dinner table for the encyclopedia, clearing new, and maintaining old, trails, counting hours—losing sleep. Nance climbed. "Watch out Dad. And Number Three, or Four or whatever we're to, do your work, do your work and your thinking if you must but prepare yourself for disappointment. Oh I forgot Number Five, I mean this movie. You're not serious about this trip I'm hearing about are you?"

"Ah," he said softly . ."why . ."

"Yes? *Dad?* "

$$= \frac{L\sqrt{1-(v^2/}}{} + \frac{L \quad 1-(v^2/}{}$$

$$= \quad \frac{1}{}$$

. . . he was distractedly nodding.

"You are? Serious about going, I mean actually—"

He nodded and said "Yes I am" as he climbed, his tone one Nancy knew to take seriously but still, snapping over a shoulder back at him she asked her question again, then stopped, waited, in annoyance, as he leaned against unforgiving stone.

"Wanna wait here while I jog Michael up the rest of the way?"

"No."

"Okay."

To her chagrin and admiration he was serious, deadly serious. He was not going to see a doctor until he had discovered universal unity and flown with his own money, what was left of it, Anther and guides and camerapeople and the Zen Masters or whatever they were—cameras lights dollies crews insanity hundreds of thousands of dollars in suitcases or might as well be. Money that could send Alan and Mike and their sister to college. She angrily started climbing. To herself, in inner argumentative silence, Nance did her frustrated thinking without looking back to see if he was all right. Or following or not. Bands of fake goddamn angels. Trademark cartoon tuna singing in the surf, hah. She could only grimly shake her inner head. It was his money, however, not hers, and the sun came out!

"Wow Michael look."

A ray of light three hundred yards in girth appeared, diagonal, the only sunshine, the hills and cloud cover everywhere else dim, the surprising beam angling grandly down illuminating distant detail of treebranches on a far hillside, glowing, radiating. Looking at it Michael said: "Is a spaceship gonna come?"

"I don't know Michael. It sure looks like it doesn't it?"

Physically suddenly Eden felt so much better it was unnerving—his heart collected and slowed, and there seemed to be no pressure anywhere, no dizziness, a solid, verveful floating, as if he were young again and could do anything. Amazed, he stood still to preserve the sensation. Then a bird in his mind twittered—short song of thought. He waited and then, coming to him, birds of thought flew and landed. It was partial, but he was already seeing beyond it . . . it was complex locally but simple overall. It was unbelievable. It was coming to him specifically and he stood listening.

"Time to go Dad."

"Do you ah . . I seem, ah, not to've brought paper."

"To *write* on?"

"Yes please."

"Are you ok?"

"Yes."

"You can have these old cards."

"Better than nothing." Leaning on the stone as if it were a work-table he started scribbling numbers. With Michael hanging on her she looked at her father who held his nose, scribbled then stopped, wrote more, leaning on the black, filthy stone, as that one beam faded.

When it was this pure all he had to do was not consciously think but simply keep relaxed and hold the moving pen to the paper. Nance's auto-body business cards, an expired health card, the white back of a previous husband's snapshot. He was so confident that even as he wrote down some not-quite-right values he didn't bother correcting them

"Dad."

because it didn't matter, he would be able to adjust later, for now just get the

"*Dad.*"

it kept coming and he kept writing, absolute velocity of ether changing quantum-sponge's roundtrip—"Dad that's *enough.* All *right?*"

"Yes," he said holding onto it and writing it—"Yes"—anything to gain another few seconds. When inspiration does come like the sex act in consummation how do you stop, no matter how embarrassed, how can you stop no matter who has caught you, no matter what glass has shattered how can you stop topological simultaneity never did preclude casual connection, *never* did, it was just

"*Daddy!*"

"Hm? Oh . . yes . ." time coordinates moving fixed as part of a base-seven genidentity grid. Not a what. Damn it a what. What was the

She stood glowering at him with her arms folded and her eyes as dark, in the dragon-lens frames, as the late-afternoon sky. She could see, by how his pen had stopped but the brown glinting eyes had not, that he was not listening to her. And then they had a shouting match there on the dark tower, while the turquoise eyes watched distance. She yelled at him that he was selfish, a monster of selfishness. He must stop writing equations right now she shrieked and he shouted, writing as fast as he could, "I'm finished!" A few wild moments more their shouts warred, she shrieking *stop,* he—scribbling—saying anything—"I'm finished! One single second! Go ahead!"—to fend her off, and then to her surprise he was finished and acted as if nothing had happened. He grinned at her. Had what he needed. In a pocket. Was ready to go back, grinning insincerely at her as if nothing had happened. Back they drove in the draining light, passing headlights. And now their excited voices, mere contours of sound at this distance, can be heard in the house and grow louder as they come toward the railroad-tie steps. They were talking animatedly. As they started down the outdoor steps their voices are sometimes understandable over the hearthfire's low crackling and unbroken inhalation . .

"—hear anything from Gwen? The real one? I mean the real-life one? I mean she . . . (indistinct, fire hissss, spat!) . . . it always seemed to me that you and she, I mean she was always your . . . (indistinct, fire shifts with a noise and new parts of wood catch . . .) . . . your—I mean the one woman you . . . am I right about that?"

"No ah, I have not seen or heard . . . (indistinct: flames, new heat, breathy hum air flying up in shimmer rolls) . . . if she would ever, which, ah, I sincerely doubt." Stare

"You doubt she—"

"I doubt she."

"Well Dad so do I. The time for that was a helluva long time ago. And Lim?"

"Lim," Lim's brother said.

"How is he?"

$$= \frac{\sqrt{1-(v^2/}}{c+v} + \frac{1-(v^2/}{c-v}$$

$$= \frac{2L}{c}\ \frac{1}{\qquad}$$

". . ah

"Lim."

"Yes."

"How is he," she reminded him.

"Yes

$$= \frac{L\sqrt{1-(v^2/}}{c+v} + \frac{L\sqrt{1-(v^2/}}{c-v}$$

$$= \frac{2L}{c}\left(\frac{1}{\sqrt{1-(v^2/}}\right)$$

"How is Lim Dad."

"Yes ah . . . Lim—"

"You drive him crazy."

"Well—"

"You do," she concluded, "and I don't blame him. Mom I know about, I mean her I don't need to ask about. Can you *believe* her?"

"Why . . . (indistinct)

"Huh?"

"Yes," he said, "I can believe her."

"I mean she's done like this total three-sixty—three-hundred-and-sixty?"

"One-hundred-and-eight—"

"Right. Turnaround. If you think it's crazy or if you think it's not maybe isn't the point, maybe the point is she's her own person for the first time. She's doing something she believes in, she's strong—did Nora tell you what she said?"

"Yes."

Front door bangs open as they arrive at the house. Stomping of outdoor shoes in the entry. Zippers, voices louder . .

"Dad now seriously." Tone lowered from animated to intense. "This movie thing."

(mumble deep, determined)

"But Dad—"

(mumble grows, the world "resolved" distinct . .)

"Hear me out though, just consider. Do you have a script? I mean a real one? Do you have any backing at all, or any encouragement at all on this thing except from yourself . . I mean are you aware of the money you're—"

"Yes," my uncle's rich tone distinctly said as they passed from the entryspace into the hall bordering the living room.

"—and more I'd say 'throwing away' than 'risking.' I mean it Dad. Are you aware of the significance of the amount, that's all I'm asking."

$$\Delta' = \frac{L\sqrt{1-(v^2/c^2)}}{c+v} + \frac{L\sqrt{1-(v^2/c^2)}}{c-v}$$

$$= \frac{2L}{c}\left(\frac{1}{\sqrt{1-(v^2/c^2)}}\right)$$

"Yes," he said. "Yes."

"Well that's all I'm—all right. Case closed," swinging Michael off her back. She was frowning like a merlin. Couldn't let go of it, it was so dumb, such a waste, such a selfish lark, spreading himself thin and to come to nothing—everyone saw it—"I just," she couldn't help but again begin. He waved her quiet with a hand-flap go-away gesture, as he dropped into his favorite gray flowers, that caught her short. That annoyed air-swat had had real anger in it! It was as if he were being patient with *her!*

So she sat down, though she hadn't given up. It wasn't the money it was the clear, total futility. A film about fishing maybe. But for her father to try to do it by himself, by himself entirely, drag poor Anther in . . she stepped back from herself in her eyes' gaze into the last pulsing, disappearing, burning-again flames to check herself—being fair? Answer was *yes.* It was madness. But perhaps, and this too was a thing she was facing for the first time, perhaps her father was genuinely crazy. "Michael?" "Yes?" "Come by the fire to warm up." "Ok," Michael surprised her by agreeing, and Eden shut his eyes a second for the tower-top flush of health was going, gone. He could feel his heart again. Laboring and bucking, feel the pressure—neck, chest, crown . .

"Hm?" he drowsily asked. "What?" "I thought you said—" "I didn't say anything." "I was dozed off."

She said: "Time to get organized." Slapping her thigh she got up and strode off into the rest of the house calling "guys," while he watched the last of the fire knowing better than to touch the numbers in his pocket until tomorrow. This was it—it might be. Or it might not be, but he was excited. Surprising connections. It was his chance. He must live it but not press it. Obey it, not be afraid, relax, wait, let it come, and when it did, when the brain window was open and the correspondences were pouring—stop everything, sacrifice anything, lose whatever sleep it was necessary to lose. Get it tamed and caged in math. Ashen, diminished shapes of themselves, the logs—branching nevermore in flame now except in quick flames released then gone, xylem tissue combining with oxygen, he yawned. Nance came back in.

Michael had found a reel and was sitting by the fire and his granddad's flowered big chair lost in countercranking, observing line loop off, learning, examining the device's action, reeling a bit back on—when it jammed. Trying to force it, thinking, with dirty white hands pulling on the line, even sometimes untangling some, but tangling it again when uncranking more, he pursed his rosepetal mouth. When it would go briefly to insipid flame the firelight moved on Michael's bald cheek and concentrating eye. Learning hands, not a word. Not a change of expression when his mom's fingers brushed the newmown raspberry hair. "They're not here," she said.

"Who Nora?"

"Yeah. They must've gone out."

The "Curtisses" stopped by dropping off jam and in their dignified way lingering, with affectionate insistence, no matter how forcefully invited, no further than the front door long enough just to chat. Flexures and scrolls of breaths on the sunset dark. Orange glow faraway through black latticing. Goodbye, thank-you, good-afternoon, good-evening good-bye. And before they stepped back inside Eden and Nancy looked at the forest and the forest was quiet, this time of year. It was quite cold. The distant orange light, through black intricacy, was almost out. They went back in but shortly afterward, after a fast conversation in the cluttered entryway, the bungalow's front door latch-cracked and whooshed open with a shove as Eden in a windbreaker pulled over his head backwards lumbered out, stood, cupped his blotchy hands.

The forest was quiet, and after his call and its flat echo, seemed quieter.

Except for the faint sound—so faint it had no character—of nearly frozen water moving over rocks, gravel, sunken branches and half-hibernating hungerless fish.

"Where do you think they would've gone?"

"If they went for a walk they could, ah, they could be anywhere. Of course when I called there was no answer—I suppose one—"

"If they were going out for longer than an hour I would've thought they would've left a note." Nance pondered, reaching—while thinking—down to pat Michael's head but getting air, as he'd moved over to the brass chest, the leviathan lid of which he was strugglingly getting open a little, then losing ground with, then, bending his small knees and pushing, starting to get open again. "She's not a note-leaver though. See Mike it's just old records, Dad what are these doing still here? Do you ever play any of these?"

"Those? Oh no, I didn't even—"

"*La Gioconda* is that right?" "*La Gioconda,* heh, yes." "You ought to give these away if you never—*Norma,* who's *Norma?* Is this stuff really any good? Look Michael here's something called *The Firebird* about a huge scary monster it looks like, a giant, someone knocked him down, look. That arm's as big as a train . ." "Monsta'," Michael granted, but wanted to get back to his reel. She spoke on her knees looking through the heavy obsolete albums with their brown paper sleeves each with a hole in the middle so you could read the burgundy circular decal in the record's middle that provided, in gold print, your information for you. "Maybe she took him for ice cream."

"In what?"

"Oh that's right. I forgot. When is she getting it back by the way? Monday? Did you find out yet how much it's gonna cost? I can take her to pick it up if I'm here. I assume she never drives yours?"

"She does actually sometimes, but I've got the only keys here—at least I thought I did. Yes."

Staring at fripperous dandies singing at each other in frock coats with frilled cuffs: "You don't have a spare set? Of keys to yours?"

"Ahhhh, such a set exists."

"Well where is it?"

"At the moment?"

Single silent chuckle—"Yes dad, at this moment."

"Underwater."

Without a word Nance got up and walked out and was back, having pushed open the door to the cold garage.

"It's here," she said. "It's overdue for inspection."

"As I said she couldn't've taken it unless heh, unless she hot-wired it, heh. She couldn't—couldn't wouldn't. Now Lim—"

"How is he dad, I mean really."

"Why, he's not as young as—"

"Seriously, is he ok?"

"Oh," he scoffed, watching for the next flame, "of course. Of course he is. Of course he's ok."

"Has he had a happy life?"

"Lim? Heh," he began, but then grew terrifically serious, or rather the seriousness that was always there came up and out decanting onto his surfaces, banishing the clown. You could see by the way the smoke wavered and changed that a flame was likely to come soon, and he watched for it—but not yet, along, around, even from within the smoldering ghost logs. "He's worked harder than he's enjoyed. He's worked very hard, my brother."

"So've you Dad."

"I have. But Lim I think even more so. He has tried hard and he continues to, er . . he doesn't ever get sad."

"Just blows up," she nodded. "What time is it?"

"Five oh-one."

"What about Gwen, she's really the one you loved isn't she."

"No. I love your mother."

"Do you think you really are figuring it out?"

"I might be."

"Dad it would be so exciting."

"It would be more than my life."

"I know it." She took the album Michael thoughtfully had brought over for her to look at but didn't look at it. "Was everything really infinitely hot at the beginning?"

He shut his eyes. Don't start talking it until it's solid.

"No," he said with his eyes shut.

"*Huh?* I mean I'm an ignoramus on the whole thing but I thought—"

"No," he said. "It was infinitely cold at the beginning."

"Since when did—"

"Since an hour ago."

"Gawd. Thanks Michael."

It came as he opened his eyes, flicker of low flame reaching—danced—sidled down the about-to-dissolve ash of a log before vanishing.

Nancy suggested calling Vanessa, a good idea. Vanessa wasn't home, Vanessa's mother said. Vanessa's mother said she couldn't be sure, but she was pretty sure Vanessa wasn't with Nora. At Eden's suggestion they made a list—Lim's house, the Bob MacAtticks, school, Duffy . . they tried these.

"I don't have his number," he said, bending to get in under the big urn table lamp and click it on. Click—brighter. Third click? He could never remember. Tried it: Click, light out. So turned it on again and click, brighter (brightest available).

"Whose number oh."

"Of course one could always . ."

"Drive up there," she snapped. "Not yet."

She picked Michael up, no light glinting in the sideways-teardrop lenses framed by her thick Rairia's sheeny straight hair. She put him down again and, as if the touching of his Velcro-strapped shoes to the rug triggered his voice, he said something. Small, pure, musical comment to himself before walking across the darkening face of the hearth to sit again with his reel.

"How long a drive is it?"

"Oh," he said, "half an hour?"

"Dad I don't know. How would I know, I'm asking you, you've been there right?"

As the clock that was the freestone stream in the dusk picking its way—low water—along the base of South Mountain alone and unheard kept the time, Nance made them tea.

Then they were idling, Michael shivering, heat gushing about their faces in the night, their feet freezing, along the curb beyond which the low-slung house was dark and Nance said in an unusually high voice: "Clearly one of us has to stay here *in* the car, *with* the engine running, *with* Michael." "I'll go," he heard himself say, "but heh, don't run away, heh, it looks deserted, there may in fact be no need even to—"

"Go," she commanded. He did.

"No one," he hissed, "nothing, not a light, not a sound." He had stolen quickly back over the lawn in and out of nimbus streetlamp indirect shine, lesions of weak, silvery reflection interrupting the general night and showing parts—windows, roof section, a chimney—of the low waiting house. "I could see," he panted, "in a window. I could see most of two rooms. There was nothing in them, not a piece of furniture, not a scrap of paper."

"What're we *doing* up here? They're prob'ly back right now and worried about *us!* Let's hit it."

"I'm cold," Michael said.

It was that—cold. In their haste to get going they'd left the front door open and it was amazing there was a glimmer of heat still left in the fireplace, but the house was raw, outdoor chilly.

"I'm cold too Michael, let's put more logs on."

Soon the firelight was everywhere in the charred hearth's firestone, dancing on three faces.

The phone rang. Electrical warble up his spine, cilia—but it was only Duffy calling back to see if there were news.

Nancy made them soup, which they ate at the breakfast-area table which she'd laid with colorful place mats and matching napkins in the shadowless bright of every light she could turn on. Michael finished his, while his mother and grandfather engaged in dialogue. If something had happened they would've heard. Useless to sit worrying, not constructive. Yes, they would call the police at some point. Maybe in half an hour, let's say half an hour, let one more half hour go by.

He sat before the fire, which had gone down. Nancy scrubbed his floors for him, then she put Michael to bed.

It was around eight.

He sat staring at the low flames, a stream rushing in his ears, feeling time's motion, aware in a way he would prefer not to be.

"I called 'em," she snapped striding in. "The sergeant on duty was very nice, very calming. They have to get this kind of thing fifty times a night. We went through the whole rigmarole of questions, names, description—vehicle? Social security number which I didn't know. There's a thing called a 'Bolo,' be-on-the-lookout. She was very soothing, sharp as a tack. I didn't say anything," Nance reported tensely, not looking at him, standing straight and talking fast, "about Nora's friend because he's gone. I mean it's over and he's gone, right? So she said probably they'll turn up soon but they have this be-on-the-lookout out and we're to call first thing in the morning if they're not back which I'm quite sure they will be, at least I do certainly hope so. I'm going to bed. I may. I may go to bed."

"I may too."

"Think they're all right?"

"Of course," he said, and was preparing to say more but took too long so that his silence, in the firelight's gaze, went on too long.

Nancy didn't go to bed at all. She didn't even remotely go to bed. She sat down. They must've dozed off.

He is looking, forward of his shoes, at a patina of lightest smoke drifting, scarcely—there being no wind in the house—forward dissipating over the oval hooked rug toward his shoes like the slowest-capering, tiniest, most infinitesimal dance of leaves there ever was . .

"Should we call them back?"

"Ah . . you mean the police?"

"Yes. Nah. But we have to do something."

"Get some rest. One way . ."

"Or another we're going to need it you mean. You're prob'ly right, I wish I had someone to call . . I have, I'm seeing someone, haven't told you."

"Oh ah," he yawned, "really?"

"More interested dad."

"No truly I'm—"

"I don't blame you."

She got up and walked out.

"He's fast asleep," she said arriving back, dropping into the chair beside his. "I see you put another log on. He's fast, fast asleep and old Emma Two's curled up on the foot of the bed."

A time passed and when he opened his eyes again he saw she was sleeping. That was good. Then, watching her oval face, he saw that her lips were moving, and he realized she wasn't resting either.

Nothing was on television at nine, at ten. She checked Michael again—same scene. Clankingly the old heating system was pouring out its baseboard breath. Emma stirred, opened a fraction of unseeing eye, and—in herself—put her muzzle between her gray forelegs where it belonged and was asleep.

"An engineer," she said sitting down. "Oh sorry you were asleep?"

"Very little, an . . engineer?"

"This guy," she said tight-jawed in the wing chair. "The guy I'm seeing."

"Oh, ah, yes."

"He's an engineer."

"Choo-choo?"

"Hanh. Structural. Nuclear tunnels, god knows. Nice guy, has a thousand books."

"That's nice."

"We," they said at the same time.

No night wind stirred the icy forest. Even the stream seemed to have gone at last to sleep—unheard utterly now through the unseen trunks under neither stars nor moon. He shivered and drew in a full lungful of the frigid air. He tarried, staring into black.

"Is it cold?"

He was back indoors again where it was light and warm and was sitting down again with her by the fire.

"Ah, it's raw, yes, cold—"

"Oh dad I never thought of this. What if they went for a walk and gawd, I don't know, a tree fell on them. Wild dogs or god knows. I mean if it's a car accident or something they find it and call you. I can't believe I'm—but I hadn't thought of it, if they're in the woods I mean—in the woods and can hear you but not, you know, respond."

He hadn't thought of it either and now she called Lim, Duffy, the "Curtisses," the MacAtticks and quite a few others. There were headlights in the trees, voices—it was cold, he was tired. His beam dancing off the vertical face of upright night-surprised trunks was stronger by far than his calling voice.

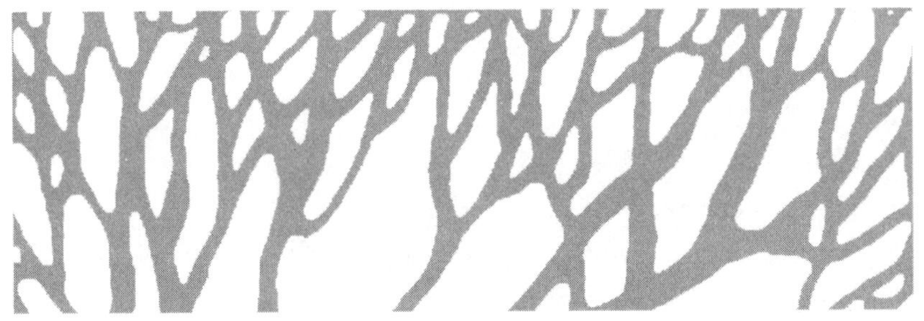

# 25

Some leaves still depend, wetly, from winter branches

you see more through forest in winter

and a quiet, defeated, hopeful, prayerful hand, running along the rim of a child's dresser, in a quiet room

such a hand falls, at the end of the dresser, into air, walk out.

An hour or five minutes or a day later she would be back, opening the door, not wanting to, opening again the door she'd shut—almost locked the last time. The room dim, each poster on the wall, each eyecorner-seen web of cape, power glove, cleat, backhoe, saurian spiked tail, hero chin and -tron's lit curve, sneakers, laces involved unneat as dropped by chair leg, bed unmade and then, with eyes almost shut, on the seventh day, made.

The Hopi rattle gourds his Gramma Rairia had sent a videotape of—picturesque, relucent—STOP frozen on the screen. No one had turned it off when they'd left. The first time into the room after arriving back she left the tape on—STOP frozen. Day, hour and minute by day, hour and minute a waste of electricity. Fingers, dustless, run the smoothwood shadow of dressertop rim, into air, handfall, walk out.

In a house of love more than disarray, and rules more than drift, a bright mind when young may be seen in gulps and spurts of time to have conjured amazing math—or it looks like it—algebra of some kind?—it's fragments—she can't even understand it—dares not touch it—it's not anything he learned in school, she's sure, looking at it on the tablet on the child-low white desk with its plastic chair.

along twig-spare lacery of branches, tear-small, circular cold drops—water—pearl the gray. They shine minutely in the soaked woods the next morning, the morning, that is, after the night Eden and she stayed up waiting, dozed, searched the woods with their sleepy friends and wandering beams, and at last, toward dawn, after sleeping in their chairs by the fire for an hour while in the dark forest it rained, heard the phone ringing.

A voice feathered and dull, hard to recognize—for a second Nancy wasn't sure who it was. Nora's voice came to them over the phone at seven-thirty a.m. bewilderedly asking someone to please come get her . . . pharmacy/bus-station two villages west—Nance knew it. When she, Michael and Eden stormed out the door and up the termitarium steps in the wet cold, circular, tiny pearls tatted the still zags and zigs and clawings of the treebranches—forget time. Forget time. She had been drugged and knew little. It was awful for them standing on the deserted early-morning sidewalk outside the windows of announcements and For-Sale signs and bus schedules to realize, without—Nance told me—ever asking the question, that Nora was alone. Dumbly they hugged her, stood back from her, who, bedraggled, squinted to focus—felt her own clay cheeks to see if they were there. She wanted to tell them, they got her into the car. But he didn't start it. They sat, getting colder, since he didn't turn the key, and waited. Michael half-asleep with his face in his mom's scarf and my uncle, hands on the impotent wheel, sitting turned to look almost at his youngest child in the front seat beside him. Nance with her firmed chin on Mike's head staring. Invisible seconds parading helplessly by.

The previous afternoon minutes after Nancy and Eden had gone for their conversation walk, in he had loped full of holiday plans, so swift in his talk, so positive in his energy—wanted to show Nora the

Christmas show in his town to the north, just that. That, just that. A fast holiday visit, an hour's positive energy. "I was glad to see him. So we—" sitting in my uncle's unstarted jalopy in the little square that senseless morning "—went." And he had eggnog, Christmas eggnog in a thermos in the car, the warm car, which she didn't know what happened to.

Not for Alan—no eggnog for Alan Q's warm voice said as he sveltely drove, snug and warm like the heat in the comfortable new—she noticed—car. Last thing she remembered noticing . .

The event bends time backward to it, bends the hours and weeks that come afterward back. By its gravity each detail, the hermetic trill of the phone, the strange voice turning into her sister's, the low, last smoke of the fire, in that morning's first light. Their earnest wasted search the night before, behind their voices, behind their blind, staggering beams. The sight of Nora standing leaning, not against anything, in her big sweater alone on the sidewalk.

In front of the just-opened pharmacy. And the days have become many, the feel, unwanted, irresistible, of the smooth travel of her hand over his dressertop, her cruising sliding fingers, drop, walk out.

Finally she locked the room so she wouldn't go into it. To have other kids to take care of was a blessing. They keep her busy and seem to understand—speak of Alan lightly, after Nancy has explained, and hold her hand. She worked with the group who contacted her, others who have gone through the same thing. She works to will, feel, share, express and discipline herself not to wake every two hours in the lorn night and sneak down the nightlight-ghost hall. Past his locked door. To peek, a long time, at each of the other two in their beds, or at a mall lose it.

Chief Airlenmacher had gotten to the FBI right away. There was ample reason to believe the tame nearby state line had been crossed. Nancy stayed eleven days baking, cleaning, hiking, waiting, talking—the dragon glasses desperately shining—to the civil grim women and men who came to talk with her, but there was nothing. The trail was as empty as the house, in that piney suburb to the north. There was no trail, no car, no sighting—vanished, impossible word, but look in a mirror. Imagine the mirror you stand looking into blink! empty. And into that emptiness, the numb frozen attention that she came to and stayed at, no time flows. Forget time. There is only one moment, the last one before it happened and, therefore, the last one during which it still might not happen . .

In a dull-gold mental locket the face. Untroubled forehead. Tundric, remote eyes. Scrambled-eggs hair is with her waking and when trying to sleep, or driving or calling Agent Worley or calling her group, FOLLO ("Friends of Lost Loved Ones"), or doing dishes or laundry or oilchange, is there—he. She has to discipline herself not to try, hours on end, to rebuild him in memory, gesture by gesture, image by image, fact by fact, the lordly overseeing of cousins, the timidity about breaking rules, then the opposite, mimicry, the bellylaugh, or concentration, watching, say, the Hopi tape. Head lowered so large forehead seems larger. Eyes clear with the tape's tiny lights dancing in them. She talked by phone to Lt. Cmdr. Elwive, kept him updated, but there was nothing. Nothing to report. She caught herself creating confusion on purpose for instance inviting too many friends for the kids to play with or letting a conflict among her children get bad or getting the wrong time for the movie they were all going to go to or telling the plumber to come when she knew the counselor and her neighbor would be there (because she'd scheduled them) merely to fill the minutes, to shovel action—any kind—into the stillness at her center, where the iron cameo glowed. Forget time. Deep at her core, where Alan was, throve a fragile arrogance. It was arrogance only if held in. Released all the way it would be crazy fear. She cunningly calculated that her FOLLO helpers, for whom on one level she was grateful, could not know what she was experiencing. The ones who had had their trial resolved either by getting their child back or another way were in a situation by definition light years distant from hers. Those still hoping, because they were still in the dark, were different too unless (her arrogant center calculated) they had been going through it for the exact same amount of time and under the precise same set of circumstances. Her iron, low-glowing cameo of him was not at her center so much as, like a headache pulsing, just behind, and to the right of, the nape of her neck as she walked and drove around. Her current boyfriend, the icthyologist, was a friendly unbookish runner who had swoopingly supplanted the engineer (she having pushed him [the icthyologist] away earlier in favor of the engineer because subconsciously she was trying to avoid a commitment), and at first he canceled numerous field trips and appointments to be with her. Then one night after the kids were in bed, over a glass of tea he invited her, gently, to talk. But she wanted to go down and sit in the cellar with him and listen to him talk about fish. He was cooperative. After a few minutes of it he stopped, in the gloam, and asked her if he might ask what they were doing. She hugged a bent leg. Sitting down here, listening to his tales of documented streams and transcontinental classification feuds, she said, caused her to feel far from Alan. But why would she want that? He said he would've thought she'd want the opposite. No, she calmly explained, she in fact was fighting for her sanity. She explained to him, in a fashion precluding misunderstanding, that given what was happening to her and what she could feel happening to her, she would do anything—anything—to preserve control of herself.

It helped to say it. Rod canceled no more field trips. One night when he was home she suddenly commanded him in a flurry to take the kids for ice cream. In a dervish whirl she got their hats on. Rod nodding, agreeing, saying even as she shooed them out that it was no problem, he'd be glad to, she slammed the door, locked it. Hearing the car start she strode upstairs and got the key out of her lowest drawer and unlocked the still, square room with its dark window. Felling the blinds so hard they clattered without turning the light on she threw herself to the floor nearly shattering her glasses and screamed, bawled and yelled, slammed—pounded the rug until her arms were tired, sat, finally, weeping freely. Even when all her energy was gone, still she sat crying and blubbering vindictive God-distrustful questions until, minutes before she heard the garage door's low drone, and got out of there, she at last was through—sat like a kid in the shadows on his rug praying your oldest, simplest prayer.

Unable to sleep, replay. If only she had dragged her father off the hill and not let him scribble his notes. If only they had simply gone for a walk around the bungalow. And exhaustingly, addictively, unwillingly would rebuild Alan trait by inclination by possession by memory again and again and again until it might get so bad she would rise, take a pill, and by the bedside nest of lamplight softly, not to wake Rod, though she half hoped to, dial the 24-hour FOLLO line. The days' routine with the kids, no matter how tired, comforted her, into-the-station-wagon out-of-the-station-wagon gulp a magazine in the dentist's waiting room shopping cart down endless aisles pump gas, friend's house, and again. All that remained during the blessed hours of hyperactivity was feeling, thoughtless feeling carried through the supermarket's electric doors like a scarcely noticed pet on one's shoulder, black unspeaking bird. If you feed a child—make a PBJ and soup—distantly or with brimming love, either way the child is fed. If you hug a child, feeling the presence of another child as you hug, does the hugged child notice? No. She didn't think so. And she did love them, and she worked very hard at her days. Feeling was hard but it was better than thinking. The feeling hurt, and sometimes weighted her down or made her have to act weirdly, but the feeling was survivable. It was thinking that at all costs had to be avoided.

There were no leads. The few crank calls proved useless; a queer silence descended. Each time she called the Bureau to check, her friendly, patient contact there said she was sorry, but there was no development. From the beginning the trail had been nonexistent: no car—no registration, no driver's license, no voter registration, no bank, no employer, no next of kin, the neighbors uniformly said they hadn't known the man, did not go there. The house was bare, spic and span, owned by a post office box. No one could locate any of his followers. The electric bill had been paid in cash! By messenger! Chief Airlenmacher threw his papers down when she phoned him. She could hear them slap desk. It would make more sense for her father, instead of her, to check in with the Norham Chief, whom Eden knew and had even talked to—before—about it, except her father had become unreliable. In fact it had become impossible to talk to him about it except in a truncated ritualized conversation that must—it seemed—go precisely the same way each time. So she would tell Chief Airlenmacher what she knew, which would be nothing, and ask him what he might've heard. The whole thing was in the hands of the Bureau of course. Rubbing his eyes the Chief spoke over the phone to her of enormous patience. Then he said he had never, ever, seen a person disappear this way. The National Crime Information Center and all the Bureau's formal and informal networks, the contacts that FOLLO had and Chief Airlenmacher's own coffee-shop, streetcorner, family-and-friends, business-card, favors-owed network in those still wooded hills, knew zero. Absolute zero, made no sense. Who had serviced the man's car? No one. Where had he bought his food? Nowhere. The Chief rubbed his eyes, though he knew he shouldn't. Where had his students come from? And where were they now? No one knew . . there's something, he told Nance rhythmically, though really he shouldn't be knuckling his eyes this way, funny . .

She was on edge, an edge that left but a slit of room for speculation about whether this lack of a single clue or scrap of information was good or bad. When she asked her contact at the Bureau about it there was a pause, a silence, that Nance's imagination pounced on. She was tough. And that was part of the danger she was in. Some parents who went through this were crushed by the experience. Blank-eyed smilers, fragile complete optimists, will-less gobs—she'd met some. That was not her problem. The threat she faced, she realized, was the opposite. She had, now, to fight to prevent her toughness from insulating her, from protecting her too well, from turning her inward forever. Seductive metallic fantasy kingdom of neurotic logic. She started a diary and for ten days dutifully entered every phone call, every scrap of speculation, every FOLLO session in intricate summary. Then one difficult evening threw the blue notebook in the trash. At one that morning, wide awake suddenly, she powered from bed in a witch's whirl and storm of covers (to—gratifyingly—the icthyologist's addled stirring), fast checked each kid in each bed in each room, tripped down the stairs, and cutting her hand on a stray can top yanked her blue diary from the trash, wiping it off with a washcloth. Replaced it on the corner of her workdesk. Squaring its angle to the desk corner angle. In a waking nightmare had thought throwing it away might bring bad luck. Decorously talked this through with her FOLLO friends. Worked through it, understood it for what it was, got a perspective on it, and some distance on it, but couldn't cry. They encouraged her to cry if she felt like crying but she didn't come close, hadn't for many days. Her FOLLO sessions were perhaps just the anesthetic required for this neurotic control-defense not to consume her.

Forget time. A moment, frozen, continuing unchanged from that surreal night, was her fate. As if a camerashutter had started to snap, but not snapped. Caught in kinetic/potential cock-slide-and-snap, snapping but never finished snapping, her hours and days continue without going anywhere. From that night and morning it is one sustained, shrill inner tone. Numb (she realized once the numbness had started to wear off ), for many days she had surprised herself and everyone by how efficiently she functioned. How composed, how swift with the kids, how reasonable in her conversations with the law and her group. Then the next stage about which she had been warned began—the numbness thinned and patched away leaving something raw that was so killingly painful that, enclosing her, it seemed to understand her, rather than the other way 'round. Memory after memory, repeated love and the touch of the dresser, guilt, frozen repeating sadness—to deal with it she had to become cold.

Through poor Nora's afterhaze of the chemicals that had been put in her, as they sat there that gray morning in the unstarted car by the pharmacy sidewalk, came, at last, the realization that her disorientation had been keeping at bay. She squirmed, looked over her shoulder, over the ratty car's back seat

"Where's Alan?"

Nancy can vividly remember the sight of her sister's mouth like a rip in cloth

Nora looking over the back seat at the knowledge that her question is the one they have silently, since arriving, been waiting for her not to ask, but to answer.

The door burst open, and the whole time her mother was there

Rairia was never still. Rairia did the laundry, the dishes, bathed the dogs, went nowhere near Alan's room, took Sala right out and bought her ballet slippers, sat Nance down, lit a cheroot. She waved it as she talked. She talked to Nance about Alan. She wouldn't let Nancy dither. Once they'd agreed on a point (take each day by itself, each hour if necessary. Make yourself distract yourself.), she wouldn't let Nancy slide conversationally away. She interrupted, comforting her daughter roughly, baked two tins of chocolate-chip cookies—not sweet enough, walked the dogs, phoned Zany at the eyrie, slept late, hugged everyone ("Ouch," a surprised Michael softly responded), boiled ham hocks, repaired both doors, snored, mightily, phoned her headquarters, gave a phone interview, mopped the kitchen floor admitting, as she toiled, that it didn't need it, bought the kids a thirty-foot-square outdoor playset, read the paper, took the 7:03. She asked about Thomas and Eden. She told of Nora, the blinding beach sun and easy sand ways odd in Rairia's barked, clipped phrases. She wrote out a check for FOLLO. Rairia on national mores, Rairia on therapy theory, Rairia on brands of garbage disposal, Rairia—kindly—on Michael's guitar playing. Rairia on Zany. She said he couldn't leave the land alone and was happy. Looking at her mother in her doublebreasted blazer and Mexican silver, Nancy realized that Rairia had gone away into another life as surely as if she had walked up a ramp of light into a spacecraft. "And beyond that," Rairia sighed—not sadly—making like a windshieldwiper or a resigned President's final wave with her second, and last, cheroot of the trip, "I will not sacrifice myself on the altar of other people's unhappiness."

The 7:03 took off at 7:03. Nancy sat in shadow. The kids were at friends'. She wanted a resolution. She wanted it finished. It was a distant, unliked part of her that wished this, a little tickle of madness, and it did not rule her, but it was there. No matter what the outcome might be, a part of her was so unable to stand it any longer that any outcome, so long as final, would be better than this . . . but this selfish madness did not rule. But it was there. And it might be—she couldn't be sure, but she suspected it might be growing. On her feet, out of the house, walking, knock on a door, any door, anything, anything to fight it . . . .

after the first numbness which was the spirit's defense against what had happened, akin to the body's nerve-vacuity in the seconds after skin has burned, she now tasted complete grief. The numbness wore off and she thought, and thought, and thought. Her despair and grieving were encompassing things. They were all mixed up now with her thought, controlling, engulfing her—she couldn't stand outside them and look at them—they subsumed her, suffocating, threatening to destroy . . it was thought, not feeling, thought—memory—image, words, moments, a voice, thinking in a gray horror that was so powerful over her, so complete, so huge and unleavened, that she did not experience so much as dwell in it, seeing him, remembering the feel of warm cheek in her neck, his organizing of other kids. The tenor voice sometimes clear in her memory, sometimes evasive—evanescent . . . lost, then out of nowhere fully heard in her mind as if in the room. Sometimes the torture was very briefly almost exquisite, almost beautiful, which was danger, danger and she would fight it. "Come on," she would say breathlessly to herself jogging, or doing the kitchen floor an hour after Rairia, "come on . . . . come on, come on." The torture of thinking about it was this taut fortissimo note held from the moment of Nora's voice on the phone that cold-pearl forest morning, a note held, pitched high, loud, unwavering, until now when, this gray morning—whatever day (the blue notebook's in the trash again)—she has one second's rest from it because, waking in the mauve strewn bedroom of her house, beside Rod (a silent lump), still partly asleep lifting her head from the pillow she has momentarily forgotten it happened.

When she tried for five consecutive minutes with her nails to break the cellophane on a quartet of cheesecrackers Michael wanted, Rod made a fast decision and picked up the phone and was able to get last-minute reservations and took her to an inn . . . the children were taken care of—Rod's parents' place in Eugene with even a retired state cop at the last minute helping out. The inn, a mountainous mountain house on a lake, gave them a candlelight dinner in their room. Halfway through, Rod answered the ringing phone. He looked exceedingly surprised, hung up, excused himself, left the room, was away several minutes, then came back and kissed her and left. The senior senator from California walked in. There was no mistaking her. Already shocked by Rod's kiss and disappearance, Nancy choked on a bean. She had a coughing fit. "Alan," she managed weakly. The senator, her small staff of two deferentially hanging back, seated herself. Looking straight at the boy's mother with a solemnity and an aggressiveness that were threatening only at first, she flashed a campaign smile geared for a few thousand people. That wasn't right. Genuinely lowering her eyes, as the smile collapsed to regret, she took a breath—there was even a shudder through the senator's body.

"First," the senator said, and her look came up and was steel, "I want to ask if you will try not to be angry. You have every right to be. I would be. I shouldn't say that. I have no idea, none, what you're going through. Your son is safe. Your son is safe," the senator said.

The light in the suite was rich gold from table lamps, from fancy ceiling fixtures and wall lamps and floor lamps and the glow, around a wide doorway, of the spacious bathroom reflecting off burnished brass, white silk and mahogany, damask sheen and the sparkly facets of mirrors and crystal drinking glasses and ponderous, immaculate ashtrays. Tabletops like dark flat ponds perfectly reflected the lamps standing on them. There were solid silver ewers, tasseled woven pulls. The lamps' light shone on the butterwhite drawn blinds, burned at, and from, every angle to make the long room with its cream ceiling and carved bed and fireplace and sitting circle shadowless, a splendid opulent chamber sealed against the lake's buffeting gales many floors below.

"Your son is safe. I mean this in the sense that we know where he is. And we know that he has not been hurt. That's the first thing. Second, he will, almost certainly, not be hurt."

You could see she wanted to say more—run the conversational table and tell Nancy in detail why this was happening and why it was happening the way it was happening and how it would turn out, but, wisely, she stopped talking just—deftly—slowly enough so Nance didn't realize, in angrily interrupting, that she'd been invited to.

"If he isn't hurt and isn't going to be I don't understand." She was sweating. No one stepped forward to help her. She might swoon. "I don't understand this. Please, just get him back. Just get him. Just . ."

"Due," the other said, "to a combination of circumstances I cannot share—"

"Won't you mean."

"No," the senator said carefully, like picking up the smallest bit of string. "I cannot. I want to. I cannot."

"Oh bullshit you—I'm sorry, I'm sorry. I believe you."

Nancy had both hands over her eyes.

Her mother was strong because Rairia had broken free, gone West, gone hog wild with zany gyrations, won through to an independence of self . . . but this woman sitting here before Nancy, this face familiar from magazine covers and TV, was strong because she had been strong from the cradle. This woman who was a senator had been strong—because her family was—the same way at five as she was now at forty-seven, had no more changed than the wood grapeclusters and garlands and carven swirling leaves of the luxurious headboards of the big beds had changed since Carver's and Hughes's and Bethune's day.

Nancy had her hands over her face and was crying. At first trying to stop. She couldn't though. A good cry was good for—oh unreal, this was unreal, unreal but it wasn't, it was real—she let go. She cried about a minute into her pink hands. While she had her hands over her face she did not see Senator Saroka reach out to the side for her man's phone, which he handed her and she put an ear to to listen, nodding.

"Sorry," Nancy flusteredly and in nervous enervation half-laughed showing them her red spectacles-askew face. "Go on, I believe you, go on."

"Due," the other said with honesty in her voice.

That honesty, a wave, met and matched in frequency-magnitude and position the opposite-engendered wave of Nancy's need. Nodes occupied the same point and there was in Nancy's heart a huge reinforced harmonic galumph of passion and relief. She believed.

"—to a set of circumstances I cannot detail, I must tell you that, though it is certain your son is not in danger, if we send our people in to get him before certain other exigencies of the situation have been addressed, then it is just as certain—in fact it is more certain—that thousands of innocent people, and perhaps an order of magnitude more than that, women and children very much among their number, will die."

Nance's voice is willed quiet by herself. Quiet and bottled and restrained when her being wants to explode, so her voice is unfamiliar, echoing reticently back to her off the room's lights' surfaces.

"Could I ask a question?"

"You certainly may. And I will answer if I possibly can."

"Is there," Nance blinks, "I mean is this—something tells me. Is there . . like a bomb in this? A nuclear . ."

High, the suite is seen from below as glowing inscrutable windows in a towerface of such windows—effulgent, resplendent and remote above such *slap*slap as a midnight chop might make against the stem of a stormanchored Deep-V.

Nance with a thrill sees the look the senator gives the staffer closest her.

"I probably can't imagine . ."

"Honey, you can't."

"Will I get Alan?" Nance asks in a small voice, ". . back?"

The senator looks straight at her and nods.

"But I'll be patient, I'll have to be. Won't I? I will. Oh I believe you, I don't know why I do but I do. Is it—of course it is."

Eyebrow.

"Complicated," Nance explains.

"Oh yes," the senator says.

"It isn't Quadros who has this . . thing."

"No."

"I can't ask you who can I."

"You could, but I wouldn't tell you. But I can tell you this. You know the name. Honey, you know the name."

"It's just," Nancy floatingly felt her way, numb-reasonable in the last moments before it hit her direct, "so odd to believe the—bad. I mean to know that all the—bad. W-what I'm trying to say is. Evil. You know what I mean, things no one would believe would—"

"They exist."

"Oh heh, well," Nance was saying to herself as Rod slipped back in, "heh. Can't tell anyone though can I, no, well, at least I know he's oh my god," she said in a bloodless voice that caused Rod to stride the carpeting to her side. She was going to cry tremendously and she looked up, recognized Rod, lifted a hand and their fingers' touch—spectacularly—Rod having taken vigorous slide-strides across the old-fashioned carpeting, is a *SNAP* of static electric spark— "Ohh," she says, "oh well." Goes forward out of her chair and onto her knees on the rich pile.

"I have put trust in you," the senator says, eating a carrot stick, "and I do believe it's not misplaced, but you will have to be patient."

"I know I will. I know that. I know and I will," Nance tearfully, joyously, chants wetly flapping her fingers from the wrist as if hope were ritual. "I know and I will. I will, I will, I will—"

"In a week or two," the senator said, "*maybe,* repeat—"

The senator meant "repeat" in the telegraphic sense of emphasis, as in *no, repeat no* . . but Nance thought it was a command and repeated, "Maybe."

The senator thought a moment. She waved her people out. She started to pull her thick collar up. "And you must not," she said, "go to the press. Of course if you did everything would be denied. The game would be changed and we would say you were unbalanced due to the loss of your son. In fact we're set up to do just that, should it prove necessary."

"I hear you," the kneeling mother said.

"I believe you do."

Nance quietly thanked her and looked up.

# 26

I downshifted coming over the hump and coasted onto the shady parking area. There the bungalow was, its low roofs quiet under the forest, its chimneys still.

Some Sufis were dancing in the treeshade in their robes. They were doing the Movements, heads, necks relaxed, all lolling left while white gowns all sway the same way, robed arms lifting in unison the other way, pivot and whirl.

I learned they do such dancing to entrance themselves and to experience by ritualizing, to ennoble, pass through, plumb and know by ritualizing, say, joy, or fear, or grief—anathema to our cult of individual uniqueness and cultural variety. That a Houston banker, an Aleut and the children of Kigali have much in common is given only lip service by us Westerners. The high priests of the old hide their terror of the new while "radicals" like my uncle by their actions give the apostles of the old all the justification they could hope for, so maybe, I thought, going down the railroad-tie steps, to have all peoples in identical white robes feeling and practicing grief or joy the same deep human way isn't such a bad idea comparatively, but it was as useless a generalization as any other and vanished with my knocking.

The door was answered by a person I'd never met. I moved in and out of a new strange group that moved easily about the bungalow. There were more white robes, a cantor, atoms on the screens of computers, someone wanted me to read a report, how fast gravity travels out from a newborn star, but I was distracted. Her turned-up nose pointing out of the waist-length fall of her hair, she—I had gotten no name—bent over a tap. Blackberry juice trickled into a glass for me. I tasted, noticing, across the living room in the unsunny western bay that was spacious and empty looking without upended tricycle or terrarium, some women smoking a water pipe. Standing on my feet feeling clumsy and somehow rudely enormous among his impressive new friends, I tried to read the thing, sipping my dark juice, but it degenerated into field equations and I was lost and carried my glass and the page around, wondering if I should leave.

A phone was ringing. It kept ringing and I picked up.

It was Tacoma.

"Fine," I said.

Lowering her voice: "What's going on? Tell me, tell me exactly. Are they all there?"

"Yes," I said, "if I understand you, er, you mean the visitors."

"Hah," she corrected. "They're permanent, mark my words. Do you know who they are?"

"Well," I said, "I would guess—"

"No one does. No one knows. Some of them are people from Boston Mom was running with. But they're from all over, stop that."

"Excuse me?"

"I said no. No means no, cleaning up half isn't acceptable. Well work it out. I'm talking to Uncle John. Excuse me where was I oh, they're loonies," she whispered. "Aren't they? And is he still going on this stupid trip?"

"He plans to."

I didn't think they were loonies.

Though I hadn't been here long, and didn't exactly feel at ease, I didn't think they were loonies. Maybe they were what he needed.

"Argh, well. Since," she said.

You could hear her eyes close

"Since," she began . .

"You don't have to."

"Yes I do. I'd rather not, but I do. Since," she said . .

I waited. Jidda, as Earth rotated, came to where Mecca had just been . .

"Since," she said, "Alan"

She was crying so softly I could barely hear it. It was quick, then over. "My father's got these odd people milling around him," she said fast. "Procedures," she said. "It's died down a lot," she said fast, "but still all the people honey stop that, thank-you. There's a person we work with who's very good. The kids are amazing, just amazing, they know exactly what the situation is, as much as any of us does." Deliberately, second by second she got hold and went on. "They know or I should say they understand what we can do, what we can control and what we can't. You," she said. "Is Mother there?"

I said I was pretty sure no.

"Out campaigning no doubt, she's coming in a week, coming to visit us. Have you seen her lately?"

"Yes she really—"

"*Doesn't* she? I mean—"

"She does."

"The best she's ever looked," she said, "and as for him I say let him do what he wants, I've thought about it. If he wants to go for this fishing film, if he believes in it, well then—"

"He believes in it," I said.

"Right," she said. "You mean he really does? Or were you finishing my sentence?"

"I think he really does."

"I do too," she snapped. "But in what?"

"Excuse me?"

"He believes in what. You think he believes in what."

"Why," I said, "the film."

"In anything that isn't real," she said, "in anything that—oh gawd I don't know, whatever isn't real yet. Have you seen him? Did you just get there? Have you seen him yet? Is he basically ok?"

I answered no, yes, no and I imagined so. We talked a little more. Out of the blue she told me I should get married.

"You should," she lectured, "look. Keep your eyes open and call me when you've been there a while. And had a chance to talk to him? My third husband's an ichthyologist. I've got him all picked out. Will you do that? Honey *no*—wait 'til I hang up, which I'm about to. Get married. I mean it. Will you?"

"Sure."

"Is Mother around?"

I said, "I don't think so."

"I've gotta get off. I'm supposed to be more forceful on the phone, 'bye."

"Good—"

"Have fun!" she yelled bravely and hung up.

In addition to Jonassen, the mystic, who sensed me though neither I nor the door made a noise, there were Amy Divine, Photo Pete, Alex Mohawk Greene, MogG 2, Farid Gwattar, the linguist, not the fighter, and Sally Celest, the brilliant reckoner, though none of these were real names. Liz Scull and her husband O came and went, as did the Zed Brothers who between them knew all there is to know about burble turbulence, and there was a round gentleman named Dr. Wan who would later become Wan the Insatiable.

They had gravitated here from various campuses and centers, a free-form exploration. Among their interests were many of the suspect realities that bat, moth-like, about the periphery of conventional academia's bright wattage. They were not doing whatever came into their heads, but neither were they not doing that. There was order, discipline of thought, and a tolerance lax in comparison with the rules of the false-tolerant thought communities they'd emigrated from.

The funny names they'd taken helped relax them socially and also intellectually, which was more important since in their other lives every last one of them—except the Sufis—was a respected dept. head or professor or head researcher. They had come at Rairia's encouragement and stayed on at Eden's, riding his horses and otherwise disporting themselves between discussions, but it did seem to me that though this was his house and it was his money feeding them he remained—eager, shabby, hopeful—rather on the outskirts of things. It didn't last long—seven weeks?—but while it did they were into some wild stuff—mind farming, telekinesis and spiritualism—but they were calm about it as Eden frenetically introduced me around. Photo Pete even sat me down, as my uncle looked gratefully on, in front of the Random-Event Generator. The Random-Event Generator (REG) is an electronic device programmed to in effect flip a coin hundreds of times a minute, absolutely objectively, binary choice. You sit before the simple green screen blinking *A50.000///B50.000, A50.000///B50.000, A50.000/// B50.000.* You are concentrating, trying to see if you can't by telepathy marginally skew the machine's normal half-heads half-tails control. When I relaxed I made the A go to 50.009. Unshaven, his last hair exploring the indoor air forlornly, he was too loud in congratulating me. He almost winced at himself but clearly couldn't help it, sputtered, to Photo Pete's affectionate chagrin, on and on about how hee, heh, a deviation of .009 was statistically significant. Wasn't it? Photo Pete (a famous astrophysical acousticist) laid a hand on my uncle's black shoulder and said well, nearly so.

His eyes' whites were not white but were traceried at their corners with vessels like networkings of elaborate sky lightning and it might seem he was looking at you but his look, if you looked closely, stopped in the air before his eyes. His ample unskilled hands, jaundice-yellow in spots, were not plunged in the black pockets of his black jeans or gesturing or wriggling in the air but hung, at his sides, trembling as he encouraged me and praised my performance on the exotic machine heh, ah, and all that it ah, implied (about my telekinetic powers I supposed but suddenly I was tired of him). The black turtleneck made him look more distinguished than he was, and with his black slacks stood in contrast to the others' lighter casual clothing or white robes.

He came looming, smiling, for me, taking my arm desperately, in great distress wanting to talk about the film and Dungeness crabs—he started right in and I think I shrank back but he wasn't deterred, if anything he was even more insistent. He was first talking about the movie, scenes themes digressions, a laundrybasket's worth of ideas. Rummaging like the broadbacked badger in a pile on a desk and staining his unreliable fingers with newsprint, he rattlingly unfolded and thrust at me, as quickly grabbing it back to read it to me out loud and explain, the Science Section Dungeness crab piece . . . apparently some scientists, setting up a simple and stable (they thought) computer model of the lifecycle over eons of a coastline population of Dungeness crabs, had run into nature's reliance on random destruction.

Assume unperturbed environment, normal generations, normal dispersal of young etc. The scientists were quite sure that all they were doing was laying down a simple grid upon which to play with environmental and other variables. But when run out over time (running his hand distractedly through hypothetical hair) . . behold! Rattle. Their simple model of crab generations showed drastic fluctuations in population, fluctuations unattributable to cause. The crab population in the scientists' model would continue steady in its predictability for thousands of years and generations and then without the slightest indication that it was going to happen suddenly the population would soar in numbers, or plummet. Why? There wasn't a reason, unless—he shook me—I don't like that—heh, *yes? Unless?* I wasn't even going to try to answer him and even in the state he was in he couldn't but see my annoyance. Unless, he answered for me, more quietly, and having let go my arm (so his hand was trembling again)—unless, he rumbled, Nature has a need for, a dependency on, inequilibrium, gratuitous destruction.

crazed, shag-bearded, the brown eyes wild with an impossible desire, he went over, his heart expanding and collapsing, to the simple machine and sat. "Imagine," he said, preparing himself before the screen's green where *A50.000///B50.000* uncaringly blinked. "The modelers devise their simplest pattern—population, genes, generations, migration—simple and then hee." He sat concentrating. "It turns out the natural ah—" stared at the display screen, it stared at him. *A50.000/// B50.000* "—the natural world is randomly destructive, may have to be, *ahem.*" The room had been cleaned and gutted of much of his library and painted an unbrilliant new hue, too airy, gentler of shadow than I remembered—thin unnatural light like a pressurized cabin floating with windless soft rush thirty-seven thousand feet above the seas' storm-scrollings. He went on talking to me, his chin lifted, eyes screen-staring, a hand—fingers splayed—very lightly atremble on either knee as he tried to think the numbers on the screen different.

He was trying. His eyes angelically shut now, his face mild, expressive and youthful in the lost world of his concentration. And he prattled on quietly about how the crab-population-model scientists would no doubt soon conclude their model had been too simple. They should have put environmental change in, they would conclude, then no doubt they would not see such a reasonless boom and bust of population, that is, they might see it, but at least now there would be a way to explain it. There would be an explanation. They would've inserted an explanation. So. Nature wasn't turmoil after all. They just had to tune their model. Nature wasn't arbitrarily destructive after all, they just—he quietly panted—had to work some new variables in. Season the ah, soup 'til it tastes the way you want. That was what was wrong with the physicist who wrote that one could be assured that when one had built a collider powerful enough to throw a pair of 20-trillion-volt proton beams dead into each other one would then discover one of two things (and these only). Either the Higgs particle or strong new forces. "They ah, don't you see? They know even before they build the thing what they'll find—they're surgically cutting out the monkey wrench, heh, but ahh, truly the." He cracked an eggy eye. "Damn," he softly said. For the numbers on the screen had not changed. He nibbled his lip at them. The tremor of the hands ball-and-clawing the black knees grew. "I don't see why the," he trailed off. The numbers on the screen were unchanged, blinking in his open eyes. It was winter but a descending autumn leaf glided, swooped and turning in a circle floated down, outside the window, not like a descending flute or our years or anything except itself, veined, brittle leaf catching sunlight, to side-slide through shadow . .

"I can't seem to get it to do it."

He sat staring at the screen, which read *A50.000///B50.000.*

Touching a thumb to his temple and the first three fingers of that hand—in the boyscout salute—to the expanse of his forehead (pinky extended), he concentrated. "I can't understand why." *A50.000///B50.000, A50.000///B50.000, A50.000///B50.000* . . "You would think er, at least I would think—" tiring a second, shuts the eyes, fingers/thumb still cogitatively pressed to forehead and temple . . *A50.000///B50.000, A50.000///B50.000,* "that," opening his eyes to resume direct visual concentration, "at least once I'd move it. Just a thousandth. Everyone who tries it gets at least some change, but why can't . ." *A50.000///B50.000, A50.000///B50.000, A50.000///B50.000, A50.000///B50.000* . . "I just don't understand why I don't get *some* change, ah . . ." Now he was sitting hunched not looking at the screen anymore with his broad black back to me and his face in a hand. He pointed with his other trembling hand (while covering his face) at what was left of his notebooks, his diaries, scraps, equations, sketches and drafts, on none of which (save the fishing film) he'd worked since the night of searchbeams and shouts against forest, and said—to me—but speaking into the palm and spread fingers of his self-blinding hand, while still pointing blindly to the side at his books (those that were left on the depleted shelves) and papers that he could not see: "I want you to have it. I want you to have it all if you want it. Not when I'm gone. Now. Make sense of it if you can." Slowly, his pointing hand fell. He continued to sit hunched, covering his face: "I cannot."

I went to bed that night feeling empty and confused.

I wanted to talk to him, to know if there were news, to ask how he was—how he was taking it, to listen if he needed to explode, to hold his hand and comfort him, to watch with him while he sobbed, if that was what he needed, and yes, out of curiosity to know what it was like. But like a metal soldier in a metal city with metal thoughts, he said nothing.

Sat in front of his random green screen staring, hands involuntarily patting his knees. Sally Celest one time had it all the way to A52.109/// B47.891 (only the "A" value could be increased by any of us, but that's just the wind of the turning world), but he could do nothing, stare, gaze and concentrate though he might. Not so much as a +0.001 took place, not in all the hours he tried, though as I've said the rest of us all moved the numbers at least a little.

His arm, lifted in mock salute as he lay on his back on the bare floor, certainly wasn't relaxed. He lay, his vast belly rounded, that arm aloft in senseless valediction, on his back in the sunlight the next morning . . I too was staring at the ceiling. I breathed, as the head Sufi asked us to, in distinct stages—from abdomen serene, the lighthearted mastervoice adjured us, up through stomach to lungs then throat. Upon each stage, in its turn, we meditated. I focused my attention on the left foot (mine), then the right. Then my lower left leg, then the right one, and up, my body—all our bodies where we lay—becoming light supposedly. Twenty of us maybe on our backs in rank and file on the ungleaming flooring as the gentle carillon voice directed us—Sufis and translators and astrophysicists, apart as individuals yet bound together in that instructing voice and the physical experience of this, such, for each of us, as it was. And my poor uncle there with his arm in the air, supine, eyes closed, lips—soft smile—barely atremble as if holding some celestially flavored lozenge on the tongue.

Our potbellied teacher, looking down, lengthily considered that saluting arm which only moments ago he—the Master—had carefully lifted to see, as he had done passing among the rest of us, if his pupil were deeply and sufficiently relaxed (if so the limb drops—flops—when released).

Centering our auras as best we could, breathing properly, thinking of light and the world under the floor at our backs, we did the exercises in the way the pleasant little man advised as he strolled around stopping by you to lift, say, your leg and let go—mine, I'm proud to say, crashed to the floor. "Good," the Master said . .

I turn my cheek and look over. The Master is bending down. My dear uncle's face, eyes shut, expression like a flower open to the sun, is trying its best.

Gingerly taking Eden's wrist and lifting, the teacher elevates the big, pallid arm and lets go.

Oh we sensed the light and loosened our muscles and became aware of the planet for about an hour. I enjoyed it. I don't make fun of it. But neither, interesting as it was, did I feel myself osmosing with it and surrendering to its peace anywhere nearly so totally as, apparently, happened to many of them. But I did take just the one class.

On the other hand, if you tried it every day for twenty years . .

What has roots that do not thirst, branches that do not flower, no leaves and stands striking and stark with crook'd, clawing arms, but does not grow

The sky lay flat under our feet. We had hiked to this high place, Eden puffing, but it was good for him. Josie MacAttick, two of Josie's kids and I had gotten him out, where Seldom Seen Pond lay windless under the frigid blue, which the still water reflected up at us. Not a cloud, the acre of currentless water like nickel. It was cold. Eden pulled his cap lower. Josie checked Roberto and Micah, who wanted to go to the pond's edge to see if she could see her reflection and was going to—her mother would let her. But first this tussling with Micah to button Micah's parka all the way up and get her left glove on. The child (as if the pond would go away) struggling against her mom and Josie's instructions . . then was free. Was told to be careful. Was standing at the water's edge.

"Why is the sky in the water?" she asked.

The reedy shoreline was not quick to devour the kindergartener's tie boots. Josie moved forward but it was Eden with a sloshy step who was at Micah's side to see that she was all right, looking, with her, down into perfectly reflected sky. The stand of burnt trees across the water, gray forever, reflected, under themselves, upsidedown against the plate blue. As a buzzard gliding slid like a bass cruising the deepness under us, that was not a deepness, of sky in water Eden rumbled in reply "The ah—" soft voiced "—sky—" bent hugely in his winter parka and mittens and scarf and tam over—but not touching—his fourth cousin thrice removed "—you know how when you look in a mirror you see yourself?"

The vermillion igloo of Micah's hat bobbed.

"Well," he said, "when water is very still, it is like a mirror."

It was.

The burnt trees.

The water was miraculously still

reflecting the sky, not the pale westering sun nor, from where Josie and her other child and I stood, Micah or Eden. The winter forest stood around us quiet. It was cold, no birds around, the reflection of the sky in the motionless pondwater a shimmer on the glass of his eye as he stood looking down at the little girl at the water's edge. We three, behind them, formed a loose amphitheater where we stood. Eden took a sloshy step back, looking at little Micah looking at the sky in the water.

"Is it the real sky?" she asked.

Tear? Something in the eye. The way he wiped it I think it was a tear. Must've wanted to answer, I guess he couldn't. He couldn't think what to say as, bending her stubby knees, leaning forward a very little bit, Micah with her mitten finger touched . .

My uncle had been grappling with the possibility that the reason gravity isn't integratable with the other fundamental forces is that there isn't any gravity. No gravity—gravity as just the twitching around of the other three forces, principally electromagnetism so that, in layman's terms, there is no such thing as matter, or mass, but only energies of all sorts. Energies combining and interacting in ways that cause our eyes and instruments to think the pond bed holds water, and the water sky, and that the boots of the people are in mud and that, concentric, out from where Micah's red, woven fingertip touched the surface, ripples fade

corrugating the image-sky, and that the academic in his bulgy parka has weight. But really we're just energies jostling, and so's the sky. And so's the sky's reflection, and so are these dissolving logs we step over, picking our way down the Sellerworths' poorly kept trail, slipping on cold rugs of leaves, our sleeky parkas scratched by twig fingernails. I had wanted to ask Eden about Alan the moment I'd arrived. But there was a wall against it. If there were a silence he would speak quickly into it, never—never—of Alan. But now, I had seen his tear. And as we walked and picked our way down through the colorless forest, all of a sudden here it came. I don't remember what he said. It was generalities, resigning oneself, the perils of the subjunctive mood, sophistry, nonsense. Clearly it was about Alan—clearly he couldn't bear it.

The subject was anathema, taboo tripwire that if touched galvanized my uncle, Nance said, into straight minutes of mannerism. First he would say, any news? Any *new* news? He had said those precise words to her the first time she'd called after flying back out to Washington, and now each time it was time again to address the dread topic he said them again. "So ah . . any news? Any *new* news?" She would report that there was none. If she should go on to say a little about FOLLO and some of the people she was meeting, or worse even remotely to allude to her own demons, his silence on the line would positively scream at her to stop. Or he might—first softly, but if she persisted he would raise the bass decibels of his voice "ahhh" to quiet her—interpose a question about some technical matter. Would ask for instance if she were still dealing with the same contact at the Bureau. Yes—her eyes shut—yes she would say, yes I am, yes.

And, he then asks, every goddamned conversation, is she (the FBI agent) "continuing to discharge her duties heh, ah, satisfactorily?"

"Yes," Nance says, holding the receiver like a stone in her mind. *Yes she is*

A pause . . he is going to ask if she needs money. He's helped nicely already, though she knows he can't afford it—contributions to FOLLO, extra household money, a hefty pledge toward the reward being offered . . . she almost hangs up, never does, taking, without thinking, the half-destroyed jelly doughnut caring Michael presses into her hand for a present . .

"And finally let me—do you, that is would additional funds help for, er, and ah, of course anything you may personally . ."

Shut your eyes. Touch smooth back of receiver to your cheek, room temperature. In the window a mountain—rare sight. "No," she says. Croak whisper. Her Adam's apple bobs as she silently downs the mucus puddle in her throat V. She composes herself and to her amazement and gratitude hears the dialtone. He has spared her and hung up on his own!

She composes herself, rights the receiver. Puts it to her ear and lips—dialhum . . . "No," she says softly, "no, thanks dad, no. We're fine in that department," she tells the empty phone.

After the meeting at the inn it is odd in a new way to tell her father again and again no news, no old news dad, no new news. The lie is easy and frictionless because it has been made very clear to her that she is to tell no one. She doesn't want to. She waits now day by day, believing. She has her resolution, her finality. She believes what the senator said. She waits, day by day, hour by hour, day and night, lying as airily and easily to her father as scissoring a string. No dad, no old news, no new news.

# 27

A distraught Chase Parr sits alone facing a mountain of pink caviar ringed with lemon slices. A dewy magnum, bedded in ice, leans toward her. Muttering to herself she's eating and drinking just as fast as her excited little system can take it.

"This is what you get yourself into," she hisses, refilling her glass and jamming the bottle back in the ice. She grabs and slurps, phantom, archimaginous eyes staring out over crystal rim. "You are so," she berates herself, "predictable." Flying about the kitchen in a cold rage her classy eyes try to set things afire, but it doesn't work. She hangs her bangs.

"They tell you you're in on it," she whispers. "From start to finish. Then they pull the rug out from under your beautiful little feet. I cannot. Believe it. I cannot believe they're doing this—to me!" Without lifting her head she points to herself. "But I guess they are. I guess they are and I guess they have. So we'd better get our little resumé out. And we'd better get our little fanny in gear while there's still time . ." An idea bulb shines. Her eyes open full and her hands are talons. Her stunning lips break into a battle-ax's cutting rim . . there is something she can do. It's unethical, even illegal. But it could solve her problem. But she can't.

It would be wrong. She hangs her head again, looking for a plot for her life. "Lordy," she genuinely sighs, her bangs, in the kitchen heat, droopy low. "My life is like this . . accumulation of disjointed episodes." She looks at her hand. Seeing it holds a strawberry, she pops the treat in her mouth, red and red—she's been popping them without thinking. She pops another. They're great with champagne. "God they're good. Oh by the way of course you can, you can do it and what's more you're going to. Or you'll be washed up in the industry forever and spend the rest of your life in Newark. In a hovel. Painting dolls. But at least you'll be able to live with yourself. These strawberries are—mmm. I can't go through with it of course." She claps her hands to her head. "But I've got to! A chance like this comes once in a lifetime! I've got to do it and that's all there is to it! But I can't," she explains in an enraged whisper, "because you have something called a conscience. C-o-n—" staring into space she puts several in a row in her mouth, licks one white spike-nailed finger after another—luscious.

"I wonder—" lick "—if I couldn't just—" lick "—*no!* My God what am I thinking I could never do such a thing unless I could be positive no one—" pensive lick "—but you can't. Oh yes you can." She rushes from the kitchen, the vista of the city's lights blurring past her in the windows. Finds her laptop and runs, legs kicking out awkwardly, back into the kitchen for one more tart-sweet pop and pringling sip. "*God* they're good." They're so good she has another and another. Each, she realizes, is a year of her life. In amazement she pops one more. Another year of her life. They're so scrumptious she eats more, seeing, as she does so, that each one she gulps is a full year of her life . .

There's just one little one left now at the bottom of the bowl.

Chase never got to try the Random-Event Generator but I'll bet she could've marvelously spoiled its randomness—Chase was a live, vigorous soul, astray but vigorous—spoiled . . vigorous though. She spent so much energy trying to take care of and call attention to and pleasure herself that you forgot how naturally, given a rod for the first time or challenged (had she been) to use her mind to break the smug machine's A50.000///B50.000 symmetry, she could just, forgetting herself, a gold bang over a gathered eye, do it. I know she could've swayed

that green screen there in my uncle's den, which was not of so high a resolution as, nor so gentle on the eye as, nor so beepingly noisy as, the digital 90, 90, 88, 91 on the lengthwise rectangular screen among such screens high on the shelf above the doll-like head drowsing on the elevated pillow

with wires taped to him, clear plastic tubes bearing strange clear liquids through needles slipped drippingly into him, and yet another tube draining his plumbing (too slowly, drippingly, into a clear sac dangling below the bed's metal foot). And with tubes in the nose and mouth—winged oxygen forced down the pinioned windpipe plastically, because he can't breathe. Not on his own. Lay in the bed in the room crammed with gear beeping and clucking and clicking and displaying in digital nonchalance on screens how his little body was working, while in a row on their scarecrow rod bodies the plastic sacs dripped their chemical help down through their meandering transparent tubes. Woke. Sagged his ebbing eyes up, toward Eden, kind of groggily nodding. Closed them again, breathed. Waited essentially. Lying there. Lifted a small hand—gesture? Probably not. Eden stepped a step closer but was still not very close. Holding his beret in both hands over his own healthy belly.

If the patient were asleep, my uncle would stand there a time then go, passing, sometimes, Lim's wife or one of the children. If he were awake, for ten minutes Eden would talk painedly and too fast delivering any scrap of news he could think of as tortuously as the clear, mysterious liquids wending their way down the conduit vines of tubing. Went through the list of news of the family and the world that he'd prepared and then, looking at the monitors, found, with difficulty, something encouraging to say about one or another of them, pulse for instance: 60 . . good. Or else about the one that had to do with measuring how much oxygen was getting into the blood . . my uncle who would easily have understood never asked a nurse or doctor to explain because, standing by the electrically malleable bed, he was panicked, concealedly, by the room and its equipment and by the presence that was day by day, hour by hour, coming into it.

Standing, wanting to go, if going wanting to come back—when

there wanting to go, when gone wanting to go back. Drive again through the breasts of the hills down into the state's second largest city to go into that room . .

The screen he watched the most often measured how successful the breathing was, hypnotizing him. 90 . . 89 . . 89 . . 89 . . 87 . . 91 . . 90 . .

90 or higher was good, one of the nurses said. Sometimes he would find, for his brother, portentous marginal cause for optimism in say several 92s in succession. With as fastidious an application of intellectual niceness as ever *philosophe* or scholar of the great Talmud brought to their endeavor, he would find, for Lim, something promising in a particular pattern. Lim, who had had a quick life—sports, St. Paul's, kids, law, the lucrative agenting for Eden, gags, six trips to Europe and one to China—said mumbling: "You're prob'ly right."

This had been in their last conversation, hours before the lungs stopped being able to go it alone and the tubes went into Lim's mouth and nose. It was a mystery just what Lim had been referring to in mumbling "You're prob'ly right," and Eden looked at him, whom Eden did love, and who had teased Eden so cruelly, so many snows ago when they were children by the MacAtticks' pasture where the pines were deep with shadow and cool when fat Eden trod off, alone, into them. Small and yellowed, Lim's fist clenches in a symbol of *fight* just before Eden leaves that night. Lim had said no more, so there was no explaining what Eden was "prob'ly right" about. A few hours later the throat tube had gone in. He passed his sister-in-law in the hall sometimes and passed rooms, during his visits, with faces—in some of them—blasted, skin draped on skull bone, eyes sunken, afraid and frozen. Statically staring, ready to go. But Lim never looked like that, mumbled, sputtered, fiddled and fussed with his IVs feebly but never, ever looked like the others Eden passed in some of the other rooms like a gallery of horrified, petrified statuary.

Lim Hope lay on his back on the hospital bed, a door between dimensions.

And sometimes, to my uncle when he came in, that efficient room of devices was like a launch lab. They hadn't had all this gear and capability a generation ago. 90 on the oxygen, 90 was good, 90 digital on the screen beeping, or 89 . . 92 . . 92 . . between comments to his brother Eden stared. Comments as hard to think of as proofs of God. He stared at the changing averaging 90899191 on the screen then stared at the window. The window showed gray streets, and that it was raining. Rain or snow or wind were the same on this side of the window. Might glance at the pulse readout: 60, good, 60, good. Though who knew how much the liquids curvingly descending their passageways were making that happen . . . . . . 93! Good! Tell him. Told him, eyes still closed. Face in mask of rest. Fair color but not the pink that raged and seemed always to Eden to have sweatbeads like a cartoon of supremest agitation flying out in all directions. Nodded. Did he? Yes. And there was a flicker of a smile around the tube in the side-sagging mouth. Yes. Desperate for one more thing to say, Eden lies. Amazes himself. He tells Lim loudly, even bending down, that he's gone back to work on the Gwen cycle. He'll end it, he shouts. It's going well! A lie! A complete, utter lie! My uncle is terribly agitated doing this. Lim's lids quiver. The chapped, bleeding-in-a-corner mouth with its tube in it forms . . . a "p" it looks like.

It was over in a couple of weeks, a bending time of late hours and hospital emergency visits, midnight ambulance trips, trips home a few days later for the little fighter in his bathrobe, a day after that, back in. His circulation was bad—trouble getting breath—fluid in the lungs, heart erratic. In retrospect they might have done something to de-clog the superhighway exit/access overpass/underpass branchwork leading from the heart, but the cancer, broken out and driving like Patton's tanks, distracted them. Earlier generations had died in hospital rooms plainer and more drab and with less electricity and machinery. You visited, but not as often. You talked about it with the healthy, but not as much. One morning you got the call. The patient had slipped away in the small hours . . but now as in certain eras distant past, close attention was paid to the process and all the players in it and they had the technology to make it stick. Their scientific ability to observe and monitor caulked shut the slightest, thinnest seam of a possibility that the undetected might occur. Here it is again, the late-afternoon visiting hour, and here you are again hovering above your poor brother like a flickering Gulliver with catheters and wires and tubes taped to him and going into and coming out of him. Does he form, a second time, "p-p-," it looks like, with his lips cut from what the docs have had to do?

Eden fled again and wondered many times afterward why he didn't stay just a couple minutes longer that rainy Tuesday. Coax Lim to try to say some words, if he wanted to. Why didn't he tell Lim to nod, or shake his head no in answer to questions he, Eden, would frame until one could triangulate in on what Lim wanted to tell him but he fled. He fled. He said: "I'll see you later, keep getting better—*fight.*" As before, the small, ochroid hand clenched in a fight/victory fist, half under the sheet.

Left the room and the hospital and went out, though it was raining, that Tuesday, and God help him went fishing.

That night he got the call from Lim's wife. He asked her, after driving—racing—over, because none of the children happened to be home—asked, standing in her and Lim's fancy drive under the starless, location-less dark sky of that night, if she were brave, could she be brave. A woman he liked and did not know well. She said yes, yes she could. Standing there, two shadows. Got there at twelve-thirty-seven a.m. with a rushing sound in his ears, the whole time the whole drive the whole time in the hospital in the room with his brother and after, a rushing sound, as if time itself were revealing the sound of its passing like the sounds of an invisible silver stream flowing somewhere out of this world. The doctor kept saying "It's *hot* in here." He explained to them. The heart had gone wild but was under control now but most everything else below the heart had quit. Quit working, he explained. Sleeves rolled up, fingers clasped, elbows on knees where he sat for them on the edge of the waiting-room sofa. But he was conscious, he said. They could see and be with him if they wanted to. He was surprisingly conscious, looking around, looking around just a very little with the pink-red swims that were his eyes. The halo of Lim's disconcertingly alive-looking face, with high color because the blood was all going to the head now at the end. The dazed eyes, life still in them in the timeless hospital light

My uncle and his sister-in-law held, squeezing them, the yellow hands and told him loudly—probably more loudly than they needed to—that they loved him, that they were proud of him, over and over

Flutteringly the overflowing sag of the mouth seemed, as he stared up at his brother, to be trying to make that "p-" again? Holding the still-squeezing hand of his brother Eden looked up at the pulse readout. It was 35. He stared at the oxygen/breathing indication. It read 45 . . 40 . .

He went out for just a short minute's respite to stride, for exercise and air, the corridors of darkened—for the most part at that hour—rooms. Made a circuit of the floor-gleaming halls and strode back.

Sally was standing with the doctor. They were at the ICU counter, looking over something. As he slowed and approached, he saw they were making arrangements.

He and Sally embraced. She did not care to go back in. He went back in. The bed was cranked flat. The nurse, the doctor, and the orderly who had hovered about at the last, were gone. It was quiet. The tubes were not only out, but most of the clear sacs on their steel trees, and also the monitor devices, had been taken away. In general you could see much more green wall.

The face was relaxed and untroubled. The eyes—eerily—were not quite shut. Slitted just the fraction.

He saluted, pivoted, and went back out to Sally. She was all right. They thanked the doctor, said goodnight. They took the elevator down, Eden having pointed at 1 and stabbed gently, but Sally reached past him and pressed 3. He found himself getting off with her. It was the

brighter, he followed her heels on the brightness of floor. Then they were at the window. They held each other's hand, looking through the glass at all the new little people in their caps

most asleep, several with tiny butts aloft. One stirred. A wizened, red face under its acrylic cap

and they went down to 1 and walked, the only sound the sound of their soles on tile, to the garage.

He tried church, avid, the picturesque face expressionless—mask of featureless surrender to the sanctuary of this stillness. As he bowed his head and murmured the words, and listened to the murmured words and sang and knelt and softly recited, his manner was privately fanatical, histrionically intense, as if he were worshiping and adoring not the deity behind the rituals but the rituals themselves, the iron beauty of the routine, the centuries' swaying censers and tilting miters and the old words worn to simple loveliness like white marble touched a billion times. The fact of the church, that women and men—animals that we are—are civilized enough at least to dream. It wasn't a golden calf or a chapel ceiling he was worshiping but the touching strivings of the human animal heart. He adored neither deity nor icon but the act. Amazing. He adored the act of worshiping. If the feeling's intense enough what difference does it make? He worships without object. It's not blasphemy or apostasy. Make *adore* intransitive. He loved, worshiped, without any final object for the act. He hadn't been in a church for fifty years and didn't go for long—two weeks—but during that time he went daily. The bishop was impressed. The Sufis were all for it. Maybe he'll go back someday . . . who knows? The bishop doesn't. The bishop hasn't an idea. Dogma says the answer's *yes,* but I wonder: Is it ever too late for God? Coming out of the valley in the first hour of darkness and beginning the climb toward the village, the rear of his car full of reels, saltwater flies and tropical cotton clothes, he finds himself slowing and turning off for the second time today into the parish lot. Alone in the medieval light and candleglow, in the echoing Alan shadows' Alan quiet before the Alan opulent altar he holds the back of the pew before him in both steadfastly trembling hands to press hard, against pew oak, the prayer inside his forehead that will not take form in words.

# 28

It was two days before they would get on the plane, Anther, Eden, a film crew from New York (schoolmates of a MacAttick-in-law) and my uncle's platoon of white-robed dervishes—I'm not certain that's the term. Down-to-earth people when they weren't devotionally swirling, the Sufis were pleased to talk sports, cook or watch network TV.

Henry's reaction to Eden's white-robed visitors was the same as it had been one time when my uncle had handed the old woodsman a golf club and suggested he try a swing. Approving, warmly distant, looking down at the seven iron, Anther had not taken it. He had not shaken his head negatively or said anything but only looked, that acknowledging way, at the club held out to him in my uncle's at that time steady hand, then, lifting his eyes to Eden's, not taken it. It wasn't a negative *no,* just a simple *no-thanks* without disapproval or disrespect, at least as far as the golf club and the Sufis were concerned. With Quadros however, Anther's reaction had from the first been a darker ignoring, the ears-flat averted glance of a dog skirting its own feces of the day before.

Henry did not ask Eden about Alan directly or otherwise. They did not speak of it, allude to it, or seem even to think of it, which as far as anyone could divine was what the grandfather wanted.

His mottled hands atremble with an even, low frequency that was almost like calm, my uncle had insisted on splurging on lightweight muslin for the Muslim, for where they were going. Nobody was sure of the plan. Flight schedules, taxis, accommodations, guides—these my uncle with that persistent tremor of the wrists had charted, phoned about, confirmed, reconfirmed, backed up and quadruplechecked, versus the perforce uncertainty of his ideas for the film which, since his study had been converted, now jammed the dressers and chairs of and lay awash on the floor of his bedroom but, he reassured her (who looked from the mess to her husband [for he still was that] and back again to his papers with a piercing eye) would tomorrow be ah, ordered and packed in boxes. The tropical wardrobe he'd bought himself, a garden of loopy colors shouting through the closet doors where her jeans and dresses once had tangled, caught her judging eye. Splashy outward manifestation of his inward mad resolve, no matter what the price, to make the film happen.

Anther was ready, he told her, as like two diplomats they strolled the bungalow's familiar rooms. The Sufis were ready. The crew was ready. The fishing resort—both guides they'd had, that glorious trip with Thomas—everyone, he said, lifting a wrist, indicating she should precede him, as they paused at the door to his study, was ready. The crewcut young man who had been working the thing stood up, stood back and explained its workings to her. She stood a moment, courtly, debriefing the white-robed boy. With intense interest she sat down to give it a try. My uncle, stopping his hands by prayer-clasping them, watched.

As she concentrated on the REG screen she started talking, to his surprise. Then admiration. Until Rairia no one but Eden, gazing at the binary green screen, had been anything but silent as they tried to make more "heads" than "tails" come up. Talking to him as naturally as if they were in a cafe while she watched the device and concentrated on it, she impressed him. It made sense. Whatever mind-beams humans can send probably tend to be set free by such chatting. He couldn't take his watering eyes off her raptor stare at the screen.

She was dressed in a skirt of leather cut flush to her roast haunches which would never go away but had been exercised to greyhound (albeit size-jumbo) sleekness. She wore a pair of low-cut chic sneakers of suede. They were almost hiking shoes, and each, on her surprisingly small feet, evoked a rocket-powered car on a track poised to break the sound barrier.

Her blazer, which she had also worn the day before, at Lim's funeral, was loden green, conservatively cut—eye-riveting the décolletage of her satiny blouse in which like porpoises lolling her 40-plus breasts smoothed and shifted, bulged like creamy dunes capsizing, scrumptious (my poor uncle) emblems of a power not principally sexual. She didn't need that—she had Zany on a thousand-acre ranch. She wasn't a bit bashful about spending Zany's money—he adored her. She took a thousand—one thousand exactly—a year for her campaign to edit the Declaration. Not a cent more, though Zany'd've done anything. Nora had not come east for the service, which everyone had understood. Nora Rairia had used her lover's bucks to whisk west without discussion or hesitation after it happened. She'd gotten Nora out of school and transferred into a special academy of beach volleyball and warm friends and real physical exhaustion that Rairia had created with Zany's bucks and that had Nora, not well—for how could she be that? But better. Much better.

Nancy had not come back either for her uncle's service (a light rain, "Onward Christian Soldiers," silken pulleys and lunch afterward), and Zany had of course stayed on the ranch because Zany never left the ranch now except by phone or minion (with Rairia's help he'd preserved his empire, at the acceptable cost of sharing a third of it with one of the Asian states), but Rairia had come and was a comfort to all, in her dramatic clothes. Her hair was longer than he remembered it and unremarkable—businesslike except, always, for the musical raven-blue lights. In the circle of friends she'd gathered for Nora there were even two full-paid therapists—incognito. Rairia told him proudly of the gathering momentum of her crusade, how the press had recently rediscovered the story, bounced and balanced it again, briefly, avidly, on their seal noses, and now, she was proud to be able to report, watching him carefully, nine states were ready to "ratify." She told him this while they were driving over to Anther's. In the night headlights passing she sat turned toward him trying to read his face, because she was worried, because of the trembling wrists, and because of what Nance had told her about how remotely and automatically he talked of it, when he did talk of it. And she was worried because when he had shown her all the things he'd bought for this ridiculous trip and tried to share with her some of his vague ideas for some of the fishing scenes, in that aquamarine paradise, not only would he not look her in the eye but seemed to shrink from her, as if she would strike him, which she had painstakingly explained was no longer necessary. He seemed to want not to finish what he was saying, as if to finish would be to face a thing he couldn't.

On reflection, after observing him, she didn't even bring Alan up. And instead of sitting Eden down and giving him the lecture on the trip and the film that had been gathering in her, she changed her mind about that too. With the pond-green screen blinking *A50.090///B49.910* behind her she looked at the varicolored rose bluish face, the beseeching brown eyes, the sag of the lips under the sag of the moustache. Reversed herself and instead of what she'd thought she was going to say, spoke soft encouragement, said the film was a fine idea, asked questions, touched the waggling wrists, supported him unconditionally, whom she no longer loved but would always—she realized—care about, and said into the puppy eyes "Yes," willingly, "Yes I'd love to" when he suggested they drive over and pay Anther a last-minute visit to sort out any last-minute problems there might be regarding the trip.

So they went over. They drove to the house with the shop connected in the former factory town with brick buildings with rows of tall windows shattered or empty of glass and deserted floors, along the bank of the dirtied trickle of a river there.

It was eight-thirty. Normally Eden would've called.

They knock. Mrs. Anther comes to the door. Her face is hurt and confused, reddened, as if she's been crying. Her eyes are unsure and unhappy though Mary Anther is a solid soul and carries the disruption of pain externally only. When Eden in mannerly embarrassment apologizing tries turning to leave, Mary Anther says "No don't go, it's better if you come in." She insists. Awkwardly, in they go. He asks does Mary remember Rairia, "my ah, heh." Yes, Mary remembers—the two women shake hands in the night shadows of the closed shop—it doesn't matter, they know, if Mary remembers Rairia or doesn't remember Rairia. Something is up. "I've seen you on television," Mary says quietly. Letting Rairia's hand drop she walks on ahead past the darkened counter and register. Rairia, politely following her hostess, is subdued. She makes herself background—this isn't for her to take charge of.

Low-ceilinged living room, frayed furniture, television set. Fake-porcelain courtiers on grainless tablewood. Resurrected from many-weeks-ago Christmas, because one of the grandkids asked for it, a winking sly Santa: lit a second, dark a second on the mantel. Henry Anther is sitting in his Naugahyde lounger staring at the living room on the flickering TV. A taunted father, his sassy wife and libertine kids are lobbing one-line putdowns at each other to the accompaniment of prerecorded hilarity and, in acknowledgment of the most genuinely unloving zingers, a vocal chorus: *OOOooooo* . . .

Please sit down, Mary invites. May I get coffee? Is it hot in here?

Thank-you no ah, we ahh, really we must go . . we've intruded . .

"No," Henry says tiredly, without taking his eyes from the screen. They all sit there, for minutes it seems. At the TV-family's youngest child's savage pornographic attack on both her parents at once, the electronic laughter like a dumped coffee can of bolts, nails, screws, clips and keys fills both the television living room and this one.

"No," Anther says again wearily.

"I was going to call," Eden says, blinking.

Mary Anther looks down, not deferentially, to smooth her sweatslacks over her knees. Takes a breath and looks up, faces Eden. "It's my fault," she says. "I've been—"

"No," Anther interrupts gently. "It ain't your fault. It ain't anybody's fault." Silence again, yet another carnivorous one-liner from the tube.

Canned laughter. A black cat appears in the livingroom doorway, looks, in front of itself, at something that isn't there, tenses around the eyes, relaxes and sits down.

Rairia thinks of speaking . . does not. She sits back. Folded arms. Unfolding them unobtrusively she sits forward, noiseless, trying to get the cat to come to her.

The cat is like truth.

"I just," Mary Anther says—

"Naw I'll tell it. I'll tell him."

My uncle on the couch with his beret on his lap and his face alert and polite is not in the peak of health. He lifts his hand to his breast to touch, without taking them out, his cigarettes in their unopened pack.

Anther looks at his old friend. Grimaces a wan thin grimace, shaking his head.

"He can't," his wife says.

"No I'll tell him," Henry says, "it's for me to tell him. I guess," Anther says, picking up the removed spring from among the disassembled reel parts on the table by his chair, "you could say I won't, but I don't want to put it that way."

Laughter . . cut dead as Mary clicks the TV.

Going back to her chair, she sits down.

"Are you sure I can't get anybody coffee? A soda?"

"No don't get 'em any coffee," Henry says wagging his head in the negative. "They don't want coffee."

"No that's right er, I mean we're grateful. But that's right, ah, please."

The doorway's empty. Rairia sits back.

Two-year-old twins, boys with big eyes, loose necks and mischief pent in them, gleefully walk straight into each other and fall down as their mother and father pick them up. Macaroons for Mary, a question for Henry before the twins' parents will leave them and their older brother here for Henry and Mary to babysit while they—Henry's son and his wife—head to the boat show in Hartford.

Henry wishes his son a good drive. There's an exchange about a bass boat, brief evaluative discussion of the status of this state as a bass state, and they're gone.

Mary excuses herself to go make sure the twins' older brother is up to handling the matching anarchists.

She hurries back to the living room which, including its three faces, is as she left it. Sitting down smooths her sweats' knees.

"Aw," Henry says fretfully . .

"— . . aw," he says, "I don't know. I don't know."

"Yes you do," Rairia offers, " and whatever it is it's all right. You can tell us."

"There's nothing wrong with it," Anther says. "I just ain't cut out for it."

"Well, Hon, yes there is," Mary says, "there is something wrong with it. You know there is."

Rairia's eyes are like tarns.

Henry, lifting thumb, first three fingers and stump fourth where the saw's slice scream toothblur blade bit as a copperhead stabs, so many autumns ago, lowers his eyes. He is shaking his head in the persistent negative again, waves Mary silent.

"I can't do it," he says.

"Heh," Eden says. "Er," my uncle says, "there's always a point in any project when your confidence fails. You can do it Henry. I know you can."

Henry Anther adjusts his nose. Something lightly passes over him, whether regret or frustration it is not possible, from the rugged face, to tell.

"Nah," he says.

Eden peers worriedly.

"No?"

"Nah," Anther explains slowly shaking his head. "It ain't got to do with confidence."

Mary Anther smiles a stiff little smile. She wants her husband to tell his friend the truth.

You can see Eden thinking. If it isn't lack of confidence, what is it? What's the problem? The project's disorganization? That the scenes and characters are still unclear? That would be reasonable . .

Annoyedly waving off his wife's encouragement Anther tries to explain. Because he wants Eden to have the truth after all, he tries to explain. He tries to explain how all his fishing knowledge went into the articles and the book Eden helped him write, which he took seriously and takes seriously. Then he tries to explain how the idea of a movie was so foreign, even embarrassing, not to say frightening, that he could not take the prospect of being involved with a film seriously, which, peculiarly, freed him in his heart to shut his eyes and hold his nose and be willing to try it, which he had wanted to do because the money it had sounded like he might make would be worth any embarrassment or discomfort—money of a magnitude he would never have been able to make otherwise, money he could use to help his family and that certain stream, money he would never again have a chance to make and would never again need to . . . but as he is working, burdensomely, to put all this into words, glancing at Eden he stops.

My uncle is stirring and fidgeting. Henry waits, calm, that masterful moment of pause, as he might let a fish he has and wants to release splash.

"Wal," the old woodsman says, "mebbe it is confidence. I guess it is. I guess it is confidence."

"Hanh? I thought you were saying you're willing to give the film a try."

"Wal," Anther says.

"Oh," my uncle says. He sits back as if he's been slapped, the playful face stricken. "Oh," he says

"See," Anther says—

"Yes I do. I believe I do. The movie would've been all right if."

"Wal—"

"The film—" my uncle holds a hand up "—would be something you would have tried if."

"Yeah," Henry says. His wife folds her arms in triumph. Anther is looking fondly at a reel part he wishes he could pick up.

"But now that, ah, now that Hollywood's out," my uncle nods, "now that there's no studio, no backing, no professional er—now that there's ah, just me, you don't think it's going to happen."

The room is quiet. Anther, handling his discomfort, sits gazing, not stirring, in his favorite chair. A disassembled reel means nothing.

"That's it," my uncle says, "isn't it. It's not the movie. It's that you think that now there isn't going to be one."

Looking at his deconstructed tackle Henry doesn't even need to nod. But when his wife who can't stand it starts to tell Eden that there might've been a movie if he, Eden, had let Henry talk to the studio people, if he, Eden, had let the movie people talk about making the movie they wanted to make instead of some impractical Eden-idea of what ought to be, Henry waves—as at a hornet buzzing the big turnip head—her quiet. But she still fumes with folded arms sitting there.

Eden is not so dumbfounded as Rairia would've thought. He sits on the edge of the couch, though there is no longer a reason for him to be on the edge of it or anything. He is staring at his friend Henry without anger. You can see the last silly light of hope draining—sundown through leafless trees—from his soul's eyes.

"Yes," he says. "Of course."

He fits his beret to his head.

Mary is standing.

"Of course," my uncle says to himself. And to Henry: "I'll take care of it. I'll take care of it all."

"Kin ya get refunds fer everything?"

In a moment of the most extreme ill ease each realizes that Anther's question has presupposed what Eden may not have meant, that the trip, without Anther, will be canceled.

The room is still. The whole night neighborhood is still, except for a car going by evenspeeded. Since Eden, in whose brown eyes not all the light is yet gone, seems unable or unwilling to answer, Rairia sternly with a pointed nod to both Anthers confirms that there will be no trip.

Slowly Henry is standing, they're all standing. Eden offers Henry his hand. It is taken. Who will say something?

No one will—well, Henry will. Anther will say something. Trying to smile and shake his head at the same time and achieving neither, Henry shakes his friend's hand. He says "Wal, see, the way I see it, the way I'm tryin' t' say it . . . it's a sport. It's just a sport. Just a outdoor sport is all it is."

Back through the shop of darkened merchandise they go, Mary following. Then he and Rairia are outside.

Mary had said nothing more—wanted to, you could see—struggled with it, but knew no. Decided no. He and Rairia are outside in the night, the shop door having shut behind them. They are picking their way carefully in the darkness pooling about this side of the house where it is hard to see whether you're going to step on uneven walkway stones or lawn.

The porchlight clicks on.

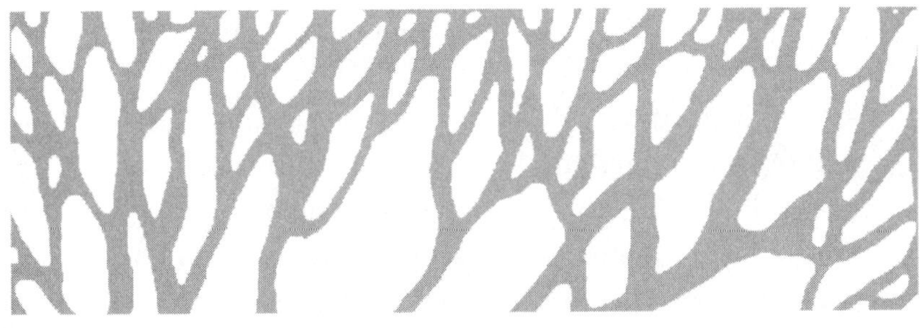

# 29

Eden, Rairia, on pitted sidewalk under the winter moon—curve sliver of—Earth's shadow lying across its face, blocking, at a tilt in space, the light of the sun where it shines ninety million miles behind them over their shoulders in their overcoats.

She steps to his side and is about to give him a hug, but, hanging her head, knows what to do, leave him a bit alone, runs a glove down his sleeve.

Fly fishing is an outdoor sport. Astronomy is a science. Chemistry and paleontology are sciences. Fly fishing is a sport. Poetry, drama, sculpture—these are arts. Fly fishing may be done artfully or practiced scientifically but it is neither art, science, nor religion. Buddhism's religion. Islam, Judaism. Zoology is a science, painting an art. Fly fishing is an outdoor sport. A trout is a fish, a rod a rod, and a stream is just a lot of water pouring downhill.

. . . his ideas were gone. He would straighten up.

Rairia was a comfort to him but not too much—she was careful not to baby him. She bade him, in his Mercator pajamas, holding his toothbrush daubed with gel, goodnight. Their last kiss is unexpected, a peck at first—"You ah, may be right," he nuzzles. Right about what, she softly wonders and asks. "Ah, about being made of particles. You may in fact not be made of them." She says: "Sh." They do close their eyes in this kiss in the shadowy hall light of the bungalow's quiet before, indistinctly saying something he misses, she turns from him in her embroidered robe, a green smear of toothpaste on her sleeve, to pad away down the hall—two doors down to the room, Thomas's once, where Duffy sleeps when she stays over.

The last light is out.

He had always believed in a few beautiful immutable rules. But his father says no, the sad eyes, the collapsed newspaper, his father's money-making ventures that never did and all the memories and traditions crushing the sad, green-eyed father from the old high house of black stone, no his dad says—bow tie, patient for the boy's first couple questions, no, the currentless green eyes say, it is eternally changing—everything—even the most fundamental laws—though this is disappointing to his father, who had hoped too to discover something permanent. There is no voice and his dad is just eyes, bow tie, 16-bore, double-barrel, skeet load, no, it is eternally changing. Everything, the lengthening face of smart verdant eyes tells him, is eternally changing. Bed, pillow, toss, hot, because asleep knows nothing, nothing of any of it. And God rising from His Throne with cataclysmic creak knees, turning a shoulder the size of a galaxy turns away. The Lord walks away across Heaven's floor as ladders, Souls, fire lakes and numbkins of the minor sins dismantle and fall, cracking back to dust. What's *sin*'s antonym? Turning away as stairways, seraph focus groups and the theologian-poet's instruments of beatification shatter, tilt, sway and crash, far below, He pads offstage.

then again to see his mother seated in a chair reading a book, every window (137) lit. Ready for a party again and again and again—*oh i know, it's most mysterious don't you think?*—waves her hand. Bent in the bones, but the sapphire-gray

eyes. Hands bad but not so arthritic she can't six days a week do some good work with them. Garden, knit, play bridge if one must—*what's my crazy son doing?* The 2-year-old who explains in pantomime how the heating system works is somebody's baby. It's Thomas, who did it at two, gravely toddling to a floor grating to hunker unsteadily and indicate with a stare that below this floor, in the house's bowels, engines of fantastic war are creating heat and then, with wonderful drama, straightening his dumpling legs in their Zouave pants, with lifting arms showing everyone how the heat comes—thus up, you see? And out? And up here and, toddler's arms flung up like launching bouquets . . . everywhere! That was how the system worked, Thomas at two had wanted them all to know. The joy of a rational system. Nothing noths antigravity so why even have it? Kosmik Konstant, Kop-out Kartoons, kan't help it . . . Nothing is the shadow Being casts. For in pushing universal accuracy the fly tyer runs into the problem of thwarted tools. Universality and infinity and stuff like that melt the bobbin, cross-eye the scissors, float the thread right up—Look! Defying gravity the thread is lifting weaving as a charmed snake's thought to. But watch out, puns can seem clever, pure A, A 440, A pure! She movie! (*gawd*) But she is—*Lady* Gwen—is off her throne. She's lifting the Sword. Finally. A Manchrave might scream up now out of the long-forgotten mines, but that's better than trying to decide forever. Gnomes in black legions might come tramping from the oleander. Catapults and 4-weight flea-flickers and tactical ground-to-air javelins might shiver her forests, but it's worth it—finally a battle, kings of old *and* new galloping toward who knows what. The Sword, slow-glowing with good and wal, you gotta have evil too—this frightens him in his half-awake tossing turning dream. Something to stay away from. The battle on the plain is immensely invigorating. Astride his dragonfowl the Night Master tries to smile but he's worried . . . her advisors in their robes, their wheels getting caught in their skirts in their excitement, are becoming more and more optimistic, are becoming frenetic in fact as they try at this late hour to serve her up the seventh and penultimate volume of their thoughts on thought. There are stunning aperceptions, and other laudable brainwork is going on too as the clangorous unlocking of dungeons, kitchens and armories pushes the very clouds in her sky along. The war preparations are so loud. Tree, delta, aorta, generations, angler in a stream, software forkings, the upsidedown organization chart of Hell (superseded 1/1/1?), hell the mind would do anything—think anything if the grief were huge enough

Later, as the first gray of day touched the black, motionless branches, as that light will do the day after you're gone, and did the day before you arrived—as the last star went out it was like driving over a rise at night to see spread before him the lights of the world's largest city. And as many stars overhead. My uncle saw his answer. He saw the system and all its laws. It changed itself as he watched. It was indescribable—he was his eyes. It was vast. As simple as a drop of water. Our genes work together holistically. Scalpel out the obese gene and scalpel out the ax-murderer gene and watch out. You're going to get more than you're left with. Eyes staring, he saw now how not only does measuring change what is measured, it changes the measurer. Some of his equations, he could see, had been right—others were taffy. How had he gotten here? Small corrections, once made, opened crevasses. Beyond lay the face of infinite possibility, a grinning skull. A lot of it was as one had expected. But there were also new games, wonderful things, whole galaxy-burst bloomings of value, and there was a cat, a cat where there had never been a cat, crouched in a viny nursery watchful.

# 30

There are always other children and we are they. Let us tell you what we did. Uncle Eden was fascinating to us, spinning his tales in the high giggle so nicely incongruous when it interrupted the rumbly bass. His unpredictable eyes and walrus moustache drew us to him as we were drawn to no other family member in that diminishing enclave of lawns, forests, meadows of special grasses, gardens, cottages, outbuildings, brown barns, skeet towers, bridle paths and condo foundation holes and surveyor's pennants and tree-eating machines with screaming metal mouths that shrill cherry or oak or pine or walnut into dust. We made the mile-long hike gladly—our parents encouraged us to, though an adult always went along and stood back, as, at the end of the journey, we would mill forward toward the shut study door. Something has happened. Our parents think we don't hear them when they go around a corner to discuss it, but we do you know. We are your children. We hear your debate about whether it's safe to visit Uncle Eden. If it's not storming we make the mile-long hike gladly, descending through groves of pines three times higher to us than to you, skipping into the sunlight again and down over the hard, frozen fields in the stinging cold to the property's southern edge where Uncle Eden's bungalow sprawls mysteriously in the shadows of the sycamores that tower by the trout stream that sweeps, under its blisters, cupolas and fairytale juts of ice, along the base of South Mountain.

Into the trees' shade, over snow with lawn under it that in the balmy months is mole-tunneled, and you can footsquish, we tiptoe. Uncle Miguel Grumman or Bey MacAttick or whoever our chaperon is sneaks us through a side door, holding our breaths lest Rairia be home. We come because it's fun but our parents say it's good for Eden too. His house is empty again. The white robes have drifted away. His visitors are gone. His study door is shut. Can you remember? You were us once. We pass through parlors. We slide by doorways curtained with the hang of his pipesmoke, a milling, shuffling colony of excited kids jostling down the glassed-in breezeway. We draw near to the study door . . . we slow now. None of us wanting to be in front. Tittering, because we know what's going on in there. He's thinking. We mill and shuffle forward in mounting excitement, until one of us braver than the rest steps forward and knocks retreating instantly.

Sometimes it takes one knock and sometimes several, but always the voice comes rumbling from the room beyond, and we open the door and go in, seeing him holding his head and glaring at the disarray of his genius.

He looks up. The brown eyes assess. We know he is sad, very sad, but here we are!

"You think," he tells us somberly, "you're going to hear a story don't you?"

We nod. We are squirming. Not a trace of a smile shows under the drooping moustache. He fascinates—his eyes are on us.

"Well." He continues staring. "You're right," he says. "You are going to hear a most amazing story. And you come right here right now and gather 'round." The adult who came with us is halfway down the breezeway hall, peeking. "Once," he begins as we go to him and stand by him and some of the smallest clamber up into his lap, "upon a time."

His pauses are part of his eloquence, and our excitement is too because we do not know, and neither does he, what he's going to say until he says it. He doesn't know what's going to happen next in the story he's telling, as we press into him and the weak, big forearms envelop us in that seven-walled room cluttered once more with his books and pipes, blotting pads, notebooks, printouts, holey old sweaters, water glasses glutted with pencils and pens, and file cards with categories of being scribbled on them.

Once the yarn is under way, whether it's a new one or a continuation of the adventures of "The Rock Who Grew a Heart," "Lydia Cymbals Incorporated" or that haunting, sporadically gallant mists-traveler known only as *The Wanderer,* it is mere seconds before we are lost in timeless enchantment. Or (and just as deliciously), if she's home in Aunt Rairia rushes sweeping like a gale to cry: "For God's sake you old windbag *scare* the children! *Scare* them!"

She was sort of a preacher. We didn't really understand. Unordained, she proceeded on an amateur basis, haranguing the tradespeople who came to her door, proselytizing the family too when given the chance, which was almost never, as she was never home except now that Eden needed her company because he was sad because of Alan which we weren't supposed to think about. "Strife's healthy!" she'd yell. "Look at history!" She was sort of famous, and we didn't really understand, but she was big and sleek with that beautiful swinging black-gray hair and her amazing belts and bracelets and armlets, and she scared us but not really. We liked her. He would smile down at us, ignoring her by continuing his tale. Trying to anger her by purposefully making it more peaceful. And she might stride out, or, if they argued, an enormous row would ensue, taken in by us without distress because—this is odd and wonderful—you know how when your parents fight? Maybe shout, raise voices? That's what Uncle Eden and his big half-former wife would do, but there was no feel of anger or bitterness or even tension—as children we know how to sense these. It was marvelous and foreign like being tickled in your mind instead of under your arms to hear her shouting at him with no bad feelings, in fact with a kind of cheerfulness to it, like swimming in a cloudburst.

One day as we were prancing, jostling, hopping and tumbling down the outdoor steps, I downshifted, coming over the hump. I coasted onto the shady parking circle and saw them. Some Sellerworth dad I didn't know was following behind the protoplasmic little company of woolen hats, scratchy scarves and half-on mittens. Down in the city I had had a dream that I was they . . . I'd heard about their visits to my uncle. I was sure it was good for him. I was lonely and in pain about Alan and could not imagine what it must be like for my uncle, let alone Nancy. But I did, that one weeknight after an admittedly Mexican dinner, have a vivid dream in which I was the kids. A friend of mine who's a counselor says impossible—practically anything can appear to happen in a dream, but not that. However vaguely or imprecisely the dreamer is always, she says, himself or herself, but I'm sorry, I remember what I remember and I was those kids.

That steelplate February day, as I parked and got out, I saw the children's colorful hats sifting and lowering as they descended the railroad-tie steps. A car was coming—I'd glimpsed it behind me. I took my glove off to shake hands with the adult Sellerworth, a quiet man—chinless—irritated rashy neck—who'd accompanied the kids. The car was lightly crunching onto the forest parking area behind us. The children were going on down in a Brownian cluster of pink cheeks and little parkas toward the dark front door under the mossy roofs under the big trees, when the cardoor slammed.

"John!" Nancy's voice rapped.

I turned and she was striding swinging her arms toward me, yellow gloves bouncing from a sleeve cuff where by their clips they were clipped. It was cold and her breath came out mistily. I think she had been through so much—had had so strenuously to discipline and control herself and repress parts of herself in order psychologically to survive—that in a strange way, because I was at some remove from it all, I was able to feel the fair, pure joy of the surprise even more straightforwardly than she must have done. I had never known him that well. But he ran to me, and I, after a second's spinning trees, to him. I can still feel the hurt, through my khaki knee, of the gravel that knee hit as I knelt and braced. He knew how I felt and nearly knocked me over. I have a son now—

two kids actually—and it was many years ago but I can still see the hair, duller gold, filling my eyes, and the big-browed shape of the head and feel the warm between unblemished cheek and manly little shoulder, where I spent my tears. Nance stood proudly, maniacally by with folded parka arms. She had her problems still, as who wouldn't. Knock on the door one vistaless morning with batter up both arms. The door opens. She is looking at adult height at first, then looks down at him. Two agents and a captivated neighbor look on. He has lost weight. She will think, in remembering it, there was an instant's terrifying caw of old age in the uplifted eyes, before all thought and wariness fled his unforgettable face. She does not remember the minutes afterward. Of course they came in and sat down. She never did clean her forearms off. She sat with Alan in her lap and her arms tight around him while in the quietest of voices they explained that he was unharmed, and mentioned that it had been a dicey operation.

The taller, senior agent shot her white cuffs. Crisply she informed Nancy that she would be Nancy's contact if there were any further questions—they would be happy to answer any that they could. No doubt she, Nancy, would want to contact Alan's father and other family members as well as, perhaps, someone from FOLLO, for help in what could, oddly enough, be almost as difficult a time. The clouded dragon glasses nod, chin mussing browngold curls. She sits there—the neighbor stays a few minutes after the government pair has left. She told me she didn't get around to thinking to call her father until that night, and when she lifted the phone to do it, she quietly hung up. "I don't know why," she tells me as I kneel in the cold on the gravel still in the hug. As I am getting to my feet her voice is hard and goes literally over my head in the cold morning—is alloyed with a streak of fear, but of course above everything she is happy. But she asks: "Why didn't I tell my father? I don't know. We just came. It'll be a surprise. We'll surprise him. But why didn't I call?"

To punish? To see his unprepared and thus ingenuous response? The drawerful of humankind's motives is as dead to the present as a fishless stream. It's what we do that counts. I was so, so glad to see him.

I learned more later, but now we were hurrying down the unsymmetrical steps. Seven or eight flakes materialized. We, the old low house and the sapless, silent forest lifted dignifiedly through them. But the children were coming back out!

"He won't tell us his stories!"

"What?"

A couple of them half-recognized Alan so it was a confused moment. They weren't sure. Nance wanted to go on in so she took charge, herding us all in. Duffy Ginty in an apron was utterly stunned. She was stunned, to see Alan. The kids were milling around. Then Duffy, her countenance pinched above the sword nose, stunned by more—clearly—than just seeing Alan, whom she didn't right away hug, took a step toward Nancy who went on guard: "Where is he?"

"In his study," Duffy answered quickly.

"Where's Grampa?"

"In his—"

"There was a stitch in time," Duffy tells us wildly.

"In his study?"

"Yes there wasn't time to call, at least we didn't call, there was time to call," Duffy struggled, "but we didn't want to add salt to injury." Nancy's back is going away from us with Alan's hand tight in hers and kids spinning and wandering around. I followed. The day was gray in the umbilical connecting hall's shutterless eyes.

Nance stopped.

"You stay here," she decided, "with Uncle John."

Duffy and Alan and I and the children drifted, as if pulled, forward a little way as Nance strode on ahead before we stopped, and were waiting.

Desperate Duffy was trying to whisper something to me as Nance opened the door and passed through. As one lofty half of a barn may at last collapse, boards-stulls-struts-roofs-studs-beams-rafters aslide so that, although the left side, while not new, and needing paint, remains upright, the right side shows sky behind it, cupola smashed, walls spoiled in sliding ruin—so with powerless eye the whole right side of the face had fallen. Worse was that side of the mouth. He sat in a chair. His hands were on the plaid of the blanket spread on his legs. The hands no longer trembled.

His left eye was bright.

We came in anyway. Nance did not cry. She walked forward slowly.

After looking at him awhile, she smoothed the bald head. She said: "Oh dad."

Dazedly she brought Alan forward and showed him to him.

He sat leaning to one side. His lips could move a little on the left side. "Dad," she said softly, "look who's here."

She touched the speckly dome again tenderly, staring down at his semi-stare. She asked, without taking her eyes off her father: "Do you think he recognizes Alan?"

It did not seem so. Nancy didn't see it because she wasn't looking at her, but Duffy Ginty was shaking her head in the negative even as she was saying "maybe . . . maybe he does . . ."

"Oh Dad."

I had never heard Nancy's voice so gentle. Duffy was taking the rest of the kids out. That was when Nance did turn, briefly to give Alan a preliminary explanation, and then she looked at me and with raised eyebrows and a headjerk asked me not in words if I would take Alan out and wait for her. Of course I would. I took Alan's hand. "*Watch* him," she blurted. "Sorry," she immediately apologized. As Alan and I were going out she was back at Eden's side in that smoke-bitter, high-minded room of windows of forest. I heard her say: "Well dad, at least you don't have to think anymore."

There are concealed cadres and coteries. There are spy schemes and the wealth to reify them. One step down the wrong alley, an hour late—or early—for your appointment, and the wrong door opens and entering a place of shadow, a world you had thought farcical, you are caught. The wizard Quadros, having established his legend[1] as a demi-

[1]Fictional identity created to mask true identity.

mad enormously hypnotic guru of (and this was key) extremely obscure background, had kept the boy many weeks with a training company of other youths, in contravention, it was said, of orders, but, possibly, even that was part of the cover. It was, from the little Nance was told, as much like a summer kids camp as a kidnapper's den. The horror had not been what Alan did while there (chores, soccer, math) but the fact that he was there. And Quadros knew it. It was a Quadros matter of pride—*Know that I can do this. I can do it without harming him, I can do it any time I want. I can do it again* . . . and the operation itself?

It hasn't started yet, Nance says. But watch Morocco.

"But how the—(muffled snigger)—how the hell would *I* know," she quickly added. A comment that as I think about it strikes me as having levels. "So," she said, not lowering her voice, "we're past it and I'm convinced Alan's not harmed. Alan's not harmed," she recited. Except there's the five-clause, three-sentence note, written in Quadros' windblown rail-under hand, that they found in Alan's pocket. "Unharmed," she repeated insistently as if tucking a whole unruly sweet-smelling household of family and animals in one by one for the night with the word. (They found it in Alan's pocket when they gingerly at last "stormed" that desert redoubt, so it must've been put there . . when? Q didn't say—one of several subjects he stayed mum on as they hustled him to the black bird.) "Nora's where she wants to be and needs to be," my phone pal recited over the midnight-clear line. "Mom's *wonderful*, Lim's dead and Dad's . . Dad. And I'm in Tacoma if you know what I mean." I waited. "My new motto which I made up the other night is this. Ready?" I said I was. Silence . . . I ventured: "Hello?" Was she still there? "Fooled ya'!" she shouted, "no seriously, seriously, I'm much better now on the phone as a result of all this. My motto is . . . Things are never as bad as you think. And occasionally they're worse."

Goodbye Nance. Take Michael to his violin lesson, then you need to buy groceries. Forgot Planned Parenthood (hah!) flyers—back to the house to get, rush in, get—don't *touch* that answering machine! Planned Parenthood HQ is locked and Alan has a temperature (103), dinner for 14 tomorrow, car in, dogs out, food for church, hymnals for the food bank. Aerobics. Daycare. Proust class. Soccer. Mammogram. Forgot Michael!—screech turnaround, back to get. Michael is watching his violin teacher's TV. A string broke—music store, new one. Late for the barbecue, phone, outdoor phone's inside so go get it, will someone please watch the charcoal while . . . literally and figuratively she drives through the years bundling kids gear and grocery bags into a car, marshally to debouch them at the trip's destination. Through all the cooked and served and planned and supervised meals she drives. Through all the airline flights, the step-aerobics classes, church committees, bake sales, gossip, benign scheming and catnaps and crab salads and flu bouts and the mall safaris and crafts magazines of her good unexamined life she drives with a fierce, cheery stubbornness and commonsense grit uncorrupted by a single philosophical gene.

Alan, long after this story ends, in telling it to his kids with a strong arm around them can scarcely remember the details, so well did he get, in time growing like an interrupted branch on upward, season by season toward the light. But that year, from the arrival in the parking circle of the elongated car of Zany Foss with its hard drives and satellite feeds and humidors and precious gems hidden behind panther doors, to the stroke that felled my uncle—that year was one of those times when a cloud seems to lie over us. The sun is behind the moon. Strange mists, wrong decisions made dreamlike and remembered only vaguely, and in perplexity . . a white hand perhaps moving slow, restlessly over white marble in an unknown room saying *very well that's enough, secure the device, get the kid out and get our deviate friend to* Fez. Or, again long afterward, decades after our story ends, a trunk of fire. Ancient wire somewhere in the old house tiring finally of carrying so much current. A column of conflagration, wild tossing branches and licks—tongues—flames loosed on the mountain night, blown leaves of sparks, a tossing pyre of candescence that destroys the bungalow and my uncle who by that time hadn't spoken in twenty years.

Left to its own devices the mind is no good. Tested by just its own standards, operating within just its own boundaries, couching its goals just in its own language, using just its own tools, the mind eventually either destroys itself or is parody. In one way or another my poor uncle thought—*thought*—about the meaning of life eight hours a day. I think in the end there was not much left over in him for anything else. The Sufis had long since drifted off. I saw the sadness of the scene, after he was struck . . . his horses, that would have to be sold off—his Random-Event Generator pulsing in a corner of the unused study, that no one had the heart to touch—the sadness of all the paraphernalia of all the ideas he'd tried, so few of which, ultimately, worked.

Helen's son the dreamer . . . I visited a few times more but the slanted face just sat, before my forced words. His hands lay unbusy on the plaid blanket Duffy or a nurse or one of his visiting children ritually spread on his knees . . .

Two things more remain in memory. The equations his pencil had hurried down onto the scrappaper on his bedside table before the artery in the neck closed (colleagues pronounce them "fascinating, and wrong"). And the staged photo of him that I found in a drawer in the first couple hours of "cleaning out" that raftered workroom before, shocked by myself, with his glossy photograph in a hand I quit forever . . . shot from the shoulders up with his shoulders squared, white shirt. Necktie (wool plaid), neat. Cheeks scrubbed and shaven. Moustache trimmed making him look young in the professionally taken portrait photo Lim had intended for use on the fourth Lady Gwen volume jacket. He looks at you, his nose dry, his mouth shut in his boyish earnestness to look responsible. Spectacles off. Hair flat. The eyes ungoggly a moment for the cameraflash, dark-encircled, serious—more serious than I could remember him ever seeming. Haunted and confident in this posed stare, even confrontational, the eyes' deep gaze seeming to challenge. To defy you to think this isn't the true he. But if it was, if it was the true he, this posed picture, then an imposter knight of happy wild vision and irresponsibility and glee had possessed him in his life, hiding this sour paragon—I don't believe it.

I don't believe it for a second.

I think this: superficially he was the knight of his gleeful visions and pleasures precisely because deeper down there was indeed a sour paragon that he wanted to hide, but step closer . . . listen, I spent a lot of time up there. The sour paragon in its turn hid, deeper still, a final, gleeful knight of wildest vision.

I'm pretty sure of this.

I took one souvenir, in addition to as many boxes of his papers as I could fit in my car. Duffy and Rairia said I could. This was a week after it happened—the earliest I was able to get away and get back up there. I walked right in, sat with, spoke—wanted to scream—stared at. Then I looked away from him where they had him sitting down at the bay end of the living room. I said something idiotic—about beauty I think—absolutely idiotic . . . he didn't make a sound or move, though they'd told me he could, if he wanted to, move his hands a little, and then I think they took pity on me. They took me to other rooms, and we sort of drifted about the bungalow, straightening up his study a little, and then we came to his bedroom, where Duffy said there was something she wanted to show me.

Quine's *Word and Object* face down like a crashed duck on his nightstand where he'd put it—open to the page where he'd stopped forever.

They let me take it. I asked to. Rairia, with a set of ringed fingers lifting the music of her hair and letting it harmoniously fall—downward harp arpeggios to her merino shoulder—said it was interesting I should want it. She didn't know why I would, but I was more than welcome . . . "*I* know," Duffy eyed the book suggestively, "he wants it cause he can't take it with him."

I stole up there one last day in November, November of the following year that is, and I walked those paths fully intending afterward to go in and visit, but as I hiked I knew how he would sit. And look. And when I came out of the trees and crossed the lower span of the meadow I went right on down through the evergreens to my car and left. Oh and I had the peculiarly immediate feeling, during my furtive hike about the forest that last day, that I was missing something in the woods, walking right past it.

From Thomas, Gwen (the nonfictional), and Joe Bitterbeer of

all people he received letters of varying frequency and length. Thomas visited once a year or so, to tug the blanket up under the expressionless face and hands. From Dr. Bright and T. Ott he received a business communication or two, all of which Duffy or a "Curtiss" or Nance or Nora would read to him, but you couldn't tell. There was no response except, sometimes, a shining in the good eye.

Duffy had a greatgranddaughter, a halcyon little girl with rifty hair and absolutely fell eyes who for several reasons Duffy took care of summers. The "Curtisses" and Wister are ageless apparently. Spring, summer and autumn they test themselves against that unchallenging mountaintop downs, so called, and continue to enter the parties of that place, to which I don't go anymore.

In an understated candlelight ceremony the Curtisses dropped the quotationmarks that had grown, in local conversation, around their "last name."

Len, whose last name *was* Curtiss, kept same while Jeff made it clear to their friends assembled on the floating dock's lake candlelight in the freezing air that he would be called, henceforth, Curtiss too, though not legally, the point of which is none of the above but rather that those two quiet souls simply made you feel better by their presence, their genuine civility, their lemon wit and kindness.

There's a new Emma, half chocolate, soft mouth like the others. She's technically Michael's—lives in Norham to keep Eden company.

Kyle Kulka, I read, has been appointed to spearhead a task force of a thousand (that's committees!) to evolve a set of working guidelines for a definition of what it is to be human. If Eden does, still, dream of his parents, how would you know? I don't go there but I get the news—there isn't much. I get reports mostly from Alan, who's become a friend, and from Nora, whose goddess torso you might recognize in the wholograph™ bright-waterdropletted-cameralens leap-bikini ad for that new nut juice, at the thought of which, tending her greatgrandkid while she gardens, Duffy just shakes her head thinking amazing things.

Duffy's eighty.

Rairia came back to take care of Eden those first crucial months, during the period handing her crusade, along with her Zany-fostering responsibilities, over to . . . Guess Who?

And so we leave Duffy at a point near her and the century's end. She's on her knees putting tulips in, wearing her ring because it won't come off. Her long nose aims at each bulb, and hole, as she plants. She is dying, not of illness but as healthily and gradually as a tree in its own good time, the baby on a blanket on the soil beside her, possibilities winking, invisible on the air, all around her in the morning sun.

# 31

Henry Anther fishes just several times a year—a few afternoons and one long weekend with Eden, on the bank in his chair, its wheels locked, a blanket over the calmed hands. Anther still has the shop. He devotes time to volunteer work for a regional conservancy society, is with his family even more than ever, reads magazines and has taken up gardening—flower—which he never did before. But these are things to fill the time during which he is not fishing. He loves the sport as much as ever, Mary says, and I think it odd, when I hear this, holding up a finger to halt the arc of her vaporous tea, that he fishes so seldom now. Of course he's older. But a change was catalyzed—grainy white cube melting to curves on my spoon in the steaming brown—by what happened to Henry's friend. Including the stroke. Especially, she thinks, the stroke, though as ever, you know my Henry, not what you'd call a talker, she says, pouring for herself.

Mary Anther's facial skin sags in lovely bags and wrinkles all the way down her cheeks but the frank blue of our first president's lordly gaze is still just that. Mary came from that town. She says that in mulling things over her husband came to understand, to his surprise, how fanatical (she uses the word) he was where catching fish was concerned.

He had always kind of thought his slow ways on the streams and lakes of his life, his low-chuckling unhurried approach and nonchalant casting, were the banner and proof of his lack of ultimate emphasis on catching trout. But no, he now saw. He'd been so super-relaxed about it precisely because that was the best way *to* catch many and big ones.

Now, Mary says, and burns her tongue.

She rattles the chipped cup into its saucer as, a door banging open, the subject of her speculation tracks into the house with mud on his shoes, perfumy spring air wafting behind him. Henry's carrying a tray of green shoots and beside him a grandkid gravely carries a smaller similar tray. With a nod through the kitchen doorway at us, and with, in his last words to me, an amiable "yup" (why not "hello?"), the old angler shuffles away down a hall to a different part of the house.

Now, Mary says. Bony finger crook'd through ear-shaped handle. Now, she tells me, when her husband does set the rare afternoon aside, preparing his equipment and driving to some coursing water to fish a fly, he finds himself in a state of unexcited gratitude. It doesn't have to do directly with the stream, though without the stream he wouldn't be able to feel it or, running a scored palm over hair that hasn't been there since four wars, have it (or it have him). Talk about such things long enough and your language gets bent like light or gravity by a huge sun. There is something special. He can't say what it is and doesn't try. He thinks of fishing most all the time in a semiconscious way like lowest, scarcely measurable seepage of amps. But he no longer becomes aroused toward winter's end. New water and old are, under it, the same as catching fish and failing to catch any. Another thing that fly fishing is not is a dance, yet he cares more now about doing it right even than he ever did, and by doing it right Anther no longer means catching trout, necessarily, though he sure prefers to catch some . . . no, he means going to the stream peacefully and without clutter or—most importantly—ambition. He means looking over the water, planning some, not a lot, and getting in and presenting his flies as best he can, which though he is eighty-nine is still very well, and informedly enough not to insult the stream though a stream cannot be insulted, yet not so scientifically as to cause even a particle of the universe he inhabits to suspect that catching trout is a priority rather than a preference. He is slow—slower. This is less from age than from hoping to be able to fish each minute of each hour not as if it were a gift (for no one gives us a stream), nor as if this moment were going to be his last but rather, with the sun setting cold scarlet to the point tips of the pines, in a cool daze of appreciation —not the grabbing kind that tries to be awake to nature every second and miss nothing thus to cram every beauty and birdsong and sunflash on the minueting currents into one's memory, but an awareness human and therefore lazy, unambitious on the outside, and, far within, also unambitious and calm, but also alert, a pilot light of natural care.

# Notes and Acknowledgments

Thanks are due the inevitable cast of characters, imagined and real, that turns the fiction writer's life into a living daydream.

Dr. Gordon Aubrecht II took a patient look at some of the "physics" herein, and David Hughes cast his skilled eye over the on-the-stream episodes, in addition to making a number of extremely perceptive criticisms in areas having nothing whatever to do with angling. Any mistakes are the author's.

Frances Moffitt reviewed the manuscript with her usual forthright insight and intelligence. Randy St. John made a course correction in philosophy. Chief Charles DelSanto gave expert testimony. The keyboard skills of Susan Guyer and Eileen Hanna, David Uhler's effective coordinating, and Tracy Patterson's smart graphic eye all helped.

As mentioned at the beginning, aberrations of spelling, diction, punctuation, capitalization and what the movies call "continuity" (a baseball that changes into a basketball, in memory's imperfect enthusiasm) remain as the author's writing ear heard them, despite Linda Lotz's and Mary McGinnis's copy-editing prowess.

My editor, Judith Schnell, is blessed with a sensibility technically professional and life wise. For her tutelage in countless small matters and not a few large ones, I am extremely grateful.

Without the patience and love of my wife Susan and our son John there would have been no book.

Department of Self-Defense. Morocco may seem a strange spot to have Nancy Elwive tell us to watch, but the author was driven there, thus: Early in 1995, in search of a country concomitantly strategically important and fairly well out of the news, staring at a map I picked Turkey. Shortly thereafter came the incursion into Iraq. Back to the map. Mindful of where a significant percentage of U.S. foreign aid quietly goes, I had Nancy tell the narrator "watch Egypt." Shortly thereafter the president of that nation visited the U.S. and there was an article or two hinting at potential instability. Back to the map. "Watch Greece," Nancy now advised. Before long there was a stir, albeit a small one, regarding the flow of contraband drilling equipment to Serbia through . . guess where? Back to the map. Egypt seemed quiet again, so in the May '95 revisions I had Nance tell us, again, to watch Egypt. On June 26 I said the hell with it and tried to pick a spot nobody should probably overly much watch.

A very minor sidelight. But in the matter of the will, and how its lack eviscerates even the best idea, the news has more than once, over the years of this book's composition, rung one sort of bell or another. Anyway this is the story of a man, a pretty good man all in all, who thinks too much.

He seeks to know God (though he doesn't know that's what he's doing) in the one place where God cannot be known: the mind.